January 1865

The southern Confederacy clings perilously to existence after four years of bloody combat with the Union armies. The northern army, under Union General Ulysses S Grant, has Confederate forces, under General Robert E Lee, pinned to the trenches of Petersburg in Virginia.

The army of Union General William Tecumseh Sherman has fought its way through Tennessee and has marched to the sea through Georgia to Savannah and now is poised to cross the river into South Carolina, the last untouched bastion of the Confederacy, and stab northward at the unprotected underbelly of the South.

Confederate forces are trying to form a defensive front as white southerners, sick of four years of suffering still cling to the hope of victory.

Hundreds of thousands of blacks, who have suffered their entire lives as slaves, forever hoping for the day of Jubilee, wonder now if that day of freedom from bondage is finally near at hand or is it merely another pipe dream that will soon evaporate.

As air rises through honey, the Union Army rises northward through South Carolina and with it rises the potential for the end of the war and freedom from slavery.

Air in the Honey is the story of four young people, two slaves, Miela and Ezekiel, Luke, a Union soldier, and Connor, a Confederate soldier, and how their hopes and lives interconnect.

Air in the Honey

Air in the Honey

PERRY TROUCHE

Air in the Honey

Copyright © 2017
by Perry Trouche

cover design by Lucy Swerdfeger

Original art work by Mrs. Emory Trouche Willis

Air in the Honey follows its prequel
The Mule Shoe
published in 2009

"...this work of southern literature functions as a wartime meditation, the book's dedication to "all those who have suffered during times of war, past and present" taken up by an author adept at coalescing historical and psychological trauma."
—Erin McKinght, *Prick of the Spindle, Journal of Literary Arts*, December 2009

Published by

~Star Cloud Press~

StarCloudPress.com

ISBN:

978-1-932842-86-9 — $ 29.95

Printed in the United States of America

Dedication

Air in the Honey is dedicated to my grandson

PERRY EDWIN TROUCHE III

and in memory of my mother,
Mrs. Paul E. Trouche III (Julie Ann Carr),

and my mother-in-law,
Mrs. John Emory Holler (Edith Wilhelmina Stuckey)

AIR: the atmosphere; that which surrounds and influences
HEIR: that which is produced; offspring;
the rightful future recipient or possessor
ERR: to deviate from the right way; to go astray, to do wrong.

"Perhaps this war will pass like the others which divided us, leaving us dead, killing us along with the killers, but the shame of this time puts its burning fingers to our faces. Who will erase the ruthlessness hidden in innocent blood?" —Pablo Neruda

"Abruptly the poker of memory stirs the ashes of recollection and uncovers a forgotten ember, still smoldering down there, still hot, still glowing, still red as red."

—William Manchester

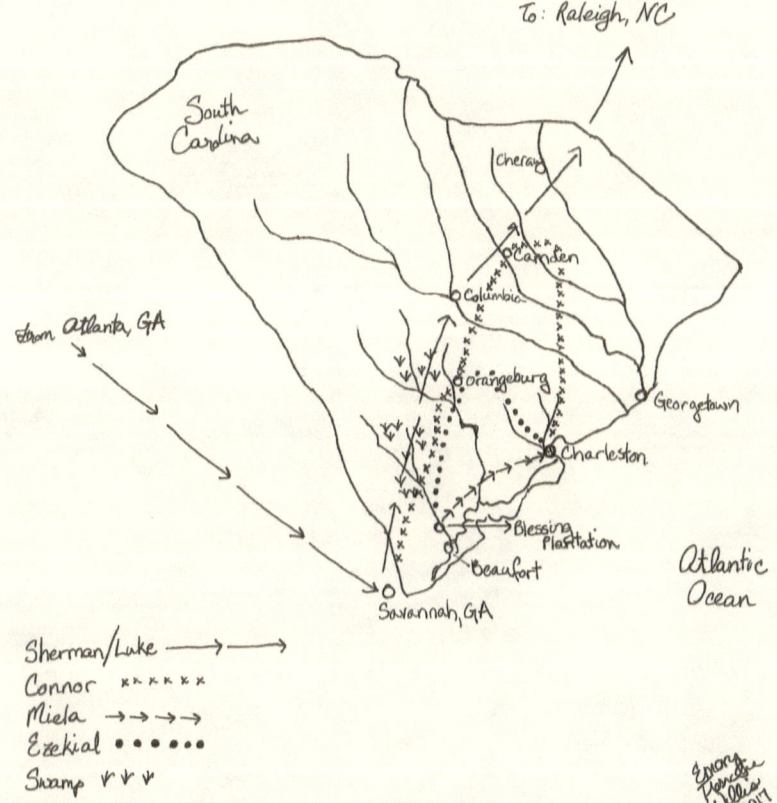

To: Raleigh, NC

South Carolina

Cheraw

Camden

Columbia

From Atlanta, GA

Orangeburg

Georgetown

Charleston

Blessing Plantation

Beaufort

Atlantic Ocean

Savannah, GA

Sherman/Luke ⟶
Connor ✕ ✕ ✕ ✕ ✕
Miela → → → →
Ezekial • • • • •
Swamp ⌄ ⌄ ⌄

BOOK 1

Jubilee Rising

"Hope is the only bee that makes honey without flowers."
— Robert Green Ingersol

CHAPTER 1 — MIELA

Miela wormed her fingers under the copper ring bolted around her neck. She sucked in air, suffocating in the baking noon sun. Sweat dripped down her back on to the wooden platform in middle of the cobblestone-lined square. She tugged at the glistening metal and grabbed the cord leash stretching from her neck-ring to the wrist of a white boy in a gray, starched jacket who pulled her to the end of a line of slaves waiting to be sold. The white boy reined her closer, whispering in her ear as a crowd of gentlemen gathered around for the sale, "Stop wiggling," he hissed. "Don't draw attention to yourself. The brokers know your value. And anyhow, slave auctions are ... well, like being with a woman. People want it, but don't like so much talking about it. They're still a bit ... well, kind of embarrassed maybe. All this out in public and all. So don't make a scene."

Miela's knees wobbled as she looked around the square at the smiling, white faces and the shops with signs advertising leather goods, cloth and lumber, and a ships' store with its peculiar sign in the shape of a bowsprit calling out 'masts, spars, blocks and pumps'. She noticed there was no sign for the slave auction. The white boy jerked her leash harder.

"The best and prettiest wait 'till the end. Keeps up the interest y'see."

"First bids," the auctioneer called out. He was a short, fat man wearing a wide straw hat. A slave girl of about twelve years old obeyed his command, stepped forward, and turned around in a full circle so all the buyers could get a view. The other slaves behind her, women and children tied together by a thick hemp rope, shuffled a step closer. Miela closed her eyes and didn't see or hear anything else.

She thought of the slave pen of the night before where she had shared a dank, brick room with sixteen other slaves, all women and children, freshly washed and wiped down with cotton seed oil to give luster for a better price. She pictured the trembling, young mother in the dark corner clutching her little boy who wiped away tears dripping down her cheeks, unaware that he would soon be separated from his mother for life.

"It's All right Momma, it'll be breakfast soon."

The mother's chest had heaved even more, and Miela remembered leaning against the cold, brick wall watching the dust particles dance on rays of sunlight from a yellow pane of the lone window high above her head. Through the dust particles she had seen a vivid image of her own mother standing beside her, smiling brighter than the sun itself, with large white teeth and thin lips pursing as she wheezed and sucked at the air. She had imagined her mother leaning forward and blowing on the little specks making them swirl into a frenzy before disappearing into the darkness.

"See there Miela. See how they're alive in the light? See how they vanish in the shadow? Do you see?" Her mother was there again for an instant, tugging at her arm, not letting go until she answered.

"Yes Momma, I see."

"It doesn't matter where they've been or where they're come from. All that matters ... and this is important Miela ... this is the most important thing for you to remember, always. All that matters is that they are alive only in the light. You see?" Her mother was holding out her hand to block the sunlight, making the particles disappear as long as her fading strength allowed, then panting for breath and finally dropping her hand, bringing the particles to life again. "Remember, your life doesn't start until the light shines. And it will someday, it will. The shadows mean nothing."

Miela imagined the feel of her mother's hug, then her hands on her cheeks and the head-kiss that she had always loved, all the while gazing into her sad eyes that even her bright smile could never make happy. But the auction bell clanged again, and the memory of her mother vanished. Miela closed her eyes again and tried to conjure up one last look at her smiling face, but all she could think of were the white men with whips and clubs bursting into the room yelling, and the young boy darting behind his mother's skirt as she stood up, wiping her face and trying to be brave. Then the pushing and shoving of trembling black women and children out the door into the bright sunshine and cobblestone streets still slippery from an earlier shower and not being allowed to walk on the smooth, slate sidewalk reserved for whites. Then lining up and marching to the brick square beside a huge, cream colored stucco building with twin marble stairs and arched windows like a church.

Miela opened her eyes and looked up at the bright blue sky then at each slave dressed in clean, white, cotton clothes with blue stripes that they had been made to change into that morning and each wearing a little red scarf around the neck, their old sweaty rags having been collected and burned.

Planters and traders gathered around closer. They wore high black hats that Miela thought looked like upside down pots. Some had brought their own slaves to sort through the 'goods'. The young mother with her little boy began sobbing uncontrollably. A white man is a yellow, silk waistcoat wanted the boy but not her. She had a deformed, claw hand that he found disgusting. He bought the boy for $700 while the screaming mother had to be dragged away by other blacks who showed no hint of emotion. Their job was to do just that, and it wasn't their first time performing it. Miela watched two other black boys innocently run about the square playing and jumping over the old howitzer barrel embedded in the bricks as a hitching post and hoped that when they were sold, they wouldn't remember their own mothers' cries.

When her time came, the auctioneer waved his leather cap and called out, "Seamstress, ironer, clear starcher. Nurse of good character and industrious habits."

He didn't say her owner, a Mr. Charles Gibbes, had just recently died of pneumonia and that his three daughters hated her. As if she could have said no when their father had come for her in the night. Miela knew better. She had seen what the 'blacksnake' whip could do to the disobedient. Better to tolerate his sweaty pounding.

A young man in a long brown coat with the tallest of all the pot hats bought her by order of the most prosperous slave broker in Charleston. The office was located just down Broad Street. The firm of Mr. Louis D. Dessalines at number 23. She made note of the number because it was her own age as far as she knew. But what she didn't know was that her sale was a source of gossip among the fancy gentlemen in the square.

After Mr. Gibbes' sudden death, his daughters had her sent off on a river packet boat the next day. Miela had spent two days on the Cooper River then four more locked in the brick room with the others. They had used one corner as the toilet and the opposite corner to eat and sleep, washing when allowed from a rain barrel in the courtyard, but the stench of the room still persisted even after the coating of cottonseed oil. The younger, white gentlemen surrounded her as she followed the Dessaline's man across the square. They laughed and called to her by name.

"Miela, your quality is evident."

"I'm sure you'll make the squire quite happy."

"Such agreeable features. And so much enthusiasm, I'm told."

The church bells of St Michael's huge steeple rang the quarter hour, and other brokers and merchants greeted each other in subdued tones. They whispered and nodded towards her, and Miela wondered why having been raped by Mr. Gibbes might be an embarrassment to her new owner but not her being held like an animal in a pen then sold as a commodity. But she had learned long ago that, although she was forced to tolerate what happened to her, it was best to remain hopeful while always keeping her eyes and ears open. Maybe Mr. Dessalines would leave her be. Slave traders commanded huge profits, so her good health would be in his best interest.

She found out later that he had immediately advertised her for resale in several states only for her to be snatched up in private sale by Mr. Dubose Blessing who matched the exorbitant bid of a red-faced Irishman, a Mr. Timms O'Conner, a commoner who had amassed a fortune in land speculation in Tennessee and who now lived comfortably in one of Charleston's finest mansions. The Dessalines firm hadn't wanted the embarrassment of their finest property being bought by someone who couldn't be considered a true gentleman. So they let her go to Mr. Blessing for the same fee without another public auction. Of course Miela knew nothing of this as she lived in her new quarters behind the courtyard of number 23 for another two weeks in a room all to her own where she had to tolerate a man probing her mouth and bottom with a wooden pointer three different times to make sure that she was free of syphilis, all while her ownership changing hands for thousands more dollars.

Then in the half light of a foggy dawn, she was taken quietly by coach to Blessing Plantation near Beaufort where she lived until Sherman came. Her official title was seamstress and maid, but her real duty was to suffer Mr. Blessing's pounding her bottom into the sacks of rice and cornmeal every night in the storeroom and once a month accompanying him to Charleston, without Mrs. Blessing. Why she didn't come with them no one ever said, but Miela knew they argued before each trip.

"It's not for me Henrietta, for Christ's sake. It's for us. For the business," he would pout, and Miela thought that he shook his head just like Mrs. Blessing's little rat terrier.

"Don't take the Lord's name in vain. It's sin enough what you do with that ..." Mrs. Blessing would always lean forward and lick her lips when she got mad, hissing a little after each word.

"I've never touched her," Mr. Blessing sputtered.

"No. Not with your hands perhaps. But ..."

"Oh, for Christ's sake!"

"Don't! I will not have ..."

"Damn it, Henrietta, you know she's been good for business." He interrupted her, holding out his hand as if to a jury. "Every broker in Charleston wants to do business with me now... with us. Since Miela has been... "

"They're all sinners too!"

"Oh, for Christ damn sake!"

"Enough!" Mrs. Blessing screamed, holding her ears and running up the stairs.

Miela always liked that part. It was always the same, the 'Christ damn sake' then the running up the stairs. The signal that a trip to Charleston was about to begin. Dirt roads would soon give way to brick and cobblestone streets lined with towering mansions shaded by huge magnolias and oaks, all heralding that her secret place was close at hand. A place where she could still feel free.

She had never been told that the cobblestones came as ballast on ships carrying rice back to England. Rice grown with slave labor at the cost of untold lives. She had always thought the round stones were a natural feature of Charleston. Perhaps in place long before the white people had come. But why the stones were lined up a certain way, she didn't know.

Mr. Blessing brought her to number 8 every month, 'to cook and clean', or so he had told a visiting minister, but she had never touched a pot or a broom. She just tolerated more of his heavy pounding every day, but at least on a soft feather bed in the first floor guest room. Then it was back to the slave quarters in the rear of the cookhouse to bathe out of a wooden bucket and further tolerate the silent glares of the other house slaves, the ones who lived in town year round and who had never been called to Mr. Blessing's bed. She knew they disliked her, hated her perhaps, especially the older cook, Thelma, who wore her hair in a tight bun that seemed to tighten even harder every time she glanced her way. And she'd heard Thelma's whispering.

"Thinks she's white. Thinks she's Miss Princess. Gonna lay up and ring that bell for me. Like I'm supposed to bring her tea on something. Hell no! She can fetch for herself."

But Miela didn't really mind Thelma, and she knew she had no choice any more than they had. It was just as her mother had said to her. The last memory she had of her as a little girl sitting on her lap. Her mother looking into her eyes saying, "Men are very powerful, Miela, and can't be trusted. They can harm you in ways a little girl can't even imagine."

But even as a small child, she could imagine a lot. She remembered thinking, exactly how were they powerful? The big men she had seen working in the rice fields certainly had rippling arm muscles. Is that what she meant?

"There are other types of power than physical, Miela." Her mother had glanced around behind her every time she whispered. "More powerful even then a young girl's inner strength."

She remembered leaning closer to her mother and whispering back, "Tell me about them, please. Tell me about their power."

She remembered her mother smiling and shaking your head. All she could ever get out of her was that men held a mysterious power that could overwhelm almost any female. She remembered watching the old men who could no longer work the rice fields and wondering if they were still powerful? Or had they lost it with old age? What about the little boys wrestling in the dirt? Were they born with it? Did all men hide it somewhere? Was there a secret place they went to retrieve it? Was it, as she expected, invisible? Most of the other things her mother taught her to believe were. God, the freedom that would come on the day of Jubilee, men's power, and even a little girl's inner strength.

But she knew as she had grown older that her mother had been wrong about men. They weren't all powerful. They couldn't ever control her mind. Even while they were on top of her and between her legs, they

6

couldn't control what she thought. Also, she was aware that the pounding brought her little bits of freedom. To be free to wander upstairs and to be left alone for hours. All day sometimes. To be able go to her secret place and relish its treasures.

Usually the pounding came early in the afternoon but sometimes morning and night. After the bucket bath, she would neaten herself up then walk right up the back stairs of the big house all the way to the fourth floor. Even the white matron, Mrs. Wilson, Mr. Blessing's cousin, would leave her be. She didn't dare trigger his disapproval and lose a potential share of inheritance. She would just call down the stairs to Thelma and the others. "Miela's taking a nap. Let her have her rest. No one is to go upstairs."

Thelma would smack her palm down on the cutting board, "Rest from what? She ain't raised a finger all day. All she's raised is Mr. Blessing's..."

"Thelma! Bring Miela a basin of fresh water."

Thelma would whack the board again and hiss loudly, "I'll stuff her princess face right in it, too."

Mrs. Wilson always turned away and pretended not to hear, but Miela heard every word. She ignored her, though, and slid out the bay window on to the high slate roof where she would sit for hours. Everyone knew where she was, but to her it was still a secret place. No one could ever know the thoughts or feelings that came from the high roof. The warm slate behind her back, the sky a different color every day. Sometimes gray and prickly damp, sometimes blue and cloudless. Other days pouring rain from low gray clouds that tried to land on her head. But the key thing being the height.

Miela felt that being so high up in the air made it all the more secret. No one else could understand, certainly no one who hadn't watched birds fly beneath them by the hundreds or hadn't seen the incredible, far horizon of blue water that some days merged with the vast expanse sky into a great bowl of blue past the promenading, sea wall they called the High Battery.

Being one with the sky, the clouds and the birds became the most important force in her life, well worth all the bed pounding. No one could ever take away what was now etched in her mind. There would never be another time in her life, from the first moment she had stepped

7

foot on the roof, that she would be trapped at ground level. She could always escape to the roof in her mind. Anytime she wanted.

Usually the trips to Charleston also meant going out on the two-masted ketch with Mr. Blessing and his nephew, Laurens. Miela remembered the first time she stepped aboard and how her heart raced when the sails flapped loudly in the breeze, lifting the thick boom as if to salute Blessing coming down the gangplank. She'd reminded herself then that the boat was not actually alive. She knew better. Haints, spells, and magic were the stuff of ignorance and superstition. She was above all that. But a sudden gust of wind swung the creaking boom, and she'd been forced to fight off doubts. Even if it were alive, and she always reminded herself that it wasn't, she would deal with it like she did with everything else. She would find out exactly what it wanted and what she could gain in return. She would just have to push away her fear, hold on to the railing and enjoy the view of the harbor, the blue water, the white sails, and the brick fort perched out on the oyster bank.

On one particular trip to Charleston and then to the ketch, she stood on the quay watching a small steamer chug slowly upriver against the ebb tide. She waved to the black man coiling rope in the stern. He waved back and for a moment she felt totally free. For that moment, she was just a person enjoying a pretty day. Maybe the boatmen felt it too. He waved back until the steamer disappeared behind the wharf. Miela smiled and looked around at the huge mansions lining East Bay Street. An old white lady was being helped up her front steps by one of her slaves. The moment of freedom vanished, evaporating in the salt air and leaving the deeper chill that she'd felt every day of her life. It pricked at her all the time, draping over her over in the quiet of the evening and in the warmth of her bed. It was a feeling like walking in the dark through a cold, misty rain. The feeling of being a slave.

She resigned herself and followed Blessing on board and down into the forward cabin as he demanded. Two slaves, Robert and Daniel, sat in the stern. Both were young men but sickly and coughing. They tended to the carriage, the horses, and the ketch on Mr. Blessing's outings. Neither one ever said a word. They struggled with the thick ropes beside a white man named Tolly, who was as big around as a barrel, and Laurens, Mr. Blessing's favorite nephew. He was pock-marked with red hair, crooked teeth, and a high-pitched nasal voice that Miela thought sounded like a little girl holding her nose. He always shared in the pounding when he came to visit from Augusta.

The boat suddenly heeled to leeward, and Miela grabbed Mr. Blessing's arm, thinking they were turning over. He pulled her to him and rubbed her bottom then led her below through the little hatch door to a triangle shelf covered with a thick quilt He undressed her, pulled down his trousers and began pounding her into the quilt against the hard wood underneath. She lay still as always and watched the blue sky through the deck hatch as his pounding intensified. Just as he finished, Lauren's upside down face appeared in the hatch above. Her heart jumped, and the startle caused her to tighten for a second. Blessing mistook it as pleasure. He sagged on top of her and buried his face in hers.

"Wonderful Miela. I've always hoped you would feel that way." He sat up, pulled out a bottle of whiskey and sucked it down.

Laurens laughed, just out of sight above the hatchway."Sailing is quite delightful actually. And so much more so, with such a cooperative crew."

Tolly laughed with him. "Yes. I believe she was cooperating nicely with Dubose just now. Perhaps she will continue cooperating well into the evening."

Laurens raised his own flask. "To a first rate crew. Here, here! Excellent effort."

Blessing let her go when Laurens called Miela to the stern. She wrapped herself in the quilt and stumbled back through the hatch as the boat rolled with the wind. She knew what to expect. Tolly and Laurens would take turns with her. She'd known it would happen as soon as she'd seen the whisky bottle in Blessing's coat pocket. He always shared her when he drank.

Laurens called to her," Come have a drink with us Miela. We can take time to get to know each other first."

Miela didn't budge, but Blessing growled at her from inside the cabin. "Go back there right now! Cooperate, damn it."

She knew she had no choice, other than tolerating a whipping. The pounding was inevitable. Tolly won the coin toss. Robert and Daniel held on to the mainsheet and tiller, turning their heads and discreetly looking away. Miela nearly suffocated under Tolley's immense abdomen until he

9

rolled off with a heel to leeward. Laurens laughed and jumped on her before Tolley could stand up. She kept her eyes open as always, fixing on the blue sky and hoping to see a bird fly past. Laurens took a long time, and it hurt badly, but a pelican swept past just above and helped her to bear it. Each of them had her twice.

When the boat returned to the dock, the wind slapped the sails, and the boom mocked her with little creaks and groans. Blessing fell asleep in the carriage, and Robert and Daniel had to carry him up to bed. He muttered to them as they tucked him under a bed sheet, "Thank you, my faithful servants."

The two slaves glanced at each other but said nothing. Miela escaped to the roof and let the sky and swooping birds heal her wounds one more time. It was the last time she had been to her secret place. The next day she had been taken back to Blessing Plantation and hadn't been back to 8 Legare Street since then.

The war had come and stayed for nearly four years. She'd heard about Fort Sumter first, then Yankees coming to Beaufort, then Hilton Head and Morris Island, and all the while, Mr. Blessing and his son Malcolm going on as if nothing had happened. She had heard the little spiel many times since.

"Grandfather survived the Indians and then the Spaniards. Father survived the British and actually made a great deal of money on the side. So don't worry, we'll survive the Yankees. They'll come to their senses when cotton prices go through the ceiling and their big looms up in New England run dry. Then we'll see how much they really care about abolition." He would chuckle and snort down a brandy. "My God, do they really think that blacks deserve a better than their own Irish? Bosh."

Miela listened but knew otherwise. She realized the world was about to change. She didn't know how she knew, but she did. Whether it was a gift to her from God like the other slaves said or whether it was due to Mr. Gibbes, her previous owner, lecturing her from the time she could talk, she couldn't say. But he had drilled into her that someday everything in the world would change, and she knew the time had come. She thought back on her time with Mr. Gibbes and thanked God that she'd always been attentive to his rambling lectures. It was her God-given awareness even as a young girl that knowledge was power. If she could understand how and why things worked, like the sluice gates for instance, she could at least know how it might affect her and the world around her. To understand a thing was to become its master or at least be better able to deal with it. The sluice gates, the plantation, the slavery laws, white society. No matter what, the process was always the same. And her main source of knowledge had been Mr. Gibbes and his ramblings until he gave her greatest gift ever. He taught her to read.

He brought her the newspapers and pamphlets from Charleston and books of all kinds. Mostly historical works, Greek and Roman history, Livingston's African Exploration, Paul Allen's History of the Expedition of Captains Lewis and Clark, but the occasional novel, such as *Gulliver's Travels*, *The Count of Monte Cristo*, and *Moby Dick*. The books all blended together, and she didn't understand most of it, but made sure to learn at least one new word every day. Mr. Gibbes was insistent she remember one thing in particular.

"You come from Africa, Miela. Do you realize that? Well, not you, but your mother or maybe hers. It's across the ocean you see. A dark continent far away." He would pat her head and, when Mrs. Gibbes wasn't around, would pull her to him and put his hands up her dress to feel her bottom. She learned to tolerate it in return for the reading. "A black girl from a dark continent. Maybe from Zanzibar. An island off the coast of Africa. Maybe I'll even take you there someday."

She halfway believed him but stayed focused on the job of reading. She knew, even then as a child, that it could be her salvation someday. Her other treat as a child was being allowed to sit quietly and listen to the visitors talk. She hung on to every word and asked Gibbes the meaning later when he came for her after the visitors left. Being able to read helped her to better understand their conversations. It allowed her to learn. No amount of abuse could take that away.

She had learned to tolerate his sweaty weight on top of her. Even as a young girl she knew it was the price for knowledge, and knowledge meant freedom someday. She knew overt resistance to his advances was useless anyway. In the end he would have his way with her just the same. The only thing that fended him off was the Asafetida bag she stuck up inside her whenever she could. An old slave named Eva showed her how.

"It's an herb. Smells worse than a skunk but won't last. See?" She put the little cotton bag tied to a loop of string to Miela's nose and it made her gag.

11

"That's awful!"

"Yes, but see, it's gone now." She tucked the bag between her sagging breasts. The smell disappeared. "It keeps for weeks. Put it up inside your bottom and ..."

"Oh, no! You're teasing."

"No, I'm not Miela. You do it like I say." Then in a whisper, "Put it up your bottom and no man will bother you." She crossed her eyes and held her nose.

Miela giggled, watching her stick out her tongue and pretend to gasp for air. "Can I smell it again?"

Eva pulled out the bag and Miela covered her nose, gagging at the awful smell that had worked so many times ever since. Mr. Gibbes would push away like he'd been splattered with horse dung. Miela always struggled not to laugh, thinking it served him right. But at least he'd given her some knowledge of the world, one talk at time, one book at a time, and the most valuable lesson of patience.

The world would change, and she would have her freedom. It was what Mr. Gibbes had predicted years ago. The world was about to turn upside down. She just knew it. The rumors had spilled from one plantation to another, from one slave hut to the next. The Yankees were just outside Savannah, just across the Savannah River, led by the great Sherman himself. A giant of a white man they said. A man with more power than anyone in the world. And he was coming.

CHAPTER 2 — CONNOR DUMONT

Brown's Mountain, Virginia, near Charlottesville

Connor packed his blanket roll with the last tins of ham, a box of hardtack crackers, a small red stone from the hillside meadow, and a few extra clothes and matches, then rolled it all up in a waxed canvas tent half. He cut a hole in the other tent half and draped it over his shoulders like a poncho, covering his gray shirt and pants that were patched with blue canvas. He cinched it down tightly with a piece of rope and at first light on a cold December morning, left his hiding place on Brown's Mountain, Virginia, walked down the hill through the apple orchard then through the woods of bare maples and chestnuts to the stone post where the hill track met the Lynchburg Road.

It took him three days to cover the forty miles to the rail station. He talked to no one and camped each night in the woods with a branch shelter and fire, relishing the cold and hunger since his conscience told him he deserved much worse. He wasn't sure why though, since he honestly couldn't remember anything of the past six months. Nothing since the carnage of Spotsylvania, something he wished he could forget. He hoped his amnesia since then was mostly due to his head wound but feared it was more than that. He kept thinking of his Uncle Paul teasing him.

"You have a weak mind my boy. Always have. It's the Irish curse you see. The potato famine and all. Left its mark for generations to come."

Maybe he was right after all. How could he not remember six months of his life? Just a week ago his eyes had opened as if he had been asleep since June. He remembered everything else about his past life. Growing up outside of Charleston, South Carolina, enlisting with McGowan's Brigade, and coming north on the train as a 'new boy' replacement just after the battle of 'The Wilderness'. And as much as he would like to forget, he remembered every detail of the slaughter in the 'Mule Shoe' parapets at Spotsylvania but nothing else until just a week ago.

He huddled by the fire inside his lean- to and fell asleep as he had every night since, trying to think of anything that would bring his memory back. He dreamed of the hut on the mountain and the fresh grave in the field of chickweed and goldenrod. But in the morning it was still a mystery. How? Why? Whose grave? He tried to put it out of his mind as he pushed on to Lynchburg, crossing the James River into the town then up its steep hills covered with red brick buildings, women bundled against the cold, thin children and old men.

The station itself was overflowing with a multitude of coughing, gagging wounded with stump arms and legs, dirty gauze bandages and mangled scarred faces, some with pneumonia and pleurisy, others with invisible wounds inside their vacant, hollow stares. The Lieutenant in charge allowed him on the train just as easily as he might have ordered him shot, swayed perhaps by his eye patch and the purple ridge down his cheek which spewed forth another splinter of wood encased in pus as it was apt to do every few weeks. His limp could have been faked, and his shoe covered up the scarred, shiny-red, half of a foot that was so ugly he'd grown almost fond of it. Still, the Lieutenant would have been within his rights to shoot him for desertion. That would have been officially the truth. But instead he wrote out a pass and said nothing but to ask his destination, adding, "Tend to that wound, son."

Son? The officer couldn't have been but nineteen or twenty, himself, but Connor just saluted,"Thank you, sir."

A toothless, old civilian with his own eye patch rode in the freight car with him and nodded towards the Lieutenant walking away down the platform, "He done turned his blind eye." He flicked open his eye patch and wriggled the scar of his torn eye socket. "It do give us certain powers, don't it." His red gums gleamed in a toothless smile then he leaned back against the plank wall and recited Psalms as the screeching car jerked out of the station and down the tracks.

No one paid him any mind during the two days and nights to Danville, creeping along in the cold, with a few brief stops for water and hardtack. The coughing ebbed and flowed in waves. Diarrhea broke out just before the change of trains at Greensboro. Stretcher bearers carried the weakest to the next car. Stops at the Haw River and Durham for wood and boiler water gave those who could walk a chance to fertilize the scrub pines that lined the tracks. Soldiers helped those who couldn't walk

14

by propping their asses out the door. It was the best they could do, but some had weakened to the point they couldn't move at all, and the car soon reeked.

A young man with the worst bowels and a deep cough seized up just before dark. He lay quiet all night, and at first light Connor found him cold and stiff, with his eyes open and a weird smile on his face. The old man next to him covered him up with a piece of canvas and led them in the Lord's Prayer.

"He was a fine boy. My sister's youngest. Two older brothers lost at Manassas and Gettysburg. Just wrote her from Danville telling her he was all right." There wasn't a hint of sorrow in his voice, and Connor thought he might have used the same tone talking about tobacco prices. "But I know Cynthia. Bet she didn't believe a word. She had a premonition back last Thanksgiving. Told me she knew Harold would get killed. Her last boy, you see. Said she knew the war and Robert E. Lee would kill all three."

He kissed his fingers then touched the boy's face under the canvas, but without emotion, as if a rote reflex, just like Connor blessing himself at Mass. His body and those from other cars were taken off at Raleigh. The worst cases of dysentery were taken off too. The cars were washed down with a lime solution and a supply of clean water and fresh bread passed out. It helped revive spirits.

Connor gobbled his half loaf of bread down as the horrible memories intruded again. The same as every day. Ever since he had awakened. They were always about Spotsylvania. The image of the Yank boy's head exploding. Pink and gray brain spraying from the back of his skull. The black hole that tore through his eye. The smoke from Connor's rifle muzzle. He breathed hard and strained down as if bracing for a stomach punch. It was the only way he had found to make it stop. But the thoughts came in another wave, trying again to wire him up in a ball. If only he hadn't pulled the trigger, the boy would still be alive. Connor strained down harder until they finally passed.

A freezing rain started up, and he submitted to the suffering along with all the others. He even relished it. Two entire days of continuous icy rain on the run to Goldsboro. It forced its way through so many holes and cracks, top and bottom, as it poured down and sloshed about the car that everyone resigned themselves to staying wet and cold. By the time they changed trains at Wilmington half the car was coughing worse than awful. Every few miles someone else picked it up. By Florence men were hocking up blood and yellowish, red phlegm. Connor remembered Doctor Tradd, a friend of his family, cupping his hands and rhythmically pounding a sick child on the chest until the pneumonia was all coughed out. He remembered what he'd said.

"The fomites can't stand a good hand thumping. Dislodges them from the alveoli most likely. Perhaps a vibratory disorientation in part. No definite scientific explanation, but it works."

Connor tried it on his neighbor, an old man wrapped in filthy wet bandages. He was so exhausted he didn't complain. The soldier next to him sat under a torn blanket tent, his crutch serving as the tent pole. His left leg was amputated above the knee, the stump encrusted in a giant scab that soaked freely in the cold puddle.

"What you doin' there?" His young face jutted out past the edge of the blanket. His eyes darted back and forth between Connors and in the old man's face.

"It's all right, Michael," the old man whispered. "It feels better now."

He coughed out a wad of phlegm and started to catch his breath better. All eyes in the car glanced up. A soldier started thumping his neighbor across from Connor. Then another and another. Pretty soon half the car was taking turns on each other.

"Don't touch me," A dark bearded soldier with a head bandage growled. "Y'all go on and kill each other. Go ahead and break your lungs loose and bleed to death." His right arm was paralyzed, and he coughed so badly he could barely get his words out. "I'll keep mine right inside me, if you don't mind."

But others kept at it most of the night. At dawn, hot soup and cornbread at the Kingstree Station revived those able to eat. The man with the paralyzed arm lay dead. His head bandage had slipped off revealing a jagged hole in its skull that oozed a maroon tar.

"Wouldn't have made no difference. Can't live with a big hole in your head like that-there." The old man coughed up more yellow phlegm and smiled at Connor. "But you got a healin' touch there, boy. Might oughta be a doctor after all this-here's over." He waved his hand at the car full of wounded. "Gonna need plenty more doctors for all this."

"Yes sir," Connor nodded, thinking only of getting home and not wanting to ever see another wounded man.

The dead man's body was taken off with six more from other cars then the train creaked away, clattering all the way to Charleston. Connor dropped his bed roll on the platform. He read the sign. 'John Street Station.' Only then did he really believe he was actually home. He propped his Spencer rifle against the wall while keeping a close eye on it. No telling who might like to trade-up to a repeater. He was glad he had it wrapped up in burlap. He showed his pass to the old officer in charge. The old man's uniform dated back to the Mexican war, and he wore a dress sword as if on parade. Connor waited while he rubbed his long white beard.

"I guess it's all right," the officer nodded slowly. "You going back?"

"Sir?"

"You staying or you planning on going back? After your furlough."

"I don't know what you mean."

"Sherman, boy! He's coming across the Savannah River any time. Militia's going down to fend him off. See?" He pointed to a page from the Charleston Courier newspaper tacked on the station wall. It was printed on old, bleached wallpaper and cut to a single sheet. It read: Militia to form at Stono Ferry. Call for volunteers. All men, 14 to 65. Wounded exempt. All requested to unite. FOR THE GLORIOUS CAUSE.

The old man wagged his finger at Connor. "General Mclaws, General Hardee, Wheeler's boys, Some of Butler's cavalry too. They're all going down. Don't see no reason for you to head back to Lee. Hell, the fight's coming here. Want me to sign you up?' '

"Sir?"

"Your pass, damn it." He leaned closer to Connor and winked at him. "Christ son. You ain't all there, are you? I'll sign your pass so you can stay with the militia. All right?"

"Yes sir," Connor nodded.

The old man rolled his eyes and scrawled illegibly on the paper. "I guess they're taking most anybody now. Even head wounds."

He handed the note back to Connor then hobbled away. One of his legs was three or four inches shorter than the other. He looked back and slapped his hip. "Mexican war. Chapultepec. Left a good piece of this leg

17

in that damn town." He shrugged and limped off towards a group of walking wounded to sign more passes.

Connor hitched a freight wagon across town then another over the new Ashley River Bridge to the Savannah Railroad Depot on the west side of the river. He took the Charleston and Savannah train as far as Adams Run then walked the last five miles. It took him most of the night, but the moon was out for a while, and the sky was clear. But no matter. He could have found his way in the pitch black. He thought about his Uncle Paul who, without the first complaint, had lived most of his adult life blind from a mule kick. The mule had died the next day and Connor remembered his Uncle Paul laughing.

"I wish that old mule had died a day earlier. Might have saved me all the bother. Poor timing for sure."

Connor heard his uncle's laugh plain as day as he walked down the oak-draped road to Younge's Island, and he laughed with him. It was good to be home and close to Uncle Paul even though he was long dead. His parents even longer. Ever since he was a small boy. He hardly remembered either of them but could feel them close by, too, and didn't think it the least bit strange. He made it to the house just before dawn and let himself in the back door.

The place had been vacant since Uncle Paul had died. Their slaves Ezekiel, Jacob, and Rosalie had been sent to Blessing plantation near Beaufort to be safe until the war was over. It was one of his uncle's last wishes. He remembered his uncle telling it was just a matter of time until all the slaves were freed, but the closest he had ever come to admitting slavery was wrong was just before Connor left for Virginia.

"A dismal failure, Connor. That's the best that can be said for it."

It was his Uncle Paul's way of admitting the truth. Connor furrowed his brow as he always did when he thought of slaves, Ezekiel in particular. He knew it was all a huge wrong. So why was he fighting? Why indeed? For slavery? He knew his efforts and those of every Confederate soldier helped keep slavery alive, at least for a while longer, and he knew it was a miserably complicated, tangled, evil mess. Yet it was his world, his heritage. He'd become aware of the absurdity of it all, just as the war started. He'd been fourteen then, but the war had ended all debate. The Yankees had become the enemy, and that was all there was to it.

He rubbed his forehead and tried to push it all away, just as he always had, but he remembered how, before the war, a few socially prominent white men, including Doctor Tradd, had dared suggest freeing the slaves. 'Freedom from within', they called it, and certainly not imposed from outside by Yankee abolitionists. Of course they'd been ridiculed as fools and their calls for 'manumission' to freedom ignored.

Connor knew now that they had been right, but he'd come to realize that despite the evil of it all, he had no chance of fighting against his home, state and every white person he'd ever known. There was no use in even trying. It would be like a salamander trying to fly. Just thinking of fighting for the Yankees was like contemplating desecrating his parents' graves.

He knew others had, though, especially upstate in the mountain areas. But he just couldn't. He didn't have the constitution for it. Fighting for South Carolina, which he felt compelled to do, meant fighting for slavery which he knew was wrong. It was indeed bitter bile to swallow. Maybe he would go to Hell for it, but so be it. He was no traitor. He'd never sensed even having a choice. It was just the only thing to do.

The best way to accomplish it was to bury all intrusive thoughts until the end of the war. It was a task he had long since mastered. The slaves would just have to wait. The war took precedence. Hadn't they waited for hundreds of years? What was another few months? So each day he contorted his brain not to think of the one evil thing that brought it all on. But opening the back door caused it to come flooding back. His protestations rang hollow, and his conscience reared up again.

He fought off tears while he ate the last of his hard-tack, curled up in a blanket from the cedar chest, and slept in a corner on the floor. The smooth, still wood felt like heaven. No mud, no splinters, no cold wind or screeching train cars. He dreamed of Ezekiel being stranded out on a marsh island and trying to get to him by putting planks down to get across the pluff mud and making it half way across then sinking down shoulder deep and not being able to budge. Black mud crept up his neck into his mouth.

"In too deep there, Connor? Like falling through the privy floor ain't it? Sticky black stuff that won't let loose." Ezekiel laughed and tossed oyster shells that splattered mud in Connor's face. "Serves you right, you piece of shit."

He woke up startled at first light. It felt like Ezekiel had just left. He got up and wandered around the old house then went out the front door and had a look at the marsh along the Stono River. He spent the whole morning lying out in the sun. The breeze off the water was chilly but nothing like the damp, cold of Virginia. He opened the old cans of ham and pork in the pantry and found them edible. Uncle's ceramic rice tierce was still full. It crawled with little white worms, but Connor didn't mind. He boiled them with the rice and decided they tasted a bit like turkey gravy. But maybe it was just his hunger talking.

He spent the rest of the day gathering what he needed. Food tins, blankets, knives, boots, clothing, a heavier coat, and Uncle Paul's rubberized poncho. He took his time to build a fire, draw water and take a long bath. Months' worth of grime reluctantly came off. Then he dressed carefully in the thickest shirts and trousers and stuffed extras into his blanket roll. He searched the attic for uncle's revolver and finally found it under the eaves, wrapped in silk, inside a round tin that oozed linseed oil. He cleaned it and counted out the cartridges. Just five. He searched all over but never found any more.

That night he lay on the floor in front of the glowing hearth and slept more soundly than ever, and without a single dream of the Ezekiel. The next morning he walked three miles down the road to Gibson's farm and found Cora Gibson cooking breakfast for her father Poppy Carr and her two little boys, Thomas and Peter. She hugged him and served him a plate of grits and ham.

"It's good to see you come home, Connor." She looked down at the plate of food. "I wish they'd all come with you."

Connor knew her husband had been killed three years before but didn't know what to say, so he ate as fast as he could, and she laughed watching him shovel it down.

"I'm sorry," he said, regaining his manners. "Didn't mean to eat so fast."

She hugged his neck and kissed his head. "You go on and eat all you can. It's good to see you again, all grown up and all."

Her little boys made faces and blew him kisses. He made faces back, and they squealed each time. Connor couldn't remember a better meal.

Afterwards, old Mr. Carr showed him where Uncle Paul was buried. Connor would have found it anyway. It was Uncle's favorite spot. A little point of land jutting out into the marsh just where the creek emptied into the sound and not far from his parents' graves and his grandmother, Mamere's. A white cross carved with Uncle's birds'-feet symbols marked his grave. Mr. Carr raked leaves from around the grave.

"Your Uncle was the only man who could read those." He nodded to the cross and the little squiggles. "Must be something important. He made me promise to print it exactly like that on his cross. Kind of like hieroglyphics. I hope he told you what they mean."

"Kind of," Connor smiled. "It's Uncle's method of telling the future. I don't know the exact translation, but it has to do with time and his belief in steering dreams."

Mr. Carr nodded. "Steering dreams, hey? Well, well. He was always a bit touched after that mule."

He shrugged and walked off to let Connor spend a while sitting on the ground at Uncle's feet until the sun sank below the oak limbs and the temperature dropped. Connor stood up and stretched, startling a flock of seagulls that swooped noisily up with the wind as if laughing at him. He said his goodbyes.

"Time to leave. Got some work to do. I'll come back…when it's over." But deep down inside he wasn't sure he ever would.

The whole world was quickly disappearing, and when it did, all of the past would evaporate with it. But for now he was home, and all around him was as it always had been. Painfully so. The seagulls laughed some more, and he pictured Uncle Paul laughing with them and saying, "Time to address the past and move on, my boy. The world keeps turning. Life goes forward. It's just the one direction. You do know that, don't you?"

Connor knew he was right. He was always right. Virginia was gone for good. He'd never go back. He couldn't. Time to move on. Time to restart his life. Maybe the best thing was not to think about it at all. Just move forward. From this day to the next. Connor knew the old man at the depot made a good point too. Every able-bodied white man would do what he could. Even those with a feeble brain. It just wasn't possible to sit idly by on Younge's Island when Sherman's entire Yank army was poised to tear across the state. He would revive his life by going south and doing what he could. It was of course hopeless, but that actually

21

appealed to him. Nothing could stop Sherman. Lee's army was pinned in the trenches of Petersburg. Old militia and teenage boys with shotguns would be just a nuisance to Sherman, like flies on an elephant. But at least he'd be one of those flies. A little, white fly. He figured having a hopeless cause might even be good for his mind.

As Uncle Paul had always said, "Everyone needs to feel a bit hopeless at one time or another. To keep dreaming of that one last long-shot. The chance miracle that turns life around. It's just that you're more hopeless than most, Connor."

The memory made him smile as he went back to the house and took his Spencer out of the burlap sleeve. He cleaned it thoroughly with turpentine and smeared it all over with some of the linseed oil. He found more in a flask and corked it tightly for later. A well oiled rifle might just save his life. He did the same with the revolver and each brass cartridge. No use dying because of a misfire. He felt the weight of the revolver in his hand and worked the hammer. The cold metal felt wonderful, like his hands had just come alive. His heart raced, and he couldn't help but laugh and thank God.

"To still be alive. To have my whole life in front of me. Thank you Lord."

He fought off another wave of thoughts of Spotsylvania and the Yank boy's head exploding then walked back to the Gibson Farm and found them in the barn. Mr. Carr had already surmised his plan, figuring it was just what he would do if he was ten years younger.

"But seventy-six is just too damn old. The Yanks would just laugh 'till they hurt. And if I bushwhack one of the bastards, what would happen to Cora and the boys?"

He handed Connor a sawed-off, double-barrel shotgun with a fresh, leather, shoulder strap, a bag of paper cartridges of buckshot, and corks to keep the powder dry and shot in the place.

"I use this on rattlesnakes. Might be worth taking with you. I got three more shotguns, if the Yanks come."

Mrs. Gibson slapped the harness down on the tack table. "No. You will not shoot at ANYONE, Poppy. No use getting yourself killed. The boys need you!"

Mr. Carr winked at Connor and whispered. "The boys need me?" He shrugged. "Maybe they need an old goat, maybe not." Then louder to

Mrs. Gibson. "Maybe they need the memory of good old granddad shooting a damn Yank!"

Cora threw up her hands. "There's no use talking to you when you're like this. Give Connor Mac's gelding." Then she walked off towards the house without turning her head.

Mr. Carr shrugged and smiled. "She's right of course, but I won't ever let on. C'mon, let's get Brig." He led Connor to the horse stall. "My son-in-law's horse." Mr. Carr sighed. "The one Mac road to Charleston to enlist with the Palmetto guard."

Connor knew Mac had been killed at Morris Island in '63 just before the big fight at Battery Wagner. Mr. Carr's oldest grandson, Will, too. A year earlier at Secessionville with the Charleston battalion. The little boys had been a late marriage surprise. Now they were all he had besides his daughter. Connor cinched the leather girth and adjusted the saddle on Brig. He made sure his picket pin and lariat were secure. Then he slid his Spencer barrel into one of the leather thimble tubes mounted on the side. Mr. Carr did the same with a shotgun. He noticed a tear in the canvas skirt and wondered how long before he would need another. Then he tied on to extra nose-bags of corn, adjusted the stirrups then checked the gelding's hock and fetlock.

"He stumbled last week crossing the big ditch in the cornfield. Better now though. Not as tender and no swelling."

Connor patted Brig's withers and admired the white shape blaze on his crest. "I'm riding a Brigadier General."

Mr. Carr nodded. "Yep. Hope he brings you luck. He did Mac. He sure loved this horse. Never once wounded while riding Brig." He paused and stared at the gelding's star. "Then he went over to Morris Island without him and got killed the very next day." He shook his head and sighed then led Brig out the barn and let Connor ride him up and down the road for a while. Mr. Carr yelled after him. "Let him run! He'll cut through the woods quicker than a fox."

Connor waved back and gently nudged Brigs flank. The horse bolted across the cornfield and jumped the ditch. Connor felt the wind in his face and yelled with delight, but Mr. Carr had already walked back behind the barn. Brig took off on a gallop across the farm and down the Rantowles road until they'd both had enough. Connor walked him back to the barn and made sure he was wiped down, fed, and watered before he joined them for supper.

They all spent a last evening together talking of the distant past and avoiding any mention of Mac or Will. Mr. Carr gave him a sheathed bowie knife as he bade farewell, but Connor liked his own better, so he accepted it with thanks then hid it back home in the attic. The next morning he rode out before dawn and made it across the Edisto River by way of the rail bridge then all the way to the Ashepoo River ferry before meeting up with a hodgepodge of straggling militia.

They were headed north towards Walterboro, Branchville and Orangeburg, but their aging Colonel couldn't explain exactly why. Connor slipped away after supper and made it across the Combahee River Bridge to the little town of Pocotaligo by midnight. Another day of more cautious riding brought him to a camp of some Georgia infantry spread out behind a flimsy parapet built beside the Charleston and Savannah Railroad. At first glance it seemed like they were facing the wrong direction, but Connor figured maybe their officer knew something he didn't.

He accepted food from a staff sergeant and told him he was on the way to join Wheeler's Cavalry. He had no intention of being cooped up behind a log parapet. Visions of Spotsylvania came flooding back. Better to keep riding south until he ran into Wheeler's boys ...or the Yanks. He knew the layout of the land fairly well and figured he could find his way, since he was sure he'd inherited Uncle's knack for direction. Plus he'd actually been down this way a few times with Uncle Paul and had even studied the maps for him after Uncle went blind. Connor remembered it all like it was yesterday. How Uncle would put his face down close and have Connor trace his fingers around the paper.

"Can't see it, but damn if I don't feel it. I can even smell it. Watch this. Turn that map upside down. Now move back. This here's the Combahee River." He would wave his hand in the air and put his finger down on the exact spot. He did it every time. Connor remembered wondering if it he really could see.

"Only a blind man has a true sense of direction," Uncle Paul would wave his arms and laugh loud enough to startle the crows.

The sergeant nodded wistfully, even pulling out his own little map from his vest pocket and pointing to several red markings. "Wish I could come with you. Slocum's coming across as Sisters Ferry. More of them coming up from Savannah and Hardeeville. Yank regiments stretched out twenty miles or more. We're tending to this end. Most of Wheeler's boys are northwest, from here to Aiken. Covering the river and keeping Kilpatrick, their bastard cavalry chief, in check, if they can."

Connor realized immediately the situation was already worse and more chaotic than he'd imagined possible. The Yanks weren't wasting any time. He rested there for the night and repacked his gear even tighter. At first light he rode off towards Savannah and, by noon, heard gunfire off to the south and again to the west. He rode on towards Blessing plantation. First things first. He would find Ezekiel, Jacob and Rosalie and do what he could for them. Fake passes. Manumission slips. Anything to help. And he'd see Miela.

He had talked to her only two times but remembered every minute, and he knew he was a damned fool to have feelings for a mulatto, slave girl. He laughed at himself. Thank God he'd met Henrietta, Dr. Tradd's daughter. Seventeen, blonde, pretty, with big green-blue eyes and a devilish smile. As wonderful a girl as he could imagine. The one who would some day save him from being such a damn fool. He remembered every minute with her, too. The time she'd come with her father to Uncle Paul's two years ago, before he'd gone to Virginia. He hadn't seen her since but thought about her all the time. Her and Miela. He shook his head at the absurdity of it all. Henrietta, the esteemed physician's blond daughter, and Miela, the mulatto slave girl. One he wanted to be his future wife, the other, a guilty but pleasurable daydream. He could just about hear Uncle Paul laughing.

"You're Catholic all right. Your mother's Rosary sessions have paid off. Nothing's pleasurable that isn't forbidden. Guilt still reigns supreme."

He smiled at the thought, and it renewed him enough to keep riding until dark. He figured he was only about ten miles away. He slept fitfully and dreamed of climbing a crumbling latticework up to Henrietta's room on the third floor and getting almost up to her window ledge when he heard Doctor Tradd yelling from below. He woke up startled. It was first light.

CHAPTER 3 — EZEKIEL DUMONT

Blessing Plantation — near Beaufort, South Carolina

E zekiel stood bare-chested in the shade of the big magnolia tree between the blacksmith shop and the barn. He washed himself from the pump well and carefully put back on his worn, patched shirt and waited until Mr. and Mrs. Blessing rode off in their finest phaeton carriage towards While Hall plantation and the engagement party for Colonel Walters' daughter, Elizabeth. He saw Miela waving goodbye to them from the front porch as the coach clattered across the little bridge over Jeremy creek and turned down the Beaufort Road.

She kept waving to the coach until it disappeared into the far pine woods. It was her way of always giving the whites what they wanted to believe, even though only a fool could remain blind to the fact that all he or any slave ever really wanted was freedom. She made him smile. Miela was good at it.

"Maybe better than me," he whispered to himself, watching Miela's performance.

But her act differed from Ezekiel's. He knew she refused to consider the one absolutely necessity of achieving the Jubilee of freedom.

"Freedom will come only by force," he had told her many times. "Peaceful waiting is just a pipedream."

"Vengeance just brings on more," Miela would always answer.

Ezekiel had learned not to argue his point since it went nowhere with her, and he knew she was right in a way. Anger for vengeance sake would accomplish nothing. It would just bring down the wrath of the whites. But violence for a specific purpose was clearly another matter. Being willing to kill for freedom was not only necessary, it was inevitable. No one, not even Miela, could convince him that any change would occur otherwise or that killing for freedom was wrong.

He walked across the back gardens past the marble fountains and the butterfly shaped ponds sculpted at high cost specifically for Mr.

26

Blessing's prized carp. All paid for with money he'd made last September by selling the chamber maid's four year old daughter, Katrina, to a Louisiana rice plantar named Lannes. A gift for Lannes' daughter, Courtney. A human doll to play with. Miela had witnessed the whole thing and had recounted it for him.

"See, Frances," Mr. Blessing had smiled at homely Mrs. Lannes sitting with Mrs. Blessing on the front porch while he patted little Katrina on her head. "A little one for Courtney to dress and fuss over."

"Thank you, Dubose,"Mrs. Lannes nodded then turned to her daughter. "She's small enough to keep upstairs, Courtney. We'll make a bed for her in the big closet by the hallway, if you like."

Six year old Courtney clapped her hands and jumped up and down. "Can we really? Oh yes. Yes. Thank you, Momma. Thank you. She's so cute." She rushed over to Katrina and touched her arm. "Hi there, little one. I'm Courtney. You'll be coming to play with me. I'll even give you one of my dolls. But I don't have a black one." She burst into giggling, and Mr. Blessing laughed with her.

"Now you do."

Mrs. Lannes smiled and put her hands together as if in prayer, "Thank you, sir. She's truly exquisite. I've never seen a cuter one."

Ezekiel stared at the fat orange and white fish gliding past and thought of Katrina's mother, Elsey, sobbing every night in her cabin, "Not my baby! Not my baby! Jesus Lord! Please! Help me Jesus! Send her back to me. Don't take her Lord. Please don't take her!"

He remembered how she'd drifted off into a trance of choking and chest-heaves before collapsing on the floor surrounded by the other slaves trying to comfort her. It was something he preferred not to think off. Roasted carp on a spit over a bonfire built with Mrs. Blessing's fine furniture was a better thought. Blessing and his son, Malcolm, with their throats cut, even better. He walked to the back steps knowing Miela would come around the side porch and meet him. They would have the evening together until Mr. Blessing returned.

He stopped and admired the flaring bricks that cascaded down from the wrap-around second floor porch. He'd always liked the exquisite workmanship. Quam, the brick mason, sure could lay brick.

Lizette, the downstairs maid, saw him standing there as she came out the pantry door at the end of the porch, rustling quickly along in her starched apron. Ezekiel called out to her.

"How's my ... "

"Shsh!" She put her fingers to her lips, "Master Malcolm's still here," she hissed, pointing to the third floor windows as Ezekiel heard him call.

"Miela! Come here. Now!"

It was the gravelly voice that Ezekiel hated. Mr. Blessing's son, Malcolm, was a bastard like no other. The architect of the Blessing Plantation policy of selling off the father of every child born to a Blessing slave, that is if the father was himself a slave. Plantation princes, of course, weren't bound by any rules at all. Selling the fathers make it easier to handle the mother and child, including their own future sale when warranted by economics, and it eliminated the possibility of an enraged father coming after Malcolm when he raped one of the women, which at one time or another over the years, he'd done to every female slave on the plantation, even the little girls. So all the adult males on the Plantation either were childless like Ezekiel or had been purchased elsewhere and brought in as needed for labor, like George and Santego. Not one slave at Blessing, child or adult, had been allowed to stay with his or her entire family for as long as anyone could remember.

Ezekiel listened to him calling Miela and had to remind himself that killing him now would jeopardize everything. He took a deep breath and held it. His time would come. There was a least some satisfaction in that. Miela appeared at the corner of the porch, and their eyes met. She looked away and slipped inside the drawing room door. There was no use waiting. Malcolm would just get drunker and meaner. The quicker she went to him the quicker it would be over. She knew it nearly killed Ezekiel. He usually walked behind the barn and hammered on the anvil the whole time hoping the noise would irritate the bastard.

She went up the back stairs and slipped into his room. Malcolm lay naked on the bed, fully aroused. She looked away and took off her clothes. She knew better than to hesitate. He loved to burn the inside of her thighs with his cigar if she kept him waiting. He motioned her over. She did as he directed and pleasured him with her mouth then her bottom. Her scarred thighs stung, but he finished with her quickly then kissed her softly on the lips. That was the worst part. To have the beast kiss her with his tongue and have to tolerate it without showing any hint of revulsion. She wondered how he could not know. How could he believe she actually liked it?

"You've got a fine brown ass, Miela. Maybe I'll have a son by you. A mulatto prince. We'll call him Hannibal. He was African you know. But more white than black." Malcolm felt her bare bottom and slipped his hands between her legs. "You like it don't you, Miela. Me up inside you." He patted her stomach then rubbed it more. "Are you pregnant? Kind of firm there." He pushed down hard. "Feels kind of full. Is there a child in there?" He put his mouth over her bottom. "Hello? Son?" Then he burst out laughing.

Miela lay still and waited for him to clean himself in a tin basin then come back to bed to hug her one last time and kiss her on the cheek, like a loving husband might his wife, before dressing and stomping off down the front stairs in his riding boots. Yarrow, the stable boy, had his charger waiting for him to gallop off to the Walters' party.

What Miela didn't know was that Edmond hated almost everything else about Blessing, except Miela's bottom. The sameness as stifling as the humidity. The heat. The insects. The boredom. He wanted nothing more than to live comfortably in Boston or New York, the deliciously cold cities of light and laughter. But of course to live there and be able to enjoy the highest social circles would require a great deal of money, and the damn war had ruined that. Even the waiver to avoid army service by being a large slaveholder was a millstone around his neck.

"A coward," ladies whispered at parties. And they were right.

He'd known it since he was seven or eight. The only two things that helped were alcohol and anger. He had long since learned to stay drunk and mad. It helped him in his quest to be the biggest bastard the state had ever known. His antidote to cowardice. To lie, steal, cheat, and abuse women, although the only women he could demean were white trash and slave girls. Abusing a proper girl meant a duel, something he had always avoided by bombast, alcohol, and playing the ne'er-do -well joker. But it was all too miserable to contemplate. At least without a brandy, that which made all things tolerable. That and Miela. Her soft brown skin, her wonderful bottom, her delicious mouth. He would take her to New York with him whenever this damn war was over. It was his one goal in life.

29

Ezekiel watched Blessing ride off and cursed as well. A bastard of a white man doing as he pleased. He glanced back at Lizette sweeping the back steps. And a black woman doing what she could. The 'loyal' house slave. Or 'servant', as the Blessings would say. She glanced up at him and smiled. Both of them knew the truth. There was no such thing as the 'loyal' slave. Only head-nodding 'yes sirs' and 'no ma'ams'. Enough to satisfy and pacify. Blacks taking advantage of what was given to them in life. Enjoying the little overt freedoms the master allowed such as Sundays off, and the covert ones when they dared, like teaching the children to read. A whipping offense still. Officially, even a capital offense. But winked at by the master.

"We're just teaching the word of God to the little ones," Lizette would smile at Mrs. Blessing and hold up her worn Bible, inscribed on the inside with: 'to loyal Lizette with affection, Mrs. Blessing.' Then she would turn the pages to a particular Psalm, "The Lord teaches obedience and service. Praise Jesus. Praise him."

Mrs. Blessing would always feel a warmth of contentment that she falsely assumed Lizette shared, believing Lizette's many years of 'service' at Blessing meant she must be loyal. "Yes Lizette. God's Holy Word teaches us that the servant shall walk in the Christian grace of the master. Both serving the Lord. His will be done."

Lizette knew exactly what to do. She'd been at Blessing Plantation longer than anyone else but old Cumseh, the withered field hand, having been bought from a North Carolina tobacco plantation when she was thirteen. Her own father had been hung for the charge of plotting insurrection when she was too young to remember, and her mother died giving birth to a sister who died as well. She imagined them all in Heaven and would think of them when dealing with Mrs. Blessing. She would raise up her hands and give Mrs. Blessing the lie that she loved hearing.

"Dear Jesus Lord. Bless this humble servant and give me strength." Mrs. Blessing would walk away with a smile, and Lizette would go teach her daughter, Grace, and all the slave children to read. Her prayer each night was, "God give us strength to throw off our shackles. Show us the promised land of freedom in the Jubilee. Let us walk in the light as free men and free women. Amen."

"Soon enough," Ezekiel would say in return. "Soon enough."

He watched another fancy carp glide past and felt the knot of the bullwhip scars on his shoulder. He smelled the turpentine smoke drifting over from the weed burn. It always calmed him. He nodded back to Lizette and felt an inner warmth. He laughed out loud then shouted over to her. "The smell of fire! The future! It's the calm before the storm!"

"What?" She looked up at him and held out her hands with that perplexed look that he always enjoyed.

He smiled back and knew the truth. Not only was loyalty a myth invented by whites, but violent insurrection was suicide. Any black who valued his own life didn't stay consumed with anger and hate very long. Ezekiel knew no one like that. Even young men like himself, whipped in the rice and cotton fields, managed to channel their anger. It just didn't accomplish anything to stay boiled up with hate. There was one thing about being a slave, a living thing for sale, valued like a horse or cow, a non-person without legal rights in a world beyond his control. It taught him how to survive. How to live in the white world where whim, ignorance, and chance dictated events.

Like all slaves, he had the awful memory of that one day in childhood, around four or five, when suddenly he became aware that he was actually owned. That he was not like the whites. That the same white children, who the day before had been playmates, were now owners. That all the other slaves' mothers and fathers, if they hadn't already been sold off, had no say in where they lived or what happened to them.

He had come to learn that his world was based on whites having the power to sell him off or even kill him anytime they wanted. And to live in such a world required developing an extraordinary ability to do what was required. To maintain obedience and subservience outwardly but to keep freedom alive in heart and mind. To overcome the immediate desire for vengeance, and turn it into watchful waiting.

"The Jubilee will come. God will send his prophet to lead us to the Promised Land," he whispered.

Every slave cabin the world over, outside of earshot of whites, recounted this fact. That freedom would come some day and that to rise up in violence before that time meant certain death at the hands of the whites. Whatever the amount of sweet revenge, it would quickly bring pain and overwhelming loss. A middle of way had to be learned.

Nodding and doing what was necessary, but all along keeping the dream of freedom alive.

Ezekiel found himself smiling. He was a bit different from the others. Not so much by what he had learned, but just by the fact that he was so damn good at it all. He just knew he was the best that ever was. He could charm the lady of the house into giving him a gold watch for his loyalty, knowing all the while that when freedom came he would be gone in seconds, with all the others following right behind. There was just no use in getting all twisted up inside. The white world was just too powerful, at least for now. But even after the Jubilee came and freed his people, he'd be happy to let the whites go. Most of them, anyhow. He would kill only those who had to die.

"Just those who merit death," he repeated slowly to himself over and over while visualizing Mr. Blessing and his son kneeling before him. "Ah, the day of Jubilee. It draws nearer to thee. "

Ezekiel waited until Malcolm had disappeared into the woods then went up the back steps to Miela before she was finished dressing. She turned and, for a second, covered her bare breasts. Tears welled up in her eyes, and she dropped her hands. She sobbed as he embraced her, kissing her tears and whispering in her ear what she had always said to him. What her mother had told her.

"The light." He wrapped his arms around her.

"I know. I know."

Her cotton slip fell off by itself, and his patched shirt and pants followed. He pulled her to him and made love to her slowly. Every gentle thrust was a soothing balm, dissipating the shame and disgust. They shared a delirium of pleasure then kissed each other for a while longer, enjoying the revenge of making love to each other on Malcolm's bed. They said their vows one more time, gazing into each other's eyes.

"To love and honor you always."

"To find you no matter where you go."

They kissed again and stayed in Malcolm's room as long as they dared. It was well after dark when they heard Lizette banging a pot and pan downstairs, the signal she had spotted the coach-lights coming up the road. They dressed quickly and kissed one last time. Miela slipped back downstairs to work in the kitchen, and Ezekiel walked over to the barn for a few hours of solitude and thought.

He knew he could have run off a thousand times. Ever since the Yankees had taken Hilton Head Island and Beaufort. Others had done just that. He didn't begrudge them. They'd done what they needed to do for themselves. But he had to look out for the other women and children who had lost all their family.

He thought back on his own childhood, his only memory of his mother being that of a frail woman on her knees screaming, "Not my son! Not my son!"

Then policemen beating her with long sticks. He could still very clearly see the pain in her eyes and those heavy sticks cracking against her back. He'd watched the whole thing and never made a peep, or so he remembered. Then buckets of water being poured over his head and a husky white man with red hair smearing him with pig grease and tying a blue handkerchief around his neck. Another white women had oiled and braided his hair then made him slip on a new, white cotton shirt. He remembered his sale price of $350 and a gray-haired woman beside him going for $50. A huge muscular man shining with grease and dressed only in a loin cloth was sold for $1600. He remembered the contorted faces around him who groaned and whimpered before being chained to a coffle of twenty slaves being sold in a group.

But why hadn't he done anything? Why hadn't he said a word? If he had prostrated himself and begged, maybe they would have let him stay with her. He knew better, but it was a thought that stabbed at him when he was off guard.

He'd never known his father and had grown up afterwards in Charleston with three other boys, Joe, Lykes, and Horatio and on old woman named Perilo. They lived in the back of the big house on Church Street, in the kitchen -slave rooms, and he'd come to think of them as his family until they all died suddenly of yellow fever when he was nine.

He remembered the doctor coming and kneeling over him in the slave cabin, how the doctor's white cheeks sagged into deep wrinkles and how his temples were covered with brown splotches.

"Come with me son. They've gone to heaven now. You come on with me and let's get you washed up."

Doctor Tradd's hands had been firm but gentle as he pulled him away from the bodies on the cot, and Ezekiel had learned at that moment that a white man could be kind. They only CHOSE not to be. Dr. Tradd had wiped him down with turpentine then washed him from a bucket of water stuffed with oleander leaves.

"It helps keep away the yellow fever," he'd whispered with some urgency. "The fomites can't stand the oleanders. It's a poison, you see. Those leaves would kill you if you ate them all. Thank God it tastes awful or we'd have children dying ..." He stopped and glanced back at the lifeless bodies.

Ezekiel watched the doctor's eyes. There was pain and fear in them. A rich white man with pain and fear? Ezekiel had always thought that the yellow fever was just another whim of the white man, until he saw the fear in Dr. Tradd's eyes. It was a wondrous, joyous revelation to a young slave boy. Whites were afraid! They weren't all- powerful. They could feel pain. They could be hurt. They had weakness. It meant there was hope after all.

He also realized how suddenly this discovery had exploded on him. That something new, something unexpected, something that he had just happened across, could change his whole world in an instant. It was the beginning of his desire to learn, and he went on to learn a great deal, about himself and the world around him. He learned that he was smarter, faster and stronger than most of the other slaves and that he was the one who could do his own chores and someone else's, too, enough so that every white man that claimed him had noticed. Each one had given him special responsibilities.

"Ezekiel. Run go get the horses"

"Ezekiel. Take the wagon up to Peter at the market."

"Ezekiel. Go down to the rice mill and tell Pompey to double thresh the number two tierce."

So on and so on. Ezekiel learned as he went. He had served at one time or another as stable boy, yard boy, carriage footman and driver, body servant to the white princes, carpenter and blacksmith. He learned to keep his eyes open and his mouth shut.

"Knowledge is power," he'd heard Mr. Brockington, one of his previous owners, brag to his son. "Blacks will remain slaves forever because they lack the ability to acquire knowledge. It's their nature you see. Only the white man has the gift of learning. Only he can truly appreciate and understand the workings of the world."

Ezekiel became determined to prove Mr. Brockington wrong. He tried to learn as much as he could every day about anything and everything, having taught himself to read by listening to the Psalms and following along with his finger. It had taken him several years, but it was worth every minute. He learned to use any and every tool and could build just about anything, and he learned to ride as well as any white man, maybe better, having learned by exercising the horses in the stable yard. He even learned how to work a rifle while on a winter hunt at Old Brass plantation. He had fired it, just to get the feel, and pretended it was by accident. The hunting party had enjoyed the spectacle.

"The boy nearly shot himself, Brockington," an older white man had laughed, wiping tears from his eyes. He was dressed in a scarlet jacket and sat comfortably on his fine, Hessian saddle sipping brandy from a pewter flask. "You better keep the guns away from the servants," he kept chuckling. "They'll kill themselves. You nearly lost a fine stable boy there."

Mr. Brockington frowned, "You just never know what they'll do." He wheeled his horse and swung at Ezekiel with his riding crop. "Damn it, Ezekiel. Haven't I told you to be careful with the guns. I'll whip your ass raw if you mess up again."

But Ezekiel knew just what to say. "Yes Mr. Brockington. I done messed up bad. Sorry sir, sorry sir. I promise I won't do it again. I promise."

"Well then", Mr. Blessing tapped his cheek with the riding crop. "You've been warned."

"Thank you, sir."

Ezekiel contented himself with the knowledge that it was just another slave duty to be performed while keeping the faith. It was no different in his eyes than feeding the horses, something that had to be done until the jubilee came. He always reminded himself, "Bide your time and keep a sharp eye. Help the others and do what you have to. And survive." He repeated it every time, and he never let on.

When he was fourteen Mr. Brockington had sold him and sent him away to Mr. Dumont's farm to pay off debts sustained when the cotton prices dropped in '54. But Mr. Dumont had died shortly thereafter, and his brother Paul took over ownership. It mattered not the slightest to Ezekiel. To him it was just another day of slavery. One owner was no

35

better or worse than another. He knew other slaves felt differently, some trying hard to stay with the men they felt were more decent or lenient, others trying to keep wives and children together, begging their owners not to sell one without the other. Ezekiel understood and felt pity for them. But to him, being considered a piece of property was the unforgivable, white sin, and all whites were guilty, no matter what else they did or didn't do. This owner or that made no difference.

He knew he was still a free man inside, and no one could ever take that away from him. He had lived at the Dumont Farm with two other slaves, Jacob and Rosalie, for almost seven years until they had all been sent "for their safety" to Blessing plantation when the war came. Jacob and Rosalie had run off to the Yankees at Hilton Head Island since then, but Ezekiel stayed put. The women and children of Blessing Plantation were his family now.

He tried to make the most of his abilities while waiting for the Jubilee, mostly by handling the horses and dealing with the white men who rode them. He'd even had some little victories that gave him pleasure. Once he had sabotaged the cinch-girth of the saddle of a visiting plantation prince by the name of Manigault, just to see if he could get away with it. The cinch had given way just as he'd figured, on one of the last series of jumps far enough away from the stable to avoid the worst suspicions. The fat prince came up to him afterwards, holding the severed cinch and demanding to know what had happened.

Ezekiel never hesitated. He examined it carefully and chewed on the letter ends. "I can tell how it snapped by the taste of the leather." The other slaves in the stable kept straight faces, and the fat prince didn't know any better. Ezekiel smelled the leather and rubbed sawdust on each severed end. "See what you got there?" He handed it over for the prince to see. "That's a scarlet fire-thorn tear. You rode through some fire-thorn's, didn't you."

The prince frowned, and for a second Ezekiel feared he'd gone too far. But the pink-faced prince had no idea what a fire-thorn was, or if they even existed, so he just nodded, "I'm sure we all rode through brambles. Couldn't be helped."

Ezekiel bowed respectfully, "That's it, all right. The sawdust draws out the sap. Gives it that sassafras flavor. You want a taste?" He held up the torn leather.

"No. That will be all right."

Ezekiel bowed again and went his way, relying on the wisdom, passed down in slave cabins for generations that a slave chewing on sawdust and leather to assist a plantation prince fit in quite nicely. The prince collected himself and walked off trying not to show his embarrassment. He'd expected subservience and a groveling apology, not a horsemanship lesson. And there was a deeper sense of uneasiness that he'd missed something, but he couldn't quite put his finger on it.

Ezekiel's fame grew as quickly as the story spread through the cabin grapevine. Here was a young black man who could outfox the princes. Ezekiel took it all in stride but continued to learn as he went, and he always remained silent. The princes, he knew, associated silence in a black man with ignorance and obedience, and Ezekiel let them.

But his patience had finally paid off. Sherman was in Georgia, just across the Savannah River, and had already made life better. Most of the white men were off fighting, so supervision had slackened off. Fewer questions were asked about slave whereabouts. He knew freedom was close. But he also knew that if he acted too soon, they could still hang him. He would have to wait a little while longer.

In the meanwhile he dressed up every Saturday in a clean shirt to take the rice or cotton to town in the wagon, making sure to talking loudly when they passed any whites. His assistants, Quam and Poins, a field hand, looked scared to death.

"It's a fine day!" He would nearly yell. "A fine day to be alive! Thank you Lord for such a wonderful day! Yeah!"
He knew it irritated the hell out of the white women in fancy dresses who shook their heads and grumbled, "He's certainly not behaving like a slave should."

They would walk off clucking like agitated hens, but as long as Ezekiel didn't cross that invisible line, he knew they'd leave him be. Old Titus, the gray-haired slave, had it right all along,

"Don't never look straight at a white woman, and for God's sake don't never touch one."

Ezekiel smiled. It was sound advice that had served him well. But the day was coming soon when all the old rules would evaporate. The Jubilee wasn't far off. With the Yanks in Hilton Head and Beaufort and Sherman in Savannah, his duty now was to protect the slaves who couldn't protect themselves. The Blessing's could pretend all they wanted. Word had spread in the slave cabins that the great Sherman, the blue general, Lincoln's anointed one, was soon coming.

"Freedom is near at hand," Lizette sang out in her cabin that night. "The whites are on the run. When they leave, we'll move into the big house and have us a fine home." She clapped and danced in a circle. "We'll make Mrs. Blessing cook for us every night."

Ezekiel laughed with her but had his own plan. Keep them together, arm them if possible, and find the right piece of land. Land that could be purchased when they were free. Big enough for a few hundred people and defended by armed black men. Families who could then live beholden to no one and free of the whims of the white princes. His mind had been swirling on the problems day and night. How to keep them together. How to get the land. He had no definite answer but had a confidence born of twenty four years of survival in the white world that he could do it. He had to. The memory of his mother on her knees would be avenged someday. But first he had to make a safe haven for his people.

He repeated his daily prayer as he coiled up in his blanket. "God grant us time to find the Promised Land. Then we'll live free in the light."

CHAPTER 4 — LUKE CONNELEY

Sisters' Ferry
45 miles north of Savannah, Georgia, on the Savannah River

From his perch on the highest limb of a towering oak, Luke could see the column of wagons emerging from a thick pine woods to the north, stretching far down the Sisters Ferry Road, and disappearing around the bend towards the Savannah River. Rows of scorched chimneys flanked the column as burning shacks in the pine woods marked its forward progress. His regiment, the 137th New York, waited in a cornfield on the bluff overlooking the dark river, now covered in swirls of vapor rising into the cold air. Luke watched it roll by in freshet, a never ending torrent sprawling through the water oaks, tupelos and cypress trees that covered the far bank.

The road behind them swarmed with blue-coated troops by the thousands. Their clothes were tattered but freshly washed, courtesy of their recent rest in Savannah. Haversacks bulged with fresh rations and extra cartridge boxes, and their Henry rifles shined in the sun. He smiled watching them move up the road. God help South Carolina.

He knew every regiment felt the same. South Carolina was the last state to conquer. North Carolina would fall like a domino. Grant had Virginia by the balls. South Carolina stood alone. It was the last vestige of rebellion. These blue-clad soldiers would conquer it and go home at last. It was the thought on everyone's mind.

His friends Dave and McMahon sat resting on the side of the road calling out to the other regiments marching by one after another, all about to be unleashed.

"Don't you go messing with South Carolina, now!" Dave smiled and wagged a finger at them. "They've promised to behave."

Men laughed back and shouted obscenities. McMahon stood up, opened his fly and thrust out his member, "I'm gonna marry me a Carolina girl."

The column laughed and cheered, and a soldier yelled back,"White or black?"

McMahon shrugged, "Don't make no difference. How about one of each?"

"Sure it matters," Dave yelled above the laughter. "White girls are easier to catch in the dark," He grabbed his crotch and shook it at the blue columns as some of Kilpatrick's cavalry rode past pulling their 12-pounder guns.

Dust rolled up through the trees like incense. Luke covered his mouth and aimed his Henry at a water oak on the far bank. He caressed the trigger guard. He lovingly wiped the barrel with his coat sleeve. His rifle stock snuggled up against his chin willingly. It had come alive since being issued in Chattanooga. He knew it was nonsense, but others told him the same story. Lots of men called their rifles by name. Luke looked down the barrel. He had never consciously named his, but one morning it just happened. Theodoric, or 'T' for short. He smiled. It was all so ridiculously silly, but T had become a friend who could read his deepest thoughts, and he knew if anything happened to him, he would grieve as if he'd lost a brother.

He admired the shiny lever action as he watched the companies crossing one at a time on a pontoon bridge. Smoke rose from the pines above the far bank and farther inland. Cheers swept the bluff again and again. He whispered into T's barrel.

"An army of good, blue-coated Union men, each with a T or one of his brothers. The rebs will melt like ice in the sun."

"First flames in South Carolina," McMahon yelled from below." The beginning of the end."

"Damn! Leave some for us!" Dave griped. "Don't burn it all just yet. We've got matches to." He relieved himself against the trunk. "And remember, the rebs promise to behave!"

Wagon after wagon rolled past pulled by teams of six mules or horses, each wagon filled to the top with crates of hard tack, sugar, salt, coffee and hundreds of boxes of Henry cartridges. Ambulance wagons followed. Most were empty, but a few men sat under the flapping canopies appearing no sicker than his friend Dave who had coughed and hocked all the way from Atlanta. But no one was griping about shirkers today. It was the first sunny day in the week, a blue sky, good

Union-man day, and a perfect day to begin the tromp through South Carolina.

Luke listened to the others laugh and cheer. Like everyone, he trembled with the anticipation of being let loose in South Carolina. The wink and nod had come from the top, from 'Uncle Billy' Sherman himself. The word had been passed. "All will be fair game in South Carolina."

Not that they hadn't laid waste to Georgia. But South Carolina! Everyone wanted to lay into it in the worst way. He knew they would destroy everything they passed, just like they'd done in Georgia. Railroads, depots, bridges, houses, barns, even whole towns. All would be wrecked or burned. South Carolina would become a wasteland. And it served them right.

"To cause all this," he whispered again to T. "To drag us all this way through four years of war. They'll get exactly what they deserve. They'll definitely reap the whirlwind."

He thought of Elmira, a thousand miles north, so different, and so much better. Was it part of the same planet? He remembered his grandfather telling him the story of the meeting at Teal's Tavern when his father was just a boy, and how the townspeople had decided to name the collection of villages at Newtown Creek, where it emptied into the Chemung River. He couldn't have been more than five or six, but he could still smell his grandfather's tobacco breath as he heard the story for the first time, one that he'd heard a thousand times since.

"Mrs. Teal's daughter, Elmira, came running in, knocking over a whiskey bottle," his grandfather would laugh, with his red face and yellow teeth, and he remembered thinking he could actually see the tavern in his grandfather's sparkling blue eyes. "Mrs. Teal yelled out, Elmira! Elmira! Elmira! And that whole room lit up with smiles. So Elmira it was. Tommy O'Kane said it was fate. And a lot of whiskey."

A thick blanket of nostalgia covered him with thoughts of the Chemung River, 'The Mighty Chemung', as his father always referred to the rocky river that flowed ice cold through town. His mind drifted to the thick snow that covered fields and draped the elms and maples and made good sledding with friends on Sullivan's Hill where his grandfather had fought under old General John Sullivan against the British and

41

Iroquois. Luke could see his father pointing to a big maple tree and reciting the same lines once again.

"Your grandfather shot that big Seneca brave right there, just as the bastard fired his flintlock. Missed him by a whisker." His father would always put his hands on his hips and nod as if grandfather was standing there counting coup.

He thought of his father and the trips with him in the warmth of spring and summer up to Seneca Lake, with the boats full of coal and lumber for the big cities in the east being pulled slowly along by mule teams on the well-worn path to the Chemung Canal. He felt the sun in his face and relished the memory until Dave called to him from below and laughed.

"What are you smiling about now? Daydreaming again? Don't fall out of that tree for God's sake!"

"Just thinking of home. The work I used to do with my father." He struck a match and tossed it down at him.

"Work, my ass. Like what?" Dave asked, fidgeting as always and looking not particularly interested.

"Hauling shingles and boards mostly. Coal for a while. But we were broke by '54. Sold the flat-boats to salt-diggers in Watkins. Been coughing up coal dust ever since." He hocked out a wad of phlegm for Dave's inspection. "See that? I'll never shovel coal again"

"We all got a cough, Luke." Dave yawned again, hocking out a wad as Luke climbed down. "It aint coal dust neither, so stop your whining."

"Stuff it up your ass."

"Screw yourself,"

Dave hocked again at him as they rejoined their company, moving up in the column towards the river where hawsers for the pontoon bridge stretched from the high bluff on the Georgia side to a smaller one across the river.

"They say it's called 'Two Sisters Bluff'," McMahon slapped his back. "And I bet those sisters are waiting for us, right over yonder."

"They should've run when they had the chance," Dave snorted. "Now thet'll get humped by good Union men."

"Maybe they want a good humping," McMahon laughed.

Luke felt it too. The rebs deserved exactly what was coming. What a damnable state. All the death and misery they'd caused. Damn them!

42

Damn them all to hell. He felt the veins in his neck pulse as a flotilla of small snags drifted down river with one huge pile of logs behind. Men hurried to get across the pontoons as the logs hit at mid-river and jammed under a section of the bridge knocking two men into the freezing water. The swimmers angled to the far bank, and both made it, dragging themselves up through the cypress stumps exhausted.

The pontoon bridge groaned and trembled. Ropes snapped overhead like cannon shots. The bridge parted in the middle and a dozen more men went into the water struggling to hold on to the free pontoons as they were swept down river around the bend. Officers called out orders for scouts to go find them, but the work kept right on. No one wanted to end up down river alone. They all knew reb cavalry lurked in the far woods waiting to pick off stragglers. The 137th waited its turn then crossed one company at the time. The pontoons bounced and swayed, and men stumbled along. More pontoon wagons, with their folding frames, canvas covers, anchors and chains, came rumbling up the road, looking like great tortoises being pulled by teams of horses. Companies of men unloaded them at the bank and manhandled them through the tupelos. Each was rowed out and anchored, and the long ropes passed along until finally a bridge again stretched across the river.

It was nearly dark before they finished and more regiments could scramble across. The river surged beneath, and all eyes warily looked up river for the next large snag. Men sang out as they touched the far bank. Knee-deep mud never felt so good. They were across the Savannah River and into South Carolina. Nothing could stop them now, and the only sign of the rebs was a warning note tacked to a tree on the bank and then passed down the line. Luke read it to the others.

"Yankees, you better leave this country. France and England have recognized the Confederacy. Lincoln is ordered to withdraw his troops from our soil."

The men howled.

"By God, he's ordered!"

"France and England, no less!"

Men grabbed at it and tore the note into bits, snatching up the pieces and stuffing them into their pockets for souvenirs. Cheers rose along the column as the words spread.

Luke laughed with them, "President Lincoln will be troubled by this."

McMahon nodded, "But he's got to follow orders. France and England, by God! They've got Kings, don't they?"

"Yes, they do. Queens, too."

"Well, the rebs shouldn't worry," Dave smiled. "We won't bother their soil. Just everything on top."

Lieutenant Whitesell rode past. "Just keep moving boys," he called out to his sergeants. "And remember! A healthy regiment is a fast regiment. The best diet in the world is living off the land. And no latrine dysentery! Let's go! Let's go!"

Luke quickened his step. Like everyone else he felt his heart race faster. "God help the southrons!"

Dave hocked out another wad and choked, "It's too late for God to help them."

McMahon slapped his back as Lieutenant Whitesell's spurred his horse up through the tupelos and yelled back at the column. "Uncle Billy says the forage liberally from the countryside. And I for one plan to take him at his word!"

Luke watched him cut through a thicket of young willow trees as men cheered all around. He felt a deep sense of pride and respect, knowing how the Lieutenant had worked his way up through the ranks by merit, like most of the officers in the 137th. He'd been wounded at Gettysburg leading a company at Culp's Hill and now was the first officer in the regiment to get across the Savannah River.

The rebs had the reputation for better officers earlier in the war, but Luke felt sure that the 137th had officers who could hold their own with anyone. Wasn't Uncle Billy's army the one alive and well and marching through South Carolina? Where was old Stonewall Jackson now? Dead, buried, and worm bait, he smiled, and it served the damn bastard right. Him and all the southron gentry who were willing to sell their souls just to keep the black man in chains.

Luke knew the regiment wouldn't let a day go by in South Carolina without destroying something. The men knew an opportunity when they saw one. Everything they came across would burn, and Luke was glad of it. They'd bring the bastards to their knees, for good, then they could go home Home! He closed his eyes and was there with his father and Uncle Jim, waiting to board the train with the other recruits.

"Better watch yourself down there," Uncle Jim whispered. "Rebs are bushwhacking devils. Hate the blacks, hate the North. Might even hate themselves. And they'll shoot a good man just because they can. Watch yourself. Don't go getting killed or coming back like this." Luke remembered how he pulled on the empty sleeve pinned across his chest. The arm lost at Bull Run. How his uncle's face tightened as he shook the stump. "Bastards. They're all Goddamn bastards."

Luke looked back at the regiments coming up through the cypress, oak, and tupelo bogs and nodded, "Good Union in will pay them back, don't you worry."

"Don't worry?" McMahon smiled. "Damn, Luke. You got to get your mind right. You're the worst daydreamer I've ever seen."

"Good Union men will pay them back!" Dave chanted, and the others took it up.

"Pay them back! Pay them back!"

Luke laughed with them. He knew they were right. He was definitely a daydreamer. But thank God for it. His daydreams had always helped him, and now more than ever as he waded along through miles of cypress swamp, hip deep in the cold black water then through thick woods of gum trees and water oaks where grassy verges marked the course of the flooded roads.

"Should have brought the canoes," Dave griped, teeth chattering.

"Tippecanoe and Tyler too?" McMahon laughed, rubbing his frozen hands.

Jack, the new boy, waded past him shivering. McMahon thought he was just cold, and Jack was glad to let him think it. He didn't want to let up on how jittery he felt, and how he hated every body of water, even the knee-deep streams that made him nauseous with fear. The bobbing pontoons over the river still had him panicked. And that ocean! He felt his stomach turn at the thought of it.

What bad luck to have been drafted into the last batch of 137th Regiment replacements just in time to be sent from Elmira by train to Brooklyn then by steamer to join the regiment in Savannah. They were the very first replacements to have come by sea. He knew he'd rather have marched a thousand miles than to have been on that ocean with water as far as he could see. His knees still shook just thinking of it. He could distinctly remember the decks rocking back-and-forth, even worse than the pontoons, with the breakers coming over the rails and trying their best to grab him, and the horror of knowing there was nothing solid beneath him for miles. It had all brought back the sickening memory of his father trying to teach him to swim off the pier at the Brooklyn Navy Yard.

He'd been just five or six but distinctly remembered how buoyant he'd felt the first few moments in the salt water, and how easy it had been to stay afloat. Then how his father had untied the rope and how he'd drifted with the current and couldn't get back. Then going under water into darkness. The pain in his lungs and the barnacles scraping his stomach and legs. Then a stranger pulling him to the pier with his father furious at him for not being able to get back by himself and forcing him back into the water to nearly drown again.

It had all come back painfully fresh on that damn troopship. Something so immense as the ocean could certainly drown a man at its whim. He tried to shake it off, but his heart still raced at the thought of possibly being ordered back on a transport. He knew he'd just have to desert. Thank God Uncle Billy had decided to march them home. He thought again of his father and tried to remember something else, something decent, but nothing much came to mind except when the family had moved to Elmira when he was ten and his father letting him handle the mules for three weeks all the way across the state. Three weeks without a whipping. The best time in his whole life.

He'd been glad to join the Army to get away from him, and the only thing he hadn't liked so far was that damn ocean. By the time the ship had reached Savannah, he'd lost fifteen pounds vomited over the side. The others teased him when he'd kissed the ground at the end of the gangplank, but he didn't care. The idea of marching a thousand miles back home didn't bother him a bit, either. Just the damn water.

"How long does this swamp go on for?" His voice cracked.

McMahon laughed, "Could be the nicest part of at South Carolina for all we know."

"Most likely," Dave agreed.

Luke looked back at Jack's pained face and winked at him, "I doubt even southrons like to live knee deep in filth."

46

Jack tried to smile but could only grit his chattering teeth. Luke shivered too, but he didn't care. He realized he was truly headed north for the first time in four years. The retreats from Virginia and the shadowing march into Pennsylvania following Lee's army were long gone. He could feel a weight lifted and could sense it in the others too. They were headed home now, and no reb army could stop them this time.

All the past years fights blended together in a swirl of smoke and noise. Chancellorsville, Gettysburg, Lookout Mountain, Missionary Ridge, Kennesaw Mountain, Peachtree Creek. Then Atlanta and the march to the sea. Now South Carolina and home. He smiled and felt rejuvenated. Not even wading through these black swamps could dampen spirits now.

He nudged McMahon, "We're headed north. Back home!"

"Damn right. Just a straight line. That a way. Home! Home!"

Dave took it up, then others, "Home! Home! Home!

"Be quiet!" Sgt. O'Keefe, the commissary sergeant, fumed. He came up alongside, with the knock-ribbed company mule, Jefferson Davis, loaded with pots and pans. "Mr. Jefferson don't like your yelling. He's been ornery this morning. Worse than usual. Gave him turnips and yams like always, but he's not appreciative. Not one bit. Just like a reb, ain't ya, Mr. Jefferson."

"Home! Home! Home!" The men kept on as the mule twitched his ears convulsively.

"See that?" The sergeant yelled back. "Mr. Jefferson always twitches like that when he's riled. He'll bite me in a minute or two"

"He's been riled since Chattanooga," Luke observed.

Sgt. O'Keefe grinned, "That's a fact. If I didn't love you, Mr. Jefferson, you'd be supper tonight. You're lucky the boys ain't hungry just yet. Not after all that food in Savannah."

The mule twitched again and nipped at him. Sergeant O'keefe swatted him on the nose and laughed, "You're a bushwacking reb mule for sure, you bastard."

Luke laughed with the others and trudged on though more swamps until dark then bedded down in a patch of soggy pines. He slept fitfully until reveille at 3 am, but marching again all the next day didn't bother him a bit. He knew the truth of it. Resting in camp wouldn't bring them home and out of this God-forsaken southland. Every day, every hour's march, brought them closer to the end.

Mr. Blessing sat in a wicker chair in the front, brick courtyard facing the cotton fields, with Miela standing behind him. Her duty was to be present for his afternoon Madeira. She didn't actually have to do anything, but he required her attendance. She watched a wagon inch down the road at the far end of the big fields. It moved almost imperceptibly. A canvas tent draped over its rough, pine frame quivered and swayed with each step of the mules. Even at that distance she recognized Ezekiel. The way he slouched over the seat with one leg cocked up on the sideboard. His little way of declaring his freedom by refusing to do what the overseer, McCallister, demanded. She remembered McCallister fuming at Ezekiel just the week before.

"I can't stand a slouching wagon driver. You want more bull on the back?"

But he had been bluffing and Ezekiel knew it. McCallister had whipped Ezekiel dozens of times before. His back looked like a pile of black snakes all twisted together. Scars upon scars. The last whipping nearly killing him, ripping an artery tangled in the scar tissue. McCallister knew Ezekiel would never give in, and it left him with an unpleasant choice. Either tolerate his behavior or kill him. Now Ezekiel was slouching down even further, turning the knife just a little more.

McCallister watched from the blacksmith shop and shook his head in disgust, muttering to himself angrily. "If there were just one other slave who could do what Ezekiel can do, I'd kill him in a second."

The bastard was good though, he had to admit. Never a runaway, always delivering the rice and cotton on schedule, always making sure the wagons and mules were properly cared for. Never sassing Mr. Blessing and always showing proper respect and courtesy to his guests. Just that one damn annoyance. That damn slouch. And gumption to die for it, the bastard.

Ezekiel smiled back at him as McCallister walked off towards the row of a slave huts, but McCallister pretended not to see. Ezekiel knew he'd

49

go straight to Elsey's cabin and that she'd do anything to protect her six year old son, Yarrow, a child who was full of life and energy and as inquisitive as could be.

Elsey knew McCallister could talk Mr. Blessing into selling him any time. To the sugarcane plantations in Louisiana like he had her daughter, Katrina, and their father, Cinder, five years ago. So she never considered saying no to his demand. The agony of losing Katrina still tore at her every day. She'd learned that the only way she could go on was to stifle all but the briefest thoughts and memories. So much so that she'd become a different person. No longer so talkative or inquisitive, and except for rare occasions, totally serious. The other adult slaves understood, but Yarrow wondered why his mother never smiled.

So every day McCallister would walk to her shack, and she'd stop whatever she was doing and lay back on in her plank bed. She was so used to it she almost felt nothing at all. Tolerating his sweating body on top of her and his thrusting between her legs. All she ever thought about, while he was humping her, was her son.

Miela stood just behind Mr. Blessing watching McCallister disappear behind the row of oaks heading to Elsey's shack and Ezekiel still slouching and holding the mules' reins as the wagon inch closer, taking twenty minutes to crawl across the big cotton fields past the oak trees and the white fence leading to the brick, sugar-house for grinding cane with its tall brick chimney and deep open hearth and iron vats for boiling the sorghum. She heard a big 'boom' in the distance and knew immediately what it meant.

Mr. Blessing's poor hearing caused him some doubt for a few seconds, but he turned and saw all the slaves looking west. Then another boom and another. Mr. Blessing watched Miela count the cannon shots on her fingers. An invisible heaviness draped over his shoulders as he looked up at her face and saw all he wanted for the rest of his life. Her skin glowed a perfect brown in the afternoon sun, and he retreated into a most delicious daydream. To escape with her. Just to take her and run. To leave Henrietta and Malcolm. To leave Blessing plantation. Just to get away. But the heaviness held him back. His legs wouldn't move towards her. His arms wouldn't rise to touch her. The cannon boomed on and on. He pictured the slaves nailing him in a coffin. Each boom another nail.

Miela saw his head bow down as if he'd fallen asleep. Then her heart surprised her again. She actually felt sorry for him. Lizette the downstairs maid had always told her she was crazy.

"You feel sympathy for Blessing? The man who owns us all? Like we're a bunch of cows or something?" Lizette would lift her top lip and make a sound like a cornered possum, a half hiss, half growl, then shake her head, thump the oak counter with a big wooden spoon. "It ain't right. And I ain't no cow."

Miela knew Lizette and the others confused her sympathy with weakness, with being an Uncle Tom. She knew for certain she was neither. She just had abilities that the others lacked. There was no conceit, though, just an appreciation of being selected for such a precious gift.

She watched Blessing slowly stand as if suddenly much older then trudge across the courtyard towards the house. She knew he wouldn't last much longer. His world was ending, and the grim reaper firing his guns in the distance warned her that any feelings of sympathy for him had a limit. She listened to the guns, wondering how he had lived an entire life in such a lie. A lie that was about to meet a violent end.

Mr. Blessing's legs felt so heavy he could barely make it up the flaring bricks of the front steps to the veranda overlooking the avenue of oaks. He rested against the freshly painted banister rail and watched the sun dart in and out of fast-moving, puffball clouds. He could have sworn one distinct ray darted down on Meila's face as she came up beside him listening to the cheer coming from the slave cabins as the guns fired on and on in the distance. Maybe God would grant a miracle.

He whispered a prayer, "May the merciful, all powerful Lord take Miela and me to a safe place. Perhaps to Charleston, then….later…. to heaven. Take us to live safely forever. Dear God, shine the sun's rays on her face as a sign. Please, take us Lord."

He said the Lord's Prayer as fervently as he could, but the sun beam moved away from Miela's face, and Blessing felt a cold wind cut its way through the oaks then across the courtyard onto the porch. Slaves danced in the fields and the children outside the huts did somersaults. He thought of his revolver. Damn all this. I'll just shoot myself. If God won't let me have her, why should He punish me further? But he knew it was a mortal sin. Having a conscience was a miserable thing. But what about the Yankees? What about losing Blessing? Losing Meila? God did allow for special circumstances didn't he? He remembered Preston Limehouse being buried in St. Philips Churchyard after hanging himself. Reverend Thomas had said, "God understands that his pain from rickets was unbearable."

Well then! His hands gripped the banister as he watched Miela's every move. If bone pain were reason enough then this awful pain would surely suffice. How could any physical pain be worse? God would just have to decide, right then and there. If the sun drops another ray down on her head, I'll know what to do. He watched her closely as the patchy clouds let loose a barrage around her. Light rays bombarded the banister rails. They landed all around her, some just inches away. But none on her. He knew God was denying him.

His stomach turned sour. Using the pistol was wrong. But by God he would do it! Unless God delivered what was due. His rightful compensation. To stand as a pillar in the Episcopal Church. To have tithed his entire life. To have served as an elder and given counsel for all those years. It must be worth something now. Worth enough to be either rewarded with Miela or forgiven for this one final act if God truly rejected him.

He stood there watching her and convinced himself it wouldn't even be a selfish thing. It would be the best thing for everyone. Hadn't he brought out the best in her? Allowing her to continue her reading. Even teaching her some mathematics, astronomy and physics. Showing her the world of Charleston. The finest events of high society. As a slave, yes, but still ... To be able to see it all. Hadn't it been his gift to her? God had to let him bring her with him now. He had to. Tears welled up as he thought of the revolver.

He let go of the banister and went inside through the french doors to his library, opening the glass door of his book cabinet and picking out volume 1 of Herodotus. He opened the book and looked at his beautiful double barrel derringer hidden in a carved out hollow. He opened the sliding breach to make sure the two shiny copper cartridges were ready. His hands trembled so hard he felt suddenly scared that he might fire it accidentally.

What am I thinking? Kill Meila? You fool. He knew he couldn't do it. Even if God allowed it. He just couldn't. He would have to suffer the pain of seeing her leave. But his hand had already picked up the pistol. He walked back out onto the veranda and rubbed the shiny barrels, feeling the world spinning beneath his feet. He sat down on the joggling board and held the pistol up with both hands. He thought of Mayan and Aztec human sacrifice and smiled. Such nonsense. Their priests holding up the sacrificial child. He looked at the barrels and knew it was pure madness. Then Miela stood in front of him.

"Miela!" He bobbled the pistol, and it fell on the porch floor "Watch out!" He cringed, waiting for it to go off, but Miela kicked it down the porch. It slid under the banister rail, over the side, down into the azaleas. "Mr. Blessing!" She touched his chin with her fingers. "Stop it!" Then she slapped him harder than he'd ever been slapped in his life.

He stood up rubbing his jaw. Blood rushed to his face in a big red whelp."Miela!" Tears flooded his eyes, and his voice left him.

Miela walked away and called to Mrs. Blessing who, as usual, sat upstairs in her sewing room engrossed in embroidery, oblivious to the world. "Ma'am! Ma'am! Mr. Blessing took a fall. He's bumped his head!" Mrs. Blessing hurried down the staircase, and Miela led her over to him and told another lie. "He must have fallen coming up the steps. For a few seconds he didn't even know who I was."

"My dear Dubose!" Mrs. Blessing hovered over him, trembling.

Miela helped her get him firmly wedged it in his leather chair in the book-lined study then gladly went for Santego, the house slave, so he could fetch Doctor Smoak from Pocotaligo. It would take all night, but she rounded up Daphne, the poultry minder, as she came in from the fields and had her stay in attendance while she went round through the back door and into the bank of azaleas beneath the veranda to find the little pistol. She didn't want Blessing to retrieve it. No telling what he might do. And it was a death sentence for a slave to get caught carrying a gun. Miela found it and threw it far under the house.

"Let it rest with the snakes and spiders," she smiled, walking quickly to Daphne's hut where she knew Ezekiel would meet her. "But Dear God, what a day. Not a Yankee in sight, and Blessing's world is already flipping over itself. Thank you Lord."

Gray-haired George, the blacksmith, was in Daphne's hut sitting on a cot. A patch work quilt lay folded neatly over layers of torn and frayed blankets. A low plank ceiling radiated heat from the fire in the brick hearth, and his leather soles steamed in the heat. On the rough table next to him lay a wedge of brown bread and a piece of cheese. An open kettle bubbling oily stew rested on the flames. A thick coating of whitewashed newspapers insulated the plank walls.

He liked Daphne, and wished he was thirty years younger. But even if she thought of him only as a kindly old man, he was still quite happy to visit her cabin when he could. He liked to imagine she looked like his mother but couldn't remember anything of his childhood except that he'd been sent off on a big boat to Blessing Plantation when he was six. He wasn't even sure from where.

Miela came inside and sat down in the pine rocker decorated with hardened wisteria vines. She snuggled on to a thick pad of beaver pelts. George handed her a cup of sassafras tea which he carefully poured from a small kettle propped at the edge of the fire.

"McCallister gave us whiskey today. Said he wanted us to have a drink with him," he said, pouring himself a cup of tea. "Everybody did but me. I just pretended to,"

"What on earth did he do that for?" Miela smiled, listening to the boom of guns in the distance. "Must be afraid of the Yankees." She smoothed her hair with a wooden comb.

"Said he was leaving in the morning. Moving his boys somewhere upstate." He stared at the plank wall and flicked a finger at the door.

"Because of the Yankees all right."

"Well that's good, isn't it?" Miela watched George's face twitch. She knew he was holding something back. "What else did he say?"

George shook his head. "He didn't say nothing else. He didn't have to." He took a deep breath. "But I know he won't leave empty-handed. He'll take all of us with him. I just know it."

"All of us? To be sold off?"

"Yep," George sighed. "I think so."

He stared at her, and the squint of his eyes said it all. Freedom might be just down the road, but they weren't safe just yet. The next few days would tell.

CHAPTER 6

SHERMAN OUTSIDE BEAUFORT, SOUTH CAROLINA

on the road inland into South Carolina

General Sherman paced up and down the muddy Beaufort rood talking incessantly. His hands ran in and out of the pockets of his old field officer's coat like fidgety field mice playing in their holes. His rusty beard glowed bright cinnamon in the sunlight filtering through the pines. His one spur clinked in rhythm as he hurried restlessly back-and-forth spewing out orders and chewing furiously on his unlit cigar which trembled with every word. So did the entourage of officers following along just behind. He stopped suddenly and called out to no one in particular, "Good Union men! Best soldiers in the world! Ready at any time for a march, a fight, or a meal. Whichever!"

He laughed then chomped back down on the cigar and strode off even quicker, shedding caked mud from his trousers with every step and pursued by a dozen couriers who dismounted from steaming, sweat drenched horses with fresh reports. Each holding out their piece of paper for him to snatch, read, and write a reply in one quick nervous twitch. He spun around and reeled off a string of orders that sent them all racing off again then called for his horse, Sam, a black gelding with a white forelock and white spots on his haunch and withers, who had the habit of walking as fast as Sherman talked. He jumped up into the saddle tapping out a nervous tattoo on the pommel. Sam responded instantly. Most of the other staff officers were forced into a trot which they knew Sherman and Sam could keep up for hours. It meant for a long, weary day, but every one of them knew they were very lucky. They'd been granted a gift from the Almighty. To be on the staff of the great William Tecumseh Sherman. Tecumseh, Shawnee for 'shooting star'. An appropriate name for the General as far as far as all of his staff were concerned.

They all loved everything about him. His tall, lean and disheveled appearance, his reddish brown hair, piercing black eyes, wrinkled face and sharp nose poking out from a droopy felt hat. A nose for tactical genius and decisive action. The kind of action that helped careers advance, which was a most important thing for all of them. Serving with 'Uncle Billy', as the men called him, was the path towards it. To enact his decisions, to carry out his direct orders and be part of the greatest conquest in American history. But only a few of them knew a secret that they used to their greater advantage. That Uncle Billy loved Charles Dickens, especially *The Pickwick Papers*. A copy circulated among a tight clique. Each privileged officer in it being able to quote a select paragraph or two as Sherman listened, amused each time.

He knew they were doing it to impress him. Some to gain favor, but some just because they loved him as much as the rebs love their dead Stonewall Jackson and Jeb Stuart, God forgive their rebel souls. He smiled each time he thought it. He didn't feel any sense of gloat, just warm pride for the men in the ranks. They did truly love him. He belonged to them. He was their Uncle Billy, the best general in the whole horrible war because he always did his best to avoid sacrificing their lives needlessly. They figured Uncle Billy could outflank the devil himself and vouched that they would follow him to Hell and back or anywhere else.

They even loved the rumors about him. That Uncle Billy didn't like his boyhood nickname 'Cump' and that he'd fought Stonewall Jackson at West Point over it and whipped him badly. That he was a genius even back then and that he'd been first in his class. The way he'd torn through Reb General Joe Johnson in Georgia was proof enough for his men. They'd all heard another rumor, too. That he hated Indians, tolerating only those who had enlisted in his army. There was a persistent story of his action in the Seminole wars in '41. How he led his men fifty miles through swamps just to massacre a certain village. What the Indians had done to deserve it, no one could say for sure, but everyone knew Indians did all kinds of awful things. So did the bastard Southrons. When Uncle Billy had them wading on and on through the cold South Carolina swamp waters, they all knew some reb town would soon be rendered to ashes.

It was no secret that Uncle Billy yearned to punish South Carolina more than any other rebel state. But he disliked newspaperman almost as much. Shirkers and liars, he called them, but just about every soldier in the army could quote his even worse contempt for the South Carolina blue-bloods.

"Worthless, motley braggarts. Pretentious, broke down, boastful, pretenders," Uncle Billy had announced one day, and the officers and men loved repeating the words over and over. It gave everyone a little boost. The swamps weren't as cold and dark anymore, the flames of burning towns, grander, and the plundered hams and beef steaks, tastier. When Sherman and Sam finally stopped just off the road in a fallow cotton field, he slouched over the saddle and chewed a cigar, watching his men tromp past. His officer staff milled about behind him as if jockeying for starting position. Every few seconds he would call out an order sending one of them galloping off up the road. The men cheered each time. They liked the idea of Uncle Billy treating his officers like servants. They thought it brought them down a notch, but the staff officers didn't care. They all knew that being treated badly by Uncle Billy was far better than being treated kindly by anyone else. His Tecumseh star had risen. It shined brighter than ever. Brighter maybe than any other star, past or present. Even Grant's.

The men in the road kept cheering, "Give 'em hell, Uncle Billy! Give 'em Hell!"

Sherman smiled. The rebs still had their heroes. Joe Wheeler, the fighter, and Wade Hampton, the braggart, were two. But they couldn't command this kind of devotion. He sat straight up and chewed the cigar butt harder and yelled out. "By God I have a better sense of humor than either of them!"

His officers looked around at each other as if an important order might be hidden in the words. Sherman chomped his cigar and continued, "My dear General Wheeler, old friend. Please let me introduce your gentry to my barbarian host!"

"Give 'em hell, Uncle Billy. Give 'em hell!" The men around him cheered some more, and Sherman responded by sending more officers galloping off in all directions with a renewed flurry of orders.

He put his hand back in his pocket and felt the flattened minie ball that he carried with him always. He liked to feel it every few minutes. It was his way of touching his youngest son, Willie. The thought of his death still stabbed him in the gut. He'd sent Willie dozens of spent minie balls and pieces of grapeshot after Shiloh, but Willie had given this particular one back to him as a birthday present. Sherman had long been past the flooding tears, but he couldn't stop touching the smooth lead. It was as if Willie was right there in his pocket.

He remembered everything about that last day on the steamer north from Vicksburg up the Mississippi. Nine-year-old Willie with the rising fever from typhoid. Red cheeks and breathing fast. Moaning and shivering as his mother dabbed his forehead with a wet towel that she dipped in a tin basin by his bed. The little double barrel shotgun on the desk in the cabin, a gift to Willie from one of his officers. The steamer creeping along slowly. Maddingly slow. The river being too low to risk speed and ripping the hull on a snag. All the while pacing a thousand miles from bedside to the main deck and back again, farther than to Helena itself where the river deepened and full steam was finally got up. And Dr. Roles of the 55th Illinois doing his best, tending to Willie the whole way from Vicksburg. But aside from cooling him with a wet sheets and listening to his racing heart, impotent to stop the inevitable.

He remembered the surge of anger and felt it even now, nearly two years later. How he'd thought seriously of shooting the poor doctor and throwing him overboard. How he'd paced and tried unsuccessfully to focus. And it all having been even worse with no orders to give, no decisions to make. Just the terrible slowness of the steamer against the current. The bastard river and its force pushing south. How he'd felt hate towards the never-ending expanse of water that flowed against them, one bend to the next. A hate he'd feel to eternity.

Then finally the dock at Memphis. Soldiers hurrying their carriage up the street to the Gayaso Hotel and a room with a cool breeze and a view of the docks. The room where Willie died just before 11 o'clock. His son's last breath a gurgle that he could still hear. His wife sitting paralyzed all night beside Willie's lifeless body with her mouth gaping open and just little movements of her chest and tiny, rasping noises. A sergeant with the 13th Battalion helping lay Willie gently into a tin casket and staying up all night with them staring at his tender little face. Then at dawn taking one last look at his son and wanting to die with him but God not allowing it then or since.

God hadn't even bothered taking away the guilt and pain of the horrible truth, that if he hadn't invited his family to come down to Vicksburg, to his encampment that summer, little Willie would still be alive. The stabbing pain kept on day after day. The pain of knowing that his bringing Willie down river caused his death. The thought of Willie on the steamer coming south with the family, smiling and innocent, but each mile bringing him closer to his death ...

Sherman stopped the awful thoughts again like he always did. He looked around at the officers busy with directing the columns of men marching northward relentlessly. His work wouldn't bring Willie back, but there would be a vengeance unmatched in history. He would see to it that the rebels, and South Carolina in particular, paid an awful price. He rode out of Beaufort with a column of regiments heading inland into rebel South Carolina, first to Gardens Corner then on to Pocotaligo at dark. A plantation house still remained standing at the end of its avenue of oaks. The regiments encamped along the road had already torn down the single -room slave huts for their cooking fires. Officers bedded down in the big house with its four big columns, and double stairway. Sherman looked back at the quickly disappearing slave huts and made note of it.

"This is why we're here boys," he said to no one in particular, but a lieutenant quickly came to his side and braced.

"Sir?"

"Nothing," Sherman smiled. He looked up at the thick, gray moss draping the oak trees beside the house. "Tillandsia Usneoides, a relative of the pineapple I've been told."

"Yes, sir," the officer saluted and retreated respectfully, making a note in a little leather book and thinking the Great Man indeed knew everything.

Sherman lay down and slept on the floor in front of the hearth but woke up cold in the middle of the night as the fire dwindled to a single puny flicker. He stood up and looked for something to burn. There were only a few things in the room. A mantel clock, a broken bedstead and a child's rocking chair. He smashed them up with his boot and piled them on the fire. They caught quickly and soon the flames roared. He sat in front of the hearth and watched the fire consume them.

"Rebs won't mind," he smiled, talking to himself while warming his hands and looking through the wavy window panes at the bitter cold outside. "Better to burn their clocks and bedsteads than kill their sons and husbands. We'll do more in the next month to end this war than all of the past year. Without many casualties I hope. Rebs are done for. They'll realize it soon enough."

He settled back down, realizing he'd destroyed private property for his own needs, something he'd promised himself he would never do, and, as he watched the little rocking chair burn, thought of Willie and had difficulty falling back asleep.

At 3 a.m. he awakened for good, as usual, quickly asking for reports from the various Divisions. He ate a piece of chicken and rode off in into the bitter cold morning with a fresh brigade to reconnoiter west towards Coosawatchie.

Rebel cavalry filtered in and out of the distant tree line, but a few Henry volleys ran them off. Sherman was just out of sight up the road when the first flames sprouted out of the second floor windows of the plantation house. The women and children who had huddled all night in the back rooms, snatched what they could before smoke and heat chased them downstairs and out into the yard.

"Thus endeth the protection of Lord Sherman," a lieutenant called out.

His men nodded and smiled. They all knew what was in store for South Carolina.

CHAPTER 7

DOCTOR HENRY TRADD

Allendale, South Carolina
Seventy miles northwest of Beaufort

D octor Tradd stepped outside his field-hospital tent. He sat down in his canvas-back chair and looked at the crowd of civilians waiting to be treated and pictured in his mind the regimental hospital in Atlanta the previous year. All the patients were soldiers back then. Men of all ages and some very young boys. He thought it strange that he could vividly and calmly remember the faces of the dead and dying despite still struggling with even the most fleeting thought of his son Alec, killed at Gaines Mill nearly three years before.

"My God has it been that long," The tears came again quickly, and he quickly talked to himself, as was his habit, bracing himself for the pain. "My boy. Given up to the Army. Fed to the slaughter for the Cause."

He wiped his face and recited the Lord's Prayer three times. The pain gradually faded as it always did, and soon he was even able to conjure a smile. It left him with a quick pang of regret for having left the Army, but he fought it off.

"I've done more than my share by any measure! Certainly by the number of men and boys treated, cured, and those delivered to the Almighty."

Pain seared his brain again.

"Damn it all! Four years of service to the regiment. Dysentery, measles, yellow fever, smallpox, pneumonia, pleurisy, empyema, and amputations by the score," he mumbled to himself, reciting it over and over, as if it were, too, a prayer, remembering the battle deaths and deaths from illness and the faces wracked with pain, and not knowing for

61

sure if it was a curse or a blessing to have been given such a powerful memory by the Almighty. He stopped and took a deep breath, aware of the waste of it all.

"Enough. That is quite enough."

He thanked God again that he had been allowed a furlough, rather than having to succumb to desertion, but he thought of his wife, Alicia, gone now some thirteen years, and how that would have bothered her nearly as much as losing her son. She had been claimed by yellow fever, damn miserable scourge. But there were no tears for her any more. No pain at all. He was all cried out for some time now. He pictured her beautiful blue-green eyes and pretty smile, and found himself smiling back. He said three Hail Mary's for her anyway, as always, thinking the Irish Papists had a damn fine prayer.

"Give them credit where due." He sighed, checking his watch then announcing loudly, but to no one in particular. "Time for the Lord's work now! The caring and healing of the unarmed!"

He looked over the crowd of poor, Irish, dirt farmers, all either elderly or crippled, with their scraggly, elderly wives and unwashed, adult daughters-in-law with their own filthy children, and felt perhaps they had been sent by the Almighty to test his resolve. Their eyes followed his every move as if he was some sort of dangerous wizard. He chuckled to himself. Perhaps he was. He smiled at them, but they all looked away, and he winced, thinking of Alec again.

"As innocent as any unarmed civilian. Maybe more so."

He glanced around at the crowd of pitiful, white refugees knowing some weren't so innocent in the first place. A group of subdued and watchful slaves followed behind. Without them there never would have been a war. But regardless of guilt or blame, he knew he couldn't have remained in Army service any longer. It wasn't that the Confederacy was near death. He'd fought for hopeless causes all his life. Another six months serving one more wouldn't have dissuaded him. Seeing the increasing suffering of the civilian population had. Guilty or not. Four years of worsening shortages and rationing was taking its toll.

"That's why I'm here in God-forsaken Allendale," he laughed to himself. "If there's anywhere else more in need of medical care, I haven't seen it. Not yet anyhow."

He stood up from his chair and stretched, watching the hint of sun peek in and out through the thickening overcast and letting it flash brightly each time into his eyes and feeling the calm it always brought. He looked over at the lines of patients, black and white, stretching from the road into the cornfield to his medical supply wagons that stood besieged by mothers with crying infants and children. A cold, misty wind lashed at the people clutching blankets and jackets and bracing themselves silently against this added punishment. Groans of pain came from his operating tent as if the canvas fabric itself was sick of it all.

"Time to get back to work," he said to himself, stretching and rubbing his hands.

He held them up into the last darting rays of sunlight hoping to feel some renewed warmth and strength, but the wind just blew colder. He walked back inside the tent, lifting the heavy double canvas flaps to be greeted by dozens of expectant faces. He smiled and nodded, having learned that although, on the one hand, being able to save a life or comfort a man on his death bed were important things, the countless little acts of comforting and reassuring the sick were perhaps just as important, if not more so, and knowing these acts radiated outward as a pebble thrown into a pond, as all of his work did.

Civilian deaths from disease and malnutrition had risen remarkably in the past four years of the war, and Sherman's march to the sea had crushed any hope that this year would be better. At least for the white South. He took a deep breath. He knew the blacks had been suffering a lot longer. In a sense forever. Slavery was not only an evil thing, but a quicksand on which the whole culture of the South was built. And tragically so, for white and black.

He'd long ago come to understand this awful fact and had done what he could to encourage freeing the slaves, but his views had never been popular. Even a respected physician could go only so far without being considered a heretic. Only his persistent, competent medical work had saved him from total ostracism. But the future was just beginning, and as he looked out at the faces of sick, black and white, he knew that every minute spent ministering to them helped build a better future for all concerned.

He stopped and drank his four ounce, daily dose of quinine and grit his teeth at the bitter taste, reasoning that keeping a supply for himself enabled him to better help others, even children wracked with malaria. There wasn't enough quinine for everyone. There wasn't enough of anything. His job was, as always, to decide who got what.

He forced himself to think about it rationally and clinically. There was no room in the practice of medicine for sentimentality. Since God Himself had created an unfair world filled with pain, sadness, and misery, it wasn't his place to wallow in worry. Just do what was possible for as many as possible. He put the bottle back into the chest, but left it unlocked and smiled with the satisfaction that, despite all the misery that countless patients had suffered, no one had ever stolen anything from his tent.

The sick and injured kept moving slowly inside one after another as he went back to work quickly with his assistant, Louisa. He had only met her four weeks prior in Savannah but had already found her to be an extraordinarily able nurse. Perhaps the best he'd ever seen. A born healer, a quick learner, and a hard worker. Never seeming to tire, day or night. And only eighteen years old. She was an orphan from a backwoods town in Georgia who had taken up caring for the village sick since she was old enough to tote a bucket of water, and who immediately had volunteered at the Wayside Railroad Hospitals once the war came.

Dr. Tradd remembered finding her late that one night in the Regimental hospital after she'd retreated with Gen. Hardee's Corp to Savannah. She was kneeling by a dying soldier giving him comfort with sips of water, and by her mere presence, and had stayed with the boy all night humming to him softly and holding his hand until he died, all the while ignoring the putrid smell of gangrene from his gaping chest wound. Dr. Tradd had seen how her hands worked. Firmly but with tenderness. He'd asked her right then to help him with his hospital wagon, and she had eagerly agreed. They had been fortunate to have made it out of Savannah before Sherman came. Now she looked up at him as he washed his hands with turpentine.

"Killing them fomites, sir?" She smiled, revealing a big gap where her front teeth had been knocked out years ago by a well-placed kick of a horse.

"Yes, Louisa. As you well know, they can't stand the turpentine."

"Yes sir. You done told me a million times."

She moved to the next patient quickly and spread her feet as if waiting to sprint for an order. He smiled at her and thanked God again that she had volunteered to come with him, knowing that with an education she could have been Matron- of- Hospital, even a physician. He had tried to teach her how to read, but she would never consent to more than a few seconds of sitting still. But even totally illiterate, she was still infinitely better at her work than most of the nurses he'd met in service. He knew it for a fact, and she did, too. Her patients did as well. Anyone could see how they just sensed it. She was truly a born healer.

He proceeded from one person to the next as usual, diagnosing and treating as quickly as his God-given abilities allowed, with Louisa right behind him to assist. A quick bloodletting for an old man with pneumonia and reddish plethora. A cinchona- bark stimulant for the little boy with erysipelas. A little girl's broken collarbone set in a figure -8 wrap. A rheumatic woman calmed with brandy, cayenne pepper and gum myrrh.

"That's the last of the gum myrrh," Dr. Tradd sighed. "Better make note of that, Louisa."

"Yes sir," she nodded.

Quinine for two blacks with malaria which he was still certain came from working in the decomposing matter of the swamp. Lime water for the black-tongued boy with pellagra and opium for the madwoman cackling behind her older brother who held a rope tied around the old woman's thin waist.

"She's been crazy in the head since '52," the man smiled, revealing a toothless upper gum. He picked at the long hairs on his ear. "Nothing bad happened to her, though. Not that we could see. Just all of a sudden started acting savage."

The old woman started for Dr. Tradd, but he stood fast and took her hand calmly and let her kiss his sleeve. He sat her down on a stool at the foot of the cot and gave her a second dose of opium. She cooperated and drank some water afterwards and kept kissing his sleeve until she nodded off.

"That will get her through the night."

"Thanks Doc," the brother smiled. "Nights usually the worst time. She don't never sleep much."

"She will tonight," he smiled, moving on to the other patients lying on pieces of blanket or burlap.

Those with yellow fever lay in a clump away from the others. All coughing, some with distended bellies, others with bright yellow eyes. Dr. Tradd gave each what he could for their pain. He fought off the regret of not having diluted the laudanum long before. Now that the bottles were nearly empty. He added some more brandy to the mix and made another round. A little pain relief for each poor soul. All likely dead in two or three days. Yellow fever killed indiscriminately. The toughest soldier or the weakest child. All yellow and bloated in death. His stomach tightened. It was the only memory of Alicia he still had to block out of his mind. "Miserable scourge!"

"Yes sir," Louisa answered obediently.

He gathered himself. "Typhoid fever can be just about as bad, but at least they have a chance with boiled pork broth and Disermus Pills of pine resin and red peppers."

"I'm sure you're right, sir," she smiled and nodded.

He moved quickly from one patient to the next, glad that most of those in the tent that day would live. Most of the black children had pellagra or scurvy, but vegetables and fruit cured them if they could just keep it down. Erysipelas flared with a few of the deeper lacerations. Dr. Tradd didn't mind the cries of pain as he probed the swollen edges and released the eruption of good white, laudable pus from every one of them. It was always a good sign. The yellow-red pus meant trouble. Swollen glands, gangrene then amputation. But none of that in this whole group. Definitely a good day.

Malaria, though, was rampant as always. Everyone suffered a bout of chills and fevers at least some of the time. Quinine was up to $400 an ounce, but he doubted there was any way of getting more, even at that price. Nothing left to do but dilute it with liquor. All but the one bottle reserved for himself. He used the broths of dogwood and willow bark too, but knew it didn't do much good. He smiled remembering how Louisa had told him she loved the taste so much she drank an entire tea kettle-full back in December. How he'd worried all night, sitting beside her and expecting something awful to happen. Then nothing but some gas.

The broths turned out to be as harmless as they were useless, but at least they were something to give sick patients a little more hope. The best medicine wasn't a mystery though. Fresh air, strict hand washing with soap or turpentine, deep latrines, well away from the water supply, and plenty of boiled water. The damn fomites hated boiled water. Could there be a more wonderful sight or sound than that of a furious boil? Fomites dissolving into nothingness. Disease on the run. If only the entire water supply of the South could be boiled at once. No fomites forever more. A disease free paradise. And a pipe dream to be sure.

He lanced another boiled and a volcano of white pus erupted. Puncture wounds and deep cuts attracted the fomites as much as flowers did bees. He fought them off with lancing then a coating of potassium iodide or silver nitrate, but always too little and too late. Never enough of anything. Defeats outnumbered victories. Maybe ten to one. Maybe a hundred to one. But a physician couldn't worry about such things, he reminded himself. Just one patient at a time. To remain professional and do what he could. But sometimes it tore at his heart no matter what, particularly children in pain.

"That's enough! That's enough!" A little black girl cried as he peeled burned skin from her arm.

He blocked out the sound of her screams. Damn the horrible pains of burns! Pain itself could go to Hell! The invisible human horror! Why did God allow it? What purpose did the agonizing suffering of a little girl serve? He let his mind wander while he went on with the repetitive work of wrapping burns and lancing boils. Work that he could do blindfolded or half asleep. He always came back to the same questions. Why did God allow it? Was He not all loving? Why did He not prevent it? Was He not all-powerful?

But he knew from years of experience that this line of inquiry went nowhere. Just to cynicism and doubt. Not anywhere a reasoning, Christian physician wished to dwell. But every time he debrided a child's burns, the questions returned, and he wondered if God might be doing it on purpose. A test for a thinking man. To see if he succumbed. Would it be obedience or retreat into agnosticism?

"Hell no! I'll remain steadfast! Being allowed to practice the art of medicine and to be a physician is reason enough to remain loyal! The great unknowns be damned! All the horrors and assaults of the universe can go to Hell, too. They have no lasting power over me!"

"No, sir. Not one bit." Louisa answered faithfully, and Dr. Tradd realized he'd been pontificating out loud again. Another bad habit.

"Thank you for believing, Louisa."

"You're welcome, sir."

He smiled at her but knew his own faith had nothing to do with church teachings or Bible study either, although he couldn't remember exactly when he'd come to that conclusion. Both were just more added mystery than much of any practical help as far as he was concerned. The key thing, God's greatest gift, was very simple. It abounded precisely in the very moments spent caring for patients. Those simple acts. The sips of medicine. The cleaning of wounds. The relief of pain. Even the wiping of a feverish brow. Each moment thus spent delivered him to God's truth.

Certainly other professions felt it too, as did mothers and loved ones helping their families. Indeed everyone had this gift at their fingertips if they chose to find it. He knew he wasn't the only one. Not by a long shot.

"But by God, I'm absolutely sure that I feel it in its most raw and powerful state!"

"I'm sure you do, sir."

Louisa held up a young boy's head. The boy shivered from debilitas. Skeletal weight loss, exhaustion, and dysenteric bowels. He'd be lucky to live more than another week. Dr. Tradd let the boy sip the last of the quinine and brandy mix then mopped his brow and had Louisa feed him spoonfuls of orange marmalade. There were only a few tins left, but no matter. He glanced up at his cedar medicine chest with its little wooden compartments inside. Most of the vials were empty, and those that weren't, useless.

"What I would give for a cure for dysentery!"

"It would be worth a lot, all right." Louisa wiped marmalade off the boy's chin.

"Son," he lay his head back down on his folded jacket. "You rest now. You'll be all right. I promise." He lied with comforting authority.

"Thank you, doctor. Thank you both." The boy's eyes teared up.

Dr. Tradd blinked hard to fight off his own, moving on to the next patient and knowing that he'd just been paid in a currency more valuable than gold. He finished up with the last of the urgent cases around 10

68

o'clock, wearily slumping down on his cot too tired to read and was just about to fade off when a sudden pain tore at his gut. For a second couldn't grasp what it was. It surged through his chest and into his throat. Tears welled up.

"Henrietta! My dearest daughter!"

How could he have not thought of her for two days now? How could the human brain allow such a lapse? Was it the work? Was it thoughts of Alec? Or even Alicia? He tried to think clinically but choked with grief.

"Henrietta! My precious Henrietta!"

The sweetest girl. The bright, shining star of his life. Gone. How could God have taken her? He fought off the memory. It was much better to forget. He tried to block the visions. Better to live with amnesia than indescribable agony. But the tears flowed harder. He could still feel the thready pulse of her thin wrist. How clammy her skin had been. How white, her face. He sat up and slapped himself.

"By God, I will not think of that!"

Yet the visions came on stronger. His beautiful Henrietta looking up at him with heavy eyelids and mouthing her last words. "I love you." Then stillness and the vacant stare that stabbed through his heart.

He staggered out the tent.

"Damn this! God damn all of this! God ... !"

He fell to his knees and remembered the worst of it. That he had allowed her to come to Savannah. From the safety of her cousin's home in Charleston to the Regimental hospital. And why? To be with her father? To help him care for the soldiers? No, only to die. Eight days after she arrived on the train! Eight days! To die in front of his eyes of biliary fever. Despite being at her side the entire time!

"What kind of worthless physician am I? How could I not save my own daughter? To bring her to a disease-filled camp then watch her die. What possessed me?"

He gagged and stumbled over to the water barrel, dipped a gourd full, and poured the cold water over his head and neck. The freezing night and the frigid water dripping down the inside of a shirt helped. He splashed more onto his face.

Henrietta was possibly ... was probably ... still in Charleston. His brain allowed him to know that she was dead yet truly hold on to a firm hope that she was still alive in Charleston. Part of him knew deep down inside that it was all nonsense, but another part of him firmly believed it. Henrietta was still in Charleston! He would see her when the war was over. The best thing until then was to put her out of his mind. To go along with his work. To work all day and stay focused. It was the only way. He walked quickly back to his tent, took out the bottle of morphine he kept in his bag, and took a big swallow then fell back into a mercifully dreamless sleep.

CHAPTER 8 — BLESSING PLANTATION

SLAVE TRADERS

zekiel and George sweated in the blacksmith shop listening to the guns boom in the distance. George nodded each time and stifled the urge to sing out. He knew what it meant. The great Sherman and the Jubilee of freedom were nearly at hand. George hammered the glowing pig iron, working the metal into a bloom until the black crust thickened with cooling then sliding it back into the roaring fire one last time laughing.

"Work that metal! Bring it to nature! See here, Ezekiel? Could be my last work as a slave. I'm gonna make me a badge of freedom."

"And I'll help you," Ezekiel smiled, hammering it again until it re-crusted and listening to Santego, the house slave, calling to George to fetch some water for Mrs. Blessing. "Mrs. Blessing still thinks Santego's too damn wonderful to fetch water," he laughed. "Thinks we look up to him, too."

"He ain't so bad," George worked the bellows and shrugged, ignoring Santego's repeated calls for water.

"He's not much of a man," Ezekiel raised his hammer. "Never tried to help Edith save Katrina."

"Mr. Blessing wouldn't ever listen to Santego, you know that."

"He might've. Santego's always been his favorite. He could have told Blessing he wouldn't work for him anymore if he sold her."

"Couldn't got himself bullwhipped too."

"A decent man would have tried. At least make Blessing think about it." Ezekiel hammered long enough for the anger to pass. Anger at George for defending Santego. Anger at the whole, horrible damn mess. He stopped and stretched and took a look outside. A line of wagons had appeared out of the far pines moving north towards the house.

"Whites from Hardeeville and Savannah." He nodded towards the scared women and children and old men sitting on sacks of bedding and clothing in overloaded wagons piled high with furniture, crates and barrels. Dozens of slaves walked along beside them keeping pace with the mules. "Most will leave quicker than a mullet can jump. As soon as they know it's safe. As soon as they know they won't be raped or lynched." He waved the hammer above his head and laughed. "When true freedom prevails! Hallelujah!"

George stopped working the bellows and looked around nervously. "That kind of talk can still mean a whipping, Ezekiel."

"I doubt it. Not anymore. The first signs of freedom are already here." Ezekiel banged on the pig iron, relishing seeing whites suffering a bit, although he didn't hold any anger towards these in particular, just a deep satisfaction knowing Sherman was coming.

He went back to his work until mid- afternoon when clouds piled up and let loose a cold rain. Thunder rumbled in the distance mingling with the ebbing cannon fire. Ezekiel knew it had to be a sign from God.

"The lightning's our freedom, George. It's coming closer by the minute."

Lightning flashed again in the distance.

"See? It's a sign from ... "

The door swung open. In burst Mr. McCallister, the overseer, and his two grandsons, Jeb and Billy, all with shotguns.

"Get down on your face, Ezekiel," McCallister nodded to the coal dust on the clay floor, ignoring George.

Ezekiel glanced at the shotguns then at McCallister's face. He knew immediately that he had no choice but to get it over with. "All right."

He prostrated himself. Jeb shackled his hands behind his back and locked his ankles to a big iron ball. McCallister kept his finger on the trigger. He knew it all had to be done exactly right. Like trapping a while boar or snaring an alligator. Any mistake could be deadly.

"There. It's done," Jeb smiled to his father. "The great Ezekiel in chains."

"Shush up," McCallister frowned, keeping his shotgun pointed at Ezekiel's head.

He knew enough about Ezekiel to believe that putting him into shackles was a death sentence to him and his grandsons if Ezekiel were ever to get free. Ezekiel was just like that. He knew it as sure as day. Not by anything violent he'd ever seen him do. Just by his eyes. His easy

72

mastery of everything. His patience. His silent watching. His waiting. McCallister would have gladly killed him right then and there if Mr. Blessing had allowed it. Damn him for being so greedy.

He knew Sherman was almost here. He wasn't deaf. He heard the gunfire down towards the Beaufort Road and knew Yank patrols had been sighted near Argyle Island and Richfield plantation just ten miles away. They could be here any minute. He looked down at Ezekiel. Soon to be sold south and end up far away in Alabama or Mississippi. Or better yet, get killed in the process. He didn't want to be looking over his shoulder with a freed Ezekiel on the loose.

Jeb and Billy rounded up the rest of the slaves while he guarded Ezekiel. They moved from one slave hut to the next, keeping them at gunpoint until bound. All except Lucy, Miela, and Santego who Blessing had promised to keep, and his own slave, Titus, who's fate he still hadn't decided. It went perfectly.

"Cut off the snake's head and the rest of it just wiggles for a while. Nothing much it can do without the head," McCallister sighed, taking a deep breath as Jeb pulled Ezekiel beneath the magnolia tree and chained him to the trunk while Billy stood a safe twenty feet away with the double-barreled shotgun trained on his head, just in case.

He hoped to God that Blessing knew what he was doing. Sending all the slaves to Columbia to be sold. What if Sherman was headed that way? Charleston was closer. He'd told Mr. Blessing exactly that the night before when he called him to his study, but the old man wouldn't budge. McCallister had suffered through his breathless ramblings.

"Better prices in Columbia." Blessing had said. "More hope for victory up there than in Charleston. And less chance the military will seize them for forced labor. And remember, Ezekiel alone is worth $1800 in gold. So don't hurt him! There's still enough time to get him to Columbia or Charlotte before the Yanks come. Maybe, just maybe, I can sell him. And all the rest, too. Give me enough to make it through the next few years at least. But it'll take a bit of luck. We've got to get them to Columbia before Sherman makes his move. Who'll buy a slave if Sherman is about to free them? But maybe Hampton and Wheeler will make a stand. They've got to. Just a temporary reprieve for a while. A little more time to broker the sale. We might have waited too long, though. Sherman's crossed Georgia quicker than anyone thought possible. I'll give him credit for that. They've already got cavalry raiding up from Beaufort. But who knows, there still just might be a decent market for my little group. And more for Ezekiel. But there's not much time. A few weeks. Maybe less. Maybe days even. Then they'll all be free. Not worth a penny. All I'm trying to do is get a decent return on my investment."

McCallister had listened and nodded all the while, but the other slaves meant nothing to him except as an exemption from the draft. Selling them might subject him and his grandsons to Army service but that wasn't definite. He knew Mr. Blessing had friends in high places. Ezekiel was the worry. A killer for sure. He was all McCallister could think about while Mr. Blessing had droned on for a while longer about his financial troubles until abruptly dismissing him. McCallister didn't hear Blessing mutter behind his back. "There goes 'poor' Mr. McCallister", which in Blessing's world meant 'white trash'. It was just as well he didn't hear, but he hadn't slept a wink all night anyhow, knowing how dangerous this could all be.

But now he was fully alert and still nervous, even with Ezekiel in chains, waiting two more hours before the slave drivers to come up the road with their wagon. A woman handled the mules and two men rode in the rear.

"I hate that woman," McCallister grumbled. "She's one mean, spiteful bitch."

But he knew once he turned Ezekiel and the others over to her, he and the boys could collect their wages and make a run for it. He hoped they'd be long gone when Sherman finally came. They could head over to Charleston and then up to Cheraw to his cousins little farm. He figured it was as decent and safe a place as any to wait for the end. Maybe, just maybe, his grandsons would survive the war. He thought of his only son, Warren, dead at Malvern Hill. It still made his heart jump even now, after nearly three years. The bile taste rose again in his throat as always. He swallowed hard. At least Billy and Jeb would be as far from the Yanks as they could get. He glanced once more at Ezekiel's emotionless eyes and prayed he'd never see them again.

Leather thongs bound the other slaves, hands and feet. A rope soon stretched along the entire line, a loop knotted to each neck then tied firmly to the rear of the wagon. The men shuffled along in extra iron ankle bracelets all chained together, but only Ezekiel had the shackles on his hands and feet. A cold wind whipped across the cornfield. The slaves shivered in the coarse burlap tunics the slavers made them wear. Each with a hole for head and arms and roughly sewn together at the sides with twine. McCallister and his grandsons kept watch with their shotguns and escorted them off the property to the Walterboro Road. They watched Ezekiel disappear around the bend with the others then turned and rode back home to pack their belongings.

The white woman sitting in the wagon was Mrs. Alma Jenkins, the slave trader's wife. Her thick quilt jacket and pants barely moved. Her red gums gleamed where she once had two front teeth. Her greasy, stiff hair remained unperturbed by the wind.

"Ya'll comfy? " She giggled, spitting a dribble into the road. Just another group of slaves to be delivered, she thought. Something she'd done for years with her husband and brother, making a decent living off the plantations between Charleston and Savannah. Delivering slaves to market and to their new life in rice or cotton fields on another plantation. She'd lost her only two children to pneumonia in infancy and, with them, any shred of compassion for anyone, tolerating her husband and her brother only because she needed them. All others meant nothing. Slaves less than nothing.

Five miles down the road she lit up her pipe and spat on the dirt road. She turned around and smiled at the slaves. Ezekiel shuffled sideways in his chains and purposely stepped on her spittle, crushing it with a little twist of his ankle. He smiled back at her, and her mouth snapped shut. She glared at him and jerked the mules to a stop.

"Patrick! Come here! Hold the mules!" She jumped down quickly and dragged the bullwhip behind her. Its knotted end slithered like a snake. She stared at Ezekiel and flicked the whip. The tip jumped in the air obediently. "I seen what you done, boy. Uppity, ain't ya." She stuck her tongue through the gap in her teeth and sucked in air. "You want me to whip your ass raw?" She spat at Ezekiel's feet. "You got the fire in your eyes. Can't whip out fire. Can kill it though. But then I'd lose my fee. Lucky for you it ain't worth it. Not just now."

Ezekiel stared back at her unblinking. His face was stone. Patrick called to her from up front where he held the mules. "Don't whip them

Alma. Mr. Blessing told us not to. He's got to sell them before the Yankees come."

"Shut up Patrick," Alma stared at Ezekiel "This one won't mind the whip." "

"Don't Alma," Patrick rubbed the mule with his glove. "Ain't much market for slaves just now. Mr. Blessing said everybody's scared the Yanks will take them."

"Take them?" Alma laughed. "Take them where? Yankee land?"

"Just don't whip 'em. Got to sell them quick like. No whipping them 'till after they're sold." He tenderly squeezed the mule's neck.

"All right I won't whip them, at least not the big ones," she laughed. "Just this little one."

She backed off a few paces and cracked the whip just over Ezekiel's head. He didn't budge. He'd suffered through whippings many times before. The scars on his back proved it. Bearing the pain had always been part of the price. He remembered every lash, though, and the face of every man who done it. He'd never been whipped by a woman, but no matter. He'd remember her, too. When freedom came he'd find every one of them. Killing them would be as easy as breaking eggs.

"Watch this, Cole," Alma pointed to Fatima, the smallest child and last in line. She cracked the whip again. It cut into her leg. She screamed and fell down. Her mother, Daphne, who was tied up front in the line closer to the wagon, screamed.

"Please no! For God's sake no!" She threw herself against the cord around her neck until it cut into her skin. The others pulled her down. Grace, the child next in line to Fatima, cringed in a ball as the whip came again and again, and blood trickled from the cuts.

"Better stop it, Alma," Cole yawned. "It'll cost us."

"Hell if it will," Alma snarled back. "State pays owners for damages to their property. All we got to say is they tried to run off."

"For God's sake, please stop!" Daphne kept begging as Fatima fell down covering her face with her bare arms while blood seeped through her burlap dress. Patrick just shook his head. He knew there was nothing he could do with Alma.

"Jesus, Alma. Just stop it. Please!" Cole pleaded. "Mr. Blessing will be mad as hell. Who's gonna buy a bleeding child? You're wasting a good profit here."

But Alma kept on until Daphne screamed herself hoarse. None of them saw the horsemen at the edge of the woods except the Ezekiel. He knew right off there were Yank soldiers. A dozen men with rifles, their saddles draped with loot and ham hocks. They rode up fast before Alma could hide the whip. She backed over to Cole and threw it under the wagon.

The lead Yank yelled from forty yards away, "Better keep that whip lady. You're gonna need it."

He pulled his horse up right in front of her. Mud caked his blue jacket, pants and boots. He wore a black felt hat adorned with two crow feathers. A shotgun and Henry repeater dangled from the saddle. His belt sported two revolvers. A thin, scraggly beard partially covered his sunburned face. Ezekiel guessed he might be eighteen or nineteen. The others gathered around and dismounted. They all carried Henrys and revolvers, and every one of them was filthy. They reeked of sweat and foul clothes.

The slaves huddled together warily until the Yanks cut them loose. Daphne bolted over to Fatima and held her in her arms. "My baby. My baby." She wiped blood from the lashes on her shoulder.

A revolver pointed to Cole's head produced the key to the ankle locks. The young Yank with the crow feather bumped his horse into Alma. "You best get going," he smiled. "We ain't supposed to incite the slaves, so I'll give you a few minutes to run. We'll tend to the girl. Uncle Billy says we shouldn't shoot civilians, so I guess we won't." The other Yanks behind him laughed. "No. We won't, really. I mean it." He waved them off. "We'll give you a few minutes start before we let these here go." He pointed to Ezekiel and the other men. "They might try to follow. No telling ..."

Patrick and Cole looked at each other then bolted down the road. Alma trotted after them, holding up her ankle length dress while the Yankees laughed as she disappeared around the bend into the trees. Ezekiel waited restlessly, his body trembling with anticipation. The Yanks took their time giving out hardtack crackers and cutting each of them pieces of cold pork. They cut a blanket into strips and wrapped Fatima's cuts as best they could. All of them had seen plenty of horrible wounds, but none had ever seen a girl bull-whipped before. They ate for a while and shared more pork and crackers then remounted and told Ezekiel and the other men to stay off the road in the daytime.

"Best work your way southeast," the crow-feather youth tossed him his ankle bracelet. "They've got land for blacks in Beaufort. So I've been told." He shrugged then sucked on a ham bone, spurring his horse and leading his men back across the field.

Ezekiel, George and the other men quickly gathered up all the leather thongs and chains and hid them in the woods. They helped Fatima into the wagon where she cuddled in her mother's lap, sobbing and holding a piece of burlap over her head. The other women and children climbed up and squeezed together in a tight ball.

"Pull the wagon off the road," Ezekiel ordered. "Over there behind that big oak. Doubt any slave patrols are around with the Yanks here, but no telling. If they come, tell them you're heading back to Blessing. And you're in charge, George, until I get back."

George didn't argue. He knew Ezekiel had the knack. Best to do what he said. He just nodded nervously as Ezekiel took off after Alma with his ankle chain in one hand and an ax from the wagon in the other. Ezekiel found Patrick first, hobbling along just a few hundred yards away. He was bent over holding his chest and wheezing loudly in long whistling breaths. He turned around when he heard Ezekiel coming and held up one hand, begging in between gulps of air, his face contorted in terror. "Please. I never ... I swear ..." He knelt down and put his hands together in prayer. "I didn't mean no harm. It was Alma. She's the one ..."

Ezekiel raised the axe. "I don't mean no harm neither."

He killed him with one chop into his forehead then dragged the body off the road and hid it under a pile of leaves. He caught up with Alma and Cole another quarter mile down the road. Alma had already cut her dress off knee-high to run faster. They saw him coming and swerved into the swampy woods. Ezekiel went after Cole next, catching him in some saw-palmettos. He pulled him down and growled in his ear.

"You stop fighting and I'll let you live," he lied, wrapping the chain around his neck and dragging him kicking and gasping to a tupelo stump. He pulled his neck across the stump and pressed down with just enough strength to kill him. Life slowly choked out of his lungs. Ezekiel put his face up close. "You're lucky. I'm in a hurry."

Cole kicked for a while then was still. Ezekiel unwrapped the chain and went after Alma. She crashed through a bramble thicket farther into the trees until the thorns stopped her. She turned and pulled out a knife. "I'll cut your black throat!" She hissed, turning through the thorns and cutting her arms and face.

Ezekiel knelt down just a few yards in front. He dropped his ax and smiled. "Take that knife of yours and cut out your eyeballs. Do that and I'll let you live." He rattled the chain.

"Bastard!" She threw a handful of dirt at him, broke free from the thorns, and ran at him screaming. He stood up and whipped the chain across her face. Teeth and blood splattered out of her mouth. She fell to her knees and Ezekiel pounced on her. He threw the knife into the briars.

"This chain is all you'll need," he whispered in her ear as she struggled to pull free. He wrapped the chain around her neck and tossed the end over a stout oak branch and hung her there kicking and gasping until blood foamed out of her mouth. He held her legs up so she could breathe and repeated the process three times until he felt enough justice had been done. Then he let her choke to death and left her chained to the tree for the raccoons.

GEORGE STOOD FROZEN behind the oaks just off the road. He felt shocked that Ezekiel had left him in charge. He watched the women care for Fatima, tenderly washing the slices of skin that flapped over bleeding cuts on her back, arms and face, with water from the wagon bucket, then rewrapping them carefully with cotton strips Daphne tore from her dress. George felt paralyzed, not knowing what to do next then he saw Ezekiel running up and felt a heaviness fall away.

"Thank God," he whispered.

Ezekiel had already wiped off the blood and hair from the axe. No need upsetting anyone. He lied to them. "Couldn't find them. Damn bastards. Probably deep in the swamp somewhere."

He knew George would be relieved. He was a good man and would stand up for a weaker person if he had to. But he was no fighter. No need to frighten him with the fact that three whites were dead just up the road in the woods. But he didn't take any chances. He had them bury all the slavers' belongings in this swamp. Just in case. Confederate cavalry and slave patrols might still be about. Freedom was here but only in sight of the Yanks soldiers. He knew this whole group could be shot or hung, and no white person would say a word. Except maybe Mr. Blessing for depriving him of his profit.

He gathered Toby, another field hand, and Pompey, the wheelwright. They were the most reliable of the men, next to George.

"We'll go back and wait at that south field. The little one that cuts through the bamboo thicket. There's a corn bin and cow shed down by the water. We can all stay dry. Blessing never sets foot back here. Doubt he even remembers he owns it. I'll scout the house. If the Yanks come, we'll regroup there. If not, I'll find Miela and the others, and we'll head towards Beaufort. Remember, Sherman's coming, so stay strong. Don't panic if we run into a slave patrol. We'll tell them we ran off to the Yanks but now we want to go back to Blessing and that we're lost. And that the Yanks whipped Fatima. Trust me. They'll want to believe us."

George's heart pounded at the thought. He stared at him with wide eyes and dry mouth. His voice trembled, "Ezekiel? What if they don't?" Ezekiel patted shoulder, "It'll be All right. I know you're scared. But listen here. We can do this. The others will follow your lead." He squeezed George's shoulder, "Just keep your fears to yourself."

His mind raced. Maybe George and Titus, McCallister's wagon driver, could take them all to Beaufort. It was time. Two men would be enough. More might make it riskier. Reb cavalry would just as soon arrest or kill ten as two. The rest of the men, Toby and Pompey, Mingo the carpenter, Esau the plowman, and Quam the brick mason could come with him. He'd heard the slave cabin rumors. That freed blacks were helping the Yanks in Georgia to build roads and bridges. They were being called 'Pioneers'. He would do the same. The men would follow him. They trusted him. But everything was changing quickly. His mind raced. What would freedom bring? What would it mean? What would the whites do? How long would they fight? Where was Sherman headed? What would happen after the Yanks left?

He gathered himself. First things first. Get the women and children to safety.

CHAPTER 9 — BLESSING PLANTATION

CONNOR

Connor rode up the Avenue of the oaks but saw no one about. The fields stood empty. Not a slave in sight. Connor felt his heart race as he trotted over to the house. Had they already left? Had Mr. Blessing already sent them off to his cousin's plantation outside Columbia? Would he see Ezekiel and Miela again?

Cows lined the pasture fence drooping their heads over the rails watching. Empty rice sheaves were scattered about. Two empty wagons waited to be loaded. One was surrounded by barrels of indigo and rice and another by turpentine kegs. The basket weavers' hut stood empty. Piles of faded sweet grass waved in the breeze. A black woman came to the doorway of the big house. It wasn't Miela.

He rode up, dismounted, and trotted up the porch steps. "Hello? Is Mr. Blessing home?" He nodded to the large black woman dressed in white who stood frowning at him with her thick arms crossed.

"He's upstairs getting ready."

"Getting ready for what?"

Lizette ignored the question and moved out of the doorway slowly to let him pass. Connor called up the front stairs. "Mr. Blessing?"

"Who's that?"

He recognized Mr. Blessing's gravel voice. "Connor Dumont. Paul Dumont's nephew."

"Right. Come on up."

Connor heard the second floor creak above him and heard the clink of Mr. Blessing setting his revolver back down on the marble table by his bed. He went up to the stairs and found the old man sitting on an ottoman poring over a pile of loose receipts and ledger pages spread out at his feet. Connor was startled by Mr. Blessing's appearance. His eyes were bright yellow and his skin a yellowish gray which made his sun-blotched, saggy face look almost reptilian. His hands rocked back and

81

forth like he was shaking dice, and he smelled of alcohol. The jovial, gracious gentleman he remembered from years past was gone. A blunted, ill humored man had taken his place.

Connor stammered for a second then forced himself to concentrate. Mr. Blessing didn't seem to notice. His open house robe hung limply from his bony shoulders. His shirt and trousers were covered in grime. Connor went up to him and held out his hand. Mr. Blessing hesitated then shook it softly.

"To what do I owe this visit." He looked back down at his papers and sighed impatiently.

"I'm on my way to join up with McLaws and Hardee. Thought I'd ..."

Mr. Blessing held out his tremulous hand. "If you don't mind." He held out a receipt. "This is what you came for. Your Uncle Paul told me you would come if you made it back from Virginia. He knew you better than you knew yourself."

Connor took the offered piece of paper and felt his heart sink. A bill of sale for nineteen slaves. He read down the names. The last on the list was Ezekiel.

"Why?" Connor felt his face flush. "Uncle Paul told me you'd let them stay here until the war ended. He said ..."

"Doesn't matter much now, does it?" Mr. Blessing stifled a yawn.

Connor saw the glint of gold fillings on his brown teeth and caught a whiff of fetid, alcohol breath. He felt his blood begin to boil. "You sold Ezekiel?"

"He was mine, wasn't he? All of them were. My rightful, lawful property." His yellow eyes constricted. "Damn if I'm going to let the Yankees tell me what I can and cannot do with my own slaves. Christ!" He waved his hand dismissively.

"But you promised Uncle Paul. He wrote to me last year and said..."

"Your uncle is dead. The promise died with him. Sherman's coming, for God's sake. What do you expect me to do? Let $15,000 worth of slaves just run off? I'm selling them fair and square to a decent broker from Winnsboro. They'll be fine. You can go see Ezekiel after it's over."

"You sold Ezekiel?"

"Yes I did. And I'd do it again. He was mine to sell, wasn't he? Didn't your uncle give him to me? Well? Didn't he?" His voice cracked and the veins on his temple pulsed.

"You God-damn old fool! Do you know what you've done?"

"Don't curse me boy!" He stood up and dropped his receipts. "Get out of my house! How dare you curse me in my own ..."

"Shut up old fool! You sold Ezekiel! Did he leave here in chains? I know he did. He couldn't have been taken otherwise. Was he? Was he in chains?"

"Get out of here!" Mr. Blessing shouted and looked at his gun.

"You touch it and I'll knock those gold teeth down your throat."

Connor grabbed the old man's shirt and jerked him closer. "Now tell me. Was he in chains?"

Mr. Blessing pulled away and snickered. "Damn right he was, the uppity black bastard! Had all the others wailing. Like he was in charge or something. Probably thought he was. With all the slack I gave him. I'm sick of his ways. Your uncle spoiled him rotten."

Connor slapped his face hard. "Do you know what's going to happen? You idiot! Ezekiel will find you and kill you. He'll burn this house down if Sherman doesn't." He cocked his fist back, and Mr. Blessing grimaced and shut his eyes. Connor pushed him back onto his ottoman and let go. "And Miela?"

The old man shook his head. "No. I kept her. Santego and Lizette too. Downstairs. Miela's in the study. We're leaving for Charleston. Not that it's any business of yours. Malcolm's already taken Mrs. Blessing. If he were here, he'd kill you." He rubbed his jaw.

Connor felt like slapping him again, but the old man wasn't worth it. He grabbed the bill of sale and went down the stairs. He knew Ezekiel would never forget. If the day came when Ezekiel stood outside this house, Connor knew that Mr. Blessing, and his son, Malcolm, would be on their way to see the Almighty. He remembered Ezekiel's one and only rule. He had been quite adamant about it, and it was very simple. That anyone who had ever whipped him or put him into shackles would someday, God willing, die by his own hands. He remembered Ezekiel's exact words.

"By my own hands, I swear. It's God's will for Justice."

"I doubt God has much to do with it," he had answered.

Ezekiel whacked him in the face, leaving a bloody lip and nose. He figured that's why he still remembered Ezekiel's exact words. "God has everything to do with it. He created slaves to inflict justice when the freedom comes."

There was no doubt that Ezekiel intended to do just that, and, in Blessing's case, Connor actually hoped he would. Uncle Paul hadn't been one to use the whip, but others had. Ezekiel had told Connor in years past the names of everyone who had whipped him, including Connor's grandmother, Mamere, but grandmother was already dead and gone.

Connor remembered her foul mouth and her snakeskin-covered stick that she used to inflict pain. Thank God the bitch-witch of Meggett was dead. He didn't have to worry about Ezekiel coming to kill her. Mr. Blessing however might live long enough to see Ezekiel up close. Connor smiled knowing it would be the last thing he would ever see, and it served the bastard right. He knew it was past time to do something. Something he should have done a long time ago. Mr. Blessing's obvious instability made it all the more imperative.

Lizette stood in the hallway at the bottom of the stairs. She nodded towards the front study."Miela's in there."

She pointed towards the study door. She knew that every man who had visited Blessing in the past three years had asked for Miela. The beautiful, brown Miela. Lizette shook her head and said her daily prayer out loud. "Lord give us strength to live till the Jubilee."

Connor blessed himself by habit, and Lizette chuckled. "Romans! Got all that crossing and kneeling."

Connor hurried past her towards the study and didn't see her mocking him with a little genuflection, but he heard Mr. Blessing upstairs picking up his pistol as he pushed open the double doors. Miela sat in a straight-backed chair with a gag in her mouth, her hands tied behind her. Blood dripped out of her nose. Connor cut her loose. She wiped away the blood and rubbed her mouth and wrists. Connor hadn't seen her for four years and felt his brain seize up. She was still the most beautiful girl he'd ever seen, then or since. Chocolate brown skin as smooth as a baby's. Brown eyes sparkling in the afternoon sun that poked through the drapes.

She stood up and took his hand in hers. "Thank you. And you are?"

"Connor. Connor Dumont."

Miela shook her head. Her green cotton dress tugged at her body. Her neck veins and collar bones moved under her skin. Connor looked away and told himself he was a fool. She's black, damn it. A slave girl for God's sake! He refocused on her eyes.

"I met you four years ago. Came here with my Uncle Paul and Ezekiel. We were ..."

"I remember!" Miela's eyes lit up. She took his hands. "I remember you. The boy on the back of the wagon with Ezekiel."

"Yes. That was me." He nodded and felt his throat go dry. He cursed himself for being such an idiot.

She came closer and looked into his face. "Yes. I remember. The white boy with the red hair and freckles."

Her hands tightened around his, and Connor felt his heart race. Damn fool. He cleared his throat and tried to focus. "Look here. This is important."

Miela let him go and smiled. "Yes, All right.

Connor quickly searched through Mr. Blessing's desk for paper. He dipped a quill pen in the inkwell and wrote out three separate letters. The first a 'manumission declaration' for Miela's freedom, as well as the others. He listed every name on Mr. Blessing's bill of sale and added "with their families" to cover anyone else. He signed it: "Connor Dumont, rightful owner of these listed slaves." A lie for a good cause. At the top and in bigger letters, he printed: "Duly freed by manumission and hereby granted freed-man status under the sponsorship of Connor Dumont." He blotted it, folded it and wrote "Freed man's manumission" on the outside. He slipped it into a thick canvas portfolio.

"This says you've been giving your freedom. The others too, if they make it back. It just might fool the slave patrols, so keep it with you."

He was sure she would leave as soon as Mr. Blessing let her out of his sight.

She took the portfolio. "How could they come back?" Her eyes pierced his. "They're on their way to Columbia."

Connor smiled. "Ezekiel will find a way. But whether or not the others come with him, this gives you some protection from slave patrols and militia. At least I hope it does." He knew that even free blacks traveling without a white person were subject to arrest and reenslavement with or without papers. The letters were just a bluff, but maybe they would help.

Miela nodded, realizing what it meant and what Mr. Blessing would do if he found out. She watched his eyes dart down to her dress then to the floor and back. She could feel his embarrassment. She smiled at his tongue-tied stuttering. It was quite useful to have another white man enthralled with her, and she figured that Mr. Blessing's dislike for him meant Connor was a decent man. Mr. Blessing disliked all decent man. It was his nature. Now to have this Connor tongue-tied over her. She certainly felt no physical attraction for him of course. He was just another white man who might be useful. That was all. And maybe a decent white man at that. She smiled at him and touched his arm.

"Thank you," she whispered.

"You're quite welcome. It's ... well ... it's just time for this. Past time," Connor stuttered, listening to the stairs for Mr. Blessing.

Miela glanced up at the ceiling. "He's been a different man since his eyes went yellow. It's been three months now. He said it was bile fever, but I've seen him drink liquor by the quarts. Nearly every day."

Connor nodded. "Be careful with him. His mind is..."

"Gone?" Miela smiled.

"Yes." He smiled back and stared at her neck then caught himself and focused on the second letter. A travel-pass for Miela and the others to go to Charleston.

"Freed men still need a travel permit. At least until the Yanks come. Then all hell will break loose. Slaves from everywhere on the run. Militia hunting them down. Yanks moving on Charleston or Columbia. It'll be chaos ... and ... opportunity."

Miela nodded. "I understand."

"Better leave here and go to Charleston. My uncle owns about fifty or so acres on a spit of land off Thomas Island. Three small cottages. A barn. A cornfield. Sweet potatoes and cabbages, too, if I remember right. The only other people who live on the Island are free blacks who run a brick kiln, so people around there are used to seeing blacks on the island. Well ... I mean ... well anyhow ... The Ferry takes you across. The place is a half mile up the road on the right. Uncle calls it Smythes. You can go there and be..." He stopped and caught his breath. He knew he couldn't promise she would be safe anywhere as a black, especially a pretty black woman. "Remember Miela. Don't tell the Yanks you're going to Smythes. The word is that they'll shoot loyal blacks."

"Loyal?" Her eyes darted at him.

"You know what I mean. Just don't tell them. But tell our boys exactly that. Our scouts and militia." He breathed deeply "They've been shooting runaways."

She took a deep breath and gathered herself. "No matter ... We'll be safe enough, God willing."

Connor hurried to write the last note. A deed of ownership to Smythes. "If the Yanks stop you, you better have a deed. Even a fake one. Just to show you're not 'Uncle Toms'."

He'd heard the stories of Sherman's men raping 'loyal' slaves in Georgia, to punish them for staying with their owners. He didn't have time to think it out anymore. He signed the deed to Smythes in his best forgery of Uncle Paul's hand writing as seller and made Miela sign as owner.

"Look. Remember this." He put his hand on her shoulder to get her attention. She smiled and leaned forward. He stammered a bit, feeling the firm muscles underneath her dress and quickly dropped his hand to his side. "Don't show the deed to the slave patrols or militia. And don't show the travel pass to the Yanks. No use setting them off. It'll be dangerous enough."

Miela nodded and whispered. "I understand. Thank you, Connor." He folded the letters and slipped them into the portfolio and tied it with string. Miela put it under her dress and backed up quickly. Connor heard the rustle behind him and knew it was Mr. Blessing. Had he seen it?

Miela held up her hand. "No. Please. Please. I'm staying with you. I'm not leaving."

Connor knew that Mr. Blessing wouldn't hurt her unless she tried to leave. He started to turn around, but a pistol barrel poked in to his neck. "Get out now!" Blessing snarled. "Get out or I'll shoot you dead. You hear me?"

Connor moved slowly. He felt the barrel inch up to his temple. "All right. I'm leaving." He backed away.

Miela nodded and mouthed the words, "I'll be all right."

"Get out! Now!" Mr. Blessing held a smaller pistol in the other hand. Connor knew he couldn't risk it. If he killed Mr. Blessing, he could be hung, and they might even blame Miela and hang her too. If they chose. They could do anything they wanted until the Yanks came. He didn't know what else to do but to leave and trust that Miela and Ezekiel could take care of themselves for just a while longer.

He backed out of the study with the pistol in his neck until Blessing poked him hard. "Get out of here! Now!"

"Yes sir." He hurried across the living room to the front porch half expecting Mr. Blessing to shoot him in the back.

He mounted up and rode off quickly across the cornfields and then down the Gillionsville Road. towards the Savannah River, reaching the bluff overlooking the south bank just before dark. He picketed Brig in a swale of cypress stumps and water oaks, wrapped up in a rubberized blanket, and waited for dawn. He told himself he'd done all he could, but it didn't help. The temperature dropped to freezing, but he didn't dare build a fire. Adding to his misery was an orange glow in the distance. He knew what it meant. Sherman's army was on the move.

CHAPTER 10 — MCCALLISTER

"When are the Yankees are coming?" McCallister's grand daughter, Helen, ran up the trail, her red hair glowing in the setting sun. "When are they ... ?

McCallister put his finger to his mouth. "Quiet Helen! I heard you."

He glanced up at her and saw her excitement fade. You old fool. Never take away a child's spirit. Even in times like this. Especially in times like this. "Tell you what Helen. How about climb up the big oak tree and keep a look at it." He watched her eyes gleam again. "Take a rag with you. Wave it when you see the Yanks come round the bend. Then come home quick. No yelling though. Quiet like a sparrow hawk."

"I'll use my red hat. Can you see that far?" Helen smiled, knowing he would wrinkle his nose and wiggle his glasses. And he did just that.

"My young lady. I can see as far as I like. If I can see the sun, the moon, and the stars, I can surely, I think, see your red hat."

Helen laughed and yelled, "Wrinkly nose can see the stars!"

Then she was off running. McCallister knew she was the brightest flower of God's whole creation, and, no matter what the Yankees did, as long as they didn't bother a ten year old girl, eventually the world would return to sanity. Everything could still be tolerable except of course that his son, Warren, wouldn't be coming back. His daughter in law either. Dead of blackwater fever some two years now. It didn't matter at all anymore that she had been a Charleston prostitute. At least she had given him Helen.

He watched her nimbly climb the oak and waved to her." Be careful!"

"All right wrinkly nose! Can you see me?"

"Perfectly well."

He kicked himself for not leaving as soon as Ezekiel and the other slaves had been taken off. He'd decided at the last minute to stay put until the Yanks had passed because he'd heard from refugees they wouldn't burn an occupied house. But that was before he'd learned from others that Hardeeville had been burned to the ground. Now the bastards were here, and it was too late to leave until morning. He realized he was risking Helen and his grandson's lives. He should have left immediately for Cheraw.

"Hell, I should have left a week ago," he mumbled to himself. "Just got to make the best of it now. Thank God, at least Ezekiel's gone."

He went over his plan again. Have the boys stay in the swamp with the mules and livestock until morning then pack up everything and make a run to his cousin's farm in Cheraw, close to North Carolina. They would be out of harm's way and maybe the damn war would end before it claimed his grandsons. If only the Yanks didn't destroy everything first. Fool! Why did you wait? To be at their mercy! Damn it, you idiot! He wondered if they would find the three silver plates he'd hidden in the dining room fireplace. Plates his mother had given him in '36. They might not mean much to the Yanks or rich white folks like the Blessings.

But they were all he had beside his wife, his grandsons, and Helen. He had a sudden sinking realization. With it being so cold, why didn't they have more than one fire going? Maybe because they didn't use that room? Not enough wood cut? He glanced down at the huge pile of firewood. They'd find it for sure. Why didn't I think of that until now? He thought for a few minutes then the best hiding place of all occurred to him with the far off howl of a hound dog in the woods.

Peanut, Helen's pet spaniel, had died just last week, and the grave down by the barn was still fresh. He jumped up, ran inside, and nearly threw himself into the dining room fireplace. He reached up into the chimney and pulled loose the canvas sack covering his coat sleeve with soot in the process. Be careful idiot. Bastard Yanks will notice that. He made sure not to track ash across the floor. His wife and her sister Wilhelmina were busy packing and baking sweet potatoes for the trip. They didn't even look up.

He grabbed a shovel from behind the empty stable, trotted over to Peanut's grave, removed the little stick cross Helen had made for him, and started digging. He made sure she was out of sight. She still cried for him every night, so he had to be careful.

"Peanut," he thought, "There's no rest for you, little pooch."

His stench greeted him as he lifted him out with a shovel and dug the grave a foot or so deeper. Just deep enough to for the sack fit under the dog. He covered up with dirt and placed peanut on top and reburied him being careful not to let the excess dirt show but not trying to hide the grave.

"Guarded by a dead dog," he said out loud, smiling."Thank you, Peanut."

He covered the grave with a piece of board, put a brick on top and stuck the cross back in place. He carefully wiped the soot off his coat sleeve with a rag then buried it in the pig pen. As he walked back to the porch, something caught his eye. He looked up. Helen was waving her red hat frantically. He waved for her to come back, and she scrambled down the oak, quick as a squirrel. She was standing on the joggling-board beside him in a few seconds, trembling enough to make it sway. He started to calm her but decided a trembling girl might be just the right thing to soften a young Yank soldier's heart.

Blue cavalry came up the road just a few minutes later. They spurred their mounts up and down the road, across the clearing and around the house.

"Any reb soldiers here, mister?" A young, blond haired Lieutenant called out, blowing his nose into a piece of dirty shirt.

"No, Lieutenant," McCallister answered as politely as he normally would. "Just us."

The Lieutenant watched his men fan out across the yard. Others dismounted and went inside the house and stable. "Do you have any gold or silver?" He yawned.

"No. Not a single piece," McCallister answered calmly.

"Bullshit," the lieutenant chuckled.

"Got a fresh grave here!" A soldier called out.

McCallister's heart leapt, but he reassured himself that only he could give it away. He glanced over at the soldiers gathering around Peanut's grave.

The Lieutenant smiled, "Let me guess. Flat trays and goblets."

"I don't have any. That's little Helen's dog, Peanut. Died last week."

He glanced at Helen squirming on the joggling board with tears in her eyes.

"Just so happened?" The lieutenant smiled. "Made of silver, I bet."

"Dead dog! That's all that's here," one of the soldiers called back. Another soldier came out of the house with this hands and arms covered in soot.

"Nothing here, Lieutenant"

The lieutenant shook his head, "If I string you up by your neck, I'll bet I'd find silver on this property."

McCallister looked the lieutenant in the eye. "No sir, you wouldn't. But we'd all know you would have abused an old man." He paused and thought better of saying anything else.

"Where are your horses and mules?" The lieutenant smiled.

"Wheeler's men took them the day before yesterday. 'Requisitioned' they said. They gave me a receipt. He pulled the note from his pocket. One that he'd asked Helen to write the day before, when the boys took all the stock and their only slave, Titus, into the swamp for safekeeping. Helen had thought it a wonderful idea and had signed it 'Lieutenant Powell,12th Tennessee cavalry'. Now he hoped she could keep a straight face. In the corner of his eye he saw her fiddling with her red hat as if she hadn't heard a word. Good girl! Smartest ten year old in the state.

"Well, well, well," Lieutenant sighed "Could you at least spare us some hams for the trip?" He never asked to see the receipt.

"I suspect you'll take what you want," he answered politely. "But could you leave us at least one hog to get us through the next week?"

"No use leaving any, mister. We're just the first boys through. I bet they'll dig up your dog a dozen times," the Lieutenant smiled and tipped his hat, trotting off as gunshots rang out from the pen. His cavalry followed with the dead pigs across their saddles. The barn, stable, and outbuildings went up in flames as they disappeared through the trees up the road.

McCallister knew it was well past time to go. "At least they didn't eat our yams and collards."

Helen wrinkled her nose at him. "Maybe I should write a note for that, too"

"Good idea."

He sat there for a while and let his heart come to rest before getting up to go retrieve the boys and Titus. It was time to leave. It couldn't wait until morning. No telling what the next bunch of Yanks would do whenever they reappeared.

The sun was setting when they got back. Everything in the house was packed into the wagon by lamplight while the mules snorted their disapproval as if they knew every minute of delay was a minute closer to them being supper for some Yank regiment. The boys helped stack bottles of rosin, jugs of turpentine, and buckets of pitch that had been hidden in the swamp. They carefully laid out the few tools they salvaged from the ashes of the barn. McCallister fought back tears as he looked around at the burned ruins of his livelihood. The vats of the tar, the turpentine distillery, the furnace and bellows of the iron works. All good money-makers for four years now. Mostly for Blessing of course, but some for his own profit, too. Mostly Confederate naval contracts. Some in hard currency but more recently in promissory notes.

He had to smile. Soon he'd own nothing but six acres of charred ruin with a promise of payment in worthless Confederate paper. He tried to remember when he'd first known it was hopeless. Thanksgiving Day for sure but probably as far back as early fall. With Lee retreating into Petersburg trenches and Johnson doing the same before Atlanta. How could they possibly win? He'd thought they were digging themselves into their graves. That was when he'd first had the awful realization that life as he knew it was ending. That his only son had died for nothing. That the day of reckoning was now finally at hand.

He covered the flammable load with a canvas tarp. Gray- haired Titus helped as best he could, limping along with a stubby wooden leg strapped to one knee. The peg leg was engraved with decorative carvings, etched into place over the lifetime of the wooden leg. He'd had only two others in twenty three years. Each also well-etched but finally wearing down with daily use. Titus wouldn't explain the markings except to say they were his own version of the coming of the Promised Land. Something that Titus knew was close at hand.

It wasn't that he felt any ill will towards McCallister. His mind didn't permit such a thought. McCallister had been a part of his life as had sunlight and rain. And how could a man be angry at the sun or the clouds? He wasn't angry. McCallister just wasn't part of it any more. That part was ending. Sherman was here. His coming had been whispered in the slave cabins for six months like incantations to 'haints'. It was something he had been waiting for his whole life.

93

When he allowed himself, he could still remember the boy who'd been tied by the neck to a pole then chained to dozens of others in the hold of a big ship. He remembered clearly a white man standing at the edge of the deck next to a cannonball that was chained to their leg irons and how he'd threatened to push it overboard and drag them all to their deaths in the ocean as penalty for any resistance. He remembered having to lie on his side between the legs of big men in front and behind. Row after row, one day after another.

After many days men began to scream deliriously and die. Then seawater was sloshed through the hold and dead bodies cut loose and dumped overboard for the sharks. There were days of being totally becalmed with a dead man slowly rotting beside him until he was finally cut loose and thrown overboard with the others. A man a few rows back went into some kind of fit and killed the man in front of him by biting through the back of his neck. He thought he remembered a black woman crying out in a strange tongue as each man died then blue sky and trying to drag bodies out of the stench to the light.

But he really didn't try to remember. He knew from experience that when he did, he felt something horrible inside that he could barely stand. It was a far greater pain than anything he'd ever known in his life, and he'd known plenty.

He'd survived the cane and rice fields in Louisiana and clearing the swamps of Mr. Blessing's new plantation, and he remembered the faces of those who hadn't. Some dying violently by accidents, some to snake bites, a few murdered by the whites, but most just withering away to sickness. Malaria, yellow fever, measles, smallpox, diphtheria and others he couldn't name. All he'd lost was the one leg to a machete cut that grew into a towering, white-crested, pus volcano before the doctor put that noxious cloth to his face. He'd awakened with the stump. He remembered feeling sad about never seeing the leg again. He still felt it could have been cured, stuffed and used again for the peg leg. But on this day, he focused on the end of the world. The lost leg didn't mean much anymore.

He knew that when freedom came, the etchings would erupt into noises. At first like ducks calling in the fog then as trumpets as the figures would take life, walking through fields of ripe corn to their families. And now that the great Sherman had come, he whispered to his etched peg every day.

"The dead will soon be free at last. We'll all live with our families in the Promised Land. Sherman's here. The great beast of a white man. The one who breathes fire and kills other whites with a huge sword of flame that towers over the treetops and roars loud enough to shake the earth itself. Sent by God to deliver all slaves to the great freedom in the New World."

Titus was sure the etchings understood him, but knew McCallister never would. But for now, all he could do was help him and his grandsons load the wagon with the last remnants of the old world.

McCallister was so distraught at leaving, that Titus had to coax him into the wagon and actually felt sorry for him. McCallister's world was ending, and his own was just beginning. He knew the snorting mules were just trying to get out of the way, but Titus whispered into their ears.

"Don't be afraid. All servants of the white man will be free. You've got to learn to live in the Jubilee."

McCallister kicked the wagon and snapped out at Titus, "Stop that damn whispering. They ain't listening. Never have."

But Titus knew otherwise. "Yes sir. Just habit is all," he smiled, backing away as the boys climbed up and McCallister took the reins.

Titus whistled the same tune as always. Just a few notes up and down but one that he liked and one that he felt calmed the mules. McCallister looked away. Titus thought he was cross again as usual, but he wasn't. McCallister was just fighting off tears. He'd decided it best to leave Titus behind. He figured there would be less risk from Yank patrols if they didn't have a slave with them. And he realized he would never hear that tune of his again.

CHAPTER 11 — BLESSING PLANTATION

EZEKIEL AND MIELA

Ezekiel led the group back to Blessing and met more Yankee cavalry along the Beaufort road. None of them spoke or offered them anything. One rider pushed right up to the women that looked them over like he might a horse or mule. Ezekiel laughed and bowed, "Thank you sir. Thank you. Hallelujah. Sweet Jesus be praised. Hallelujah."

He knew white soldiers could just take what they wanted anytime. Rebs or Yanks. Any resistance could mean death. Best to keep laughing and keep the women together and moving. And it worked, thank God. The Yanks moved on, and they made it to Blessing by supper time. Ezekiel had them hide in the backfield while he scouted the plantation. Yank troops were already coming across the cornfield. The barn was in flames.

"Jubilee has come early," Ezekiel laughed.

Poins, a field hand, trotted off through the woods to take a look. He came running back yelling, "Them other Yanks are just white folks too. They ain't animals like Toby said! He lied to us."

George told him to shush. "You should know better than to listen to Toby. He's always fibbing."

Poins stopped and took a deep breathe and smiled. He squared his shoulders and puffed out his chest, thinking it made him look older. "I knew that," he shrugged. "Just wanted you to know it, too."

George chuckled. "Thank you. Now we know."

Little Grace, Lizette's child, smiled at him, and Poins felt his heart beat out nearly out of his chest. His breath went short, and he bumped into the wagon. He couldn't think of another thing to say so he sucked in air in a little whistle. George stared at him. He remembered Poins' mother doing just that before she'd been sold down to an Alabama cotton plantation when Poins was seven or eight. She hadn't been mentioned in his presence since. His father was either Malcolm Blessing or one of the Middleton princes. No one ever laid claim.

Poins' friend Gage stood behind them listening. He still didn't believe that Toby was lying. His mind worked differently than anyone else. He'd come to Blessing plantation from a tobacco plantation in Virginia five years before after he'd been nearly suffocated to death in a barn fire.

"The smoke messed with his brain," Mr. McCallister had announced to the others when he'd arrived in the wagon with six other slaves headed for Bonny Hall plantation. There had never been any mention of his mother or any family, and Gage certainly didn't know anything. He couldn't remember one day to the next. But he was big, affable, and strong.

"And cheap," McCallister had laughed, showing young Malcolm the bill of sale. "Best buy of a young buck I've ever made."

"And just that little bit of smoke damage?" Malcolm nodded, impressed at the low price.

"Can't work in the big house, though," McCallister shrugged. "Can't be taught, you see. But we'll have Daphne mind him in the fields."
Gage had done field work tasks ever since, as long as someone was directing him, and he grew up to be the strongest man on the plantation. Big, gentle, and quiet. He followed Ezekiel through the trees to watch the blue columns come across the fields. A river of white men emerging from the pine woods at one and then disappearing at the other. Gage looked at their necks and how their Adam's apple's always moved up and down. He'd never liked white men's Adam's apple's. There was something sinister about the big white bump that moved when they swallowed. His throat went dry at the sight of thousands white soldiers and all those Adam's apples.

Ezekiel focused on the rifles. He stood there transfixed by the awesome power. Just these men in the field, he thought. Just these here would be enough to rule every black he ever knew. How many more of them were there? He knew Yanks were up and down the coast. In other states, too. But how many white men with rifles could there be? He kept watching for an hour. The column never stopped. He walked up and nodded to the soldiers as they hurried along. He wanted to have a close look. Thousands and thousands of rifles. His head began to spin. What could be done? Freedom was here, quicker than anyone imagined. But Sherman was on the move. Blacks left behind lost their protection. The Yanks were the only guarantee. Until his men had rifles of their own. But how to get them? He knew that question would have to wait. First things first.

He started to walk back across the field when a young officer rode over and handed him a piece of paper. "Special order number 15. Land for you blacks. You're free now,"

Ezekiel read it and felt his eyes water up. He swallowed hard. No use letting on that he was soft at heart. He knew he'd have to explain it to the others since most of them couldn't read. He knew it was something they needed to learn how to do, but it would just have to wait until freedom was here for good. He smiled remembering what Pompey had said when he'd heard Sherman was about to cross the Savannah River. The nonsense that he believed. That when the Yanks crossed into South Carolina, blacks would wake up that morning knowing how to read anything written by white men. It would be part of the gift of freedom. The ability to read, all the food you could eat, a new house for each of them, land for everyone, and never having to work again. He laughed as he ran back to them holding up the paper and calling out,

"Look here! The Yanks have taken Blessing. And there's an order from General Sherman. It's called Special Order number 15. Says we can have the land from Charleston to Savannah. All of it!"

But they all just stared silently, not knowing what he meant.

"You hear me?" Ezekiel laughed. "Are y'all deaf or something? Sherman says it's the special order! Number 15! It gives us our land!"

No one said a word.

"All the land from Charleston to Savannah!" Ezekiel laughed until his sides ached.

Toby nodded and understood, but the others just kept looking at him. Most had never been off the plantation, had certainly never seen a map, and had no real knowledge of their surroundings. They'd just worked each day, moving across one field or swamp to another. The world they could comprehend was the horizon across the marsh, the pine thicket ahead, or the creek they'd just crossed. The rest of it was just a tale to listen to by the fire at night. Charleston to Savannah meant as much to them as Canaan to the Jordan River.

Ezekiel Laughed and chanted, "Special order! Special order! Number 15! Say it with me."

The children loved watching him laugh. They had never seen him this happy. They started chanting with him and clapping hands. "Special order! Special order! Number 15!"

Ezekiel laughed until he choked. He read the piece of paper a dozen times to be sure his eyes weren't playing tricks then he took George, Toby, and Pompey aside. "We've got two rattle snakes fighting each other," he caught his breath. "All we've got to do is get the women and children out of the way. The land in this order is their safe haven. When it's over we'll skin the dead snake."

Toby nodded as he wiped his round face with his sleeve. "Looks like the gray snake's just about dead already," he smiled. "Might be time to chop his head off now."

Pompey scratched his head. "If the Yanks are here and the rebs are leaving. Ain't it time to get us blue uniforms and rifles."

Ezekiel shook his head, "No. Not yet. Best we just help them for now. The rebs are still about. If they caught you, they'd kill you for sure. They don't take kindly to blacks wearing the blue."

"Well I don't take kindly to what they done to Fatima," Toby answered. They all turned and looked at Ezekiel.

"We'll help them, don't you worry. But not with a rifle. Not just yet. We can clear trees, build roads, drive wagons. Anybody know a better wagon driver than Pompey?"

He knew Miela might have a different idea, but whatever they decided, they would have to move fast. He led them back towards the main house, coming around the bamboo thicket and into the big field.

"My God, look," Elsey pointed down across the field to a swarm of blacks coming out of the far woods following the Yank wagon train. They had their hands out begging, and Ezekiel felt a tinge of anger but told himself it was wrong. He knew most blacks had never known anything but slavery and these had probably run away from the plantations down towards Savannah with nothing to eat and nowhere to go and no sense yet of what freedom meant. He realized it would take a while. When you're whole life in the white world has been worth the same as a cow or horse, well ... How could that prepare a man for freedom? He figured these same beggars would soon understand that eventually.

Pompey sat on a stump beside him and chewed on a sassafras stem. He'd never seen more than a dozen or so whites in one place, ever. He'd never seen more than two dozen different whites his entire life. Now there were thousands of white soldiers with guns walking just past him. He was not only stunned but reassured. It all made sense to him now. There wasn't anything divine about whites' power over blacks like he'd been told. There were just a lot more of them. And they all had guns.

Ezekiel spotted Miela, Lizette and Santego crouched together out in a cornfield watching the plantation burn. He ran to her and hugged her, picking her up by the feet and twirling her around in the air. The Yank soldiers walking past ignored them. Ezekiel had a feeling of being almost invisible. Lizette laughed and clapped.

"Malcolm and the Missus done run off to Charleston, and Mr. Blessing's gone to hide in the swamp. He said he'd shoot us if we didn't come. Miela said go ahead and do it and just walked right up to him. He put that pistol right to her chest, and she just shook her head and said go ahead and shoot. She said it right to his face." She laughed harder and held her side. "Should have seen his face. Red as a camellia. Just stuttered for a while then huffed off."

Miela hung on to the Ezekiel's neck as he spun her around, and Lizette clapped and sang out. "See what she's done? Miela's the one! See what she's done! She's got the power, I tell you. More than any haint or root. Made Blessing all red-faced and stuttering."

Ezekiel held Miela and kissed her. Lizette caught her breath and looked away. She hugged little Grace and Yarrow who had run up behind Ezekiel. They giggled and tried to squirm loose, but Lizette held them tight.

Miela laughed with the children, and Ezekiel enjoyed watching her, but he knew this first night would be the dangerous. He gathered the group together in the cornfield off the Beaufort Road and stayed close as twilight fell. Toby, Pompey, and Titus sat right beside the women and Miela had each girl smear herself with mud and soot.

"Best look filthy. No telling what the Yanks might do, come dark."

Ezekiel made Gage and Jemps, the livestock tender, drop their shovels. "A shovel might tempt a Yank to shoot. Just keep walking around the women. If the Yanks cause trouble just laugh and clap and sing out loud. It's the best chance."

He knew Jemps was the smartest sixteen year-old he'd ever known, except for himself. Competent at all sorts of tasks. A young man who could be trusted to do the right thing in an emergency. Jemps nodded back eagerly, nearly bursting with excitement as rifle fire erupted from the barn with the Yank shooting all the pigs.

"All right, Ezekiel. We can handle it."

"I know you can. And don't worry. I'll be right back. I'll stay close enough to come running if anything happens." He shook hands with both boys. "Thank God, we've got strong men like you two. I know we'll be all right."

Jemps and Gage beamed. "Yes sir!"

Ezekiel took a sharpening stone, a knife, and a rag soaked in linseed oil from the slaver's wagon, and slipped off as darkness fell while Miela was busy helping Daphne tend to Fatima, and Lizette was cooking up a molasses taffy to let the children pull, thinking it would give them all something reassuring to do. He walked behind the big house. He could see Mr. Blessing talking with Yank officers. It made him smile. Mr. Blessing's new found friends. Ezekiel watched him from out in the dark field. He made sure to stay well out of the firelight.

"So Blessing's come back out of the swamp. Never one to rough it. I should have guessed it. He thinks the Yanks might be decent after all. Certainly better than a night sleeping on a cypress stump." He laughed loud enough for Blessing to hear. "There will be no Mr. Blessing by morning!"

Blessing couldn't see Ezekiel in the dark, but his heart fluttered when he heard the laugh. "It can't be him," he reassured himself. "The slave drivers must be all the way to Walterboro by now. Ezekiel's long gone. Just my nerves." He looked around at the soldiers and the dozens of cooking fires sprouting up across the field. He sighed. "Who wouldn't have a case of nerves?" He opened his brandy flask and imbibed heavily.

The Yanks were busy all around him. Burning the out buildings first. The dairy, the chicken coops, the pig pens, the stables, the carpenter shop, the blacksmith shop and the smoke house. The coach house and big house were swarming with officers. Saved, at least for now. The flaming out-buildings lit up the grounds and reflected off the tents spreading across the field. The whole oak avenue glowed red while soldiers laughed and cheered.

Ezekiel could barely keep from cheering with them. It was like a grand picnic. Whole roasted pigs sizzled on many a bonfire. The swarm of freed slaves milled around on the edges of the shadows to see what the white Yanks would leave them. Miela's group waited in the cornfield in a circle, eating cornbread and ham from the slavers' wagon. Ezekiel watched from the shadow of an oak tree.

He knew what he had to do. It wasn't even revenge. It was just pure justice. Nothing could be true in the coming world if Mr. Blessing and Malcolm were allowed to live. Nothing would ever truly be real. Their death would mark a beginning. The old world was ending. The world of slaves and human property to be sold like so many goats, chickens or horses, to be raped or murdered at the whim of an angry owner without the slightest thought of punishment. The old world of all that would be gone forever. For Mr. Blessing to live in the new world would be a lie. An injustice that couldn't be tolerated. He must die.

Mr. Blessing sat wrapped in blankets shivering on the open ground, dispossessed from the big house and surrounded by the few possessions he had been allowed to carry out the front door. Ezekiel knew he had to wait until Blessing was alone. The Yanks would soon leave, and if Mrs. Blessing found out he was the one, she'd have him hunted down if it took until the end of time. He'd just wait. The old man would have to walk out into the shadows at some point. Nature would call eventually, and when it did, the bastard would die. He thought of Mr. Blessing sitting there worrying about his future, and he had to stifle another laugh. He ran his thumb over the knife in his pocket. He felt the sharp edge.

"A wonderful thing that sharpening stone," he smiled.

Mr. Blessing stood up, and Ezekiel's heart went to his throat. He watched the old man walk away from the house towards the glowing embers of the blacksmith shop and out into the darkness. Ezekiel followed, being careful to keep his face in the shadow of his hooded cloak. Blessing walked on and on, and Ezekiel smiled.

"Too proud to do his business in front of the Yanks. Well, thank you, sir."

Finally Mr. Blessing stopped and stooped down, dropping his pants in the dark. He squatted down, and Ezekiel came out quickly behind him. The Yanks yelling in the field drowned out his footsteps. Mr. Blessing never heard a thing. Ezekiel walked right up, grabbed the old man's hair, and pushed him down into his own excrement. He carved open his throat with a hard pull on the knife. The severed windpipe gushed its last few breaths. Then he pulled Blessing's head around so he could see who killed him.

"Yes it's me. Ezekiel. Who else?"

Mr. Blessing's mouth gaped open as if trying to yell. His torn throat gurgled blood until he was still. Ezekiel cleaned off the knife and wiped the blood carefully off his arms and hands with the oil rag then stuffed it in the old man's open mouth. He kicked the body and admired his handiwork.

"So much for you, Mr. Blessing. Dead with your pants down. A fine way for a gentleman to die."

CHAPTER 12 — CONNOR

Savannah River — South Carolina
15 miles from Sister's Ferry

T he Savannah River was swollen in flood. Connor lay on an island of frozen leaves shivering in the winter cold. It was as cold a morning as he could remember. Sparrows lay frozen in the leaves. Squirrels hid in their nests. Oaks and cypress trees stood naked in the oily water that had crept two hundred yards closer in the night under patches of ice. Water stretched as far as the eye could see through the trees. In just a half-hour, he watched the river rise enough to sneak around and cut him off from the woods behind. Here and there a patch of pines stood on an icy island as a fleet of freshly uprooted trees swept steadily down with the current.

Connor shivered harder. His legs and shoes were wrapped tightly with thick waxed canvas, and his poncho cut from a rubber tent half kept him warm. The bitter cold was actually a comfort of sorts. He kept thinking how much better it was than the nightmare of the fight at the Muleshoe at Spotsylvania. Visions swirled in his mind. The blood and brains churning into the mud, heads exploding, men screaming. He pushed the thoughts away and looked up. A line of Yank cavalry waded through the trees on the other side of the river. Each with a Henry rifle and saddle bags loaded with sacks of food, ammunition, extra boots and blankets. Some with a spare rifle or shotgun strapped alongside.

Crows cawed in the distance, and the Yanks disappeared back into the far woods. Upriver, metal glinted in the morning sun. They'd be crossing soon. He could hear wagons rumbling over log-corduroyed roads. He lay still, quietly watching. His Spencer rifle was loaded and ready. Thoughts bombarded him. Why exactly had he come? What was he doing? What difference would one Spencer rifle make? He thought of Uncle Paul and what he would say.

"You're here because you didn't want to miss the biggest damn thing that ever happened in South Carolina! A sort of history in the making. Isn't that it?"

Uncle was right. But it was hard for him to think. His brain kept going off on tangents. He rubbed his frozen hands together watching the glint of steel across the river. He took a deep breath and refocused. Better at least to bother them a bit. It wasn't right letting the Yanks come across unmolested. Metal flashed directly across from him. He adjusted the rear sight of his Spencer, never taking his eyes off the spot. Just like shooting turkeys. He aimed carefully and waited for another glint. A man in blue appeared across the river, visible only by his movement. Then others appeared next to him wading through the flooded trees near the bank.

Connor picked out the first man, centered and fired. He watched the lot of them go down. Two seconds later the bark exploded just beside his head. He heard the shot as he quickly turned on his back. Yank sharpshooter. The thought came with another clipped piece of bark and another shot. Connor rolled way to cover behind a little hillock. He tied a holly branch to a wisteria vine then slowly crawled away and shook it. A volley erupted at the shaking bush. He fired back and another bullet clipped past his ear as he crawled through freezing water until he was out of sight. Then he ran for it.

Connor spurred Brig up through the swampy woods. Across a cornfield, a troop of cavalry trotted out from the pines lining the field. They were all wrapped in soggy gray blankets that draped down over their saddles and their homespun clothes dyed yellow -brown. Every man had a sheaf of hay or oats slung from his saddle and most pulled along an extra horse or mule. They trotted up with rifles leveled at his chest and circled him. Others fanned out up across the field and into the woods behind him.

One was pockmarked and dressed in black with an extra double barrel shotgun strapped across his back. Connor thought of his friend, Snake, at Spotsylvania. He could still see his brains coming out of his smashed head. He pushed the thought away. Another lanky, sharp jawed rider sat on his gelding draped in a rubberized blanket, poncho style, his carbine draped across the saddle, two revolvers and a long hunting knife in his belt. Cartridge boxes dangled to each side. He nodded at Connor's Spencer, his blue eyes squinting into slits.

"Nice rifle. Want to trade for a Sharps carbine?" He smiled.

"No thanks. It's brought me some luck so far. Yanks haven't got me yet." He glanced around at the others circling behind him. A motley bunch. No two were outfitted the same. Piano covers and curtains served as saddle blankets, and each man carried an assortment of pistols, carbines, shotguns, and Bowie knives.

"Who you with?" The lanky one asked.

"Came down from Charleston to join the militia. On furlough from McGowan's brigade. Names Connor. Sniped at the Yanks across the river just now. They sniped back too. Just missed me. Guess they'll be coming across ..."

"McGowan? Up with Lee?" The lanky man smiled. "You've come a long way just to join the militia."

The others laughed.

"I've got papers signed by ..." Connor reached into his saddle bag as the men around him snickered.

"Don't matter to us. We're scouting for Wheeler. Just making sure you weren't one of them Alabama Yanks riding with Sherman. Names JB." He tipped his hat as a rider came trotting up from the woods.

"Yanks done laid pontoons. Down at Sisters Ferry," the rider said matter-of-factly. "They're across and sniping something awful. Already hooked up with them others coming up from Beaufort."

JB pointed to Connor and smiled. "See boys. Connor knows what he's talking about. Best get a move on." He wheeled his gelding and called out orders. "Spread out, up and down the river. Connor, come with me if you want. We're short a man. Could use a Carolina boy."

"Be glad to," Connor nodded and followed along with three others.

"We got some from all over," JB shrugged. "First Alabama mostly. But it's a mix really. Mostly we ride in scouts like this here. Fifty or so. Five or six in each group. Spread out, nip at the Yanks. Keep an eye out. Wheeler don't care so much where we are or what we do, so long as we snipe at the bastards every day." He spurred ahead, across the field with Connor and the three others following behind.

The pockmarked man rode up beside Connor. "Name's Bucky." He tapped his carbine and laughed. "JB's got a mind of his own. Just does what he pleases. Thinks the officers are afraid of him. Could be he's right."

The next man on a huge mule nodded, "They should be. Four Lieutenants dead in six months."

"Wasn't JB's fault, Norton," Bucky grunted.

"I know. But still…" Norton brandished a thick spar of sawmill iron sharpened on one edge, swinging it overhead for Connor's benefit.

"Better than the sword. Cleaves a man's head off. I don't mind a Yank with no head," he smiled.

He carried a sawed off rifle and two shiny navy revolvers. The belt across the shoulder held a dozen brass cartridges. "Got to find me a dead Yank officer. Get me some more of these bastards. Getting harder to come by for sure." He pulled up, listening to a burst of gunfire towards the river. "Might get my chance real soon."

The man next to him introduced himself as Barry. Hair dangled from one side of his head, but his scalp was shaved clean on the other. His jaw jutted out, swollen and bright purple. His tunic was open and his gray shirt smeared with grease. He carried a shotgun and a Sharps rifle strapped to his saddle and a brace of single shot pistols that he reloaded as he rode, stuffing each with fresh powder, buckshot and a piece of cork.

"Keeps it tight and dry. Best invention I ever thought of."

Connor reached in his shell bag and pulled out his own cork. "I agree."

Barry shrugged. "See? It's already catching on." He twirled his bowie knife effortlessly on his fingertips as he trotted along. "Better than a juggler at the county fair. What you think?" He tossed the knife up, caught up by the handle and shaved his scalp stubble with the shiny blade. "Never once ever even nicked myself."

"Some talent," Connor answered, admiring his gray mare's new silver-etched saddle. "Pretty fancy mount there too."

"Got it off the Mayor back there in Savannah. He was riding out to surrender you see. Didn't make much sense giving the Yanks such a fine horse and saddle. Can't say the Mayor was too enthusiastic about my plan. But that's what you get for surrendering." He smiled and licked the gap where he is his front teeth had once been. "Knocked out by a Yank rifle butt. Just north of Atlanta, the bastards. They shot my horse too.

Norton here came back to get me. Killed the one that knocked my teeth out. Three others too. He's hell with them pistols."

"This here's what ya'll need," the third man rode up and nodded to Connor. He wore a Russian style Navy cap that looked like an upside down flower vase embroidered with gold leaves. He held up a big, double barrel pistol. "It's a LeMat. Good enough for Jeb Stuart, God rest his soul. Damn more than I deserve."

Norton held out his Navy revolver and laughed. "Get yourself a regular pistol like this here, Cheshire. You shoot that cannon and no telling who you'll hit."

Cheshire also carried a Henry repeater, and Connor couldn't help but stare. He'd never seen a finer rifle.

Cheshire nodded, "Yep. Bought it myself. Home on furlough after Chickamauga. Won't never tote a muzzleloader again. Best $48 I ever spent. All the boys should too. Sixteen shots, you know. Yep. $48 in gold wins the war. Nothing stops a regiment with Henrys. Too bad the Yanks got thousands of them."

"Thanks for the good news." Norton laughed. "Don't pay him no mind, Connor. He just loves bragging on that rifle."

Cheshire rubbed the rifle's lever and shrugged, "Say what you want, but it's a new war with this here."

"Norton!" JB called. "You and Connor take that woods there." He pointed down a track through the scrub pines to a low spot of water oaks and tupelos. Norton turned and trotted off without a word. Connor followed. He didn't consider otherwise. At least this group seemed to have some energy. They came to a stand of cypress and walked their horses slowly through the roots and cypress knees in a swamp that stretched as far as they could see.

"River's up." Norton whispered. "Listen!"

Connor heard it too. Rumbling of wagons over planking. "Bastards must love their pontoon bridges."

Norton shook his head smiling. "Good at it too." He sighed and stretched. "We've got some fighting coming soon." He checked his rifle, pulled some burned pieces of ham from his saddlebag and tossed one to Connor. "You're from around here eh?"

Connor nodded. "Charleston. And you?"

"Louisiana. Been with the first Alabama since '62. Skirmished all over Kentucky and Tennessee."

He gulped down a hunk of meat. "Murfreesboro, Chickamauga, Decatur, back down to Savannah, now this side of the river. We got a mix now. Tennessee. Mississippi. Texas boys, too. Some of us Caddo Lake boys with them. All having fun now, eh?" He checked his cartridge belt. "Caddo Lake? I knew someone from there. Shreveport right? Texas line."

"Yeah that's it." Norton's jaw dropped. "Well damn, who's your friend?"

"Name was McFadden. He's dead now. Up at Spotsylvania." Connor pictured McFadden with his eyes shot out.

Norton rubbed his chin. "Never knew a McFadden at Caddo. There was one at Chattanooga, I think. No, maybe it was McNulty." He smiled and kept chewing. "Your friend's dead?"

"Yep, he's gone." Connor focused on the rumbling noise in the distance.

"He's in good company." Norton swallowed another mouthful. "We lost a bunch. Can't think of it for too long though. Got to keep going." He stretched and tossed Connor some more ham then started to say something else but stopped. He fiddled with his iron spar and looked off into the trees listening to the rumbling of wagons on planking that came and went with the breeze. Then he cocked his head and seemed to come to. "Not a mile off. Best get on up there."

The temperature dropped as they rode. A ceiling of low, gray clouds hovered overhead. Cold, drizzling rain soon followed and with it, rifle fire from up and down the river. They picked their way through the woods to a narrow wagon track where they came up on more of Wheeler's cavalry.

"A raggy ass bunch, aren't we," Norton smiled.

Connor glanced at the frayed slouch hats, grease smeared coats, rotted out saddles, and sickly horses and mules. A young lieutenant with his hair cut short in front and a pony tail in back rode up through the pines carrying a saber and calling out to the troopers. "Pass the word. We're moving north towards the Salkehatchie River."

Norton smiled and pointed to the lieutenant's sword. "Might cut your self, Lieutenant."

One fresh faced, skinny boy following behind the officer beamed. "It's for sticking hams and honey trees." He was riding a mule loaded down with shotguns, blanket rolls and a wicker basket filled with honeycombs.

Norton turned to Connor. "General Wheeler loves his honey. He'll ride fifty miles a day but always makes time for a honey tree. They say he can spot a bee hive from a quarter-mile. The boys always try to beat him to it." He shared some more ham and they listened while the lieutenant dismounted to confer with another officer. "Heard the Yanks burned about every plantation in Georgia." Norton whispered. "Gonna do the same here. Giving the land to the slaves." He scratched his scalp. "Don't bother me none. Bunch of rich boys gonna lose their silver spoons to the bummers. I'm real sorry."

The officers mounted up and ordered everyone to follow. They rode towards the river where they came to a muddy landing in the trees. Mounted troopers had already been cutting down pines and piling them up to make rafts to float down river on to the Yank pontoons. Rifle fire sputtered on the breeze. Connor and Norton dismounted and helped the others pull the trees down to the river. Shivering men stood shoulder-deep lashing the trees together into bundles. They pushed them out with poles to catch the current. One after another the rafts went downstream and around the bend.

"Maybe that'll slow them down a bit." The lieutenant stood up in the stirrups at the water's edge and peered down river with his telescope as the last of the logs went downriver with the current and disappeared.

Rifle fire erupted to the rear. Men quickly remounted and rode off through the trees. Connor and Norton swung back the direction they'd come hoping to find JB before dark. They came to a lone farmhouse in a small clearing at the edge of a thick woods and took cover as blue clad bummers rode into view on the other side. They both froze, and the bummers didn't see them.

Norton whispered. "Stay still. The Yanks are moving fast today. We'll break back towards the river then around. Wait till I move."

Connor watched the bummers encircle the farmhouse where a woman with three children stood on the tiny porch. His heart raced. The first Yanks he'd seen up close since Spotsylvania. Two of them dismounted from their mules. Each carried a shovel and an iron rod. They ignored the house and family and walked out into the stubble field, poking into the ground a few times then started to dig. Another big Yank grabbed a young boy out of his mother's arms and held him by the hair. He held a knife to the boy's throat. The other Yanks leveled their Henrys at the woman and her two daughters. Another Yank tied a coil of rope around the quivering boy's neck and tossed it over a ceiling beam. The bummers jerked the boy up. The woman crawled towards her son, choking and kicking at the end of the taut rope. Another bummer kicked the screaming women away. The boy convulsed in the air.

"In the corn bin!" The woman yelled. "The silver's into corn bin!"

The bummer let go of the rope, and the boy crumpled to the porch coughing. The woman and her daughters locked arms around him. The bummer re-coiled his rope, went over to the corn bin with the others and dug up to silver.

"Pretty damned pitiful," he called back to the woman. "About get your boy killed over four candlesticks and one damned pewter bowl."

The Yanks split up the loot and trotted off across the clearing. Norton hissed at Connor and motioned him to follow him back into the woods.

"We should have shot the bastards," he whispered. "Shit." He felt like a coward.

Norton just shook his head and rode off through the woods. Connor followed reluctantly until they caught up with another of JB's scout groups and followed them north through the flooded river woods with gunfire creeping up behind them on the cold wind.

"Just keep them moving," Norton grinned. "We'll stand soon enough. Let them come. You ever read about Napoleon?"

Connor actually had, but didn't let on. It was easier just to listen. They crossed a little finger- creek in the cypress swamp. Norton pushed ahead and called back smiling.

"Napoleon thought he had the Russkys whipped. Burned Moscow. Then what?" He paused, waiting for Connor to say something. But Connor just shrugged. "They retreated the way they came. That's what. The winter snow and Cossacks killed most of them. Same thing here. Winter time. Deep swamps. Sniping at their flanks. We'll draw them in and kill the lot. Wait and see."

Connor had heard that idea before. The vast expanse of the south. A slow death to the invaders by wearing them down and picking them off at the edges. But it was all just a pipe dream. "They've got Henrys. And there's plenty enough food, as long as they don't mind eating horses and dogs."

Norton didn't answer. He was already trotting farther ahead, listening to rifle fire. But one young rider close by called over to him, "Dog meat ain't bad if it's boiled first then cooked black. Some breeds are better than others, though."

The man beside him nodded. "Collie dogs sure taste better than the bloodhounds."

"Come on Connor! Stay close," Norton waved to him to follow. "I bet JB's found a good spot for an ambush."

The Connor's spurred Brig out to the woods as the scout spread out along the edge of the cypress and tupelo swamp. He tried to calm his racing heart but couldn't. There was no escaping the fact that he was just a lowly fly about to bite the elephant.

Miela stood with the other adult slaves and children at the edge of the cornfield wondering where Ezekiel had gone. He was nowhere to be seen in the fire-lit fields. She felt a shiver thinking of what he might be doing. Everyone else's eyes were fixed on the flames shooting out of the second floor windows of the big house. Fire whipped up into the night sky shooting out a comet of sparks that vied with the stars. Each eruption of flame sent glowing red embers rising above a dark cloud of smoke that roiled in the firelight. The children squealed with each new eruption of fireworks. It was better than Mr. Blessing's gaudiest New Year's rockets. Nothing could rival this.

"Watch and remember children," Miela patted each one on they're head. "The night that freedom came." But as she spoke, she saw Lizette walk up the front steps of the burning house and run inside with an ax.

"No! Lizette! No!"

Miela ran towards the house and could clearly see Lizette inside the glowing dining room. Flames poured from the second-floor bay windows and crawled along the ceiling of Mr. Blessing's study. Lizette climbed up on the dining room table. She stood there as the smoke began to fill the room. She lifted the axe up high and hacked down with all her strength. The blade went all the way through the mahogany. She left the ax sticking out of the table, climbed down, arranged the china cups around the table as it is preparing for Mrs. Blessing's afternoon tea then backed her way to the door and smiled as the flames raced up the back stairs. She stared for a while at the axe in the table. It was a sight she would always remember. One that would warm her heart forever. Miela came up panting and grabbed her, thinking Lizette might try to go back inside.

"Don't worry child. I ain't that crazy. Just had to do this. For the children. And for me."

Miela relaxed her grip and nudged her quickly through the mass of soldiers over to the group of slaves now sitting in a tight circle farther out into the field. A Yank officer on horseback was looking down at them pointing to the east across the field.

"Why are you here? They're the ones that made you slaves. Leave this plantation. Free yourselves. Go to Beaufort. They've got land for you there."

"Yes, sir," Lizette smiled and nodded, waiting for Miela to say something. But Miela knew the less said the better. Let the Yanks think that they wanted. She kept smiling as the Yank officer rode off.

"White men like to give blacks orders," she whispered to Lizette. "I guess it doesn't really matter where they come from. It's in their blood."

She watched the same officer lecture Daphne, who just kept nodding and saying, "Thank you sir, thank you sir. We will. Yes sir. That's right."

She could picture the Yanks words going in one ear and out the other. Daphne was never one to listen well even when she tried to. Miela figured it was the reason she'd never learned to read. She just couldn't focus long enough to spell out a word. She watched Daphne walk back to the wagons and climb up to clean Fatima's wounds, re-dressing them with blanket strips while Santego lectured them all.

"We need to stay put!" Santego tapped his fingers on the wagon wheel. "Mr. McCallister and those bastard boys of his are long gone. There's gonna be peace now at Blessing." He nodded towards the flames roaring from the roof of the big house. "No need to leave as far as I'm concerned. The longer we take care of ourselves, the deeper the roots of freedom grow. The harder it'll be for any white men to rip them out. The Yanks will leave us alone and the rebs think we're being 'loyal'. You watch," he smiled. "Even after all they've done ..." he started laughing. "I'm 'grateful' All right. Anyhow, the home guards and slave patrols are still out there. If we leave Blessing we're fair game to every reb patrol that wanders by. They can shoot every one of us if they want. A black man on the run in open country is asking to be killed by the rebs. Best chance is to stay put until the Yanks beat them. The Yanks are here to help us. We stay put here and help ourselves."

"I don't trust them," Pompey shook his head. "White men ain't gonna take sides with blacks against other whites. Ain't gonna happen. When the war's over, we'll be the losers. The whites won't fight each other forever."

"Best to look out for ourselves," Santego kept on, trying to ignore Pompey. "Stay put on Blessing. Work the land for ourselves and lay claim to it. The Yanks might even give it to us."

But he had the nagging thought that Pompey might be right. That when the Yanks went back up north, they would be slaves again. Maybe they would call it something different, but it would be slavery just the same. He kept that thought to himself, though, and focused on the burning house.

Miela fetched a glass jar of honey from the back of the wagon. She pressed the wooden lid tight and tapped it firmly into place with the handle of big iron spoon. "You're wrong Santego! Look here a everybody! This is what you're up against. Now watch." Her voice trembled with irritation. They all knew it wasn't like her. She held up the honey jar so it glowed amber in the light of the flaming house. "See this?" She turned the jar upside down and the air bubble started to rise slowly. "See the honey? See how it parts as the air rises? See it?"

The children shuffled closer to watch. What was Miela up to? All eyes were on the air bubble. It had come to life in Miela's hands. They watched it rise up through the honey.

"See? The air is freedom. It rises up in the honey. See? The honey is ..."

"Can I have some?" little Agnes squeezed up front. "I like honey."

"Yes you can, Agnes," Miela smiled and patted her head. "You can have some when it gets to the top." She turned the jar over again in the bubble rose again. Agnes pulled at her arm and strained to see. The others crowded closer. "The honey is all around us. We're like ants in the air bubble. If we stay inside it we are free. If we fall back in the honey. We're ..."

"Stuck?" Agnes asked. "Stuck in the sticky stuff?"

"That's right," Miela laughed. "Stuck in the sticky stuff."

"You mean Sherman?" Pompey scratched his unshaven neck then picked Agnes up so she could see. "Sherman is the sticky stuff?"

"No, Pompey," Toby poked his shoulder. "Sherman is freedom, and he's on the move north. When he's gone, freedom's gone too. Sherman is the air bubble. Right Miela?"

Miela turned the jar over again and nodded, "Yep, that's it. We've got to stay close. All the way to Charleston."

Agnes pulled on her arm again, "It's got to the top. Can I have some now?" She wiped her sniffles onto her sleeve.

"Yes, you can." Miela pried open the lid and let in each of the children have a dripping, sticky, finger full.

"Just got to stay in the air," Toby nodded. "Don't get too far ahead and can't fall behind. The rebs are all around sure enough."

Miela looked up at him and smiled, "That's it all right."

Santego frowned and crossed his arms."What is if Sherman ain't headed to Charleston? What if he's going somewhere else?"

"Like where?" Lizette put her hands on her hips and stepped towards him like she might slap him.

"I don't know. Anywhere. Just not to Charleston."

Agnes begged for more honey, but Miela just patted her shoulder and smiled. "Then we'll stay close, as long as we can. Then make a run for Charleston."

"But why Charleston?" Santego kept on.

"Shush up," Lizette raised her hand, but Miela held her back.

"Because we've got a Promised Land waiting for us there, that's why. A place called Smythes on an island outside of Charleston. On Thomas island. I've got the deed in my pocket," she smiled and patted her hip. Santego squinted at her in disbelief. "How did you ... ?"

Lizette pushed him back. "No! Don't you say nothing bad about Miela."

"I didn't say nothing," he protested. "Just wondering how."

"You know damn well how," Quam laughed.

Lizette darted at him and back handed him hard. "You be quiet!"

"Stop it. Both of you," Miela wagged a finger at them and smiled. "I have a friend who arranged it. And it's not what you think. I trust him." She cut her eyes towards the burning house. "Ezekiel will explain. Where is he anyhow?"

"Don't you know they'll kill you Miela, if they think you're inciting," Santego ignored Lizette's hissing at him and walked up to Miela. He stood with his arms crossed."Best we all stay put here. Safest thing for the little ones."

"Don't worry Santego," Miela smiled back disarmingly. "They won't hang a woman with child. They don't want to waste new property." She tapped her stomach and smiled at Lizette. "That's right. I'm expecting."

Lizette quickly smothered her. "Dear Lord! Bless this mother and child."

"Praise the Lord! Bless them," Daphne answered, hugging Miela so hard she could hardly breath.

Santego frowned, "Maybe not. But they can take the baby and hang you after." He widened his stance and dug his feet into the dark soil.

Miela laughed. "The war will end soon. Didn't the Yankees just burn Blessing?" She pointed to the flames. "I bet the rebs won't be selling babies much longer."

Santego said nothing but didn't budge for quite a while. Miela blew kisses at him until he finally shook his head and walked off waving his hands over his head. "There's no talking sense to you, Miela. You'll get them all killed sure enough."

Old white haired Cumseh sat on an overturned bucket listening. She had just finished boiling a crow soup for future ailments and was holding her heart-shaped planchette board in her lap. She knew Miela had knowledge beyond her years and that it was probably the right thing to go with her, but she was deeply jealous of Miela. Her beauty, her intelligence, her charm, her innate goodness, her obvious power over everyone, black or white. And now a deed to the Promised Land.

She fingered her planchette, her most prized possession and her only link to a distant past that she remembered now as if a dream. She could still see the stiff corpse of her mother with her neck grossly swollen from the water-mocassin bite in the rice field. The other slave children gathered around her and the adults comforting her. Then Grandfather Blessing and the rest of the white folks coming back from a picnic and acting as if nothing had happened. The only other thing she could remember from childhood was a wagon-load of black men being hauled off to market. Her father with them, at least that's what she'd been told. She'd tried for years to remember his face but had long since given up. Working the fields of Blessing Plantation had been all she'd known since then.

Many slaves had come and gone. Men sold off, women dead with sickness, children born to servitude. But she thanked God for her planchette. It was only thing that she truly needed. She would take with her where ever they were going. Without it she was just a shriveled up potion mixer. With it, she was Cumseh, the conjurer, the last of the 'juju' women, master of spells and charms and conduit to the world of 'haints' and demons. Someone the other slaves had always respected due to her powers. They paid homage not so much for her help but to avoid the evil root. The planchette board made her Miela's equal. At least in Cumseh's mind it did.

"But how does she do it?" Cumseh whispered to her board.

Miela irritated her to no end. Always something special, damn her. But she still had to admit that she liked Miela, even loved her, like everyone else, despite considering her a rival. She knew Miela had magical powers, too. Some said it was her rich, brown skin. Others said it was special words she used. Cumseh figured it might be an ancient code of sorts, like the Egyptians and Romans that Miela talked about. Words that could make a slave disappear, or send a warning by rabbit or killdeer bird, or produce a twisted root or tiny turtle in the throat to choke an overseer to death. And she'd heard Lizette tell everyone a hundred times about what Miela did to Mr. Dinwiddie, the white overseer from Bannockburn plantation who'd come last year to buy some field hands.

"She just curtsied to him then he grabbed his chest and turned beet red." Lizette always acted out the part, clutching her chest and holding her breath. "Then he coughed up a pink froth, started shaking all over and crawled back up in his wagon. Ain't never come back again. Miela put a bad root on him, sure enough. Thank you, Jesus."

Everyone knew Miela had done it. Juju women, like Cumseh and Miela, could cause people to waste away with marasmus, or die horribly with the tetanus. A week or so of clenched jaws, stiff neck, back arched and rigid, and intense pain leading to insanity and death. It was just part of their power. Cumseh had it, so everyone gave her a wide berth. Miela was different. She was treated with love and respect and always surrounded by children. Cumseh darted her eyes at Miela and fought off a moment of jealous peevishness then went back to work.

She dropped a piece in slate on the board and barely touched the edge. It moved quickly to a letter. Cumseh touched it again. It moved to another letter. Then another and another. Lizette and Daphne watched in silent awe. Cumseh touched it one last time, and the slate spun onto the black edge and stopped. She stepped back. Lizette and

Daphne did too, watching her closely. They waited for a long while. Daphne spoke up, afraid that Cumseh would summon up a haint.

"What does it mean, Cumseh?"

Cumseh shook her head as if she'd just awakened from a trance then rolled her eyes back, raised her hands and cried out, "Heir!"

"Are you talking to Stonewall Jackson again?" Daphne squinted at her.

She wasn't quite sure about Cumseh. Why did she always want to talk with the ghost of the greatest reb of all time? Why did she always want to conjure him up? Especially now, after what the slavers did to Fatima. Hadn't Stonewall helped keep them in bondage? Keep them from the Jubilee?

Everyone waited breathlessly until Cumseh dropped her hands. "Don't ya'll worry. Stonewall ain't coming back from the dead just yet. He says not this year." Then she called out again. "He's got a message for Miela! He's on the planchette right now!"

Grace ran up and pushed closer. "What? Let me see!"

Cumseh shook her head, "It's for Miela only. "

"Is he really there?" Daphne asked. "Stonewall Jackson's ghost?" She leaned over Cumseh's shoulder and stared at the letters on the planchette. Her eyes opened wide as Cumseh's fingers moved to another letter.

"He's here All right. He's waiting for you to leave. Says he won't talk if you're watching."

"What?" Daphne stomped her feet. "That ain't right." She frowned but Cumseh wouldn't relent. "Ain't he like a reb saint or something? Ain't saints supposed to give us signs? Appear to us in visions and such?" She waited for Cumseh to answer, but she just shook her head and watched the slate a move at her fingertips. Daphne frowned deeper and went to sit by the fire.

"Daphne!" Cumseh called after her, "Stonewall says he's got a message for you, too. He wants you to tell Fatima that her wounds will soon disappear. Stonewall says his arm grew back too ... In heaven."

"He said he wanted ME to tell her?" Daphne beamed, suddenly more appreciative of Cumseh's power.

"Yes," she bowed. "He wants you to do it."

119

"Thank you, Cumseh." She turned to walk away. "And he's in heaven? You sure? Stonewall the reb?"

Cumseh nodded as the slate moved again, "Yes, he is. And he says be quick."

Daphne nodded and hurried over to Fatima while Miela laughed, enjoying the theatrics. Cumseh glared back.

"Be careful Miela. Laugh if you want but I got powers too. More than any haint-man ever. I know all sorts of things. Lemon juice for corns. Sassafras tea for blindness. Chicken gizzards in fresh rain water for colic." She held up a bulging leather pouch. "My conjure-bag gets stronger every day. Grave yard dirt, white man's fingernails, purple beetles, a jay birds head, a squirrel jaw, and dried rattlesnake fangs." She whirled the bag and threw it up in the air catching it in her palm. "See? It always lands just like a butterfly."

"What's that message again?" Quam asked, ignoring her bag and looking down at the pieces of slate.

"Heir," Miela smiled, trying to keep a straight face and not wanting to irritate Cumseh any more than usual. "It's a person who inherits."

"So what's 'inherit'?" Quam asked, dreaming of Miela naked in his bed, his favorite fantasy.

"It means getting something from someone when they die."

"Huh?" He cocked his head and squinted at her but still didn't understand. No one had ever given him anything. Dead or alive.

"Well, who is it?" Lizeytte glanced at Cumseh. "Come on, who?"

Cumseh raised her trembling hand and pointed her bony finger at Miela. "The heir's inside her, right now."

Lizette and Daphne patted her stomach again gently. Quam shook his head. "Miela's got air in her stomach? So what? I do too, sometimes."

Miela looked at up at him and tried to say something but just laughed as Ezekiel appeared out of the darkness, pulling on a long piece of taffy and pretending as if nothing had happened.

CHAPTER 14 — LUKE, SOUTH CAROLINA

Salkehatchie Swamp — 75 miles north of Beaufort

The morning brought more cold and rain. Luke stumbled along through the swamp wrapped in a soggy blanket trying to shake off the chill and chewing on a piece of hardtack. He wondered how some awful place like the swamps of South Carolina could be this cold. The whole company splashed forward in the chest-deep, freezing water. Everyone dangled cartridge boxes around their necks.

Reb muskets and shotguns opened up in front, but volley after volley of return fire into the far tree line caused the rebs to tuck and run just as Luke knew they would. Any reb foolish enough to stand their ground was a dead man. His New York boys knew how to fight. Outflank and outgun. Move, pivot, move again. Blast the rebs into rout.

A few hundred yards into the trees at the edge of a clearing stood an abandoned reb artillery wagon, alone and still. A few old flintlock rifles and shotguns lay strewn about. A boy lay dead with a hole in one temple. The other side of his head was torn open.

"Shit." McMahon kicked the boy's barefoot. They were still pink. "Look at this."

"Yep, just a boy." Jack, who wasn't much older, knelt and collected the boy's long hunting knife and cow hide sheath.

Dave spit on the boy's stomach. "A rebel shit. Boy or not."

"Amen to that," McMahon agreed.

Luke looked down at the boy and felt nothing. Movement in the leaves caught his eye. A squirrel lay on its back struggling to crawl away. Its back legs didn't move and blood covered his stomach. The other regiments were moving up fast through the woods. He broke off a piece of hardtack and sprinkled the crumbs around the squirrel then poured water into the hollow of the cypress root next to it. He saw the eyes watching him, expecting death. Luke knew it would come soon enough. At least he'd done what he could.

121

He hurried to catch up, knowing it was the war that made a man care more for a squirrel than a boy. But a rebel boy who had a choice. A boy who sacrificed his own life. And for what? He shook it off and was soon waist deep in another swamp.

The company was ordered to stop for the night as temperature dropped and the rain came down harder. The gray clouds parted just enough to unleash more cold wind then they piled back up to rip off another torrent. It was the worst winter rain Luke could ever remember. At least in New York, when it got cold, it snowed. Better to deal with snow than rain any day. It was so miserable Luke had to laugh.

"How can anyone live in such a godforsaken place?"

"Because they're rebel scum. Carolina swamp scum." Dave relieved himself into an oak hollow, and no one disagreed.

"Rebs are animals. Carolina rebs are the worst. Live like pigs, smell like skunks. Ever seen two skunks go at it?" Dave grunted. He walked to the edge of the woods and screamed as he tried to urinate. He dropped to his knees groaning. "Caught something bad from that whore in Savannah. Lying bitch said she was clean."

He dabbed himself with the little vial of mercury the doctor had given him and groaned as it burned. Tears filled his eyes, and it wasn't just the pain. To be so stupid. To let this happen. To dread taking a drink of water for fear of having to piss. He shook his head in disgust and yelled out, "You damn idiot!"

"Better get off your knees there, Dave. Some big old rattlesnake might bite your dick off," McMahon called over to him laughing.

Dave tried to laugh back, but the vision of the biggest rattlesnake he'd ever seen swarmed over him as the rest of them talked and built a fire. It stabbed into his brain more painful than the worst clap.

"No! By God, No!," he yelled.

Damn if I'll think of that again. He half listened to McMahon laughing at him, but it was no use. The burning pain in his groin brought it all back in an instant. Crouching by a log pile back home in New Ulm, Minnesota, with his mother standing in the snow by the wagon, his father cutting another tree in a rising blizzard, and the dark, foreboding forest encroaching around the clearing. Then his mother screaming and him hiding in the logs when the Indians appeared. How their faces looked so jagged with black and red lines. How they'd held his mother's hair as they cut her throat. His father on his stomach with a spear in his back. His sister's head smashed on a tree trunk. Having to stay perfectly still as the flames consumed the cabin and the log pile around him. How the Indians vanished into the woods. Then the big snake crawling over his back and out into the snow while he trembled in terror underneath the logs with his clothes on fire.

Dave caught his breath and looked around. McMahon was passing around a bottle of Madeira he'd liberated in Savannah. No one was looking at him. He tried to put it all out of his mind. It wasn't something he ever wanted to remember again, much less share with anyone else.

"I will never think of it again. Never," he whispered to himself, dabbing himself one last time with the mercury then cleaning himself up and joining the others, tolerating McMahon's teasing.

"Never trust a whore, Dave. Especially the reb kind."

Dave nodded and refocused. He took a deep breath and felt the stabbing pain evaporate. He rubbed his swollen shoulder where he'd been nicked by a reb sniper outside of Savannah. The ache brought a pleasant memory. He thought of how his Uncle George always rubbed his arm when he needed a drink, which was most all the time. The man who had adopted him and taken him back east to Elmira. He sipped Madeira and thought back on those good years of working with him on the canal boats, until the railroad came and put them out of business. Then working on the stagecoach with him on the Oswego -Elmira line. His uncle, drunk as usual, letting him crack the whip and set the reins for a full cantor on the long descent into town.

He remembered him being drunk when he'd taken him to the recruiting office, on his 16th birthday, lying to the officer that he was 18 and signing him up for the $677 bounty and a $15 finder's fee, enough money to buy Uncle several kegs of decent whisky.

"To join the army and fight the slavers," was Uncle's official reason, even though Uncle had never mentioned slavery before. Not until they'd offered the enlistment bounty. The only blacks they'd ever met were a dozen or so runaway slaves making their way up to Canada through the underground railroad and a boatman by the name of Swales who worked on the canal. But Uncle surely needed the money. No tavern owner between Elmira and Williamsport would give him any more credit. Dave remembered Uncle taking the enlistment money and immediately buying a jug of whiskey which he promptly sucked down. How he'd patted his protruding abdomen afterwards.

"The liver must be s fed. It's an Irish curse." Then downing another half and letting out a big 'Ahhh' and sending him on his way. "Run on Davey boy. The liver is still hungry."

He remembered his Uncle laughing as he closed the tavern door behind him. Dave hadn't seen him since. He hadn't even come to see his regiment off. But Dave didn't mind. To the contrary, he figured it might have even been a good thing. The Army had, in a lot of ways, made him a man, and he knew he was good at soldiering. He looked around at the others shivering by the fire and felt at peace again. The bad memories were gone. At least for the moment. Even the pain in his dick felt better. He downed his share of the Madeira and reminded himself that he'd made it through Chancellorsville and Gettysburg without a scratch. While others trembled with fear he'd always felt a cold chill in his chest and throat. Like he'd just swallowed ice water. It always steadied his aim. It made his ears ring too. So much so that he couldn't hear anything else. The volleys, the guns firing, men screaming. It all became a muffled hum in the distance. He knew it was a gift from God.

The only things he'd missed from home were the little things. Not having seen a porcupine for three years, the red and yellow of the sugar maples, poplars, elms, and birch trees in the fall, the goldenrod coating the fallow fields before first frost. But God willing, he'd see them again soon. First things first, though. And the first thing on the list was damnable South Carolina.

McMahon had downed most of the bottle and suddenly held forth, talking fast between belly-laughs. "Father worked on the Niagara. The ship that laid the cable in '58 to England," He wiped his eyes as if he'd told the funniest joke. "Worked for six months on that last trip. Three men lost at sea. They finally got back to New York, and the damned cable parted two weeks later. Two weeks! Three men dead for two weeks of telegraph to London."

Luke tossed him a scorched sweet potato. "Where's he now?"

"Father? Works at the Brooklyn Navy Yard. Runs the cordage wagons. Haven't seen him since the riots in '63. Was on furlough, remember? Helluva time to go home. Troops fired on the mob. They

124

burned the draft office and that fancy Brooks Brothers store on Cherry Street. Hung some black men they found. About two dozen or so. Just minding their own business, but in the wrong place for damn sure. Ain't no love for blacks in New York. Not in my family neither." He chewed one end of the sweet potato then finished off the Madeira. "Momma had to scavenge back in '58 before father got home. Rotten food from the markets and such. Couldn't make enough money to live off. Took to picking rags in the lower East side. We lived behind the Lewis Ambrotype Company off Chatham Square. Not far from the Five Points." He stopped and slapped his leg. "Any time a black man showed his face, some Irish boy or another would beat the tar out of him. Momma said blacks caused all our troubles. She never liked 'em for damn sure. Can't say I ever understood why. They never done nothing bad to me."

"Well the blacks did cause the war," Jack pitched in. "Without slavery there wouldn't be no war."

"Christ Jack," Luke cut his eyes at him. "It wasn't their fault they were born into slavery."

"Well, no, but still..." he shrugged.

McMahon tossed the empty bottle in the fire. "Jack might be right in a way. Just think of all the boys we've lost. Schmidt and Ellison at Chancellorsville. Maloney, Van Fleet, Rodgers and Foessel at Gettysburg. Jim Jones at Lookout Mountain. Coakley at Missionary Ridge. Hare and Wilcox with dysentery in Chattanooga. That new boy last week." He stopped and stared at the fire. "What was his name? Bill somebody. From Horse Heads."

Luke felt a wave of anger rush over him. A new boy dead and buried in Georgia, and they couldn't even remember his name. He'd just arrived in Savannah with Jack's group of replacements and had apparently forgotten Henry rifles didn't have a safety. Shot himself crossing a fence. Dropped his rifle and blew his head off.

"The rebs are to blame for all this, Jack. Not the blacks." Luke wrapped himself tighter in his blanket and shuffled closer to the fire.

"All right. I know. I know."

"Yep. And Carolina rebs are gonna know it real soon too," Dave swatted Jack's cap off his head, getting up to piss again. "We're sure gonna educate them."

125

Maybe he was right, Luke thought. Maybe the horror was really over. The wild terror of reb charges at Culp's Hill. The slaughter at Chancellorsville, the bitter fighting at Missionary Ridge. Maybe now, since Savannah fell, since turning north, it was truly over. Just a walk home. The smiles and joking said it all. He slept as best he could through a cold, wet night, but the morning brought more cannon fire in the distance. It wasn't over quite yet.

The regiment pushed on a few more miles up the road to another clearing with four rough pine shacks in a row. The first three were already in flames. An old man stood on the porch of the last shack wrapped in a blanket and refusing to move. A soldier stepped up to him.

"Move away mister."

A shotgun poked out from the blanket and fired into the soldier's chest. Luke and Dave fired back with dozens of others. The old man crumpled on the porch. The soldier was already dead, eyes and mouth open like he was about to finish a sentence. His friends buried him there in the cornfield next to the house and everyone was thinking the same thing. There was still a war on, and it could have been any of them.

They marched on and at twilight came to the little crossroads of Lawtonville and burned what little was left. A sturdy log smokehouse at the edge of the cotton field was the last dwelling left standing. All the hams were long gone, but the house itself was saved for the officers. A lone piglet darted out of the cotton field and scampered safely to the woods before soldiers could shoot.

McMahon nodded to some of the officers gathering around a pretty slave girl behind the smokehouse. "That girl there would be smart to run off too. While she still can."

She had a huge halo of hair down to her shoulders, and as twilight descended, her lips glowed red in the firelight. The officers led her into the smokehouse. Her shoulders were wrapped in a thick quilt, but Luke could see her bare legs poking out underneath. Her ankles were thin and delicate. Her whole body trembled so badly she could barely walk up the steps. A dozen or so officers pressed closer. Luke could hear her moaning. He thought of the wounded deer he'd shot years ago back home. How it had watched him walk up with his rifle. How its bloodied body quivered in terror. The moan it made as he aimed the rifle at its head and fired. He'd sworn afterwards he would never shoot another deer.

The girl moaned until the plank door shut behind her. The shack was lit with a candle and Luke could hear the floor creak. Officers laughed just outside by the fire and, one after another, made their way up the steps. Luke strained to hear the girl, but there wasn't any other sound. Just laughter and the sound the floor squeaking as they each went inside. He tried to stay awake to see what happened, but then it was morning, and he was wrapped in his rubber tent half in a drizzle.

He got up and wolfed down a quick breakfast of the last pieces of ham and hardback as the officers torched the smokehouse then mounted up to leave. He never saw the black girl come out. He asked Jack and McMahon, but they hadn't seen her either.

"Maybe they took her off in the wagons last night." They stood next to him as flames engulfed the shack and roared up through the split log roof and out of the door.

"Yeah, maybe," Dave shrugged,

The forest ahead burned brightly and lit up the overcast. The tall pines hissed and screeched as the roaring fire leapt from one tree to the next, exploding into huge torches and forcing the column to stay in the road while cavalry rode up on each flank looking like dark shadows between pillars of flame. The horsemen carried buckets of resin from the stills and painted the pine trunks ahead of the fire and letting the wind-driven flames do the rest.

Clouds of black smoke rose from the pitch pines and blotted out the sun. Dense coils of it drifted across the road, thick enough at times for Luke and his company to have to lie flat to breathe. They groped their way forward following sentinels of blackened brick chimneys standing guard over more charred ruins along a dike in the middle of the woods. It didn't seem to serve any purpose, but on it lay four dead blacks.

"See? Just what I said. Bushwhacked. Freed by us, killed by the Johnny's," Dave commented dryly, rubbing his frozen legs. "Look there." He pointed ahead, and from the thick stand of willows came eight shivering black men wrapped in wet, mud-drenched blankets. Their young leader was a huge man with coal black eyes and skin. His legs and feet were wrapped in pieces of canvas tied with twine. He draped his blanket over the dead man and knelt down beside them.

"Thank y'all. Taylor's the name. We all thank you. These four here were from Bannockburn Plantation." He pointed to the bodies. "Told

127

'em to wait till y'all was closer. Wouldn't listen. Now we got just eight. We were fifteen yesterday. Three shot by white cavalry. Now this here. But we still got eight."

Luke offered him his canteen, and he accepted it with a forced smile. Jack gave him a blanket. Dave and McMahon shared theirs with two others. Other men gathered around. Soon all eight were wrapped in blankets and eating hardtack crackers. Two of them wept openly and couldn't say a word. The rest thanked the soldiers.

"God bless y'all. God protect you too."

Each black man took his turn kneeling next to the bodies and praying silently. A message in the flesh to all gathered on that dike. The reason they'd fought all this way. They all felt it. No decent Union man could stay put forever up north and let the bastard rebs go on killing innocent human beings at their will. It had to stop. And they were the men who would do it.

They left the blacks hardtack and food tins then pushed on for miles through more swamp until it was too dark to see, but no one complained. They all knew they were lucky to be Uncle Billy's boys and a hell of a lot better off than most. Regimental foragers brought in more food, and everyone had a decent supper. Guinea fowls, roasted pumpkins, boiled cabbages, carrots, hams, and bottles of peach brandy. The last remaining farmhouse burned at dawn after men lit a big fire in the middle of the main room to boil their coffee. They left it burning when the march resumed.

"Where'd you find the brandy?" McMahon yelled to a rider tossing out more bottles from a basket strapped to his mule.

"The rebs had another little town over there." He pointed back into the woods. "It's gone now, but they were happy to share."

"Well, thank you kindly. The day sure looks a lot more promising.

"McMahon took a sip and passed it around. "The rain's letting up, my belly's full, and I slept well. And now peach brandy. And looky there." A general's headquarters-wagon rolled past with two more mulatto girls sitting on the back giggling. McMahon rolled his eyes. "His 'cooks'. Two young ones, no less."

"Maybe they cook better as a team," Dave laughed.

Luke watched their brown bosoms jiggle along in the bouncing wagon until they disappeared through the trees and wondered what would become of them when the war ended. He shook it off. No one else seemed bothered, so why should he.

CHAPTER 15 — JESSE'S BUMMERS

The blue regiments splashed through freezing water, chest high in places. Luke held his Henry and shell bag above his head while reb snipers took potshots from the far oaks across the cypress and tupelo bogs. A man down the line in another company fell backwards into waist deep water with a hole in his forehead. Luke's whole regiment fired back. Another old-timer got hit in the chin. It blew out most of his lower teeth and part of his tongue and jawbone. He bled a good pint into the black water, cursing and feeling around in the mud for his lost piece of bone. Luke helped him back to a shallow spot where stretcher bearers carried him off to the surgeons. What bastards, he thought. To do this to an old man! To come this far just to get maimed like that. Especially this close to the end. The bastard johnnies know it's over too. They had to know. Luke fired off his entire magazine into the far oaks and felt better for it, but all he wanted right that moment was to be back in Elmira. To walk down to the Chemung River and be able to enjoy the sound of water churning over boulders in midstream.

But why did God allow all this? Was He toying with them? Luke knew it was blasphemous to think it, but was God taunting them? More good Union men dead, and for what? Bullets cut through the branches just above his head. He figured God might be giving him a warning.

Another regiment moved to the front and the reb snipers stopped. Dave trotted up ahead and squatted over a dead reb.

"Not a whisker on this one, neither, Armed with a damn squirrel rifle again. For God's sake! Are they crazy? Sending these boys to fight with flintlocks?"

Luke felt no pity though. Just the opposite. The bastards were done, yet they still fought on. Still trying to kill good Union man. "Christ, just give it up!" he yelled. "Bastard rebs!"

Dave spat on the reb boy's face."They're bastards all right. Serves you right boy, goddamn you."

Luke sipped on his canteen as another group of foragers come up from the rear through the swamp. All were loaded down with loot and pulling along spare mules. They rode right past a colonel and his officers who were busy studying a map on a little table beside a smoking house. The officers never even looked up.

"They're invisible," Jack laughed. "Damn it, that's the life. Time for me to join up. There'll never be another chance like this. Riding, scouting, chasing rebs, doing what you please. Hell yes."

"It's still pillaging," Luke shook his head. "As much as South Carolina deserves it. Wheeler's cavalry hangs pillagers."

"Hell you say. They bushwhack us whether we pillage or not, Luke. Just like today. Hell, any of us could get shot tomorrow. I'll take my chances," Jack shrugged. "It's got to be easy enough to do it. Ain't never seen an officer ever say a word. Anyhow, the more men riding up front makes it easier for everybody."

Luke knew he had a point. Their own company's officers considered any man riding off on a captured horse or mule just on extended duty and still part of the regiment. Just off scouting. And Jack wasn't in a mood to listen to any of Luke's warnings. He was convinced it was his destiny to 'scout'. Around midnight he had his chance. Another group of bummers rode in,= and he decided to act. He felt like he'd just been given a promotion.

The leader of the group rode a mule loaded down with turpentine jugs and wore a poncho made of a tent half. In addition to his Henry, he carried a revolver in his belt and a shotgun strapped to the saddle. Luke recognized the man from one of the other companies. A man from Binghamton. Near Elmira. Jessie Long. A blacksmith with a reputation of being tough and mean.

He remembered what Jesse had done at Chancellorsville, after the battle, when the army was retreating north across the Rappahannock River. He'd walked into a farmhouse and killed an old man and three young boys. He'd come out covered in blood and told the Captain that they'd tried to stab him. He'd made it seem like self-defense, but everyone knew otherwise. Jesse had murdered them plain and simple, but the retreat went on all day and night, and nothing else was said. No one really cared about an old reb farmer and his boys when thousands of Union soldiers lay dead just a mile down the road.

The rumor was that his sister had married a Pennsylvania man who'd moved her to Harpers Ferry, Virginia, to become an innkeeper. They were pro-union and had flown the Union flag when Stonewall Jackson's men seized the town in '62. Rebel soldiers threw bricks through the windows and when the last of A. P. Hill's division marched out towards Antietam, a fire broke out and his sister burned to death. Jesse had vowed revenge. He had made it clear that he viewed all southerners as murderers. His hate demanded revenge. Foraging through Georgia and South Carolina had given him a means to that end, and he'd been riding unrestrained across South Carolina with a few other men now for a week. Luke tried to talk Jack out of it.

"He's a killer, Jack. And he enjoys it. Watch out. He'll kick the hornets' nest and have reb bushwhackers on your tail."

"Maybe, maybe not. Looks like he's holding his own so far." Jack checked his Henry, stuck a newly found butcher knife in his belt and tipped his hat. " You boys be careful now," he smiled, as he went over to join Jesse's group.

"Sure you can," Jesse croaked while relieving himself against a tree. "We're a man short. Just one rule. Do as I say." He buttoned up his trousers, jumped up on his mule, and rode off across the field and into the dark pine woods. His dark complexion blended in with the shadows. Four other men rode mules behind him in single file. All were draped in tent half ponchos with saddles bristling with shotguns and Henrys.

The last in line, a huge man with long blonde hair and a bull neck, tossed Jack the reins of a spare mule. "Name's Tom. This old hag will get you to the next town. But remember. Do what Jesse says. He don't mind shooting a man who won't listen," he laughed. "Trust me on that."

The others never said a word. Jack cinched up the rope bridle and stirrups, mounted up, and followed along. He turned at the edge of the field and waved to Luke, and Luke waved back, saying a quick Hail Mary on his behalf and hoping he'd see him again. Alive.

IN THE MORNING, just after dawn, a white flag on a bamboo pole appeared at the far side of a fallow corn field. Men crouched and aimed their Henrys expecting a reb trick. A black man in rags rose up. Then another. Then twenty or so. Women and children too, young and old. All with their hands up as if surrendering. Another swarm of blacks

132

appeared behind them. Then another. More across the field and more in the woods.

"Well I'll be damned," Luke lowered his rifle.

"Hundreds of them," McMahon sipped the last of the liquor. "Maybe thousands."

"Thank you! Thank you!" The crowd chanted as they crossed the field towards them waving their hands and crying in joy. "Praise Jesus, Praise Jesus! Lord protect y'all."

Luke felt his skin tingle. To see them that jubilant. The realization that they were no longer someone's property. That they were free. He listened to them laughing and felt a rush of pride. Freed by good Union men marching through South Carolina to crush the rebellion.

"This is something. By God, this is something!"

"Damn right it is," McMahon agreed. "Just look at them!"

A group of young black men trotted up the road in front of the women and children. Their clothes were in tatters, but all of them looked bright eyed and strong. McMahon scratched himself. "You think they'd make good soldiers?"

"They look pretty raggy to me," Dave laughed

"I don't know," Luke shrugged. "Heard they fought well at Battery Wagner last year. Fought reb veterans too. Heard they did All right."

"Maybe so," Dave remembered the rag tag lines of butternut and gray rebs coming out of the woods at Chancellorsville and up that hill at Gettysburg. They hadn't looked like much either. Not until they broke the whole Union line. He knew appearances could deceive. But he still had his doubts as the column pushed on and left most of the blacks swarming in the rear.

"Got to give them credit," McMahon nodded towards another group of black men trotting through the woods on the flank. "They're keeping up with the best army since Caesar."

"Yeah. Maybe we should give 'em guns. Let them fight for us. Give them Henrys. The rebs worst nightmare," Luke laughed.

"They ain't bashful, are they," Dave snorted, watching a young black mother nurse her baby on a full breast without the slightest attempt to cover herself.

"Where's she supposed to go?" Luke laughed.

"I don't give a damn where any of them go. You remember what Hitchens said?" Dave snapped back.

Luke did indeed remember. Every word. And he knew immediately there was no sense in arguing with Dave. Dave's friend from Ithaca had died at Missionary Ridge. After two days of agony, oozing pus and feces from the hole in his stomach and side. He remembered exactly what he'd said. He could still see it as if it were yesterday. His blue eyes staring at him and his stomach muscles knotted into a vice. He could still hear his teeth grinding and his groans that whole long awful night as he died. His last words whispered to them.

"I got to die so some shit slave can live? It ain't fair. It ain't fair at all." Then the blank, fixed stare as life ebbed a way.

Dave cursed at another black man sitting on the stump and three black girls skipping rope. "Hell with them all. It ain't fair all right. Not one damn bit of it."

Luke let him be and said nothing. What could he say? That that war was just? That every man's death had a purpose? He knew it was useless to think so. Hitchens was dead, and the blacks on this road had nothing to do with it. But Dave would never see it that way.

JESSE HAD HIS MEN PUSH NORTH through more pine barrens until just before dusk when they came up another farm with two slave cabins in a cotton field. A dozen blacks cowered at the edge of the field. An old white man, a middle-aged woman and her three young daughters stood on the porch of the house.

"No fighting age men about it," Jesse laughed. "Guess they don't want to go at it. Not right yet."

He dismounted and asked the old man politely where they had hidden their valuables. The old man said they had nothing. Jesse punched him in the face, dragged him across the porch, and strung him up by his neck over the porch. He let him dangle there with his feet barely touching the ground below.

"Tell us where you hid it, old man," he laughed. "We'll spare the house if you do. Won't bother the girls, neither."

The other stared impassively. Raping young white girls might have caused some hesitation, but each knew that if the others did, so would he. Except Jack. He decided right then, he would ride back to the regiment if Jesse crossed that line. The rest of it he could do. The price that Carolina needed to pay. Reaping the whirlwind and all. He was determined to prove to Jesse that he did indeed have the stomach for it. But not raping young girls. He wouldn't go that far. Not yet anyhow. He watched the old man kicking in the air until his face turned blue then Jesse dropping him like a sack. He gasped for air and started to cry on his knees.

"Just like a reb. Crying like a shittin' baby," Jesse laughed. "Now you gonna tell? Or which girl do you want done first? We'll give you the pleasure of screwing them right in front of you."

The old man waved his hand and begged, "Please, no! I'll tell. For God's sake, not my granddaughters." He caught his breath and wiped his face, but the terror was still there. "It's down in the pigsty. Under the trough. Three or four feet down under a board. Gold coins in a cypress chest. And a big set of serving trays, under the horse trough. Please just spare my granddaughters." He knelt there holding his hands in prayer. Jesse smiled, "If it's there ... well ..."

He nodded to the others in his group, Cord, Jack and Kennedy. They went over and dug it out.

"A fortune!" Cord yelled. "The old man done gave us a fortune! Just like he said. Gold coins. Some might be a hundred years old." He fired his revolver in the air, and all of them filled their haversacks with coins. Jack took his share.

Jesse untied the old man. "We'll spare your granddaughters. All but one, that is. You get to pick her out," he laughed.

"No! No, please! You promised!" the old man grabbed his legs.

Jesse backhanded him and pulled his revolver. He fired past his face. "You touch me again old reb, and we'll do them all, then gut-shoot you and dump you in the swamp. Bring me one!" He screamed to his men. Big Tom grabbed one of the girls kicking and screaming from the porch and dragged her inside, throwing her down the floor on a thick woven reed mat between two rocking chairs in front of the brick hearth. The others huddled screaming. The chosen one was the youngest. Blonde hair and beet-red face from screaming. He gagged her, tied her hands and ripped off her dress and underclothes. The two other girls were held at gunpoint on the porch.

Jesse fired into the wall just past their heads to make his point. "Don't you come inside or you'll be next. You understand me?"

They sobbed, but saw it was hopeless. The old man stood up, pushed past Jesse, and jumped on top of the girl to protect her. Jesse walked up behind and kicked him in the head. Cord and Kennedy dragged him into their yard and left him face down in the mud. The old woman ran and knelt beside him and pulled him into her lap crying.

Jesse was the first to rape the girl. When he finished, he pulled his pants back up and yelled out to the shivering man lying in the drizzle of rain, "See old man? See how fair we are. The others won't be touched."

The other girls on the porch kept sobbing uncontrollably, their faces contorted with horror as Tim, Cord, and Big Tom took turns with their sister. They watched her kick and struggle, but her muffled screams gradually grew weaker until she finally went limp, silently trembling in shock like a deer set on by a pack of dogs. The rain began to come down harder. Jack watched from yard until Jesse shoved him towards the porch.

"Take your turn or get the hell out of here."

Jack's heart raced. He stepped inside the door and his hands shook as he looked at the trembling girl the floor with her bare legs spread and Big Tom still on top of her. He thought of his little sister. How could any decent man do this? Big Tom stopped humping and stood up. There was blood all over his groin and all over the reed mat and the floorboards. The girl's bottom bled profusely. Jack felt totally frozen. He couldn't move. Kennedy jumped in front of him. He dropped his pants and humped her until finished then pulled away on his knees. Her trembling hands had stopped moving. Bright red blood covered the mats.

"Shit!" He pulled away in disgust. "She's bleeding like shit! God damn artery. Shit!"

Cord and Tim laughed nervously. Big Tom rolled up a piece of oilcloth and stuck it up her bottom.

"There, that's better now. Bleeding all over the damn floor. Like you're all hurt up or something. Shit," he laughed and gagged her, but blank eyes stared back. Her body was still and limp.

"Oh for God's sake," Kennedy kicked her leg. "Just like a reb bitch to faint after a little humpin'."

Tim felt her neck. "She ain't fainted. She's dead. "

136

Kennedy fell back against the wall. The realization hit him that he'd just done his business inside a dead body. He started to gag. The others just stared. Jesse knelt over her and listened to her chest.

"The little shit." He kicked the rocking chair across the room into the hearth and fired his revolver into the ceiling, "Can you believe that? A few humps and she goes and dies. Bull shit!"

Jack reminded himself he hadn't been part of it. He hadn't touched her and certainly couldn't have stopped it. He backed off the porch past the two sobbing sisters. Jesse followed and punched him in the back and started screaming again.

"Burn the house! Burn the body! Do it now!"

He grabbed the other girls and pulled them out into the pouring rain beside the woman and the old man. Big Tom drenched the dead girl's body and the whole room with turpentine and lit a match. The rest of them backed off.

The girls outside wailed in terror, and the woman crawled towards the house screaming, "Catherine! No! Not my Catherine!"

Jesse kicked her down into the mud and snatched a lock and chain from the woman's neck as she wailed. He cocked her head back by the hair. "Shut up, you rebel hag. You want your little bitch? Then go get her."

He tossed the locket into the roaring fire, and the woman crawled towards the flames, moaning, "No! No! Not my Catherine!"

Big Tom grabbed her by the shoulders and dragged her back through the mud to the others. Jesse walked over and snatched Jack by the collar. "You didn't take your turn, did you?"

Jack jerked free, but Jesse stuck his revolver into his face."You're going to take your turn," he grunted, nodding towards the slave huts.

Cord stood in the rain with a shotgun leveled at the blacks huddled between the two slave cabins. Tim put his pistol to a young girl's head and pulled her away from the others. The other women and children wailed. Five black man locked arms in a circle around them. The oldest man knelt in the rain in front of the others.

"Please don't harm her, sir. She ain't but a child."

Tim ignored him and pulled the girl into one of shacks. Cord fired over the others' heads, and the whole group went face down in the mud. Jesse shoved Jack towards the door,

"You'd better go screw that black girl. You ain't a boy-lover are you?" He fired again into the mud between Jack's feet and laughed, "I won't stand for that!"

Jack stumbled backwards. He told himself there was no choice but to do it. He felt sick as he stepped inside the little shack. Tim pushed the girl onto a plank bed covered with a burlap mattress.

"You think you can handle this one girl?" He chuckled. "Best do it quick before Jesse gets mad. You ain't seen him mad. Not like I have. Trust me."

He went outside and shut the door. Jack heard them laughing. The girl said nothing but trembled all over. She pulled up her dress and spread her legs, knowing better than to resist. Men who would kill a white girl surely wouldn't spare a slave. Her mother, now huddled with the others in the mud, had always taught her to keep her mouth shut and to submit to whites when necessary. It was the only way to survive.

The door flew open and Jesse stood there laughing, "Go on! Do it!"

Jack felt cornered. He didn't know what else to do. Jesse might shoot the girl. He told himself that was the only reason he would do it. He dropped his pants and lay down on top of terrified girl, but as soon as he touched her, he knew he couldn't. He just pretended to hump her. But well enough to convince Jesse. Then he buttoned up his trousers and pushed past him out the door.

"Jack's all right, boys," Jesse yelled, following him outside. "He just likes the black ones better."

He fired his pistol again and jumped up on his mule. The others mounted up, and Jack rode behind them, leaving the clump of blacks and the white family all wailing in the mud. He wasn't sure why he followed along. Part of it was fear of Jesse and part fear of being branded soft.

"I'm no coward," he muttered to himself over and over.

But he struggled with one nagging feeling. Something harder to admit. Much harder. That even after witnessing Jesse's brutality and the terror he'd inflicted, that there was something worse. A loathsome awareness deep down inside. The awful realization that he'd enjoyed it.

Chapter 16 — Miela and Ezekiel

Blessing Plantation

Miela slept with Ezekiel on a mattress of corn stalks. The thin blanket on a cold night didn't bother them. Each felt alive with the other's warmth. Ezekiel resisted sleep as long as he could, savoring being with her in the open for, all the world to see. His first taste of freedom.

When he finally succumbed, he dreamed of hiding from slave patrols in the corn bin. The morning sunlight jabbed at his face. He opened his eyes from his dream. The slave patrol disappeared. He turned his head and the sun seemed to follow. It scurried along through the pine trees at the edge of the field darting out in golden rays across the cornfield stubble. Ezekiel turned over and wondered if God was playing with him again.

He knew God had a sense of humor. He was sure he had met Him once, when he was a boy. God had appeared to him then in a dream as a small white man with a gray mustache and an ivory-handled cane. He'd sat Ezekiel on a gristmill stone and lectured him on the benefits of the obedience. Ezekiel smiled at the memory of exactly what he'd said in reply.

"You say everyone benefits from obedience? Well, All right Sir. I'll obey Mr. Brockington, if he obeys me."

He remembered, as that long ago dream began to fade, that God had tapped his cane on the grist stone, shaking his head and laughing, "You have quite a while yet for that, young man. Quite a while."

Ezekiel wondered if God was sending him another message. Or could it be just the plain old morning sun shining through the trees? Would he know one from the other? The slave patrol dream came back for a little while, and he hid some more under the corn. He felt different though. He was holding a knife and, if necessary, would kill the patrol. He woke up again, and the sun was no longer in his eyes. Morning had come.

"God has spoken," he smiled. "Maybe 'quite a while' is now." He felt Miela's warmth and melted against her.

She opened her eyes and smiled, "Good morning Ezekiel." She kissed him and propped up on an elbow to look down at his face while he focused on her smooth, brown shoulder. "Listen," she held his chin in her hand. "Mr. Dumont has a place in Charleston. Connor Dumont was here the other day. When was it ... ?" She looked up and made a face.

Ezekiel pulled her to him. "Connor Dumont? Here? What for?" His brain raced. "What did he ... ?"

"Shush. He came to help," Miela smiled. "He wrote me out a deed to Mr. Dumont's farm and a pass for the reb patrols."

"What the ... ?" Ezekiel was stunned. He figured she'd go with the others to Beaufort. Now Connor Dumont. The only white boy he'd ever considered a friend. But that was years ago when he was just a boy himself, and he hadn't seen Connor since ... He couldn't remember how long it had been, but he remembered the day Connor had left the farm to go to Virginia for the war. Connor's eyes had welled up when he'd said goodbye. Ezekiel remembered that awful feeling he'd stifled ever since. The slave owner's nephew. The white boy who would someday own him and the others. The awful, detestable, unforgivable feeling that he'd struggled to snuff out. The feeling of ... even now, even with Miela beside him on the first day of freedom, he couldn't say the word without it making his stomach tighten up. But he looked at Miela's face and saw it right there in her loving eyes. He quickly stifled the thought and regained himself.

"I might have whipped his ass. Probably should shoot him. Just for what his uncle did."

"His Uncle Paul's dead," Miela touched his lips.

Ezekiel just shrugged. "Saves me from having to do it. Still ... that damn Connor."

"He's trying to help." She kissed his nose.

"A bit late for that, don't you think?" Ezekiel held her tightly by the waist.

"It's never too late for goodness, Ezekiel," Miela smiled, her eyes sparkling in the morning light. "Connor said the safest thing was to go there with the deed. It's legally ours even when the Yanks leave. He doubts that will be the case down in Beaufort when Sherman's gone. All this talk of Freedman's land. It'll all be taken away as soon as they're out of sight. But not with a real deed signed by Connor. He's legally granting us the land. They can't take that away because the Yanks didn't give it to us. And it's big enough for all of us to live there, and Mr. Blessing can't make trouble either. Not with the deed and all."

Ezekiel smiled back. She didn't know, and he wouldn't tell her about Mr. Blessing. He nodded as if he believed it, but he knew the deed was worthless if any white man decided he wanted the land. But now that Mr. Blessing was dead, maybe it would be All right. Maybe there was a chance it would work. "All right, I'll have George and Titus take ya'll there. They'll ... "

"Wait. What do you mean?" Her eyes widened. Fear caught her throat. "You have to come too. We're all going with Sherman to Charleston."

"Listen Miela," Ezekiel smoothed down her hair and kissed her forehead. "I've got to help the Yank soldiers. It's for our freedom. I've got to do what I can. To fight for my own freedom, for OUR freedom. I can't let white men do it for me. And I can't be with you if I'm working for the Yanks. Maybe we'll be close by, but maybe not. Y'all will have to fend for yourselves."

"But ... " Miela knew immediately there was nothing she could do. She knew Ezekiel. When he'd made up his mind there was no talking him out of it. She buried her face in his chest and cried for a while. "All right ... " She sat up and wiped her face. This would be just one more burden to bear. And just for a little while, God willing.

Ezekiel took a deep breath. "Look, just stay close enough to the Yank soldiers to stay safe from slave patrols, but don't get in their way. I don't trust them."

Grace and Agnes ran over squealing. "Ezekiel and Miela under the blankets together." They giggled and pointed. "Going to get married. Love and kisses." They hugged themselves and kissed the air then ran off laughing.

Ezekiel sighed, "I WILL marry you."

Miela wiped away the last of her tears. "We're already married. Don't you know that?"

Ezekiel nodded, "Yes I do."

They kissed for a while longer then got up to do what was necessary. Ezekiel told George and Titus that the plan was the same, but with Charleston the destination instead of Beaufort. Both just shrugged. It made no difference to them. They'd heard of Beaufort and Charleston but neither had any definite idea of their whereabouts. Only Santego continued to disagree.

He scuffed his shoe at last year's dried-up cornstalks in the field. "I'm not going nowhere. Heard slave patrols shot runaways from Old Brass plantation just last week. Anyhow, freedom's here right now. We don't need to leave. Don't have to go find it in Charleston. It's already dropped down right on top of us. Why go get ourselves killed? Just wait here and let the freedom to take root. Right here." He sipped from a gourd of water then turned to George and Titus. "You're crazy to runoff. Can Ezekiel promise that you'll be safe? Can he promise no white man with the gun won't blow your heads off? It ain't nothing to them to kill a slave. Ya'll know it's true. Just got to stay put. Ride it out here. Take the land. Stay together. Let the whites fight it out. We'll be alive and free when it's over."

"Don't have to lift a finger, eh?" Ezekiel smiled. "Freedom will drop down on us from Mr. Lincoln."

"That's right. We just have to wait and ... "

"Let the white man free us?" Ezekiel cocked an eye at him.

"It's freedom, Ezekiel. Don't matter how we get there," Santego frowned. "This ain't about you being some kind of hero. It's about all of them being free." He waved his hand at the women and children.

"It DOES matter how we get there, Santego. It matters that they'll all know it, too. That we worked and fought for our own freedom. It's gonna come because of what WE'VE done. At least partly. And they'll know that for the rest of their lives. "

"What you gonna do, Ezekiel?" Santego laughed. "Fight the whole reb army by yourself."

"I'll do my part. As a free man. Helping the Yanks anyway I can. It IS a fight, Santego. A fight to free ALL blacks."

"I see. You're gonna free everybody."

"I'll do my part. And when it's over, I won't have to live the rest of my life knowing that I did nothing for my own freedom."

142

Santego glared at him. "I never said ... " He glanced around at the silent faces of George and Titus. "We can be safe here, that's all."

"We can be MEN out there. Free men fighting for all blacks everywhere."

Santego shook his head and walked off. He couldn't out-argue Ezekiel and didn't want to think Ezekiel just might be right. He told himself he was only looking out for the women and children. "Staying put is just the safe thing to do," he mumbled to himself, sitting down alone out in the field to wait and watch.

The rest of them followed Ezekiel's orders. They spent the whole day gathering what was left of food stores in the still partially-intact barn and what wasn't burned in the charred cellar of the big house. George had managed to hold onto the two slavers' mules and the wagon by keeping them walking in circles in the field. Maybe the Yanks had thought he was working for them or maybe they thought he was crazy, but the wagon and mules were saved. They would get them to Charleston.

CHAPTER 17 – BLESSING PLANTATION

MIELA AND EZEKIEL

The next morning brought misty rain, low gray sky, and a sharper cold on the northwest wind. Miela was up at first light to help them all get going. The bleak weather matched the dreary desolation of once beautiful Blessing. Black smoke billowed from a raging fire at the turpentine distillery in the far pine woods. It raced with the wind across the field over the smoldering ruins of the big house, stables, dairy and blacksmith shop. Only two slave huts and the threshing mill had survived the second night.

Titus raked through the muddy ashes for prizes, bending over every so often to pick up something and put it in his pocket. Elsey shivered in wet blankets covered with ash as she made her way from Daphne's hut to the outhouse in the woods. Columns of blue soldiers still marched steadily northwards along the road, with the chance of freedom moving along with them.

Miela quickly gathered up George, Pompey, Quam, and Lizette and gave them tasks. Quam, the water barrels; Lizette, clothing; George, food; and Pompey, the mules, wagon and feed. She prefaced each command with 'would you please?' But it wasn't necessary. They would have followed her orders even if barked at them like the Yank sergeants yelling at the stragglers scurrying across the corn fields. They knew Miela was their shining star and had anticipated these very orders. Pompey already had the wagon ready to load barrels. Lizette had Yarrow and Gage rounding up all the children to help them pack up what clothing and blankets hadn't been torched or stolen. Mingo had stood guard all night at the threshing mill guarding what was left of the rice and corn. Meila smiled and thanked them as they went on with their jobs. She tried to help but stooped over with morning sickness and had to sit down in the field until the nausea passed. She watched an ant struggle its way over the cornstalks carrying a piece of a wasp's wing. She blew on it and the ant braced itself but didn't let go of the wing. She thought of God looking down at this littlest of his creatures and granting it protection. She wanted to believe in it all. God's mercy and love and such. It pained her to admit that she had her doubts despite endless Bible lessons.

Mrs. Blessing always had the visiting white clergy instruct them, but it was always the same thing. Obedience of servant to master. She'd heard them say that God loved all his creatures, masters and slaves, but she never figured out why God would allow white slavers to take precious children from their mothers and sell them off to a plantations in Louisiana. She tried to block out the thoughts that always came when she remembered the seamstress, Moll, screaming at the sight of her six-year-old son, Jack, being carted off on the slave traders' wagon. She had the recurrent intrusive thought of Jesus being sold off to the sugar cane fields.

"But that's exactly what God did," Mrs. Blessing would say. "He gave us his only child. So we can all live in grace forever. Free of original sin."

It still didn't make sense to Miela. She'd always thought that freedom from slavery was much more important than freedom from sin. If God was so powerful, so full of love and mercy, why were blacks still kept as slaves? Why did children still get taken away? Why all the pain and suffering? Why would an all-powerful and loving Supreme Being allow this to happen? There was always the recurrent thought that God was either cruel or incompetent, or at least not nearly as powerful as preached in the Bible. But it always caused her to cringe, and she always tried to block it out. She still kept the faith, but the cold morning, nausea, and gagging, made it harder.

"Enough of this," she sighed, gathering herself up and going over to Pompey to help load the wagon.

Yarrow, Jemps and Poins helped load too. Yarrow thought the curve of the wagon, front and back, looked just like the rice boats he'd seen in years past sailing up the river in the distance. He daydreamed that the wagon had a mast of slim pine and sails made of bedspreads. He knew Jemps could figure out how to waterproof the bottom with tar and help him caulk the seams with string and pine resin. He figured they could all float out with the tide down the Combahee River, with him standing tall in the stern like a rice boat captain listening to the gurgle of water in the hull and the cries of gulls and shore birds. He remembered Toby saying the river went out to the ocean.

"The ocean is bigger than any river anywhere," he'd said. "Tilts back and forth like a big washtub. Sends the water rushing back up river twice a day. Runs like a clock. Up and back twice a day."

Yarrow stood in the wagon dressed neatly in his green tow-cotton vest and brown pants. The same ones he worn for the past year. He thought for a while about the river and the ocean tilting back and forth and decided it had to be his future. He wedged a sack of corn in the wagon and announced it to Jemps, "I'll have my own boat now that I'm free. I'll build a house right over there by the river. Go up and back with the tide."

Jemps shook his head and tossed up a sack of bedding, "Nope. We'll soon be leaving this place. Miela says we got land of our own. It's up near Charleston."

"I want mine right here," Yarrow frowned. "Don't want any other."

"Well, you can't. Sorry. Got to move away. Freedom's come. Ain't gonna live on a slave plantation no more. This here's still Mr. Blessing's land."

Yarrow crossed his arms and squatted down in the wagon. "Ain't moving. Heard Toby said we get forty acres each. I'll take mine right here."

"Jemps is right, Yarrow." Pompey stooped beside the wagon checking the ropes holding the water barrel in place. "Maybe you can have a boat over yonder. In Charleston." He waved toward the far tree line.

"But why not here?"

"Listen to Jemps, freedom's here so we ... "

"He done told me. Freedom just means we've got to leave and go somewhere else. What's so good about that?" He buried his face in his knees.

Pompey slapped him with a bundle of blankets. "Damn it boy! Freedom means nobody can take you away. Or take the other children away. Can't take YOUR young'uns away when you have 'em. They can't sell you like them mules. Can't you understand that?" He slapped him again.

Jemps saw the tears in Yarrow's eyes, and allowed himself a brief memory of a screaming woman being led off in a coffle of slaves for market in Charleston, but he didn't try to remember more. He had long ago learned that no amount of wishful thinking gave him back his mother. She was just that stinging wisp of a memory. Anyhow, he had a bunch of mothers now. All the women of Blessing.

Yarrow looked up and wiped away his tears. He knew Jemps and Pompey wouldn't lie to him, and he sure didn't want to be owned like a horse or mule. But he still felt sad. He couldn't help it. He figured his best chance at having his own boat was staying put right there on Blessing plantation. Not in Charleston or anywhere else.

"Why can't Sherman just give us this? Let Mr. Blessing and his wife be our slaves."

He glanced over Jemps who just shook his head. "I don't want to argue anymore."

Pompey sighed. "Look here, Yarrow. I'm sorry but ... "

Yarrow cut him off. "All right. But the ocean's tilting too strong. That'll mess us all up." He jumped on Pompey's back, and Pompey twirled him around until George came up and told them to stop.

"C'mon ya'll. Do what Miela says. Let's get this wagon loaded up."

"All right. Keep your pants on."

They all pitched in to help load sacks of corn, millet and rice. The only one, besides Santego, who refused to follow Miela's plan was Dye, who had been serving as an upstairs maid at the Big House. She'd made up her mind to go to Beaufort and wouldn't let Miela talk her out of it. "I'm headed to the Free-man's land in Beaufort, Miela. I know you say it's wrong, but that's where I'm headed. That's all there is to it."

Miela tried for hours to convince her otherwise until morning sickness made her sit down again. Dye kissed her head. "I love you too. I know you're just trying to do what's best. But this here's best for me. I've got to go. "

"Why not come with us?"

"The same reason you're not coming with me. It's what you think is best. I'm doing just the same."

Miela gave up and watched her pack. An extra dress, a thick piece of quilt, some sweet potatoes, corn meal, a jar of molasses, and some matches she'd saved from the big house before it burned. Then she hugged everyone goodbye, shouldered her pole with the sacks at each end and walked off down the Beaufort Road, throwing kisses to everyone.

"Be careful Dye. Jesus protect you," Elsey knelt down crying.

Dye wiped away her own tears. She knew it was a big risk, but she had to try. Beaufort was real. Freed men lived there with their own land. She knew George wouldn't lie to her. Maybe Miela was right heading to Charleston with Sherman, but maybe not. Who knew what the Yanks would do or how long they'd stay? Freedom was already happening in Beaufort. She felt strength surging to her legs and strode away before she started crying again.

The children followed her across the field tugging at her burlap apron while the rest of the women huddled together in tears. Agnes was the last to let go. She felt the apron slip out of her fingers and started to sob. Dye had always been the one who had brought her prizes. Buttons, bits of lace and cloth, brightly colored pieces of paper and porcelain. All from the big house that now lay in ashes.

"Don't leave, Dye. Don't leave."

Dye turned and waved. "I'll come back, Agnes. I'll bring you something special."

Agnes stood there watching her walk away, her shoulders heaving, until Dye disappeared around the far bend in the road. Fatima and Grace stood behind her waiting for her to stop crying. Grace gave her a rag from her pocket to wipe her nose, and Agnes turned around and walked back with them, still bursting into tears every few minutes until Titus gave her a little stringer of lead flashing from the floor of the wagon.

"The last piece left," he smiled. "Rest of it melted when the roof burned." He nodded towards the smoldering ruins. "See? You can twist it into a bracelet or necklace if you like."

Agnes wiped the last of her sniffles away and coiled the stringer around her wrist. "Thank you Titus. I'll give it to Dye when she comes back."

"I know she'll like it. Now come help me check the wagon." He showed her how to drip more linseed and peanut oil along the axle bed. "Be careful not to waste any. Has to last 'til we reach Charleston. Maybe longer. No telling when we'll find more."

"I'll be careful."

Titus figured no one else except maybe Miela and Ezekiel appreciated how much worse things could get. A worn out hub, a broken rim, the wagon overturned, the children having to walk, the adults having to carry all the provisions. He wiped the springs gently with his oil rag and patted the wheel. Old but still strong. Just like me. He latched the jockey box that brimmed with extra blankets, tapped down the covers on the water barrels that sloshed full and tightened the rope loops on the side holding picks, hatchets, axes and shovels. "Good work, Agnes. Now go help Lizette packed up the salt from the meat cellar."

"All you can carry," Lizette smiled at her. "I bet it's worth $200 a sack. We can use it for barter. Thank God the Yankees didn't take it. Thank you Lord for protecting us."

Lizette had already dug up the charred dirt under the burned smokehouse and boiled it down to a salty residue the night before. She wanted everyone to know that she was the one Miela had entrusted to guard it all. She let Quam have a taste, on a piece of greasy cornbread. He wolfed it down and smiled in a way that reminded her of the day he'd came back from the Lunatic Asylum in Columbia years ago.

She remembered a cold wind had blowing in off the fields when the wagon had arrived loaded with barrels and crates, with Quam sitting on a piece of iron machinery for the cotton press. The wagon driver had stepped down and directed the field hands to unload cargo, leaving Quam to climb down by himself. He'd been gone for six months after he'd come down with the scarlet fever that caused him to talk out of his head and bark and growl like a dog. Mr. McCallister tied him up an in a thick burlap girdle and had him carted him off to Columbia. Lizette remembered how he'd smiled that same smile and how Gage had said that he thought it marvelous than a lunatic could still be happy. She remembered Toby running up to hug him and Cumseh rubbing peanut oil in his hair.

"It's All right Quam," Cumseh had looked around the plantation grounds. "One asylum is pretty much like another. Except it's easier getting released from Columbia."

Now she watched Quam help little Agnes carefully stuff burlap padding between the baked clay pots full of cornmeal, each with a deep patina of glaze and its own waxed, wicker top. Agnes averted her eyes as she tied to water jugs to their spots on each side of the wagon. She still didn't like the faces Titus had carved into the clay.

"Like demons," she thought. "Maybe a 'plateye', the worst demon of all. Best not to even to think the word and certainly not to look them in the eye."

Quam teased her. "That one's winking at you. Gonna creep down from there tonight and bite you on the neck." He held his hands to his ears and wiggled his fingers, but Agnes knew he was teasing.

"Oh shut up. I'm not scared of no pot." She waved him off but still wouldn't look at the faces.

Ezekiel called for the men to top off each wagon with sacks of sweet potatoes and hogsheads of sorghum syrup. The food and provisions that the Yank soldiers had missed. "Enough to keep you going for two weeks if you're careful."

Quam helped Toby finish with the last sacks then went with Jemps to whack the four big pecan trees with long bamboo poles as high as they could reach while the rest of the children scooped them up. While they weren't looking, Titus gave Agnes another prize. A gold 'US' button he'd found in the ruins of the barn.

"It'll help her get over Dye,"he whispered to Toby.

Grace saw Agnes cleaning it off with her tongue. She didn't mind not getting one herself, not really, but she already missed her cozy room under the back stairs where Mrs. Blessing had let her sleep. She liked having been allowed to sleep in the big house and cried when it burned. She'd learned to steer clear of Malcolm Blessing with his backhand slaps and cursing, but it wasn't hard to do since Mrs. Blessing had let her play in her daughter's room, the one who had died many years ago of diphtheria. Sometimes she would even hide from her mother, Lizette, when she called her for another errand.

She hadn't realized that Lizette knew exactly where she was all the while, but allowed it knowing that at least Mrs. Blessing treated her decently and protected her from Malcolm. Grace thought her hiding was quite clever and had no sense of others' perspectives. She loved the comforts of the big house as any six year-old would. That the others slaves' lives were harsh and miserable was not something she ever really thought about. It never even entered my mind. All that counted until now was that Mrs. Blessing let her stay inside and play. She looked at the

150

mud on her shoes as she trudged along behind the others through the ashes and felt the cold damp cutting through her blanket coat and cried again until Lizette comforted her with a big hug.

The men finished loading everything of value, and everyone gathered around a fire for a supper together of ham fat and cornmeal pancakes. The next morning they all said their goodbyes. George and Titus were to go with the women and children. All the rest of the men. Toby, Quam, Pompey, Esau, and Mingo volunteered to go with Ezekiel.

Ezekiel hugged Miela. "Take care of yourself. Stay close to the Yank column, but make camp far enough away at night. No telling what soldiers might do."

"I know, I know. We'll be invisible all the way."

"It's not funny, Miela. You've got to do it just right. Reb patrols could hang all of you."

"They don't hang children. Never have."

"Damn it, you know what I mean."

She put a finger to her lips and smiled, "All right, we'll be careful." She grabbed his head and squeezed his cheeks, kissing him hard on the mouth. The children squealed and giggled.

"Be careful, please," Ezekiel held her by the waist and pulled her tightly against him.

"I will. I promise I will."

Ezekiel made doubly sure the wagon was evenly loaded and the mules properly harnessed. He waved to them as they walked off under the avenue of oaks past the rubble of the big house. Titus blew his conch shell as they moved on down the road. His way of saying goodbye to all he'd ever known. Miela walked behind the wagon and waved every three or four steps until she disappeared into the far pines. Ezekiel fought off an urge to cry, but his eyes still watered up. He turned away and wiped them off.

"By God, I will not," he thought.

Toby came ups beside him punched him on the shoulder. "She'll be All right. Miela's got the gift. Just like you. As Miela goes, goes the Jubilee."

Ezekiel regained himself. "Yep. She'll be fine. Pity the rebs who try to stop her."

151

Toby smiled. Ezekiel was back. The world could proceed. "C'mon Ezekiel, let's find ourselves a Yank officer ... To enlist."

CHAPTER 18 – EZEKIEL

on the Swamp Road north from Blessing Plantation

An officer from the quartermaster Corps accepted Ezekiel's offer to work and put them in with a group of freed black men, mostly from Georgia, who had built log 'corduroy' roads through the swamps outside Savannah. As they marched off into the woods behind the white regiments, they looked back at scorched Blessing, and all felt a bit stunned. Pompey and Quam started singing 'Now thank we all Our God', and most of the black men joined in. Ezekiel listened and tolerated it, but all the hymns he'd ever heard seemed in some way to give thanks for the world of slavery. The others loved it though, and it was indeed a fine hymn, as much as any could be, and despite being Mr. Blessing's favorite. But he couldn't bring himself to sing along. Not yet.

They walked on for miles and miles until axes and sharpening stones were finally handed out. Ezekiel and his crew were set to work with the others to 'corduroy' a swamp road for a brigade of commissary wagons. Ezekiel was glad for the work since he didn't have time to think any more of Miela. Anything could happen to her, no matter what gifts she possessed.

Doubts bombarded him as trees were cut down, carried into place, and pegged down in the mud through the swamp for the wagons. Would she be all right? Would something happen to her? Would he regret forever not going with her? He forced himself to focus on the task at hand, working all that day and halfway into the night before rest was called and then sleeping as best he could on piles of logs. He dreamed of Miela calling him from across a river and not being able to get to her and woke up with a start.

Dawn greeted him with a cold drizzle. Men were already crowding around a commissary wagon to get hardtack crackers and chunks of cold ham. It all went down too quickly, but Quam saved a piece of ham fat to smear on a big boil festering on his elbow.

"It'll draw out the pus as it dries," He laughed, rolling his sleeve back down.

"Pigs' fat is just superstition," Toby said. "God you're dumb."

"Maybe." Quam laughed rubbing his greasy hands through his hair. "But I like the way it feels. Anyhow, ain't I free now? To do what I want? Ain't I?"

"Free men still need to work," Ezekiel picked up an axe and nodded to the Georgia men heading into the swamp. "Come on boys, time to get to it."

Quam followed the others for another day of cutting trees, pegging down stringers and cross logs, and helping wrestle pontoons over the deepest stream in the swamp. The last brackets were hammered shut, and they all cheered as the white wagon drivers crossed over the creaking pontoon bridge. Ezekiel and the others stood aside, shivering hip deep in the cold water as wagon after wagon passed over the submerged corduroy then across the pontoons. Most of the drivers ignored them but a few nodded, and one red bearded, flush-faced wagoner actually thanked them.

"Not a bad corduroy, boys. I've crossed worse." He flicked the reins and his mule team plodded along knee deep, picking their footing in the water as the wheels of the wagon kept up a thunking cadence over the submerged logs. "Gitup mules! Gitup and cross this miserable reb swamp."

Toby rested against his axe and yelled out, "We'll corduroy as far as y'all need to go! No swamp can stop us. We'll get you...."

A rifle shot exploded close by. Every one dropped.

"What the hell!" Ezekiel glanced over at Quam. He was face down in the mud."No!"

He jumped to him and pulled him up. There was a red hole in his forehead. He had never made a sound. Esau, Ezekiel and Mingo dropped to his side stunned, but he was already dead. Brain poured out the back of his head. The wagons stopped. A young Yank soldier fiddled with his rifle. An older driver slapped his head and cursed.

"What did I tell you? Don't load the damn Henry when we're causing corduroy. See what happens!" He looked back, shook his head then snapped the reins and kept on. A dead black man was no reason to slow down the column. Uncle Billy's order was to always keep moving.

154

Stopping just to get mixed up with an accidental killing was certainly not in his plan for the day. He pulled at his whiskers and looked Ezekiel in the eye.

"Sorry."

He flecked the reins and his mules went on. No one else said a word, and no other wagon stopped. Ezekiel watched the soldiers file past. Another dead black man meant nothing to them. Their concerns lay somewhere up ahead. Getting home in one piece, mostly.

Ezekiel waited there on his knees half expecting Quam to stand up and tell them he was all right. He made himself feel the hole in his forehead and in the back of his skull. Seeing the blood and brains in his fingers forced him to his feet.

"C'mon lets bury him. Get up, let' go."

Esau, Toby, Mingo, and Pompey rose out of their daze and helped carry Quam up to a patch of dry ground where they buried him as best they could, all realizing it could have been any one of them in the ground.

"You go on to the promised land, Quam," Esau cried. "We'll get there too, someday."

Ezekiel laid his shovel next to him on the grave and wiped the blood off his face before they wrapped him in a blanket and covered him with dirt. Toby made a little cross from sticks tied with strips of palm fronds and stuck it in the ground at his feet.

"Here lies a good man. Deserving better than most. We can ... " he started to say something else but couldn't.

Ezekiel finished for him. "We can keep him in our hearts. But we've got to go on."

He waded back through the swamp and the others followed and went back to work. It was the only thing he knew. Work soaked up the gagging bile in his throat. Had his pride killed Quam? Would he be death to them all? And Miela ... ? He hacked away at the trees and carried logs until his arms and back screamed, and it helped. He had to see it through. It was the only way now to honor Quam.

He kept them working hard all day in the waist deep water. They all shivered enough to rock the corduroy logs, but no one backed off. They are felt the same. Quam was gone. Vanished in the swamp. Killed by the whites just as freedom knocked. The rest of them were still alive and free, working to be men and maybe help others be free. Nothing could stop them now. Not Quam's death. Not the freezing water. Not hunger or exhaustion. Not even the taunting of some of the white Yankee soldiers crossing over their road.

"Better watch it in there, boy," a grinning sergeant on horseback called out. "Alligators will chase a black man. They like that dark meat."

The rest of his cavalry troop laughed as they splashed by. Ezekiel glanced up long enough to get a look at his face. Just in case, he thought. Maybe we'll meet again. But outwardly he ignored the white soldiers' taunts as did the others. He knew it had to be tolerated, even now with Quam in a hole in the swamp. Blue whites, gray whites. It didn't matter much. He smiled back at them knowing it was best. Knowing whites never knew exactly what to think of a smiling black man. He would keep on helping the Yanks with the corduroy and pontoons even if they cursed and abused him, because he knew they were still on the best possible road to freedom. Some day he would live beholden to no one. Free to do as he pleased. To go wherever and whenever he chose. To be able to decide for himself how he lived his own life.

He knew he could take anything the Yanks could throw at him. But what about the others. Toby was tough and a jack of all trades. As good a carpenter as Mingo and equal to George as a blacksmith. He could lay brick, plow a field, handle a team of mules as well as Ezekiel himself. He would do fine. Esau was hard too. Years behind the plow. Sturdy and strong. Mingo and Pompey were the ones that worried him. Too used to working in a dry, warm, carpenter-wheelwright shop. And always waiting to be told what to do. But how bad could it be?

He thought of the whippings and the steamy hot, malarial rice fields. Nothing much could top that. Then Quam. Dead and gone after one day. A strong, hard-working, black man, killed by the whites as soon as he stepped foot off Blessing plantation.

Maybe they should all have stayed put. He shook off the surge of guilt and looked around at the black pioneers chopping trees and carrying logs. He reminded himself that he didn't kill Quam, slavery did. And anyhow, death didn't scare him. It never really had. He knew he had nothing to lose. But if he had to die, better it be while working for freedom. But the doubts still lingered. Could the others do it? Could Miela?

Toby followed Ezekiel's every move. He knew Ezekiel was his best chance. What happened to Quam could happen to any slave, anytime. He thought of his mother and father dead in Louisiana, or so George had told him a long time ago. He remembered George saying that his parents were both buried in the same graveyard down in Baton Rouge.

"Dead of yellow fever. Mr. Blessing's cousin down there sold you when you are just three. Said the wagon left before the fever game. Killed eighteen others on the plantation. Blessing said it meant you were born lucky."

Toby grunted. Lucky! He chopped harder. The only luck he needed now was a chance to seek justice. Ezekiel was the key. He'd follow him to his last breath. If he had brothers and sisters somewhere, he figured they'd be thinking the same way. It was time to fight back. If the Yanks won, he was free. If the rebs won, they'd just have to kill him. In the meantime he'd work until he dropped.

The temperature plummeted by midday, and the swamp iced up. Ezekiel led the way, stepping through the ice and finding footholds in the roots and tangles in the swamp bottom. The cold stabbed at his feet through the strip of rubberized blanket tied over his shoes. Mingo and Pompey groaned but followed the others across. Each trying to suffer the frigid water as bravely as the man in front. The wind piercing the gaps in the trees didn't help.

Ezekiel kept his mind busy. It helped with the cold. He felt proud that he'd always thought of himself as a free man, even before the war. But he knew the others hadn't. Pompey let it slip that even now he still considered himself a slave. Ezekiel had patience with him. Some men had so little confidence in themselves. Perhaps most. It was just a product of slavery. It was so difficult for some to look at themselves as men rather than property since that was all they'd experienced their entire lives. Fathers, mothers, brothers, sisters and children sold and taken away, never to be seen again. And knowing every day that one's food and shelter was at the whim of the owner. Watching hunting dogs eat better food and having the run of the big house. Seeing old men and women worked to death in rice fields while strong healthy white heirs lay about on the veranda. It was a white world and it didn't belong to them. Not yet, anyhow.

Ezekiel knew it would take time, but he also knew he would work towards it as long as it took. Forever, if he had to. The same self doubting ex-slaves would, someday, realize they were free men, and the world was just as much theirs as any whites.

He still carried his brass, diamond shaped slave badge, stamped number 615 that read 'Servant 1859.' Just as a reminder. He would wear it the rest of his life. A mark of how far he'd come, and where he was headed.

They worked the next three days in freezing rain and bitter cold, cutting down trees, sectioning each into logs, and carrying them through the swamp to the end of the corduroy road and wedging them into place with stakes so more wagons could bump across. But it was still dangerous for the mules and horses. Three broken legs in the first ten wagons that first morning. Wagon drivers cursed and soldiers wrestled braying animals out of their harnesses and shot them right there in the swamp.

Ezekiel's men swarmed the culprit holes and filled them as best they could with bundles of smaller cut branches. Soldiers pulling extra mules came up from the rear and the wagons soon moved on. Hardly a word was spoken between the wagoneers and Ezekiel's men. The occasional nod sufficed. They knew these soldiers' forward progress meant their freedom, and the wagoneers knew the pioneers' backbreaking work was work that they would otherwise have had to do themselves. They knew how hard it was to fight a full wagon through a bog. The corduroy saved them plenty of misery. Sharing a box of hardtack, a sack of cornmeal or a few tins of beef seemed more than fair. There were those who didn't though. Cynical, bitter, or maybe just beyond caring. Ezekiel knew better than to argue. Free man or not. Better to keep his mouth shut.

Each night he made sure everyone had something to eat, with extra to Mingo and Pompey who shivered the worst, but only after saying a prayer for Quam and another asking God to let the rest of them survive.

CHAPTER 19— DYE ON THE BEAUFORT ROAD

south from Blessing Plantation and
Miela's group east to Charleston

Dye made it twelve miles to the Tulifinny River the first day and slept in a burned off cornfield wrapped in her quilt She never lit a fire, and stayed just off the edge of the road always glancing behind and up at the next bend. Twice horsemen appeared out of the woods crossing the road in front. Each time she dropped flat and froze. They disappeared, and she walked through the trees for a few miles just to be sure. She slept in a smoldering ruin of a burned farm on the second night figuring no one would bother it again. She saw horsemen three more times that day, twice across the fields as she skirted the edges, the third time coming up from behind on the road. She jumped behind a clump of saw palmettos and watched a troop of gray and brown cavalry cantor by. They looked right at her but none stopped. She waited for them to disappear around the far bend then ran deeper into the woods and hid until dark. She figured they might come back the way they come, and she knew they had seen her.

Noises in this swamp nearby kept her up nearly all night. It sounded like two cats ready to fight. She never saw anything though, just her imagination running wild in the blackness. At dawn, she waited until any horsemen would already be up and about. She heard nothing but birds singing, so she crept slowly back to the road, crossing the narrow plank bridge and following the meandering Gardens Corner Road all day without seeing a soul and sleeping that night behind a cypress stump in the woods.

The next morning, she ate her last cornmeal square and found some sassafras roots to suck on then pushed on through some woods by a salt marsh and saw smoke. A black woman walked along the marsh edge with two children. Dye didn't wait. She cut straight through the thicket

159

towards her, and, when the woman turned at the noise, she called out and raised her hands.

"I'm alone. Will you help me?"

The woman grabbed the children and pushed them behind her. Dye struggled through the last batch of saplings and briars to the clearing by the marsh. She waved to the woman.

"I'm Dye from Blessing. I'm trying to get to Beaufort. To freedman's land. Can you spare some food?"

God smiled down on her. The woman hesitated but nodded. The two girls behind her peered around and giggled.

"I'm Tenah."

The woman let the children run along towards the smoke. She pulled her burlap jacket tight across her wide hips. Her face was creased and scarred on one side but soft and smooth on the other. Dye saw that she was blind in one eye. It was just a white ball that didn't move.

"Come with me child. We don't have much, but we'll share what we can." She motioned Dye over.

The woman's neck bulged with a goiter as she spoke. Her body odor permeated the air around her. A sickly-sweet mix of sweat, unwashed bottom, and little dabs of turpentine under her arms and below her pendulous breasts.

"We're heading there, too." She pointed across the mile-wide marsh. "It's just there. See? The trees over there. Freedman's land."

Dye stopped and looked across the expanse of green marsh and the blue inlet that separated them from freedom. "How do we get across?" She shifted her pole and walked up beside Tenah. Tenah shook her head and smiled. "I don't know, but we'll find a way. We've come this far. God will lead us the rest of the way." She waved both hands at the river and the far pines. "To the Promised Land!"

Then she hugged Dye as if she'd known her all of her life.

THE ENDLESS BLUE COLUMNS still pushed north along the Pocotaligo Road. It took Miela's group an hour to get to the North Creek boundary of Blessing Plantation. When they were finally across the little bridge and off the plantation, they grouped beside the wagons. All eyes were on her as she led them in the Lord's prayer.

" ... And deliver us from evil. For thine is the kingdom and the power and the glory."

"Amen."

Miela patted the children's heads and rubbed her stomach. "It's time to move on. The future is up ahead, and with children like you it's bound to be wonderful. We'll cut around and follow alongside the Yankees as far as we can. Stay close enough to be safe."

No one argued. Everyone figured Miela must know what she was doing. She was always the one who knew the answer to just about everything. Definitely she was their best chance. They followed her across a little hillock, and Miela looked back, down towards the plantation fields, and forward, up into the pine woods ahead. She saw the plumes of black smoke in a long arc from the southwest to the northeast marking the Yankees' progress. She knew it meant that nothing would ever be the same and felt her stomach tighten again into a ball. She had to remind herself that it was a good thing. She told George to lead the mules and wagon down the east road that ran towards the town of Salkehatchie and then on to Charleston.

Yank cavalry patrols crisscrossed the road in front and back all day long, but the big columns of soldiers disappeared as their little group plodded on towards Charleston. Miela prayed they would at least stay close enough to scare off the slave patrols. They made it eight miles through a cold drizzle to the Salkehatchie River before dark, but found the bridge destroyed. Nothing was left but charred timbers. The river was up, surging through the trees and over the causeway. The mules stopped a few yard short of the rising water, and everyone gathered around.

Jemps sized it up quickly. "Too deep to ford without losing all the provisions, and the nearest bridge might be miles away. What we need is boat. Big enough for the wagon and mules."

"What we gonna do?" George shook his head. "Two axes working as fast as we can ... Six good-sized logs ... Maybe a day's work. Maybe two."

Fatima sat in the wagon next to the corn barrels. "What if the water gets in the corn? We won't have nothing to eat."

"Don't worry, it's watertight," Poins tapped the barrels.

Jemps glanced up at him. "I seen the flat boats use barrels for their heaviest loads. Two barrels lashed on each side. Took on another ton of rice. Maybe we can do the same."

Miela hugged him. "He's right. It just might work. Come on Titus, Gage. Help get this one down. It'll work I tell you," Miela beamed. "The barrels will get us across.""

They all helped unload the barrels at the back of the wagon then roll them down to the river. Jemps stood shivering at the bank. "We'll wedge the barrels under the wagon as it goes down into the river."

Titus shook his head. "No guide rope. How we gonna get it across."

"Gage and I can swim across with a rope," Jemps answered. "Then ya'll can cross together by holding on. We'll all pull the wagon across. The mules will swim behind."

"That water's cold," Lizette frowned, not wanting to have to admit that, like most of the others, she couldn't swim.

"That's right," Miela snapped back. "It's cold as ice water. Just get in the wagon and hold tight until it gets across. Unless you have a better idea."

Lizette glared back at her but held her tongue. No one else dissented and Jemps and Gage stripped down to their pants then helped George guide the wagon back down over the barrels.

"Damn! It floats!"

"All right then. Let's get working."

The wagons floated just enough to keep the shivering women and children and provisions from washing away. Jemps and Gage splashed cold water on each other and posed waist deep to make the children laugh then took the rope and swam across, playing out the line as they went. They tied it off on a stout pine on the far side.

Jemps yelled back across. "Come on y'all. It'll work."

Titus tied his end to the wagon, and the men pulled themselves across the river single file. Titus could never remember being so cold before, but all he thought about was his wooden leg. He made sure it was strapped on tightly before he went in.

Jemps called to him. "C'mon Titus, you're leg floats better than mine."

Titus didn't answer. He'd heard every joke in the world over the years. No one else could ever know what the leg meant to him. Once across, he checked the straps just to be sure then tapped the carved wood.

"Thank you, sir. You've served me well."

He helped the others pull the wagon across the river. Nothing was lost but one shovel that decided to untie itself in midstream. Miela made all the men dry themselves off as best they could with blankets then they pushed on to higher ground as darkness fell, making camp in the pine woods. Miela knew it was dangerous to build a fire that could be spotted by home guard or slave patrols, but she figured the Yanks were close enough to keep the rebs occupied and most everyone was wet and cold. She let the men dig a pit and soon a large fire was roaring.

Daphne quickly had cornmeal pancakes and ham slices sizzling. The children laughed and played, even Fatima. She was quickly running around as if nothing had happened. It was all a great lark. Even George, the most serious one, felt a sense of relief. They were together, away from Blessing, and on the road to freedom

"That pig fat's good ain't it," Daphne laughed, re-dressing Fatima's bandages that had come loose with her playing and watching Elsey begin her nightly ritual of rubbing fat drippings from the supper meat all over her skin and hair. "Elsey's going to be safe now. No Yank's gonna rape a greasy woman. She's still got that asafetida between her legs too."

Elsey shrugged, "Best get one for Miela, too. Let her dangle it between her pretty brown titties." She held up the rancid cloth sack tied to a string around her neck.

Miela smiled. "Should I have one in my crotch, too? Or just one between my missies?"

Everyone laughed but Lizette. She shook her head sternly wondering how Miela could laugh and joke after having been abused by Malcolm for so long.

"Don't be joking about that. You know as well as anybody. A white man will rape a black girl quick as they please. Ain't nobody gonna stop them. No protection except grease and asafetida. You better mind and tend to it nightly." She folded her arms across her huge breasts and glared down her double chin at Miela.

"You're right Lizette. I'll do it. I believe you. Nobody messes with asafetida and a grease." She smiled to Elsey and Daphne.

Lizette kept glaring at her. "You mocking me, Miela? Remember you're brown skinned! White men on both sides will rape you if you don't mind yourself."

"No ma'am," Miela smiled and pleaded, "I'm not mocking you. I promise. I'm really not."

Daphne laughed. "Miela knows you're right, Lizette. Brown skin, like hers, is what all white men want."

"I'm not brown skinned. I'm cinnamon. Mrs. Blessing told me so."

Cumseh spat in the fire then curled up in a blanket. "Well cinnamon or brown. Whatever you call it. You're going to get rebs and Yanks between your legs if you don't mind Lizette. You can't have too much grease and 'fetida."

Miela laughed but knew that no matter what any of them did or didn't do, it would take a lot of good luck to make it to Smythe's safely. She slept fitfully and had them up the next morning at first light for a quick breakfast of corn cakes and molasses and sassafras tea then on the road towards Charleston until dark. The adults tried to keep the children's spirits up even when they were hungry and cold. Elsey taught Agnes how to balance a basket on her head. She gave her a smaller one of twisted corn shucks and straw just right for her size.

"See? I kept it inside the big one all this time."

Agnes smiled and clapped her hands as if the miracle had occurred. Elsey rearranged the extra clothes she carried in her basket along with her prizes from over the years.

"See here. My blue bottle, four nails, an arrowhead, leastways it looks like one to me. Fat lighter and a decent leather sole."

She showed them all to Agnes then tucked them back into her basket and casually flung it on top of her head. She walked along effortlessly with it tilting back and forth with her stride as if glued to her scalp with her prized hoe perched over her shoulder. The long bamboo handle, sharpened on the end, stuck out ahead of her as she walked.

"No telling when we might see Mr. Snake." She stuck the sharp end into the dirt and twirled the hoe blade around. "But he don't got no chance with Elsey's hoe."

Miela watched Fatima and Agnes holding hands in their matching black and white plaid dresses that Daphne had made them from a bolt of calico. She smiled and felt the big roll of paper bills in her pocket.

Confederate dollar bills from Mr. Blessing's study. Maybe they could buy some more clothes. If only they could get to Smythes safely.

Titus walked ahead of her wearing a yellow coffee sack as a shirt, and singing the same verse of his favorite song over and over. She joined in, glad for the distraction,

"Old Satan's mad and I am glad. Send them angels down. He missed the soul he thought he had. Oh send them angels down."

He gathered up poke leaves and sheep-sorrel greens for supper and stuffed them into a small croaker sack. "Too small to wear," he whispered to Agnes shaking the sack full of greens. "But it makes a good gather-bag."

Agnes looked in the bag. "Just them weeds? Nothing else?"

Titus just laughed. "Nobody thinks much of greens 'till the belly starts growling. C'mon and help me find some more, or I just might put you in it."

"I wouldn't fit," she laughed.

"If I cut you up, you will." He tapped his little whittling knife. "We can eat you for supper."

"Stop It. Miela won't let you cut me up."

"She might if she's hungry enough."

"Will you Miela?"

"No. He's just teasing." She cut an eye at him. "He didn't mean to scare you."

"I ain't scared. I swear I ain't."

"Then help me pick greens,"Titus smiled.

She helped for a while until the rain picked up again. A cold, driving rain that fell heavier for an hour or so then lightened to a steady drizzle that never let up. Everyone shivered in the wet cold, pulling soaked blankets tighter around their necks. Agnes pulled her quilt hat down to her nose and hid under Miela's arm.

"I'm sick of the rain, Miela. Why's it got to rain every day? I want to get somewhere warm and dry. Can we go back to Blessing?"

Jemps walked up behind and bent forward into the cold rain that came suddenly heavier again, whipping in sheets with the rising wind. "It's damn cold All right, Agnes. Wet and cold. But we're free. Remember? You'll be warm and dry at the slave market if you go back."

165

Miela squeezed her shoulder. "You'll be All right, Agnes. It won't rain forever. It just seems that way. We'll get somewhere dry for supper, I promise."

She said a quick prayer to herself that her promise would hold true, and by late afternoon the rain finally stopped.

"Thank you Lord," Lizette called out from the rear.

Miela snuggled Agnes's neck and whispered, "See? I told you."

Agnes kissed her on the cheek and ran up ahead, leading them on another two miles down the path before coming to a clearing in the pines bathed in sunlight. Everyone rested, relishing the warmth until Yank horseman burst from the trees. The girls screamed and contracted quickly into a ball around Jemps and Miela.

An officer rode up to them with two troopers in tow."Listen here!" He called out. "Land is waiting for you back towards Beaufort. From the coast inland thirty miles. Forty acres for every three families. No whites will be permitted to take it from me." He repeated it again and watched the silent faces stare back at him.

"I don't think they understand, sir? A trooper spit out a wad of tobacco.

"Go back!" The officer ignored the trooper. "Go get your land. It's yours now!" He rode around the group repeating it over and over, but none of them budged. Miela held her burlap cloak close to her face and glanced up at the officer.

"Excuse me sir, but we'd rather go with General Sherman to Charleston."

She knew that none of them had any intention of going back. No matter what a blue soldier on horseback said. As soon as he was gone with the rest of the soldiers, the whites would come back. All the Yankees had done to smack the hornets' nest. She knew that the only the force of the Yank guns would give her people land. As soon as those guns disappeared, so would the land and probably their lives. Better to keep going. Follow General Sherman to Charleston and get to Thomas Island. At least Connor's deed would mean something. Maybe.

The Yank officer wiped his brow and looked exasperated. "We're not heading to Charleston. We're heading to Columbia. You all need to move away from this column. Go to Beaufort. Do it now."

He didn't wait for an answer, wheeling his horse and riding off as an entire regiment followed through the clearing, helping themselves to all the sweet potatoes, pecans and corn meal. One soldier even took Elsey's hoe and one of the axes off the wagon.

"Keep together. Don't resist," Miela whispered.

"What do you think, Miela?" Gage tugged at her sleeve and whispered back. "Forty acres. What's that mean exactly?"

Miela patted his head ignoring the sudden hollow pit in her stomach. She felt stunned. The entire plan was unraveling. If General Sherman wasn't headed to Charleston, could they get there safely? She felt a tightness in her chest and a sudden shortness of breath but tried to fake that she was calm.

"We have our own Promised Land, Gage," she whispered back. "It's waiting for us. We'll get there soon enough. Clean water and good land." Gage shrugged and scratched his chin. "If you say so."

They moved on quickly, everyone looking over their shoulder half expecting something worse. The oak woods gave way to higher ground with pines and another clearing ringed with blooming camellias. A three story, white washed house, with a red, shingled roof and surrounded by an open wooden deck, stood in the cornfield. A huge iron pot stood on a layer of bricks on the deck. It held a roaring fire. A dozen or so white children ran back and forth to a woodpile in the field bringing small loads to feed the flames. Three women, dressed head to toe in black, knelt in the front doorway chanting a foreign tongue. As Miela's group came out of the trees and across the open field, they could see an open coffin by the back of the house. An ax was embedded in its side.

"What the hell?" George whispered to Miela.

The three women turned and yelled in their strange tongue. "Deixar agora! Deixar agora!"

The middle woman stood up, raised her hand, and let loose a high pitch scream. All the white children ran inside and peered out from the second-floor windows.

"What y'all saying?" Jemps yelled back. "Can't y'all speak plain?"

Lizette quickly pulled at his arm. "Shush! They're whites for Gods' sake!"

"My God," Titus flicked the reins. "They're mad women. Crazy people. Let's get on around."

Cumseh relieved herself, squatting in the stubble corn row, and one of the women stopped her chanting and called out. "What you doing there in my corn?"

"Y'all CAN speak plain!" Jemps called back. Then he whispered to the rest. "They're crazy for sure. Rabid maybe. Watch yourselves."

Miela ignored him and walked up to the house. "Good afternoon ma'am. We're on our way to Charleston. Could you spare some food. We can pay ... "

"Begone ye devils! Be gone! Cast ye out and fire ye into infernal parts!" The woman reached into the pouch of her black dress and threw a handful of white powder at Miela.

"I'm just asking to buy food ma'am." Miela bowed slightly and backed off. "If you can't spare it, we understand."

"Begone! You are rebuked!" She knelt back down again with the others and started back with the chanting.

"Be careful, Miela," Jemps whispered. "They're rabid."

Miela backed away. "I doubt it. Just scared is all."

"Scared? Don't think so," Jemps shook his head. "They're rabid, I tell you. No use haggling with crazy people."

Miela waved to the women and had Titus lead the mules across the field and past the house. Soon they were out of sight in the woods. Everyone was silent, listening to the women's continued chanting in the distance, now magnified by the gloom of the woods. They came to a narrow foot bridge over a branch creek and went across single file as Titus and George plowed the wagon across upstream. Poins was last in line when he heard a stick crack behind him. A little boy and girl came running towards them through the trees.

"Watch out! They're coming!"

He ran across the foot bridge and gathered himself besides Jemps and Gage. Fatima hid behind Miela's skirt. The two white children ran to the foot bridge and smiled, panting for breath. They each carried a bundle over their shoulder. The taller boy had curly, reddish brown hair with bright blue eyes, and the girl, long black hair and dark brown eyes.

"We brought ya'll some ham and biscuits. Momma, Aunt Georgia, and Mary Helen ... " The boy wheezed deeply, bending over to rest his hand on his knees. The bundle dropped to his feet. "They're just scared, that's all. Missouri Yanks came yesterday. Dug up Uncle Joe ... Split open his coffin looking for gold and silver. They had a white girl with them. Took her inside and ... " He shook his head. "I don't know what, but they did something to her. Momma , Aunt Georgia and Mary Helen went up in the attic ... Came down chanting that old Portuguese that Aunt Therese taught them last year. They threw powder all about too. Scared them Missouri boys off ... They took the girl, though. Mama had us build a fire in the kettle. Said it was our only hope to act crazy." He paused and smiled. "When they saw ya'll coming, they started up with the chanting again."

Miela walked over the foot bridge to them. Cumseh hissed at her. "No, Miela. No."

"Thank you, son." Miela smiled and patted the boy's curly hair. She turned and waved a hand slowly towards the wagon and the wary group. "Now, because of two brave and decent children, we have a pleasant evening ahead. Don't we?" She clapped and nodded to the others. Everyone hesitated then clapped halfheartedly. "Thank you both. Thank you. Now tell us your names." She tried to hug the little girl, but she pulled free and hid behind the boy.

"I'm Perry," the boy said. "She's my sister, Emory. She don't talk much."

Emory quickly swatted his shoulder and spoke up. "I do too. Why would you say that?"

Perry pushed her away. "Stop it."

Miela laughed. "As long as they're children like you and Emory, there's hope for us all." She hugged Perry first, then Emory, and they tolerated it then each handed over their bundles and ran off silently, disappearing through the trees like ghosts.

Cumseh chewed on a pinecone and spit into her palm. She swirled the spittle around with a piece of oyster shell then raised her hand. "I've seen the future, and it ain't what you'd expect."

Miela laughed, "Never has been."

Cumseh darted her eyes at her and didn't say another word until Miela let them stop for the night. She refused to eat a biscuit and carefully put all the bits of chewed cone into a small hollow in an oak tree then covered it in moss and whispered loudly to Grace. "It's the spirit that needs nourishing, not the body."

Miela ignored her, knowing Cumseh had to have her little spiels. She hadn't planned to say anything to them about General Sherman heading to Columbia either, but decided since their lives were at stake, she had to be honest. She gathered the adults around and told them what the officer said.

"What does it mean?" Daphne asked.

"I'm not exactly sure, but it might be more of a risk. Slave patrols and all."

"Oh my God," Daphne trembled, glancing over to Fatima."Not again!"

"I swear we can make it. Fatima will be All right."

"But how do you know?"

"Yep. Maybe we should've gone to Beaufort," Jemps said almost apologetically.

"Maybe. But I think it'll work out." Miela patted Fatima's head while everyone else stared at her in silence. "Smythe's is ours. We just have to find a way to get there."

Cumseh cleared her throat. "The Divine will guide us and help us," she smiled, suddenly buoyed by the knowledge that Miela had been wrong about something.

"Yes, indeed He will," Miela smiled back. "But we'll have to stick together and help ourselves too."

Cumseh fetched herself a biscuit and devoured it. "Don't y'all worry, I'm sure we'll be just fine."

CHAPTER 20 — EZEKIEL

in the Salkehatchie Swamp

By midday a cold rain poured down through the swamp canopy. Ezekiel's group waited by their section of corduroy ready to stake down loose logs that sprung up here and there as if trying to ambush and impale passing wagons. Fresh logs were put down on loose spots and hammered tight. Regiment after regiment splashed by knee-deep and hundreds of wagons rumbled over the logs. Another quartermaster officer came along and ordered Ezekiel's group to climb aboard the wagons. The officer passed the word to the other wagon drivers to share rations while they rode forward. Ezekiel and the others gulped hard tack and canned beef. The wagons move past long lines of infantry waiting their turn to slosh through the swamp. A string of insults flew their way.

"Hey slave boys! You headed to market?"

"Why you boys to get to ride while good Union men have to walk?"

"Pampered blacks! You better keep going, you sons of bitches. Wait till they drop you off. We'll catch up with you soon enough."

They all knew better than to say anything back. "Never sass a white man," Ezekiel whispered, smiling at the others who nodded back. They knew what he meant. They could think anything they wanted, just don't say it out loud. It would just bring more pain and suffering, at best. Ezekiel looked around at the men and felt a surge of pride that they all silently took it. They signaled to each other by tapping their feet. Little taps to each other that said 'We've seen worse. This here's nothing'. Mingo started humming the 'Hallelujah' song and the rest of them took it up. The wagon driver and his assistant started singing along, then next and the next. Some of the soldiers along the corduroy joined in.

"Glory, glory hallelujah! Glory, glory hallelujah!"

The worst of the animosity dissipated with the rising chorus. Ezekiel felt goose bumps and had to restrain a yell. He tapped Pompey's foot as

171

he started to raise his voice. "Best you let the white soldiers do the singing for now."

The others smiled, and everyone hummed louder as the wagons rolled on, another ten miles or so before stopping just before dark to camp at the edge of another swamp needing more corduroy. They ate their rations supplied by the wagoneers and bedded down for the night on a patch of solid ground around a clump of pines. Dozens of small fires sprang up through the swamp where the other pioneer groups were gathered. Ezekiel stayed up until well past midnight to make sure his group was safe then he lay down and dreamed of digging out a rice dike. He woke up a few times, but all was quiet and he fell back to sleep until, somewhere in the middle of the night, a rifle shot exploded near his face. He rolled quickly into the darkness away from the faint glow of smoldering fire.

"Never ride a wagon when white men are walking!" A voice screamed. "You hear that! Only good Union men! White men. Wisconsin men! You think they're dying by the thousands just so you bastard blacks can ride by us in wagons? Bull shit!"

Another shot rang out. Ezekiel saw shadows retreating into the woods behind the flash. He ran after them with a shovel, ready to kill the bastards in the dark before anyone saw him. But the soldiers were gone just as quickly. More Yank soldiers came running up through the trees. Ezekiel saw his opportunity vanish.

He picked his way back to the camp where Toby had the embers flaming up with fresh wood and dried palm fronds. Esau and Mingo stood silently looking down at a body on the ground. An officer walked up out of the darkness with a squad of rifleman. He knelt down to inspect the body.

"He's been shot. An accident I expect. Men with rifles at night in enemy country. It happens. Best bury your man there." He walked off quickly, and the soldiers backed away, keeping their eyes on Ezekiel's group until they were just shadows in the dark woods.

"Pompey," Toby said before Ezekiel could see his face. "Shot in the chest while he slept. Damn bastards. Hell if I'll corduroy another swamp. Not for them. No sir."

Mingo sniffled then sobbed, but Esau didn't make a sound Ezekiel knelt beside Pompey and patted his forehead for a while then helped

172

Toby carry him back into the trees away from the road. They dug a grave and gently laid him to rest. Esau made him a little cross.

"Here lies a good man." Ezekiel blessed himself like he'd seen the Catholics do. He'd come to feel it was fitting for a good prayer.

The others did the same and repeated it after him in unison, "Here lies a good man."

They all sat down together around a grave and waited for dawn. All of them kept their shovels ready while the wind picked up and the temperature dropped. They shivered together under their blankets until first light then Ezekiel stood up stiff and cold. He made them all eat a breakfast of more hard tack and ham fat although none of them felt like eating. But Ezekiel insisted.

"Eat it down. Every bite of it. We have to go on. For Pompey and Quam. It's the right thing to do. It's the only thing to do. The only way we can honor them."

Toby nodded. "Ezekiel's right, damn it. We've got to see it through. Work for the Jubilee or die trying." He sprang up like a frog and grabbed Esau and Mingo by their collars. "Come on. Y'all ain't getting lazy on me. I'll bet Pompey would be glad to change places with you." He led them off to work mumbling curses under his breath all morning, angry that Quam and Pompey were dead and angry that there was nothing he could do about it except follow Ezekiel's lead. If he could just get his hands on the bastard that shot him. But the regiments kept marching past all day as if nothing had happened. He daydreamed of choking the soldier to death as they cut small pines all morning while other groups dragged them into place in the swamp.

About mid-day captain reined in his horse as he passed and pulled out a little book and pencil. Soldiers kept marching along while he wrote in his book. "You men. Are you freed men?" The red faced captain jotted a note in his little book.

Toby stared at him, wanting to yell out that his bastard soldiers had just killed Pompey. He slowly nodded. "Yes, we're free."

"Well then, tell me. What about the great attachment they speak of? Between master and slave. Did you have that?" He smiled and waited to jot down the answer.

"They sure don't speak for us. No sir." Toby swung his ax and chopped a fallen pine which jumped up and brushed the horse's hindquarters. The horse reared. The captain flew off and landed on his back. The book plopped in a mud puddle.

"Damn it!" He stood up gingerly, rubbing his bruised ribs and wiping off his book. The lines of marching soldiers laughed, but Ezekiel ran up and knew just how to respond.

"Are you All right sir?" He quickly bowed and handed the officer his hat.

"I'm just fine," he growled.

"There's no attachment, sir," Toby grabbed the horse's reins and lead it back to the captain. "Just a myth is all. Rebs like you to think it. But it ain't true. Never was."

The captain wiped mud off his sleeves then winced as he remounted. "I see. But of course you can't speak for all slaves." He wrote something down.

"Well, yes ... Yes, I can. I can speak for anyone who's been property to be bought and sold. Only a free man can have attachment."

The captain nodded. "I see. Maybe those of you who've run off feel differently. Some stayed though, didn't they?"

Ezekiel rested on his ax. "The others are just trying to survive, that's all."

The captain wrote some more in his book and put the pencil away. "Attachment too, I think."

Ezekiel squinted at him as he rode off. What a fool. Life as a slave, Ezekiel thought, wasn't really life at all. He thought of his few days of actual freedom and began to consider them the beginning of his true life. He couldn't count the years of slavery any longer. They meant nothing now. He remembered them as if being in prison. Maybe Quam and Pompey would trade places, but nothing good had come from those years. He smelled the pines as the breeze pushed patchy clouds overhead. They smelled better than ever before, and guns rumbled in the distance. "A sign from God, boys. Sherman's army is still on the move." He smiled thinking of it. "Come on. Time to build another road for the avenging angels. For Quam and Pompey, too." He lead them through the woods to another swamp where more corduroy was built and laid by another pioneer group. Ezekiel felt the cold water stabbing at his feet and relished every second. "We're free man boys. Free men working for the Jubilee."

Toby felt it too and laughed with him, shaking off the angry thoughts about Pompey and Quam. "Helping the avenging Angels get where they need to get. To smite the rebs. Lay 'em to waste. Come on Mingo, Esau. Y'all can smile too. Quam and Pompey would! They're looking down on you right now laughing with us. Come on."

Esau and Mingo did their best to join in but didn't quite grasp it yet. Freedom was still just a word. It meant nothing more than a time to follow Ezekiel. All that mattered was to follow. To see what each day brought. And what had it brought Pompey and Quam?

Ezekiel started laughing punch drunk. He kept thinking about how he'd changed from a kept object, a possession, physically valued like a horse or mule, to a free person. How he'd granted himself freedom from slavery long before he'd heard the guns in the distance. No one else had the right to declare him free, any more than they had the right to make him a slave. They only had the power. But Yank guns had ended that. He took a deep breath and remembered every detail about killing Mr. Blessing. The only fitting end for a jailer and slaver. He looked over at his men carrying logs and felt another rush of pride knowing they could corduroy as fast as any men anywhere. Their work, black freed-men's work, might help Sherman as much as a fresh regiment. Maybe more. Every swamp they corduroyed helped the Yanks tear the slave world apart. Every day brought freedom to more blacks. Quam and Pompey had given their lives for it.

He promised himself that before the end came, when their work was nearly over, when the slave world was destroyed, that he would somehow manage to arm himself. All the others too. He knew it had to be done just right. Whether it was an enlistment into a unit or just helping themselves to captured reb weapons, it didn't really matter to him. As long as his men were armed when the end came. And as many others as he could muster. So that no matter what happened after the war, he would never have to take orders from white men again.

"Black men with rifles," he chanted under his breath, nudging Toby. "Black men with rifles. Black men with rifles."

Toby nodded and took it up. "Black men with lots of rifles. Hell yes." They kept it up all day, working in a driving rain pushing corduroy over a wide swamp with a hundred or so other men and finishing just before dawn. The first few regiments marching past cheered their work, but others in the rear ignored them or threw out more insults. Their group stood aside quietly until ordered to fall in behind a New York Regiment then tramped along most of the day with shovels and picks on their shoulders. That night they were given a side of beef to cook over the fire and each three men were given a blanket or tent section to keep warm. They stood around the flames and talked. Mingo gobbled down as much as he was allowed and could have eaten more. He patted his stomach and laughed.

"I could eat me a whole mule. I betcha."

Ezekiel bear-hugged him from behind. "Tell us about the Charleston jail Mingo. You been there, ain't you?" He knew talking would help them get past Quam and Pompey.

Mingo bent forward and lifted Ezekiel off his feet. Everyone laughed.

"Yep. I've been in the Charleston jail all right. Every day pushing the oak poles of that big millstone. Around and around in a circle. With three others. Milling corn. Wagons full. All day, dawn to dark. Pushing the millstone . A break to eat corn bread and drink water. Any slacking off meant the 'black snake'. The guards called it 'giving us sugar'. That's why they called it the sugar house." He gulped swamp water that Toby had boiled and let cool. "I seen a man so down that he put his head in the stone trough." He paused and looked away. "The keepers couldn't get there fast enough. We couldn't stop it neither. That big stone wheel took half a circle to stop. Squashed his head like stomping on a frog." He shivered at the memory. "Made his legs twitch like one too. For a long while. Like he was still living. We all had to look see. Like maybe his head was still there. But nope. Just a grease spot. I'll never go back there again. No sir. They can shoot me, hang me, whatever. I'm never going back."

"Amen." They all nodded in agreement.

"Amen is right. Your turn, Esau," Ezekiel tossed him a hardtack cracker. "Tell us something. You've seen some things ain't you?"

Esau reluctantly spoke up. He was the least interested in Sherman or freedom since he thought he'd been about half free already. "I done spent weeks at a time in the Savannah River dredging driftwood snags and getting paid by the barge- load. That was something. Back when Mr. Blessing hired me out to the Savannah men working on the channel. A few of the others ran off as soon as they heard the Yanks was in Beaufort, but I stayed put. I done cleared swamp for rice fields and picked cotton before. I knew there was worse things than dredge work."

"A slave's a slave. No matter what kind of work." Ezekiel squeezed him from behind.

Esau laughed and tried to fight him off but couldn't. "Well a master is a master too. Ain't Sherman just the new master?"

Ezekiel let him go. "You don't understand. There's no master anymore."

"I know, but..."

"But nothing. It's freedom, Esau, freedom. You're a free man," Ezekiel laughed.

Esau scratched his head and nodded as if he understood. He warmed his soggy disintegrated shoes by the fire and rewrapped them with strips of blanket. But he still couldn't quite grasp the idea of not being owned by someone. He still saw 'the freedom' as being owned by the new master, 'the Sherman'.

Toby chewed on a piece of gristle beside him. "I remember working at Hobonny Plantation before I made it to Blessing. It was hell back there. Most of the others had come from indoor work in Charleston. Sewing or cleaning, that sort of thing. They couldn't stand it. Clearing swamp for rice fields is hell for sure. Maybe worse. Some of them died that first week. Just keeled over in the swamp and died. Couldn't stand it y'see. But not me. I worked my way up to foreman then got sold to Blessing."

"You've made a fine slave," Ezekiel teased him.

"Don't you worry, Ezekiel. I'll be a rich man after all this here." He waved his arm at the trees.

"What are you gonna do, Toby ? When you're free?" Esau asked.

"He IS free, Esau," Ezekiel shook his head. "We ALL are."

"All right, Ezekiel. All right."

Toby laughed. "Don't you worry. I'll work whatever. I'll do anything. Heard a free man gets a dollar a day. That'll do me just fine."

"A dollar?" Mingo shook his head. "I doubt it."

"I tell you they do. All free men do. Right now. Irish mostly. Work in the rice mills and salt works, gas works too. They've even taken over the crabbing. So I've heard. They say the Irish will do about anything. Charleston rich folks calling them 'white slaves'."

"I've been a free slave before I got sold to Blessing," Mingo raised his hands as if giving praise. "Hired out by Mr. Cutler as a carpenter. Lived on my own in Charleston back then. Had a room on Montagu Street. Worked in Mr. Hazel's carpenter shop. He said I was the best he'd ever had."

"A slave's a slave," Ezekiel spat on the fire.

"But I had my own room and...."

"Bullshit on your room! I don't give a shit. What counts is freedom. For all blacks, everywhere. Not some bullshit code that lets you think you're free because you got your own room."

"Well All right, Ezekiel. Don't get mad," Mingo sunk down on to his knees and poked at the fire."But it was a really nice room."

Toby laughed. "Did you ever get with any of them free black women?

Mingo shook his head nervously, eyes darting up at Ezekiel who still glared at him. "No. Free blacks like them don't like to be seen with slaves."

"Well shit on them then," Toby jumped up. "Guess I'll have to follow Ezekiel to the end." He grabbed Esau and twirled him around.

Mingo glanced around to make sure no soldiers were about. "Joke if you want, but look here. There's this one man I swear I'll kill if I get my hands on him. That bastard overseer at Fort Sumter, name of DeBurgh. Back when they made me work at the fort last year. Yanks shooting them big cannons at us all the time. Us digging ditches and building walls for the white soldiers. A fine job ain't it? Men getting their heads blown off too. Samuel from Old Brass plantation got shot right in half. Big cannon ball blew his legs back under a board lean-to. DeBurgh saw the legs sticking out and thought somebody was sleeping. Started whipping them dead legs." He gulped a cup of swamp water and caught his breath. "That bastard started laughing. Laughing! I swear. Can you believe that? Laughing at Samuel getting chopped in half. But don't you worry. I'll find DeBurgh all right. I find him and kill him just as sweet as...." He looked at the Ezekiel and smiled. "You know what I mean. I kill him, I swear."

Ezekiel tossed more branches of the fire. "It's all right, Mingo. Anyhow, it's the right thing to do. Listen here!" He sat down beside Toby and made sure he had everyone's attention. "Can't let bastards like that live. Once this war's over, they'll be a bill to be paid. Some scores to settle. DeBurgh's one of them for sure."

"Damn right," Mingo shivered. "By God in Heaven, damn right."

CHAPTER 21— EZEKIEL AND LUKE

in the Salkehatchie Swamp

In the morning, cheering regiments announced that Sherman's entourage had appeared across the swamp. The yelling came closer until the band of officers surrounding the great man came up on Ezekiel's crew cutting pines for corduroy. Sherman himself called out to them.

"You men! Tell me ... " He stood up in the stirrups. Ezekiel and the others stopped in mid stride and waited, the weight of the logs pressing down every second on their shoulders. "Will you do this for us every day?" Sherman waved his hand to encompass the swamp they had just crossed.

"Yes sir!" They all answered as one.

Ezekiel dripped streams of sweat as he lifted the log up over his head so he could see Sherman better. He grinned at the sight. Just a skinny, red-headed, white man in a dirty, rumpled coat. "But General, sir." He called to the great man. "The day we get guns is the day the war's over." All the blacks in earshot cheered. Sherman he noticed none of the white troops cheered with them. He knew there was no love lost on freed slaves, no matter what the official policy. A few black regiments wouldn't make a difference anyway. It was too late for that.

He nodded to Ezekiel then nudged Sam who trotted forward quickly, making his entourage scurry to keep up. More officers came and went around him like bees around their queen as he rode up to a line of wagons in a tunnel-like opening in the water oaks and willows. He dismounted quickly, and walked to a wagon covered with a canvas tent. Soldiers stood guard at each end. Sherman stepped up and pulled back the tent flap.

Two hundred yards away, Luke stood in line with the rest of his regiment, waiting to move forward. He saw a black woman's face and her bare arms behind the tent flap for just a second. Ezekiel caught a glimpse of her too but focused on his work, trying not to let his worry about Miela consume him. The tent flap closed, and the guards shuffled off.

"A discreet distance," Dave smiled. "A couple should have their privacy."

Uncle Billy's got his own needs," Luke nodded approvingly. "Like any man."

"No, he ain't like other men," McMahon stood up as the regiment came to life. "Nope, he's more like the devil himself. Devil to the rebs that for sure."

"Maybe so," Dave shouldered his Henry. "But if he's the Devil, I'll damn well follow him to Hell."

"And if he isn't the devil then Satan sure better watch out," Luke smiled. "Uncle Billy will whip his ass too."

McMahon nodded. "I'll bet even God Almighty is just a bit afraid of him."

The entourage of officers milled about for half an hour while the regiment waited and watched. The tent flap reopened. Sherman jumped down with his open coat blowing in the breeze. He wiped his brow and put a fresh cigar in his mouth as orderlies brought up Sam. Then he remounted and trotted off. The tent flap peeked open again, and a black girl glanced out for a second but quickly retreated back inside.

Luke wondered for a second what would happen to her, but shook it off. There was no use worrying about that, he sighed. There was only one real worry. The same worry that was on every soldier's mind. The war was coming to a close. Who would be the last unlucky bastard to die? The last casualty of the war. Someone had to be. But everyone thought it would be someone else. And what a waste. Everyone else marching home and that last man dead in a hole.

Luke pushed that thought away, too, as sergeants screamed out orders and the regiment moved on, marching north for ten more miles through smoky woods to a patchwork of little clearings with a cluster of ramshackle plank houses. The men spread out and burned the houses as they passed. Luke walked up to the door of one shack and kicked it in. He jumped to the side. No telling if another old reb with a shotgun wanted to die for the Cause. He glanced inside. A stiff corpse of a woman lay on the packed dirt floor. By the smell, Luke knew the woman had been dead for days.

Crying came from the corner cupboard. Just a plank wall across a corner of the room with a small hatch in the bottom. It was bolted shut. Luke pulled out the rusty nail that held the iron rungs. He held his rifle ready and opened the hatch, gagging at the smell.

Two children stuck their heads out the opening. Feces and vomit covered their urine-soaked burlap tunics. The bigger one, maybe four, crawled past gagging and scraping feces off his back on the board hatchway. The smaller one got halfway out and wriggled like a fish pulled to a mud bank. Luke felt his heart in his throat.

McMahon stood beside him calling his name "Luke! Luke!" He pushed Luke's rifle barrel away. "Don't shoot! They're children!"

Luke gathered himself and covered his nose with his sleeve. He knelt and touched the big one and wiped feces off his face. He pulled the little one up and his stomach turned at the sight of a huge bleeding ulcer on its rear. He wiped the face. A girl. Blonde hair glistened under the filth. Dave came up with a bottle of turpentine and a flask of whiskey. Luke soaked a rag and wiped their faces. They shivered but didn't resist. McMahon pulled off their tunics and wiped them down head to toe. Dave gave them hardtack and wrapped them in blankets.

They carried the children outside to a well pump and properly washed them, wiping them down again with whiskey afterwards. Luke knew they had a better chance against dysentery and pneumonia with a good whiskey bath. The children stared back at him silently, their faces still contorted in terror. They tolerated his touch though, as he wrapped their wounds and bandaged the big ulcer on the little girl's rear.

McMahon picked them up and put them on a passing wagon, perching them on blankets and folded tent canvas with crackers and a canteen of water beside them. He showed them how to pull the cork to sip it. The boy nodded as the wagon moved on with the column.

They went back and burned the house with the women's corpse inside before the regiment moved on to camp on little hillock of pines. Luke went over to the wagon-park to check on the children and found them by a campfire next to a commissary Sergeant who had them well tended to. The boy started talking for the first time.

"Momma put us in the cupboard when she heard the Yankees were coming. She just never let us out." His face had relaxed a bit. He was a little boy again.

"Momma smells bad," the little girl giggled, her white teeth shining in the firelight as the boy's face hardened. He began to sob.

"Don't cry, Reese," the little girl patted her brother on the shoulder.

"Momma will be here in the morning. She'll kiss you and make it better."

The sergeant glanced up at Luke, his brow furrowed deeply. He handed the girl a cup of water. "I'm sure she will. Now let's get you both to bed."

He made a blanket roost for them in the wagon, and Luke stayed to help. Both children cried out in the night and had to be comforted, the little girl especially. Luke piled more blankets around her each time and smoothed her hair until she went back to sleep. In the morning, both children wolfed down tins of ham and beef. They both looked much brighter. Color had returned to their faces. They were children again.

Luke walked across the clearing to an old man and two women idling on the porch of their partially destroyed shack. Their barn had already been burned to the ground and their cows and pigs slaughtered, but they agreed to take the children. The commissary sergeant gave them two crates of hardtack, a sack of cornmeal, and two raw hams before the regiment moved on. The children shivered hard enough to rattle the porch rail, but the women knelt beside them whispering and stroking their hair. They both waved to Luke and the sergeant as they walked away.

Luke thought of home and his family. He could see his mother bent over her sewing table, his sister standing beside her, his mother's nimble fingers working on a seam, her brown hair with a touch of gray, the polished, turtle shell comb in her bun. The blue dots on her apron. Gray cotton slippers worn at a heel. He remembered as a boy watching her fingers work with the needle and thimble thinking they looked like a family of worms, all coming and going in a jumble of activity. The seams nearly flew out behind them. His mother would look up and smile and crinkle her nose. The worms would keep on tussling back-and-forth. Then his father would call from outside near the barn. Luke could still hear the rasp in his voice and smelled him as if he was standing right there in his face. Alcohol and cow dung. Maybe a hint of linseed oil.

"What the hell you doing boy?" Luke felt his heart jump. "Are you a momma's boy? Get out here and be a man. Get the stalls cleaned." His scarred face was always beet red. His breath reeked of tobacco juice that stained his teeth brown, and he was always dressed in black pants that hid the dirt well. Luke smiled as the details came flooding back. He knew his father was a hard man to put up with. How did his mother live with him all those years? Why had she married him in the first place?

"You listening to me boy?"

His father seemed right behind them. He felt his ear sting like it had a thousand times before. His father being good at inflicting pain. He could picture his mother looking up and motioning him to come closer. She would rub his ear and whisper that she loved him, but as he remembered it all, he felt a tightness deep in his gut. Not because his father was such an ass. But something worse. It was hard for him to admit it even now, even to himself. It hurt just thinking it. But he knew that despite all of his father's meanness and all of his mother's kindness, the one parent that meant the most to him was his father. But it was even worse than that. Even as a twelve year old boy, he'd come not only to dislike his mother, he'd come to hate her. There was no good reason. Just a boy, a young man, not wanting to be cared for by a doting, loving mother. It all seemed backwards. The kind person, hated. The mean person, loved. He didn't understand it, but he knew it was the truth. At least it had been until the war came. He thanked God he didn't feel that way anymore. Not since that first awful day at Chancellorsville. He truly didn't. And it was about the only good thing to have come from it all.

The regiment fell in behind them through smoky woods past burning turpentine stills then on to an open field with a white-washed farmhouse and a dozen small out-buildings and shacks. An old woman sat in a rocking chair on her little porch watching the blue soldiers swarmed across her property.

"Miracle it ain't burned yet." McMahon nodded towards soldiers kicking in the empty hen-house door. "Bet them chickens are long gone."

"Don't worry ma'am. Nobody's going to mess with your house." Dave walked up to the porch and dropped his arms over the banister.

"My uncle's got that same goose." He pointed up to the weathervane on the barn. A white goose with twirling wings, nose into the breeze, and flying hard.

184

"Best take the damn goose down then, if you want it, Dave. Before the boys light it up," McMahon called to him.

Soldiers spread out across the yard towards the barn, outbuildings and cotton field beyond, smoke rising from each shack as they passed. Dave held his Henry tightly across his chest. He knew he couldn't save the barn or the goose. By the time he climbed up, they'd have the house on fire. Maybe the barn beneath him too. All he could do was stand on the porch for a while, and buy the old woman some time.

"This house stays put." Dave rubbed his trigger guard and glared at McMahon.

"All right then Dave." McMahon raised his hands and backed off. He'd seen that look before. He yelled at the soldiers torching the barn. "Leave the house alone!"

The soldiers glanced at Dave with his Henry and nodded. McMahon knew Dave was a spinning top at times. No telling what he might do. He remembered him in action at Missionary Ridge. Shooting the wounded rebs in a trench line. One at a time. Putting his foot on their necks then the barrel to each skull. He remembered the splash of brains into Dave's peaceful face. He glanced back at him on the porch. Dave just stood there, eyes fixed on the barn roof as smoke engulfed the goose, its wings flapping harder in the intense heat as flames burst through the roof then twirling in the flames as if looking for an escape. Then the roof collapsing and the goose vanishing in the smoke.

Dave knelt down and felt his stomach turn. His face burst into sweat. The woman knelt beside him and may have been praying. Luke and McMahon stood guard with him until everything but the house was a smoldering ruin and the regiment was moving on following the column north. Luke nudged Dave off the porch. The old woman didn't want to let him go, holding his hand and kissing it before Luke pulled him along. They looked back and waved to the old woman who sat back down in her rocking chair looking over at another blue regiment coming across the field behind them towards the house.

McMahon and Luke hurried Dave along to catch up with the company farther up in the pines where a dozen or so white woman next to a burned-out shack stood in a circle with arms linked around a clump of children. The children sat a little pile of crates and kegs. All the women had left in the world.

"White buffalo circling their young. Must be inbred. Keeping the wolves at bay and all. Not much use against rifles though." McMahon sipped his canteen. "Doubt reb bitches are much brighter than buffalo anyhow."

"And they smell worse," Dave nodded, feeling back to his old self as orders were called out to stop for the night.

Luke felt relieved and ate quickly then sunk into sleep. He dreamed of camping with a red-haired girl at Glenn Eldridge on Seneca Lake, on the pebble beach downwind of the bottom spray of a cold waterfall. At dawn he tried to remember the girl's face, but she vanished in the cold early light.

They marched on without breakfast and came across three dead black men in blue uniforms. Each shot in the back of the head. No one stopped to inquire. No officer made a fuss. And there were no rebs in sight. Luke knew what it meant. White boys from another regiment had killed them. For what reason, he didn't know. But being black was reason enough for some. Hatred grew hotter the farther they marched on through the swamps. The more misery they suffered, the more the fires of hate took on a life of their own. The war just fanned the flames. Hatred towards rebs, towards this damnable state, even towards the blacks whose own misery at the hands of slavers caused this whole stinking war. Luke knew it wasn't right to feel that way and fought it off. But he knew others embraced it. He'd heard the western regiments made it a point to hate all blacks as much as any reb bushwhacker. They would gladly crush the rebs but would be quite happy to kill the blacks too. Luke figured the three dead men in the woods might be some proof that some of these the rumors were true.

CHAPTER 22— MIELA

*on the road east from Blessing Plantation
towards Charleston*

The morning sun peeked through the low gray clouds racing off to the northeast and brought a better mood to Miela's group shivering in their blankets around a small cooking fire, waiting for their breakfast of boiled rice. Lisette gulped a handful of half-cooked mush then squeezed Agnes.

"The Lord brings us hope. The sun's shining girl! Smile back at it." She turned to swing her around and saw the horsemen coming through the trees. She knew right off it was more trouble.

"Slave patrol!" She said as softly as she could, and all the adults froze. The children looked at their wide-eyed faces and then around at the horsemen, none of them knowing exactly what it all meant. The riders came slowly across the field. Four boys with shotguns and pistols.

"The worst kind," Miela whispered to Jemps. "Boys!"

She remembered a similar group a few months back. They'd whipped Gage. Right on Blessing Plantation. Broke into his cabin and torched all his clothes and shoes. Charged Mr. Blessing for their time. Said they were off duty but had spotted an 'insubordinate'. Blessing had refused to pay so they came back one night and tossed a torch into Elsey's cabin. Little Yarrow had been burned on the back. Elsey had doused his flaming shirt with a pitcher of water she'd just fetched. Miela could still smell his burned skin. It made her jaw tighten so much she had to consciously force it open. If only Ezekiel was here. With one of those new Yank rifles.

The horses were just forty yards distant when Daphne grabbed Fatima and started crying. Miela tried to shush her up. It was always best to be calm and act stupid. Any emotion made it worse. The four boys came up and leveled guns at them. They all looked just the same to Miela. All ruddy faced with blond hair. And none more than fourteen or fifteen. Having fun with guns and horses. Out hunting slaves. Never mind Sherman.

"Y'all got passes?" One boy asked.

"Yes sir, got it right here," she nodded respectfully, showing it to the boys. Thank God for Connor. It was good for the whole month.

"Nope," the boy spurred his horse into Cumseh, knocking her to the ground. "This ain't no good."

"But sir we got ... " Miela held out her hand

"Shut up girl or I'll blow your black head off." Another boy leveled a shotgun at her while the first boy waved the pass in her face.

"This here's for yesterday and it ain't yesterday."

"But sir, if you please, it's for ... "

"Shut up!" Another spurred his horse forward towards Cumseh who had just made it up to her knees. She lay back down quickly and stayed calm. The horse stopped, and the boy got furious. He drew his pistol and fired in the air. Miela's heart raced. Why is he so angry? Most slave patrols were usually quite matter-of-fact in their cruelty. But she really didn't care. He was just another white boy with a gun. Even if she had known that the boy's father had been killed at Chickamauga, his uncle, in Elmira prison camp, and two brothers of dysentery at Petersburg, it wouldn't have made any difference. The whites were the ones that started all this. All she cared about was living long enough to have her baby and get her people to freedom. The thought went by as quick as it took the boy to spur the horse towards Gage who had no idea what to do.

He instinctively grabbed the horses bridle and shouted out, "Stop!"

The boy's face turned red as an apple. He swung at Gage with a short club. Gage fell to his knees for a second then lurched forward, grabbed the boy's leg, and pulled him out of the saddle. Before the boy hit the ground, a shotgun fired. Gage fell on his side and crawled away terrified. Blood was everywhere. His sleeve was torn and red meat stuck out of his shoulder. Another blast hit him square in the back. He stopped crawling, sank slowly into the weeds, twitching like a frog. Then he was still. The boys regrouped, and the dismounted one checked his horse.

His hands trembled, and he puffed out his cheeks."Bastard blacks. You just can't trust 'em."

Fatima shook violently, and Daphne held on tighter. Everyone else crouched down terrified. Miela looked up at the four boys' taut faces and their leveled guns and knew what they were thinking. That it was better to have a dozen dead blacks than even one live witness. She held shivering Fatima tightly in her arms. Then she gambled everything.

"I'm pregnant, sir. Mr. Malcolm Blessing knows it, too. He wants us to go to Smythes on Daniel Island. Near Charleston, sir. Said we had to go there and wait for him. Sherman's army is coming y'see. Mr. Malcolm says the Yankees will hurt us. Poor Gage there was feebleminded, sir. He didn't know what he was doing. I'm so sorry, but he was just ... Please help us get to Smythes."

The boys rode around them for a while talking in whispers. One of them gagged and wiped tears from his eyes. Another looked terrified, but Miela's gamble worked. The moment passed. Shotguns were averted. The boy who fired was trembling all over.

"The bastard tried to jump Peter," he yelled, his voice cracking. "Deserved what he got. Every bit."

Miela could tell he was about to cry, but he rode off before it showed. Another boy reeled off a string of curses that made his face turn purple, "Ain't the county gonna to pay your owner back? Owner gets reimbursed by the county ... for blacks killed by patrol." He spun his horse around, and Miela nodded and waved her hands in the air.

"Yes sir. It's not your fault, sir. It's Gage's fault. We just want to get to Charleston, sir."

The other three boys rode one more circle around the group then bolted back off through the woods. No one moved until they were out of sight. Daphne fell to her knees with Fatima shaking even harder. "Why? Why? Oh Lord, why poor Gage?" She sobbed until overcome by the realization that it could have been Fatima. Miela knelt on the ground by Gage and wept.

"What have I done?" She whispered. "What have I done?"

"You ain't done nothing, Miela," Lizette knelt beside her and hugged her, breaking into tears.. "Nothing but give us love and hope. You ain't the one who killed Gage. Them patrol boys did."

Jemps came up and held them both, and the others gathered around. Elsey and Daphne covered Gage with a blanket. Miela wiped her face and caught her breath. She thought of Blessing being 'reimbursed'.

"We must ... bury ... " Tears came again, and she let Lizette finish for her.

"We'll bury him in a decent grave with a marker. He'd do the same for us."

George pulled out the shovel and started digging. Titus, Jemps and Poins took turns. All the women and children helped with spoons and cups. It took them two hours to do it right. A deep grave. A neatly folded blanket. Gage's face and hands washed, his hair combed. With Miela leading them in a prayer and Lizette singing the Hallelujah song. Then they all say goodbye to Gage and moved on down the little track in the woods. No one wanted to stay in that field a second longer than necessary.

A mile further they came to the Charleston Road and followed it for a few more miles to a fork in the road at the crossroads called Blue House. Miela guessed it best to go right, but a wave of nausea bent her over. She gagged until Lizette sat her down on an overturned bucket and gave her some water.

"I guess it's that way. I don't know for sure," Miela felt her eyes well up again "What if I'm wrong? What if something else happens?"

Cumseh came over and rubbed her back, "Something bad's gonna happen, either way. Best we move on and trust the Divine."

"Oh my God!" Daphne pointed through the trees. A troop of gray cavalry were coming towards them in a long arc. "Look! Oh my God! Not again!"

Daphne grabbed Fatima and crawled under the wagon. The cavalry quickly surrounded them and a sunburned man came forward on his twitching mule.

"Who's been shooting!" His carbine dangled over the mule's neck. Both of his legs were wrapped in blue canvas leggings tied with twine. Miela couldn't think of anything else but the truth.

"Four boys back there. Slave patrol. They shot Gage. He was simpleminded and didn't know what he was doing. But we've got papers ... " She reached into her pocket to get the passes.

"Where y'all belong?" The sunburned man asked Elsey, purposely ignoring Miela, but Elsey was too scared to talk. The sunburned reb dismounted, held her by the shoulder and whispered softly, "Where y'all belong?"

It was more terrifying to Elsey than the loudest scream. Her throat closed shut until Miela stepped forward. "We belong to Mr. Blessing. He

190

told us to go to Charleston. To Smythes. We're heading where his nephew told us to go." She said it all quickly but clearly, and it was nearly the whole truth.

"My ass," one of the gray horsemen laughed. "Gonna join the Yanks, ain't ya."

The sunburned man let Elsey go and gently patted Yarrow on the head. Yarrow kept still. He thought of the time he'd crawled under the smokehouse after guinea hen and came face to face with a big rattlesnake with the hen in its mouth. He remembered staying frozen for a while then crawling back out, hoping the rattler was satisfied with his meal. Thank God it had been. Maybe the reb would be too.

"You been freed, eh?" He smiled and brushed Miela's shoulders.

"Yes sir," she bowed respectfully.

"And you're going down to Charleston?" The reb sighed and touched her on the nose.

"Yes sir. Mr. Blessing's place. Smythes." Her eyes glanced quickly at terrified Elsey who stared straight at the ground. The reb grabbed Miela's chin.

"Don't look at her no more. I'm talking to you."

"Yes sir," she answered quickly, feeling her heart straining in her throat.

"You said Mr. Blessing? Smythes?"

"Yes sir." She stood rigidly still, not daring even to cross her fingers.

"I tell you what we'll do then. Philip! Come here," he called to a young horseman. "Get that little one there." He pointed to Grace who clung in terror to Lizette's skirt. "We'll take her with us. We'll get her to Smythes and give her back, IF ... IF you show up." He rubbed Grace's head then jumped up on his mule. Grace was snatched up by a skinny teenage boy with a pock marked face and draped over his pommel.

"Please sir! Please!" Lizette screamed. "Please let her stay! She's my little girl! For god's sake, please!"

Another trooper cocked a shotgun and jabbed her in the neck with the barrel. Lizette kept screaming and clutched at Grace's leg, but Jemps held her back, whispering in her ear, "Don't fight. They'll kill you Lizette."

191

The young trooper holding Grace twisted his face into a grimace as if steeling himself while Lizette kept screaming. "Please! Oh please God, no!"

The other women stood mute and terrified. Even Miela was stunned dumb. George pushed forward and grabbed at Grace's legs. Titus and Poins jumped to his side. Horsemen rode into them, knocking all three to the ground. Poins jumped back up and went for her leg again.

The sunburned man whirled his mule around and yelled out, "You touch her again and we'll take another! Lucky we don't blow your heads off." He pointed his gun at Poins then spurred off with the others into the woods with Grace.

Yarrow ran after them, dodging in between horseman and hurtling over stumps. Jemps tried to catch him, but a rider wheeled in front of him waving a pistol. Yarrow vaulted a log pile with another trooper's horse right behind him. He kept his eyes focused on Grace bouncing across the young trooper's saddle. All he could hear was her screaming until a rifle butt knocked him senseless. His head thudded into a small pine, and he lay still.

The cavalry rode off with Grace still screaming for her mother. Miela ran up and held Yarrow in her lap, and Jemps fetched water to rinse his head. Miela dabbed the rising knot with her skirt as Yarrow came to with a start. She tried to hold him, but he wouldn't let her.

"Grace!" He wobbled to his feet and looked around, trembling with his hands clenched until realizing she was gone. "Grace! Grace!" He shook his head and sobbed, "I'll find her. If it takes until I die, I swear on the Bible, I'll find her."

Miela looked up at the fork in the road, picked up a clod of mud, and threw it. "Damn this! Damn it to hell! Why? Why? Damn it! Do you hear me?" She looked at the sky "Where are you Lord?"

The others, except Lizette, stood for a while in the profound silence that fell on all of them, as it had at some time or another in their lives, when they had witnessed murder, rape, or the 'blacksnake' at the hands of the whites. Lizette let out a wail that sounded like saw blades cutting iron. Only her wailing and Miela's cursing penetrated the silence. None of the group had ever seen either of them like this. Cumseh pulled out a dried chicken bone from her apron then bent over and scooped a handful of dirt.

"This here's an evil day, but the Divine has plans we can't see." She spat on the bone and tossed it over her head then stomped it in the dirt and buried it in a little hole. "Leave this sorrow. Let the crows have this bone." She rolled her eyes back and wiped dirt across her forehead. "If we leave right now, Grace will find us. If we stay, we'll never see her again."

"Cumseh's right," Jemps wiped his face. "We'll find Grace, Lizette! Don't you worry, Yarrow. We'll find her. Even rebs won't hurt a little girl."

Lizette gagged and went on wailing. Jemps patted her shoulder. "We got to go one. Ain't nothing else to do. C'mon Poins, George. Let's go."

They did as he said and helped Lizette into the wagon. She flopped on her side trembling all over. Yarrow curled up next to her in a ball. Titus rubbed his wooden leg for a while before getting the mules moving forward. Everyone else followed. Miela stopped cursing. Her vision contracted into a dark tunnel. A pain tore at her stomach, and a voice in her head said, "You don't deserve a child of your own." She threw up and stumbled to her knees until Elsey pulled her back to her feet and helped her along.

They camped a few miles down the road just as darkness fell, but they didn't even build a fire. No one slept much. Lizette wailed all night. They were all still in a daze in the morning. Lizette was unable to eat or walk. She didn't say a word. The others weren't much better. It took them all day to go five miles to another fork in the road where the sun flashed out from behind a solid line of gray overcast that raced northward. Blue sky chased it along.

George made them stop and watch. He led them in the Lord's Prayer then made a fire to cook more of the rice. He forced everyone to eat as much as they could. Daphne got Lizette to take a few mouthfuls. George was the last to stop eating. He wiped his mouth then stood up on the highest box in the wagon and spread his arms.

"The Lord has given us a sign. Behold the bright blue sky. It chases away the gray darkness. It's a new day of freedom. Time to let the Lord provide." He jumped down from the wagon and hugged Miela. "You've got to take them to Smythes. You'll find it. I know it. God is with you. Jemps, too."

"What are you doing?" Miela pulled at his sleeves. 'No ... "

193

"I'm going to Sherman. I been called. It's God's way. He done told me by taking Grace, and I ain't turning my back on the Lord."

"No George. You come with us. Let's stay together. We're almost there."

"YA'LL are. Not me. I'm going north. See the clouds running? They're showing me the way."

"But why?" She wiped away tears. "Come with us. Please, don't do this." She held her arms out pleading.

"I know. I love y'all too. All of you. But you're almost there. I ain't been able to protect Gage or Grace. Y'all can do this without me."

Miela grabbed his shirt. "Stay with us please. For the children's sake."

"No!" He pushed her way "You want me to go against the Lord?"

"But George, you might be mistaken. You know how the Lord is ... It's just so hard to know." She knelt down with her hands clasped in prayer.

"Yep. He's real hard to know All right." Jemps stood behind her with a hand on Miela's shoulder nodding. "And I ain't seen no sign from God. You need to stay with us."

George ignored him. He packed a sack full of rice, slid a jar of molasses in his pocket, rolled up a blanket and tied it over his shoulder, rebel style, then hugged each of them. He picked up a shovel.

"I'll be needing this for snakes and such." He took a deep breath. "And remember, I love y'all. We'll be together soon, I bet. Freedom is almost here." Then he walked off knowing there was no use prolonging it. None of the others would ever agree with him. "See y'all in the Jubilee."

Miela's shoulders sank. She felt anger more than anything. Why was this happening? Was it not meant to be? Daphne came up behind her.

"Don't worry the Miela, we'll make it." She squeezed Miela's shoulder. "We'll be fine." But she had to avert his eyes from Lizette sitting up in the wagon wailing again.

Miela wiped her eyes and tried to believe her. "Yes, of course we will."

No one else knew any other way. Only to follow Miela. They all stood there in shock. What was George thinking? Poins ran after him and hugged him again. His tears dripped onto his coat. Elsey followed with more rice and another blanket. Daphne sang the Hallelujah song as

194

he walked away up the road that curved north through the pines. He waved back until finally out of sight. Lizette fell back into the wagon wailing even louder. Cumseh fanned her with a rag. She clenched her other fist around some sparrow feathers.

"By the power of the Divine above and the bent roots below, we'll find Grace." She tossed the feathers into the air and cackled like a crow. Lizette looked up and stopped her wailing. She clutched her stomach as if she'd been impaled, and Cumseh smiled. "The Divine's inside you now."

Jemps helped her snuggle up beside Yarrow and got the rest of them moving again. They walked on to the railway and followed it to a trestle over the Ashepoo River. No one was about and Miela was in a trance. Jemps decided to risk it. The wagon clattered across, rattling and vibrating hard enough to crack a sorghum jar and leaving a sticky trail across the timbers. All the while Jemps prayed to God that the train wouldn't come.

When they made it, he knelt and promised God he would never doubt Him again. They moved on into the woods on the other side then another half mile down the road beside the track before a troop of gray cavalry came down the rail embankment. Agnes started crying. Everyone froze as the troopers glanced over at them but rode off the way they'd come.

Miela woke from her daze, "I swear to God."

"See? Agnes?" Daphne patted her head. "They left us alone! It's truly the Jubilee."

They moved on and camped at the edge of a fallow cornfield next to a thick stand of bamboo towering thirty feet or so. Yarrow came to life and collected dozens of bamboo poles and lashed them to the side of the wagon.

"Spears!" He yelled. "I'll stab them in the eye if they come back. I'll kill every one of them!"

Miela sat by the small fire that Jemps built in a hole deep enough to hide the flame. She took a jar of honey and turned it over and over. Daphne tended to Lizette who had stopped wailing enough to accept some rice mush in sassafras tea. Yarrow came back with his last bundle of bamboo spears and sat down beside her. "What are you doing Miela?"

Miela quickly glanced up and nodded. "This is the truth. See this? See? The air rises. See? Watch this. This is the future. Now watch." She held the jar up over her head then smashed it on the ground. The jar disintegrated, and honey poured out into the dirt. "See? The air is free now. The jar can't trap it anymore."

Daphne and Elsey quickly scooped up what they could into waxed gourd bowls. Agnes and Fatima dipped pieces of bamboo and licked it up, grime and all. Cumseh grunted, rubbing a piece of oyster shell through her hair, "It ain't like you to be wasteful, Miela."

Miela picked up a piece of broken glass that nicked her finger. She sucked on it and sighed. "Freedom comes with a price."

Yarrow shook his head, "What about Grace? Where's her freedom?"

"She'll come back, Yarrow. It's the end of slavery now. Freedom's here. They'll have to let her go. Grace is smart, too. She knows where we're headed. The name at least. Smythes. And remember, she loves you as much as you love her. She'll find you or we'll find her. I promise."

Yarrow stuck his fingers into the honey and licked them clean. He stared out into the darkening woods as the last of the twilight faded and started crying but pulled his jacket over his head so the girls couldn't see. Miela hugged him and held him close, feeling his chest heave for a long time.

"Miela," he whispered. "They better not hurt her. I swear to God they better not. I'll kill them if they do."

Miela squeezed him harder. "She'll be all right. I promise. God won't allow ... " She felt her throat close up. Yarrow looked up at her wide-eyed, but what could she say? That God didn't allow horrible things to happen? She looked into his tear- streaked, tender face and knew what she had to do. She shook off her fears and smiled at him.

"Yes, Yarrow. She'll be all right. God in heaven will protect her. He's just testing us. She'll be all right. I swear she will."

As he fell asleep in her arms, she prayed to God that He wouldn't make her a liar.

Chapter 23 — Miela

on the road to Charleston

In the morning Miela kept them headed down the Charleston Road. Dead horses and mules littered the fields. Flies swarmed everywhere. The stench of rotting flesh hung in the air like an oily mist. The only living things were dozens of chicken roosting in the trees around a burning shack.

"Damn miasma," Jemps covered his nose. "Kill enough horses and mules. Miasma, I tell you. Enough to sicken a man. Maim the spirit."

"Here. Rub some sassafras on your nose," Elsey handed him some dried up stems.

"No thanks. We just need to keep on moving. Get away from all this."

"Yanks kill them horses?" Lizette held her nose.

"Maybe. Or the rebs. So the Yanks couldn't use 'em."

"Well, that ain't right."

"But look there. Even the Yanks can't kill gamecock chickens fast enough," Titus laughed. He took careful aim with one of Yarrow's bamboo spears and threw it up into one of the oak trees. A bird dropped flapping and kicking, and Daphne retrieved it.

"Get two more, Titus," she beamed, holding the bird up her by the neck and judging its weight. "Ain't enough meat on this one."

Titus and Jemps kept trying, but the rest of the chickens were too quick, flying to where the road disappeared into the swamp. The mules pulled the wagon across flooded bogs with wheels sinking deep into the mud before finding drier footing on a little dike cutting across through the trees. Everyone rested on its dry top, glad to be out of the water and away from the stench. No one saw the black man with a shotgun standing in the cypress hollow just ten feet from them. He'd been perfectly still, remaining invisible until he stepped forward.

"What y'all doing here!" His voice rolled across the dike. Elsey grabbed the children and pulled them behind the wagon. Even Jemps was face down on the dike until he got a grip on himself. Hell, it was just one black man, he thought, even if he had a shotgun.

"What y'all doing?" The man asked again a little calmer. He seemed scared himself but breathed easier, seeing that they weren't armed.

Miela spoke up, "Going to Charleston. Just doing the best we can. Don't mean no harm to nobody."

The black man stepped forward and pulled the brown canvas hood off his head. His face was pulled taut over sharp cheekbones. His legs and feet were wrapped in grease-coated canvas. A sarape of mud-covered burlap, cinched up with a piece of rope, covered his shoulders. He tucked the shotgun barrel under the rope as if into a holster.

"Y'all are lucky I ain't shot you. Name's Scipio. Been running for three days. Patrol found our camp back yonder. Killed most of us. Took the others off. Ain't seen nobody since." He eyed the sacks of rice. "Ain't had nothing but bugs to eat." He glanced over his shoulder and took a knee. "Was gonna cook this snake when it was safe. Didn't want to get shot because of building a fire." He pulled out a large copperhead from a fold in the serape. Fatima shrieked, and Daphne covered her mouth.

"Don't worry none," the man smiled. His upper teeth were brown with grime. "Cut his head off awhile back, so he won't bite nobody."

"Here," Jemps gave him a rice sack. The man ate a handful raw.

"Thanks." He scooped water out of the hollow in the cypress root. "Been hiding in the swamp for over a year now. With other runaways. We been living trapping 'possums and raccoons, some wild pigs too." He gulped more rice. "The shotgun's from a reb scout. Got stuck in the swamp after dark with a lame horse. Heard him splashing around and waited until he settled down. Mr. Cyrus cut his throat. He kept the gun until the patrol came. Got shot in the neck. I grabbed a gun and ran for it. Ain't never going back to Pon Pon Plantation. They can kill me if they like." He gulped more water and came up for air. "I'll show y'all the quickest way around, if you want."

Miela agreed to follow his lead, but she knew a gun was big trouble. Slave patrols would shoot any armed slaves, and the vision of the shotgun blast into Gage's back flashed in her mind. She pushed it away and took a deep breath. Gun or no gun, there was no guarantee. She kept her fingers crossed until they reached higher ground. Scipio took payment of another sack of rice and a blanket and went his own way, disappearing in seconds into a thicket of sycamores and water oaks.

"Good luck," Jemps called behind him.

"And to y'all,"Scipio answered from deeper in the woods.

Miela had them push on quickly, not wanting to linger around a shotgun. They followed the road a few miles into higher pine woods then across cornfields to a row of slave huts backing up to more woods and shielded from the still intact plantation house by a row of magnolia trees. An old black man sat on the log bench and silently watched them approach. He was dressed in dirty rags.

Miela spoke up first, "We come from Blessing Plantation. Headed up Charleston way. Looking for a place to rest tonight ... in peace. Got our own food. Share it with you too, if you need some. Needing only some rest in return. We've got everything else."

The old man nodded, "Ain't got nothing to eat."

Jemps handed over another sack of rice and the old man smiled, "Heard Yanks is coming, but ain't seen none. Y'all seen any?"

Miela nodded and went over to whisper their story in his ear as not to upset Lizette and Yarrow. The own man sighed deeply, "The Jubilee ain't an easy thing, is it?"

"No it isn't," Miela tried not to wince at his smell. Like a dead possum, but tangier, like rancid turtle soup.

"Name's Cork. Mr. Walker left a week ago. Took all the other slaves with him. Except those that ran off. And me. I hid under my hut 'till they left."

"I'm Miela."

Cork bent close and whispered to her, "What about the Yanks? Y'all really seen some?

"A ways back. None since the other side of the rail bridge." Miela figured he was just anxious for the freedom like the rest. She didn't tell Cork that she was perfectly happy with never seeing another Yank the rest of her life. If everyone would just leave her and the others alone. Cork sighed and scratched his gray beard then told them to set up camp between the two closest huts. He walked off to the last hut and stayed inside until after dark. Daphne cooked rice and molasses, and Jemps took

199

Cork a big bowl. Lizette climbed down from the wagon and sat by the fire. The children surrounded her and gave her hugs and kisses.

"Grace will be all right, Lizette. She'll be just fine."

Lizette wiped away her tears and hugged them back. "I know. I know. The Lord's just testing us." She tried to smile but couldn't.

Poins ands Titus sat beside her and made her eat. She cried for a while afterwards but not as hard as before, and she let the children cuddle with her underneath a blanket. When everyone else was bedded down, Cork came back out of the dark and found Miela.

"Come with me."

He walked off and Miela followed. What now? Some payment was do, for sure. Was nothing ever free? Even kindness from fellow blacks? Cork waved for her to hurry up. He held the door of the last hut open and pushed Miela inside. It was pitch black until Cork lit a match. Miela almost fainted. Her heart leapt right into her mouth. There in front of her crouched two white men. Both skeletal and dressed in blue rags. One short with dark hair, the other taller with a badly cut face and lip. They squatted on the sand floor next to a sink hole in the middle of the room. A tall wooden stool stood over the hole dangling flypaper beneath it. A box at the bottom of the hole held empty tins of sardines and condensed milk covered by a cotton mesh. The shorter skeleton spoke first. His lips were pulled tightly across his rotting teeth.

"We jumped from a prison train three days ago. Rebs are moving all the prisoners from Charleston to upstate somewhere. We figured we were just about dead anyhow. Jumped into the swamp. The train never stopped. Guards in the last car shot Billy, the bastards. Billy Grooms from Elmira. Dead in some stinking South Carolina's swamp."

"That's enough, Frank," The taller skeleton lisped and winced as he spoke.

Frank nodded. "We ain't going back. Just tell us where you saw our boys. Point us in the right direction. We'll walk 'till we drop. Could use some more food, though."

Miela glanced down at the empty rice bowl, "Yes of course. We've got more."

It all ran through her mind in a second. She knew what the rebs would do to them if they came tonight. If they caught them harboring Yank prisoners. What had the old man done? Why involve an innocent group of runaways? She knew they should get away right now, but she knew she couldn't. She went back and told Jemps to quickly gather clothing, and she woke Daphne to cook a dozen more rice cakes which the Yanks gobbled. Their stomachs finally stopped gnawing for the first time since the jump from the prison train. In the candle light, Miela saw they were just boys. Skeletal boys.

"Captured at Battery Wagner," the tall one lisped, but he wouldn't say anymore. As if he didn't really trust her. But why should he, Miela thought. She let them be and went back to the others, praying that no reb cavalry came along. Daphne cooked more rice cakes until well past midnight, and Miela wrapped them in a piece of canvas. At first light she gave some to Cork and some to the Yank boys.

"If y'all got to run. These here will give you strength. Help you keep going."

The taller boy took the bundle and stuffed inside his shirt. Lizette helped Daphne cook dozens more for breakfast. The soldiers ate again as if they hadn't ever eaten before. With renewed energy they wrapped themselves in blankets that Jemps gave them. They thanked Cork and Miela for their help then walked off northwest.

"We'll find Sherman or die trying," the tall one called back, limping and waving at them.

Miela waved back then had the group pack up quickly. She didn't want to linger anywhere close by, just in case. What if another slave patrol or more reb cavalry scouts surprised them? She had them push on all that day through thick woods, keeping off the road as much as they could, using it only when the swamp was impassable. At dark they found another bamboo thicket where the men cut a path into the middle so that they could hide the wagon. They dug a hole for the fire so it couldn't be seen and cooked a meal of more rice cakes and molasses. Miela bedded down for the night more relaxed, knowing the two Yanks had to be miles away.

in the Salkehatchie Swamp

The wind cut through Connor's rubber poncho as he squatted with numb feet on the frosty ground watching Yank bummers come walking around the bend in the causeway road. Connor thought they looked too relaxed. Like they were back up north somewhere, Iowa or Maine maybe, wandering over to friend's farm. Men fired from behind the trees up the road and killed two of them right off.

"Poor bastards," Barry chuckled. "Gonna let you stay in South Carolina now. Gonna fertilize that there swamp a while. Gators and coon's gonna love your innards. Should've known better than to ... "

Firing broke loose up the causeway, drowning him out, then all through the swamp as more Yanks came up on the flanks and peppered the air with their Henrys. The ambush answered with three volleys. Powder-smoke raced through the trees with a north wind. Bullets whined above. Two boys in the saw -palmettos at the roads edge lurched back in a spray of blood as Yanks' 12 pounders roared. The whole line fired again then pulled back past the swamp through scrub oaks, willows and a patchwork of fallow, stump strewn fields to rest on high ground on the other side while the wounded were bandaged up, as well as possible, behind a bamboo thicket in the pine woods. Norton passed around his 'fear tonic' like nothing had happened. It tasted like sweetened turpentine and made Connor gag.

"Don't you like good gin?" Barry laughed.

Rifle fire started up to the right before he could answer, and riders came galloping through the trees yelling, "Yanks are past the creek yonder!"

Everyone was quickly off, following JB to the rear as rifle fire crept closer. They rode through another cypress and water-oak swamp to higher ground where pines led to open field at least a half mile across. A huge mansion stood formidably at the end of an avenue of oaks. Symmetrical crescent shaped ponds, bigger than Blessing's, cut into a sloping, terraced hillside of azaleas. An ornate, gold-inlaid carriage stood abandoned on the avenue.

A shadow came from a third-floor dormer window. Everyone looked up at a gray-haired man, dressed in a white, ruffled shirt, protruding far enough through the open dormer window that Connor felt surely he would fall to his death.

"You men! Turn around and fight! How dare you run away!" His frail body shivered in fury. His voice rasped across the field. "I've lost two sons in Virginia! Two sons given to the Cause! How dare you run!" The old man gripped the ledge with white knuckles. The sun flashed on his gold watch and opal ring.

Norton poked Barry and nodded towards a dozen slaves, all women and children, peering around the corner of the house. "Yes sir!" He called out loud enough for the old man and the blacks to hear. "Better to see your own sons die than give up your slaves!"
The old man kept yelling until his face turned red. "Turn around! Damn you! Turn around!"

"It sure don't make sense. Boys dying so old men can be tended to by blacks." Barry rubbed his scalp. "Guess you just can't pry a rich planter loose from his slaves."

"This states crazy all right," JB laughed. "You know what they say about South Carolina. Too small to be a republic and too large to be an insane asylum. No offense Conner."

"None taken," he shrugged, remembering Uncle Paul laughing when he'd first heard it. Some fellow named Pettigru, he remembered. A man who may have been more honest than diplomatic.

"Don't leave! Stand and fight! Don't leave!" The old man in the window kept yelling as they followed JB across the corn and cotton fields into the far woods and out of sight.

THEY RODE ON FOR MILES as the rifle fire in the rear petered out then camped in a clearing in the woods beside a little farm house. Connor peered through the yellow window at a woman sitting inside on a low stool by the fire stirring a simmering kettle of lard that hung by a chain over the fire. A black streak of soot extended from one dark eyebrow around to her ear. She rested the long wooden ladle on the kettle top and nervously picked her eyebrow with her soot blackened hand, widening the streak even more. Her other hand was just a scared nub of badly burned fingers that shook rhythmically.

She looked up and motioned for Connor to come inside. Others followed him into the warmth. On the coarsely-hewn, oak mantle was a daguerreotype of two men and a teenage boy, all dressed in Confederate gray. She saw Connor looking at them.

"Been gone since Shiloh in '62. No word since Atlanta. Since they went back into Tennessee with Hood." She stopped stirring and puffed out her cheeks. "But why? Why go to Tennessee? Can anybody answer me that? What in God's name is he doing? Taking my men into Tennessee! Why, for Christ's sake. Forgive me Lord for taking thy name in vain. But why? Sherman's here! The bastard Yanks are here!" Her face scrunched up like she had smelled a skunk. "Hood! Christ almighty. He's a fool. No, that's too kind. He's a lunatic, an imbecile." She stifled tears and started stirring the kettle again.

Connor felt the need to do something but wasn't sure what. "Maybe so ma'am, maybe so."

Her face snapped up at him, but she looked away just as quickly "That's my husband, Jake." She pointed to the daguerreotype. "My son, Peter, and my brother, Timothy. All gone with Hood." Her hand slipped down the handle almost to the bubbling hot lard.

"Ma'am!"

"It's all right. I guess God knows what he's doing? Doesn't He?" She tried to laugh. "It's the worry y'see. Every day since '62. If I worry too much then I count the trees across the field, the big oak first, then back to the dogwood at the edge of the pine woods. Thirty five trees you see. I count them all six times. All three came home and '65. So don't say nothing. It's my way. And it's worked so far. Shiloh, Murfreesboro, Perryville, Chickamauga, Kennesaw Mountain, Atlanta. I got letters after each one. You know how many dead they mentioned in those letters? 72! Just from their company. 72! They've seen so many come and go ... My little boy is a sergeant now. He's one of the old-timers." She wiped more soot onto her face and kept stirring. "I'll count those trees six times a day until they come walking up the road from Rivers Bridge."

Connor put his hand on her shoulder. "Ma'am. I sure hope they'll be all right."

She pulled away for a second then relaxed and stared up at him with tears in her eyes. She wiped her face some more and touched his arm with her nub hand. "They say all my good luck's because of this. Turpentine fire y'see. My glove lit up like a torch. Couldn't get it off. Jake saved me. Made me stick it under the ice. The stream was frozen that winter. It's never been since, until now. It might have been God's work." She raised the nub. "It's a magic hand now. One touch on the forehead will keep a man whole. In one piece that is. No holes.... in your shirt.... from lead balls or pieces of metal. I truly believe it. You might as well bend down here and take some."

Connor didn't hesitate. He knelt as if at the altar. "Thank you. No harm in a bit of magic."

Norton walked over and did the same, thinking, "Why not give it a chance. Maybe she had real magic, maybe not, but what's the harm."

"God bless you all. Keep you whole." She touched their foreheads with the web of ice cold fingers.

"Thank you ma'am," Connor blessed himself by habit.

"You're welcome. You're both welcome."

She went back to stirring her lard, and they retreated outside to the porch where a ponderous barefoot girl, fat enough to crush a mule, walked slowly back and forth smiling at the troopers. Her face was perfectly round and as pretty as her triple chin would allow, but the porch creaked under her weight. She wore wide brimmed stiff felt hat and was draped in a bed spread with a rope around her enormous abdomen.

"Any of you boys know Colonel Capers? The 24th South Carolina. Or my husband Dickey Jones?" Her eyes widened for a second as they all shook their hands 'no'.

"No ma'am. Wheeler's boys. What's left of us." Barry held his hat over his chest for a moment and glanced at her pink toes.

She smiled back and wiggled them. "Don't worry. Haven't felt 'em since I was sixteen. It's the one good thing about my size. I could wade the Salkehatchie today if I had to. They turn purple sometimes, but it don't hurt. A good thing since there ain't enough shoes to go around."

"Yep. A good thing indeed," Barry laughed with her and tipped his hat as he backed away.

The woman with the nub hand came out with a basket of cornbread squares drizzled with molasses, and they were promptly wolfed down. She returned again with a jug of sweet apple cider and a platter of fried red breasts on slices of sweet potatoes. Men gathered around eating them up as fast as she brought them out until every stomach had at least something then everyone bedded down by the fires to quickly succumb to sleep.

BUCKY WOKE UP before everyone else as always. He loved the smell of the cold earth in the dark, a smell no one else ever seemed to appreciate. He loved everything about mornings. Cold, dark, wet. It didn't matter. They were just as beautiful to him as warm sunshine and blue sky. He saddled his mule Maloney and made sure no one else saw him hug his neck. He couldn't hide his smile though. He thanked God as he always did. For the new day and for the pure joy of his life. He looked around at men stumbling up to the crackling fire and at the row of picketed horses blowing steamy breath and getting restless with the dawn light that triggered a sudden chorus of birds. He felt his bowie knife and slid his double-barrel shotgun out of its leather sling, just enough to feel the trigger guard and the twin hammers. He slid it back into the Yank saddle on Maloney and said his prayer. The same as always.

"Thank you Lord for letting me have such a big old time."

Then he gobbled a breakfast of a few slices of cold ham and followed JB and the others north through flooded rice fields that stretched half a mile down to a big swamp.

Connor rode up ahead imagining what it had been like, digging out cypress and tupelo stumps in mosquito infested swamps. Bad enough for a free man. He couldn't fathom what it must have been like for the slaves. The wrongness of it slapped him again, but he didn't want to think it, even for a second. He didn't want any doubts at all. To be able to believe all that he'd been brought up with. That slavery was a good thing, for blacks and whites. That it was ordained by the Almighty. The natural, correct, way of things. In harmony with God's world. Or so the preachers said. But no wonder the slaves ran off to fight for the Yanks. He'd have done just the same. Just for being owned. The thought of it all made his growing hunger even more miserable. He could imagine his Uncle Paul laughing at him.

"Hell of a time to conclude that you're fighting for the wrong side! For God's sake, boy! It's your own State!"

Connor blocked it all out, first by thinking of food, then by what he would say back to his uncle, as if he were standing in front of him.

"I'm no traitor. No Judas turncoat. No galvanized Yankee. I'll fight side by side with the others. No matter right or wrong. By God, it IS my State!"

All morning long he kept repeating it to himself, but his thoughts always went back to his Uncle laughing at him. Rifle fire finally refocused his mind as he followed the others across a causeway in the swamp to a hillock of pines where an officer ordered the whole scout to support the line of infantry already forming up. A log parapet stretched through the trees facing the swamp. Shallow trenches and rifle pits behind the works were already filling up with more teenage boys and gray-haired man with flintlock rifles and shotguns. Only the older militia-men seemed nervous and twitchy, fumbling with their makeshift cartridge pouches and old rifles. They knew what was coming, what they were about to face. The boys were all smiles and joking around.

"Blissfully ignorant boys on a lark," Norton nodded towards them. "No sour old men can tell them otherwise. It's pure fun. The best game ever, 'til the Henrys range in."

Connor saw it too. It was in their eyes. To be out after Sherman, free from all other chores, with no mother hovering over them. It might have been a slice of heaven. Knowing that it was about to end didn't hurt their mood either. Better to get in at the tail end. Fight the Yanks as long as permitted then go home satisfied and safe. They'd have these days for the rest of their lives. To be boys in gray and to have fought the Yanks. All of them planned to survive too. And Connor figured most would. They could outrun the old men.

JB rode up and had them follow him down the line taking messages and orders back and forth to different scouts on both flanks. No one seemed to be in charge. Men dug rifle pits wherever they pleased with whatever they had. Cups and bowls mostly.

"This here won't last long," JB flicked his hand at the raggy trench line. "Yanks will cut through right or left. Always best to know what's in the rear. Always have a plan."

"The plan is to run like hell," Chesire laughed.

JB cut his eyes at him and smiled. "Could be. C'mon."

He led the whole scout down through a swale to an oak bog then up through more pine woods past more ditches and earthworks that were still spreading up and down the bluff overlooking the swamp, helped along by slave labor. A party of fifty or so more, guarded by overseers armed with shotguns, cleared some of the trees in front so the 12-pounder guns could bear on the causeway. They were watched warily by the closest company of infantry as rifle fire crackled right and left through the woods.

"Would have been better to do what General Cleburne said," Norton nodded towards them. "Free the slaves and let them fight for us as free men."

"That'll be the day," Barry grunted.

Connor had heard that talk before but knew Cleburne was dead now and that no one else high at the government had ever pushed his idea further. He watched the blacks cut trees knee-deep in swamp all the while glancing back at their white guards. Connor knew they'd run for if they could. Even if Robert E. Lee in the flesh rode up and handed out freedom badges, they'd go to the Yanks as quick as mockingbirds after a cat. It was too late for all that. It had always been too late, even from the first day. The first day someone brought a man in chains to a slave market. The handwriting was on the wall. Connor thought about it as he helped dig another deeper hole. One day a slave, a piece of property, the next a free man being asked to fight for his former owners. It was all just too absurd.

He could picture his Uncle Paul snickering at him again. It was almost a relief that the Yanks were here. He could focus on the job at hand. No time to ponder right or wrong. Just fight for his State. Or at least that's what he told himself. If he went to Hell for his part in it all, then so be it. But as he looked down the trench line at the white faces of boys and old man, he knew he could never have fought against them. He might as well have tried cutting off his own hands or plucking out his eyes.

208

"But Connor," he could hear his Uncle laughing again. "Doesn't the good book say it's better to gouge out an eye than to burn in hell? Answer me! Doesn't it?"

He smiled at the thought and refocused on the digging, feeling thankful for the task and finishing just before dark, sleeping where he dropped as the scattered rifle fire in the distance finally died out.

At first light it started back up heavier, and the wind picked up along with it, driving the cold drizzle that found its way under Connor's hat and collar. The moon was still up, trying to peek through the clouds. The Yanks' rifle fire crackled louder as they came down the causeway, and it wasn't long before blue shapes weaved in and out between the trees.

Connor kept low and waited for the others. More shots rang out to the right. Rapid Henry fire erupted, and bullets whined overhead. The whole line opened up in return. Smoke blended with the ground fog to cover the swamp. The Yank muzzle flashes marked their positions. Connor aimed carefully and adjusted for range downhill. He fired then listened to the Henry fire shift to the right.

"They ain't wasting anytime. Flanking us quick today, the bastards," JB fired then dropped lower to reload his Sharps. "We might be moving sooner than I thought."

Connor fired again. The flanks were someone else's problem. He remembered that awful night at Spotsylvania. Yanks coming straight at them in the dark. Men dying all around him. He fired over the logs, and it helped. Spotsylvania disappeared as the rifle fire ebbed and flowed. First one flank, then the other. Sometimes the whole line. It went on all day while the hazy sun rose overhead through the smoke then slowly settled back down into the trees to the west as the Henrys crept louder and closer.

The battery of 12 pounders behind them fired blindly into the mist. The gun teams kept up a steady pace. Each concussion ringing ears up and down the line. The Yank guns returned fire, echoing in the distance and shells crashing through the branches above. Smoke drifted thicker through the trees. The bastards. He knew there was no way to stop them. He stood straight up and fired off all seven rounds from the Spencer magazine then dropped behind the logs to reload. Norton and Barry cheered. A bullet clipped the head log just between him and Barry.

"Best not do that again Connor," Norton fired under the head log.

"Yanks don't amuse easy." As he spoke a mass of Henrys erupted to the far left. "Now see!" Norton poked him "See what you done."

Barry laughed and propped his hat up on a stake and waited. "They'll shoot it off for sure. Any second now." Everyone reloaded and watched. The hat just swayed in the breeze. A few minutes passed and nothing. Barry frowned. "Damn Yanks. They ain't right."

The 12 pounders behind them fired again in unison. The concussion sent a covey of officers galloping off. A young boy fell backwards a few paces from Connor. His big hat went flying, and he crawled a few feet with part of his brain dangling out. He fell on his side and felt his scalp and the bulging gray mass. Connor tried to help him.

"Scalp's swollen bad, eh?" His eyes filled with tears as looked up..

"You can make it. Come on." Conner helped drag him to the rear.

They made it to the trees twenty yards back with the Yanks shooting just over their heads when the boy dropped to the ground convulsing. His eyes rolled up into his head, and he stopped moving. Connor shook him and realized he was gone. No one else looked back from the trench line. Connor went through his pockets and found a letter addressed to a Mrs. Wilson in Charleston. He put it in his pocket and crawled back to the trench. He made a vow to let her know that at least he hadn't died alone.

Blue jackets, barely visible in the smoke, darted between the trees in the swamp. Rifle fire roared continuously. Bullets whined overhead and clipped the log parapet. More men dropped up and down the line. Shells landed front and back. Solid shots crashed into the trees. Another explosive shell killed men down to the left. The staccato rhythm of Yank Henry fire crackled towards the left rear. Everyone knew they were flanking. It was just a matter of time. How long would the line hold? When should they break for the rear?

JB shook his head. "Not yet."

Bucky went back to the rear to check on the horses and came running back. He ducked down beside JB panting. "Yanks coming across on both flanks. They'll be rolling up the militia soon enough."

"Get back to the horses and wait for us," JB fired over the logs, and Bucky winked at Connor then ran back to the trees.

Officers conferred behind the gun parapet as a Yank rifle fire grew to a continuous roar. The militia mostly kept their heads down and fired blindly over the logs. Connor watched the muzzles pointing to the treetops fire over and over. He reloaded his Spencer with one of his last four cartridge tubes, tapped the smooth copper for good luck, cocked the hammer and rose up to fire three shots level with the swamp. He dropped to cover just as the logs splintered close to his head. Norton waited for a few seconds then fired over the top. His hat flew off and he ducked down and crawled to relieve it.

"Shit on this JB. Time to git."

JB shook his head. "Militia's good for a few more volleys. And no Yank cavalry's getting across that swamp. Just their infantry flanking now. But it'll take another hour or so." He rose, carefully aimed and fired, then sat back down with his back to the parapet and reloaded.

The big guns behind them fired a salvo just as the gunners' horse teams galloped up with limbers. The gun crews seem to race each other to be the first to hitch up. JB shook his head, "Well shit. Just watch the militia now. They'll run for it now, sure enough. As soon as those guns pull out."

Officers up and down the line called to each other and waved their swords. The gun teams limbered up and pulled off with their 12 pounders, the gun carriages bouncing over ruts and fallen branches. The militia line wavered for a few seconds, most heads turning to the rear, watching their artillery support disappear into the rear woods.

More officers rode up through the trees. One raised his telescope as a shell exploded underneath his horse, disemboweling the mare and catapulting him headfirst into a pine tree. The horse brayed and kicked savagely until life drained out her open belly. Soldiers helped the man back to the rear while the militia still waited for a signal. Three shells exploded just in front of the trench line. That was it. The whole line broke and ran as if one.

Cheshire waited, crouched against the logs, just down the line from Connor. He stood up to shoot one last time. His Henry fired, and he fell on his rear from a great whack, like a mule kick in the sternum. A hole had appeared in his chest. He felt the hole and the flowing blood and looked at Connor with his mouth wide open as if trying to say out loud that he wanted to live. That this wasn't right at all. That it was all indeed

211

just a lark. It was fun hunting Yanks. This wasn't supposed to happen. Not this close to the end of the war. Why me? He mouthed the words to Connor then wondered if God would answer his prayer.

"Why me Lord?" He said it out loud, and tried to say more, but the lancing spasm in his back took his breath away. He wondered if he'd been shot twice and couldn't help crying, "Spare me, Lord."

He felt the hole again. It had stopped bleeding. He thought it might be a good sign, but he knew otherwise. He'd seen plenty of men shot at Chickamauga. He'd watched some of them die slowly over a few days. Painful, swollen abdomens, pale and sweaty faces. Then delirium and death. He tried to stop crying, to keep a brave face, but he couldn't.

"Be a man!" He could hear his father yelling at him. "Be a man!" It was his grandfather too. "Be a man!" But he couldn't stop the tears.

"Spare me, dear Lord." He wasn't sure if he'd said it out loud, but Connor heard him and crawled to him with rifle fire clipping the head-log and ripping the branches above him. He put his arm around Chesire's head and wiped his face. Connor gave him a sip of water. His tongue was suddenly so dry it stuck to the roof of his mouth

"Thanks," he whispered then cried, "But not like this."

He felt a warmth creep over him, and he knew he'd be dead soon. The last thing he saw through the tears was Connor's face and a dark cloud overhead. He lay on his back and watched it roll by. It would rain soon. At least by dark. He wanted to live to see the rain. But the dark cloud descended over him, and Connor's face disappeared in a shadow. Then all was still.

Connor watched him take his last breath and closed his eyes. He lay his head down and checked his pockets. Nothing but crumbling cornbread and Henry cartridges. Barry and Norton ran up.

"Christ almighty! Not Cheshire," Norton screwed up his face like he'd had a boil lanced.

Barry grunted and thumped Cheshire's shoulder, "Damn this! The bastards."

Henry fire raked the logs in front and JB yelled at them, "Let's go! Time to git! Come on damn it! It's time!"

They left Cheshire's body and ran for it, stooping low and listening to bullets cut into the tree trunks right and left. Norton carried Cheshire's Henry. They made it to the horses picketed behind a little rise and rode off towards the southeast where the fire grew louder and closer. Connor couldn't tell how many they'd lost, but quite a few wounded had to be helped along, and he said another Hail Mary that the Yanks didn't follow too quickly.

Their scout joined up with the others along the flank until a new line was formed. They advanced enough to fire off a few volleys into the Yank skirmishers who eventually came across a little clearing in the woods. Henrys barked back at them by the hundreds. A few men were hit and had to be left. Everyone else rode off through the woods for several more miles then across another swamp where they came up on another line of Wheeler's cavalry.

JB had them post pickets and rest in a cut-over clearing of pine stumps. Horses were watered and fed. Men shared what food they had by small fires beside the stumps. JB had them all gather to say the Lord's Prayer for Cheshire.

"He was a good man to ride with, a good scout, and fine company in camp. I was glad to have him with me. I know y'all feel the same." He paused and took a deep breath. "Now he's gone, so close to the end. It ain't fair at all, but it's done. Time for all of us to move on. We owe it to him. And all the others. To get through this shit and remember it all."

"Just never figured it would be Cheshire," Norton shook his head. "Thought he'd go home to Selma with that Henry of his."

"It ain't right at all," Bucky sighed. "Just leaving him there like that. Shit."

"It ain't right for any of 'em. Remember Ferguson at..." Barry paused, looked up at the twilight sky, and walked off.

The others didn't say anything. They were all used to putting death out of their minds. The quicker the better. Men dying wasn't something new for any of them, but all hoped Chesire would be the last. Connor saw the tears in their eyes and made it a point to do most of the work in camp that night. He said a few more Hail Marys, hoping God would at least see that the Yanks were decent enough to bury him.

Everyone started wrapping up in blankets and ponchos to bed down around the fire as the temperature dropped and the wind picked up. Barry opened his leather case that he had strapped over his shoulder inside his tunic and motioned Connor over. He wanted to show him his

213

ized collection that he kept inside his little leather-bound Bible wrapped in a piece of cloth.

"32 feathers, 47 stamps. See?" He turned each page slowly, showing off his prizes one at a time. Connor did his part in turn, looking at each feather and stamp carefully. It knew it was the least he could do. Barry didn't have much else. "Got this one here in Kentucky. It was Chesire's favorite. See how the lines cross the gold. See that?" Barry shivered as he held the stamp up in the light of the fire. "They send a message, don't they? One's for courting and the other's for going anywhere in the world. Ain't it something?" Barry took a deep breath and turned to a certain page. "But this one's best. A peacock. See? What a feather."

"Yes it is. It certainly is." Connor watched Barry's eyes water as he caressed the purple feather

"All that we seen, all that we done. Them that got killed. Chesire, old Mr. Collins with his legs ... " He stopped and wiped his eyes. "Then this here. All this beauty. Got it right in my pocket. Every day. Anytime I want it. And it's better than fear tonic." He paused, closed the book and looked up at Connor. "You think I'm crazy, don't you."

Connor shook his head and tapped the leather cover with his finger.

"No, it's really something, Barry. It really is."

"Yep. Maybe so."

As they bundled up next to the fire, Connor figured most of the others had something similar. Something that each man carried with him. Something he needed. Maybe just in his thoughts or memories. Something that was as real and beautiful as the stamps and feathers were to Barry. And as he inched closer to the fire, he thought of Henrietta. It made the cold a lot more bearable. He could picture how her cheeks dimpled when she talked, how her eyes sparkled green in the morning light, how her skin felt when she gripped his hand. And how it all caused him to be a bit of a fool when he'd gone to visit her. How she'd come to the door a grownup sixteen year old, not the tomboy he'd known in years past.

It had been on a visit with Uncle Paul to Dr. Tradd's cousin in Columbia, shortly before he'd gone off to the war. Henrietta lived there for a while after her mother died while Dr. Tradd was serving in the Army. He remembered his embarrassment and how he just couldn't find anything to say and how his uncle had put a hand on the shoulder and made it worse.

"Don't worry Connor. Women often make men speechless."

He remembered just standing there, red-faced, while Henrietta smiled at him then took his hand and pulled him inside. JB stepped past his head and threw another log on the fire. Connor pulled his blanket tighter and fought to continue the memory. The touch of Henrietta's hand, her face, her voice. He felt sleep racing towards him and whispered, "I damn well WILL marry her, by God. As soon as this damn war is over."

BOOK 2

Sanctuary

*No man can put a chain about the ankle of his fellow man
without at last finding the other fastened about his own neck.*
— Frederick Douglass

CHAPTER 25 — DR. TRADD

Allendale, South Carolina
and the road to Orangeburg, 50 miles north

D r. Tradd watched Louisa boil his operating instruments in the kettle over the fire outside his tent while he busied himself mixing more of his latest malaria remedy in a smaller pot. The hollowness in his gut receded as he focused on the daily routine.

"Three parts dogwood bark, three parts poplar," He mumbled to himself. "Four parts willow, 1 quart of whiskey, then soak for two weeks." He wasn't sure if it would work any better than the last batch but felt it might just be better than nothing. All the quinine would soon be gone and he knew those little infective particles from the swamp could attack with a shaking chills anytime.

He called them fomites because he was convinced his theory that miasmatic vapors gave life to the dust particles. If he could just decipher how. He had learned by experience before the war that there was no use tempting fate. In the summer time it was better to stay close to a sea breeze or escape to the pine forests or better yet to the mountains up near Flat Rock, North Carolina. The miasmas of summer didn't discriminate. They killed whites and blacks alike.

Dr. Tradd's professional opinion had been widely publicized. Swamp decay and degenerate matter caused fomites that crept as high as the wind would take them, turning hot, humid, summer air into deadly miasmas. City life in Charleston was no safer. Decayed meat, as well as animal and human waste, did the same, unleashing fomites in the salt breezes that poisoned the air even up to third-floor verandas facing the sea. Fomites and their miasmas killed those most susceptible first, the elderly and tiny infants, but anyone, even the young and healthy, where potential victims. And although his theory was not accepted by most physicians, he knew for certain that no one had conceived of a better one.

But the real question was treatment. Could fomites be prevented? How could they be killed? Nothing so far had ever seemed to help. His mind wandered as he watched his instruments boil. Iodine helped slow the spread of gangrene, but the question was how to keep the damn fomites from starting up in the first place. Onions helped the scurvy, but what on earth caused all the bruising and the internal hemorrhage? Typhus was even harder. Headache, fever, the skin rash then delirium and death. Nothing but a sinapism of mustard seed paste had ever seemed to work, but it smelled awful, like putrefaction , and some died anyway. And that awful jaw-clenching, neck-twisting death by tetanus. He caught his breath and tried to block out the memory of the little girl whose jaw snapped in half before she died. He could still hear the muffled screams through her locked teeth and the look of terror in her eyes as he had begged God for forgiveness for the act of holding the ether rag over her nose until she had stopped breathing. Fortunately his brain would not allow the memory to last more than a few seconds.

He watched the malaria remedy boil down to a brownish broth. It might even work better for skin infections. Maybe even better than pure alcohol. Maybe it will kill the fomites too. In recent months, with alcohol in short supply, he'd been rubbing it all over affected skin, letting it dry then incising as necessary. He thought he was seeing a lower rate of erysipelas and purulence. At least he thought so. It was hard to tell sometimes. He smiled as he stirred the broth. Maybe fomites of all types hated the dogwood.

That day he lanced eleven boils, cleaned and dressed seven burns, amputated a gangrenous big toe before dinner, and, all along, kept inoculating for smallpox as he went. He kept the crusts of cow pox scabs to use for vaccinations. He always added more to his saline jar whenever he came across a fresh case, trying to keep enough for a least a few dozen patients. Most veteran regiments had already been vaccinated, but not civilians, slaves, home guard units, or militia groups. All it took was one case of smallpox to decimate all those in contact. Every day he scraped arms with his rasp and rubbed a little piece of crusty scab into the raw wound. No one ever complained. Only an imbecile or someone totally insane would purposely choose the risk of small pox.

He ate some collards and rice that Louisa had prepared then treated a little girl's pneumonia with camphor and paregoric. A boy with seizures was next. He was seven, according to his mother. A skinny, poor white boy with scraggly unwashed brown hair and a dirty face. The boy looked healthy otherwise. He glanced back at the mother. Her clothes were filthy, and she reeked of body odor. Her hair looked as if it hadn't been washed in months and her breathe was putrid.

"You want him to stop having seizures?"

She looked up with eyes as big as a saucer. "Yes sir."

"Then take care of yourself. Eat more, and keep clean. It will help calm his nerves."

Her jaw dropped, and she stood there staring at him with a gaping mouth.

"You hear me?"

She nodded then crossed her arms and pouted just as the boy began violently convulsing on his back. Saliva driblets foamed from his mouth. Dr. Tradd sent Louisa down to the creek along the edge of the woods for a bucket of cold water. He turned the boy on his side and stuck a wooden spoon in his mouth. Louisa trotted back up through the trees panting and sloshing water all over her jacket and dress. Dr. Tradd turned the boy on his stomach as he convulsed with rigid, rhythmic jerks. He poured cold water over the boy's head and chest, and the seizures instantly stopped.

"Praise the Lord!" The boy's mother wailed. "Thank you, Jesus."

"Best thank Dr. Tradd, too." Louisa knelt beside the boy, turning him on his side and wiping his face.

Dr. Tradd sighed. "Seizures stop by themselves, but cold water sometimes helps it along quicker."

He had seen plenty of seizures over the years. Some real, some put on by clever malingerers. More of the latter in recent years with soldiers desperate to get home, away from the horror of war. And willing to fake just about anything. Seizures, paralysis, blindness. He smiled as he remembered the young man from Hagood's Brigade who had been invalided home to Charleston with paraplegia. How he'd pushed himself around in a little four-wheel cart accepting sympathy from all who witnessed his daily struggle. Dr. Tradd remembered how he'd spotted the man just last year while he was home on furlough from his regimental duties. The young man was climbing down a ladder on Limehouse Street as Dr. Tradd was passing by in his carriage. He'd reined in the horse and stopped just to have a little fun with him. He smiled as he remembered the conversation.

"Hello Reeves, how are you doing there? How are the legs?"

The young man's eyes had widened, and he'd let out an audible gasp. Suddenly his legs went limp again as he'd lowered himself down the rest of the ladder using just his arms.

"No better at all. Worse maybe. The pain is something awful." Reeves let himself fall the last few rungs and sprawled on the cobblestones moaning and groaning.

"The sacrifices you soldiers have made!" Dr. Tradd tipped his hat and bowed. "I truly admire your prevarication."

He laughed to himself as he remembered the tears welling up in Reeve's eyes and how he'd nodded back appreciatively, "Thank you doctor, sir. That means a lot to me. You're too kind."

Dr. Tradd chuckled every time he thought of Reeves. It still gave him a boost. Something that was in too short of a supply these days like every thing else.

He refocused on his work, watching Louisa quickly dry the boy and wrap him tightly in a blanket. She told the boy's mother to keep him on his side."And if the seizures come back, pour more water on his neck."

The woman nodded and knelt beside her son as Dr. Tradd went over to the next patient. A thin, coughing black woman. He took a small blue bottle from his case and measured out an ounce of brown liquid in a little silver cup then held it to the woman's mouth and nodded.

"Sip is slowly."

"What is it?" She smelled it, held her nose, and pulled away. She shook her head. "I can't drink that."

Dr. Tradd rubbed his chin. "Listen here. This is Swain's Panacea. The last bottle in all of South Carolina. That smell is Sarsparilla and oil of wintergreen. It won't hurt you. It's the best cure yet for consumption. You drink it right now or I'll tell the others you're too scared to take your medicine."

The black woman frowned and lapsed into a worse bout of coughing.

"See?" Dr. Tradd patted the woman's shoulder. "You need it worse than ever."

She smelled it again and nodded, letting Dr. Tradd hold the cup and pour it in her mouth.

"One hard swallow then you're done."

She gulped it down and coughed for a long time. Dr. Tradd let her have some water and put the bottle back in its place.

"Just takes a while for it to work. Cures the general debility. The diseases of the liver and skin, too. And rheumatism. Works well for scurvy too," he smiled, knowing she wasn't in the least interested in anything other than her cough.

"All right," she gasped for air.

He gave her some more water, but she kept on coughing until she gagged. He patted her head until the fits finally passed then moved on to the next patient. A white woman with legs so swollen they looked like they might burst open any second.

"Worse case of anasarca I've ever seen." He shook his head as he pressed his finger into the edematous elephantiasis of the groaning woman's legs. The distension began at the knee and swelled into a huge mass of weeping flesh all the way to the ankle. Lord have mercy. As big as a watermelon. Nothing could help her now. The old treatments with calomel and castor oil did nothing. Surgical incision was useless. The best thing was a good diet, laudanum for the pain, and a tight wrap to help contain the inevitable swelling.

Louisa helped him wrap the leg with a freshly cut cotton sheet.

"What did you call it doctor? What was that name?"

"Anasarca. Elephantiasis of the limb. Glandular swelling and distention of the skin. Probably fomite in origin. Miasmas and such. Bodily humors may also play a part."

Louisa nodded, "I knew in Anna Cathcart once. She wasn't a fat girl though. Skinny as a bone."

Dr. Tradd stopped wrapping and looked up at her for a second then laughed until his side ached. "Thank you for that, Louisa."

"You're welcome," she shrugged, not knowing what was so funny. "But you best keep moving." She pulled him along to the next patient as he regained himself, rationing out a blackberry, jimson weed, and rum cordial to an elderly man with diarrhea.

"Contagious fomites embedded in the bowel. How they hate the jimson weed."

"Maybe ... If you say so," the old man agreed.

"I do indeed."

He also prescribed a sip of his brandy and camphor mix. "Best potion in the world for the inflammatory diseases."

The man sucked it down, squinching his face up with the awful taste. He gagged, wiped his mouth and nodded.

"Yes sir, doc. Powerful good stuff."

Dr. Tradd smiled back. "Such honesty from the patients is always gratifying."

"Glad to do my part," the old man coughed and sucked down a cup of water.

The last patient was a large black man with a bad back. His paraspinous muscles felt hard as wood. The culprit being a puncture wound from a wagon spoke two weeks prior. The initial erysipelas had formed into a boil that burst ten days before, but the spasm and pain persisted.

"A perfect subject for my electric therapy," Dr Tradd smiled. "Louisa, bring out the equipment from the wagon."

"Yes sir. Right away."

He carefully examined the man's back until Louisa returned with the acid-filled, copper Daniel cell that looked like an artillery shell embedded in a ceramic pot. He gently took it from her, set it on the ground by the man's blanket, and fastened the copper wires securely to their lead mounts.

"Electricity from zinc and copper sulfate! It's indeed a modern world!" Dr Tradd announced.

The black man twisted in bed trying to see behind him. "What's that sizzling noise?"

"Lie still!" Dr. Tradd nudged his head over with his elbow. He felt guilty knowing he was about to inflict pain, and that a black man, no matter how large and powerful, usually obeyed a white man out of fear of punishment.

"Yes sir," the black man sighed, listening to the rising hiss from the jar. "But what you gonna do with that wire thing?"

Dr. Tradd touched the wires together, felt the electric shock up to his elbows, and smiled. It had to be curative.

"I'm about to relieve you of all your back pain." He touched the wires to the back and the man's head arched straight up.

"Damn it! Don't do that!" He reached around and started to grab Dr. Tradd but stopped instinctively. "Don't do that, PLEASE SIR."

Louisa took hold of his arm. "Lie back down please. He's trying to help you"

The black man glared at her as if he'd been slapped. He knew better than to resist, much less harm, a white woman or doctor, even with the great Sherman's army coming soon. It could still be a death sentence. The best thing, as all slaves knew, was to endure. He buried his face in the blanket and bit on the reed mat.

Dr. Tradd ignored him, touching the wires again to his back and holding them fast. His hands vibrated with the shock, and the man screamed until out of breath.

"Hold tight there." Dr. Tradd encouraged. "The fomites can't stand the electricity."

The black man's muscles twitched, but Dr. Tradd knew the benefits were mostly invisible. Those damn fomites. How much pain and suffering they caused. If only the electricity would work. What a breakthrough it would be. Medical science finally having a cure for all the common afflictions. Fevers, jaundice, stones, tumors, erysipelas, malaria. The list went on and on. All due to the damnable fomites. But soon to be on the run, he smiled. Such pioneering work could change medical history!

The black man groaned and raised his hand, unable to tolerate another second. Dr. Tradd pulled away. "See? It's over. Your back will heal now. Lie down and get some sleep."

The black man lay there hoping that his pain and suffering was not just another punishment casually inflicted by a white man but actually some real treatment for his back. He lay still but stayed tense until he saw Louisa pack up the jar and wire. Dr. Tradd gave him half a cup of brandy which he had never tasted before. It burned his throat and made him feel warm, and it helped him to relax enough to doze off.

Louisa covered the man back up with a blanket and Dr. Tradd went back to his medicine cabinet to make sure all the other little bottles were corked tightly. He checked each one. Glauber salts, paregoric, mercury, opium, castor oil, quinine, calomel, Epsom salts, chloride of lime in mint water. Stimulants of snake root, partridge berry, sassafras and lavender. Astringents of rosemary, sumac and white oak bark. Tonics of

225

persimmon, wild cherry, sage, and willow. He treasured them all as a collector might treasure coins or stamps or pistols. But in his heart he knew they were all 99% worthless. Still he kept them gently tucked away in their cases and packed securely in the wagon. He touched each bottle as he would a child. And he always had the same thought. Mozart's fingers touching his violin. It always made him chuckle, but there was just the hint of truth.

He knew he had indeed performed a miracle or two. The slave girl with the breach twins and placenta previa last year who had bled so much that blood had stained ceiling plaster on the floor below. Three lives saved when none should have been. Perry Dumont, his old friend, God rest his soul, seizing with a brain hemorrhage from a fall down the stairs while drunk. The drill, heated red hot over the fire, that he'd used to bore a hole through his skull. The geyser of blood-clot that had erupted. And him sitting up in talking with the drill still poking out of his head. He remembered it all vividly and smiled as he closed his leather case. There were other miracles too. Cures by deft touch and pleasant to remember as well. A salve for the pain of all the failures and deaths. He sighed and went out to wash his hands one last time before bed, knowing misery always returned and death always won. But no matter. A life devoted to alleviating pain and temporarily thwarting death was a life well spent.

Louisa made sure every patient in the big tent had clean water and at least one family member in attendance. Then she went to her own little canvas tent from across from Dr. Tradd's, bathed from her little tin basin, and slept between double- sewn blankets backed with a canvas lining. She said her same prayer as she did every night.

"Dear God, please bless and protect Dr. Tradd and give us another day of doing Your work."

Dr. Tradd lay on his cot reading by lamp light. He enjoyed reading in the evening, if workload and fatigue permitted. Besides his medical books, he carried a few favorite volumes in the wagon. Among them, Schlegel's *Lectures on Modern History*, Lamartine's *History of the French Revolution* ,and his treasure, a first edition of *Modern British Eloquence*, Harper and Brothers, 1852. He guarded them all as he might the crown jewels. But this night Dr. Tradd splurged and rewarded himself with a full hour of studying his prize. Charles Darwin's, *The Origin of the Species*.

A present from his cousin in Bermuda. He let page after page of detail into natural selection sweep away the ubiquitous guilt of not using the time specifically for more alleviation of suffering. It was the only way he knew to deal with guilt. Sweep it away into a corner. There would always be more suffering and illness than there was time to help, and always more guilt to sweep away. But as he read, he told himself that it would just have to wait until morning.

It wasn't the theory of evolution so much that appealed to him so much, more the pleasure in Darwin's studious observations and details. He loved to dream of a life devoted to pure study and learning. How different a life it would have been. Certainly not a daily battle against sickness and death, for sure. He read on and escaped for a while longer. But he knew that time spent reading by candlelight was just a respite. Life's ongoing battle would erupt again in the morning, and he would again dive headfirst into it at first light. There was a certain satisfaction in that to be sure, and he thanked God for allowing him the perspective and understanding.

"Ah, to know one's place in the universe," he repeated over and over until he lapsed into dreams and slept soundly.

In the morning a rumor had spread that Sherman was across the Savannah River and headed north towards them. Dr. Tradd and Louisa decided to move on towards Columbia despite the driving rain. Hundreds of refugees camped around them decided to do the same. The road rutted into a deep bog past Buford's Bridge over the Salkehatchie River. Dr. Tradd studied his own state map which his niece had hand-painted on a piece of canvas back in '62, compiled from a slew of available documents at the Charleston Library Society. It showed every major road, town, bridge, and river and several dozen of the smaller byways and villages. He decided to move north to Midway and Bamberg, set up his clinic, and wait to see where Sherman was headed. They followed the unmarked road through the pine woods as the map dictated coming to a fallow cornfield where a yellow rag waved from an old battered farm house.

"It's the sign for typhoid," Dr. Tradd whispered, handing the reins to Louisa. "I wonder who knew? Maybe they're wrong."

He climbed down, unstrapped his bigger kit from the wagon, and walked slowly across the field toward the open door. Louisa started to follow.

"Best stay where you are Louisa. Just in case"

He stepped inside and found three dead children stiff on the floor of the first room. A woman shivered with fever and coughed up blood of a narrow bed in the second. A baby gasped agonally on a plank crib. Dr. Tradd felt the baby's stomach. Hard as a brick. He shook his head and opened the bottle of laudanum. The woman turned and stared with red hollow eyes. She watched him drip laudanum into the baby's mouth then heard the child's breathing slowly fade into quiet. She coughed up more blood and cried for a while as Dr. Tradd mixed up a potion of resin, red pepper, and a few drops of mercury in a cup of water.

"Drink this." He held the woman's head up. She closed her eyes and groaned. Her limp arms twitched. "Drink this or die." He fought back a yawn of fatigue and scolded himself, repeating his mantra to himself. 'Always behave as if all the world observes.'

"Please." He shook the woman's head gently and she groaned some more. "Drink it now."

She opened her red eyes and tried to nod. He held the cup to her lips, and she swallowed it down a little dribble at a time. He propped her head up a bit on a folded quilt jacket pulled from under the bed. She groaned louder and tried to lift her arm. The coughing started back up. She gagged a few times then vomited up a quart of blood.

Dr. Tradd considered using the silver catheter and the rubber tubing to give a saline infusion. He'd read the reports of cholera in India being treated with such. Maybe it would work for typhoid. But he knew also that the results showed remarkable improvement for only 24 to 48 hours then rapid decline and 98% fatality. Worse than letting the disease run its course. But had they tried boiling the saline and cooling it before injecting? Should he try it now? Maybe ... but 98% fatality. 98%! He pondered and searched his heart. God remained silent. Not the slightest help. She vomited up another quart and Dr. Tradd wiped the blood away with a blanket hanging from the side of bed. It was no use. Too late. He could only keep vigil with her until she died. But each time her red eyes opened, he made a point to smile and nod. Better to die looking into a caring face than at her dead children. She may have even tried to smile back before she suddenly stopped breathing and grew still.

He wrote 'Typhoid' on the front of the house with a piece of chalk then he moved up the road until dark. Louisa fried corn fritters for supper and again for breakfast, and they made it to Bamberg the next day. He helped her set up the clinic in a half empty warehouse. Only a few patients came in that afternoon, but more refugee families, too tired to walk another mile, came in at dusk and bedded down. All the while Dr. Tradd guessed correctly that most white refugees were intent on getting to Columbia, and the blacks, to Sherman.

He treated two infants with colic that night, an old man with a tooth abscess, a young girl with jaundice, a boy with a broken wrist, and a woman in labor. Louisa delivered a fine healthy baby girl, and when she cried out her first breaths loud and clear, everyone in the warehouse applauded. The young mother had two other children by her side and was quite adept at nursing her infant. The baby made hardly a sound all night and everyone including Dr. Tradd slept soundly.

CHAPTER 26 — CONNOR

on the road north to Orangeburg

JB led them northward through more pine woods and swamp toward the Orangeburg Road where other scouts joined them. The lieutenant in charge called him over. "Got to get across the Edisto right here. The whole regiment's gathering up the railroad. Past the main junction in Branchville. Got to make a stand at Orangeburg."

Connor remembered it from his trip with Uncle Paul to Columbia. Just warehouses, an engine yard, depot and a few shacks, but it was the main junction of the railroad, the link between Atlanta and Lee's army in Virginia. They rode on through swampy woods for miles meeting other scouts and listening to scattered rifle fire behind them and to the southwest. Their band grew to company size and not another officer among them. Groups peeled off as they pleased and more riders joined up. Connor looked around at the mix and realized that whatever order and cohesion there may have been in the past was now long gone. Thank the Lord for JB. He exuded more confidence than any battery of 12 pounders and gave them all a purpose. And he had a nose for direction, finding his way through one dense bog or woods after another. The men gladly followed. Connor, too. They stayed one step ahead of the Yanks all day long. The rifle fire in the distance helped them all stay focused.

More horsemen rode up with a black man in a blue uniform. He was hog-tied to a mule. They led him into a clearing in the pines and circled around him. Connor and the others knew what would happen. One of the men fired his revolver over the mules head. The mule bolted and bucked the black man off. The troopers around him howled. Connor felt a wave of guilt, but it receded quickly like a piece of the dream at first light. No time for that. He didn't know this man, so his death wasn't anything to fret over.

A blond boy in a green coat jumped his mount over the prisoner, showing off his horsemanship and scaring the terrified black man into a fetal ball. "Y'all think Captain Jones will let me keep him?" The boy smiled, dismounting to help his prize up to his feet. He walked him in a circle to display him like he would a horse or cow. "I found him yonder, past that last bog. Said he'd been forced to pioneer. Said he'd run for it last night. Wanted to get back home. To Cedar Grove Plantation."

"Bull shit. Just shoot him, Cletus," a tall man with a thick black beard yawned as he spoke.

"Can't we just wait and see?" The boy walked the prisoner faster in a tighter circle as if that might help. The black man began to sob.

The tall man shook his head slowly. "You know what they say. Black-wearing-blue is black-rot-dead."

"Maybe so, but listen here. One more thing," the boy haggled. "He says he can cook up a storm. Sews real good too." He kept walking him in circles. But it was no use. Another young trooper walked his horse up and pointed his shotgun at the man's chest. The black turned his head away shaking in terror. The shotgun fired and the man's body slumped to the ground. Connor looked away as the boy took the man's broghans. The shooter spurred his horse. "Next time, Cletus, just bring in the shoes."

The others laughed, but Connor felt nauseous and forced himself to think of the bummers he'd seen choking the boy at the farm. He looked down at the dead man and felt the nausea give way to a hollowness inside, like his innards were paralyzed. It was worse than any pain he'd ever felt What if it had been Ezekiel? What could he have done? What SHOULD he have done? A train whistle blew and roused him. He thanked God he wasn't forced to act and reminded himself that it wasn't his place to decide any of this, but it didn't help much.

He swung into line behind JB and followed him down towards the Edisto River. The rail bridge was blocked by another train full of sick and wounded. They all had to swim their horses and mules across. Other cavalry regiments clumped up with him. More Tennessee and Alabama boys and some South Carolina militia. The train rolled slowly across the bridge as it began to drizzle. It gave off an awful stench, reeking of feces, gangrene and vomit as it came to a halt on the other side. Orderlies dragged two bodies to the door. They pulled them stiffly off into the weeds beside the track and left them covered with blankets.

A dozen or so women waiting beside the tracks in a wagon covered their noses with handkerchiefs then went aboard the cars. They ladled out water and passed out cornbread squares to those who could still eat. There wasn't a doctor to be seen. Connor and the others helped with the water buckets and the women did the best they could. The whistle blew and everyone hopped off just as the cars jolted forward. The wails and groans of the wounded rose up with the rocking motion of the train. The screeching of rusty wheels and the clatter of loose bed rail bed timbers partially drowned them out. Connor and Norton were the last to jump off. One of the ladies waved them over to help load the stiff bodies into the back of the wagon pulled along by two mules. The wagon started off down a dirt track into the thick woods leaving Connor in a daze staring at the dead men's bare feet bouncing with each jolt of the wagon until JB yelled and hurried them off northwards along the rail-bed.

They reached the little town of Orangeburg at dark. Lamps lit up the row of houses and campfires spread up and down the tracks and on the main street. Men clumped for warmth and food. JB's group found a spot next to the rail depot to picket horses and build their own fire as it started to drizzle. Norton explored the depot and stumbled across three crates of oyster tins and a new officer's jacket with a major's insignia. He traded in his raggy coat and smeared ham grease and soot over the insignia. Connor and Bucky helped him pass the tins around. Every man in the entire scout ate his full and there was still plenty left over. Connor stuffed as many tins as he could into his jacket pockets and haversack. Others did the same. Bucky came out of the dark holding two jugs.

"Whiskey! Found it in that house yonder." He nodded towards a lamp burning in the second-floor window. "Nobody was home," he smiled. "At least not on the first floor."

"Fear tonic's as valuable as food," Norton laughed, as everyone lined up and filled bottles and flasks.

"More so." Connor gulped down a cupful.

"That's the spirit. You hear that, Bucky?"

Bucky grunted from underneath his blanket, and Connor drank enough to numb his paralyzed gut then slept on the bare floor of the depot. At least it felt good to be out of the rain.

In the morning, they helped the militia dig more rifle pits facing a clearing two hundred yards from the river. Another log wall was partially complete on one side of the clearing beside a patch of oaks and pines. A few old citizens with hunting rifles and a couple of boys armed with small shotguns crouched behind one section.

Barry called over to them. "Y'all gonna stop Sherman right here? God bless you! And good luck to you too!" He stood at attention and saluted as seriously as he could, but the boys just laughed.

The old men stared back silently as Connor took his place behind a stump next to them. The rest spread out across the little ridge behind the logs and rifle pits. Connor looked down at the river. Another parapet, another fight, another flank. It was useless, but the river at least was in front, and there was a little swag to the rear that gave them a chance to get away. They might get off two or three volleys before the Yanks pinned them down with Henry fire. If they were lucky. The Yanks could just charge the ford, but probably they'd keep up the rifle fire and a work around each side. The swag behind the parapet would help Connor's scout escape, if they timed it right. Unless a Henry bullet caught one of them looking.

JB rode off with Bucky just as Henry fire crackled up across the river. Yanks appeared along the far bank, dodging from tree to tree and firing as they came. They blasted the whole clearing, and the militia and infantry went to ground.

"They ain't so dumb after all," Barry nodded towards the militiamen lying face down in the field.

"A bullet coming at your nose gets a man's attention pretty quick."

"That it does."

Connor emptied his Spencer and moved around as much as he could between shots. No use letting a marksman get a bead. One of the old men down from him caught one between the eyes. It blew out the bald spot on the back of his head. The boys nearest him fired once then ducked down and ran for it. The rest of the old men crouched behind the wall and fired into the sky. None of them dared look over the top. Connor didn't blame them. He listened to the Henry fire creep along the river west and east then more in front. Bullets clipped branches in the trees behind him and smacked against the pine trunks of the parapet. It intensified steadily, sounding like a great humming noise above their heads.

"You hear that?" Norton laughed. "They're singing to us."

"Let's sing along," Barry yelled back, blindly emptying his LeMat over the logs.

The infantry to the right volleyed and Connor fired with them. He reloaded, watching old men fire another volley into the sky. "The militia boys are good for ten more minutes. Maybe fifteen. What you think?"

Norton fired then laughed so hard he couldn't reload. "They'll be shitting and running before that, I bet. Quicker since they ain't burned that last bridge up yonder."

"Are you shitting me?" Barry's jaw dropped. "They haven't burned all the bridges?"

"Nope," Norton sipped from a flask. "JB said the Mayor didn't want to. Guess we should've put him in charge."

They all volleyed again at a Yank skirmish line pushing into the willows closer to the river. The Yanks fired back faster than Connor thought humanly possible.

"Damn Henrys!"

He reloaded his Spencer tubes and fired blindly into the smoke, keeping up a steady rhythm with Barry and Norton.. The infantry line did the same, their officers looking calm and confident, directing alternate sections to fire volleys while the others reloaded. A few men dropped, but the head logs kept most alive. The Yanks were in check for a while until Henrys closed in on each flank then moved farther to the left rear.

"Games up," Norton nodded to the officers yelling at his men as they fired and started to fall back one section at a time. "Not a bad show. Getting better at it."

"Same result though," Barry fired one last time. "Time to skedaddle. So much for the battle of Orangeburg."

Connor followed them to the safety of the woods to the rear where Bucky held the horses and mules on the reverse slope of the little swag. JB rode up with the rest of the scout. "Come on quick!" He yelled. "We're holding the left flank 'till these here have time to git."

Shells exploded along the river and Norton swung up into the saddle. A bullet hit him in the gut, knocking him off his mule onto a jagged pine

234

stump. Connor heard the bone in his arm crack. Barry and JB helped him back up. They strapped his arm in a shirt sleeve sling and propped him in the saddle then pulled his mule along, riding on each side, bracing him as he slumped over the mule's neck.

Norton was aware enough to try to hold on, but each bounce in the saddle bought a spasm of pain. He felt the bone grind under the bandage and prayed that it wouldn't cut an artery. His stomach ached, but not terribly, and his mind drifted off to his friend Barkley, back at Perryville. How he'd kept a smile on his face after the bouncing shell smashed his shoulder. Norton remembered how his hand was turned out at an impossible angle. How his shoulder ballooned purple from the blood within. Then the tourniquet, the doctor at a field hospital setting the arm, the pallor of his face, and the stillness after his last breath, and Norton's disbelief that his friend had died with just a trickle of visible blood. He looked down at his swollen hand and blood-covered stomach and knew this was just as bad, if not worse.

The scout rode on through oak and hickory woods for miles then across a little creek to a pine thicket where they made camp behind a regiment of Georgia militia. Barry and Connor helped Norton off his mule and carried him to the shelter of a lone granddaddy oak. They gave him water, but he drank only a mouthful. Blood glistened his tunic and pants while JB checked his wound. He unbuttoned his blood-soaked shirt while Norton grit his teeth and groaned. Maroon filth had already congealed over the bleeding belly wound. It looked like a hole filled with a wet plum pudding. JB covered it gently with a piece of shirt and gave Norton a sip from a small bottle of whiskey. Norton bent double in pain for a while then closed his eyes and slid off into a fitful sleep.

Connor bedded down next to him, exhaustion overwhelming hunger, thirst, and worry. He dreamed of a waterfall and trees with gold and red leaves. A cold breeze rustling through the branches and over the churning waterfall made him shiver. He woke up in the night and listened. Norton was quiet. Men snored in the darkness. A small fire crackled by the picket line. Everything was still. Stars shined through the pine trees, sparkling all the way to the ground. Not a sliver of moonlight disturbed them. Was it a ridge line? He drifted back off to sleep before he knew, and in the morning's first light, woke up next to Norton.

His body was hard and stiff. He was still slumped against the oak. His eyes were open. Connor fought off tears and covered him with a blanket. Bucky came up but didn't say a word, his face squished into a tense frown. He walked off and came back with a small spade and started digging a grave right there by the oak. "It's as good a place as any to be buried."

Barry joined him without speaking, helping dig with his cup. Connor forced himself to stand up. He staggered, feeling a weight on his neck. His legs felt like pudding. He dug beside them using his knife and hands, but with no more feeling than he'd had as a boy when planting a garden. None of it seemed the least bit real. When they were finished digging, Barry said a prayer. "Keep an eye out on Norton, Lord. Just don't forget about him. He's gonna be right here by this tree for a long time."

Bucky started shaking. "They got no right." He couldn't catch his breath. "They got no right to kill Norton. The bastards!" He threw the shovel into the scrub pines. "Bastards! They got no right!"

Barry retrieved the shovel and whacked it against the oak behind Norton's body. "It's all shit! We kill them and they kill ours!"

"The hell with that!" Bucky dove at him swinging fists into his head. Barry jabbed the spade into his gut and pushed him down. Blood dripped from his nose.

Bucky came at him again screaming. "Bastard!"

JB ran up and threw him down and shouted in his face. "Stop it dammit! Save it for the Yanks."

He let them take a while to calm down then gathered the others and led them again in the Lord's prayer. They laid Norton in the hole, covered him with a blanket, piled dirt on top and packed it down. Connor jammed Norton's iron spar at his feet. Barry laid his Enfield on top and put a peacock feather above his head. "Norton told me he liked that one."

"I can see why," Connor nodded, knowing it was the right thing to say.

"Yes, sir, Norton's got wings to fly now. He'll be waitin' for us all in heaven."

"Amen," Bucky hid his furrowed face in his sleeve for a while then gave Connor one of Norton's revolvers and kept the other. They divided up the cartridges. Norton's big mule went to a boy with a wounded horse.

"What's done is done," JB tossed a handful of dirt on top and walked off.

Connor wiped off his hands and thought of Chesire and how he'd been talking one second then gone the next. And now Norton. Consumed by the earth of a freshly dug grave. A grave that could have been meant for any of the rest of them, and could still happen any time. Graves that could appear anywhere, any day. He pictured a coarse, muddy pit waiting for him after his last breath and could just hear his Uncle Paul laughing at him again. "You just figured that out? Christ, Connor, don't you ever use your brain?"

JB poked Connor and roused him. "No time for that now. Stay focused. We got work to do," he nodded to the rifle fire crackling in the distance. "The Yanks are still on the move. C'mon."

Connor followed him over to a group of officers peering down at a map spread on a log. Bucky and Barry came over and shared a turkey leg, hardtack and slices of pork, but Connor felt the hollowness worsen in his gut despite the food. He didn't want to look back at the grave, either, but forced himself to. Had his eyes deceived him? Maybe Norton had just walked off somewhere. Maybe he'd dreamed the whole thing.

"C'mon Connor! Stay sharp! Norton would if it was you over there!" JB was standing right in front of him, shouting in his face. "Got to screen the retreat to Columbia, C'mon!"

Connor glanced back at the grave and felt dizzy but braced himself. "Yes. All right ... Ok."

"We'll ride over to Bull swamp, then north. To the Congaree Creek. The whole army's pulling back. Here, drink this," he handed Connor a small bottle of whisky. "It'll help your jitters."

Connor took a big drink and looked around at the few dozen fires surrounded by clumps of wet and dirty cavalrymen and the scraggly thin lines of exhausted infantry sitting in the road waiting for orders. He glanced back at the big oak and the fresh grave hoping to see Norton walking up out of the pines. JB yelled at him again and he came out of the haze. He took another swallow, and it helped.

"I'm coming."

The warmth of the whiskey soothed his gut. He tossed the bottle to Barry, trotted back to the grave, and scooped a handful of dirt into his pocket but wasn't sure why. Then he followed the others off through the woods only half aware of the men around him, riding on all morning through pine forests and hardwood swamps before catching two Yank cavalry pickets in a clearing about noon. Both were shot down as they ran for a hillock in the thick woods where, from the rise, they could see a crowd of slaves down by a river ford. A Yank cavalry skirmish line was holding them back until their main troop crossed.

"Heading towards Columbia. Half of them across already. Wish we had the rest of the regiment now." JB looked back at the scout coming up through the trees. He took a deep, noisy breath then scratched his neck and exhaled with a long growl. "Damn it. We don't have enough. We'd just be killing ourselves." He shook his head and cursed. "And a bunch of slaves too."

Connor watched the black mass force itself past the wheeling Yank horsemen. Men, women, and children plunged into the river. They were screaming. Most of it was unintelligible, but Connor could hear "Help us!" and "Please, God!" The cavalry fired into the air then gave up and rode across the ford leaving the slaves behind. Blacks flailed in the high water and dozens were swept down river bobbing up and down in the dark water until their heads disappeared.

JB waved at the trembling, wailing mass at the river's edge and at the drowning blacks being swept around the far bend. "Remember that rumor about slaves joining the army? Well, that's your answer."

Connor watched the spectacle and felt helpless. If they rode forward, more slaves would try to swim across, out of fear of capture. But if they didn't keep close to the Yanks.....? Then again, what would it matter now? He was glad he didn't have to make the decision.

JB thought for a while then asked Connor to climb an oak tree for a better look. He scrambled up to the top branches and could see miles down the river across the far cotton and corn fields. Everywhere he looked he saw columns of bluecoats and glinting metal. All of them surrounded by black swarms that spread out on both sides of each column as if they were herding the Yanks along. He shimmied down, told JB what he'd seen then mounted up and followed the rest north.

Connor kept thinking of Cheshire and Norton. Why had they been singled out? Why did the Lord take some lives and spare others? All he'd ever heard was 'God works in mysterious ways' which was to him the same as 'I don't know'. He tried to shake it off and keep his mind focused on the job at hand, but he couldn't keep from picturing his Uncle Paul still laughing at him.

Barry noticed him lagging and gave him more shots of whiskey until it eventually passed. JB kept the scout moving until well after dark and that night they slept in a dry barn and ate the rest of the oyster tins. Another whiskey bottle was conjured and emptied quickly. Sleep came easily. No one talked at all. At dawn, an officer riding past in another scout ordered JB to swing southeast.

"Find out if Sherman's sending any regiments back towards Charleston. Doubt it, but he's wily. Maybe Columbia's just a feint. The Colonel says Wheeler wants to be sure." The tone of voice said that he knew it was a waste of time, but JB didn't hesitate. He saluted and turned to the men. "We're gonna get to Columbia the long way, boys. Today's gonna be a big ride."

He gulped some cornbread crumbs and was quickly mounted up. Everyone else did the same. Connor was glad for it. He didn't really care where they were headed as long as they were on the move, keeping his mind from wandering, and staying at least one step ahead of the Yanks.

THE TOWN OF ORANGEBURG was already in flames when Luke's New York Regiment came out of the woods. Fires roared up in the depot warehouse across the road, bursting through the roof as cases of liquor and bottles of resin formed a river of fire that roared into houses and sheds nearby. It was quickly a crackling inferno that consumed most of the town into one big fireball. Through the smoke, Luke could see a mass of children huddled around a gray-haired man. There must have been fifty or sixty of them. Mostly young boys but a few scraggly-haired girls clumped together on the grass, out of reach of the flames and heat. The building behind them was burning too.

The children looked around at the flames nervously, chewing on hunks of molasses -soaked cornbread from buckets in the center. Many were crying. Those closest to the old man clutched at his pants and coat sleeves while he remained perfectly still, holding a broken piece of banister rail like a staff. Soldiers rushed past, some throwing cans of food, others ignoring them. A very young private with a head bandage, a Henry strapped to his back, and a shotgun over his shoulder walked up to the old man.

Luke caught the soldier's eye and realized he was only a few years older than the children, but as different from them as a Chinaman. The young soldier adjusted his head bandage. He checked his shotgun then he gave them the last of his hardtack from his haversack. Others joined him but some passing soldiers jeered.

"Hey Moses! Them Israelite's eating mighty fast there. Might better make it last. Might be slim pickings coming your way."

"They're just little rebel shits. Give 'em a few years. They'll be the worst bushwhackers yet, rebel lover!"

The young soldier ignored them, and the children stuffed the hardtack into their pockets. None thanked him, but the old man opened his mouth as if trying to, until billowing smoke covered the road and caused him to lapse into a coughing fit. Luke coughed with him then wrapped his face in a blanket strip like hundreds of others. He was tired South Carolina smoke. What he wanted was clear, crisp, blue sky day with a north wind to refresh his spirit.

He trudged along with the regiment up the road, and the wind picked up as if by command. Luke smiled. Maybe God was finally listening. And nothing else burned in front, for a change. Maybe there was nothing left to burn. Nothing but shacks and little crossroads anyway. Not until they reached Columbia. It was just a matter of days. Poor bastards, he sighed. Their largest city would soon be a blackened ruin. Did they know what was coming?

Shouts came down the column as the regiment came to a halt. A rider recaptured his attention, coming down the line and pulling up in front of a group of officers. The rider saluted to a Colonel and handed him piece of paper. The Colonel read the order then rose up in the stirrups and called out.

"Two prisoners to be shot immediately." He put his hand to his chin and took a deep breath. "General Sherman says do it now. Lieutenant Weitzel, bring me two prisoners now. Let them draw straws for it." The lieutenant rode up beside him. "To be shot?"

"Yes!" The Colonel snapped back. "Orders from General Sherman! Do you hear me?"

"Yes sir!" the lieutenant held the salute a few seconds longer hoping something else would happen. Anything else.

"Now!"

Luke watched and wondered why he felt sick. Hadn't he seen men slaughtered at Chickamauga? Young boys dying with their guts shot out? Wasn't this the same? He stifled the lump in his throat as two reb prisoners were culled from the group. Both were wounded. They were led out into the field under the guard of a rifle squad and offered blindfolds. Both declined. They shook hands and said the Lord's prayer together.

The Lieutenant called back to the Colonel. "Are you sure, sir?" He wanted everyone to hear.

"Yes! Sherman says two reb prisoners will be shot for every Union prisoner murdered."

Every man in the regiment saw it very clearly. Uncle Billy valued their lives a lot more than any damn reb. He would shoot reb prisoners until Hell froze over if he had to. If it helped save his own men. Luke felt the same as most everyone else. Too bad for the two prisoners, but thank God for Uncle Billy. He loved him even more. If he made it home alive, God willing, it was due to the Lord's mercy and Uncle Billy's genius. A general who refused to needlessly sacrifice soldiers and who would punish reb bushwhackers and murderers with unwavering determination. As the rifles fired, Luke said a string of Hail Marys for the dead rebs and another for Uncle Billy.

The regiment moved on quickly, in silence, through more pine woods until just before dark then climbed up a sloping field to the edge of a bluff above the smoking ruins of a railroad bridge and, beyond it, a carpet of trees stretching miles and miles.

"Christ," Dave groaned, "We still got a long way to go."

JESSE'S GROUP was ten miles away. Jack helped Big Tom gut a goat carcass he'd been carrying on his saddle, and they all gathered around while it cooked. The woman in a little cabin across the clearing walked up and stood just outside the circle of men around the fire. Jack thought that her cheekbones might burst through her skin. The young girls clung to her filthy skirt. Their hollow eyes stared at the roasting goat, but

241

everyone ignored them. All except Cord. He sliced off a piece of half-cooked meat and tossed it in the dirt at their feet. The children pounced on it, tearing it apart and wolfing it down, dirt and all. They licked their hands and glued their eyes back on the sizzling meat. The woman never budged.

Cord smiled at her and sliced another piece. "You want some?" He smiled, holding it up on the point of his knife.

The women knew what he meant. She knew she had no choice. Her children were hungry. They hadn't eaten in two days. Another bummer group had already eaten the last of their chickens, pigs and corn, and Mr. Crawford, their neighbor, hadn't come back from Orangeburg with the pigs he promised. The choice was clear. Either submit and eat, or struggle to find more food in the wet cold for her children.

She thought again about walking to the Crawford's farm in the morning. Maybe they still had food. Maybe the Yanks hadn't come that way. But it was a good twelve miles, and if more Yanks came while she was gone, they would surely burn the house. It wasn't much, but it kept the girls warm and dry. As long as they stayed inside, the bummers weren't apt to burn it down. At least that's what she told herself and tried to believe. She looked down at her shivering girls. Meagan, the youngest, hadn't spoken a word in two days, since the first bummers had come. Her glassy eyes looked unreal, like dolls eyes. How much longer could she last? The woman stared at the piece of meat on the knife and nodded.

"You boys watch the young'uns," Cord flicked the meat to the little girls and watched them gobbled it down. Momma's coming with me." He touched her shoulder and the girls clutched closer to her skirt.

"They'll stay with me," the woman whispered hoarsely, her fingers caressing their hair.

"Suit yourself," Cord led the way back inside the shack and threw a blanket over a couple of chairs, making a little tent.

"Get in there. The girls can sit just outside. They won't see a thing," he smiled, reaching for the buttons on her bodice.

She let him unbutton her then crawled inside the tent and lay down on the floor. She put her hands out the sides of the blanket so her shivering girls could hold them. Cord knelt over her, lifted her dress and mounted her. When he finished, he crawled out from under the blanket, walked back out to the fire, and cut off three hunks of goat meat. When he went back inside, the woman was on her knees wiping herself with the edge of her dress. The younger girl sobbed. The older one shivered and stared blankly. Cord tossed the meat in her lap and the three of them tore it apart with their fingers.

Tim called from outside. "Don't feed her so much, Cord. I want to share some with her, too."

Kennedy, Big Tom, and Tim took turns with the mother, piling more hunks of meat around her little blanket tent. The girls shivered the whole time but never let go of her hand. Tim buttoned up his pants and stepped down from the little porch, "Your turn, Jack." He passed a liquor bottle around, and Jack took a big enough gulp to calm his nerves and summon up some gumption.

"Go to hell, Tim. I'm not poking anybody after you," he tried to chuckle, knowing it had to come across just right.

"Go to hell yourself," Tim gulped a piece of meat and laughed. "I still think you're a rebel lover."

Jack grabbed his crotch and made Jesse laugh then shared more of the bottle and played along, trying not to glance back at the cabin. But all along thinking that if the rebs did anything like this in Chemung County that they'd be lucky not to be hacked to death by outraged fathers, brothers, and sons. Men just like these same men laughing around the fire. Men with their own sisters and mothers. Men who before the war, wouldn't have dreamed of doing what they considered normal behavior now. He went through his litany again. The war, the bastard reb scum, the evils of the South, good Union men ... Then he thought of the blue and gold fields of Elmira again until it was time to bed down for the night.

North from Orangeburg, South Carolina to Columbia

D r. Tradd listened to a pouring rain at dawn, but the ware house roof was largely intact and everyone remained dry and some still slept soundly. The refugee patients and families were exhausted from travel and even the newborn baby cooperated, waking up only long enough to breast-feed before falling back to sleep. By mid-morning the rain let up and Louisa had the mules watered, fed and harnessed. They pushed on and made it to Orangeburg just after dark.

The little town bristled with young confederate infantry and elderly home guard who crowded every dry space to escape another cold drizzle. Dr. Tradd and Louisa picked their way through the crowded road and found shelter at the far end of town in a broken railroad car that quickly filled up with three refugee families. Rumors followed closely behind them. Sherman was moving faster than anyone had thought possible, but the Army would make a stand in the morning. Sherman's marauders would dash themselves to bits against determined opposition. A pipedream to be sure but nevertheless a real fight, however one-sided. And one that he had no desire to witness, having seen more than enough bloodbaths over the last four years. He decided it best to push on to Columbia first thing in the morning knowing it had to be overflowing already with ill refugees, and certain that whatever wounded who escaped capture would be taken there for help.

They left at dawn and slogged through a hard day and evening of rain squalls that slackened off only as they made their way across the Congaree River Bridge into the outskirts of Columbia well after dark. They camped for the rest of the night alongside the road with hundreds of other refugees and at dawn followed the hilly road up towards town. Louisa had never known that so many people existed outside of the Army. Vast crowds, white and black, hustled about everywhere. Some pushing their way to the Charlotte Railroad Depot. Others making their way up the streets into town. Dr. Tradd asked for directions to the closest hospital, and a lady dressed in a fine green velvet dress answered quickly as if she'd been waiting for someone to ask.

"Up there five or six blocks then left at Sumter and right at Washington ... I think." She paused and leaned closer. "And don't worry. Sherman's going to Charleston. My daughter's friend, Anne Pinckney, is a personal acquaintance of General Hardee. She heard, on his authority, that there is no possible way for Sherman to get all the way up here. These people know nothing." She dismissed the nervous crowd waiting for the Charlotte train with a wave of her shriveled hand. "She said Stewart's Corps is coming from Tennessee. That devil Sherman will wish he was back in Hell."

Dr. Tradd nodded and smiled. "I appreciate your help."

He decided not to remind her that Sherman had managed to get all the way from Chattanooga to Savannah through the entire army of General Joe Johnson and that he now had 60,000 veterans marching this way fast and that he doubted, even if Robert E. Lee appeared in the flesh and conjured up another whole army, that they could stop them now. He tipped his hat to the lady as her two slaves helped her into her surrey. She stuck her head out the window and pointed a finger at him.

"He's the Devil all right. But God will smite him down soon enough."

"I'm sure someone of your obvious character must be correct," Dr. Tradd bowed as her blacks flicked the horse's reins and her coach moved off through the crowd.

"You're welcome, sir ... and young lady."

Louisa smiled back but kept the mules headed up the hill past a constantly moving throng of civilian refugees, mostly elderly and women with children, who crowded around the depot hoping to find room on the last few trains to safety. Most looked as if they, too, had been on the road for weeks. Dr. Tradd saw it in their faces. Fear and disbelief stemming from keeping ahead of the Yanks and wondering every day if they would have a dry place to rest and food to eat. He watched a young mother herding her three tired children past a crowd of drunks and knew exactly what she wanted. Food and shelter for her little ones. And survival.

Two old men argued on a street corner behind her. One held forth loudly that a Confederate counterattack was imminent, the other shaking his head.

"It's too late. Too late. The time for that has passed."

"No it's not. Hampton will whip them back to Georgia. Just you wait. God will give his boys strength."

"They're boys All right. Got fifteen year olds now." He tipped his hat to Louisa and lowered his voice enough that Dr. Tradd couldn't hear the rest as their wagon passed a rail siding between warehouse rows that housed weary refugee families trying to escape another cold rain shower. Civilians, young and old, packed the railroad sheds and slept under the eaves of platforms and store porches. The occasional military- aged man crouched with them. Dr. Tradd figured most were shirkers or deserters, changed into civilian clothes, but no matter. There weren't enough to make a difference anyway, and when it was all over, they were the ones who would have to live with themselves. He watched one man pick up two little girls from the street and carry them into a half collapsed cattle car on a siding. The man glanced over as he set the girls down, wiped mud off their foreheads and gave them each a hug. Dr. Tradd smiled back. At least some men had better reasons than others.

Hogs and piglets roamed the streets rooting out pannage from gutters and fence lines. Here and there children chased them squealing through yards and alleyways. Chickens and guinea hens flew about in agitation. Old men and women, mothers with children, and gangs of young teens hurried everywhere. Boisterous groups of blacks gathered on side streets smiling and laughing, all knowing Sherman was coming and that their world was about to change.

A few blocks further up the hill, two black men sold potatoes, turnips, collard greens and field peas from the back of the wagon at the steps of the state house. They accepted Confederate paper currency but at a 10 to 1 exchange rate to coins or barter. A haggard young mother with two children in rags put a silver goblet on the wagon seat and left with three big sacks of beans. An older woman paid out a handful of bills for two little bags of peas and greens then cursed the blacks who just shrugged and smiled back. An old man sat beside a sign that read 'hot showers $.25.' Two teenage blacks dipped buckets into a simmering cauldron and poured them gently into a wooden chute propped up on timbers that emptied into a bath house draped with chest high canvas for privacy. Their ball of lye soap, suspended on a rope, gradually shrank in size.

Other stalls which had been recently used for the State Bazaar still lined the Statehouse grounds. A few purveyors hawked roast venison, turtle soup, and a green paste of salted artichokes over stewed chickens. Dr. Tradd and Louisa paid Confederate currency for all they could eat then moved on through the throng and stopped to pay respects to Dr. Tradd's cousin Harriet, her elderly husband Edward, and their fifteen-year-old daughter Emily, who lived just up a gradual rise past the towering steeple of Trinity Episcopal Church.

After appropriate greetings, they sat together for a while on soft chairs in the living room and then moved to the porch overlooking a geometric garden blooming with red and white camellias. Louisa sat in the kitchen all the while, resting and knitting. Garlands of pine boughs tied with twine festooned the porch. The white painted chairs were appointed in rich red damask and gathered around an oak table inlaid with blue cut-glass. A lemon cake, a bowl of charlotte russe, and a platter of brown sugar cookies, waited to be consumed. A pitcher of sangria and another of ginger tea glistened next to little porcelain cups. They proceeded to drink the tea and the sangria, exchanging niceties while catching up with each other's lives over the past year. Harriett spoke of Columbia's wartime bustle and Dr. Tradd about his service with the regiment in Georgia. He felt the empty feeling grabbing his gut but didn't let on.

Emily brought out the doll she had purchased at the State Bazaar. "For the care of the wounded. A good cause of course. That's why we bid so high. $2000." She paused and held up the flaxen- haired, wax beauty and added, "Confederate. Not gold."

"$2000? Well, well." Dr. Tradd squinted at the doll knowing two slaves could have been set free with the $2000 but kept it to himself. Emily quickly served them sorghum pudding with melted butter as Edward's red face grew redder. "We're calling it 'Sherman pudding' now," Emily smiled, making her long nose look even longer. "Better eat up fast. Yanks will be here soon enough."

Her father darted his eyes at her as if she had raised her voice during church. The Yankee tidal wave that surged on the horizon was not to be

247

mentioned. Edward and Harriet felt the slightest word would surely bring bad luck, and Dr. Tradd didn't want to disturb them further. Harriett rang the servants' bell for more ginger tea, and Dr. Tradd took it as his cue to move on. Only then did anyone ask about Henrietta.

As soon as Dr. Tradd heard her name, a sudden detachment overcame him. The same as he felt observing a surgery in the hospital amphitheater. Curiosity and professional interest, but no emotional investment. A hollowness expanded inside as if he'd taken morphine or laudanum. He pictured Henrietta running through the living room, clapping her hands and twirling about, then stopping at his chair, dropping to her knees wide-eyed and breathless,"Father you just won't believe what I just saw."

He could see every detail of her face: the dimples on her cheeks, the way her nose wrinkled with the bright smile, the way her lips pursed when she said 'you'. An extraordinarily calm settled over him and he wondered for a moment if he had indeed taken morphine after breakfast. He stopped and thought. No, nothing but quinine and weak tea. But as he heard Harriet speaking, he knew he was dealing with a strange effect of the mind that occurred with severe grief. He thought about it coldly and clinically, as if someone else's child had died, effortlessly able to separate himself completely from any noxious feeling at all.

"I'm sorry to have to tell you that ... well there's no way to make it easy for you. Henrietta died in December in Savannah. A type of biliary fever."

Harriet's and Emily's mouths gaped open simultaneously and each raised her right hand as if about to give testimony.

"Oh my God!" Harriet covered her mouth.

"No lord, no!" Emily held her mother. Edward stood silently in the corner, his jaw contracting grimly.

Dr. Tradd patted Emily's head and was able to tell them the entire story only because of the morphine-like, painless warmth that surged through his chest and neck. He watched her tears flow but thought Harriet's gasping for air was a bit forced. He had to remind himself not to be too judgmental. After all, Henrietta was just a distant cousin. Emily knelt beside him and hugged him while Edward stood cross-armed.

"We're so sorry, Henry. And after all you've suffered," Harriet cried, gripping his arm. "Oh my dear, dear cousin. Poor Henrietta."

Only then did Dr. Tradd feel the first glimmer of pain. "Now, now," he thought to himself quickly, "No time for that. Not just this minute. There's work to be done, the caring for the sick and wounded. Good work to be sure. Even if it's done at least as much for my own benefit as that of my patients."

He excused himself with brief hugs and handshakes, and the morphine feeling lasted long enough for him to gather Louisa and move up the street to the Wayside hospital as if there had been no mention of Henrietta at all.

The hospital was just then serving patients fresh bread and stew that smelled of onions and sizzling fat. Wounded and sick soldiers lounged all over the tracks and platforms of the rail station next door. They sipped on sassafras tea scented with lemon and apples and sweetened with molasses. Nuns from the Ursuline Convent ladled out pitchers from on iron pot suspended by chains over a make shift brick hearth next to the tracks. An orderly spoon-fed a young soldier whose arms had been amputated at the elbow.

Neither Dr. Tradd or Louisa could manage more than a glance at the boy's peach-fuzz face as they went inside and were quickly put to work by the surgeon in charge, assigned to a large ward of civilians and soldiers jumbled together on blankets and pieces of canvas. The stench was awful, but Dr. Tradd felt suddenly refreshed as if he'd been swimming in the ice cold streams of the North Carolina highlands near Flat Rock. His brain never allowed the mention of Henrietta again all that day, as usual, and he again thanked God for his work.

His first patient was a veteran soldier with a draining hip wound. The soldier's wife knelt beside him exhausted but determined to help. Dr. Tradd examined the festering wound. Maggots poked in and out of purulent tissue. The soldier and his wife had already covered their faces with rags dampened with turpentine to ward off the rotting stench.

"Doctor, please ... those maggots ... "

His wife began to cry. Dr. Tradd knew better than to argue. He had yet to meet a patient willing to tolerate maggots wiggling and squirming in their wound. He knew to say something comforting then cover the wound with cotton. Out of sight, out of mind. He also knew the maggots were God's gift to wound care, turning a festering, purulent ulcer into pink, firm, healing flesh within days. Somehow the maggots destroyed the fomites that caused the purulence. Maybe by consuming them or perhaps by a protective toxin. He didn't know how, and of course, since the fomites weren't visible, no one could know. But, by God, maggots could clean a wound better than any team of doctors.

"Just leave it wrapped up for three to four days. You will observe a miraculous healing," he smiled as he finished wrapping the soldier's hip. "The gauze is impregnated with calomel and arsenic," he lied. "It helps with the healing. So does this." He gave the soldier a dose of a persimmon astringent that actually did nothing but help patients to believe. They both just squinted back at him hoping it could possibly be true. He smiled to himself. Faith was a healing power in its own right. Stronger even than maggots. Stronger than many wanted to admit. He figured it had more to do with conjuring up a person's inner resolve than any external Divine presence. But who knew for sure?

He moved on to the next patient and used what was available, painting an erysipelas leg with a warm creosote then dabbing it with permanganate. The man groaned with pain. Dr. Tradd relented and let him sip the tincture of morphia. He moved on and sprinkled several wounds with a sulfate of iron disinfectant. He cleaned a deep chest wound, extracting bits of comb, half of a pencil, pieces of coat wadding, and a good cupful of pus.

"Noxious effluvium," he muttered to himself. "Detrimenta Fomita." The young soldier took the pain silently but spoke out as Dr. Tradd wrapped fresh lint gauze and covered it all with a piece of cotton sheet.

"Hey Doc? Can I have that pencil back?"

"Yes, indeed you can," Dr. Tradd first cleaned it with turpentine then presented it to the boy who accepted it with tears in his eyes.

"Only pencil I ever had."

"Well now you still have one."

"I wish the Yanks hadn't broke it though."

"Yes. I'm sorry they did too. If I find another, I'll bring it to you."

"Would you?" His eyes lit up.

"Yes indeed I will. If I find one. Now you rest and let that wound heal."

He patted the boy's head and moved on to the next patient as orderlies lit more lamps. A red haired boy named O'Malley with a hugely swollen leg wound. He tried to smile at Louisa as she prepared him, "You're an angel from heaven, missy."

Louisa smiled back, "I'm just doing the Lord's work."

"Yes, but you do it so very well indeed," he winced.

She blushed and scrunched her shoulder, "You're just being kind to me."

"When I get better, I'd like to be a lot kinder," he groaned.

She smiled and held up a bottle of chloroform, deftly dropping just enough on the sponge as she held it to the boy's nose before he could say more. He struggled for a few seconds then succumbed and slept deeply. Dr. Tradd poured alcohol over the festering leg and then more on his best knife. He made the incision lengthways up the leg and pus erupted behind the blade.

"Ah, the blessings of youth," he smiled. "Mount Vesuvius." He squeezed the calf and pus poured out in a wave. "Such vitality in this leg. It's a wonderful sign."

He went back along the incision a second time probing for more pus pockets and wiping away smaller eruptions. When satisfied that he'd found them all, he irrigated the wound with boiled water, first making sure that it had cooled enough not to burn. Then he put some of his bamboo tubes in place. Half a dozen sticking straight out the incision. He sutured it as loosely as he could. Just enough to let the red muscle granulated together from the inside. The tubes would let air go in and pus out. It was the boy's only chance. As he put the last sutures in place, he felt the pulse on the boy's foot. Good, much stronger. The foot just might be saved!

He smiled and winked at Louisa. "The wonders of modern surgery. Saving a leg that would have been amputated in '62. How far we've come."

Louisa nodded back, "Yes sir, but it's always been hard to kill an Irishman."

"Yes, yes," he laughed. "You're correct in that. They're a tough lot. The years of struggle, I suppose. They are indeed hard to kill."

251

Orderlies took O'Malley away and another young soldier was brought in with a horribly mutilated knee and open fracture of the femur.

"Shot at Rivers Bridge last week," the sergeant in charge read a report that came with the boy. "Dressed at a field station and changed at Orangeburg." He scratched his head. "This boy's lucky to still be alive."

Dr. Tradd nodded. The sergeant was right. Thigh amputations ran a 50 to 60% mortality rate. He checked his watch and nodded to Louisa. She dripped chloroform on the cloth cone. Always better than ether, Dr. Tradd smiled, glancing up at the open flames of the lamps. Less combustible. The soldier was soon insensible and flaccid. Dr. Tradd wasted no time. Louisa held up the leg. The tourniquet was tightened. He incised the skin in one circumferential cut. Then he freed the subcutaneous fascia and pulled the skin back as much as he could. Then through the muscle, all the way to the bone. He folded the muscles like he might a shirt sleeve, ligating the arteries with silk thread. Then he cut through the protruding bone quickly with his catling knife. The shattered leg detached itself, and Louisa put it on the floor. Dr. Tradd pulled the muscle flaps back across the bone and sewed them together, leaving all the sutures protruding a good 6 inches. Then he checked his watch. Twelve minutes. He shook his head. Too long. Too much time. The fomites in the open air loved bone ends. God help this man if pyemia set in. And too much chloroform inflamed the lungs.

He dabbed the sutured skin with bromide solution then covered it with a thick paste of phenolic acid. He knew that both could cure some cases of gangrene so why not use it to prevent and protect. There were no medical reports of such, but he knew in his heart it must work. He wrapped the stump in the last of the clean gauze then made it fast with another piece of clean cotton sheet and covered it all in a cerate of wax. Louisa stopped dripping the chloroform and the soldier awakened quickly. He shivered and coughed then groaned as the pain set back in. When fully awake and crying in agony, Dr. Tradd injected his hip with the syringe of opium liquid.

"There you are young man. That'll keep you comfortable for a few hours."

252

In seconds, the boy relaxed and purred like a kitten as Louisa readied a half dozen opium pills for later and cleaned up the blood. She propped the stump on a blanket roll while Dr. Tradd listened to the boy's heart and lungs then examined the amputated leg. The femur stuck straight through the knee joint. Dr. Tradd shook his head. How did the boy make it all the way here? How could anyone stand such pain? The power of human endurance. The brute process of self-preservation. He handed the leg to Louisa to dispose of then sat down and took a sip of brandy. How did God dream up such a complicated existence?

He walked through the other wards to acquaint himself before retiring and found them packed with soldiers suffering with chicken pox. Some of them were too sick to eat, others scared it would turn into smallpox. The young surgeon in charge was trying to reassure them.

"It's not smallpox. It's just chicken pox. They're two completely different illnesses."

The look on their faces said they wanted to believe him but didn't. The surgeon took off his bloodied apron and carefully adjusted his collar and neatly folded down his sleeves.

"Perhaps if I can confer with a colleague," he nodded to Dr. Tradd and winked. They shook hands and Dr. Tradd turned to the room full of feverish men.

"You all have the chicken pox. It's a common illness. It will last two or three days and be gone. It will not, I repeat not, turn into smallpox." One old timer held up a bottle. "Ipecac and sarsaparilla. Makes the stomach vomit up the bad biles and humors. Cured me of the smallpox when I was twelve."

Soldiers turned to him, and he happily obliged, passing it around and inducing a wave of puking until the young surgeon confiscated the bottle. "That will not help! It will just make you weaker."

He frowned at the old man who pulled out another little bottle and clutched it tightly to his chest. "I'll have to fight ya doc, if you come for this one."

The doctor rubbed his temples then threw up his hands and walked out, cursing under his breath. Dr. Tradd knew better than to interfere. These men, like all the others, believed what they wanted, and it didn't really matter what the surgeon said or did. Dysentery was about the only disease a physician could truly prevent. The rest was just a bit of luck.

"Good evening to you, gentlemen. But it really is just the chicken pox."

"Thank you, Doc. We'll take it from here," the old timer took a swig and passed his bottle to outstretched hands. "The bad biles don't stand a chance."

Louisa came up behind Dr. Tradd and pulled him along to the staff rooms next-door where a quick supper of chicken and rice nourished them both enough to keep working well past midnight. Then as he collapsed on a cot, he thanked God again for His Divine gift.

"As You know, Lord, it's much better even than morphine."

CHAPTER 28 — EZEKIEL AND CONNOR

The next morning Ezekiel waited for orders that never came. He sat with the others on a little ridge of pines listening to the rifle fire to the north and west as more regiments moved down the road through the woods. After an hour of waiting he searched out an officer to find out what he could.

"Excuse me sir. But no one's given us orders yet. Could you please ..."

"We don't need you anymore," the Lieutenant replied curtly and walked away through the stumps. He stopped after a few paces and came back.

"Listen here. You boys ... men ... have done a good job for us. But orders are to cut all pioneer groups loose. We're headed into Columbia in a day on two. No need for corduroy now that we're out of the swamps."

"Cut us loose? What ... ?" Ezekiel focused in the Lieutenant's face trying to glean what he could.

"Look here. After Columbia we'll be heading up to North Carolina. The war's almost over. We're getting rumors that General Hardee's pulling out of Charleston. Doesn't want to be trapped, you see. The whole coast, Charleston included, is being occupied by the Navy."

Ezekiel felt his heart skip. "Charleston is free? You mean there no rebs left?

"That's the rumor." The Lieutenant pulled out money from his satchel.

"Here. This is $30 in U.S. currency. It's all I have." He held out the wad of bills. "Take it and head back to the coast. Tell the others too. Best stay put there until the war's over. It won't be long now."

Ezekiel hesitated for a second, fighting off the thought that the lives of Quam, Mingo, and Pompey were worth $30, then nodded. "Thank you sir."

He quickly stuffed the money inside his jacket. The Lieutenant held out his hand. Ezekiel looked at his empty palm then smiled and shook hands man to man. The Lieutenant nodded. "I truly thank you ... and your men ... for what you've done. I wish ... " His face flushed and he cleared his throat. "Well ... Reb cavalry is about. But they'll be after us, not blacks headed to the coast. But still ... "

Ezekiel understood. "We'll be careful, Lieutenant. Thanks, and good luck to you, too." He saluted then ran back and told Esau, Mingo, and Toby the news. He gave each of them $10. The other pioneers gathered around. Some sang out, a few grumbled and cursed, but most just stood there in bewildered silence. They looked at each other waiting for something else to happen.

Ezekiel raised his voice. "Any man who wants to come with me to Charleston, be ready in one hour."

"Is Sherman going to Charleston?" A tall man from another group asked.

"Nope. The officer said he's headed north with the whole army."

"Ain't the rebs back there?"

"The Lieutenant said ... "

The tall man leaned on his axe. "I wouldn't trust him. What does he know about slave patrols? Best we stay close to Sherman. No matter what they say."

Men nodded and agreed. None of them wanted any part of Charleston. A man with braided hair raised his shovel. "I ain't never going back. Never."

"Damn right."

"Amen to that."

The tall man raised his axe, and others did the same. "I ain't come this far to give up. I'm headed north with Uncle Billy! Let's go!" He let out a big yell.

Others cheered with him and followed him off through the trees, but some stood there looking at Ezekiel. Even the men who barely knew him sensed that he was different from all the others. Someone they could rely on. Someone they would be sad to lose. But they were used to that, and each of them knew that this was a beginning of sorts. A start down a new path, and, for once in their lives, maybe a chosen path.

Ezekiel didn't try to persuade them. He knew the others might be right. The Union Army was still the only true guarantee of freedom. And they could all clearly see the blue lines marching off north. Everything else was a risk. He didn't know what was behind them or what the rebs would do after the Yanks left, so he didn't say anything else but helped them divide up what was left of the hardtack, beef tins, and Lucifer matches. He shook hands with each man.

"Enough to last three or four days if you're careful. And Godspeed to freedom, all of you. But before we split up, let's say a prayer together. Everyone! Please. It'll be the last time." He bowed his head and men gathered around in silence to listen. "May God bless these free black men who have struggled to help win their freedom. God grant them protection. For them and all their people. For the rest of their lives. Where ever they go. God bless us all."

"Amen."

Esau blessed himself like Ezekiel then sat down on a stump in shock.

"Cast off like worn out shoes. To hell with the Yanks."

Toby looked up at the blue sky and the patchy clouds racing above the pine tops. He gave Ezekiel a bear-hug. "I'll miss you Ezekiel."

"What? You're not coming with me?"

Toby squeezed the air out of his lungs then laughed and let him go. "Nope, I'm headed wherever Sherman's headed." He nodded to the marching columns. "North, I guess. I think my chances are better to stick with them."

"But Toby, if we stay together we..."

"You can come with me of you like," he smiled. "But I know you won't. I believe there's a certain young lady down that way ...

"Miela," Esau wiped his eyes. "You mean you really ain't coming with us?"

"I'm sorry Esau but ... "

Esau waved him off. "You're going with them?" He bent over with his head in his hands and cried.

Toby knelt beside him. "I've got to follow my dream, Esau, and it's up north. Somewhere where there's snow."

Toby's eyes darted up at him, tears running down his face. "But it's snowed here. I seen it. Just two years ago. Remember? It covered all the fields. Won't that do? Why not stay here Toby? It'll snow again. I know it will."

"I'm sorry Esau, but I've got to go."

257

"Me too," Mingo bowed his head. "I hate to leave y'all, but I'm going as far as I can go with Sherman. I come this far. Can't stop halfway. I'll keep an eye on Toby. Don't you worry none, Esau."

Esau's shoulders seemed to melt. "But ... Will I ever see y'all ... again?" He sobbed louder.

"I'll come back when ever it's over. I promise." Mingo pleaded.

Ezekiel rubbed his face in his sleeve. "Damn it."

Toby's eyes watered up. He found it hard to breath. "Damn all of this."

They are cried together under the pine trees until Ezekiel finally gathered himself up. "Damn you, Toby." He smacked his shoulder. "You'll probably end up a rich plantation prince. With about twenty women hanging all over you. You too, Mingo."

"Nope. One good woman's all I want. I'll bring her back with me when I come. You'll see."

Toby caught his breath and tried to say something but couldn't.

Esau looked up with a flicker of hope. "Couldn't y'all find women in Charleston? What about Daphme and Elsey?"

"I'm sorry, Esau,"Toby wiped his eyes. Mingo said nothing but looked down at his feet. .

Esau realized there was nothing he else could say. His chest heaved some more, and Toby and Mingo comforted him until he was all cried out. Others around them welled up and some sobbed openly. Ezekiel gave Mingo and Toby bear hugs in return and got some of the men laughing. Toby tried to smile but couldn't. He gathered his belongings and started off after the column with the others. Mingo followed behind. Ezekiel and Esau waved goodbye, and Ezekiel called to them.

"When it's over, come back down to Charleston. We'll soon be set up in a big way. Give y'all the time of your life."

Toby waved back. "I'll be there," His voice cracked. "And I'll make sure you keep your promise."

"Goodbye friends!" Mingo yelled and waved, following Toby and his group through the pines.

They both turned and waved one last time then disappeared in the trees. Ezekiel didn't waste any time. He pulled Esau off in the opposite direction in a hurry so he wouldn't have time to tear up again. But Esau was so stunned he went willingly, figuring he had no other choice anyhow.

They walked east through the woods past the last groups of Yank soldiers. It took them all afternoon to come to a road where they came up on a passing group of blacks headed the opposite direction and found out that they were on the State Road that ran towards Charleston. They headed southeast and pushed hard, well into the evening, twice running into Yank cavalry and bummer groups headed the other way, towards Columbia, but no one bothered them. Even the white refugees camped along the roadside left them alone. Ezekiel figured the secret was to travel light. The less they carried, the less they had available to steal and the lower risk of being stopped.

They pressed on until after dark when they came to the little crossroads called Jamison and rested in the shelter of a half burned barn. Ezekiel didn't allow a fire but let Esau eat more than he thought he needed. Better to keep his belly full for now. The next few days would be crucial. They would soon be out of range of Yank cavalry and headed straight through reb territory until they reached Charleston. And there was no way to know how far the Yanks had come up from the coast. Was it just the city? Or were they pushing out farther every day? He hoped three or four days of hard walking would bring them to safety. But no telling.

He lay down on his blanket, looked up at the stars, and was quickly dreaming of Miela. She was yelling at him out of the third floor window at Blessing Plantation Then a white arm pulled her back inside. Ezekiel could hear her being slapped. He struggled to get to her, but his feet sunk into deep mud. He woke up with a start. Esau was snoring loudly, but all else was quiet. An owl hooted close by. Ezekiel watched the moon race through scraggly clouds for a while until exhaustion overwhelmed him.

At dawn he washed off the 'US' from his shirt and made Esau do the same. Better chance of not getting shot by any rebs they might happen across. They walked fast and made it another five miles or so to a burned out bridge over a deep creek in the swamp. Ezekiel stopped at the scrub oaks at the water's edge and listened. Esau squatted behind him. Ezekiel cocked his head and turned around.

259

"Shit. They're coming." He glanced back at the black water as a cold wind rose up and drowned out whatever he'd heard.

"Who is ... ?"

"Shhh ... Sit tight." He squatted down and turned his head sideways, covering one ear then the other. "They're behind us ... I think ... wait."

Esau stooped behind him trembling. "What is it?"

"Now! Now!" Ezekiel jumped up and ran through the last clump of scrub oaks then splashed into the water. Esau followed right behind, ducking as branches snapped back past his head. Ezekiel saw the glint of metal as he reached midstream.

"Damn. They're on both sides," he whispered, as gray horsemen came through the trees. He felt his heart jump. Esau stood behind him shaking uncontrollably. He had no idea what to think or do. Only to follow Ezekiel.

Connor spurred Brig down through the woods to the ford. The rest of the scout covered both banks. He saw two black men standing chest deep in midstream surrounded by troopers who gathered in a circle around the men, rifles leveled. JB walked his horse towards them and drew his revolver. "Y'all been working for the Yanks?" He aimed his pistol at Ezekiel's head.

"No sir!" Ezekiel called out for all to hear. "We're just trying to get to Charleston. Mr. Blessing said we could wait there 'till the Yanks leave."

Connor's heart went to his throat when he heard Ezekiel's voice. His mind raced as he trotted Brig into the creek, and listened to JB yell out, "Going to Charleston, eh? Y'all here that boys? They're gonna walk to Charleston to help General Hardee retreat."

"Shoot 'em and be done with it," Barry called out from the south bank.

"No, wait!" Connor wheeled Brig in front of Ezekiel.

Ezekiel looked up and couldn't believe his eyes. Connor Dumont. What the hell ... ? But he didn't let on. What could he say? That he'd run away? That they'd been working for the Yanks? It wouldn't take much for rebs to shoot a runaway much less a pioneer. Connor did the same. He didn't acknowledge Ezekiel. Best to keep his mouth shut. Better to not let them know. There was nothing he could say that would help. He was sure of that. Best to just make sure JB let them go. He thought about risking a wink to Ezekiel but in a split-second decided it wasn't worth it. What if someone noticed? Still, it was hard not to. Ezekiel watched his eyes and played along.

"It's not right to shoot them. You know it's not," Connor pushed Brig right up to Ezekiel.

"Hell with that," Barry motioned with his revolver. "They're headed to Charleston to join the Yanks."

"It's not right. These two don't matter. The Yanks have plenty already. Leave them be. Let's move on. We've got plenty of bummers to deal with."

Esau seized up with cold and fear, groaning loudly as if in pain. Ezekiel focused on Barry's revolver. If he fired, he knew he'd have to dive to the bottom and try to swim away through the stumps. It was only chest deep, but the black water might hide him long enough to have a chance. And maybe Connor would help.

Connor kept on quickly with whatever he could think of. "The Yanks are moving north, JB. They'll be gone in a week or two. These two here won't matter, and we've all got to live with what we do. Let them go. It's the right thing to do."

"The right thing? That's a fine speech, Connor," Barry laughed. "But I say shoot them. Seems right to me."

"No, we'll leave them be," JB slid his pistol back in his belt. "They're unarmed runaways. Best save our ammunition for bummers and looters."

"After they done killed Norton? You going soft JB? Who gives a damn about these here?" Barry cursed and swung his revolver towards Ezekiel's face.

"No, damn it! These here didn't shoot Norton. Now leave 'em be!" He wheeled his horse and rode off through the trees.

Barry cocked his pistol. "Bullshit."

"Don't do it, Barry!" Connor nudged Brig between him and Ezekiel. "Listen to JB."

Barry fired the revolver into the air. Esau dropped underwater for a few seconds then surfaced and covered his head. Ezekiel shivered all over, his legs so numb with cold that he could barely stand, but he was determined to stay on his feet. Barry spat at him. "Come on boys! Leave these good Confederates alone! They're going down to Charleston to join up," he laughed. "Black Confederates! It's a new world!"

He spurred his mount across the stream, and the others followed. Connor waited for a few seconds to make sure none of the other troopers disobeyed. He glanced back at Ezekiel but said nothing as he rode off. He didn't want anyone to notice. Ezekiel watched Connor and the last of the gray horsemen disappear in the trees and felt his whole body go numb. He couldn't stop shaking, and it wasn't just the cold. He waded across, through the chest deep freezing water and helped Esau up the bank.

"Stay down," his teeth chattered audibly. His arms shook like an epileptic.

Esau lay down in the leaves groaning and shivering. Ezekiel sat beside him and felt a wave of nausea then a hollow gnawing, worse than any belly ache ever. Not only had he made a mistake that might have cost them their lives, but they'd been saved by Connor Dumont. Damn him. Of all the ...

He thought of Miela and knew what she would say, "It's God's hand at work. Just His way of teaching you humility."

He felt the trembling getting worse and lay down on his back. He strained down and tightened his stomach until it passed. Then he started to chuckle. It was too absurd. It had to be God's work all right. God was messing with them for sure. He kept on chuckling until he had Esau smiling along with him.

Esau didn't think for a second that Ezekiel had made a mistake. He had just taken him across a river full of reb cavalry for God's sake. And neither of them with so much as a scratch. He felt as he'd always felt. Ezekiel was without a doubt the greatest man he'd ever known. He didn't even consider complaining when Ezekiel had him push on wet and cold another fifteen miles. He wanted more than anything to get away from that stream and any other rebs that might be about.

Just before dark their lucked held, finding a half eaten, roasted pig in a field just off the road. Ezekiel cut out the parts that hadn't been chewed on by the raccoons and washed them off in a creek. He allowed a small fire in a pine thicket but only after they'd dug a deep hole. They huddled around it with their coats and blankets popped on sticks drying over the flames and wolfed down the rest of the pig. Ezekiel let the fire burn as long as Esau wanted. He didn't fall asleep until the wee hours.

His brain clouded up with memories. Rowing a leaking skiff through marsh creeks with Mr. Dumont's other slaves, Jacob and Jacob's sister, Rosalie. He remembered telling them he'd be free someday and how Jacob had looked away. His way of saying he didn't believe it. As sleep descended, he herded a glut of emotion into a corner and shut the door. No use living in the past. Esau was snoring again. He smothered the fire and slept well, waking up just before dawn and thinking for just a second as his eyes focused that Jacob and Rosalie were there with him. A fleeting second of joy that evaporated in the cold morning air. But it breathed an intense energy into his lungs.

"By God we're freemen, Esau." He poked him awake. "Stand up." He pulled Esau to his feet and roared out. "We're free men!"

Esau winced and ducked down, expecting the worst. "What if the rebs are still around?"

Ezekiel ignored him and yelled it over and over and finally got him to yell with him, but Esau was glad to stop. No sense taking such a risk in reb country. But Ezekiel chuckled all morning while they trotted along for miles and miles, keeping just off the road and far enough into the woods to not be easily spotted. They found corn at an abandoned barn in the afternoon and packed their blanket rolls with as much as they could carry. By dark they crossed an intact bridge over a swamp. A sign post at the crossroads at the far end read: Ridgeville-12, Monck's Corner-14, Northeastern RR.-17. Ezekiel figured they had to be close. With luck they'd be in Yank territory in the morning. The clear night air brought a canopy of stars followed by a crescent moon with the tinge of orange just before dawn. Ezekiel knew it had to be a good omen.

JB LED HIS SCOUT NORTH towards Columbia. They rode ten miles and came to a crossroads where two men rode up and introduced themselves to JB.

"Name's Joe Sanders. Stono Scouts. Guess I'm the last. Ain't seen Captain Walpole are Major Gilchrist since last week. Some of 'em headed back towards Kingstree or so I've heard. Was on picket duty when word came to pull out." He wolfed down pork chunks and gulped his canteen. He wiped his hair down with the grease then stuffed it back under his cap. He wore one boot, the other foot wrapped in blanket strips. His companion rode a mule and wore a tall straw hat with a tiny brim.

263

"Is that a basket?" Bucky laughed, nodding to his hat.

The boy nodded. He took it off and pulled out a little bible and a daguerreotype of a woman. "That's my bible and my momma's picture. All I got left." He put them back in his hat and smiled. "No Yank's gonna shoot through God's word. No Christian anyhow. Name's Fitts. 3rd South Carolina cavalry. Ain't seen the rest of them since Rivers Bridge. Scattered north and west, I think. Thought my double-barrel could be of some use somewhere else." He patted the barrel that stuck through a sleeve of canvas tied to the saddle.

JB nodded. "Might as well join up with us."

"Thanks. Much obliged. Might as well, 'till we find our boys ... IF we find them, that is."

Barry shared some 'fear tonic' with them and JB scrounged up half a gutted pig that quickly sizzled on a skewer then disappeared. Yank rifle fire opened up to the west as the scout bedded down. 12 pounders and howitzers started dueling to the east. It went on until well after dark, and everyone slept fitfully expecting the morning would bring a fight.

Before dawn, a Yank skirmish line pushed in from the west. Within an hour everyone was retreating up the Columbia Road. JB's scout kept up a steady fire at the Yanks coming across a flooded cotton field covered with green slime and bounded to the west by sandy, pine-skirted hills. They pulled back with the others, heading north toward Columbia with rifle fire keeping pace behind them and on both flanks. Two hours of riding through sand hills and pine thickets brought them to a wide, unintended cornfield with last years withered stalks drying in the sun as it dodged in and out between rows of gray clouds that looked to Connor like fish scales.

JB and Bucky scouted around the edges of the field while the rest of them waited in the cover of the trees. Barry and Connor shared some watered-down whiskey and the last of a nearly rotten turkey leg, enjoying the splotchy sunlight as they ate. "It's better with the whiskey, ain't it." Barry crunched on a bone. "Next time we outta ... "

A shotgun blasted from the far end of the field. Connor and Barry dropped their morsels and jumped to their mounts. Rapid Henry fire followed. JB galloped up around the edge of the trees. "Bummer's!" He yelled, pointing his revolver to the rear. "They got Bucky!"

He fired blindly behind him. Henry's answered from deeper in the woods. Everyone followed quickly. Down the edge of the field through the pines then across a little stump clearing that tapered into a bog of water oaks. Rifle fire erupted from the trees as they crossed the clearing. Barry's mare went down. Connor whirled around to help him. Barry pulled his leg free from under the horse just as a bummer rode up out of the smoke and fired at him. He emptied Chesire's LeMat in return, and the bummer rode back into the trees. Barry grabbed the Henry and jumped up on Brig behind Connor.

"Go!"

He slapped Brig's rear, and they galloped across the clearing into the far trees where the scout had spread out. They waited for the bummers to enter the clearing then opened up. One bummers dropped, and the rest rode off through the woods the way they'd come. Connor quickly counted thirty or more of the bastards. All with Henrys. JB held the men back figuring they'd just be riding into another ambush then led the scout up a little rise to a stand of cane where they regrouped along a sandy road. A wounded trooper was tended to while flankers watched for the bummers. No one knew that Bucky was still alive

BUCKY HAD COME TO after being shot off his mount just as the bummers rode up. He shot the closest with his carbine then tried to stand but his legs wouldn't work. He felt blood in his throat. More of it bubbled from a hole in his shirt. He pulled himself into the high weeds of the cornfield and waited. Another Yank rode up from behind, firing his Henry and nearly trampling him. Bucky shot him off his horse with Norton's revolver. The rest of them backed off and lit up the field with turpentine fires. Bucky knew what was happening. He tried to crawl away, but his arms were too weak. The bummers surrounded him and tossed jugs of turpentine into the flames. He pushed away from the burning weeds and cornstalks as long as he could, but the smoke choked him so much he never saw the bummer behind him. A jug broke on his shoulder, and a roaring flame engulfed him. He felt his breath go short and saw his legs on fire but couldn't feel them. He rolled over on his back and reached down to reload Norton's revolver as the fire burned into his shell pouch. His paper shotgun cartridges exploded and buckshot cut into his heart. The sky turned red then a weight smothered him into blackness.

The wind picked up and rustled the trees. JB listened to the rifle fire, his face glowing red in the cold. "By God we'll kill some of those bastards. Set up along here. Some of y'all get in the cane. Some along the road in the trees there. Take the horses yonder past the ridge."

Everyone was happy to oblige. Connor hoped the Yanks would too. He stationed himself at the end of the line with Barry, hiding in the saw palmettos behind a thick stand of cane. The rest of the line followed the curvature of the road. The cold wind in the trees masked any restless noise while they waited. But it didn't take long. The first bummer trotted around the bend like he owned the property. Connor smiled and felt a wave of pleasure. The joy of revenge. For Bucky, for Cheshire, for Norton. For all the rest. The Yanks trotted up in a clump. A dozen of them. All lugging hams, chickens, and bags of loot on their saddles. One with a small lamp, another with a rocking chair, and two with braces of geese hanging by the necks like gray -feathered saddle bags. Connor realized these couldn't be the same ones. But it didn't matter. Barry's shotgun opened up, and a bloody hole ripped through the last Yank's head. He was dead before he hit the ground. The whole line fired. All but two of the bummers went down. The lead man and one other ducked and galloped up the road. The men in the bamboo thicket blasted them both off their horses.

The firing stopped just as fast as it started. Everyone reloaded and waited for JB's signal as the wind blew the smoke away. They crept forward, all watching for bummers playing dead. JB poked the lead Yank with a stick, and he flipped over quick as a cottonmouth. JB fired into the Yank's face before he could get off a shot. The rest of the men stopped in their tracks as if standing on thin ice. They glanced at each other then opened up, killing four wounded Yanks and shooting each dead body in the head just to be sure. JB turned the lead bummer over on his back. He cut off a piece of palmetto and jabbed the stem into the red, pulpy hole in the man's face. Then he urinated on him.

"This is for Bucky, Norton and Cheshire."

Connor had to look away even though he knew the bastard felt nothing. Every other Yank soon had a palmetto frond sticking out of a bullet hole. Fitts laughed and spat tobacco juice on each body. "Serves the bastards right. Betcha that ain't what they were expecting eh? South Carolina didn't turn out to be as much fun as they thought."

More Henry fire came from farther down the road, and JB called for the horses. They followed him north before the other Yanks came up, but rifle fire followed them on the breeze all afternoon. They made it to the Saluda River Bridge outside of Columbia just before dark. JB found an officer and gave his report, and Barry took a look around, happening across another scout butchering a cow and trading some fear tonic for a haunch. JB waited until everyone had eaten their full then took off his cap.

"What's there to say about Bucky. I figured he'd be heading back home after all this shit. Figured he'd be wearing that same black outfit of his ... for years. Maybe he would've been a good undertaker. Who knows? Never figured he'd get hit. Not bad anyhow. Not after all he's been through." He took a deep breath. "Shit. Shit on all of this."

"Amen," Barry nodded. "Bucky was special all right. And shit it is." Everyone shared a drink in his honor then bedded down exhausted. Connor drifted off wondering who would be next. Would the bastards get them all? Would any of them ever be heading home? He dreamed of wild dogs stalking him inside Uncle Paul's house and woke up just as they had him cornered.

In the morning the scout was quickly on the move, riding north, crossing the Saluda River and fanning out into the woods to the east of the prison camp just up the hill. They followed JB to the stockade where he conferred with officers. The camp reeked of human waste and rotting bodies. Barry and Connor dismounted and climbed up to the firing step up the parapet to have a look. Inside the log stockade, skeletal Yank prisoners stumbled about squatting to relieve their bowels into a ditch running across the grounds. Guards were trying to herd them into a line. Men scooped water from puddles nearby. Cadaverous bodies lay wrapped in blankets all around. Raggy tent halves on sticks covered clumps of shivering men in filthy burrows in the mud. Others waited for a thin, watery gruel ladled rudely by a pair of soldiers who wore handkerchiefs over their noses. A wind shift brought the full assault of the camp's smell. Connor told himself that barbaric conditions were just a part of war. It couldn't be helped. But the groans of the half-naked skeletons squatting in the ditch said otherwise.

An old man on the firing step nodded to him. He was dressed in a Mexican war uniform. Connor figured he had to be seventy. His shotgun was aimed down at the other coughing skeletons.

"Easier just to let them die inside their holes then cave them in. Don't have to dig a fresh grave. Most of us don't like shooting the poor bastards. Even when they cross the deadline. It just means more grave digging. Some of the younger boys love it though. Taunting the Yanks with bits of food. Kind of like a sport. Half of a baked sweet potato makes a fine bait. Toss it into the dead zone and wait for one of them skeletons to go for it." He paused and caught his breath. "Then shoot him down."

One of the boys on the firing step heard what he'd said and walked over, laughing. "Yep. That's right. And what of it? At first I wouldn't shoot a crawling man, but the other fellas showed me it was all just a Yank trick, y'see. They crawl on purpose."

Barry grabbed the boy's collar and jerked him off his feet. "How bout I throw you down there. Let you crawl on your own damn knees for a while."

The boy dropped his rifle and pulled free. "What the hell?"

Barry swatted his head, sending his hat flying down into the dead zone. "Shooting starving prisoners? How bout we give the Yanks rifles and let them shoot back? A little more sporting, eh?"

Connor held Barry back as two more boy-guards with shotguns ran up the firing step. "Come on Barry, we don't need to fight our own ... not just yet anyhow."

"Hell you say," Barry jerked free. "Maybe it's time we did." The veins of his shaved head pulsed hard enough to burst. "Y'all want to be soldiers! Then come fight the damn bummers! We lost good men back yonder! And for what? So little boys like you can torment starving men? Hell with you all!"

An old militia officer scurried out from the log guard-hut. "Y'all go on now. Leave the boys be. They're just doing their job."

Barry spat at his feet as he climbed down. "Hell with you, too."

Connor followed him down the ladder. He thought of the terrified black man and the wounded Yank bummers but told himself that this was something entirely different. He glanced back at the scarecrows in line jostling for a sip of grayish slop before being herded off. He couldn't picture them as soldiers. They were barely human anymore. The fruits of war. He thought of Norton and Bucky and looked back at the boyish guards with their shotguns, each still quite ready to shoot any skeleton that crossed the wire marker.

"Why not just go ahead and shoot 'em now," Barry cursed."Better than letting starving men shit to death. It's a sin, I tell you. Worse than anything we ever did."

"Damn right," Connor quickly agreed. "Way worse."

JB rode up and called to them, "C'mon y'all. Stop dawdling. We've been ordered to help guard the prisoners. They're moving 'em across the bridge to the rail depot."

Men grumbled. No one liked the idea. They followed grudgingly, covering the rear of the prisoner column as they shuffled and stumbled from the stockade across the bridge and up the hill where more militia took over. Officers and orderlies galloped about it with reports and orders, but no one seemed to have a real plan. JB had the scout rest their horses behind some trees overlooking the fields stretching down towards the river and took a squad, including Barry, Connor and Fitts, with him up the road towards town to reconnoiter.

THE CITY BURST AT THE SEAMS with crowds of civilians, and raggedy groups of soldiers who milled about everywhere. No one seemed to have given it much thought about what they'd do once they'd made it to Columbia, only that nothing else mattered except to get there, and away from Sherman. Connor had heard the rumors. Twenty thousand refugees by some counts. So many that there were no homes left to rent. They said the banks were so packed full of treasures from all over that the nervous bank clerks held shotguns in their laps.

The troops wandering the streets looked to like children eyeing candy. The blacks in the streets and alleyways stared back silently. They could have been statues. A few civilians stood in their yards nervously waving Confederate flags as if to proclaim themselves friends while raggy Tennessee, Mississippi, and Georgia boys consumed free flowing alcohol that had emerged everywhere, from the finest brandy to hog-swill moonshine. The remnants of the Army of the Tennessee was perfectly happy to drink all that Columbia had to offer.

JB had them dismount and post a guard over the horses while he searched out officers for further orders. The rest of them milled about the warehouse row. Connor talked with a barefoot boy from a Mississippi regiment. He was missing two fingers on his right hand and had trouble trying the shoes he'd found in a pile next to a row of broken crates. He sat in the middle of the street with warehouses on one side and cutler-shops on the other. Soldiers all around were helping themselves to government goods that had been declared free to all. Some things they needed, like shoes. Some things they wanted, like whiskey and tinned meats. And some things they were just curious about, like a big grandfather clock that chimed for one group of soldiers beside a fire they'd built in a big black kettle on the loading platform next to the train tracks. They threw pieces of the broken crates into the kettle fire and sipped whiskey, taking turns resetting the clock and listening to it chime over and over as the throng of soldiers started breaking open more crates.

"Liquor!" Someone yelled.

Barry darted into the mix and came back shortly with three bottles. The crowd grew larger and rowdier with soldiers and civilians growing increasingly emboldened with alcohol. A shop window was smashed, and the crowd hauled away bolts of cloth and boxes of canned food. Officers ignored the looting, but one captain rode up and ordered all the milling soldiers to help pile cotton bales in the street. No one even grumbled. At least it was something constructive to do.

"Building a fort, I guess," Barry winked. "I guess they think we'll hold them here 'till Lee or Johnson come. The civilians just don't know it yet." He motioned to the jammed train station and the panicked mob of townspeople trying to wedge themselves on board the overloaded cars. Connor sucked down a mouthful of spirit then went to work with the others, laughing punch drunk and piling up bales until a ten foot wall blocked the entire street and caused even more agitation in the crowds of refugees. Another officer came up as they ran out of cotton bales and just as quickly ordered the street reopened. The heavy bales were dutifully dragged back out of the way but with less enthusiasm.

Connor and Barry finished off their bottles then walked up the street between warehouse rows listening to the talk. Rumors flew everywhere. Lee was marching south to reinforce Wheeler and Hampton. Thousands of men from Hood's army were coming from Augusta. Hardee was bringing 20,000 up from Charleston.

"People believe what they want to believe," Barry shared an oyster tin. "And these Columbia folks sure as hell don't want to listen to bad news."

They finished off the tins just as JB pushed through the crowd. "They're giving all the Army stores away. Everything. Hampton's orders. Gonna open all these warehouses. Figure it's better that the folks here take it than Sherman. Best go get the rest of the boys, Barry. Those that are still sober that is."

Barry trotted off a bit wobbly but with renewed purpose, and Connor followed JB. Within minutes, commissary officers came pushing their way through the crowd throwing open the doors of the warehouses across the street. The effect was instantaneous. A mob surged inside. Row after row of boxes and barrels were smashed and grabbed. People pulled out blankets, cans of food, tanned hides, boxes of peas and potatoes, clothing, bridles and yolks, barrels of sorghum molasses, and crate after crate of liquor that bobbed for a few moments above the mob then disappeared, quickly spiraling the throng into a riot. Blacks and whites, soldiers and civilians, most drunk, all shoved in and out of warehouse rows on both sides of the street, carrying off boxes, sacks, crates and barrels. Connor saw Barry and most of the scout pinned by the mob against a wall down the street. He and JB squirmed their way over and found Fitts stuffing his blanket rolls with tins of food.

"Look here. Oysters and ham. Got enough here to get us home. If we ain't trampled to death."

"Yes sir. The last morsels of the Confederacy," JB forced a laugh.

"Enjoy every bite, boys."

Warehouse after warehouse was ransacked until an artillery company fired pistols over their heads and rolled through with their guns. The mob waited until the horses and caissons passed then went back at it as if starving, breaking into more stores and helping themselves to warmer clothing, blankets and more liquor. Every man emerged with prizes stuffed in pockets and haversacks. The liquor flowed more freely than ever from bottles of all shapes and sizes. JB helped Fitts pull open another locked store-front door.

"Come on boys. Help yourself!" Fitts yelled.

271

Wine and brandy bottles lined the shop walls. Stacked crates of ham and oyster tins formed a little fort in the middle of the room. The crowd surged in behind them, stuffing bottles and tins into their haversacks as an old man limped up out the basement door. He carried a huge sword. JB saluted him immediately. "We're requisitioning, sir. Don't mind us." The old man raised his sword then thought better of it. Connor steadied himself, took a pen and paper from the corner, and quickly wrote out a receipt. "Here, Sir. They'll surely to pay you back."

The man took the note, crumpled it up in a ball, and threw it at Connor's feet. "You're damn vultures. You're worse than the Yanks."

"No sir, we ain't," JB snorted back. "We ain't strung you up by your balls and lit a fire under you, just to find your gold and silver, now have we?"

The old man took a step towards him, but Connor held his arm until he snatched it away. "Go to hell!" He stuck the sword into a sack of sweet potatoes then limped back down the steps to the basement and slammed the door.

"Secession's not quite as pretty as he'd imagined," Fitts laughed, pushing his way back into the street. Connor felt the liquor talking too. He followed JB, Barry, and the others who had forced their way through the mob that was getting drunker by the minute. All order had vanished. No other officers were to be seen anywhere. Soldiers all around were laughing and smashing empty bottles in the street as they stumbled along from one store to another until the thud of 12-pounders suddenly echoed in the distance. All heads turned as one.

JB washed his face in a water barrel. "God damn this shit. Sherman's here already," hurriedly wolfing down a last bite of cheese he pulled from his pocket. "He's about as restless as Wheeler. Best we get a move on. I'm sure the boys would like us to requisition a wagon ....and as much as we can carry. Come on."

He led them up the crowded streets to the rail depot where the mob swarmed towards a train backing in to the station. Old men and women fought with soldiers and government clerks for spots in each car. Bags, boxes, furniture, children and pets were tossed up through car windows. More sacks, chests, and crates were lashed to each car roof or left dangling precariously from doors and windows like saddlebags. Connor watched an old man dive headfirst through an open window. The train started rolling with his legs sticking out. The crowd ran along with the train, piling onto each car roof and hanging from each side as it moved down the tracks. A boy lost his footing and fell between the moving cars then just as quickly emerged on the next car roof where he sat down and munched on a carrot. Connor smiled. Only a twelve-year-old could be that nimble.

The train jerked to a stop. More of the mob pressed around the cars, jamming inside to suffocation. Women and crying children tried to stay together. More climbed through windows to fight for spots while blacks danced at the edge of the depot carrying off more loot from nearby stores. The train lurched forward again through the swirls of people as a locomotive screeched and belched smoke. A small girl fell from her mother arms onto the track. The wheel rolled over her foot. She screamed and jerked backwards. The foot was gone. Her bare ankle spurted blood. A man jumped down from the window and pulled her to the siding as people surged past, stumbling over them and ignoring the child.

Connor fought his way through the crowd to help the man tie a tourniquet on her leg. Her mother shivered uncontrollably, wailing a high-pitched noise like a tea kettle. Connor helped carry her back to line of ambulance wagons already brimming with sick and wounded. A doctor staggered down from his spot on one of the wagons and worked on the girl right there on the siding. The girl screamed until the doctor held an ether rag tightly to her face and put her to sleep. He cauterized the wound with silver nitrate, ligated the bleeding vessels then wrapped the stump in gauze and cotton. The mother kept shivering in a state of shock the whole time until the doctor gave her a big drink from a brown bottle he pulled out of his bag.

"Laudenum," he winked at Connor. "The best thing for pain, physical or otherwise."

"Yes sir. I believe you," Connor nodded, helping lift the sleeping girl and her mother into the hospital wagon.

The train whistle screeched, and the cars lurched a few feet then stopped again. A young officer stood on a boxcar roof with his shirt sleeves rolled up shouting out orders to men carrying boxes from a line of wagons into one car door and throwing suitcases and bags of clothing out the other. No one else seemed to be in charge. The train pushed forward again, wedging through the crowd on the tracks ahead. The lieutenant and his men jumped aboard. A huge vent of black smoke belched out the stack and the locomotive crawled away screeching and moaning. The mob surged on to the tracks behind, waiting for another train that never came.

JB stole one of the Lieutenant's deserted wagons, with its pair of thin mules, from the siding before anyone else claimed them. He had them fill it up with barrels of salt pork, cornmeal, and tins of ham and oysters. No one interfered. Barry came up with the rest of the men and horses, and they all took what provisions they could carry then followed JB back the way they'd come.

Tins of ham and oysters were plentiful, and everyone ate their fill. They camped down towards the river, listening to guns firing in the distance, but no one slept well. Everyone knew what tomorrow would bring.

CHAPTER 29 — MIELA TO CHARLESTON

Thunder whipped through the pre-dawn chill. Miela watched for heat lightning, but there was none. Jemps stood up after lighting the morning fire, "Cannons?" He cocked his head as more rumbles drifted faintly through the trees, "Sounds like it's coming from the east. More Yanks maybe?"

"Could be. Or rebs. No way to tell."

"Then how do we know it's safe."

"We don't," Miela furrowed her brow. White men and their guns. Damn them all. Where was the promise of a peaceful tomorrow? She felt her stomach cramp but managed to help Daphne cook breakfast for the others. Jemps hurried everyone along so that at first light they were ready to move on up the road towards Charleston. By noon they reached the Ashley River, crossing at Bees Ferry and walking the five miles to the junction with the State Road heading into town. Lines of gray infantry walked northward. She had Titus pull the wagons off the road behind a pine thicket and had Poins cover the mules with a good coating of mud.

"Better they looked nasty. Less temptation."

"What about us?" Jemps asked. "The children?"

Miela cracked a smile, "You're all dirty enough."

"What about Daphne, and Elsey? They're pretty clean."

"No. That's All right." The way he said it made her want to laugh. "Don't worry. They've got asafetida if they need it."

Elsey shook her head, "I ain't wearing it no more. But I ain't as pretty as you."

Cumseh grunted at her and tried to talk her into making another, but Elsey wouldn't budge. "Am I pretty? Answer me, Cumseh. Am I?"

"Don't matter. If they ... "

"I ain't wearing it. You can save your breath."

Cumseh kept on for an hour or so but to no avail while they all waited for a break in the line of troops. It never came. After an hour, Miela decided

275

to risk moving on, figuring staying put didn't offer any more safety anyway. "C'mon. Let's go."

"Are you sure?" Jemps asked.

Miela didn't answer, and Titus cracked the whip. The mules came to life, pulling the wagon out of the thicket while the girls all huddled in the back of the wagon terrified. Yarrow walked beside them with a sharpened bamboo stick, but Jemps told him not to say or do anything. Miela kept her fingers crossed, but none of the soldiers seem to even notice them. They all looked exhausted and their officers, worried. Jemps noticed that most of their horses and mules looked surprisingly fresh and well fed.

He sighed in relief. "I think we're all right. They won't be needing our mules just yet."

"God willing," Miela whispered back.

She looked at the hodgepodge of white men plodding along and knew her group was at their mercy. Units of cavalry came along and mixed with assortments of infantry, artillery units, home guard, cadets, militia, and stragglers of all ages and armament. Boys with freshly washed church clothes and old men with faded butternut field jackets mixed together in a retreating stew. Walking wounded joined the remnants of regiments trudging up the road behind teams of horses pulling caissons and cannon.

None of Miela's group had ever seen a cannon before. Yarrow looked at the shiny bronze barrel in awe. It pointed backwards towards the men marching behind. What if it went off, he wondered. Why walk behind it like that? Miela called to him when he stopped to gawk, and he hurried to catch up. She kept them all off the road as much as possible while thousands more soldiers passed them. An endless line of gray and brown, all headed northwest. Only once did anyone stop them. An officer wearing a beautifully embroidered gray coat trotted over. He inquired where they were headed, and Miela told him. He nodded, touched his brown and red cap, and rode off. No one else said a word.

"It's like we're indivisible," Cumseh whispered to the children.

"Invisible?" Agnes asked. "What's that?"

"It means they can't see us."

"Really?" Agnes waved at her. "But I can still see my hands."

276

Cumseh grunted, "But they can't see us. I tell you the Divine's working His magic."

Fatima jumped up from her perch in front of the wagon, "You mean they can't see my backside?" She started to lift her dress.

"No!" Lizette grabbed her and pulled her down.

Miela turned and signaled for them to keep quiet, and the girls realized Cumseh was just teasing. Agnes lay back down and watched the treetops move past, "Shoot. I want to be invisible."

"Me too," Fatima looked at the back of her hand hoping to see right through it.

Cumseh hissed at them. "I ain't lying. Them troopers can't even see Miela. She's invisible to them too. Like a haint in the fog."

"But, I can see her."

"Me too."

Cumseh hissed again and waved them off. Yarrow walked behind them bringing up the rear with his bamboo spear. The girls called to him to come stand in the wagon beside them. They liked pretending with him. The wagon wasn't ever a ship until he stood in the back with his bamboo tiller between the barrels. But Yarrow just shook his head. He was past pretending. All he could think of was Grace. He wouldn't play with the others anymore. Not until he found her. He wouldn't even talk to the girls until they camped at dark in a patch of scrub oaks beside a pile of oyster shells and ate the last of the rice. Titus held up the last bag of millet and one last jar of molasses.

"It's all right. We'll be in Charleston tomorrow," Miela sighed. "It can't be more than seven or eight more miles."

"Praise the Lord," Daphne answered. She helped Titus boil all the millet, saving half for the next day, then helped get Lizette to eat. Afterwards she took her time tending to Fatima's healing cuts while the others watched wagons and carriages crossing a field on the other side of the road.

Dozens of white families were following along behind the army. A few of them glanced their way, but no one came over to bother them. Jemps and Miela stayed up most of the night to keep watch anyway. They roused everyone at first light and were off without breakfast, reaching the outskirts of Charleston by afternoon. Explosions thundered closer than before. Thousands of people were on the move. Groups of blacks on foot headed towards town, just like them, and whites in wagons and carriages headed the other way. By midafternoon it was chaos.

Young black men ran along the road past them, singing and drinking from jugs. White families huddled low in wagons as if expecting to be assaulted. More bands of Confederate cavalry and straggling infantry moved up the State Road ignoring other groups of blacks rummaging through a dry goods store across from the race track. Miela kept them headed into the city proper where the streets formed into a grid, and houses lined each block. Crowds of blacks were all about yelling and singing and waving flags made of sheets and blankets.

"Sherman and Lincoln are coming!' A group of girls sang out in unison waving pieces of red and blue cloth. "We're going to the Jubilee!" Daphne sang with them as the girls ran around the wagon then off down a side street. Fatima and Agnes wanted to run off behind them, but Miela held them back and kept Titus headed down Rutledge Avenue past the last of the fleeing white families. They came to a pond that merged with marsh grass and the larger river beyond. A bridge stretched across to the far bank. Soldiers were dousing the timbers with turpentine. They scurried off, and an officer lit a torch. Flames exploded, and the east wind did the rest. The fire raced across the bridge to the far side. The entire structure of fresh pine timbers coated with tar, roared in a long flame. Black smoke boiled up, obscuring the view down river. Concussions echoed across the city. More plumes of smoke rose in the distance, and more crowds of blacks, mostly women and children surged down the street.

"We'll follow them." Miela called to Titus. "Steer the mules along behind them . They must be headed towards the Yanks. Once we're safe we can go find the ferry to Smythe's. It has to be along the river somewhere."

The memory of being raped on Mr. Blessing's boat stabbed at her but quickly disappeared. She looked around at the wide-eyed children staring at the surging crowds of free blacks and patted their heads. "It's all right. They're just a bit wild since freedom's here."

"This is freedom?" Yarrow waved his bamboo stick at the yelling and singing throng.

"Yes, it is. The beginnings of it anyhow."

He held his bamboo stick up over his head, "Well, I guess I'm ready for it."

"Me too," Agnes squealed.

Titus kept the mules moving along with the crowd as they drifted east along a wide street to a train depot where a locomotive inched slowly out of the station pulling along a line of cars covered with Confederate soldiers and white civilians clinging to every square inch. Most were flat beds, but a few were coal and cattle cars with two decrepit passenger cars bringing up the rear, bursting at the seams with men clinging to the roof and holding onto each other in a web of arms and legs. The train moved slowly through a crowd of terrified white civilians. Young black men ran through the crowd yelling and drinking pillaged liquor. Women wailed and old men scowled.

A group of black women confiscated a dozen or so abandoned hand carts to carry off piles of discarded belongings. The white civilians who couldn't find a place on the train began to move off into the side streets as it started to rain. Black teens laughed, impervious to the cold. To them it was all part of a glorious new celebration, but the soldiers hanging on to overload cars, as the train moved up the track, bore it as just another torment to be tolerated. The civilians moving off up the streets wrapped themselves in coats and blankets as if warding off more than they could fathom. Daphne and Elsey nodded to each other and stripped to their undergarments, letting the cold rain wash their shivering bodies.

Explosions a few blocks away rocked the air. Smoke drifted down the street and mixed with the rain. Titus started to sing the 'hallelujah song' and all the girls joined in. Lizette huddled in a blanket with Cumseh, mouthing the words as her tears mingled with the rain. They all watched in awe as a crowd of cheering blacks looted the depot round-house and the railroad machine -shop. Fires began to sprout up in the huge woodpile of the lumber yard a block away. Thousands of marooned cotton bales stood in tall rows in the storage yard. Smashed barrels lay everywhere. A group of white children threw handfuls of black powder onto a small fire, laughing as it roared up into a big fireball. Miela saw that no white adults were close by. She yelled at them.

"Get away from that! It'll burn you!"

They glanced over at her and hesitated for a second then went back to their game, throwing more handfuls onto the fires that began to spread to the cotton bales. Older blacks poured turpentine on some of the cotton bales down towards the loading dock, and, despite the drizzle, the fire spread quickly in the fresh, cold breeze. Hundreds of freed slaves and white civilians began to loot through the abandoned boxes and kegs alongside the tracks and in the warehouse rows along side the depot. Everything worth eating or trading was carried off. Tins of oysters, kegs of nails, barrels of molasses, bolts of cloth, rolls of burlap. All dusted with loose cotton blackened with engines soot. Explosions from the direction of the harbor again rocked the air. The children playing with the powder grew bolder, throwing handfuls onto the turpentine fires.

Miela yelled at them again, "For God's sake stop it!"

None of them paid her any mind. Two black men behind them tossed a keg onto the tracks, breaking it open to see what was inside. Black powder seeped out. They ignored it and grabbed another keg then another, breaking them open on the tracks. Miela could see what was about to happen.

"Come on quick, Titus!" She grabbed the reins and pulled the mules. "Come on, right now! Jemps, Poins, now! Go! Go!"

They all heard the fear in her voice and didn't hesitate, all of them helping to pull the mules quickly around the corner behind a brick warehouse row. The children behind them threw more black powder at the burning bales. The flash ignited the powder kegs, and the entire warehouse erupted into a ball of flame. The explosion knocked bricks off the warehouse roof, just missing Miela, but the main blast went down the tracks behind the thick brick walls. Hundreds of people were caught in the flames. All those trapped inside the gutted station were immolated. Lizette covered Fatima's eyes as a woman staggered out a few steps through the raging fire to the tracks then collapsed with a blackened, burning baby in her arms. Miela held Jemps back.

"They're dead. There's nothing you can do. C'mon!" She pushed Titus. "Move!"

He pulled the braying mules along, listening to the screams of the burned and wounded behind him as another last section of depot exploded. Miela looked away, hurrying the rest along away from the danger. "Go! Go! Who knows what else will blow!"

"We should go back and help!" Jemps pulled free as the smoke from the blast swirled around him.

Miela hesitated knowing he was right, but another explosion erupted a block away. Rifle fire and pistol shots crackled from close by. "We can't risk it! It's too dangerous!" Her mind raced. What to do? To come all this way and then this! Should they go back and help or get to safety? Titus held the reins looking into her eyes, "They need help Miela."

"I know, but ... " She glanced at the terrified, crying children while Titus waited for her to give an order. Burned civilians wandered past them in a daze. She felt it too. Dazed and unsure. "All right, let's ... "

A squad of gray soldiers came up past them through the smoke. They stopped, leveled their rifles at a group of black looters just up the street, and fired. Several men fell. The soldiers began to reload.

"For Gods sake! Come on! Go!" Miela yelled, wrapping her arms around Agnes.

Titus snapped the reins sending the mules into a trot and the wagon rumbling down to Meeting Street away from the shooting. Miela felt sick to her stomach. Jemps and Poins hung their heads ashamed as they wandered in a daze past the parade grounds of the Citadel Barracks now full of cheering and singing blacks who seemed oblivious to the rifle fire and the continuing explosions just up the street. The last of the Confederate garrison trotted out from the barracks with rifles ready as more cannon fire echoed from the direction of the harbor.

Miela kept them all moving as crowds began to run towards the sound of the guns. Everyone was cheering and singing and ignoring the rebel officer riding ahead of his reargaurd infantry. A group of young black men came out of a huge white -columned building carrying a table and chandelier.

The officer pointed his sword and yelled, "Hibernian Hall!"

The soldiers swung into line, leveled rifles, and fired at the blacks running off in all directions. The powder smoke rolled off into the breeze, and two more black men lay dead on the marble steps. The soldiers quickly followed the officer off through the crowds. Young blacks picked up stones and ran up close enough to pelt them. The soldiers fired back over their heads and made their escape. Scattered rifle fire continued to crackle up from all around, but Miela hurried Jemps and Titus along.

They made it to the wharves of the harbor-front as the cold wind picked up. A vast expanse of water spread out before them. Dozens of ships lay at anchor a few miles out. They watched rowboats push off from three big gunboats anchored closer in. The wind and tide brought the little boats quickly towards the sea wall, and as the sailors climbed up a rickety ladder, one of the gunboats suddenly disappeared in a red ball of flame. It rose up above the water suspended by a plume of smoke and surrounded by a huge splash. A second later the explosion rocked the waterfront. Iron plate rained down on the granite quay. Everyone took cover under the wagon. Flames and smoke billow up, and what was left of the gunboat quickly disappeared underwater. The other two gunboats followed suit, erupting in fireballs that hurled debris over the sea wall. A big piece of iron plate crushed the roof of a nearby warehouse.

"Fireworks!" Agnes clapped and squirmed around in delight.

"Shush!" Miela grabbed her arm, motioning to the Confederate seamen making their way up the street as more explosions erupted from smaller boats blowing up in the distance. "No use making them mad on the last day of their war."

The children held hands, itching to yell out and dance around, but Miela held firm. "Just wait," she whispered. "Just wait."

"It looks like a big gray lizard!" Yarrow called out, ignoring her and pointing his bamboo stick towards the next wharf where flames roared from a stranded, wrecked gunboat. "Goodbye Mr. Lizard!"

"Shhh!" Miela glanced back at the last of the Confederate seaman making their way on foot up the quay.

Yarrow obeyed reluctantly, now fascinated with the four steamers coming across the harbor. He watched them turn into the ebb tide and drop anchor. Blue-uniformed troops were lowered into dozens of boats with oars that looked to him like giant crabs' legs. Men began pulling methodically towards the wharves as the last rebel seaman disappeared around the warehouse row. Miela cautiously looked around for any more Confederates, "They're gone! They're all gone."

"Then we're free! We're free!" Jemps shouted out.

Everyone crawled out from under the wagon and broke into a yell. Even Cumseh smiled and cheered, waving a crow feather, "Freedom! Freedom!"

The rowboats came closer and Titus and Daphne, yelled out simultaneously, "They're black! They're black!" Both of them pointed and jumped up and down. Everyone else stood transfixed. They were indeed black men in blue uniforms.

"The Lord has brought the Jubilee for sure!" Titus yelled. "Black soldiers come to free the slaves!"

Miela and Elsey knelt and cried. They couldn't help it. Jemps knelt beside them and hugged Miela."You did it! You've got us to freedom. See? See right there? Those men. Those beautiful black men."

Jemps squeezed Fatima and spun her around, making her squeal. Everyone else kept clapping and cheering, watching the black troops land all along the waterfront up and down the river. A few white civilians watched from half shuttered windows with numb expressions of disbelief. Black troops in blue uniforms were marching up their street, and the whole wharf area was quickly teaming with even larger crowds of freed men.

Cheers and screams of delight filled the air while white Yank officers led the troops into town, proudly calling out the names of their regiments above the din.

"The 21st US!"

"The 55th Massachusetts!"

"The 3rd South Carolina Regiment!"

Rousing hallelujahs erupted each time and echoed after them through the streets. It grew to a cacophony of noise. Boys beating iron skillet's on cobblestones, women shrieking, and men blowing horns and conch shells without fear. Blacks by the thousands celebrating the Promised Land. Charleston, now a free city. Now protected by black soldiers. It was the most wonderful thing any freed slave could imagine.

Yarrow trembled with excitement watching another company of black men in fresh blue uniforms with bayonets of the 3rd South Carolina Regiment marched by. He joined Jemps and Poins in a smart salute. Wonderful thoughts went through his mind. That red-faced reb, the one who'd taken Glace, now skewered on a bayonet begging for his life, and Grace standing beside him laughing. He felt his bamboo stick and looked closely at the shiny rifles moving past. "I got to get me one of them."

Jemps hugged him, "We'll get a bunch of them, Yarrow, and we'll get Grace back too. Don't you worry."

Yarrow fought off tears. He didn't want to cry in front of the black soldiers, so he put on a brave face and shouldered his stick just like the marching men in the ranks. A sergeant glanced over and saluted him. He saluted back and felt his heart soar. He broke out in a big smile. "Did you see that, Jemps? He saluted me."

"I saw it, Yarrow. He sure did. You're a real soldier now."

Yarrow felt a warmth run through his chest and couldn't tell for a while if he was actually floating on air. He yelled and clapped with everyone else until the last of the soldiers had passed by. Miela had to pull him along with the others, leading the way to the end of a tabby wharf where they huddled together while she inquired about the ferry to Thomas Island. The men standing there shook their heads.

"There's one up by Five-Mile. Up by the River Road. Doubt that it's still runnin' though. All the rebs done left. White boys sank our steamers, too. We can row ya'll up with the tide tomorrow," he nodded to the two long boats bobbing along the quay. "But not that big wagon. Not them mules neither."

Miela thanked them then went back to the wagon. "We've passed the ferry, and it s too late to try to reach it today. We need to find a place in town for tonight." She thought that a minute while all eyes followed every movement of her face and hands. "Legare Street. The Blessing's home. We're free now and we can pay our way if we have too. We're gonna stay there tonight."

Titus frowned and Jemps grimaced like he had been stung by a wasp. "I don't know. What if Mr. Malcolm comes back. He might ... "

"We're free!" Miela raised her voice. "Those black troops guarantee it. He can't do anything to us anymore." She touched his shoulder gently and smiled, "Don't worry. It's the safest place to go. He won't set foot back here anyway. Not yet. Not with all these troops around."

Jemps took a deep breath and held it. He still wasn't sure, but had no idea what else to do. He just hoped to God that she was right. "I guess so. All right then."

"C'mon."

Miela led the way down East Bay Street to Broad Street just past the slave auction square and fought off a wave of painful memories. She knew the Blessing's home was only a few blocks down Broad Street, away from the water. She remembered the carriage rides to Blessing's boat and how

284

short a ride it seemed. But the walk seemed much longer. She led them over to the burned-out Catholic Church at the corner of Legare Street and Broad where she had them wait by the rubble while she took Jemps with her down the two blocks to the Blessing home. She found it exactly as she remembered. Four floors of towering light-brown stucco. She peeked inside the gate and came face to face with a tall Yank officer.

"Can I help you?"

Miela froze. "I'm sorry. We're trying to find out if Mr. Blessing's home."

The officer shrugged. "No civilian's here. No rebs about," he yawned.

"Are you a ... former slave?"

She smiled with relief. "Yes sir. We're a group of freed slaves looking for safe lodging. I figured our former owner might be willing to ... "

"I guess you can stay in the back. The officers from the 21st Regiment are taking this one here. There's a cookhouse back there and slave ... what used to be ... slave quarters. Help yourself but best do it before more refugees show up." He yawned again then turned quickly and went inside, slamming the massive door behind him.

"Thank you sir."

She led them around back and found the slave quarters empty.

"Thank God. Malcolm sure won't come back here with the Yanks about." She smiled at the thought of Mrs. Blessing's prized and 'loyal' town slaves having all runoff. She went inside. Both floors were in disarray as if they'd left in a hurry. Pots and pans, bedding, and old torn clothing lay in piles on the floor. She worked the thick sliding bolts on the inside of the door and figured they would be as safe here as anywhere, then quickly went back and retrieved the rest of the group.

That night they all slept soundly behind locked doors and under a roof for the first time since leaving Blessing. How long it had been? She tried to remember but it all blurred together. It couldn't have been more than ten days, she thought, but in a way, it seemed like an eternity.

CHAPTER 30 — DR. TRADD / CONNOR

Columbia, South Carolina

A t dawn a huge explosion rattled the walls and windows of the Hospital and silenced the barking dogs in the street. Dr. Tradd quickly dressed and went outside. Smoke rose over the railroad depot a few blocks away. Scores of bodies, smashed wagons, trunks and barrels were strewn in the rubble. Officers ran up as the smoke cleared, but more explosions rocked the warehouse rows towards the river. A Yank shell hit the third floor windows of a warehouse spraying brick fragments into the street. Dr. Tradd crouched behind a hitching post watching officers yell out orders to their cavalry guard. Troopers struggled to regain control of jumpy horses and mules as another group of officers came out of the front door of the house across the street guarding a dark haired general closely as if the Yanks were waiting for him in the next alley. Dr. Tradd smiled. There were more officers than men.

"Make Way for General Beauregard. Make way."

Dr. Tradd caught a quick glimpse of the famous man as his entourage hustled him around the corner to the lee of the building. Dark hair, olive skin and a waxed mustache, hurrying along crouched behind his escort as more shells landed just down the street cutting a wagon in half and killing the driver. More soldiers came running around the corner headed downhill towards the river and the Yanks. General Beauregard and his officers peaked out from behind the building and headed the other way.

Shells screeched overhead and more explosions echoed across the Capitol grounds two blocks away. Fleeing civilians and jubilant slaves hurried past a group of South Carolina militia, mostly teens and old men, crouched behind abandoned cotton bales alongside the brick walls of the Army Medical and Chemical Lab across the street. Men emerged from the broken door carrying bottles of medicinal alcohol. A militiaman called to his company.

"Better we finish it off before the Yanks, eh boys?"

Men cheered while others pulled out crates from inside the warehouse and pried them open. They handed out bottles while their officers clumped together on the far side of the road with backs carefully turned. Louisa came looking for him as the militia marched off swigging it all down as fast as they could. She looked them over and felt jealous. Many of them just young boys, mostly smiling and excited. Boys on a lark. One big lark. She wondered if the war meant anything to them. Didn't they know that their mothers would suffer an eternity if they died? It wasn't fair, she frowned. Men were totally thoughtless. So much so that they couldn't be even remotely related to women. They were closer to animals. She smiled to herself. Undomesticated, wild animals. So why did she have the sudden urge to go with them? She watched them disappear down the street yelling and whooping. It wasn't fair at all. And it never had been. Another mystery of life for sure. One of many. She saw Dr. Tradd coming back up the street towards the hospital and reminded herself to write it down in her diary.

"We need to pack up quickly. Get Emily, Edward and Harriet and go to the Asylum. They'll need help there for sure and it'll be the safest place in town when the Yanks come." He checked his watch. "The Yanks will be here within the hour I suppose."

He went inside and found the staff and surgeons gathering up the sick and wounded into the rooms closest to the courtyard.

"Just in case the hospital burns." The young surgeon sighed. He had a pistol in his belt

Dr. Tradd nodded in agreement. "We're going to the asylum. We'll take as many as we can in the wagon."

"No. They're safer all together in one place. Even Sherman wouldn't murder 65 sick and wounded in cold blood."

"Then you best put that pistol away. It will just tempt the Yanks."

"They'll damn well have to take it from me."

Dr. Tradd shrugged and walked away but turned at the door and said sternly, "Remember, your physician first. Your duty is to protect your patients."

He walked away without waiting for a response. Louisa quickly had the wagon hitched, and they rode up the street towards his cousin's house. Edward had climbed up the ladder to the roof with buckets of water and blankets and stationed himself there ready to stamp out any flaming embers or firebrands. Emily and Harriet had both put on three dresses and filled each pocket with silver spoons and forks, each wrapped in cotton so they wouldn't clink together.

Harriet's eyes were red and puffy from crying. "Why don't we just let them march through. Let them have Columbia. Let them have the whole state. They can't rule us forever. Certainly they won't stay for long." She waited for Dr. Tradd to say something, but he didn't, so she kept on with more of an edge. "They won't stay. You'll see. I just know they won't. Michigan boys want to be in Michigan. Pennsylvania boys, in Pennsylvania. Iowa, in Iowa. And so on, and so on. They'll leave and we'll get back to running things just like we left off. All we have to do is just pay them no mind."

"Best do it at the Asylum." Dr. Tradd motioned to Louisa and the wagon. "We'll be safer there."

"I'm definitely not leaving my house. I doubt they'll bother us if we stay inside."

"I don't know. This is Sherman. From what I've heard, his bunch is ... well, different."

"They're Christians aren't they? So are we. Certainly they'll respect that. We're absolutely not leaving. The Lord will protect us."

"Well I hope so. I hope He'll protect us all."

A squad of Confederate cavalry came up the street and stopped at the empty lot next door. They strained in their saddles to get a glimpse of the rifle fire down by the river. Harriet snapped at them. "Y'all better leave too. You're not doing us any good if the Yanks come, except getting yourselves killed and getting my house burned down. We have a better chance without you."

The troopers shrugged and moved on to the next a block where they had a better view and where no other civilians bothered them. None of them cared in the least if some rich lady's house burned down, but they did care a lot about being in the best spot to high-tail it when the time came.

Cannon fire rumbled closer as Lizzy, Harriet's house slave, walked slowly across the side yard with a bucket of freshly washed clothes. "I've already cooked supper, ma'am. Chicken stew, collards and sweet potatoes. Don't want y'all to go hungry." She walked back towards the kitchen, retrieved her things then went down the back steps with their bundle tied to a broom handle over her shoulder.

Harriet yelled at her from the living room window. "Lizzy, where are you going?"

"I'm leaving, Mrs. Walker. It's the time of the Jubilee. Don't you hear that? Mr. Sherman's coming. Everyone's free now."

"You can't just leave! I haven't given you permission."

"I'm sorry ma'am, but I have to."

"Why ... ? What ... ingratitude! Do you hear me? Ingratitude! Never ... never have I seen such! You want to leave me now? Why it's just ... just ... "

"Freedom!" Lizzy called out as she walked off down the street never looking back.

"Unbelievable," Harriet held out her hands to Dr. Tradd as if beseeching his support. "As well as we've treated her. To just walk off. Can you believe that?"

"Well ... Best come with us now."

"We'll stay put right here, Henry," she sighed. "God willing, we'll be all right. You go on if you must."

Dr. Tradd knew he didn't have time to wait for her stubbornness to budge. He climbed up the ladder and pleaded with Edward. "Please listen to reason. You'll all be safer at the Asylum."

"No, thank you. I'll stay right here. They can burn me alive if they choose, but God will know what they've done."

He refused to leave, and Dr. Tradd knew he'd run out of time. Louisa pulled the wagon around, and they hurried the mules up the hill towards the asylum.

THE COOL, BLUE SKY, DAY sprouted a rising wind. Rifle fire crackled in the distance and rose steadily to a continuous roar. The Yanks were coming across to the north. It was plain to everyone. The whole scout was soon up and mounted and riding up the road towards the gunfire. Other troops of cavalry rode past going the other way towards the city.

"The Yanks are moving across the Broad River," a courier yelled, as he reined in his horse. "Got a pontoon bridge down already."

Rifle fire erupted in the distance as he spoke. JB hurried the scout on to a covered bridge where gray infantry still held the far bank in the swirl of powder smoke and rifle fire. A Yanks skirmish line was pushing closer to the river on the far side. JB galloped down as close to the river as cover allowed, then lined up with the other scouts behind the willows and water oaks and took aim at the Yank infantry swarming down the far hills. Rifle fire soon made both banks disappear in clouds of smoke. They fired off a few volleys and slipped away.

Connor fired one last time as tree bark stung his face. He knew it was no use. Nothing could stop the Yanks. It was over. Killing a few more meant nothing. So why do it? He fired off another magazine and pictured his mother by the hearth cooking supper and lecturing him, her eyes cutting deep into his pride.

"Just forgive them Connor. Just forgive them."

He loaded another Spencer tube and fired off another seven shots. He could picture his mother shaking her head. "Be a good Christian. Turn the other cheek. Blessed be the peacemaker."

An officer trotted up and yelled to them, rousing him out of his trance. "Orders to burn the bridge! We need some volunteers!"

JB didn't hesitate. "Come on boys. That's us."

Barry, Connor and a dozen others followed him down a little swag a hundred yards or so from the bridge where they found a sunken road cutting down through the willows to the water's edge. Other troopers were already spreading out pine straw inside the near end of the bridge and dousing it with turpentine. The last of the retreating gray infantry were crossing back towards them under fire, running ran past more piles of pine straw bales that hadn't been spread out or soaked. Rifle fire erupted from the far end.

"Light them bales!" JB yelled. But the soldiers just hurried past.

"I'll do it," Barry ran inside before anyone could think. Men were already lighting fires behind him. Smoke filled the bridge.

"Get back here, Barry!" JB yelled. "What the hell are you doing?" A huge wall of flame shot up inside the bridge. Barry was barely visible beyond the flames, tossing more pine straw and turpentine. The Yanks were coming into the far end firing their Henrys.

"Get back here, Barry!" JB screamed.

The fire roared, engulfing the entire width of the bridge. Connor saw in an instant that Barry's only chance was to jump. JB saw it too.

"Jump! Jump into the river! Barry!"

JB and Connor tried to get closer but the heat push them back. The Yanks kept firing and they watched Barry cover his head with his coat and run towards them through the flames.

"Jump! Jump!' JB yelled, unable to do a thing.

Barry stumbled and disappeared in the inferno and reappeared twirling in the flames and slapping at his face. He fell through the bridge railing headfirst onto an island of boulders below. Blood trickled down the rocks from his back of his head. JB yelled at him, but Connor knew he was already dead. The Yanks volleyed and bullets thudded into the timbers around them. Connor and JB emptied their revolvers at the Yanks through the flames then pulled back to the road.

More volleys chipped at the rocks around Barry's body. JB groaned like he'd been gut shot. The bridge housing collapsed in a fireball on to the road bed and stopped the Yank skirmishers. Connor and the others dropped to the cover of the sunken road. Everyone knew Barry was dead, but no one wanted to admit it. No one wanted to give up a last hope just yet. They waited to be sure, watching the timbers burn for half an hour until the bottom fell out of the bridge into the roaring Broad River below. One big, flaming section fell on Barry's body and buried him. JB stood up and screamed.

"You God-damn bastards!"

He emptied his revolver again and dropped down groaning louder. He vomited between his legs then held onto his knees and sobbed. The men around him volleyed one last time then helped him back to the horses. Connor followed in a daze. It had all happened too fast. Why had Barry done it? What had possessed him? To do that this close to the end. He looked back at the bridge. Nothing was left but the stone pillars underneath and a few dangling flaming timbers.

Everyone remounted as the Yanks began paddling flatboats across the rocky shallows that splashed all around with rifle shots. The Yanks in front fired their Henrys at the tree line along the bank as the scout rode up the hill, stopped and spread out along a fence line about 200 yards above the willows. They vollied, but Henrys fired back faster than ever. The Yank boats came ashore. Blue jackets swarmed the trees, and a blue skirmish line pushed ahead. The Yanks already had a rope stretched across the river and pontoons were being dumped on the far bank, one after another. The pontoon bridge edged closer and men around Connor were already running for the rear.

"Come on Connor, it's time to git!" JB yelled from horseback beside him. "They've got another bridge down. The game's up."

Connor glanced up at his face. He was smiling as if nothing had happened.

JB fired his revolver. "This is shit! You hear me, Connor? Let's git!"

As they retreated, another gray line formed up and fired a volley at the blue skirmishers coming up the field. Connor felt a wave of nauseating, cold sweats. There was no reason for Barry to have died.....to have killed himself. It was useless. Christ! Why? But there was no time to understand any of it as they pushed up the road packed with retreating cavalry. Henry fire was picking up all around. Connor looked up at the half-finished State House dominating the far hill. He wondered if it would survive until morning.

BLACK SMOKE FROM THE TURPENTINE KINDLING poured out of every window of the railroad depot. It came straight through the solid brick walls in great exhaled puffs as Connor's entire scout and a mingling of other cavalry units pulled back through town. Nervous civilians peered out of windows. Others fled on foot by wagon north towards the Winnsboro Road. All firing ceased for a while. A thin picket line of horsemen stretched through a patch of pines and across a corn field down to thicker willows by the river where another butternut company appeared as if out of the ground, walking their horses into the willows only to disappear again. Connor realized his scout wouldn't be the last unit to pull out. An honor lost.

Other scouts clumped in the street beside the University and the Wayside Hospital waiting for a line of wagons and other cavalry regiments to move out of the way. Connor saw a familiar face in the crowd of civilians hurrying north along the side of the street beside the horsemen. Dr. Preston Wilson, Dr. Tradd's cousin, the man he'd met at Uncle Paul's three years ago before his uncle had died and before he had gone north to Spotsylvania. He weaved through the horsemen, dismounted, and tied Brig to a dogwood tree then caught up with Dr. Wilson tending to wounded in front of the hospital door. Orderlies carried litters of more sick and wounded to the nearby wagons. Anyone who had the strength to travel would escape capture. The rest would be at the Yanks' mercy. Connor thought of the skeletons at Sorghum and wondered how merciful they'd be.

Dr. Wilson didn't recognize him. Connor had to re-introduce himself then inquired about Dr. Tradd, wanting really to know about Henrietta.

"Do you know where he is? I mean is he safe?"

"He was right inside there, a while ago," Dr. Wilson jerked his thumb to this two-story white house surrounded by dozens more litters of broken men. "Might have gone up to the Asylum."

"He's here? In Columbia?" Connor's heart kept. It couldn't be. Henrietta? He scanned the crowd. Was she here?

"Yes. He must have evacuated Savannah just before Sherman came because he got here before me," Dr. Wilson tapped his foot impatiently, annoyed that he was wasting precious time.

"And his daughter Henrietta? Is she here too?" Connor's mouth went dry.

Dr. Wilson paused, squinted unpleasantly then shook his head. "No. She's not ... here."

Connor felt a wave of panic that got his heart racing even faster. Was something wrong? Had something happened to Henrietta? "Where is she?" His mouth was so dry he could barely get the words out. He watched Dr. Wilson take his time to form his reply while squinting hard and furrowing his brow.

"She's dead," he grimaced, knowing it had come out too harshly, a reaction to his own grief. Henrietta being the only member of the Tradd family, besides Dr. Tradd himself, who he'd ever cared for.

"Dead?" Connor's mind raced for an alternative. The word itself didn't absorb. Had he heard wrong? Had he said something else? "What do you mean?" He felt himself on a precipice.

Dr. Wilson's face stiffened a bit, suddenly aware that he was about to inflict deep pain. "She died in Savannah last month. Went down to visit Dr. Tradd. Died of biliary fever. Caught it from the wounded soldiers."

293

"Henrietta?" Connor couldn't fathom what he heard. "Surely not Henrietta."

"Yes, I'm afraid so. Henry had her buried there in Savannah. Couldn't even get her body home before the Yanks came."

Dr. Wilson's mouth kept moving, but Connor heard nothing else. He may have even said something in return, but he couldn't be sure. Then Dr. Wilson stopped talking suddenly and slipped away through the litters of wounded. A shell exploded somewhere in the distance, the concussion reverberating through the canyon-like warehouse rows and echoing off the red brick walls into Connor's chest and throat. He felt nauseous and squatted down behind the dogwood tree, the pit of his stomach ripped open. He bent forward until his head touched the brick sidewalk and threw up.

The horror of it screamed at him. Spasms of pain lanced through his chest. Henrietta ... dead. The words welled up like acid on his tongue. He focused for a while on the throng of refugees and horsemen pushing through the bottleneck of wagons overloaded with wounded. He waited for someone, Dr. Tradd perhaps, to run up, hug him, and say it was all a terrible mistake. That she was all right, that she wasn't dead. But there was no relief. Dr. Tradd never came to hug him. The pain lanced again, and the words kept slashing and stabbing. Henrietta, dead! He felt himself being lifted to his feet. JB and Fitts were standing beside him.

"What's wrong Connor? You sick? You been hit?" Fitts smiled nervously.

JB pulled his arm, "Come on Connor we've got to move. The scouts gonna screen the Winnsboro Road."

"No!" Connor jerked free. "I'm not leaving."

"Not leaving? Hell you say." JB leaned into his face, "You best come on. This here's where fevers are catching." He pointed to the yard full of litters as another shell exploded closer up the hill towards the Capitol.

"No time to waste neither."

"I'm not leaving, JB. Sorry, but I can't." He summoned up a reserve and spoke as if he were someone else. "A friend of mine died. I've got to stay. I've got to ... "

"We done lost a lot of friends," JB answered quickly, but restraining himself. "More than you know. No time for that now though. Come on and ride."

"No." Conner felt a calm warmth fill his stomach. "I don't care what happens to me. I'm just not leaving."

Fitts poked his shoulder, "Damn. I think the boy means it."

"I do."

JB grabbed his arm but just as quickly let go. He squinted and balled his fist, then let out a big, deep sigh. "Back in '61 or '62, the Major might've had you shot." He paused and smiled. "But... well...I guess things haven't worked out exactly like we planned, have they? Guess a man can choose when he's had enough."

"I've got to stay, JB." Connor's eyes teared up. "For what they've done ... to my friend."

Fitts offered his hand, "Well then ... Good luck to you Connor. Come look me up in Walterboro when this here's all over." His eyes were filling up too.

"And you ... in Charleston."

JB took Connor's hand as well. "I guess it's the living afterwards that's gonna be harder ... Harder than most people realize." He waved his hand at the crowds of fleeing civilians. "You take care of yourself, Connor. Like Fitts says, come see me in Tuscaloosa."

"Thanks JB. Good luck to you."

"You too, Connor." He turned quickly, his face squinting into pain, then jumped up in the saddle and trotted off without looking back. Connor retrieved his Spencer revolver and the last of his ammunition from his saddle. Fitts took Brig's reins and tried to say something else, but all he could do was nod and wave. Sam rode behind him and shouted out.

"Give 'em hell, Connor!"

Connor waved to them and felt another spasm of pain in his gut. But he knew what he had to do. All that mattered now was to avenge Henrietta. It didn't make any sense, but he didn't really care. It was the only thought that helped ease the pain. To do what he could to inflict punishment. On someone. Anyone. It didn't really matter who. And it didn't really matter what had happened before. The undercurrents of doubt were easily deflected. It wasn't the time to debate who was to blame or who caused what to happen or even who caused the war or why. None of that mattered now. Only to avenge her. To exact a suitable price. There was no question of why. That could wait. There was only the matter of how. It was the only important thing, and he knew the opportunity was at hand.

He never considered going inside the hospital to see Dr. Tradd. The idea of it made him sick. There wasn't room in his chest for any more pain. It already felt about to burst. Like a nest of snakes inside striking constantly as he stumbled down the hill to the taller warehouses, watching the last of the gray cavalry ride past. Any more pain would double him over in the street. As it was, he could barely walk. It felt just like he was hip deep in the surf.

He was vaguely aware of the crowds around him. Blacks began to outnumber whites. Connor saw their smiles and how they watched him carefully as he slowly moved past. He knew there was just a small window of opportunity. In a matter of minutes they would no longer be fearful of a white man with a rifle. The Yanks were close behind and the blacks knew that today was the beginning of their freedom. The gray jackets like Connor were no longer in control of their lives.

CHAPTER 31— LUKE / CONNOR

Columbia

The day of retribution had arrived. The day they'd all been waiting for. A clear blue sky, brisk north wind, and the beautiful view of a reb city of Columbia across the river. A city waiting to be devoured. To be served up for dinner lock, stock and barrel. Luke doubted that there was a hesitant soldier in the entire army. Columbia would be a luscious picnic lunch then destroyed like Carthage and not a tear shed. It would happen this very day. He felt a clarity of purpose he hadn't felt since the regiment first mustered in '61. All the death and suffering had led to this. It was a day to be savored. Every minute's worth.

The regiment moved down to the Broad River that swept along over a bed of rocks and boulders, churning itself in places into a yellow brown mush. Rapids in the river were a wonderful sight after all the dismal swamps. They could see the church spires of Columbia in the distance rising above the morning mist. A pontoon bridge inched closer to the far bank. Blue clad skirmishers crossed in rafts and rock-hopped the smaller section of river. More regiments fanned out into the woods down the hill stopping long enough to spray Henry fire at the rebel infantry hiding in the willow trees along the far bank. Pontoons and planking kept dropping into place until men were pouring across.

A burned bridge still smoldered just downstream. A black man was out in his little boat beside it, pulling up fish traps between the boulders as if nothing was happening. The blue soldiers crossing upstream cheered him. He gave them a brief wave in return then went back to pulling his traps and dumping fish into his boat. Luke felt a wave of homesickness. To be a working man again. To be carefree, back home, and away from all this. To live just for the beauty of the day. He took a deep breath. It was a comfort of sorts to know that at least one freed black man was already doing just that.

Their company crossed the shallows to a small island with a jumble of logs and willow trees that afforded scant cover from the reb snipers. Several soldiers were hit. One fell with a bullet to his neck. McMahon pulled him behind the logs and wrapped the wound tightly with a blanket strip as more shots spit at them. "Bastard rebs! Trying to shoot a wounded man? God damn you!"

Luke and Dave sprayed the far bank with their Henrys from behind a rock ledge. They watched rebs run back up the hill then drop behind a huge brick wall. More men were hit coming across the last of the shallows, but others were already climbing up the bank to higher ground, firing as they went. Everyone else quickly followed, up to a canal carved into the hillside paralleling the river.

"Christ almighty," Dave peered out at the brick wall where the rebs had retreated. "They've got us pinned."

"Hell you say," McMahon pointed to men already running across the open field beyond. "The rebs will disappear faster than groundhogs. Just you wait."

Luke reloaded and enjoyed a brief rest while other companies came across the shallows behind them. He liked the idea of the canal around the rapids. The rebs hadn't done so badly with this. Not a bad design at all. Cut right into the hillside, too. Maybe there were some good tow-boat men like his uncle right behind that brick wall up there. He stopped himself. They were damnable rebels nevertheless. Bastard bushwhackers, slavers, and traitors. He repeated it several times then followed the others across the narrow plank bridge over the canal and up a grassy hill to the brick wall.

He thanked God the bastards didn't stand and fight, remembering Fredericksburg and the slaughter that awful December morning. He could still see the row of gray and brown hats and the phalanx of rifles moving up and down behind that wall on Marye's Heights. The thought of it still gave him chills and a hollow nausea in his gut. Thank God for today. The wind in his face. The blue sky chasing the clouds along. It felt like a good Elmira spring day. Brought down to South Carolina on the north wind!

Their company led the brigade up the hill past the wall through corn and cotton fields. The reb Capitol stood a mile to the east. The reb flag still flew on the roof. Luke knew it wouldn't for long. They dropped down into a swag that ran straight up from the river between the higher land on both sides, coming out on a meadow of dandelions that stretched towards rows of brick warehouses sprawling down the slope towards the confluence of the two rivers. Up the hill, stately houses, churches, and tree-lined streets looked as well-kept as the situation allowed, but the ranks of soldiers were already surging towards them. Luke knew their orders. Don't loot or burn any occupied dwelling. But what white civilian would stay and face a frenzied army?

Men fired at rebel cavalry sneaking through a clump of willows past the rail depot in the distance. Luke knelt to take aim. He got off one shot before officers waved them forward towards town. Smoke and wisps of cotton floated on the rising north wind that grew stronger with the full morning sun.

"Like a picnic at first snow," Luke crumpled up a dandelion and let it fly in the wind.

"We'll have a picnic all right," Dave grinned. "A feast on Columbia."

The blizzard of loose cotton continued to fly about on the brisk wind that carried off the thin, gray smoke burning his eyes. "There's something chemical in it. Maybe the johnnies are burning hospital medicine or war machinery."

"No matter," McMahon shrugged. "They can burn all they want. Save us the trouble."

He pointed to a side street where white women and old men wore bandanas over their faces, hurrying gaggles of bundled up children away from the sprawling blue mob. The refugees looked back over their shoulders and flinched at the gunshots. A few pitiful slaves followed them, toting huge loads of family belongings and ignoring the growing crowds of singing blacks. Luke wondered. Didn't they know they were free now? Didn't they understand?

When he reached the crest of a hill, he could see long lines of civilians making their way to the north and west through the smoky windswept streets. Flames burst through the roof of a red brick building just up the hill. Billowing black smoke mixed with the white cotton snow and the gray haze from more distant fires. Another huge explosion rocked the town, followed by another even louder blast. Entire regiments flattened as one. Men all around looked up and cheered as they realized they were alive and unhurt. Brick fragments rained down and stung hard, but it all seemed part of a great celebration.

"Fireworks from the Johnnies!" McMahon yelled.

"We'll give them fireworks back!" Dave fired in the air.

The men around him howled and did the same. Luke knew what it meant. Columbia had an hour, maybe two. Then it would cease to exist. He pushed on with the others, reaching the new Capitol building at the top of the hill and finding a huge construction yard filled with slabs of marble, blocks of granite, piles of wooden trusses, and an assortment of wagons with blocks and pulleys. A tall wooden crane leaned up all the way to the unfinished roof where blue clad soldiers from another regiment were already ensconced under a flapping Union flag.

"Damn their hides," McMahon cursed. "They beat us to it."

"Well, let's go join them." Luke's head swirled. "Must be more room in the inn."

The rooftop boys fired a volley into the far streets, and all heads turned quickly to find their target. All that could be seen were more throngs of white civilians scurrying away from the approaching surge. They fired again, and a bucket was lowered from the roof to a group of soldiers on the ground, who filled it with wine and brandy bottles from cases stacked in two wheelbarrows. The bucket went up quickly to the men on the roof, and Dave grabbed two wine bottles left in the dirt. Luke picked his way through the piles of marble blocks then past a huge copper sculpture of a palmetto tree embedded in a granite base. Soldiers took turns urinating on it. Luke joined them, laughing. What a joy. To piss on the state symbol. The bastard state that started the whole damn thing.

"What the hell?" McMahon flinched at another volley close by."Drinking and picking off civilians?" He shook his head and smiled. "That ain't right."

"Don't bother me none," Dave shrugged. "Should've had enough sense to leave before all this."

Luke pushed him from behind. "C'mon. Let's get up there,"
Dave led the way, up ladders to the main balcony then inside to a staircase that led to another series of ladders to the roof. Soldiers were sprawled everywhere inside, rapidly getting drunk. They stepped over them and climbed out onto the open roof which was bordered on the

edges by a three foot, granite wall. A group of eight men were kneeling and shooting over it towards the north.

"Got one!" A dark bearded drunk yelled out. "Picked him off his horse, clean."

"Cavalry?" One of the others jumped up to look.

"Nope, just a reb lover. Should've stayed home." He eyed McMahon and Dave. "What you fellas want?" He swigged a bottle of wine and wiped his face.

"We've got orders to take the building." McMahon glanced over the roof edge and felt dizzy at the height.

"Put those orders up your ass," the dark beard answered then spat over the side. His friends all laughed. "You boys can visit with us for a while, though. Name's Webster." He swung his Henry around and fired into the air.

"That's fine," Luke nodded, knowing that a drunk soldier with a Henry was not a man to cross. "We appreciate your hospitality."

Webster laughed. "Yep, we got a lot to offer too. We're herding rebs y' see. Up yonder." He waved his hand to the west and sat back down.

"I see you brought your own bottles, too. That's good planning."

Dave passed one to him. "Here's to herding rebs.'

"To herding rebs!"

They shared the bottle and another of Webster's then joined them with a volley into the air.

"You boys are all right." Webster took another gulp.

Luke urinated over the side. "Do you mind if we stay here all month?"

Webster coughed up liquor through his nose. "No, not one bit."

ABOUT 500 YARDS AWAY, Connor had climbed up to a ware house attic. He checked his cartridges, squeezed his head out of a vent window and took a look down the street. The riverfront and the fields beyond the warehouse-district swarmed with the Yank soldiers. Thousands of blacks followed them clapping their hands, jumping up and down, and screaming. He could see a Union flag fluttering above blue jackets on the unfinished Capitol roof to the northwest. The soldiers' heads poked up above the roof edge. It would be a long shot, but he'd try. The slats would help steady the barrel, and no one below in the streets would pay much mind to another rifle shot. Chaos and random firing continued everywhere. He elevated the rear sight for maximum range, took a deep breath then squeezed off a round. Nothing happened. He fired a dozen more times until all of the rooftop blue jackets suddenly disappeared.

A PIECE OF GRANITE chipped off the wall by Luke's head and ricocheted across the roof.

"What the hell? Was that one of our boys?" McMahon leaned over the wall to get a view.

"Got to be a sniper," Dave whispered, as if the reb was listening.

Another bullet smacked the granite as a volley of gunshots erupted below.

McMahon pointed over the edge. "Just stray shots, I bet. The johnnies aren't suicidal." He put his hat on his rifle barrel and held it up. Nothing happened.

"I don't know. I bet he's over yonder. See that warehouse row?" Luke stayed down, pointing with his rifle barrel.

"You boys are too scaredy-cat," Webster stood up and waved his hands. "Johnny! Up here. Got your Capitol! What you gonna do about it?"

All the drunks laughed as he danced a jig and undid his pants to give Columbia a view of his privates.

CONNOR SAW THE BLUEJACKET on the roof jumping up and down.

"Thank you," he smiled and squeezed off another round. The soldier disappeared.

"Not much fun getting shot, is it?"

Thoughts of Norton and Chesire bombarded him until he swatted them away. He told himself this was entirely different. Bastard Yanks deserved what they got. They could all rot in hell. He was merely the avenging angel that would send them there. He thought of Henrietta and the pain impaled him until he doubled over.

THERE WAS NO SOUND when the bullet hit Webster's arm. At first everyone laughed. He spun down and yelled as blood splattered over the granite.

"Shit! Dammit!" He sat down and felt his elbow. The bone was splintered and a piece stuck out the back of his torn sleeve. One of his friends tied a tourniquet and two others helped him down the ladder. Luke figured he'd be minus an arm by dark, but the alcohol kept him from caring too much.

"Bastards," Dave whispered. "We'll make them pay for that. Columbia will keep us warm tonight."

"No doubt about that," McMahon agreed, finishing off another bottle.

They kept their heads down below the roof wall except to rise up to fire randomly towards the north. Luke bobbed his hat up and down on his bayonet just above the wall, but nothing happened. McMahon stood up, dropped his pants, and pissed over the wall. He took his time to finish then sat down untouched.

CONNOR HEARD COMMOTION BELOW in the warehouse and mens' voices getting closer. Time to run for it. He ditched the rifle and his gray cap, and stuffed his revolver under a shirt, then slid out onto the roof and shimmied down a telegraph pole to the alleyway where he rummaged through a pile of discarded clothes. In less than a minute, he was cloaked in an oversized black jacket and walking beside the columns of the infantry, along with the cheering blacks and the white Unionists who had appeared out of nowhere. He even grabbed a little homemade Union flag that floated to him on the wind. It's got to be God's Will, he smiled. His chance to avenge Henrietta's death before making it back to Wheeler, if he could. He winced at another knife stabbing into his gut but strained down and fought it off.

"By God," he whispered. "I swear I'll kill me at least one more of the bastards before the night's over." And his smile was the only part of his act that he didn't have to fake.

CHAPTER 32 — THE ASYLUM

Columbia

Smoke drifted through the air. Cannon fire rumbled in the distance. The north wind quickened, cutting a chill through Dr. Tradd's heavy coat. Rifle fire crackled closer towards the west. The wagon clattered past a group of children climbing an oak tree for a better view. A line of civilian wagons stuffed with men, women and children, and their assorted bags, trunks, and crates, were already moving past the Asylum towards the Winnsboro Road. The big, iron gate stood unperturbed at the end of a dirt lane, thick bars firmly shut tight against unwanted entry. The word 'Asylum' was imprinted in the mortar above the six towering white columns of the main red brick building. A skinny old man dressed in a yellow jacket and green pants sat on a stool in a small wooden hut by the gate. A whistle dangled from his neck. He stood up as the wagon approached.

"Yes Sir?" The man scratched himself.

"I'm Dr. Tradd from Charleston. I've come to assist Dr. Parker."

The old man nodded, wrote something on a piece of paper and then blew his whistle, making the mules jump. He smiled at Louisa.

"It just lets them know I'm opening the gate."

Louisa smiled back. "Yes, I'm sure that's quite necessary."

"Don't want them inmates running loose, do we?" The old man turned to Dr. Tradd. "You'll find Dr. Parker down past the nitre beds, over yonder."

Dr. Tradd helped him open the gates wide enough to allow the wagon to pass under the brick arch. Louisa drove the mules and wagon to the rear of the main building past the salt works, a collection of long low sheds with rows of small vats that sat over fire pits. He found Dr. Parker coming out the next building that housed the nitre beds and greeted his old friend. The pungent ammonia smell drifted over them with the breeze.

"The Army's work," Dr. Parker nodded towards the nitre beds inside the double door. "Never enough of anything anymore, especially nitrogen for powder ... but maybe there never was."

Dr. Tradd caught a deep whiff and snorted reflexively. Dr. Parker laughed. "Patients don't seem to mind. They get used to it. Some even like it after a while. Maybe someday the right odor will help cure insanity. You never know."

"Fomites of the brain? " Dr. Tradd knew his friend shared his own curiosity regarding infectious disease. "The etiology of the deranged mind?"

Dr. Parker shrugged, "Only the Lord knows. But my, my....it's good to see you, old friend."

He stood just a bit over five feet tall. His stance cocked a bit to the side, with his hands on his hips, dark hair, clean-shaven and bright twinkling blue eyes. He was trim and fit even at age 60 and looked to Dr. Tradd as if he could have been a blockade runner or bull fighter just as well as a thoroughly decent guardian of the insane, a man who had done everything in his power to protect and provide for his patients, even with the war shortages. They walked together to his office in the main building listening to more explosions in the distance. Louisa tended to the mules.

"It'll be hell for a few days. Might even get myself shot," Dr. Parker opened his office door and laughed.

"I doubt Sherman wants to shoot Asylum superintendent's. He'd have to take care of the inmates, wouldn't he?"

Dr. Parker shook his head. "Yank prisoners. Seventeen of them. In the basement. The Army took the rest by train to Charlotte just yesterday." He took a deep breath. "Skeletons mostly. Walking skeletons. See the fences behind the male dormitory?" He pointed out his window. "We had a thousand of them out there for the past few days. The Army decided to move them all when Sherman got past the Salkehatchie. The last seventeen are down in the basement. It's warmer down there."

"Too weak to move?"

"Most of them, yes. A couple of brave souls stayed to help." His eyes sparkled. "God, I hate this damn war. I doubt Sherman will be too happy about it either. Sure wish the Army had just let him have his sick men back. Parole them for God's sake." Dr. Parker sighed and stretched his muscular arms. "Men kept in prisons to rot because the politicians can't come to an agreement. But what the hell. There's no use whining."

"Well, you've done what you could." Dr. Tradd looked out the window at the fenced yard.

"I think so, yes,"Dr. Parker nodded. "We bathed and fed those last seventeen. Got them all new clothes. But it won't be enough for most of them. Dysentery and starvation for the past few months in other camps. I doubt half of them will live another week."

"Can I help?"

"You can help me with the milk and bread. What's left of it. We have just enough for the next week. Most of the orderlies have gone. No telling what who'll be left by morning. If the Asylum still here, that is."

Dr. Parker sat down and wrote something in the asylum ledger and smiled. "And do you know who has given us the money to keep going this long?"

Dr. Tradd shook his head.

"General Wade Hampton himself. He doesn't want his name mentioned. It's his only request in return for years of financial support. So you're now sworn to secrecy. And you know what else? He insisted that we omit the names of all patients from any official report ... to protect their privacy. I tell you, he's a thoroughly decent gentleman. He's kept these patients clothed and fed with a bit left over for medicines for the last two years. Of course he didn't anticipate all these prisoners, so there was less to go around ... But still ... "

"Wade Hampton?" Dr. Tradd had heard the rumors of his generosity while in Savannah, but he hadn't believed it.

"Yes. But remember, you're sworn to secrecy," Dr. Parker smiled. "For a good cause."

Dr. Tradd nodded and followed him downstairs to help with the boxes of stale, hard bread.

"Well, at least today the inmates will eat well." Dr. Parker broke off a chunk from one of the hard loaves. "The prisoners too." He stuck his head out the door and called to someone in the dark archway down the hall. "Milk and bread! Let's go!"

A young man appeared in the doorway dressed in a long brown coat. He staggered with exhaustion and barely noticed Dr. Tradd. "Yes sir, Dr. Parker."

Two older men appeared behind him and helped carry the boxes of bread down the hallway. Two others came from outside carrying buckets of milk. Dr. Tradd followed along to the patient wards and helped them feed the inmates. They sat on low wooden cots with thin cotton mattresses, eight to ten to a room with a young boy and an old man tending to the men, and two young nurses to the women. The patients were dressed in gray-night shirts. Dr. Tradd noticed that they were at least clean and decently nourished. Most picked at the bread sullenly. Only the agitated insane, who were chained in dark rooms and guarded by larger boys, refused to eat anything.

Dr. Parker sighed and shook his head. "We've tried everything. Cold water. Hot baths. Tight blanket wraps. Exercise. Sleep deprivation. Bed rest. But none of it works. Once they get agitated into delirium, they wither and die within weeks. Sometimes days."

A frail, elderly woman thrashed on a chair, her wrists and ankles bound by thick leather belts, her face contorted into a fierce grimace, her mouth opened as if yelling but without making any sound.

Dr. Parker patted her foot. "She'll die in the next few days. Forced feeding just agitates them worse. We always try ... What else can we do, but ... someday. Someday."

He led Dr. Tradd and two orderlies down the corridor to the basement steps. "We'll take the rest of the milk and bread to the prisoners. They're locked up down here." He pointed down the cold stone steps. A stench rose up the dark stairwell past the two, home-guard sentry boys with shotguns who squatted on the stairs playing cards.

Dr. Parker stepped between their card game. "Boys, we're taking the prisoners some food."

"Hey doc, Are these last ones going up to Charlotte too?" The bigger boy asked.

"Doubt it," the smaller one chuckled and made a face behind Dr. Parker's back. "I bet they'll croak right here."

Dr. Parker stopped and looked down at them with a pained face, "Boys, listen here. These men are prisoners of war and deserve to be treated like human beings." He slid the big iron bolt loose and opened

307

the door. Two prisoners just inside the door stood up. The others didn't move at all. The stench of excrement assaulted Dr. Tradd. He reflexly gagged, but stopped himself. Damn it, be calm. These are human beings by God!

Dr. Parker shook his head. "We've bathed them yesterday and gave them beef broth and bread since the others left. Fresh clothes too. But as you can see ... Damn dysentery."

Dr. Tradd saw it all too well. Men lay in their own filth, arms, hands, and faces covered with sores and boils. Men who'd been kept in open fields without shelter in winter, half starved to death and left to rot in their own extrement, then moved here already half dead. He knew it wasn't Dr. Parker's fault He could barely care for his own patients, and these men were already too far gone. He covered his nose with his sleeve, stooped down and wiped vomitus from a man's cheek and put a clean piece of cloth from a milk crate under his head.

"There were a thousand more?" Dr. Tradd asked, passing out milk and bread.

"Yes. At least there were three days ago. No telling how many are left now."

Dr. Parker helped a man who couldn't lift his head drink a cup of milk. "I'm Dr. Parker. This is fresh bread and milk. It's all we have. Drink. C'mon now, drink."

An orderly fetched soap and water and washed off some of his filth. Dr. Tradd made sure that the other weaker prisoners got at least as much milk as they could manage then left the rest of the bread and milk on the floor by the door.

The two standing men thanked him then gulped down more mouthfuls. They went back around and gave more milk and bread slices to all the rest you could eat. A few shook their heads. Others didn't move at all.

"Nearly dead," one of the standing Yanks said. "These two ain't moved for three days. Ain't pissed neither. Just the diarrhea."

Dr. Tradd went over and knelt beside them. He felt each man's thready pulse. Barely alive indeed. He knew they wouldn't live more than a few more hours. He glanced back at Dr. Parker and shook his head. Dr. Parker rubbed his temple then called up the stairs to the sentries.

"Come down here and help us with these men. Damn it, I will not let them die in this damn basement."

The boys came down the stairs cautiously with their shotguns leveled at the Yanks.

"Help us carry these two," he ordered.

The smaller boy obeyed, but the big one just stood there holding his shotgun ready while the rest of them managed to get the wafer thin Yanks out the narrow doorway. The small boy frowned.

"He stinks like shit. Light as a feather, too."

"Yes. The Army's starved him to death," Dr. Tradd replied icily.

The big boy locked the bolt behind them and made another face at Dr. Parker as one of the Yanks called to them from the other side of the door.

"Thank you doc. I won't forget it. Never."

Dr. Parker started to answer but just shook his head and went up the stairs. He had them carry the Yanks to spare beds in one of the wards and had a nurse wash them again and dress them in clean night shirts. Dr. Tradd saw the anguish in his friend's face as he looked up at him.

"I wish to God we'd had them sooner. Maybe Sherman will offer a hand." He glanced up to the window and listened to the rifle fire getting closer. "Henry!" He called out.

A young blond haired boy came running up the hallway. "Yes sir!"

"Tell everyone to get away from the windows. And tell Martha and John to check the yard and garden and make sure everyone's inside."

"Yes sir!" He smiled eagerly and ran off yelling for the others.

Dr. Parker smiled. "War is always such a great lark for teenage boys. As long as they don't get dysentery or get shot."

"That's it All right," Dr. Tradd smiled, helping dress the Yanks' boils and sores. "War is designed for boys."

"By old men like us."

"Cantankerous old men?"

"Exactly."

When they were finished, he followed Dr. Parker outside where they watched the last of Wheeler's cavalry ride past headed towards the Winnsboro Road. Dr. Parker had the staff hand out a bit of the milk and bread to the passing gray -coats. He considered delving into the patient's last week of supplies but held firm. He figured it might take longer than he'd planned for more supplies to come.

"Maybe we should have kept more in reserve," he sighed. "But ... No, I will not have this Asylum run by fear. We will prevail. By God. Supplies will come. A week will be long enough."

Dr. Tradd nodded, but knew his friend was taking a big chance. He watched the last of the cavalry ride off then followed him back to the infirmary and helped tend to three inmates with pneumonia, cupping them with warm glasses and helping them swallow milk spiked with brandy. Four more had jaundice and fever. He hoped it wasn't the biliary type.

Pain stabbed at him and nearly doubled him over. For a second his brain wouldn't even allow the thought, but then it slashed at him harder than ever. Henrietta. He remembered her swollen belly, yellow eyes and raging fever. Nothing had relieved her agony but opium and death. He caught his breath and refocused on the patient in front of him. It was the only way to go on. He barely heard Dr. Parker talking.

"Everything's in short supply, but we have twenty crates of madeira in the basement, courtesy of The Charleston Jockey Club. We've been using it to dilute the last of the laudanum and opium. I'm sure the Jockey Club would approve."

"Yes ... I'm sure they would," Dr. Tradd gathered himself and felt the icy knife in his chest slowly melt away.

The gatekeeper's whistle blew, and Dr. Parker had Louisa and the orderlies finish tending to them. Dr. Tradd followed him outside, taking deep breathes as if surfacing from underwater. A troop of blue cavalry was already swarming through the gate and surrounding the main building. Dr. Parker spoke with an officer and led him and a squad of soldiers down to the basement to the prisoners. He ordered a hospital wagon to be brought up. The orderlies, nurses and the two home guard boys, now disarmed, helped load the prisoners into the wagon. Dr. Tradd could hear the cavalrymen cursing.

"Bastard Rebs. They should all be shot."

The Yank officer spoke with Dr. Parker on the front steps then nodded and mounted back up. The troopers around him continued to grumble until a burly, red-haired sergeant yelled at them.

"Shut up and follow orders. The lieutenant says spare the hospital and that's what we're gonna do."

The troopers obeyed, but Dr. Tradd realized it was a close thing. The Yanks rode off with the prisoners and the gate was then locked shut behind them. Dr. Tradd breathed easier. The pain in his chest was dissipating, and he had patients to care for, thank God. He went back to on the wards, helping tend to the inmates, and by afternoon they could smell the smoke getting thicker and saw fires less than a mile away. They all knew Columbia was doomed. Saving the Asylum was the key. Every orderly and nurse was ordered to carry a water bucket and blanket. Dr. Tradd made sure Louisa was safe and well protected in a ground floor staff room.

"Thank the Lord the Asylum is fireproof," Dr. Parker tapped the thick stucco walls.

Dr. Tradd smiled, "Let's hope it's also Sherman proof."

"A much harder feat of engineering to be sure," Dr. Parker laughed.

They went up to the roof-top balcony and sat down on a bench. A column of smoke rose from the western part of the city. Within an hour, they could see flames rising up from several different places in an arc from west to south. They watched for a while then went back down, checked on the inmates, and helped the orderlies and nurses, then climbed back up the stairs to watch some more. Both of them went up and down the stairs a dozen times or so. Others did the same. Everyone wanted to see what was happening. Each trip to the roof brought the flames closer. Rifle shots and bigger explosions ripped the smoky air. Occasional stray bullets hit the front facade. A window on a landing facing town exploded in shards of glass cutting Louisa on her nose and cheek. Dr. Tradd grabbed her and pulled her down below the sill.

"I'm All right," she said, panting and trembling.

Dr. Tradd felt her head and neck to make sure. "No bullet wound, thank God."

He wiped her nose and cheek with his handkerchief and waited there with her until the closest rifle fire subsided then led her down the stairs to the infirmary where he cleaned and bandaged her cheeks and bloody nose.

She smiled at him as his hands held her face. "I guess God doesn't want me up on that roof."

311

Dr. Tradd wiped off a trickle of blood from her nose and fought off a swarm of visions of Henrietta. He patted Louisa's temple and neck and nodded, "The Lord wants to protect you." Tears filled his eyes. "And rightfully so. You more than anyone else." He caressed her hair. She was such a good person. God would certainly not allow her to be harmed.

"I swear I'm All right. But God sure does work in mysterious ways, don't he." She squeezed his hand. "I guess all we can do is trust in His mercy and do the best we can ... Like you do every day, Dr. Tradd. You're heaven sent for sure."

For a second, she was Henrietta. His heart flipped over on its side. Dr. Tradd turned away so she wouldn't see him crying then he walked out of the room quickly. If he didn't look back, Henrietta would be alive. He knew it was nonsense but didn't dare turn around even when Louisa called to him.

"I'll rest here for a few minutes and then go help the nurses. You be careful, sir."

"You too," he answered over his shoulder, hurrying back up the stairs to the shattered window and looking out at the swath of fires burning across town. Rifle fire crackled in the distance, but he refused to move from the open window.

"God, you can take me anytime you please. Just protect Louisa. You know it's the right thing to do." He said it out loud and waited until the rifle fire ended. Nothing came close though, so he went up to the roof and watched the fires until Dr. Parker retrieved him.

"C'mon Henry. Best eat a meal. They've got rice and fried chicken ready. We'll eat then make last rounds for the night. God willing."

Dr. Tradd roused himself. "I think you're right. No telling what will be left by breakfast. Better eat that chicken while we can."

CHAPTER 33 — CONNOR

Columbia

Connor had no idea which way to head, but figured uphill was best. He found another old patched jacket in the street and helped himself to wine bottles from the smashed storefront. He broke one bottle and poured it all over himself then gulped down a few mouthfuls of another and cracked open the third. Another two-fisted drunk civilian wouldn't matter to the Yanks.

What he was about to do was wrong, but he didn't give a damn. He would go to his deathbed knowing he'd done what he needed to avenge Henrietta. At least one Yank would pay with his life. Uncle would say 'Brave talk' but he didn't care. He walked up through an empty field towards the Capitol building and the center of town. Smoke swirled in the wind. Houses just past the warehouse row burst into flames. Drunk soldiers with firebrands ran down the alleyways and side streets. The heat was intense as he walked past, but he didn't mind. The only people fool enough to push straight into Columbia's Inferno were Yank soldiers and drunks. Every sober civilian was headed the other way, dragging along bundles and bags or pushing overladen carts like the families he saw headed back down toward the river.

He staggered along pretending to swig the bottles, keeping watch for the right target, having made up his mind he wouldn't kill a just any raging drunk. He'd find at least one bastard clear enough in the head to know better ... and make him pay.

Yanks howled and sang up and down the street, but most were staggering along with half empty liquor bottles themselves. Here and there men laughed and urinated at the flames, others whipped with each other with cut-off pieces of fire hoses. The city burned around them. Soldiers danced and yelled in the firelight. Connor waved his bottles and danced with them from street to street. A few soldiers cheered him along, but none had much reason to think about him at all. He was just like

313

everyone else. Drunk and enjoying the evening immensely. The bottles made him part of the mob, and he knew better than to open his mouth and give away his accent.

He caught his breath and moved away quickly. Fires roared from every house up the street. Connor kept to the shadows and watched Yanks drift by in twos and threes, all drunk and yelling, with torches in hand and pillowcases full of loot. Two more emerged from a doorway holding a naked black girl by her wrists. The rest of the Yanks disappeared further up the street in the smoke.

Connor looked around. No other Yanks were visible. He didn't stop to think. He picked up a brick, leaped over the wall, and ran towards them. The roar of the fires drowned out his footsteps. The Yanks never saw him coming. He smashed the brick into the first Yank's head at full speed. He crumpled instantly. He fired his revolver point-blank into the other Yank's chest. The man fell backwards over the fence. The black girl crouched down terrified and mute. Blood dripped down her legs and from her mouth and nose. Her hands were tied at the wrist. Connor pulled his knife to cut her loose toward the flames beginning to lick out the doorway behind her.

"No! Please don't," she begged on her knees.

"I won't hurt you." Connor knelt beside her and touched her arm.

"No, please!" She shivered and trembled, moaning in terror.

He grabbed her hands and cut her loose before she could pull way then pulled out a blanket from one of the Yank's packs and wrapped her up. She sobbed in heaves but let him lead her away to a dark spot in the field where two walls merged beside a gully. A small lean-to hut stood in the corner over a wood pile.

"Hide here. Cover up in the blanket. No one will find you. I'll get you some food. I'll be right back."

She shivered all over and squatted down in the shadows, nearly invisible with the blanket covering her. Connor went back to the dead Yanks and took their tins, hardtack and canteens. He left everything else. He knew the penalty for wearing captured Yank clothes or equipment. A quick death, if he was lucky. Better to leave it. He found a discarded quilt along the edge of the field and went back to the girl. She put her hand up again as if he might attack her.

"It's all right. You're safe." He patted her arm, and she calmed down a bit. He wrapped her in the quilt and opened the tins with his knife. "Stay here until the Yanks leave. They'll be gone tomorrow or the next day. Just stay here until they're gone."

She nodded and wiped blood from her nose. "Thank you Mister." Her hands trembled. Tears ran down her face.

Connor patted her shoulder again and trotted off keeping to the shadows. His brain was a big jumble. It wasn't guilt or remorse or shame. Not anger either, and certainly not satisfaction. Just a cold emptiness that felt like ice melting in his gut. He remembered what his uncle had said to him before he'd left for Virginia and Spotsylvania. About revenge and hate.

"It's the devil's finger, my boy. One finger is all you should ever allow inside. Well, maybe two at the most ... some of us, three ... but I don't recommend it. Especially not you. You're a bit weak minded for that. And If he gets his whole hand inside, you're dead meat ... down his path forever. A man has to have the backbone to say 'no' when the time comes. When he starts slipping in the whole hand ... watch out ... it's too late. Way too risky for you, my boy. Hail Mary's won't suffice, either. Sometimes even a lifetime's worth of rosary recitals aren't enough. Yep, I think one finger is plenty ... for you."

Connor felt the ice-melt inside his gut. It moved slowly, wormlike, up his throat. He choked for a few seconds and spit out a mouthful of dark bile. Maybe Uncle Paul was right. One finger was enough. Connor thought about the men he'd killed and had a moment of regret. Were they the right sort to kill? Maybe an officer would have been better? Maybe there was still time for more. He looked back and watched the flames quickly lick up to the roof of a three story house. The walls of the house trembled and slowly bent inward. The roof sagged and collapsed in a fireball.

The heat baked his face and, as he watched the flames, it occurred to him that Henrietta lived in a three-story house. Pain quickly snatched at his throat, and he braced himself, but it wasn't as bad as he'd feared. He relaxed his guard and wondered if maybe this was a sign. A new beginning. Maybe God was telling him something. Maybe she was still alive. He knew it was nonsense but latched onto the thought. She was still alive. Dr. Wilson was mistaken. He'd seen the pain in his eyes, and he knew the truth deep down, but still... As long as the fires raged, maybe his dream would still come true, and the longer he watched the more convinced he became.

He waited for a while until another group of soldiers had moved on then walked along for an hour or so past block after block of burning houses. He thought about killing another Yank or two. Guilt and doubt were still easily kept at bay. Four cartridges were left and easy targets abounded everywhere. Drunks staggering along in twos and threes loaded down with loot. He could kill them and quickly disappear to smoke. No one would ever know.

"Do it, boy," he could just about hear his uncle urging him.

"No don't," his mother cried, as if both were standing in front of him arguing. "Let your heart be at peace. Let them go, Connor. Do you hear me? Blessed be the peacemaker."

"Kill them first," Uncle laughed. "Then have all the peace you want."

"No! Save your soul!"

"Don't worry about that. It's long beyond saving."

He turned into a blazing street listening to his uncle's laughter then down past a brick wall surrounding a church cemetery. The firelight danced on the graves making shadows like ghosts rising up to watch the inferno. A lone Yank holding a wine bottle stood on top of a marble crypt urinating down on a stone angel that looked like a little girl with wings. Connor walked up to him as a buttoned up his trousers. The wine bottle flashed red then purple as thick smoke covered the graveyard. The Yank jumped down and nodded then saw the revolver pointed to his chest and dropped the bottle. Connor fired. The Yank fell back over the angel. His hat flew off, and the smoke cleared for a second. A burst of flame from the house across the street lit his face. Connor saw he was just a boy. Maybe seventeen or so. His face smooth and pink in the firelight. Connor knelt down quickly, feeling a sudden weight on his shoulders. He looked around. No one was there, just as he'd expected. But the sudden shame if it surprised him. He dropped the revolver. Had it just burned his hand? He touched it again and it felt ice cold. He could hear his uncle whispering in his ear.

"Don't be a fool. Keep the pistol. He might be a boy, but he was no cherub."

Then he could have sworn he heard his mother saying Hail Mary's. He picked up the pistol, stuck it back in his belt and hurried away. He refused to look back. He told himself as long as he didn't, the boy would be all right and that he'd done no more than was required for Henrietta. But deep inside, he knew the truth. He found a brick staircase standing alone over a smoldering ruin and crawled underneath exhausted. Sleep descended fitfully bringing a dream of two little boys playing with the huge revolver that fell to the floor and fired into the younger boy's forehead. It startled him awake for a while, and he felt the icy snow-melt in his gut slowly rise again to his face and cover him in darkness.

CHAPTER 34 — LUKE

Columbia

Luke waited on the roof with the others until just before dark, drinking wine and enjoying the view. No one seemed to be in charge below. Bonfires had sprouted out in several spots to the northwest, and smoke had thickened into a fast-moving fog. They all decided it was time to go back down and join the chaos in town.

They walked up the hill towards a burning church steeple that roared like a giant torch. The houses on both sides of the street next to it quickly lit up like a string of fireworks in the wind-whipped inferno. Soldiers manned a steam powered pump engine that began throwing out a stream of water into the blaze until a mob of drunks surrounded them, slashing every hose with their bayonets, and blasting the water barrels with their Henrys. Men cheered as the water poured out into the street. Others tied down the steam release valve and ran for cover, laughing and drinking. They watched from a safe distance until the boiler blew up, sending shrapnel clattering against the burning houses.

House after house erupted in flames. The fire spread to the roof of a red brick building on one side of the wide lawn of the South Carolina College flying a yellow reb hospital flag. Wounded reb soldiers screamed from inside as smoke and flames quickly spread. Doctors, nurses and a few Union soldiers fought the blaze with wet blankets while others worked a hand-pump water wagon. An officer stood guard warding off drunken soldiers bent on stabbing the hoses. Two badly burned rebs crawled out of the hospital door as flames sprouted from the eaves above them. The roof collapsed into the second story. Luke and Dave help the rebs to the safety of the open square then stepped back and watched, knowing no one left upstairs could still be alive.

Just off the grassy square, another brick building swarmed with hundreds more Confederate wounded. Drunk cavalrymen were yelling at the nurses to get out of the way. An older nurse stood in the doorway.

Her white apron was bloodstained. Her hands rested on her hips. "These are wounded prisoners. All they want is to go home. You will not go in there and harm them." Her voice was strong and clear, but one stumbling cavalryman just laughed.

"We ain't gonna hurt them. We're gonna shoot them." He fired his carbine into the ground at her feet.

She spread her arms across the doorway. "You'll have to shoot me first."

"All right then," he smiled, turning to the others while reloading his rifle. "See? See what she's making me do?"

"Stop!" An officer rode up on horseback. "General Howard says leave all prisoners alone." He nudged his horse past the drunk cavalry man who backed off and took a long swig from a bottle for the officer's benefit.

"Yes sir," he saluted, weaving back and forth. "But can we at least burn something else?"

The officer wheeled his horse in a circle and smiled. "He didn't say anything about the library," pointing across the lawn to men carrying arm loads of books down from a columned portico. The drunks cheered and surged over to help. A huge bonfire of books soon raged, spreading to the entire library building as thousands of books fed the flames. The old nurse wiped her brow and watched unperturbed. She figured they could always get more books.

She and the other nurses and nuns helped tend to more badly burned rebs that Luke and others helped carry to safer spots on the grass by a cistern. One man was charred all over. The nuns doused him with cold water to try to help ease the pain. Luke gave him a sip of brandy, but the reb coughed up blood and died. The nuns blessed themselves and whispered a prayer in his ear while other burned, wounded, or sick soldiers begged for help. Luke gave an old reb another sip of brandy. The bone of his leg glistened white through an open wound.

"There weren't no joy in that," he hissed. "Names Patrick. From just up the road in Winnsboro. Hell of a mess, ain't it."

"That it is."

Luke gave him more brandy. He looked around at the carpet of filthy, wounded men and remembered the awful days back at Chattanooga after the carnage at Chickamauga. Men spread out on a field much like this. All begging for water. Flies covering their gangrenous wounds. Bones sticking out. Faces hideously torn. One man with no lower jaw. Another with half of his head gone and still babbling on. Another with no legs. Just the open wound of his torn hip-sockets with something glistening underneath that poked in and out like a wet squirrel's head as he cried in agony. The vivid memory came back in a wave of nausea. He remembered the doctor covering the man's nose with the chloroform sponge and slipping him off to sleep and death. He remembered thinking if not for the chloroform maybe they should have shot him. He looked around at the men on the grass in front of him. They looked much the same.

"C'mon Luke," McMahon pulled his collar. "Kilpatrick's riding through. Must be the rear guard. We don't want to get caught here by Wheeler's cavalry."

Luke pushed him away. He knew the Army wasn't leaving Columbia anytime soon. He took a drink from the brandy bottle then gave Patrick another sip. He held up the bottle and laughed. "Wheeler can't have Patrick's brandy."

"Come on Luke. Let the nuns take care of Patrick."

"The old reb wiped his eyes. "Where you from, Yank?"

"New York."

"I heard of New York. It's way up past Raleigh, ain't it?"

"Yep. Way past."

"Well good luck to you."

Patrick squeezed his hand, and Luke felt like he was saying goodbye to an old friend. He picked his way carefully over the groaning men to the edge of the lawn. Flames raced down the blocks of houses on the next street, setting off multiple explosions.

"Sounds like ammunition. Rebs must be hiding powder," Dave grabbed more whiskey bottles from drunk with a wheelbarrow full. The drunk just wobbled on.

"Won't do them no good," McMahon took a drink, listening to more explosions. "The wrath of God is a powerful sight, ain't it?"

Cows trapped in the burning stalls behind the flaming houses bellowed in terror. Soldiers wrapped themselves in blankets to get close enough to knock open the gates. Three cows come running down the alley. Men cheered while flaming house across the street collapsed on a drunk urinating in the doorway. Other drunks tried to pull him free, but the intense heat pushed them back. The man burned to death. The

320

drunks stood there watching for a while then went over and gathered their wheelbarrow and walked off as if nothing had happened. They ignored the old man, with a little girl holding on to his coat-tails, calling to them from the next yard and waving a bible.

"War is begotten of Satan and born in Hell. You'll all burn in Hellfire for eternity!"

Dave genuflected back and blessed himself. "You've got a right to be riled. Best summon up the chivalry and give us a whipping."

"Mock me if you want," the old man put his hand over the Bible. "But I'll pray that God wreaks vengeance upon you and your friends."

"He done that already. He sent us to this shithole." Dave walked over and tried to kiss the man's Bible, but the old man pulled away and retreated behind a broken picket fence.

Luke and McMahon pulled Dave along behind a mob of soldiers who carried Henrys in one hand and sacks of loot in the other. A few freed slaves joined the crowd. Mostly young men yelling out that they were ready to fight the rebs. Luke saw very few black women and all of them, very old. He figured most were hiding as best they could. Everyone knew white women were mostly safe as long as they didn't put up a fight for silver or gold. But black women were fair game. Luke had seen it happen ever since they'd reached Tennessee. The boys didn't think twice about raping a black girl. It wasn't much of a sin to them. Some had even told him they figured it was just part of their pay. A way of making things even for all they'd been through. Of course any half decent looking black or mulatto girl was usually snatched up into some officers' wagon first. To be 'utilized'.

Soldiers smashed the front door of the home across the street. They went inside and quickly emerged with picture frames, a large clock and a huge blue vase. They stopped in the yard, casually lit torches and tossed them through the second-floor windows. A woman with two small boys and an old man came running out coughing. Luke drank his share from the wine bottle and told himself ALL rebs deserved their fate, even these.

"Reap the whirlwind," he called out again out loudly, repeating it twice more when the old man fell to his knees sobbing, staring at the flames consuming his house. Luke watched the taller boy pat the old man's hand and kiss his ear.

"It's all right, Grampa," the boy kissed him again on his bald head. "I'll help you build another house."

"Damn them all!" Luke heard himself shout.

Dave and McMahon nodded next to him, "Damn right!"

"Hell yes!"

"How many good union men dead?" Luke kept yelling. "How many slaves shackled and sold like cattle?" He sucked down more wine. "How many miles from home have they dragged us into this shit country of theirs? They can all go to Hell. Shit on them. ALL of them!"

"Tell it Luke! Tell it!" McMahon danced in a circle.

Dave whistled and clapped, "Preach to us, Luke! Apostle Luke!"

Luke felt his head spin and thought of Taylor, the new boy, with his legs blown off at Gettysburg. How his eyes filled with tears as he realized he would die on that mangled little Culps Hill. That he would never see his family again in Elmira. Luke felt something stick inside his chest like tar. Yelling soldiers in the street couldn't quite drown out the smaller boy in the smoke-filled yard who knelt beside his brother and called out in a high pitched voice as clear as blue sky.

"That's enough. That's enough!" It was as if he was calling only to Luke. "That's enough."

He kept crying out as Luke stepped over the little fence and walked up to the old man. He gave him $10 of US currency. All that he had. The old man stared at him with hollow eyes then crumpled the bills up in his fist. The boy cried out again, "That's enough."

Luke knew words were useless. He walked back out to the street and felt clearly for the first time that it was indeed enough. It was time to go home. The rest was only the means to the end.

"The war's over."

Dave looked at him funny. "Are you all right?"

McMahon tapped Luke's shoulder. "What you talking about, Luke?"

"I just want to go home." He fought off a sudden welling up of tears. McMahon didn't let on. "Amen to that."

He'd seen good men than Luke cry like babies. Especially at Fredericksburg and Gettysburg. He knew it was something that war did to a man. To any good, decent man, that is. The ones that didn't ever cry were either imbeciles or bastards. Luke was as fine and decent a sort as anyone he'd ever met.

322

"Amen and hallelujah to that." Dave poked Luke's shoulder and conjured a smile out of him.

McMahon opened another bottle and made Luke take a drink. "To home."

"To home."

"Damn right, to home."

He pulled Luke on through the smoke, and they finished off the bottle. Luke's head spun, but it felt good to walk. He decided he'd walk all night if he had to. He just didn't want that tar feeling to come back. They went on for several blocks through thick smoke until they came up on a group of nuns kneeling in the doorway of a brick convent just off the street. An older nun stood in the front, facing down another mob of soldiers.

"I'm Sister Baptista Lynch! Mother Superior of Ursuline Convent. I taught General Sherman's daughter, Minnie, back in Ohio. Now you men leave here and let father O'Connell and the nuns be."

The soldiers laughed and jeered her. A young soldier pushed his way toward the door, lit a match, and held it close to her face, "We ain't Roman Catholics, and nothing's gonna save this convent, sister."

McMahon ran forward. "You're not burning a convent! The nuns aren't the ones who started this war. There's plenty left to burn down the street anyway. This ain't right and you know it. Good Union men don't burn convents!"

"Hell you say." A red haired drunk yelled whiskey breathy in his face. "Heard they've got some sort of Bishop inside. Been preaching that the Pope blessed Lee and Johnson. We're gonna burn him out."

Luke and Dave pushed to McMahon's side, standing with him between the mob and the nuns. McMahon took a long swig from the drunk's whiskey bottle just to let the soldiers know he was one of them.

"If Uncle Billy was here, he'd tell you to move on. Let the nuns be."

"Well Uncle Billy ain't here," the red head laughed. "If you don't want to burn them out, then don't. We've got plenty here that will."

Shots rang out across the street, and the mob surged forward. Drunks in the front raised their rifles. Luke stepped in front of him and stood his ground. The mob hesitated, and Luke let the closest man poke his Henry barrel into his chin.

He looked the drunk in the eye."Leave the nuns be."

"Move out of the way or burn with them," the redhead yelled. Another man poked a rifle into McMahon's ear. Others covered Dave.

"Move now or you're dead men. I mean it." He sloshed turpentine on Luke's shoes.

Dave grabbed Luke's collar and pulled him and McMahon to the side. "No use burning to death. These boys mean business. Anyhow, you did what you could."

Soldiers pushed through the door with torches. The rest of the nuns came out quickly, huddling behind the Mother Superior and saying the rosary faster than Luke thought possible. Mother Superior kept up a constant barrage. "You'll all burn in Hell for this. Burn in Hell forever. You're doing the Devil's work."

"No ma'am." A laughing soldier blessed himself and genuflected in front of her. "Worse than that. We're doing Uncle Billy's work."

Flames quickly licked out the convent windows, and the nun's moved farther away between their Hail Mary's. Another squad of soldiers tried to help with a pump engine, but they never got close to the convent. Men hacked the fire hoses to bits and watched the convent burn. Dave pulled Luke along, but McMahon lagged behind dragging his Henry in the dirt.

"That's not right. Not right at all, by God." He stopped and blessed himself then lifted his rifle and cocked it. "I'm gonna shoot that red-haired bastard, right now."

Luke grabbed his collar. "And get killed in return? No. Dave's right. The convent's gone. There's nothing else you can do about it now. Let the bastard go. Let's get through this ... to the end."

Dave stood behind him just in case. They both knew McMahon was stubborn and just not capable of feeling fear. He'd kill whoever he pleased, whenever he made his mind up. But McMahon just stood there for a while thinking then smiled. "All right, Luke. You're right as usual. Even when you're drunk. The little bastard ain't worth dying for. Not this close to the end."

"Damn right. Not this close." Dave snorted agreement and pulled him away.

They walked on and found a company of men shooting signal rockets. Red, white and blue starbursts soared high above the flames. The towering hulk of the State Capitol turned color with each explosion. Luke realized that he was all turned around and that they'd walked almost in a complete circle in the smoke. Men cheered and pointed down the street to the next hill where more fires sprang to life, crackling and roaring up to the swirling reddish-brown clouds that quivered and flowed like molten copper. Sparks and embers flew in the wind, and Luke knew he was watching something that he would never see again. Something that no one should ever see again. A city being destroyed.

A pistol shot rang out close by. Everyone ducked. An officer rode up the dragging a dead soldier behind his horse. The man was face down and tied by the feet. His arms flailed behind him and his face furrowed through the dirt. The officer yelled out, "He raped a white woman! This is what he gets!" Then he trotted off, pulling the corpse up the hill towards another huge wall of flames.

Dave spat in the dirt. "Punish him sure. If he really screwed a white woman. But don't shoot him. That ain't right. Not this far along. That officer's taking a real bad chance. Some friends of that boy might just shoot him back."

"Just part of the butcher's bill," McMahon fired his rifle in the air as the dead man disappeared in the smoke. "Payment necessary for the rest of us to make it home."

"Still ... ," Dave threw a brick into a flaming house. "I hope that officer gets a bullet up his ass."

on the State Road southeast towards Charleston

Ezekiel and Esau walked on for another five or six miles until they saw a column of blue infantry coming up the road. "We made it! We made it!" Esau shouted out, running into the road waving and cheering. Ezekiel followed. The Yank soldiers mostly ignored them but a few waved back. Esau danced and clapped. "We're free. We're free. Aren't we?"

"Yes sir, we are. We are indeed." Ezekiel let him celebrate. A wagon driver tossed them a hardtack box, and Esau tore into to it fast enough to make the soldiers laugh. Ezekiel stood behind him watching him eat and didn't care what the soldiers thought as long as there were enough of them to keep the rebs at bay. That's all they needed.

Esau finished off the hardtack, and they walked on to a series of diked, rice fields then across to higher ground where a square rice-winnowing house perched on a dozen thick stilts like some giant spider crab. It hadn't been touched. Ezekiel smiled as he went inside.

The iron boiler squatted heavily on a huge brick fireplace smack in the middle of the room. Next to it was a pile of bone-dry pine knots. The chimney narrowed like a pyramid as it ascended above the boiler through the opening in the wood shingle roof. The steam powered rollers with the long leather straps lay still and quiet. Piles of rice covered the floor next to the fly wheel and gear mechanism. Baskets a clean kernels lined one side of the room. More empty canvas sacks dangled through three large holes in the floor as if still waiting to be packed by slaves. On the ground below, a cast-iron pump perched an iron pipe sticking up through bricks glistening with algae from years of endless dripping.

"How many buckets do you think carried up? Over the years I mean? How many do you guess?" Ezekiel kicked a loose board.

"I guess about as many as they needed."

"No. That's not what I mean," Ezekiel laughed. "Just think of it. All the slaves. All the hours. All the work. Right here. For all those years. All day every day."

Esau shrugged, "Yep, except for dinner break. And Sundays."

Ezekiel hugged him. "Well I'm gonna give them exactly what they've always needed. What this winnow house always needed."

Esau wondered what he was up to. There was no telling with Ezekiel. He climbed up the ladder to watch him, sitting down in the open door, dangling his legs in the air, and tossing rice kernels from one hand to the other. Ezekiel kept laughing as he began stuffing pine knots into the hearth below, then lighting a strip of canvas and tossing it in. Smoke began to pour from the chimney, faster and lighter as the heat built up. The boiler started to vibrate. He threw another armload of pine knots into the roaring fire. The steam escape valve whistled louder and louder, turning into a screech then a wail that made both of them cover their ears. Ezekiel tied the valve down tightly with a piece of copper wire he found dangling around the pump handle.

"Better get out of here, Esau. It's gonna blow."

"What the ... !" Esau scrambled down the ladder quickly and retreated across the road.

The copper wire began to glow red hot. Ezekiel jumped out the door, ran across the road and pulled Esau down into a ditch. The wail of the steam stopped for a second as the entire house appeared to expand. Then it splintered into thin air. They both saw the explosion before they heard it. The concussion knocked them both on their backs. Boards, shingles, pieces of metal, and a blizzard of rice kernels rained down on them. As the smoke cleared, Ezekiel looked up and cheered. The chimney stood unperturbed next to a tangled pile of timbers, iron machine parts and a few scorched sacks of rice .

"Now that there's a sight." He slapped Esau's back, then, in an afterthought, felt his neck and shoulders. "Are you hurt?"

"Nope." He felt his face just to be sure. "But damn, Ezekiel. What've you done?"

"Just trying to even things up a bit, that's all." He stood up and wiped himself off. "Fair is fair. C'mon."

They helped themselves to as much rice as they could carry then hurried off through the pine woods. No use staying around and asking for trouble. Another mile or so up, they cut across a fallow cornfield as a dozen or so wagons slowly moved into the open, along a road that skirted the far edge. They were filled to the brim with white women and children, piles of furniture, sacks of belongings, and kegs of food and water. As soon as Esau saw them, he immediately squatted down in the weeds. Ezekiel kept walking towards the wagons.

"Must be almost to Charleston. I'll just go and ask," he winked.

"Ezekiel, wait ... " Esau thought he must be crazy.

"You there!" An old man called out as he saw Ezekiel approaching. The ridges of his cheek bones cut through his greyish skin, and his head trembled in rhythm with the creak of a wagon wheels. He pointed a hammer at the Ezekiel. "What do you want?" He pulled on the reins, and the line of wagons behind him came to a stop.

Ezekiel walked across the field right up to the man who sat high on a molasses barrel tied to the wagon seat. "Is this the Charleston Road?"He asked.

"Yes," the old man glared down at him.

"How far to town?"

"Maybe six miles."

A blond haired boy in the wagon behind cocked a musket. Ezekiel looked down the line. 11 wagons, each with six or seven whites. Women and children and old men. All running away from the Yanks in Charleston. Rifle barrels rose from the other wagons, and Ezekiel knew it was time for his act. He tipped his hat and bowed.

"Thank you, sir. Were just looking for some food, please sir. "

"Well, we don't have any to spare," the man grunted, flicking the reins. The wagon rolled off, and Ezekiel stood beside the road, bowing to each following wagon. No use tempting a 12-year-old with a cocked shotgun. But once they were out of sight, he laughed and twirled Esau in the circle.

"It's just a few more miles! C'mon."

"We're almost there?"

"Yes indeed." He thought of Miela waiting for him and pushed on hard the rest of the day, making it to the northern outskirts of the city by dark and sleeping in an abandoned turpentine still. In the morning they walked into Charleston past the outer earthworks and the Potters

Field, then past the race track and a huge camp of refugees and freed-men near an empty, log stockade and hundreds of fresh graves.

"Yank prisoners of war," a gray-haired, freed slave nodded towards the graves. "The rebs killed a bunch of 'em. Marched the last few off just the other day."

"Are they all gone? The rebs, I mean," Ezekiel looked around the wide field to the trees and houses beyond.

"Yep. Not one left in town. We're all free men now."

"Yes sir, that we are," Ezekiel smiled. "Good luck to you."

"And to you."

Ezekiel and Esau kept on into town past lines of Yank troops everywhere. There were the only whites to be seen. Jubilant blacks filled the streets and the weather cooperated with a warm day, a glorious blue sky, and a wonderful breeze. Food was everywhere. Courtesy of the departed whites. Every deserted pantry was now open for all.. Tables of bread, pies, canned meats, milk, and eggs lined the sidewalks. People laughed and shared with them as they walked past. No one asked them for anything. The bounty of freedom shined down upon them.

Ezekiel and Esau gorged themselves all the way down Meeting Street past the massive, still intact, Charleston Hotel with its row of gray columns, then past block after block of burned out buildings, charred brick steps to nowhere, and the ash -covered remains of the Congregational Church. They stopped to rest in the shade of the row of loquat trees surrounded by little picket fences to protect them from horses. A group of black men staggered past, each man armed with two whiskey bottles. Behind them, a pregnant woman ran up and hugged Esau.

"It's the Jubilee!" She shouted in his face.

Another younger girl poked him with the skewer of roasted meat. "Come on and eat. It's freedom, can't you see? Everything s free now. Everything you want." She ran into the front yard of a huge, stuccoed-brick mansion. "Come on out here Roxanne! Bring these men ... these fine free-men ... some of Mr. Ramsay's wine and canned fish."

A few seconds later, two women came out with silver platters stacked with an assortment of smoked lamb, oysters, beef, and salted fish. A third followed with two wine bottles. "Mr. Ramsay is happy to share," she laughed. "Well ... he would be ... if he was here."

"Well, thank you. Thank you kindly. And Mr. Ramsey too," Ezekiel laughed, opening the bottles by knocking them against the wooden door frame until the corks popped out. Another useful bit of knowledge gleaned from observing the white man, he smiled to himself. "Here Esau. Have a taste."

"Yes, thank you," Esau swallowed a mouthful. "It's fine wine. The best. So very fine," He didn't let on that he'd never tasted wine before and that the musty, rooty taste was a bit unpleasant to him. Nevertheless he knew it was the right thing to drink it, on the day of jubilee, and Ezekiel was just the right person to help him finish off a bottle while they stuffed themselves with lamb and oysters. They took the other bottle with them after thanking the women.

"Y'all come back for more, anytime you want," the pregnant woman smiled, waving after them. "Mr.Ramsey said he was going to Columbia. Didn't know when he would be back. Best we drink it up while we can."

"Thank you kindly," Esau waved, feeling a bit queezy but following Ezekiel down the street then across town where they spent the entire day trying to find out the whereabouts of Miela and the others. Ezekiel figured she might have gone to Blessing's since the Yanks would protect her, but he had never been to Blessing's Charleston home and had no idea where it was. His luck held when they met a freed slave from Hobonny Plantation who knew the location.

"Name's Juma," he nodded, pointing towards Legare Street. "I'll bet that's where she is all right. At least while it's safe around here." He waved a sharpened broomstick at the white faces that had begun to peer out from shuttered second-floor windows. "No telling what they'll do when the Yanks leave. Best to ... "

Juma started to say something else, but Ezekiel didnt hear another word. He was already running down the street leaving Esau to say thanks and hurry after him. Ezekiel felt his breath going short, and his eyes watering up. He had to find her, now. He raced on and found the house just as Juma had described. A massive mansion towering four stories high, with what looked like a stucco ladder cut into the corners. He stood there looking up when he heard a voice calling him. His heart jumped to his throat.

Miela saw him outside the gate, standing like he always did. Hands on his hips, one knee slightly bent, head cocked to the side. "Ezekiel!" Her breath with short as she ran out of the gate. "Ezekiel!"

His head snapped towards her. "Miela!"

Then his face was buried in her neck and his arms wrapped around her as if he'd never let her go. Neither of them could feel the ground. The clouds spun around above. Miela holding onto him tight enough to keep him from disappearing and not releasing her grip for a good ten minutes. He did the same. Neither spoke. Words were useless. He felt her firm belly as they stood there in the gateway in each other's arms, neither wanting to move or break the spell until Fatima ran up and broke it for them.

"Why are y'all so kissy?" she squealed.

Miela looked around at her then kissed Ezekiel again. She pulled him inside the gate as Esau came up panting behind them. Fatima gave him a hug and they followed Miela and Ezekiel behind the Big House to the slave quarters in the rear where they found the whole group. Everyone was in tears for a while until Cumseh swatted at them with a braided palm frond.

"It ain't like he's the Holy Ghost or nothing. It's just Ezekiel ... and Esau. Anyhow, I'm hungry."

Jemps and Poins lifted her up and carried her across the yard while she kicked and whipped them with her palm braid. The others followed behind Ezekiel, laughing and jostling to be closest to him until Miela told them to give him space. Supper was prepared, and they all gave thanks to God to be together again. Ezekiel told them what had happened except he lied about Mingo, Pompey, and Quam. He told them they'd gone north with Toby. He figured that was plenty sad enough for everyone, and he was right. Esau played along. He was glad his friends were all still alive in their minds. It truly helped him feel better.

The children made them tell all about what they'd seen and done, but it all seemed suddenly like a distant dream. Miela let Daphne tell Ezekiel and Esau about the wagon trip and, after Yarrow and Lizette fell asleep, about Gage and Grace. Finally when everyone had heard enough, Miela led Ezekiel upstairs. They slept together on a thin cotton mattress in a closet off the end of the long room, making love and holding on to each other into the wee hours. Nothing else mattered. Nothing that had ever happened mattered. Only that he was with her and her with him. They spent the next two days resting, eating, sleeping, and enjoying just being together while everyone went about the tasks of collecting supplies and clothing. The plan was still to go to Thomas Island. To the land Connor had deeded to them at Smythe's. Miela was insistent upon it.

"It's our only hope. Once the Yank troops leave ... We need someplace we can take care of ourselves."

Ezekiel knew she was right. The city would be no place to live once the Yanks left. They needed their own land to grow food, make shelter, and be able to protect each other. He decided he had to go look for himself though. To make sure that it would all work out. Miela told him what Connor had said about free -blacks living on the island. And that was all fine and good. But what Connor said was one thing. True safety, another. He just wanted to find out if the island was clear of rebs.

He took one of the mules and found his way, by stopping and asking freemen a dozen times, up to the Thomas Island Ferry on the Cooper River about five miles outside of town. The only trouble he ran into was with one picket of Yank infantry who questioned him riding a mule.

"You're not one of them loyal blacks working for the rebs, are you?" A huge, red faced Irishman sneered.

"There's no such thing. Never was," Ezekiel answered calmly. "When I see my old master, Mr. Blessing, I'll stick this knife up his ass." He smiled, pulled the blade out of the leather sheath and pretended to stick it where it belonged.

The Irishman laughed and slapped his back. "I believe you, boy." He turned and yelled to the other troops. "This boy's all right. He has a special gift for his master's ass. Let him through."

Ezekiel kept smiling, ignoring being called 'boy'. He knew one dead black man meant nothing to them. All it would take was one smirk then a bullet in the back and some lie about reb bushwhackers. But they let him pass, and he rode up to the ferry landing and caught the last trip across for the day. He said nothing to the old boat captain or the young boys serving as deckhands and kept a close grip on the mule. When the ferry nudged into the small Thomas Island landing, he pulled the mule down the gangplank and watched the ferry move on up the creek to the larger landings at Daniel Island and the Calais Tavern and Cainhoy Road.

He followed Miela 's directions up the muddy landing road and found the turn to the farm just where she said it would be. Directions given to her by Connor Dumont. Christ. He shook his head. He still couldn't quite believe the bastard had saved his life. And now he was accepting help from him. Help from the nephew of his old owner. The only white man who didn't fit his notion of the world. The only one who gave him second thoughts. And what was it that he felt exactly? He shivered and had to laugh as he rode further up the narrow track through the pines that filtered down to a salt marsh on one side then across a large fallow cornfield overgrown with trumpet vines, honeysuckle, and yellow jasmine.

In a copse of oaks and willows, stood four cabins aligned with the curvature of the woods. Several smaller out- buildings and a cattle stockade bordered the pines across the field along with a pigsty, blacksmith shop, cookhouse, dairy, corn bin, and turpentine still. He took it all in. The cornfield, the line of oaks and pines along with marsh bank, the blue water of the river sparkling in the distance in the through gaps in the trees, and the marsh stretching for two miles to the far bank. He tied the mule in the stockade and walked quietly along the entire perimeter of the clearing and then into the woods beyond. He wanted to make sure that it was safe. White civilians might be a problem. Reb cavalry scouts, worse. He found a brick kiln and small house in a cornfield on the other side of the woods, but no one was about, not a soul. He knocked on the door, but there was no one home. He looked in the window in the porch. The interior was covered in cobwebs. No one had been there for months at least.

He walked back through the woods and smelled smoke. It came drifting over the marsh across a narrow section of creek from a patch of woods where he spotted horses and four men in the far trees. He dropped and hid quickly and watched then until nearly dark. They were definitely Confederate cavalry. He was sure of it. Damn. It wasn't going to be as easy as Miela thought. He crept quietly back and slept in the barn without building a fire. Just in case. The next day, he caught the ferry back and didn't say a word to anyone on the boat or at the landing then made his way back to Legare Street and gave Miela the bad news. Smythe's would definitely have to wait for a while. At least a couple more weeks until all the rebs were gone and the Yanks were fully in control.

CHAPTER 36 — DR. TRADD / LUKE / CONNOR

Columbia and the road to Winnsboro

D r. Tradd startled awake at first light to the acrid smell of thick smoke. He had fallen asleep in a chair in the hallway outside the men's ward. He roused himself and climbed the stairwell to the roof looking down from highest point at the charred ruins of block after block of the city. A stillness had descended. He stood there for a while in shock not believing his eyes. Columbia was gone. Ruins. Nothing but ruins. His legs went wobbly, and he staggered down to find Dr. Parker. The nurses and orderlies were already helping groups of families who had been burned out of their homes. They were all terrified and exhausted and gladly accepted the spare rooms for shelter from the cold and wolfed down a breakfast of hot cornmeal porridge. Dr. Tradd and Louisa helped the staff pass out blankets and hot sassafras tea then he had her fetch the wagon and mules. He knew he had to go back for his cousin and her family. Surely they would leave now unless they were already. .. he refused to think it. He ordered Louisa to stay inside the gate but she refused.

"I'm coming with you, sir and there's nothing you can do about it," she smiled.

He could see that she was exhausted, but he knew he couldn't make her stay. He really didn't want her to either. He stood up in the wagon and looked down the lane towards the burned out lower part of the city. Where was General Hampton? Why hadn't the Army defended Columbia? Why had God let this happen? He already knew the answer but didn't want to think about it anymore. Rifle fire burst out nearby. Gray troopers rode through a patch of trees beyond the last rows of still-intact houses to the north. Yankee infantry darted through smoldering ruins to the west behind them. A bullet hit the brick gatepost.

"Damn them all. They're still at it," he shook his head, turning to Louisa. "Better get down."

She looked up and nodded but saw his face freeze into a distant stare. He leaned over and clutched his chest then fell limply back into the wagon.

"Dr. Tradd! What's wrong!"

Blood glistened through his shirt and jacket. He felt a sudden chill then a much deeper cold as if he'd been immersed in a mountain stream.

"Oh my god! You've been shot!" She ripped open his shirt. A bullet hole poured blood above his left nipple. His eyes opened wider, and the frozen stare relaxed. He lost his breath and felt himself sinking under-water. The light above him on the surface dimmed then flickered out.

"Dr. Tradd! Dr. Tradd!" She clutched his limp body to hers. Dr.Parker came running.

"No! Merciful God! No!" He jumped up into the wagon and stuck his finger into the bullet hole. His other hand felt Dr. Tradd's neck then opened his eyelids wide. He knew immediately that his friend was dead.

Louisa kept crying, "No, please! No, no, please no!"

Dr. Parker slumped down in the wagon seat. He sat there for a while looking around at the Asylum gate and the courtyard beyond, thinking of all his friend's work and effort. "All that he's done and now this? Why? Why would the good Lord allow this? Speak to me, Lord."

Louisa kept sobbing, "No, please God, no."

Two orderlies came up, and Dr.Parker signaled them to take her away. She tried to hold on to Dr. Tradd, but she trembled so hard she couldn't control her arms. She fell to her knees beside the wagon, and they had to carry her inside. Dr. Parker gathered himself up and touched Dr. Tradd's shoulder.

"Goodbye my good friend." He wiped away his tears. "If this is God's work then there must be a reason. Some damn good reason. Why else would He ... "

He caught his breath and sat there for a while looking up at the hazy sky and smelling the ashes of the burned city. "You're just showing me the way, aren't you, Henry. You know I'll be along soon enough ... " He tried to smile. "But, if you don't mind, there are a few more things I have to tend to first. The same kinds of things you'd do if ... Well I don't have to explain to you. I'll see you in good time. We can discuss it all then.

Perhaps we'll find the answers we're looking for ... Actually I'm sure of it."

LUKE'S REGIMENT MARCHED UP THE HILL as the sun rose blood-red through heavy smoke. Dazed people wandered through the desolation. The air reeked of charred carcasses that lay in the ruins. Mostly dogs, but here and there, cows, goats and a few horses. A worse smell drifted in the breeze from block after block of blackened houses. The nauseatingly sick smell of burned human flesh. Luke knew that his family back home would never truly understand this. No one would. No one who hadn't been here. But maybe everyone should come look. Blackened, gutted houses, charred brick walls and chimneys, as far as the eye could see. A world of ash, smoke, and burned out shells of buildings.

"Sherman's brickyard."

"Helluva sight, isn't it Luke," Dave drained his canteen feeling the after effects of the evening.

"It is indeed. It is indeed. I'll bet if they'd seen this in '61, the war would have ended a lot quicker."

"Amen again."

Bugles sounded and regiments congealed along the soot- covered streets, but it took all morning for any semblance of order to return. Luke's company stood for hours in a graveyard next to a burned church. He read the names of the deceased. Walker, Pickens, Chestnut, Harding. He wondered if they were looking down on the ruins of the city. Would they have counseled peace? Or were these some of the men who had led them to the brink? He wiped off the coating of ash from a marble lamb at the head of a grave that read 'Teresa Sortain'. He pictured her funeral with mourners, family, and friends. The churchyard of oaks, now scorched and bare, but at the time providing shade and perhaps comfort. He wiped off his hands as sergeants yelled for the company to form up. He tried to put any feeling of pity out of his mind. It wasn't hard to do. Who could feel pity for people who started a war such as this? Just to keep their damn slaves.

The column started north along a gradual rise through town. Children scrambled beside them through the rubble, picking up parched kernels of corn and licking scorched meat off bricks and boards. The fruit of their Elders way of life, he thought. Some of the older children's faces

336

were contorted in hate, but the younger ones, especially those with something to eat, watched the army moved past as if it were an Easter Parade. A few soldiers tossed tins of food and quickly children were running alongside begging for more, their smiles and laughter cutting through the smoke like a fresh breeze. But they may have hardened the faces of the adult civilians even more. Thousands of them stood like statues in the ruins as the last of the rear regiments marched out of the burnt district followed by supply wagons and behind them the rear-guard cavalry and scouts.

Fifty or so civilian wagons of all kinds and shapes, struggled to keep close. Blacks and whites, Tories and Union sympathizers, freed slaves, escaped convicts and a few Asylum dwellers, profiteers, deserters, some fearful of the coming chaos, and some whites just fed up with it all. The wagon train rattled along, paralleling the columns along the Winnsboro Road, through a rising chorus of boos and hisses from the crowd. But catcalls were all they dared hurl. No one lifted a hand. The blue ranks were well armed and watching closely.

"Wheeler will find you, traitors," a soot-blackened woman brandishing a long, iron ladle yelled out. "He'll string you up by your throats."

"Get out of here Yankee lovers," an old man with one trouser leg torn off yelled and spat at a passing wagon. "Go live with the blacks, you white trash."

None of those leaving argued back. No use stirring up the mob. And there was certainly no compromise. Just those who stayed and those who left. Pipers in one regiment didn't help by playing 'Yankee Doodle' as they marched. Some in the crowd sang 'Dixie' in return, but most just continued to stare silently as the blue column walked away.

CHARRED RUINS STRETCHED as far as Connor could see in the dim first light. Slender brick chimneys stood alone or in small clumps like gravestones across the blackened hillsides. The sun rose red through the smoke, shining light on two soot covered clay figurines standing like sentinels in the middle of the street watching him. The bare scorched brick walls behind them looked like ancient ruins. Like Carthage. He remembered Dr. Tradd telling him the story of Hannibal.

"He fought for twenty years until the Romans finally beat him. Then he just ran off and let his country be ravaged. No excuse in my book. Should have stood firm. Better to die at the gates of his home than live forever in shame."

Smoke formed a halo around the rising sun, and Connor wondered if he would live in shame too. He went back to the cemetery, but the Yank's body was gone. Had he dreamed the whole thing? He hoped he had. But he knew otherwise. He couldn't take it back either. The rage of vengeance was all gone, but nothing could be changed ... About anything he'd done. He walked quickly away from the cemetery towards the open fields past the State Asylum and found an intact corn bin behind a burned-out house and hid inside. His brain whirled around. Henrietta, the dead Yanks, Barry, Norton, Chesire, and Bucky, the black girl he'd saved. He waited inside the bin all day and that night, nibbling at raw corn and trying not to think about Henrietta or the last Yank boy's pink face.

He woke early the next morning and smelled the bitter smoke. It reminded him of the slave girl he'd seen in Charleston years ago being held down on her knees while a root doctor held smoldering moss under her nose. The girl had been possessed by an evil root for days, crawling on her knees and barking like a dog. The smoke of the moss brought her out of her trance. He remembered how she looked around at the crowd of curious onlookers then suddenly cried out, "Oh Lord Jesus, what have I done!"

Connor felt the same. The rage of boiling blood had subsided in the acrid haze. He thought of the night of the fire. The anger, the desire to kill. He looked around at the morning light falling like a translucent stage curtain through the evaporating smoke. The trance was over. Maybe Henrietta was dead. But maybe not. Maybe Dr. Wilson was just lying. Just trying to inflict pain. War did strange things to people. Misery and death worked on the mind in curious ways. But he'd find out soon enough ... when it was all over. Anyhow, he'd done his part. He'd taken revenge. It was more than enough for now.

"It's time to put her out of my mind," he whispered, repeating it over and over until he began to believe it.

It was time to move on. Time to let the war take its course. He told himself to get up, but he lingered there in the bin watching a few dazed civilians poke through the charred rubble. The tinge of shame and guilt passed quickly. Too quickly, he thought, for any decent man. And what about today? Would he do the same? He told himself no.

"I'll do only what is necessary to survive." He repeated it out loud several times. "Just to survive."

Only then did he rouse himself, stiff and sore, from his bed of cold cornstalks. He walked to the edge of town and spotted Yank cavalry coming up the hill, so he hid in a wood shed the rest of the day while blue soldiers roamed about destroying the remaining government buildings. Sleep came easily, and he was glad just to lie there and let them do as they pleased. The night was quiet, still, and cold.

The following morning, the last of the Union army pulled out heading north. Weary citizens emerged from blanket tents and half burned sheds and barns. The private homes still standing swarmed with burned out neighbors and stunned refugees glad to have even a porch roof over their heads. Connor walked around the ruins looking for a horse, but there were none left. He found a group of women cooking soup and cornbread pancakes in the middle of the street. A big kettle hung on a chain over a fire fueled by the remnants of scorched houses. Four little boys ran up and down the street bringing back scorched timbers one at a time.

"Help yourself, young man," a plain looking woman ladling out bowls of redish soup called to him. "The Lord giveth and taketh away. Got to face it. C'mon."

"Yes ma'am," he answered, his voice sounding to him like he was talking into a conch shell.

He wolfed it all down and accepted seconds of soup and more pancakes. The woman didn't ask any questions and none of her friends seemed to even notice that the city was gone. They focused only on the fire, the bubbling soup, and the cornbread pancakes, inviting every person that straggled by to have breakfast. Connor felt a bit ashamed to eat a third bowl full, but he did. He drank water from a wooden bucket that hung from an iron pump handle at the corner. He thanked the ladies then walked on through street after street of smoldering blackened ruins.

Stunned civilians stood wrapped in blankets looking at their destroyed homes as if their eyes were deceiving them. The bright morning sun and blue sky only made it worse. Connor hurried along northward, knowing in his heart he couldn't face another day in Columbia, and figuring he would eventually run into somebody with a horse. He could ride with whatever scout he came across. Maybe he would run into JB and Fitts up the road.

A few miles outside the city on the Winnsboro Road, a group of fifty or so gray and brown horsemen came up behind him. Connor waved them down and a few of them stopped. They kept their rifles leveled at his chest. Connor saw that three of them pulled along spare mules.

"Name's Connor. Been riding with JB's scout, Wheelers cavalry. Got separated in Columbia. And lost my horse," he said quickly, eyeing the extra mounts.

A man with a black beard, greasy hair, and dark complexion smiled at him. "Been hiding out in town eh, with all the Yanks about? And now you ain't got no ride." He laughed. "You from Charleston?"

Connor nodded.

"Your accent," the man smiled. "Name's Billy Powell. From Winnsboro. We been riding with Cheatam's Division. Most of the others come from Tennessee and Alabama. We're riding up towards my home ... if it's still there ... we'll see what we can do." He waved to a boy with bushy blonde hair sprouting out the side of his cap in ringlets. He held the reins of a spare mule and squinted back at Powell.

"You sure?"

"Yes, Selby. The man's with Wheeler. Remember Aiken? Wheeler's boys saved our ass." He turned to Connor. "You've been there? At Aiken?"

Connor shook his head and Selby's eyes lit up for a second. Maybe he didn't have to give up his spare after all.

"Give Connor the mule, Selby... Please," Powell winked at Connor, and Selby obeyed with an audible sigh.

"Much obliged," Connor tipped his cap and took the reins.

"See? It feels good to be charitable, don't it Selby?'

"I guess so," he shrugged.

"Ain't got no gun neither there Connor?" Powell chuckled. "What was you doin'? Throwing rocks at 'em?"

He held up the small revolver and swung up onto the worn Yank saddle. "Could use a rifle ... Or shotgun."

"Don't worry. We'll find you ... "

"Well looky here! Damn if it ain't Connor."

Connor recognized JB's voice immediately. He turned to see JB and Fitts ride up beside him, Fitts still on Brig, and both draped with their rifles and cartridge boxes.

"Risen from the dead and all. Like a Lazarus man," JB shook his head and grinned. "Damn my eyes, Connor. It's good to see you. Went into the burning fury and came out in one piece. Resurrected, I guess."

"It seems so," Connor smiled and felt a tear in his eye.

"JB said he just wouldn't leave you," Fitts poked at him. "Made me hide out west of town for two days. Said you'd show up. Damn if he weren't right. Sam wouldn't stay, though. Rode off with Butler's cavalry."

"Seemed like the right thing to do, that's all," JB shrugged. "Made sense to me. I figured if we just waited long enough, you'd pop out. I doubted seriously that the good Lord would take Barry, Bucky, Norton, Chesire, AND Connor Dumont. Figured he'd let one of you go, so it had to be you."

"I thought he was just crazy in the head. What with Barry and all ..." He stopped and thought better of it.

JB bowed his head, took a deep breath and shook it off. "Well it's a new day now, ain't it. And these here boys are crazy as any of Wheeler's scouts." He waved his hand at Powell and Selby then cramped up and gripped his side. "Anyhow, I knew the good Lord was looking out for us when we found two Yanks asleep with Henry rifles out of reach. Didn't even have to wake 'em. Just rode off with their All right and cartridge boxes. Now tell me that ain't a sign from above."

"The man has a point," Fitts agreed. "But you didn't tell me this old war horse was so temperamental, Connor. Bucked me into a barrel of green apples back yonder. Had to let him eat about half a ton before he'd move. Bound to have a mean bellyful about now. But I ain't giving him back."

"You keep him," Connor settled in on his mule. "Might disturb him if we change ownership too many times. Could use your shotgun though. If you can spare it."

"Sure can. I'm a Henry man now, for sure."

"See?" Powell beamed. "Now everybody's happy, c'mon."

341

He spurred his horse and they all followed the rest of the group up the road, riding a good twenty miles towards Winnsboro, stopping to rest midafternoon at a shabby little farmhouse on a sandy pine ridge. Men cautiously spread out around the house and yard, on the lookout for bummers. Smoke rose from the chimney. A horse cart was unhitched by the well. Two mules were tied to a small pine beside the house. Four black women dressed in dirty rags came out on the porch and waved, but their faces showed terror.

A sergeant with a sawed off shotgun and a straw hat called to them. "Where y'all from?" Flakes of peeling sunburned skin dangled from the end of his red nose.

The lightest skinned black woman called back with a big smile. "Right here. This is our place. We've been free blacks for ... "

The sergeant raised his hand. "Get your men out here. I'll talk to them."

The women slipped back behind the plank door and disappeared. Two black men slowly emerged. Both were visibly trembling.

"Where you from?" The sergeant asked.

"Right here. We be from right here," one of the black men answered, suddenly standing as still as a statue.

"Right here?" The sergeant smiled. "Where exactly is right here? What's the name of that town right over yonder?" He pointed up the road that disappeared over a little rise.

"We ain't been ... we never been up there. We've just been right here." The man was shaking so hard he could barely stand. The other man began to sob, his face contorted in fear.

Powell rode up and laughed. "Sgt. Massey, I've living in these parts before the war. My uncle's place is right over yonder. Ain't never been blacks living anywhere near here except on Monticello Plantation. No free blacks ever lived in these parts."

"Go see." The sergeant nodded towards the house. Powell tied his horse to the railing right in front of the stiff, terrified blacks and went inside. He yelled from inside the house.

"I have something!" He trotted out and held up a framed daguerreotype. "I know him. He's my uncle's friend, Mr. Weigel. He tends to the gristmill and runs a cooperage in Winnsboro. This ain't their place." He nodded to the blacks. "They don't belong here."

342

"So be it," the sergeant shook his head and sighed. "Take 'em over to the tree line."

The women came out wailing as troopers pulled the two men across the yard. "Please don't. We don't mean nothing," the taller one sobbed.

"We're just trying to live. Yanks burned Monticello. We just been trying to live. That's all. I swear that's all."

"The Yanks been mean to us," the woman's eyes lit up like she'd remembered the one thing that would save them. "That's right! They said we were worthless rebel-lovers because we wouldn't follow them. And we DIDN'T follow them. We didn't! Please God! We stayed! We just want to live."

Sergeant Massey listened then looked over at the soldiers with the two black men. "Shoot them."

"Wait!" Connor called out. "Maybe Mr. Weigel gave them permission."

Powell glanced back and shrugged. "Doubt it."

The troopers raised their rifles as the black women screamed. They fired, and the black men fell backwards into the weeds. All four women fell to the porch floor crying and shaking like epileptics. Sergeant Massey was unperturbed.

"Let that be a lesson," he looked back at Connor. "And don't you never ... " He shook his head and rode off past the house with the rest of the troop following behind.

Connor glanced back at the bodies and at the bawling, gasping women knew what the lesson would be. A lesson that would live with these people and their children forever. What other lesson could it be? He rode after them trying to block it all out of his mind.

A mile of two further down the road, men had stopped to help a white woman who sobbed on her knees in a stubble cornfield. Her dress was torn into strips that she had tied back together with twine. Caked blood covered her upper lip and stained the front of her blouse. She looked up at the troopers and clinched her fist.

"They were Alabama men," she pounded the dirt and trembled. "Alabama men riding with Sherman. The worst. The worst."

"Alabama? Are you sure?" JB offered her some water.

"What?" Her lip curled into a snarl. "You think I don't know who done this to me?" She gripped a handful of bloody dress. "US 1st

343

Alabama. They made sure I knew. Called me a rebel bitch and held me down." She sobbed uncontrollably, pacing up and down the field clutching the front of her dress and wringing it into a knot.

Sergeant Massey called to her. "We'll find them and kill them if they ain't run for it."

She looked at him quickly and her eyes widened. Then slowly her forehead furrowed deeper and harder until she fell to her knees again. Selby whispered to Connor, "Who's gonna want her now? You know what I mean. A woman who's been ... "

"Raped," Connor whispered back

"Yep," Selby nodded. "We just got to kill the bastards before they get a second chance."

Powell cursed under his breath. "We need to do more than that."

CHAPTER 37— CONNOR / JESSE

Powell kept the group headed northward towards Winnsboro, flanking the rear of the Union columns. In a driving rain, they came up on bummers camping in a farmhouse. The Yanks didn't hear them coming but were plainly visible through the smashed windows. All the troopers spread out and waited in the rain for the order to fire.

Jesse, Jack and the others were inside drying off in front of a fire built with furniture in the middle of the biggest first floor room. Big Tom cooked freshly cut steaks on spits over the and laughed as the fire slowly ate his way through the charred floor. Connor's group crept close enough to the house in the rain to hear them talking.

"See, Jack. I told you it would be fun," Jesse spoke through a mouthful of bloody meat. "Them other boys were shits anyhow. Glad they split off. Hope they get their asses shot to hell."

Cord carved off a big chunk and gulped it down. "Jack's all right," he smiled. "Just took him a while to find the spirit."

"That's it all right," Big Tom tore off long piece of dripping fat and sucked on it. "Jack's seen the wisdom of Jesse's way."

Jesse just shrugged, "Rebs are generous, that's all."

Tim choked laughing. "Yep. They've been pretty damn generous all right. Especially the women."

Kennedy laughed with him. "Bet you this fire burns up the wall before it goes through the floor," he held out a gold coin.

"I'll take that bet," Jesse nodded.

"It'll go up the wall. I know it will," Kennedy stomped on the floor.

"This is thick pine. Won't burn through this here."

"Hell if it won't," Jesse laughed, spewing out chewed meat.

But Kennedy was right. That pitch pine boards did just as he said, leading the fire sideways and up the far wall. Jack quickly finished his steak as the fire spread up to the plank ceiling, the heat suddenly becoming unbearable. They all backed out to the porch then over to the barn through the pouring rain. They never had a chance to build another fire.

They were too busy laughing and breaking up the stalls for firewood to hear the reb troopers coming closer in the rain. The first thing they noticed was a turpentine fire raging in back of the barn. For a few seconds, Jesse kept laughing, thinking Kennedy was still outside playing a joke. Then the flaming turpentine jars came flying through the bigger front door, and Kennedy staggered into view engulfed in fire. He screamed as the flames roared over his face then rifles fired and his head exploded. The rest of them scrambled to the back door. More turpentine jars crashed against the rough plank walls dripping liquid fire into the hay.

"Keep low. Fire as you run. We'll get to the woods and circle up." Jesse fired through the slats emptying his Henry in all directions. Big Tom, Cord and Tim joined in. Jack knelt beside them frozen, his eyes fixed on Kennedy's burning body outside.

"Load up damn it," Jesse backhanded him. "We've been in worse than this here. Rebs won't stand up to Henrys. Never have, never will." Jack cocked his rifle as another turpentine jar crashed against the pine planks splashing on Jesse's boot. Jesse just grinned as the flames licked up his ankle. "This ain't nothing, I tell you. Nothing at all. We'll gut some damn rebs for that, Sure as Hell. C'mon!"

Jack followed Jesse and the others out the door, firing his Henry blindly. Connor and the whole scout were waiting with shotguns and rifles. One volley cut them all down. Jesse's head exploded. Blood splattered from Cord's neck. Tim curled up on his side as if sleeping. Big Tom made it as far as the trees then fell on his face and was still.

Jack felt a pressure his chest and heard a roar in his ears. He cringed, thinking, why did I go with him? Why didn't I leave when I could? For God's sake, it was all just a lark. He lay on his back in the rain, and the roar abruptly stopped. He was startled at the quiet. There wasn't a sound. The night sky was just pitch blackness. It slowly descended on him like a heavy quilt, and he died before another thought could form. Sergeant Massey walked up cautiously and shot all of them in the head with his revolver. "Can't be too careful. Just like rattlesnakes."

Powell laughed. "Yep. Might still get you after they're dead."

The men stripped the bodies of weapons, food and equipment, gathered up their horses, and rode on until past midnight. Rest was finally called. Connor curled up in a blanket in the rain. He figured the Yanks got what they deserved. All the others too. Or at least that's what he told himself as he drifted off to sleep, trying not to think of the Yank in the cemetery ... or Henrietta.

In the morning they rode on a few miles towards Winnsboro, and the local boys like Powell and Selby rode off quickly to check on their parents' houses. Everyone else dismounted and scraped up flower that covered the streets, courtesy of the Yanks. Men watered their horses, adjusted saddles, and checked weapons. Everyone knew the Yanks' rearguard couldn't be too far ahead now. They pushed on quickly several more miles towards the Wateree River until a scout galloped out of the pine woods in front.

"Yanks up at Poplar Springs! Burning everything. Got infantry and wagons straggling for miles."

Sergeant Massey nodded and pointed to the woods. "Show us."

The trooper led them down a cart path through rolling, sandy hills of scrub pines following the trail of smoldering farmhouses northeast until they came up on a small rearguard of Yank cavalry about a mile behind the last of their infantry regiments. Four Yank stragglers with dysentery who couldn't keep up with their regiment tried to surrender at the edge of the patch of willows. Powell and Selby reappeared, galloping up through the trees, right up to the four men, three who could barely stand and one squatting down bare-assed with the squirts. They pulled out revolvers and shot the three standing. The squatting man covered his face with his arms and screamed , 'No!' Powell shot him in the gut and again in the head. He reloaded and trotted off without a word.

"You think they were the ones?' Fitts elbowed Connor. "The ones that ...did ... the woman."

"I doubt it. Not with the shits and all. Maybe the bummers back in the barn."

Connor looked down at the smooth, peach fuzz on the youngest Yank's face. He thought of the boy's family never knowing what happened, and he wasn't sure exactly why this one particular Yank meant anything to him. He found himself dismounting, holding the mule's reins in one hand and rifling through the boy's pockets for something with his name on it. Some of the troopers rode up and watched from their saddles. All he found was a little black prayer book with the handwritten note on the inside cover that read, 'George. May God bless you and protect you. Your loving father, Andrew.'

"Got anything good?" A boy about the same age and wearing a Yank officer's hat smiled, his cheek sticking out with a wad of tobacco.

"Nope," Connor shook his head, leaving the prayer book with the body and remounting.

"Shit on him then. Ain't nothin' more worthless than a dead Yank with empty pockets." The boy spat a brown squirt on the dead Yanks boot as more gray horsemen came out of the woods with three bummers died across their saddles like sacks of cornmeal.

"We killed the others," a trooper called out dismounting. "Ten or so. Bastards shot six of ours,"

The men around him just stared blankly as he tossed the groaning Yank prisoners to the ground. One turned on his side and spit at him. His bald head glistened with sweat. "South Carolina ain't worth a good shit. Go ahead and shoot us. Our boys will give it back to double. Probably poking your mommas and sisters right now." He spit again and howled until a trooper kicked him hard in the mouth. Another Yank tried to get to his knees. He was just a boy.

"But I didn't do nothing! I weren't meaning no harm! I ain't the kind that takes to hurting people. Never took nothing that weren't mine." He caught his breath and kept on, his mouth so dry it was hard for him to talk. "This here's different. The Army and all. They said it weren't a bad thing. What I mean is ... they TOLD us to do it. Said it was for the Army. That Uncle Billy said it was all right. That it would help end the war. I swear didn't mean no harm. I didn't, I swear I didn't. What I mean is ... I'm a Christian. I swear I'll never raise a hand against nobody, never again. I mean it. I swear I mean it!"

His blue eyes sparkled in the afternoon sunlight that streamed in hazy rays through the trees. Then he began to cry. He knew it was hopeless. The troops around him stared back expressionless. He wasn't a human being in their eyes. Just a cornered animal. On equal terms with a possum or skunk. He knew his life was about to end. It was so horribly absurd and unfair that he couldn't hold back the tears. "Why me? Plenty of others never got caught. Plenty did worse. I'm different than the others. We was just passing the time. That was all it ever was to me. I don't got nothing against you. Never cared if the South went its own way. Never cared nothing about the blacks. They're your business, not mine. I just did what they told me ... and I'm just 17 for God's sake ... I'm just 17. Please don't kill me. The war's nearly over. My momma ... she's expecting me to ... "

A trooper walked up behind him as he spoke, put his revolver to the back of the boy's neck and fired. His body slumped in the dirt. The bald Yank got up to his knees again, spit out blood, and laughed. "He'll be seeing his momma in heaven about now. But you reb shits can go straight to Hell. Uncle Billy sent plenty there already." He looked around at the troopers and smiled. "Hey there, mister. What's the difference between Hell and South Carolina anyhow? Looks about the same to me. Reb shits infesting both."

Another kick to the head silenced him. Not another word was spoken. Rope was cut into short sections. Just long enough for tight knots around the neck and just high enough up the small pines so their feet wouldn't touch. The two Yanks were hung up and left kicking in their last moments.

JB tossed Connor a half of a sweet potato. "There won't be any prisoners from now on," he spoke in a low voice. "Not after Columbia."

"What?" Fitt's squinted, puzzled and holding out his hands. "We got to kill all prisoners? All of them? Even soldiers?"

"We've been shooting bummers ain't we? What's the difference," JB barked back.

"There's a big difference," Connor snapped at him. "Bummers are criminals. Soldiers are soldiers. Just like us."

Selby rode up next to him and shrugged. "Hell you say. They're all the same to me. I'll be glad to shoot them if y'all don't want to. Don't mind it at all. The boys in town heard Hampton killed 18 of 'em. Right in front of Kilpatrick's troopers. Slit their throats and dropped them off a bridge." He took a swig from his canteen and chuckled. "Y'all want any crackers?"

"This here's just murder, plain and simple," Connor squinted harder at the Yanks dangling from the ropes.

"Nope. You're wrong, Connor," JB replied calmly. "Ain't no murder when it's war."

"Damn right," Selby answered, spitting out hardtack crumbs. "That's what I say."

Connor kept his mouth shut. It was horribly wrong, but he realized, now that his blood had finally stopped boiling, that he was just as guilty, maybe more so. He tried to think of the last few days, but it was all just a jumbled mess. Best not to think at all, he reminded himself as troopers riding across the field started singing the 'Bonnie Blue Flag'. A teen in a red shirt galloped past him, swinging at the dead Yanks with a bamboo stick. Others took it up, whacking the bodies like they were piñatas, all laughing like they were at a picnic.

"Hell, Connor. The bastards scared the hell out of my parents. They deserve what they get," Selby laughed as another band of gray cavalry pummeled the hanging bodies.

"Well, maybe they ... "

"Maybe nothing!" Selby spat a wad of tobacco as more companies of troopers came up the road behind them.

Powell yelled over to them. "Y'all with Butler or Wheeler?"

"Ain't with neither," a mud-covered rider yelled back with a thick mountain accent. "Third Kentucky,"

"Heard anything?"

"Yep. Some of the Yanks got stuck up yonder. A ford called Mickle's Ferry. The river's too high. The bastards can't get across. We're gonna nick off a piece or two. Or so we've been told."

Connor listened but figured otherwise. If they could have been 'nicked', it would've already happened. He shook off the pain in his gut and looked up at the blue sky through the pines. What the hell. Maybe miracles were still possible. He followed along as they moved on toward the river and camped that night in a cotton field surrounded by woods. A trooper brought in a dog carcass. JB and Selby skinned and cleaned it, before sticking it on the spit over the fire. All eyes focused on the sizzling meat.

"It beats another night of parched corn," Powell slapped Selby on the back. "I ate a beagle dog once in Tennessee. It weren't bad neither," He produced a brown bottle, took a swig and passed it around as the wind picked up and the temperature dropped to near freezing.

"A motley bunch we are indeed," JB smiled, looking over at the troopers bedding down through the trees.

"Always have been," Fitts shrugged, finishing off his piece of dog leg then helping Selby bake the corn batter over the fire until toasted and firm.

Everyone ate their fill, and another bottle appeared from JB's blanket roll. They all shared, warming themselves up by the fire before bedding down. In the morning, troopers rode up with a captured Yank wagon and everyone helped themselves to tins of food and boxes of hardtack. The temperature fell even lower, and the cold wind blew straight through Connor's jacket. He wrapped his blanket tighter and shivered steadily underneath as the scout rode north through sandy pine barrens dotted with untended and overgrown cotton fields. Rifle fire drifted briefly on the cold wind then vanished.

On the next rise a dead Yank sat propped up against the base of a tree as if taking a nap. Connor thought of Norton and looked over at JB. Neither said a word. They followed in the rear of the scout another two or three miles through the pine trees and came up on a line of mounted militia stretched across the hardwood bottom. A dozen dead Yanks littered the ground. A big trooper with a head bandage had a live Yank plopped over his saddle and rode off with him like he might a prized calf. Others took turns shooting each Yank body, just to be sure, before quickly eating the Yanks' ham and hardtack.

One gray trooper lay on his back with a smile on his face. A hole in his forehead dripped a few drops of blood. Selby dismounted and listened to his chest. He gently lifted his head to feel the back of his neck and scalp. "It didn't go all the way through. The bullet's still in there. It's still in his brain. Hey you? Can you hear me?"

"He's dead, Selby," Powell said gently.

"Yep, maybe. But can he still hear? He's smiling. See? Remember Wallace at Dalton. Got his forehead blown off, but he smiled and talked for a long time until ... "

"But that boy there ain't talking. He's dead," Powell laughed.

"Can you hear me?" Selby yelled in his ear as firing erupted on all sides and the whole troop started to fall back in disorder across a cut-over clearing.

"C'mon! He's dead!"

351

Yank infantry came up the road from the east, firing as they spread out through the pine woods on both sides. The big trooper with the head bandage carried the Yank prisoner out into the open so that the Yank infantry in the far woods could clearly see him. He had a rope tied to the Yank's ankle and a note pinned on the man's chest. He gently laid him down on the ground then pulled his revolver from his belt and shot the Yank in the back of the head. The Yank infantry across the field roared and opened up with their Henrys. The trooper galloped back across the field dragging the dead man behind him, stopping at the edge of the pines and screaming like he was in agony. He wheeled his horse and fired his shotgun into the dead Yank's chest. Henry fire cut through the pines around him, but he was oblivious. The rest of them took cover behind the sandy ridge.

"Damn," JB rode up next to Connor. "The boys are getting meaner."

"It's not meanness. It's madness. This whole damn thing," Connor shook his head. "Got any more brandy?"

"Not a drop."

Another trooper pulled up next to them. His sharp cheek bones glistened with sweat. He wiped his brow with a soggy black felt hat. "Wiggins there was as right-minded as anybody back in '60. I knew him from before the war. He was a blacksmith in Kingstree. A good man."

"Was," Connor nodded.

The trooper's smile vanished. "Back off boy," he snapped back.

"Wiggins' is a decent man. Just last year, on furlough, he helped rebuild my barn. I'll cut him some slack. You better too."

Connor said nothing. He knew the trooper was right. Even a decent person could tolerate only so much for so long. Eventually something broke inside. He fought off more thoughts of the Yank boy on the grave in Columbia and watched Wiggins ride off through the trees, still dragging the body.

"He does have a burr up his ass now, don't he," Fitts laughed.

Wiggins' friend darted his eyes at him then rode off. Fitts glanced at Connor and shrugged then offered him a drink from one of the wine bottles as they pulled back through the woods. Connor drank more than his share and felt some better.

"Must have a big burr. Big as Hell."

The scout rode another fifteen miles until well after dark then went into camp along a road already bristling with other troops. JB went over to another scout and scrounged up enough food for everyone to get at least something. The night was clear and cold. Everyone crowded around the fire wrapped in their blankets. Powell offered up a bottle of whiskey that he'd been saving since Columbia, and everyone warmed up a little more. Connor gulped a mouthful that pleasantly burned his throat then bedded down by the fire for the night. Selby threw more wood on the fire as the wind picked up and the temperature dropped further. Men curled up as close to the fire as they could.

Connor didn't see a single sentry on duty but was too tired and drunk to care. He slept fitfully despite the alcohol, dreaming of a fire in the back pew at Mass. First light brought a dry mouth and a worse headache, but as he looked around at the clumps of brown and gray men rising up out of their blanket rolls, he didn't hear a single complaint. Damn if he would be the first. He shared a tin of Yank ham with Fitts then rode north with the troop towards Cheraw.

Chapter 38 — Luke and Connor

marching northeast to Camden and Cheraw

Luke's regiment waded on through more swamps for miles, burning every pitiful hamlet or cabin they happened across and skirmishing bastard reb bushwhackers dozens of times before coming up to what was left the town of Camden. A scattering of reb cavalry appeared behind a railroad embankment, but another regiment of blue coats kept them at bay. Rumors spread that the rebel General Hardee had 20,000 gray backs marching their way from Cheraw. Luke smiled as he watched the town burn. He didn't pay much attention to rumors anymore, not since crossing the Savannah River.

"We haven't seen but a few hundred rebs the whole trip. So let the rumors fly. Uncle Billy will just keep burning towns until the bastards give it up."

"Hell yes," Dave patted his back, watching the rail depot collapse into a fireball. "That's my Luke there."

"And for what?" Luke kept on. "For God's sake! Stop fighting, you bastards. Just surrender and let us go home."

"Or we'll just whip some more reb ass!" McMahon walked over with a half cooked side of bacon and tore into it. Luke and Dave joined in and, between the three of them, ate the whole thing.

"We're doing our part, eh Luke?" Dave grinned, wiping bacon grease off his beard.

"Yep. Hell with them all." Luke forced down the last few bites as officers called the regiment to reform. "To Hell with the whole damn war."

"You're dead-on now. But best we just finish it. C'mon."

The column was quickly on the move again, every haversack brimming with bottles and loot. They pushed on another ten miles. Luke's company camped that evening in a well tended cotton field. McMahon passed around a wine bottle. "What do you think happened to Jack? We ain't heard from him since he left with them bummers. When was that anyhow? Had to be before Orangeburg."

Luke stared across the field towards a burning turpentine still. "Either they're holed up with wine and women, or the rebs got them."

"Hope they don't end up in like those two we saw ... you know, those two hanging from the tree."

Luke pictured the gutted men hanging upside down with their intestines dangling to the ground and covered with ants. He quickly forced the image at his mind. "No sense in going missing in these parts. Not with bushwhacking rebs about."

McMahon rubbed his Henry and sighed. "Hell, they're probably drunk and bagging some pretty black ass right about now."

"Probably," Luke nodded, but thinking otherwise.

He figured they would have heard something by now. But, maybe not. As he bedded down he told himself Jack was all right. He wanted to believe it, and that night he dreamed of climbing a rock ledge with him at Glen Eldridge, on Seneca Lake. Jack was above him, almost to the top, and Luke's fingers were slipping on the algae-covered cliff below when he woke up just before dawn. Gunfire crackled in the distance and crept closer by first light.

"Shotguns and pistols," McMahon rolled his tent-half and checked his rifle. "Reb cavalry's on the move."

"Bastards just won't give it up, will they," Dave rewrapped his worn out shoes with strips of canvas.

"Nope. Not until we make them."

The gunfire came closer as the column moved out, and Luke's regiment was sent to picket the right flank. They spread out and wandered through a tangle of oaks, willows, and water oaks before coming to a bamboo thicket. Luke forced his way into the stalks, but couldn't get through. He moved back and around and lost sight of Dave and McMahon. The two men nearest him were from another company. He knew one of them. A small Italian, named Ferrico. The only man in the regiment to have escaped a rebel prison camp after being captured at Gettysburg.

Luke pulled himself up over a brier tangle as shotguns opened up. Ferrico went down, the other man too. Luke dropped to his knees in the bog and lifted his rifle. A huge reb soldier stood above him swinging his shotgun down at his head. Luke fired and felt his head split. When he came to, he was bouncing along on a mule.

The reb pulled up and dumped him on the ground. "Git up, Yank. You're awake now. You can run with the rest."

A young, wiry cavalryman with a scraggly black beard tied a rope to his wrist. Five other bound, blue-jackets trotted along behind other riders. Luke stumbled along, struggling to stay on his feet over pine stumps into a sandy field then down into another bog and across a shallow black-water creek past a cane thicket then into a cut over clearing full of more rebel cavalry.

Connor was there resting on his mule, along with dozens of other men from JB's troop, after riding on a big morning loop through pine then through low tracts of cane. He listened to the rifle fire erupt from the woods to the west and grow louder as more brown and gray troopers came riding across the creek. He saw the six prisoners being pulled along by ropes held by the horsemen and knew what was about to happen.

"Shoot the prisoners," a sergeant yelled.

Connor reacted immediately. He rode up and grabbed the nearest rope. "I'll kill him," he called out loud enough for everyone to hear.

The young rider hesitated, scratched his beard, then let go and rode off. Luke glanced up at his new captor. A boy with a scarred face, an eye patch, and a soot-covered, black jacket. He glanced at the double-barrel shotgun and Bowie knife. He thought of the men hanging from the tree. His mind raced. The five other blue jackets were dragged away and quickly shot at the edge of the clearing. Connor pulled Luke the other way. He crossed a stream where Luke lost his footing and went underwater.

Connor spurred his mule and yelled, "Like it boy?"

He had to make it look good. The last of the gray troopers riding past barely took notice. Just another Yank bummer being dragged to his death. Connor let Luke get to his feet then pulled him to the far bank and down into a swag in the woods. JB rode up behind and kept a lookout on the little ridge. Connor pulled Luke behind a big oak tree.

"Sit down and stay quiet!"

Luke knelt down and felt his heart jump. He gasped for air and looked around for any chance. Connor lowered his shotgun and fired into the ground. He paused and fired once more then backed off and reloaded.

"They'll think I put one in your head."

He looked into Luke's face. His mouth was wide open as if about to yell. His jaw trembled, and his eyes darted back and forth as he rose up to a crouch. Luke stammered for words, his eyes still searching for an escape. Was the reb just toying with him? His heart jumped higher into his throat.

"Just stay down, damn it," Connor snapped.

"Come on Connor! Everybody's leaving," JB yelled from the ridge.

"I'm coming!" He backed off, keeping Luke covered with the shotgun just in case. "Just keep still and be quiet. There might be another scout further back. Wait a while then head north. You'll find your column about a mile up."

"Thank you ... " Luke answered hesitantly. He rubbed his wrists, still not yet sure whether to believe. "God protect you," he added, thinking it was best to say more.

Connor shrugged. "Maybe. I hope so." But he immediately regretted letting on. Why was he talking to some Yank shit? Just spare his life and move on. It was the one thing that might make up for the boy in the cemetery.

JB fired into the air and yelled, "Come on Connor! The boys are pulling out." He wheeled about and trotted off with the others through the pines, yelling over his shoulder. "Damn it, come on! Let's go!"

Connor looked around. No one else was in sight. "Where you from Yank?" He felt a sudden, strange enjoyment at the absurdity of the moment but kept his shotgun ready.

"From Elmira. Elmira , New York," Luke stood up slowly, and Connor backed away another step.

"Elmira. I've heard of it. Near the Finger Lakes right? Real deep ones. Gorges. Glens. Real cold water. Right?"

"Yes ... ," Luke almost smiled. He couldn't believe it. What was happening? Who was this reb? "You've been there?"

"No. Had a friend though. He'd been up there before the war. His uncle lived in a place called Glenn Eldridge at Seneca Lake. He said it was the prettiest place he'd ever seen."

"I know it well," Luke shook his head in amazement. A rebel who knows about Seneca Lake and Glenn Eldridge. My God! Thoughts swirled his head. He wanted to believe he was being spared, but the shotgun was still pointed at his chest. He tried to think of something else to say. "Well I hope your friend gets back up there ... when the war's over."

Connor shook his head, his vision blurring for a second by the image of William's head exploding at Spotsylvania. "No ... He can't. He's dead. At the Mule Shoe ... at Spotsylvania." He backed away and fought off a sudden shortness of breath.

"Sorry," Luke held up his hands. Now I've done it. The reb will shoot me sure as Hell. What else to say? Quick. His brain clouded up. "This war is shit. Total shit," he stammered.

"That's for damn sure."

Luke caught his breath. "What's your name?"

"My name?" He hesitated. "Connor Dumont." What the Hell am I doing?

"Mine's Luke Conneley." He bowed stiffly and thought of adding 'thank you for sparing my life', but the shotgun was still pointed at his chest.

Connor nodded back. "I hope you make it home, Yank ... Luke."

"You too ... Connor." Luke hoped saying his name would help.

Connor felt an urge to even shake hands and talk more about Seneca and the Glen but knew it was insane. JB screamed at him from further down through the woods. Connor backed off, jumped up in the saddle, and trotted off quickly, glancing back to make sure Luke wasn't pulling a hidden revolver on him. Luke waved and Connor almost waved back. He chuckled to himself. Waving at a Yank. A dead one no less.

Luke hid in the cane thicket long enough to convince himself that no other rebs were lurking about then he made his way north, coming out of the bog into a stump clearing. Blue jacket cavalry passing through the pines on the other side leveled their carbines at him. He raised his hands.

"137th New York!"

The blue cavalrymen trotted up, keeping him covered until they were convinced then hoisted him up behind a young trooper wrapped in an oilcloth poncho. "You're one lucky son of a bitch. We're the last of the rearguard," the trooper smiled. "Nothing behind us but Wheeler's jackals."

"You don't know how lucky."

Luke held on tight as the boy spurred his horse and followed the rest of the troopers up through the woods, riding north for a few miles listening to rifle fire to the east and west. He found his regiment's camp just before dark. Dave slapped his back and opened the last bottle of wine in his honor. "Thought you were a dead man for sure," he laughed. "Them rebs bushwhacked us good. Two men missing from H company. That Italian fella ... "

"Ferrico," Luke nodded. "He's dead. They caught five others too. Shot them all. A reb boy took me back into the swamp and let me go."

McMahon's jaw dropped. "They caught you and let you go? The rebs?"

"Yep, just turned me loose."

Luke had to tell them the whole story a dozen times before they let him bed down, but he was glad to do it. It still didn't seem at all real. He slept fitfully and dreamed of crawling naked along a rocky creek bed. Each time, as the water came up over his face, he would wake up with a start. At dawn he felt more exhausted than any time since Gettysburg and was thankful for a slow start that morning. Dave brought him a cup of root coffee, and McMahon made sure he had a full ration of fatback and hardtack.

"You worried us yesterday, Luke. You're not gonna do that again are you?" McMahon faked a frown.

Luke gulped down the coffee and food. "No. I think one miracle is quite enough. I'll just head on home now ... if you don't mind."

"I'm right behind you," Dave laughed and pointed north. "About 600 miles that way."

THE REST OF LUKE'S MARCH to Cheraw was uneventful. Two good days and no reb cavalry raids. He was pleasantly surprised by the town. Most of the civilians had fled so the forage opportunities abounded everywhere. Whiskey, wine, gold and silver were the first priorities, but every house nearly burst with loot. Persian rugs, crystal chandeliers, fine china, all sorts of exquisite furniture. Officers laughed and enjoyed the better pickings that their rank entailed. The men contented themselves with as much liquor and wine as they would carry or drink. Regimental wagons creaked and groaned under the loads of kegs and barrels.

Luke stuck his head inside St. David's Episcopal church down the street. The reality of the war slapped him in the face. The church was packed with Confederate sick and wounded on blankets on the floor or in the pews. It smelled of dysentery and gangrene. An old man ladled out water to those who had strength enough to sip. His oversized, homespun coat drooped over his shoulders and arms. He smiled at Luke and eyed his wine bottles. Luke gave him one, and the old man opened it and took a sip.

"Thank you, son," he nodded. "Mighty fine. Best medicine there is … Along with peace and quiet."

He carried the bottle over to a sobbing boy whose nose had been shot off and helped a nurse put a fresh piece of gauze over the hole. He gave him a drink of the wine then looked back at Luke. "Y'all sure beat us to hell. Gave us a whipping, that's for damn sure." He turned and bent over the crying boy to let him sip more wine. "Hell, maybe we even deserved it. But it's over now. Except for this here. It won't never be over for the likes of him."

Luke took another bottle from his haversack and put it beside the boy's blanket. The nurse nodded, and the old man gave the boy another sip. Luke went outside. He'd seen enough men maimed and dying. He didn't feel like looking at any more on such a fine day. The wine flushed his face, and he stumbled down the church steps out into the sun following Dave and McMahon to the edge of town where they sat down on porch chairs of an abandoned house with a view of cotton fields stretching down to the river.

McMahon gulped down two whole wine bottles and wiped his face. Luke saw the tears in his eyes. It was the first time he'd ever seen him cry. "It's over Luke. We all know it's over now, yet … ," he slurred his words as he waved his hand back towards the river. "All those others that … "

"I know. I know."

"It's all shit, and there's nothing we can do about it."

"No, but it's all over now."

"No, that's not what I mean ... you aren't listening," McMahon struggled to open another bottle. "All those boys ... dead and maimed. And for what?"

"They won't be the last, I don't think," Dave shrugged unperturbed. "Might have a bit yet more to go."

"Hell you say," McMahon snapped back. "It's damn well over."

Dave put his hands up and backed off, "All right, all right. It's over."

"The whole stinking war's been one big shit-hole," McMahon ripped out the cork.

"Damn right," Luke patted him in the back. He felt it too. The waste of it all.

"I'm not crazy, Luke. It's just the wine, that's all," McMahon wiped his face. "It's just the wine."

Luke and Dave glanced at each other. "Of course it's the wine. No reason to ... "

McMahon cursed some more then took a deep breath and gathered himself. "I guess I'm gonna have to drink a whole lot more, eh?"

"Yes indeed," Luke nodded.

"Hell yes," Dave opened another bottle. "Here's to the three of us ... all crazy as shit."

SHERMAN'S ENTOURAGE ARRIVED IN CHERAW shortly afterwards. His officers led him to a decent house that hadn't been ransacked. A colonel brought him a Persian rug and asked if he could cut him a new tent bottom and saddle cloth. General Sherman nodded, and the colonel and his lieutenants went to work with sharpened knives and scissors. Sherman accepted a drink of Madeira then walked outside and up the street to the river, followed by other officers and a company of rifleman. He stopped to watch the high, raging water eat away at the bank.

"There goes another little piece of South Carolina," he smiled, tossing his chewed cigar stub into the black water and stooping down to pick up a little piece of brick. "Well look here, boys. It's shaped just like Ohio. This might be a sign," he laughed. "Time to get on home."

He turned around and looked back at the town, now swarming with blue troops, and at the rain clouds rolling in over cotton fields to the south bordered by a green wall of pine trees. He put the piece of brick in his pocket next to Willie's bullet then felt a tingle down his spine. "Yes. We're just about done here. It'll soon be time ... very soon."

He conjured up a fresh cigar, lit it up, and paused to enjoy a hearty puff. His fingers found the bullet again. As he smelled the sweet cigar smoke, it suddenly reminded him of Christmas dinner with his family back home. His chest sagged for just a moment then he recovered himself and looked around at his entourage who encircled him, watching his every move. He smiled at them. "It's a fine day indeed, isn't it?"

"Yes sir," they all answered.

Then he thought of several things that needed to be done and reeled off another flurry of orders.

CHAPTER 39 — MIELA / EZEKIEL

Charleston

The two upstairs rooms of the slave quarters at Legare St. were lined with cots. The downstairs, consisting of a laundry room and pantry, now empty except for kegs of parched corn, were used as the living and eating area. Everyone slept upstairs except Poins and Jemps who slept in the garden hut after draping it over with mosquito netting they'd found inside. Neither could quite grasp the idea that things would never be the same. They would come out of the hut every morning half expecting the Yankee troops to have disappeared and for Mr. Blessing to be waiting for his breakfast on the second floor veranda. Every morning they would look up and smile at the blue coats up on the porch who in turn would ignore them.

Miela kept to herself, hoping things would improve as the city settled down under military rule. She went out every morning looking for food while Ezekiel went up to the ferry landing every other day or so to see if things were getting safe enough to go to Smythes. Miela found a little to eat here and there, but it still not enough for all of them. The Union supplies saved them. Crates and barrels kept piling up along the wharf front and the officers doled out rations to those not too proud to beg. Just enough food to keep them all going.

Miela feared that if they took the ferry over to Smythe's with less than a few weeks' worth of food, they might run at before they could find or gather more. Then what? She watched the civilian whites whispering as she helped Jemps and Poins load a few sacks of corn onto the wagon to take back to Legare Street. She knew clearly that when the Union troops left, the whites would quickly regain control. Even if the Yanks stayed, if they stopped giving out food, what would they do? She figured it was best to stay at Legare St. only as long as necessary to gather up enough supplies to last them.

"But how much do we need?" Jemps asked.

"I really don't know," Miela sighed. "As much as we can find, I guess."

She knew there was no promise that a freedman would have enough to eat or to be truly free to do what he chose even though slavery had officially ended. She kept hoping that the each day would be better though. That peace would bring in a new world. That the city would rebuild, and that everyone, blacks and white, would somehow learn to get along as free people. But every day it was the same. The Union troops patrolling the streets, the white civilians whispering and waiting, and food always in short supply despite the daily dole of rations.

Thousands of other freed blacks were doing just the same. Each day the crowd waiting for bags of corn grew larger. It was hardly worth leaving the house, even before the yellow fever broke out. The rumor was that it was caused by recently opened drains in the streets that hadn't been purified by thunderstorms. Others said it came from a ship from Nassau docked at Adger's wharf. Whatever the cause, within one week 67 people had died. Elsey got sick with chills and fever, and Miela quarantined her in the garden hut and made Poins and Jemps sleep in the pantry. She stayed delirious with fever for three days, but lived. A Union officer in the main house wasn't so lucky. They could hear him coughing up on the third floor for the same three days then he screamed all night and died just after dawn of the fourth day.

The other Yank officers had him buried behind the kitchen house in a space between the woodshed and the rear property wall. Miela and the others watched the soldiers dig the grave down eight feet to the water table. They lined the bottom with bricks, oyster shells and lime, and wrapped him in a red velvet drape from the main house and sewed it tight. The men lowered him gently into the grave. Miela hugged Lizette and they all joined the soldiers in 'Amazing Grace', singing together as the soldiers filled in the grave then lining the top with slate shingles and bricks and hammering a wooden cross into the ground about his head. An older officer knelt by the grave.

"Now Andrew has gone on before us. He'll always be up there in Heaven reminding God that good Union men are still dying in this godforsaken place. So Lord, please listen to him. We're still needing some more help down here."

The Yank soldiers said the Lord's Prayer and finished paying their respects then went back to the main house. Lizette knelt down and helped carefully rearrange all the pieces of slate and bricks into even lines. Yarrow climbed up the big magnolia tree in the backyard and tossed down enough blossoms to cover the grave. A yellow cat appeared on the back wall, jumped down, then curled up right next to the cross as if part of the ceremony.

Cumseh scattered pieces of white blossoms over the grave, "A yellow cat is a sign from God. We need to go to Smythe's. It's time. Food or no food. We'll just have to make do." She crossed her arms and glared at Miela.

Miela nodded back, "Cumseh's right. Absolutely right. We'll go as soon as Ezekiel says it's safe."

Cumseh cocked her head and wondered if Miela was playing with her, but Miela came over and gave her a hug. Cumseh smiled, "Maybe it really is a sign from God."

Miela squeezed her hand, "It has to be."

Late that night, Ezekiel came back from his trip to the ferry and announced to everyone that it was indeed time to go. "I went over and scouted the island. There's no reb cavalry anywhere to be seen. No one at the ferry has seen any sign of them for a week. I say let's take tomorrow to pack up and get ready. It's time to go to Smythe's."

He counted their money. Twenty-three dollars in coins and three Yank dollar bills. And they had just enough food for another two weeks. But after that ... ? Neither he nor Miela knew exactly what to think. They really didn't want to think about it at all. They both knew it was a risk. But to stay in the city was a risk, too. To survive in the city meant making money, and Miela knew what kind of 'work' was available for a woman. She knew that staying at Legare Street with drunk soldiers in the street at night and food running low was no one's first choice.

The next day all of them went to work. Elsey and Daphne packed up the food, Jemps and Poins the wagons and team, and Titus the clothing and equipment. The children pitched in and Lizette gathered herself enough to cook corn cakes for the journey. Cumseh helped her and even gave her a hug, the first anyone remembered. Miela walked down to the Ashley River to buy fresh fish from the returning skiffs that rowed back to shore in the evening.

The boats pulled up next to the bathhouse built on pilings and now swarming with blacks who had never been allowed to use it before freedom came. The Mosquito Fleet, she smiled, thinking of the name they were being called. Twenty or more skiffs of all shapes and sizes with homemade, jerry-rigged spars and sails. And every fisherman among them black and free. She gladly paid the asking price for a dozen spot tail bass, croackers, dogfish and flounder, all wrapped in a little piece of burlap and still kicking.

"It's still a free meal,"she laughed. "Fish caught by free men and eaten by a free family."

The fishermen laughed with her but still made her pay. She went home and Daphne cooked all the fish in cornmeal batter. They ate half for supper and saved the rest of the trip. That night she curled up with Ezekiel in their little closet room and made love for a long time. God had blessed them. If only He would continue to bless them for a little while longer.

In the morning the wagon was loaded to the brim with everything they could carry. They made their way as a group up past the city market and Miela bought four goats to go with them. They tied them to the back of the wagon and moved on up Meeting Street. The children rode in the wagon with Titus and Cumseh. Jemps and Poins walked up front beside Ezekiel. Miela and Daphne were right behind. Elsey and Lizette brought up the rear.

Off-duty soldiers lounged in the street. Homeless, hungry blacks wandered this way and that. Whites sat silently on brick piles watching them. More than just a week before. Miela felt their stares and saw the black soldiers staring back. Two soldiers walked right into a group of white men of army age and cursed at them.

"Get off my sidewalk, reb. And stop looking at black women."

One white man with a dark beard and scar across his forehead jumped up and started to raise his fist, but his friends held him back. They all stepped out of the soldier's way, but Miela knew exactly what would happen when the soldiers were gone. She thanked God Connor had written them the deed to Smythe's.

An old white man, obviously drunk, staggered up to the wagon and smiled at the children. "How're my little bitties doing? Where y'all taking my little ones?" He produced a liquor bottle, sucking down a

mouthful. "Jules Luden's the name. Sail-maker for the high and mighty."
He bowed and almost fell down, bumping his head on the side of the
wagon. The children all laughed, but Daphne and Elsey quickly stood
between him and the wagon.

A black soldier came up and put his face right in the man's nose.
"What are you smiling at grandpa? You think they're still your slaves?"
He poked his shoulder. Other soldiers surrounded them and bumped him
harder in the back. One knocked his hat off. Luden stooped to pick it up
and a soldier pushed him down.

"That's right old man. Get on your knees and get used to it. Black
men with guns are here to stay."

All of the soldiers laughed. Mr. Luden got up slowly. His knees and
hips ached. His brain went blank. Nothing came to mind. What could
he say? What could he do? His whole life and everything he'd known
were gone. Black Yanks, rudely tormenting him in broad daylight on one
of Charleston's finest streets, were proof positive of that. There was
nothing to do now but wait for the end. Then a gentle hand took his
arm. Miela had pushed through the soldiers and was helping steady him
get to his feet. "Are you all right?"

He looked up into her pretty, brown face and stammered, "Yes ...
thank you."

A soldier touched her thick black hair and laughed behind her back.
"Are you his mistress? You sure ain't no society girl."

Miela hesitated but saw Ezekiel stepping forward out of the corner
of her eye. She knew there would be big trouble in just a second. "Nope,"
she smiled to the soldier. "He's my slave now. I own him lock, stock, and
barrel." She laughed, and the crowd of soldiers whooped, having expected
to see fear or anger not a laughing, confident, and very pretty black
woman. It turned the tide and Ezekiel backed off.

"Well now. So that's it." The black soldier wiped Luden's face with
a dirty handkerchief and patted his head. "We better not harm this nice
lady's property."

Miela pulled him behind her and laughed, "Now y'all leave my white
man alone."

Luden nodded and managed to bow towards the soldier before
holding on to the moving wagon. "Thank you ... sir."

"Get out of here grand dad and don't thank me. You best thank God ... old man," the soldier laughed. "If we hear your missus say one bad thing about you, we'll cut your balls off."

Miela laughed louder and hugged the soldier's neck. "Now don't you worry about Luden ... He'll be the best servant I'll ever have." She took his hand and patted it, blinking her eyes at him as if making fun. "Won't you?"

Luden staggered, feeling the bourbon wrack his brain. He tried to salute the white Yank officer who rode up and ordered the soldiers to reform into lines and march on. Miela held his hand and smiled, waving until they all disappeared safely around the next corner. She looked over at Ezekiel and saw the brick in his hand. She knew she'd been lucky.

"Thank you Miss ... ,"Luden wobbled. Miela grabbed his arm.
"My name's Miela ... From Blessing Plantation. " She squeezed his hand. Luden felt his eyes water up. He couldn't help it. He looked up at his battered house with the shell hole in the third-floor wall, the shutters broken and hanging loose, the window panes all broken out, and chest-high weeds on the lawn.

"Thank you." He let go of the wagon, wobbled into the gate of his yard, knelt down, and sobbed. Agnes and Fatima jumped out of the wagon, clapping like it was a game. Miela gently pulled them back to the moving wagon.

"Mr. Luden here has some pain to heal up. It's his time just now, not ours. We've got to get to Smythe's before dark."
Luden looked up through his alcohol haze and called out to them, "God bless all the children ... ALL of them." He hiccoughed and knew it wasn't even a lie.

Even before the war, as a sailmaker, he'd taken pride in always looking out for the children, black or white. Giving them candy or molasses pancakes and making them bracelets that he knotted out of bits of cloth. He'd always figured that children were more decent and deserving of charity. Perhaps the perfect age being about ten. It was only when they got older that they became unpleasant. At least that's how it had appeared in his eyes.

He waved to Miela as her group pushed past more black regiments drilling in the street. She waved back, but Ezekiel kept them walking along quickly. Only Yarrow lagged behind, wanting a blue uniform with a rifle more than ever, so he could go find Grace and kill the bastard rebs that took her. Ezekiel wanted one too but kept it to himself for now. He fetched Yarrow and had him stay by his side, looking around at Miela and the darting eyes of the silent whites walking past.

He knew the rebs would never accept defeat. They would never let blacks be free. At least not totally. Their war would never end. He daydreamed of black regiments staying in Charleston forever. Maybe Sherman wouldn't disarm his army. At least for many years. A blue army made up of black men with rifles. The only way to stay free. Otherwise the whites would just wink to each other, and the black man would be back on the plantation, if not in chains then at the very least in servitude. As soon as Sherman went home.

Yarrow pulled free and jumped into the wagon to play boat captain. Ezekiel refocused and kept them moving faster than they were used to with Miela. They covered the six miles to the ferry by suppertime. The boat was just getting ready to leave for the last trip of the day. Ezekiel shook his head. "Best that we cross in the morning. So we can get our bearings while it's daylight."

No one questioned his decision, not even Miela. They all figured if anyone could pull it off, it was Ezekiel. He went inside the tavern. Yarrow watched him through a dirty yellow window. Ezekiel stood at a corner of the plank bar talking with the white ferryman. White union officers sat at a table with other white civilians. Two other black men sat on stools by the fire. One of them glanced up at Yarrow in the window and shook his head. Just then Miela pulled him away.

"Come back with us, Yarrow. Men don't like being spied on."

"I wasn't spying, just looking," he frowned, jerking his arm free. "What exactly is spying anyhow?"

"Never mind, just come on."

She had them build a fire across the road where they camped for the night. Lizette baked sweet potatoes in the coals, and they ate the rest of the fish. Ezekiel came back and said everything was set for the morning.

"What's today?" Cumseh suddenly asked, warming her hands over the fire.

"Don't have no idea," Daphne laughed. "What day is it Miela?"

"I'm really not sure."

Cumseh looked up at the sliver of moon, her eyes filled with wonder. "Well I'll tell you this, there'll be no full moon this month," she smiled. "Have you ever heard of a month with no full moon?" She looked up at the sky and raised her hands.

"Well there must've been one," Elsey said with a mouthful of fish. "There ain't no month with no full moon."

"Nope. There won't be none. It's a sign from God. A sign that Grace will come back. That she'll be all right. One way or another. She'll come back or we'll find her." She cupped her hands and held them up, holding the sliver of moon in her palms. She could almost feel it. Soft, like Grace's hand. And bright as her smile. Tears started to roll down her cheeks before she could stop them. They were all speechless. No one had ever seen Cumseh cry before. She coughed and rubbed her eyes, and Miela pretended not to see.

"It is a good sign All right, Cumseh. God's looking out for Grace, I know it. You're right. And he's looking out for you too."

Cumseh wiped her face and regained herself. She pulled out two little pieces of iron. Two bits of shrapnel she'd found back at Legare Street. She rubbed them together with a little grinding noise then buried in the dirt and covered the little mound with ashes from the fire. "The bad times are gone now. The Divine is with us. Grace will soon be too. In the promised land across the river."

"It's Thomas Island, or Smythes, not 'the promised land," Ezekiel sighed, but Daphne kept chanting it out in a ditty the rest of the evening.

"Tomorrow brings the promised land, the promised land.

Tomorrow brings the promised land, it BRINGS the promised land." Ezekiel ate some fish and decided it best to stay out of it. He stayed up all night keeping watch with an axe and a brick by his side. It was a clear night, and the rising breeze off the water kept the mosquitoes away. He listened carefully all the while, but after they all bedded down and the tavern closed, the only sound was the breeze, the lapping water of the Cooper River, and Titus snoring.

Chapter 40 — Thomas Island

Charleston

In the morning Ezekiel went over to speak to Mr. Montague, a 'free black' and one of the ferry crew, who lived in a small log cabin behind Dover's Tavern. He wanted to find out the truth. Would they be safe going over to Thomas Island? Mr. Montague said yes, then lowered his voice and came closer. "The free blacks who lived there ran off. Been gone now for about two years. Not a soul on Thomas Island. Rebel cavalry's been coming down the Cainhoy Road, but I heard they pulled out. But they never come across the creek over to the island. Not that I've ever seen. No reason to, y'see. Nothing's there."

"Why did they leave? The people who lived there."

"You know why," Mr. Montague smiled. "But I can see you're man who's willing to work hard for what the whites will allow."

"What do you mean?"

"What I mean is ... that they left because they were afraid. Afraid the whites would take everything away. Their freedom, too. Make them slaves again. Heard they done went to Florida. Thought it was safer. Figured if they fought back they'd be killed."

"A fight don't bother me. I'd fight the devil himself if it would help my family."

Mr. Montague raised his hands and shook his head. "I believe you. You look like you might. But that's not what I mean. What I'm saying is the whites will let you own a little piece of property. That's what 'free-black' means. Just that it still depends on their good graces. No more, no less. They've always had the power. Always will."

What he didn't tell Ezekiel was that if the South had won, it would have helped him work his way up in the ferry business since he had long known the secret for success in living with the whites was to be openly and vocally 'loyal.' He'd done just that. For years. But now that the North had won, he was glad on the one hand that the uppity whites had

371

been brought down a peg it, but on the other, the price he'd paid was dear. He was no longer anything special in the black community. Everyone was a 'free black' now. If anything, he was looked down upon. An Uncle Tom. A half traitor.

It riled him because he hadn't done any of it for himself. His wife and children were his life. He'd worked only to protect them, and he always would. To hell with anyone who didn't understand that. And he was savvy enough about the white man's world to foresee that freedom might not be all that freed-men thought it would be. The main problem, he knew, would be land. White's owned most of it and wouldn't part with it for long. Just until the last blue coat marched off out of sight. Blacks would be free, but penniless, landless, and totally dependent on their previous masters, now their bosses. He knew they'd all have to deal with white society after the Yanks left, and he knew they wouldn't stay forever. The trick would be to appear still loyal to one and yet not be a traitor to the other.

Ezekiel nodded and seemed to read his mind. "I'll do what I have to, to help my family. And I wouldn't trust any man who didn't. The first thing for me though is to get them across the river. Over to the farm." He waved at the wide Cooper River and the marsh beyond. "Can I trust Captain O'Neill? I don't want everyone knowing our business. Who we are, how many, and such as that."

Montague nodded. "I understand completely. It just might work too. You've got some money, you say? Captain O'Neill keeps his mouth shut for money. A paying customer's business is his own."

Ezekiel nodded. "We've got some. Enough I hope. How much do they normally charge?"

"Fifty cents a person. A dollar for a horse mule or cow. Wagons depend on the weight. You'll need about $20-$30. And I doubt they'll take Confederate." He pulled out a wad of Confederate bills from his pocket. "I wish I'd spent all this last month."

"I think we have enough."

Montague shook his hand. "Well then, maybe I'll come visit you ... when you're set up."

"Be glad to have you."

He went inside the little shack office and paid for the ferry transport, using up almost all of the money for the trip over. The white-haired ferry owner, Mr. O'Neill, stepped back outside with him and directed the whole group and the wagon down to the landing where the large flat-boat ferry waited in its slip between two sets of pilings. A square steering-cabin, iron boiler, soot-covered funnel, and pulsing steam engine, enclosed in a wooden protective cage, sat in the stern. The bow area was open for cargo.

"My boys down there will help you load up," O'Neill waved dismissively.

Ezekiel tipped his hat and shuffled his feet a bit. Miela glanced at him and smiled. They both knew how to act. Just the way the whites liked. And it worked every time. Mr. O'Neill just snorted and smiled.

"Boy, you got no idea what you're doing, do you?" He bent closer to Ezekiel, pointed across the river and whispered. "It ain't the 'promised land' like them women was singing last night. It's just Thomas Island."

He kept leaning forward and Ezekiel bowed his head, trying to look as obedient as he could. Mr. O'Neill shook his head and walked back inside the cabin. "God help us."

"Thank you sir," Ezekiel tipped his hat, smiling at the good fortune of a high tide that had the ferry pushed right up close to the bank.

He had everyone help pull the wagon on board by hand, and the two white deck hands, boys about 16 years old he guessed, helped with surprising enthusiasm. Even the mules cooperated, thanks to Titus covering their eyes with blankets before loading. It all went easier than he'd expected. Mr. O'Neill and Montague came aboard as the boys were about to cast off, and the engine was given full steam. The ferry boys let go of the ropes and the boat chugged away from the bank then across the Cooper River towards the Thomas Island landing.

The day was mostly clear but windy and cold. Fish-scale clouds came in rows from the east. The river churned past, chop rising harder as the tide began to turn to ebb and push back at full strength. The women and children huddled against the aft cabin in the lee of the wind, but Ezekiel stood in the bow relishing every second. The only thing possibly more wonderful on this crisp, glorious day would have been the river parting itself at the wave of his hands. He smiled at the thought and Miela saw it.

"What?" She smiled back.

"You know," he waved his hands at the river. "All this." He glanced over his shoulder at the white dock hands then leaned closer to her and whispered. "Our freedom."

Miela understood. No use boasting in front of whites. Their world had turned upside down. For now. But it could happen again, in reverse. She stood by his side and held his hand as they came up on the entrance to a small creek and churned up a channel that snaked through the marsh grass. Yarrow stood in the wagon amidships watching everything. The big bow pushing up the creek, the stern -wake rippling the marsh grass and stirring up annoyed herons and egrets into sudden flight, the line of moss-covered oaks overhanging the bends and waving at them from the Island bank, and a lone osprey eyeing them unperturbed in his nest high in a dead pine tree. Everything about being on a boat was exactly as he'd imagined it would be, only better.

They came up to the deserted landing. Just a clearing in the trees with two rows of pilings lining the pluff mud along the bank. The ferry slowed down then edged into the pilings and swung into the slot between them and up against the bank. The deck hand boys quickly tied the bow to an oak tree and lowered the gangplank. The unloading process took much longer. The mules didn't want to leave the boat, and the wagon had to be unloaded completely before it could be manhandled up the ramp. Mr. O'Neill came out at the aft cabin to watch, but neither he nor the boys helped. Only Mr. Montague lent a hand.

It took all of their strength and the help of the mules pulling a tow rope from up on the bank to get the wagon safely up to land. Everyone helped reload the crates and barrels as Mr. O'Neill reversed the engine and pulled back into the wide creek, turning slowly towards the Cooper River. Jemps and Yarrow waved, but neither of the white boys on the bow waved back. Mr. O'Neill just shook his head and said something inaudible against the thump-thump of the steam piston.

The ferry dropped back down the creek with the ebb tide, finally disappearing around the far bend in the high marsh grass. Ezekiel and Miela waved too, knowing the value of feigned pleasantries. No telling what the local whites would do. The deed signed by Connor meant nothing if some white person, Yank or reb, decided to take exception. Both knew that blacks might be free according to President Lincoln's proclamation and the force of the Union Army, but blacks still had virtually no rights. Certainly none versus a white man. The best thing to do was to get settled in as fast as possible on the property. There had to be some safety in numbers. The death of one or two blacks might be nothing, but killing off the whole group would be a bit more difficult. They followed Connor's little map which led them a quarter mile up the overgrown road to a smaller track through a stand of pines. The trees opened up as the road cut across a clearing. A row of thatched-roof huts lined the road, each with walls made of bamboo poles woven over a pine frame and packed with clay. Two larger shacks stood by themselves close to the back edge of the pine trees. Ezekiel and Miela walked over. The larger one was made of pine logs and had a cast-iron stove with a tin stovepipe rising through the tabby wall. A plank bed was built into one corner. An empty water basin waited to be filled beside a cast-iron coffee pot. A row of skillets of different sizes hung from wooden pegs on the wall. One entire wall was painted with an odd shaped white horse that reminded Miela of the cave drawings she'd seen in Mr. Blessings *New York Times* paper. She remembered him saying it was an article about ancient cave dwellers in Spain and southern France.

"You like that? Ezekiel asked, nodding towards the painting.

"I do. There's something about it. Something spiritual."

"Maybe it's a Spirit horse. The Holy Spirit and all. Heard it takes different shapes. Like a ... "

Miela laughed. "You know all kinds of things, but I doubt you can tell me much about the Holy Spirit."

He shrugged and smiled. "I guess not."

Agnes stuck her head into the flap door. "Poins found a dozen rattlesnake skins," she beamed.

Yarrow bumped in behind her holding up deer antlers. "A bunch of these too."

They darted back out in search of more treasures, and Ezekiel and Miela followed behind, over to the smaller shack made of rough pine planks daubed with tabby. There were no windows or chimney, just a fire pit sunk into the middle of the floor, a tarred canvas flap for a door and a hole in the roof to let out smoke.

"We can make do," Ezekiel scuffed at the worn floor boards.

"We can do more than that. We can ... what's that word ... the one Blessing used to ... "

Ezekiel grunted. "Please don't mention him ... I'd rather you not ..."

"Flourish," Miela ignored him. "We'll flourish. You just wait and see."

"All right," he sighed. "Flourish it is. C'mon."

They walked to the end of the road where an open shed stood on a dozen palmetto log pilings with a plank roof that covered hog pens and horse stalls. A corn crib was built into the outside wall next to a tabby brick well and cistern. Jemps and Titus were already unloading the wagon, making a perimeter of sacks, kegs, and boxes like a little fort. Ezekiel helped them get everything situated then everyone took a break to eat some cold, left- over corn cakes.

He walked off by himself to scout the woods around the field all the way to the marsh that stretched a mile or so to the river. He found two campsites fairly recently used and an empty hardtack box. Horse tracks led him through the woods to the north, to more marsh stretching nearly a half a mile to the far bank. A ribbon of blue water snaked through the green marsh grass, disappearing around a small island of palmetto trees in the distance.

He followed the tracks along the marsh until he found a spot where the creek came right up to the high bank. The tracks disappeared. It seemed too far to swim horses though. At least he hoped it was too far. Maybe a boat had landed? He waited and watched for an hour but saw no movement anywhere along the distant bank. He retraced his steps, being careful to brush over his foot prints. At several spots where the tracks cut between thickets, he cut saplings and wedged them between the trees forming a crude fence of branches. Nothing that would stop a determined horseman for too long, but it might dissuade someone who was just curious.

By the time he got back to the clearing, Lizette had a fire going in the stove and smoke was rising from the big shack. Titus had the mules watered and resting in the stalls under the shed. Jemps and Poins pulled more water up from the well with a leaky wooden bucket they'd found. They filled up the trough and empty kegs and arranged them in a row beside the well as Yarrow chased the squealing girls in circles in the field. Puffy white clouds drifted overhead with the wind. The bright blue sky sparkled in the smiles of the children. In Miela's too as she walked towards him. Her brown skin glowing richer in the sunlight. Ezekiel knelt down and took off his cap. In a few weeks or so, he knew they'd be well entrenched. More cabins would go up. The fields would be plowed. Gardens planted. Laundry would hang from cloth- lines. The whites could still remove them by force, but the longer they stayed, the more it became home and the better their chances.

He blessed himself. He had come to enjoy doing it. It just seemed right. He gave thanks to God, silently in his heart for the gift that He had bestowed on them. He stayed kneeling there for a while just appreciating the moment. He thought of Quam, Pompey and Mingo. And of Toby on his way north. Tears came to his eyes. He blessed himself again then wiped his eyes and stood up. He turned around and saw the entire group on their knees behind him watching. A wave of tears washed over his face. He couldn't stop it. He sobbed into the back of his arm until Miela was there holding his face in her hands and kissing his cheeks. Then he was surrounded by everyone. The children tugging at his sleeves, the women hugging him, and the men patting his shoulder. No one said anything for a while until Miela kissed him and turned to the others.

"Ezekiel's a good man. As good as a man can be. Let's all try to be as good as him."

"Thank you Jesus!" Daphne called out.

"Thank you Lord," the rest of them answered.

Miela led Ezekiel to the big cabin and pulled him inside. He lay down on the blankets she had already placed on the bed, and she lay down next to him. He slept for hours. When he woke up, he let Miela and Jemps know about the horse tracks, but they all decided not to tell the others. Lizette cooked a supper of more corn cakes and the last of the molasses then Jemps stood guard at the edge of the field until well past midnight. Everything remained calm. There was just the wind in the trees and the roar of the crickets. Ezekiel finally decided they were as safe as they could be and gathered Jemps in. He went back inside and lay against Miela's warmth but slept fitfully. It didn't surprise him though. The first night in Jubilee and all. It was bound to have his blood up.

Chapter 41 — Mr. Luden

Charleston

Mr. Luden went inside and poured himself the last of his Madeira. He didn't even savor it, gulping it down instead in one large swallow. Fortification, he thought. Time to face the painful truth. His known world was gone. The new world in Charleston would be something totally foreign. He listened to the black soldiers singing out their marching cadences as they stomped up the street then pictured Miela's smiling face and wished that he was a capable artist. If only it could be painted properly and shared. A smile of hope for the future. A smile that meant decency in return for decency, no matter what the new world brought, To treat people as one would want to be treated. A behavior that surely would always be valued. Unless ... he allowed himself a brief glimpse of hell ... unless the freed slaves who had never been treated as human beings would now return the favor. If so, would the pendulum ever stop swinging? He let the last few drops from the bottle drip onto his tongue then wobbled off up to the Freedman's Bureau. By God, he would take a stand today.

He knew that there were hundreds, maybe thousands of blacks, women and children mostly, without food or shelter and completely dependent on the Yank troops. It was time for him to do something decent for them, his neighbors be damned. He thought of his two sons, dead from dysentery and buried in Virginia. And for what? The damn war? The cause? A wave of nausea washed over him, but he fought it off. He took $10 in gold coins out of the cash drawer and a bill of lading that proved that he was a sailmaker then walked up Meeting Street to the Freedman's Bureau and stood across from the entrance watching hundreds of blacks milling about. He wasn't exactly sure what to expect but figured God would show him the way. And he was right. A black women and a young girl came around the corner, huddled together under a torn blanket. The woman's only garment, an empty croaker sack, dangling from her neck. The girl's patched clothes were covered in mud and her feet wrapped in muddy rags. Why these two and not the others? It caused his heart to flutter. Was he doing the right thing? He didn't really know but figured God did.

That the Lord could take his only two sons in war, and his wife years ago to yellow fever, and still command his respect and love, showed His enormous power. That He could deliver a sign for Luden's future in the form of a black woman and child was, by that measure, easily believable. It was the only way to make sense of his loss. Especially his boys. God was showing him the right path to take.

He walked over and spoke to the woman. "My name's Luden. I can offer you a safe place to live with your daughter. We can go inside the bureau now and make it official. So you'll know it'll be safe." He backed away and held out his hands, watching the woman's jaw tighten as she eyed him suspiciously, just as he'd expected. "I'm just doing the Lord's work. I swear."

The woman squinted at him for a while like she'd just seen something but wasn't sure exactly what then took a deep breath and puffed out her cheeks. Her face slowly softened and tears formed up in her eyes. "I been praying to the Lord for help. We sure could use some." She nodded to the little girl. "She ain't mine. Just looking after her 'till I find her people. Some reb horsemen had her. Riding her on the back of the big ol'mule. Just swung her down and rode off. Never said a word to me, and she ain't neither. Not a word since. Not a one. Don't even know her name. I been calling her Sunshine."

Luden bent over to look into the little girl's face. Under a layer of dirt and grime, he saw a pretty child of eight or nine years old. The woman pulled the blanket back a bit, and the girl clutched her side tighter. "She's real afraid of letting me go. Real scared. Got reason to be, I reckon."

"No doubt that's so. But now it's time to be safe. And don't you worry. I'll help find her people. By God, if it's the last thing I do." He held out his hand. "The name's Jules. Jules Luden."

"Laura." They shook hands. "From Wassamsaw Plantation. Had four others with me, but they all went off with Sherman. Ain't seen them since."

"Come with me inside then. We'll get the necessary papers. C'mon."

He felt queasy but told himself not to dally. He didn't want doubt to get a foothold.

Laura had huge misgivings too, but hunger dictated no other option, and she desperately wanted to believe in just this kind of behavior from whites in the new Jubilee. So she followed him inside with Sunshine stumbling along with her, fists clutching her dress too tightly to be pried loose. They stood in line behind hundreds of others waiting to get to a desk where Union officers filled out mounds of paperwork. The officers were so overwhelmed with requests for help, that they never questioned Luden's motives. Focusing only on the fact that a white civilian was offering to take two refugees off their hands. One officer had Luden sign papers that required him to provide food and shelter and to allow a visit from a government clerk to check on the home situation. A visit that the officer knew would never be made. There just wasn't the time or manpower to do it.

Luden signed where he was directed, and Laura made her mark. The officer gave each of them a little piece of blue paper with a number printed in red ink. "In case there's a problem. Just come back and show this number. Good luck." Then he called the next person in line.

Luden took a deep breath and led Laura and Sunshine out the door and back to his house. Laura followed, holding on to Sunshine and praying to God it wasn't a trap. The first thing Luden did at home was cook one of his last chickens with sweet potatoes and a tin of cherries. Laura and Sunshine ate it all. Not a morsel was left. Luden went back to the pantry and retrieved two tins of peaches. They wolfed those down too. Then he cooked up a platter full of cornmeal pancakes, and only after a half-dozen each did they finally fill up.

"We ain't eaten much in a week. A dead squirrel we found. Some pecans. Some mushrooms. I heard they can kill you, but figured we was about dead anyhow. No harm done I guess." She smiled and tapped her stomach. Sunshine sat beside her holding on to her dress. Laura felt her fist relax just a bit. She knew it would take time. Especially since she felt just about as tense as Sunshine. The thought that Luden might still turn out to be a devil wouldn't die easily.

Luden showed them to the small bedroom behind the washroom on the first floor. It was his oldest son's room and still had his portrait on the wall. "The Lord took my boy. He's up in Heaven now looking down on us ... But I know he'd like to see his room be put to good use."

"What's his name?" Laura nodded to the portrait.

"Jasper. His brother, Ross, is up there in Heaven, too." He jerked his thumb towards the ceiling. "But Ross never liked people in his room upstairs," he shrugged. "Just the way he was. A good boy at heart but liked his privacy. Jasper though ... he'd ... " He smiled and cleared his throat. "Anyhow, this here's your room now. Make yourselves comfortable." He showed them the washroom and the privy then walked off and left them alone.

Laura sat on the bed with Sunshine and hugged her."We got an angel watching over us," pointing to Jasper's portrait. "A white angel with an angel brother." She squeezed her hard enough to make her smile. "C'mon let's get ourselves a bath."

Luden came back down with blankets and an assortment of old clothes then set out to inquire about the others in Laura's party from Wassamsaw, but there was no word. It took several more days for Sunshine to relax enough to talk. Having enough to eat and sleeping on a soft bed helped. At breakfast one morning, she stopped eating her cornmeal cakes. "My name's Grace," she whispered. "From Blessing Plantation."

"Praise the Lord!" Laura cried, hearing her speak for the first time. "Praise Him!"

Luden's eyes lit up. "My God!"

Laura looked up at him. "What?"

"The Lord has truly spoken."

"Praise God!" Laura held up her hands to give praise. She was quite ready for the Lord to speak. She figured He was long overdue.

"I've MET them. Her people. From Blessing Plantation. A woman named Miela."

"Miela!" Grace cried out. "Miela ! Where is she? I want her, please!" She pushed back away from the table and started trembling.

"All right Sunshine ... Grace," Laura hugged her. "We'll find her. Don't you worry none. I promise we'll ... "

"Yes, of course we will." Luden thought of his boys and fought off tears. "We'll definitely find her."

"By the grace of God!" Laura waved her hands and clapped them above her head.

"And Yarrow?" Grace cried, shaking so hard that she dropped her fork. "Can you find him too?" Her eyes implored him.

"I guarantee it. By God's Holy Name." He felt tears welling up as if from a gushing spring deep inside him. He thought of his wife, his boys, and all the other dead sons and husbands whose names had been read aloud at St. Michael's Church Sunday after Sunday for four years. His tears swelled into sobs, and his chest heaved. Then he felt strong arms around him, and little hands caressing his face. For a full minute, it was his wife and boys from a distant time as he watched water dripping onto his patched pants. Laura's tears. Her black face streaked wet. Her arms around him.

And beautiful little Grace gently wiping his face and hugging his neck. "It's All right Mr. Luden I know you'll find them. I'll help you, I swear."

Luden sucked up enough air in between sobs to answer, "Yes, we will ... by God, yes we will."

"Thank you Jesus!" Laura knelt beside him trembling with the Spirit. Luden caught his breath and patted her shoulder. "Yes indeed. The Lord is with us today."

"Hallelujah."

A WEEK LATER A WHITE MAN with a black woman and a little girl appeared on the road at the edge of the woods at Smythe's. Yarrow was helping Poins and Jemps cut firewood and spotted them first. He knew right off it was Grace. He dropped his hatchet and ran to her yelling, "Grace! Grace!"

Grace relaxed her grip on Laura's dress and ran to him, "Yarrow ! Yarrow!"

Yarrow flew into her and grabbed her, swooping her around and around, screaming the whole time, "Grace ! Grace!"

Grace cried so hard she could barely breathe and had to sit down. Yarrow hovered over her, his trembling hands touching her face and hair and then her shoulders, wanting to feel her, to make sure she was really there. "You're here! You just dropped down from heaven!" He knelt down and squeezed her harder.

Lizette was out weeding her tomatoes and cabbages when she heard Yarrow shout. Her heart leapt into her throat. She dropped her hoe. She took a deep breath and turned around slowly, expecting the worst. Her eyes watered up so fast she could barely see Grace running across the field, but she knew it was her, instantly. The way her baby girl's knees almost knocked together as she ran. She felt her chest heave and her own knees go weak. She could barely breathe. Then Titus was holding on to her and leading her to her daughter.

Yarrow was kneeling beside her with his arm around her as the others ran up shouting and praising God. Everyone was in tears. Yarrow whispered into Grace's ear,"No one will ever take you away again, I swear. You're mine now. You'll be my wife. My family."

She smiled in between sobs. "I know. I know. And you'll be my husband. Then we get to stay together night and day. We've just got to be husband and wife."

He squeezed her again, hard enough to let her know he meant it, and the only other person she was aware of for the next few seconds was Miela who knelt in front of her and kissed her forehead. "Welcome home Grace. Welcome home."

Then a voice called to her. A voice like no other. "Grace!"

"Momma!" She looked up and threw herself into Lizette's bosom. "Momma!"

Lizette sobbed and heaved uncontrollably, pulling Grace tightly into her arms and pressing her as close as she could, totally unable to speak and surrounded by everyone else, all crying and holding on to each other. Lizette rubbed her back and caressed her hair, still half expecting her to vanish, but finally in between sobs, she held her chin up and kissed her on the forehead. "My dear, precious girl. My baby girl."

"Thank you Lord above!" Cumseh dropped wisteria blossoms on Grace's head.

MR. LUDEN WIPED AWAY TEARS himself. He tried to tell them the story about how he first met Grace and Laura, but he couldn't catch his breath. Laura cried with him, sharing hugs with everyone as if she'd been part of their family for a long time. Mr. Luden tried to say something else in between his chest heaves. "My two sons ... " Then he cried even harder.

Miela kissed him on the cheek, and he blushed red. Agnes laughed, and Cumseh pinched her ear. Luden wiped his face and gathered himself then gave Miela a handkerchief tied around a roll of gold coins. "My two sons ... died for the Confederacy ... This represents their pay for three years of service. I had it changed to coins. I figured the boys would enjoy seeing something good come of it." He blushed even redder when Miela kissed him but felt a weight drop off his shoulders.

"You're redder than a red bird," Agnes squealed.

"Shush there," Elsey jerked her shoulder. "He's a good man. See that?" She pointed to his flushed face. "Good white men can flush red like that. Bad men can't. Never laugh at a good man's red face, you hear?"

She let her go, but Agnes ran off singing out. "Redbird! Redbird!"

Lizette pulled him to her and gave him a big hug. "In Jesus Name, thank you. Thank you. You brought my baby ... " She couldn't say anymore through her tears. She put her arms back around Grace.

Miela kissed her head and pulled Luden along. "Let them have a minute. Come on everyone." They left Lizette and Yarrow holding Grace while Titus stood guard above them. Miela escorted Luden to the big cabin hoping to have time to share cornmeal cakes and honey, but the ferry whistle sounded in the distance.

"You'll always have a place to come in Charleston, anytime. All of you." Luden squeezed Miela's hand then he gave Laura a big hug. "Laura knows where."

"Stop that Mr. Luden," Laura said laughing. "You'll make me blush too."

"Redbird! Redbird!" Agnes squealed, dodging Elsey swatting at her then running off yelling louder. "Got us a big old redbird!"

Luden wiped his face again then felt a laugh erupt out of nowhere. It was the best laugh he could ever remember.

CHAPTER 42 — CONNOR

on the road southeast towards Charleston

Connor's troop rode through a swamp dotted with makeshift tents and log hovels. Gaunt gray and butternut soldiers stood by each little fire. All were armed and staring nervously at the horsemen riding by.

"You boys with General Mclaws?" JB called out, already sure they weren't. The men in the swamp said nothing back. "They're deserters sure as hell," he whispered to Powell. "As many or more than our whole troop, and some better armed too. Look. Henrys."

Powell stood up in the stirrups. "We're headed up past Cheraw. Trying to get there before the Yanks cross the PeeDee. Gonna make a stand somewhere up yonder. Anybody who's got a mule or a horse can join us if you want."

None of the deserters answered him, but all watched closely as if expecting a fight. Connor saw it in their faces. Men who had been through plenty enough already. Men who would fight now only to stay alive. Not many would be coming with them. Maybe none at all.

Selby whispered to Connor. "No use getting all riled up about deserters. Heard a rumor from some of Butler's boys. Most everybody's gone from Petersburg now. Lee's down to a handful or two."

"I wouldn't doubt it," Connor glanced back through the trees at the dozens of deserters still watching them from around their fires.

"Wait a minute," a man called out from behind them, riding up through the cypress trees on a mule. "What the hell. Might as well have a last go," the rider laughed. His young face looked skeletal, but his brown eyes were full of life. He carried an Enfield rifle and a Yank canvas backpack bulging with a rubber tent half. "Gonna be over soon enough. Chandler's my name. Was up at Petersburg until ... well I just had enough for a while ... But I guess I can ride with you boys, now that I've got this mule."

385

"Connor. 12th South Carolina. Well I was, anyhow." He watched Chandler lift his head and smile. His gold teeth shined in the morning light.

"That's what we'll all be saying in a couple of months. WAS with ... whoever ... You ain't got any more food by chance, do you."

Connor tossed him a Yank beef-tin and Chandler wolfed it down and licked his fingers. "Ain't ate much since crossing the Peedee. Just some dog meat ... some raccoon. I guess I'd eat this mule of they'd give me another." He patted of the mule's neck. "No offense there Mr. Mule. I've been hungry for weeks. Took me two weeks just to get to Raleigh. My wife's cousin got me this mule. I rode all night. Hid in the woods by day. Couple more weeks to get here. I don't rightly relish the trenches no more. I guess I lost my gumption last month. Saw a swarm of rats eating a corpse in a shell hole. They came at us when we tried to run them off. Killed a mess of 'em with shovels ... Anyhow, boys are leaving every day. Call it desertion if you want. I call it facing the facts. This here war's over ... And we done lost. The rest of all this ... hell, it's just pride."

No one argued with him as they rode on single file through the trees. Everyone knew that nothing had slowed Sherman since Atlanta, and Lee was pinned down in Virginia. It was indeed over and no one wanted to be the last man killed, but surrender was a nauseating word.

They rode on for ten miles or so until dark then camped on higher ground in some pine woods. Connor helped Chandler and Selby boil corn while Powell and Fitts conjured up two more bottles of whiskey which helped everyone sleep soundly. Morning brought a glorious spring day. Not a cloud in the sky. Just a hint of breeze stirred the pines. They all gulped down more corn mush before the whole scout rode north with remnants of other regiments.

The sun warmed Connor enough to shed his poncho, "It's too pretty a day to fight."

Fitts tied his jacket around his waist. "Yep. Maybe the Yanks will take a rest." But as he spoke, rifle fire crackled faintly on the breeze. "Or maybe not.

They galloped off through more pine barrens glimpsing Yank cavalry on the next little rise paralleling a narrow stream that lay between them. Skirmishing commenced quickly. Rifles and shotguns fired up and down the line. The Yanks fired back, but no one was hit. The troop moved quickly north along the edge of the woods taking potshots at Yank cavalry and receiving them in return. It went on well past dark. A running fight along the stream bed in the pitch black. Every time quiet tried to take hold, a shot or two rang out, and by dawn the troop was strung out for miles.

It went again the next day then for two more weeks. Everyday flanking and tailing the Yank columns and sniping at them when possible. Then word came that Sherman's whole army was across the Pee Dee River and into North Carolina. The bastards were gone, and Connor, like a lot of the men from South Carolina figured he was somebody else's problem now. Everyone knew the war had to be nearly over, but most didn't want to desert Wheeler's Cavalry, unless they had to.

Their commanding officer, a colonel of the 1st Alabama but from South Carolina himself, gave them another option. He mounted his horse and wiped his long brown hair behind his ears, sitting up as straight as he could in the saddle but shivering uncontrollably. He wiped his eyes with the back of his yellowish leather glove. His other hand was wrapped in a big wad of bloody gauze. Another wave of shivering made his head bob. He cleared his throat and called out to the men.

"I'm going up to Goldsboro to join up with General Johnson. Any man who wants to follow can come with me." He wiped his face again with his glove. "Any man who wants to stay ... to help fight the Yank troops down by the coast ... will be allowed to leave. No questions asked. Go protect your homes and families. You've served honorably. No one could ask for more." He cleared his throat for a long time and wiped his face some more, then shivered so much he had to tighten his knees on the saddle. "God protect you all. I won't ever forget what you've given. And the others ... "

His men stood around him with bowed heads. Some wiped their faces. Most just stood in silence for a while. It was the first time any of them had heard an officer give them official permission to leave ... for good. They turned and looked at each other in shock and disbelief. It was just beginning to dawn on them that it was the beginning of the end. For many it meant the war was truly over. An officer telling each man to decide for himself what he wanted to do.

The effect was immediate. Some of the younger men decided to go north with the colonel to find Gen. Joe Johnson. Most of the others were headed home, but no one argued. Neither group begrudged the other. Now it was just a matter of exactly how and when it would end. To those staying, it was already over. To those going north, the ending would be one last fight, fueled indeed by pride. One last gathering of the Confederate Army. Some of them just not wanting to live the rest of their lives with the regret, and maybe that of their families, that they hadn't been there at the very end. But men in both groups already felt a sinking pit inside. The awareness that the biggest thing in their lives, the biggest thing that they'd ever been part of, was about to end. And very few thought that peace would bring anything better.

But Connor did. The war was over for him too. Sherman was no longer in South Carolina. It was time to go home and rebuild. Time to go find a peace that might work, that might actually last. If he could get back to Charleston, he might do some good. Check on Poppy Carr and Cora Gibson and do what he could for Miela and Ezekiel. If HE didn't then who would? It was his duty for sure. It had to be.

JB went over and spoke with the colonel then mounted up. "Are you coming, Connor?

"No. I'm going home."

"You sure?"

"I am. It's something I've got to do."

JB took his hat off and rubbed his head then walked his horse over, bent down and offered Connor his hand. "I ain't saying goodbye again. You'll turn up eventually."

Fitts followed behind and shook his hand too. "You sure you don't want Brig back?"

"No, you keep him. I think he's been good luck for both of us."

Selby and Powell followed behind. "Take care of yourself, Connor. Watch out for straggling bummers."

"Y'all too," Connor's eyes welled up, but he fought it off.

"Hey Connor!" JB wheeled his horse around. "Keep an eye on Norton's grave. Maybe when you get a chance you can ... Well you know what I mean. Might not be anybody else to tend to it. And ... well ... the others too."

"Don't you worry. I'll look after them. I'll do what needs to be done."

JB started to say something else but choked up and just waved. He turned his horse up the road and trotted off after the others. Powell called back as he rode off. "Remember to come visit me in Winnsboro. We'll have a fine drunk some day. Eat some big old catfish." He waved then spurred his horse after JB.

"I'll be there. Don't you worry." Connor waved back and watched the remnant of the scout disappear around the far bend in the pines then joined the others headed home.

He made his way southeast towards Bishopville and in two days rode 60 miles through cotton fields and farmland full of lazy cattle and barking dogs. A sign that Sherman's bummers had spared at least part of the State.

Two little gray terriers ambushed his mule just past the bridge over the Black River, causing the mule to buck Connor off into a split-rail fence. The terriers nipped at his pants and elbows until he kicked them away laughing. "Y'all don't know how lucky you are." He stood up and brushed himself off. "But I sure wouldn't mind introducing you to the Union Army."

He retreated a safe distance until the terriers ran back underneath a farm house. No one was about. Hiding, he guessed, and he didn't blame them. Maybe the terriers helped in the way. An early warning of sorts. Not a good time to meet strangers on the road. Deserters were everywhere. Every one of them armed and their discipline suspect at best. He rode on until dark and camped just off the road in an apple orchard. In the middle of the night he woke up with severe stomach cramps, and chills. By dawn he was shaking so hard he could hardly walk. He tried to ride on, but his gut tightened up in a ball and doubled him over. He woke up in the dirt with his mule nibbling green apples just off the road. Every time he tried to stand up the world spun around and threw him back down. Waves of cramps tore through his gut, balling him up into fetal position. It went on for hours. He vomited up blood and lay shivering on his side. How idiotic it was to suddenly get this sick after all he'd been through.

Just before dark it began to rain. He tried to crawl over to an oak tree at the edge of the road but everything went black. When he woke up, it was daylight and he was on a straw-filled mattress with a woman's face hovering above him. It was his mother for a full minute or two until she came into focus. A homely looking woman smiled at him. She was gap-toothed with a huge mole on her upper lip sprouting two long hairs.

"You got chills and fever. Colic too. Maybe you ate some bad apples. My name's Blair Lowry and I'll take care of you, don't you worry."

Connor tried to tell her it was probably dysentery, but his mouth was bone dry, and his lips felt stuck with glue. She spoon-fed him beef broth, but he threw it up and started coughing up more blood. He lost consciousness and remembered nothing else of the next few days except for her face coming closer and something that tasted like licorice dripping on to his lips. He found out later that he had spiked a high fever and stayed delirious for three days. When he came to, he was too weak to stand. He lay on the mattress in the woman's two-room cabin for three more weeks sipping beef broth and licorice-tasting paregoric that she offered for his unrelenting cramps.

"You ain't fit to walk much less ride that old mule." She laughed hard enough to reveal a mouthful of blackened, decaying teeth. "You'd best not be in no hurry to get it out of here neither. You'll be crawling on your belly in no time."

"Thank you ma'am," Connor managed to whisper back.

"That's all right. My boy's been up with A.P. Hill in Virginia. Name's Chester. He got bad sick last year, but he's all right now. He'll be coming home soon." She patted his clammy brow and smiled. "Mr. Belton came over last night. He said it's almost over. Yep. Chester's coming home. I know he will. Would've heard if he was ... She took a deep breath and sighed. "Well anyhow, you'll be staying right here 'till your better."

"Yes ma'am. Thank you."

Connor felt his stomach tighten up again and sipped more paregoric. She checked on him off and on all night to cover his chest in wet towels and give him sips of broth, but the coughing got worse before dawn. Shaking chills again wracked his body. It felt like he was falling into a tunnel. He was in and out of consciousness for a few more days, coughing up hunks of bloody, yellowish pus. Several times he thought he saw Henrietta at the door waving to him and whistling like a mockingbird, but she never spoke.

When the regained full awareness, he felt so totally drained that he couldn't sit or stand. It took two more weeks of Mrs. Lowry's beef broth, sips of paregoric, and a tincture of sassafras and huckleberry tea mixed with a few drops of turpentine, to get him on his feet. He slowly regained his strength until he felt able to ride. It was past time to get a move on. Connor thanked her and promised to come visit when he had money to pay her for her kindness.

"That ain't necessary. Keeping you alive means Chester's coming home," she smiled. "As God reigns in Heaven, I know he will."

"Yes ma'am. I'm sure he's all right. Thank you for your kindness."

She gave him a big hug and wouldn't let him go for a while. He was surprised at the strength of her arms around him and tolerated her kissing his cheek before she led him outside to help him saddle the mule. He mounted up and started off down the road towards Charleston. At the first bend in the road, turned to wave goodbye, but she had already gone back inside.

CHAPTER 43— EZEKIEL AND CONNOR

to Charleston, and the raid inland from the coast

Everyone at Smythe's went about their chores as usual. Planting corn and sweet potatoes, cutting firewood, fetching water, patching cabin walls and roofs, and building a fence around the entire field. Ezekiel decided to wait there for a while to make sure they were safe. They had plenty of raccoon meat and fish to eat, and Titus found two huge pecan trees deep in the woods and brought in two big baskets full. They still had some corn meal left and hadn't touched one keg of molasses. Most importantly to Ezekiel, no one had bothered them. They hadn't seen a soul since they'd landed. The ferry went back and forth up the Cooper River each day stopping at the Thomas Island Creek on its way upriver to take on the firewood that Poins, Titus, and Jemps cut for a dime a cord. But no one ever got off at Thomas Island the entire month. Ezekiel began to relax. He decided to go back to Charleston to look into enlisting. He knew better than to tell Miela. His story was that he wanted to find out what was happening, but also that they needed a few things. And that it was better and cheaper for him to travel alone. So one bright, clear morning he took the ferry across, walked all the way to Charleston, and slept on the racetrack grounds with hundreds of other blacks who'd come in from all over the state. Word spread to the camp that night that recruits were being sought for a new black regiment, and Ezekiel knew it was meant to be. All the other young men were excited too. To be fully armed and trained. To be able to go fight the rebel forces still roaming the countryside upstate. He knew immediately that he had to join up. He found out the details the next morning then obtained the things he needed for Smythe's. Sewing needles, cotton cloth, sugar, and some tar for the skiff that Jemps wanted to build. He made his way back to the landing by dark, slept under the porch and took the ferry across in the morning.

Miela knew as soon as she saw him coming up the road that something else that happened. He wouldn't have come back in one day otherwise. Ezekiel had already decided he wouldn't tell her until the next morning, just before he was about to leave, but she'd already guessed it.

He sat down and ate some fish that Poins had caught the night before. Miela came up behind him and put her hands on his shoulders.

"You're joining the Army, aren't you?"

He swallowed hard and looked up at her in shock. "How did you know?"

She wiped away tears. "It's what I would do, if I were a man."

He nodded. His mind raced. There was no use trying to keep secrets from her. She truly was a sorceress. A mind reader. "A black regiment's being formed. Fully armed too. Full service with the Army. No log cutting or bridge building. A real infantry Regiment."

"And?" Miela waited.

"To fight the rebs up by Florence."

"Where's Florence?"

Ezekiel sighed. "I'm not exactly sure, but ... "

"Then why not just let them have it?"

"Look ... ," he said harshly, then raised his hands in apology. "They're still at it. It's not over yet."

"It's over if you let it be over."

Ezekiel darted his eyes at her but said nothing else. Miela knew there was nothing she could do once he'd made up his mind. She would just have to stay put while he was gone and help the others the best she could. "So how long?"

"I'm not sure. A month or two maybe. The rebs are nearly finished, so ... "

"Then why go?"

He tried to put his arms around her, but she brushed him aside.

"C'mon Miela, you know I have too. It's not right for ... "

"What's right is whatever you decide is right. Isn't that true?" She felt anger welling up. "I swear to God, if you get yourself killed, I'll ... " She stopped, took a deep breath and hugged him. "I just want you to be here ... safe and with us ... with me. Please be careful."

"I will. I swear it."

Miela stayed right beside him all that evening but, to avoid a fight, didn't say anything else. She couldn't bear the thought of him leaving with anger between them, and maybe never coming home. In the morning at the ferry landing, Ezekiel hugged her for a long time, kissed her before boarding then slipped downstream with the tide, waving until out of sight. Esau went with him. They walked from the ferry landing back to Charleston and, in the morning, waited with hundreds of others swarming the partially burned train depot on John Street to join the new regiment. All blacks, aged 18 to 45, were accepted. Ezekiel waited in line with Esau and nodded to the officer, a handsome, well groomed black man dressed in a brand-new, blue uniform.

"Sir, my name's Ezekiel. This is Esau," he saluted. "We've been pioneers with General Sherman. We want to serve together."

"I see," the officer nodded. "You 've been with Sherman?"

"Yes sir, from the Salkehatchie to the Congaree. Laying corduroy mostly. Then we came back here. We heard y'all was forming black regiments," he smiled. "To fight."

The officer nodded. "All right. Sign here. Both of you."

He pushed forward a ledger with signatures and marks of all kinds. Ezekiel wrote out his name in capital letters, like Miela had taught him long ago with chalk on pieces slate. He made each letter as big as the ledger would allow so his name would stand out. His first time writing out his name as a free man. Esau made his mark like a bird's foot, and the officer nodded and signed his name beside theirs.

"Congratulations. You just signed up with the 102nd US infantry. My name's Delaney. Major Martin Delaney. Take this to Lieutenant Swails rolls over there. He'll get you uniforms and weapons." He wrote on a piece of paper and handed it to him. Ezekiel stood there for a few seconds more restraining himself then saluted the Major who returned it.

He felt his heart flip over. He turned to Esau.

"We're in the 102nd!"

Esau clapped his hands then poked Ezekiel's arm. "Is that good?"

Ezekiel just yelled in his face, "102nd! C'mon!"

They hurried into a line of other freedmen waiting for equipment and weapons. Lieutenant Swails, a trim black man in a crisp, blue uniform sat at a desk under a canvas awning in front of stacks of rifles and uniforms being issued to squads of soldiers. When it was Ezekiel and Esau's turn, they were given new blue pants and jackets, with backpacks, leather belts, and stiff leather shoes that had never been worn. Neither one of them had ever before worn new shoes or new clothes. They quickly changed out of their rags behind the awning and laughed at each other's appearance then followed the line over to Lieutenant Swails to get a rifle. The Lieutenant lapsed into a fit of coughing that wouldn't stop until he took a long drink from a jar of whisky. He caught his breath. "You're to be issued rifles that we've recently captured." His cough erupted again.

"Militia and such ... " He gasped for air and drank more from the jar. "Not the finest weapons, but they'll do. The regiment's going up to Georgetown ... General Potter is up there now. "

"Yes sir," Ezekiel quickly saluted again, smiling.

The cough seized the Lieutenant again, and he waved them off. A sergeant by the name of Taylor took over. He was well over 6 feet tall with wide shoulders, and he looked serious. He issued them the rifles. Old Enfields. A bit rusty but with full cartridge pouches and cap boxes. Enough for the entire company of 60 blacks that formed part of the regiment now swarming around the wagons. Esau pointed his rifle at Ezekiel and laughed.

"Surrender, you damn rebel."

"Don't do that," Ezekiel swatted the barrel away. "You could shoot somebody."

"It ain't loaded, is it?"

"Just don't point it at me. And pretend it's always about to go off." Esau blew on the rifle's trigger guard. "Is it? About to?"

"Listen here! Don't load the rifles yet," Sergeant Taylor yelled to the whole group, "Just keep them pointed up in the air."

Ezekiel glanced at Esau who sheepishly nodded back. Most of the others, like him, had never held, much less loaded, a gun before. They just stood there looking around at the next man, trying to figure out what to do until Sgt. Taylor had them march over to the Ashley River and line up facing the marsh. He showed each man how to load the rifle, cock and aim. It took most of them a while to figure out how to ram home the Minie-Ball cartridge and put the percussion cap on just right, but Ezekiel did it like it was old hat. He went over and conferred with the sergeant then stepped out in front of the clump of men.

"Listen here! Point your rifles out at the marsh. Line up here." He pushed and prodded them and to a line facing the Ashley River, but a few kept laughing and joking around. Ezekiel fired his rifle in the air.

"Now aim your rifles at the river!" He put his rifle up to his shoulder so that the others could see how to do it. Sergeant Taylor smiled and nodded beside him. He knew he'd found his first platoon sergeant.

"Ready! Aim!" Ezekiel called out to the trembling line of rifles pointing towards the marsh. Men looked around at each other and strained nervously to hold their rifles steady as the wind gusted towards them off the river.

"Fire!"

The line of rifles roared and smoke blew back into the men's faces. They all smelled the gunpowder and looked at each other in a daze. A moment of silence passed then a yell erupted from every man. They all felt it. The power of a new age that had dawned for each of them.

Sgt. Taylor kept them at it all afternoon until every man's shoulder was sore. But it was a wonderful soreness. They marched back in jubilation to a new camp at the racetrack where they slept that night in new canvas tents with a big black US painted on each front flap. White orderlies cooked them a huge feast of boiled beef, sweet potatoes, and cornbread. They all ate as much as they could. No one could sleep though. They were US soldiers now. The ecstasy of it felt like a cauldron of strong coffee.

For three days they marched around the race track and practiced firing their rifles into the marsh. Then on a bright sunny morning, they broke camp, marched off across town with another black regiment to a wharf on the Cooper River and boarded a steamer. None of them had ever been on anything but a flatboat in a tidal creek so when the steamer made its way out of the harbor in a rising northeast wind and chop, most of them stood on deck smiling nervously and trying to act as bravely as the next man. They watched dozens of pelicans diving for fish and men tossed hard tack crumbs to flights of begging gulls, but as night fell, the swell worsened and seasickness spread like a contagion. Even Ezekiel heaved his breakfast over the side. They all thanked God that by dawn the ship had steamed up into the calm Winyah Bay up the coast, followed by a squadron of porpoises that kept pace along the starboard side. They disembarked on to firm, dry ground upriver in the little town of Georgetown.

"I swear I wasn't scared a bit," Esau laughed.

Ezekiel smiled back. "I know. I know. And I'm Jeff Davis."

"Well, maybe a little," Esau shrugged as officers barked out commands to form up.

Their regiment quickly disembarked, marched a few miles past the town that already swarmed with Union troops then camped for the night in a corn field surrounded by woods. Men regained their stomachs and practiced marching some more in a big circle around the field. The next day they joined a column of white regiments and marched off up the Black River Road. Ezekiel walked alongside his platoon, as ordered by Sergeant Taylor. He spread the word up and down the line. No men were to be left behind. Wounded or otherwise.

"Rebs kill blacks. Wounded or captured. It don't matter. So don't straggle behind. No matter what."

Most of them figured as much. They'd all heard the rumors, but their spirits were up and nothing could dampen their mood. They were Union soldiers now. All of them felt on top of the world as they marched on for two more days through woods and recently plowed fields to a crossroads on the Black River. All of the farmhouses in the little hamlet were already burning. Courtesy of the white regiments in front. Their regiment was allowed only to watch. Ezekiel asked Lieutenant Delaney why.

Delaney leaned over and whispered, "Don't want to stir things up. Burning out whites in front of other whites? Nope. Even with our own white troops it's a risk. One step at a time ... for now."

Ezekiel knew he was right. He nodded and accepted it. "Yes sir. For now."

THE NEXT DAY brought Conner as far as Sumter and the railroad. Rifle fire crackled lightly in the distance. He kept on and found militia scattered across a cotton field in total disarray. No one saw him coming until he was up on them. Connor saw that they were just boys and old men. He realized a single company of Yank cavalry would slaughter them. A faint tapping and tearing sound came across the fallow cornfield followed by the grumble and thud of cannon in the distance. It not quite over after all. An officer with a white beard down to his stomach and a slight hunchback twirled the last lock of hair on his balding head and puffed his cheeks out like he'd just run all the way across the field. He might have been Moses' brother. Two hatless boy-soldiers stood beside him, eyes darting back and forth, exchanging unspoken worry. The old man seemed paralyzed.

"What to do?" He muttered finally, sighing in relief as if, by merely asking the question, he'd been relieved of a great load.

"We should move up towards Manning," one of the boys smiled, as he would to his grandfather. "Up towards the shooting. Probably it's them Yanks we heard about coming up from Georgetown." He wore a brand-new gray jacket over neatly ironed blue pants and carried two old flintlock pistols in his belt. His red hair seemed to stiffen against the breeze.

The other boy nodded quickly. He was dressed in homespun butternut covered over with an ankle length brown duster. "Yes sir. Let's go on up. Time to move." His eyes widened as if he had been called on to do a reading in church, and he stuttered a bit. "Best we go ... go ... Forward." He gulped air and saluted. "Sir!"

The old man nodded, twirled his hair into a knot, and took a deep breath. His face turned beet red then he let out a high pitched squeal that sounded like 'Yee - wah!' The boys took it as an order and trotted off, gathered up their 'men,' herding them into three bunches and facing them southeast towards the shooting.

"Let's go!" The red-haired boy waved a pistol above his head and in afterthought decided to shoot. He cocked it, held it out at arms length, and flinched as he pulled the trigger. The pan flashed and a half second later the old pistol fired into the dirt halfway across the field. Connor rode up behind them still unnoticed. He figured that after one good Yank volley, those still standing and untouched would be running home, content that they'd stood their ground as long as possible and glad that they'd been there at the very end. He startled them all by calling out to the old officer, but they recovered quickly and accepted Connor's offer to come along with the militia as they moved down the road toward the shooting.

A ways up the road they met more militia and a group of officers who seemed to know what they were doing. The old man sighed audibly, and his scrunched shoulders seemed to relax as he gladly relinquished command. Horses and mules were ordered to be picketed in the rear. Connor grabbed his shotgun and haversack and took his place in line, knowing it was all useless if the Yanks came their way, but figuring he couldn't just stand by and watch.

The whole line moved behind a millpond where a smooth-cheeked lieutenant in a fresh uniform limped along with bandaged leg and directed them to a ditch bank with a few logs for a parapet. They didn't have long to wait. Yank rifle fire crept closer. The lieutenant called out to them.

"The Yanks are raiding up from the coast, men. Some blue belly named Potter. We'll stop the bastards right here." He waved his spotless dress sword and limped down the line.

The red-haired boy winked at Connor. "Weren't Sherman enough?"

"Plenty enough for sure."

"Bastards are just gloating now, ain't they."

"Maybe so."

Gray horsemen appeared across the pond, quickly retreated across a narrow earthen dam that formed a causeway over the swamp to the right then took cover in a pine thicket to the rear. Following closely behind them was a line of blue soldiers who crested a small rise on the other side of the mill pond and moved steadily towards the causeway. Yank guns opened up right and left from the far trees. The lieutenant hurried along dragging his injured foot.

"You men better get ... "

A Yank shot decapitated him in mid-sentence. Blood spurted from his open neck and Connor thought he saw the lieutenant's lips mouth one last word. Half of the trembling boy-militiamen ran for it. The others fired a volley and ducked. The Yank column stopped briefly halfway across the dam as blue soldiers took cover in the ditch rows to either side before coming on again yelling. More gray cavalry came up from the right and stopped them for the moment with a well aimed volley, but Connor knew it wouldn't be for long.

He dared the buzzing Henry fire to take a peek over the log in front of him. He could see other Yanks wading across more swamp to the left. A railroad bridge crossing the swamp 300 yards past the left flank had been partially torn up to prevent crossing, and two guns covered the bridge area and the far bank. Blue troops peeked in and out of the trees past the bridge, and all the soldiers were black.

A tall man led the way. He walked bent over a little to the right, just like Ezekiel. Wouldn't that be fitting, Connor smiled. To come this far and get shot by Ezekiel himself. Connor could see them carrying logs to make a footpath across the swamp. He watched the tall soldier stand up on the stump and wave his arms for all to see. Connor found himself smiling. That had to be Ezekiel's dream. If only he could see this. But Henry fire ripped into the dirt beside him, and he crouched lower to wait for the little farce of a battle to unfold.

EZEKIEL'S REGIMENT marched up just as the reb militia fired on the column from behind the millpond. Heavy return fire broke out as each regiment came up and went into line. Ezekiel 's regiment was ordered to flank the rebs by putting down logs across the swamp to the right under the burned railroad bridge. The men went to it, quickly working their way halfway across the bog.

Ezekiel stood up on a stump and waved his arms at the rebs across the pond. "Y'all done burned it before WE could!" He yelled, firing his rifle at the hats bobbing up behind a little ditch line and log parapet. Bullets cut into the leaves about his head. He turned and dropped his pants.

"Look here! How 'bout kiss my big black ass!"

Bullets cut closer. Ezekiel jumped down to cover, and the men around him howled. Every one of them beginning to think what Esau already knew. That he was anointed by God.

A COLONEL RODE UP WITH A BAND of Kentucky cavalry and called to Connor's section. "Push those Yanks out of the woods yonder! Make them bunch on the causeway!" He ducked low as a Yank 12-pounder bounced over the logs to the right.

The red-haired boy yelled back. "We ain't got but 20 men left, sir. How we gonna stop them?

"Damn it. Move to the left. Follow orders son. You need to ... "

A gun fired from the rear drowning him out. It lobbed a shell over the trees into the swamp to the left. The boy saluted, and the rest of his bunch followed him down the ditch line behind the logs and around the back of the mill pond. Connor went with them. He knew what was about to happen. They spread out across the road behind the cover of a bramble thicket laced with wisteria vines and watched the Yanks come up fast. Hundreds of them. Connor fired first then everyone volleyed. The Yanks dropped to cover. They opened back up with Henry fire and everyone hugged the dirt. More men moved to the left around the last of the log works. Another Yank volley cut half of them down. The rest of them fired one more time then pulled back across the road.

The boy with the red hair was hit in the shoulder and chest. He hobbled back to the pine woods in the rear where the militia was starting to bunch up and said he was all right but promptly coughed up a pint of blood and collapsed. Connor tried to help him up, but blood poured out of his mouth and nose and the hole in his chest. His breathing stopped, and he stared open-eyed into the sun. Connor closed his eyelids and lay him gently on a bed of pine-straw but didn't feel much of anything except the waste of it all. He went back to find his mule and saw the last of the militia already riding away towards the rear. Someone had made off with him. A saddled was just too much of a temptation for boys running from Yank bullets. The whole line was pulling back past another creek and mill pond, and Connor felt there was no choice but to join them.

EZEKIEL'S MEN fired a volley and watched the reb line run for it. They cheered and carried Ezekiel on their shoulders back up the bank, embellishing the story until they had him shooting lightning bolts out his ass at the rebs. Everyone joined in singing 'John Brown's Body' until their throats were sore. It was clearly a time to rejoice. The Jubilee was with them in that swamp, and it was a glorious sight to see. They all kept cheering as their regiment pushed on to another pond, another reb line, and another flanking move through a swamp. As Ezekiel waded forward through the muck, a reb shell clipped a water oak right over his head. He caught the branch as it fell, held it up and waved it at the rebs.

"You can't hit shit, you bastards!"

His men again went wild again. Ezekiel was their new-found god.

Officers lined the retreating gray militia behind the ditch row flanking the next road. More Kentucky cavalry, mounted on scraggly mules, came up behind them. An old cannon stood in the middle of the road. Men were trying to reload it, but the rest of the shells wouldn't fit. Connor started laughing punch-drunk. He couldn't help it.

"The hand of God!" He shouted. The boys around him stared at him like he was a crazy man. But Connor kept on. "Yanks with Henrys, boys with shotguns, and a cannon that won't shoot! Why the Hell not!"

An officer turned to say something, but rifle fire ripped into the ditch line. Everyone dropped to cover. Yank infantry were coming on fast through the trees below the bridge. More of them were sniping from across the pond and beyond the smoldering ruins of the mill house. Thank God someone had thought to burn it, he thought. Yank guns opened up from the far trees. Connor watched an officer direct return fire. Two 12-pounders got off three rounds before Yank shells bracketed them and blood splashed everywhere. The officer's shoulder and half his chest disappeared. He fell dead over the gun wheel. The gun crew fired one last time then ran for it. The line of militia melted with them towards the rear.

Connor's crouched low as a bullet smacked the man next to him in the back. He ran across the road and slipped into the woods with the others. The Yank shells crashed through the branches above, but everyone else made it back to another bridge over a little creek where yet another stand was planned. They waited there until dark, but the Yanks didn't follow.

Connor thanked the Lord and took his place in line behind a pile of fence rails where he slept fitfully, listening to his stomach growl. At dawn some women from Sumter came up with a wagon full of cornmeal platters, pots of grits, and four large hams. Everyone had at least a few mouthfuls. Connor washed it down with muddy creek water and watched most of the remaining militia slip away to the rear. The mounted Kentucky men stood guard until they all disappeared. Connor understood. No use getting killed just to slow the Yanks down for half an hour. Better to tuck and run and maybe find a better spot, if any.

His little group joined the retreat, pulling back a few miles to the shelter of another ditch bank behind a little road through open fields. They waited there all day but nothing happened until just after dark when a house across the field went up in flames. It lit up the field all night like a Christmas bonfire. No one claimed responsibility, but the house just so happened to be full of sides of beef, and militia boys took turns jumping inside to pull out scorched, sizzling meat. Others came out with sacks of flour just as the front portico collapsed behind them in a volcano of flames. Connor ate half-cooked beef dipped in flour with the rest of them until collapsing into sleep. In the morning, just shortly before dawn, the Yanks came again and, after a volley on two, the whole line melted away again to the rear.

Connor followed the others through a pine woods and across a little bog into a bamboo thicket while Yank guns fired behind them. Someone yelled out next to him and bamboo shafts exploded into his face. It was the last thing he remembered until he woke up five days later.

THE REBS ran quicker than before. Ezekiel's company barely made it out past the swamp to the left when the firing stopped, and the whole reb line disappeared into the far trees across a corn field leaving a half dozen dead behind. Ezekiel found one bloody body along a ditch line and grabbed the brace of revolvers from the man's belt along with a belt of brass cartridges. He kept the better pistol and gave the other to Esau.

"Might not be a bad thing to have ... in reserve."

"Thanks Ezekiel. You mean I can keep it? For good?"

"Damn right. Spoils of war. Ain't that what they say?"

"Spoils? I don't know."

"Just keep it out of sight for now. Somebody might want it."

White officers rode up as he spoke. They glanced around at the dead rebels then ordered the regiment to help with the destruction of the surrounding countryside, assigning a certain section of fields and woods. They brought up a wagon full of turpentine kegs to do the job, The men all hesitated for a while, wanting to make sure it was safe to join in, but Lieutenant Swails gave them the go-ahead. "The time has come, boys. It's all right. Do as you're ordered."

Men yelled and fired rifles in the air until Major Delaney had them stop. "Enough! Just get to work."

They set about it slowly at first, still hesitating, even Ezekiel, until they all saw that none of the white regiments seemed to mind. Then they put their hearts in it, burning everything they came across. Cotton

403

presses, gin houses, barns, stables, farmhouses, fodder, cotton bales. They 'requisitioned' every healthy horse or mule, and shot everything else. Cows, goats, dogs, donkeys.

Ezekiel enjoyed every minute of it. So did the others. They tore up railroad tracks and burned the bridge across the Black River, along with a depot, train cars and locomotives. Ezekiel watched the flames and the pillars of smoke and knew that God was alive and well. He couldn't restrain a yell.

"His will be done!"

Men yelled back, "Jubilee! Jubilee!

And it went on for days. Marching 10 to 15 miles at a time and burning everything in their path. Ezekiel made sure to keep count on the trip. 30 locomotives, 98 railcars, three depots, and two bridges. He never got tired of watching them all go up in flames. It was truly a celebration of the Jubilee.

Every night they would bivouac as equals with the other soldiers. White regiments from New York, Ohio and Massachusetts along with the blacks of the 54th Massachusetts and the 32nd and 102nd South Carolina. Freed slaves of the south fighting for their freedom along with northern whites. Ezekiel hardly slept a wink for three weeks. His brain went from one joy to the next. To be able to fight as a black regiment. And win! The feeling overwhelmed him and kept him awake and tingling to the wee hours. He didn't want to miss a second.

CHAPTER 44 – LUKE AND EZEKIEL

Luke's regiment crossed the Pee Dee River on a pontoon bridge and began a more leisurely tromp through North Carolina. Days were filled with long, boring marches and no complaints. There wasn't the first hint of trouble and not a rifle shot was to be heard. Luke felt quite content. It was fine to be bored. He'd pushed his luck and was happy to march quietly all the way home. The peace and quiet helped him and everyone else to relax.

Then one lazy afternoon at a ten minute rest stop, the distant boom of cannon fire rumbled through the trees, "Damn it! Shit on this," Dave threw his canteen into the dirt. "Christ, give it up! You bastards!"

McMahon covered his eyes and groaned, "How much longer? What the hell are they thinking?"

Luke felt it too. The sinking fear in the pit of the stomach that something awful was waiting up the road, yet again. And it was. Near Averasboro, North Carolina. The rebs attacked Luke's column through dense woods. Cannon fire raged close by in the pines. Thick clouds of powder smoke drifted through the trees. His regiment moved forward slowly, picking its way through brambles and thick underbrush then up over a little hillock where they come under intense rifle fire from the invisible reb line further up in the forest.

Luke felt a sting on his forearm and couldn't hold up his rifle. Lieutenant Weitzel went down with a shot to the neck. Luke grabbed the lieutenant's revolver. He emptied it at a line of rebs charging out of the smoke and yelled for McMahon and Dave to follow. He ran forward without thinking, The whole company went with them, and the rest of the regiment followed. The hodgepodge line of reb militiamen turned and scurried back through the trees. Officers came up and took charge, but snipers kept everyone down. The fighting sputtered in front then moved off to the distance.

Luke felt his arm throb and rolled up his sleeve. A white piece of bone stuck out just below his elbow. His hand trembled and turned blue.

It doubled in size as he watched. Dave and McMahon looked at each other and knew what it meant. So did Luke, but no one said a word. They helped him back to the dressing station where stretcher bearers took him to the field hospital set up in a little crossroads. A surgeon examined him.

"The arm's got to come off, son. Too much damage to the arteries. You'll die of infection or gangrene if we don't amputate."

"Wait," Luke felt short of breath. "Give it chance. Put a splint on it. Let's see how it ... "

"It's coming off ... Now." The doctor was gruff. His job was to save lives not limbs. A pile of arms and legs bore witness just behind him. And he didn't have the luxury of time to debate with a wounded private. Dozens more waited their turn just outside the tent.

Luke argued with him as his breath went short then orderlies picked him up and put him on an operating table. His mouth went bone dry and the tent spun around. He felt a cloth on his nose and a quick noxious blast of ether then everything went dark. He woke up on a blanket with his left arm gone below the elbow. The bandaged stump twitched as the ether wore off. He struggled not to cry. He hadn't when others had died, and he told himself he damn well wouldn't now.

A young captain came up and pinned a blue ribbon on his shirt. "You're a sergeant now. But first you need to heal up. Rest for a while."

Luke looked down at the stump. "But ... How ... ?"

"Don't you worry," the captain waved his hand dismissively. "We've got plenty missing an arm or leg. You'll do All right." He walked off with a limp, his wooden peg leg sticking out where his right foot should have been.

An orderly followed behind and gave Luke a dose of laudanum. He drifted off to sleep and stayed half aware for four narcotic days. When he came to, he found he'd been moved to the big camp at Goldsboro and that he'd missed the larger battle at Bentonville. He prayed that Dave and McMahon were All right. God surely wouldn't take them now. Not this close to the end. He couldn't be that cruel. A few Hail Mary's seemed appropriate though, just in case.

Fever set in that afternoon, and when he tried to get up, he felt nauseous and weak. The doctors found a deep pus pocket at the end of his stump. A black orderly come and dug into it with a metal probe while Luke bit on his belt. It went on twice daily for a week, the digging then rinsing with soapy water that caused enough pain to make him cry, then packing with cotton gauze that was Yanked out before the next torture. Each time feeling like he'd been bullwhipped. But it was a torture that worked. The fever relented, and he knew he would live. Luke thanked the orderly.

"I can see now that the pain was worth it," he nodded, watching him wipe the probe off with a piece of dirty rag.

"Yep. A man can bear 'bout anything if he's got no choice." He smiled and went to work on another man's seeping leg stump.

"Maybe. But I doubt I could have stood that another week."

"You'd be surprised. Had a sergeant help me pull a piece of fence post out of his own gut then hold the hole open so I could fill it up with iodine. Bit clear through his belt but not a sound." The orderly laughed. "All that just to die a week later. No tellin' with the Almighty, eh?"

Luke's arm throbbed badly. He didn't want to think of any worse agony but couldn't help but watch as the orderly dug into the next man's leg stump, thankful at least that it was someone else who had to bear it for a while. Sleep came after more laudanum, and, in the morning, his appetite returned.

Over the next few days, he regained enough strength to walk about the sprawling encampment admiring the different regimental flags flying over the city of tents. His own 137th New York wasn't there, and no one seemed to know anything, or at least they wouldn't say. Then one afternoon a few days later, while sitting on a bench by the camp headquarters enjoying the warmth of the spring sun, a dispatch rider galloped up, jumped off, and just let his horse go. He ran into the Headquarters tent and shouted,

"It's over! Lee surrendered! His whole army! Everything! Two days ago at Appomattox. In Virginia!"

All the officers stood up and looked at each other speechless. The rider waited for a second then yelled louder as if they hadn't heard him.

"It's over! The war's over! Lee surrendered!" He saluted again then burst into tears as if wanting too for a long time.

A Colonel read his dispatch over and over. He wanted to be absolutely sure. No use getting the men's hopes up if it was just rumor. Finally he looked up at the other officers gathered around him, all of them wide-eyed and holding their breath.

"It's true. Lee surrendered." He held up the orders and yelled. "The wars over!"

Everyone within ear shot fought off tears. The word spread faster than a breaking wave. A roar went up and down the tent lines as men stopped what they were doing and, after a moment of disbelief, felt something seer into their brains. The crystalized moment of awareness that they were no longer fighters, only soldiers waiting to be disbanded to go home. The disbelief evaporating instantly into cheering, singing, and dancing arm in arm. Veterans who had never shed a tear on the worst battlefields, or afterwards, wept like children. Rifles volleyed into the air.

Luke realized at that moment that the old world had suddenly disappeared. A second ago he had been part of a conquering army. Now it was all over. He was just a man among many others in a strange place, suddenly aware of how far they'd come…and how far they were from home.

EZEKIEL'S MEN heard the news of Lee's had surrender in Virginia and listened to the white regiments whoop and cheer. Men ran through the camp's firing into the air and passing around bottles of liquor that miraculously appeared from under blanket rolls. The black regiments all stood quietly. They all felt the same thing. They didn't want it to be over. Not quite yet. Not until they'd whipped the white rebs just a little more. Punished them some more for what they'd done. For what their fathers and grandfathers had done.

"Lord. Give us just one more good fight," Ezekiel prayed with the others, and God heard them.

Gunfire rang out the next morning. One last reb militia stand at a little pond called Boykin's. Ezekiel and his men laughed as the morning light showed them the way. The rebs on the higher ground behind another millpond. A big swamp on both sides of a flooded road. A log parapet across the one high causeway. Two more reb guns barking at them. Shells clipping branches above their heads, but not a hesitant man among them. God was on their side, and Ezekiel, their leader, was invincible.

They were ordered to the right and waded through the swamp water about a quarter mile to another bridge. Ezekiel led the men across on logs laid over the bridge remnants. Reb militiamen came out and lined the far bank, firing as soon as they came into range. Lieutenant Swails appeared, waving his sword above his head. "Come on, boys! Send them bastards to hell!"

Ezekiel ran up beside him and fired his rifle as bullets thumped into the bridge timbers. The men followed as quickly as their footing allowed. The charred timbers supports gave way twice, and several men fell down into the swamp. They waved that they were all right except for one man with a broken wrist.

"Come on boys!" The lieutenant fired his revolver at the rebs then fell down as if he'd twisted his ankle. Ezekiel helped him up and saw blood running down his leg into his boot. The lieutenant felt his knee and winced. "Shit."

"They last wound of the war probably," Ezekiel smiled.

"Yep. Could be. Better help me back."

Ezekiel strapped his rifle over his shoulder and carried him to the safety of the trees while the rest of the men kept up rifle fire until the rebs pulled back into the far woods. Lieutenant Swails felt the hole in his calf and his hands trembled. "Got to walk all the way back to Elmira on this?" He tried to laugh.

"Where's that?" Ezekiel helped him up.

"New York. It's where I'm from."

"I've heard of New York."

He tried picturing in his mind the globe on the iron stand he'd seen in Mr. Blessing study. New York surely was one of those black dots that swirled by when he'd spun it as fast as he could. He smiled, realizing that the globe and everything else of Blessing's was now just ashes. Then he thought of Toby on his way north to the snow and that he might never see him again. He knew it was the price he had to pay.

The lieutenant groaned some more and felt faint. Ezekiel gave him water to drink and waited with him until orderlies came up and took him off on a litter. Swails clenched his teeth and tried to smile. "Come up and visit me after the war, Ezekiel. I'll return the favor, God willing."

"Yes sir," he saluted. "I'd like that." He held his salute until the Lieutenant's head bobbed out of sight through the trees. Joy filled his heart. To salute a black officer. "The dawn of a new day!"He called out to his men. "The Jubilee!"

"The Jubilee!" They yelled back. Then men all around started howling like hunting dogs.

Ezekiel led them back across the bridge remnants to high ground where they opened up on the rebs. The gray militia line melted away into the far woods. Ezekiel ran after them firing, and his men followed. They all loved it. Chasing and shooting at white rebs. Something they could only have dreamed about just a few weeks before. They made it across another cotton field and into a thick woods before bugles sounded the recall. Officers shouted out orders to fall back. Men cursed. They wanted to keep going.

"Damn that," Ezekiel had them form a quick skirmish line and fire one last volley into the woods. "At least they got the message, eh boys?" Men howled some more and fired one last time. None of them knowing if they would ever have another chance. They pulled back across the field and over the rail bridge and formed up. Other regiments were doing the same. Then waiting most of the afternoon for orders before the entire column turned and headed back towards Georgetown. Their war was over.

The march back was nothing but a big lark. No fighting at all. But it didn't suit Ezekiel or his men. They would have much preferred blasting militia, but it was all over. They were now being forced to content themselves with what they'd done. To be part of a black army that had conquered the rebs. It wasn't as much fun as chasing the bastards, but it was still a damn good feeling.

A huge crowd of freed slaves followed the column back. Ezekiel tried counting how many. One cotton field alone held over a thousand. He gave up and counted his blessings instead. Thank God he'd been part of it and not like the younger boys staring at them, longing to be a soldier and sad that it would all be over before they were of age.

It took five more days to make it back to Georgetown where they waited for transport back to Charleston. Ezekiel wandered the streets by the river with Esau. Relaxed soldiers lounged everywhere, but sentries were posted on every block.

"I guess we ain't burning Georgetown," Ezekiel smiled.

"Not yet anyhow." Esau lit a match and flicked it into the dirt street.

"Nope. If it ain't burning now, it won't ever."

He gazed up al a stately red brick building with massive white columns holding up a wide balcony. Esau followed him inside and up the dual flanking staircase to a second floor ball room. 'Indigo Exchange', read the brass tablet on the wall. They peered inside the french doors and marveled at the curvature of the wide plaster ceiling. A cool breeze off the river swept through the open windows and, for a second, Ezekiel imagined what the plantation princes had felt, coming up the stairs in all their finery for an Easter Ball, then waltzing in with rich debutantes gowned in silk and diamonds. He laughed and grabbed Esau by the arm.

"Dance with me. Come on." He bowed and tried to hum a tune but couldn't. Esau backed away.

"You better watch out." He looked around at the sound of footsteps on the stairs. "They might not want us dancing."

"Who?" Ezekiel laughed and lit a match. "Think of all the slaves that built this hall. Let's dance this once then burn it down. Come on Esau let's burn it."

"Well ... I don't know. I kind of like how the ceiling curves."

Ezekiel looked up. "Me too, I have to admit it. But I still want to burn it down." He lit another match as the posted sentry walked up. The young, red-faced soldier shrugged.

"I'd just as soon burn the whole town, but the Captain says no. At least, not today. Hell, if it was up to me I'd burn every southron shit hole."

Ezekiel nodded. "All right, by me."

Esau smiled. "South-ron." He said it very slowly. "South-ron. I like that."

"Come on Esau," Ezekiel grabbed him and twirled him around. "One dance before we go."

Esau fought him off. "You're crazy."

The sentry laughed. "Who ain't in this hell-hole."

He pulled out a tin flask and offered them a drink. They accepted the whiskey and lounged on the veranda for the rest of the afternoon enjoying the peace and quiet until just before dark when transports came up the river and the regiment was called to load up.

The weather gods were merciful with calm seas and a light breeze. A double ration of hardtack, ham tins, and rum was handed out, and men bedded down on deck. Ezekiel couldn't sleep though. He realized that life as a free man waited for him in Charleston. He stayed up on deck all night enjoying the canopy of stars that dipped into the ocean on the horizon, figuring it was God's way of talking to him. Every star representing a future blessing. A way to make sense of what he'd been through. And he damn well was ready for it.

Chapter 45 — Celebration

Charleston

Poins ran back from the ferry landing with a copy of the Union Mercury newspaper that a black man had tossed to him from the ferry as it went past. "It says that a parade's planned in Charleston," he panted. "To celebrate freedom ... at least that's what the man yelled to me."

Miela read it out loud,"A parade to celebrate Union victory and freedom for all blacks in South Carolina'. It starts in two days."

"We've got to go, please," Daphne begged.

"Yes please," Elsey grabbed her from behind.

"A parade! A parade!" The children yelled, gathering around, all eyes on Miela,

"All right! All right. Of course we'll go."

How could they not, she thought. The Jubilee was here. It was the most important time of their lives. They had to go see it. Especially the children. They needed to remember. Everyone shouted, and the children danced in a circle. Titus was the only one quite content to stay put and tend to the farm. Everyone else raced to finish up their chores and ready themselves for the trip the next morning. That night the children could hardly sleep, and everyone was ready at dawn. Miela decided to take the wagon and the mules and go back to Legare Street.

"We'll stay a few days. Maybe a week or so. We'll watch the parade then make a trip to the market. Jemps and Poins can fish."

"I'll bring the raccoon hides," Jemps trotted off towards the barn. "I can sell them for ... "

"What ever the family needs," Miela called after him. "Bring the salted meat too."

Jemps stopped running and sighed, "All right," He walked slowly inside the barn door. "But I'm buying myself something with any fish that I catch."

"Fair enough," Miela smiled.

She doubted Malcolm Blessing would be there since the Yanks were in the big house, and the Jubilee going on. But if he was, she still had Jemps and Poins with her. Surely they would be safe enough as long as they stuck together. If there was any sign of trouble, they could take Mr. Luden up on his offer to stay with him. So they took the ferry and made good time on the road into town, getting to Legare Street before dark and sleeping in their quarters in the back. There were fewer Yank officers in the big house, but enough to keep Blessing away. The parade started early the next morning, and everyone was up early in anticipation.

They walked up Meeting Street past the huge, ornate Charleston Orphan House, still magnificent even with the shell holes in the portico, with its towering cupola, and neat geometric garden complete with ornamental statues. Throngs of other blacks surged past them singing and dancing in the streets. The parade stretched for a mile past the Citadel square. Mock mourners walked alongside a horse-drawn hearse with signs that read: 'The body of slavery', 'Slavery is dead,' 'Who owns him? No one.'

Thousands of freed blacks stood along the sidewalks cheering continuously as a black cavalry unit rode past with blue sashes and red, white, and blue rosettes. Miela and the others jumped up and down, shouting and clapping just like the children. The 21st Union Regimental Band marched up behind them playing the Hallelujah Song, and little girls in front carried a banner that read: 'We know no masters but ourselves.'

One group after another followed. All shouting and singing. Butchers, tailors, coopers, painters, carpenters, blacksmiths, wheelwrights. All black and all with banners that read: 'No caste or color, just free.' A wagon painted blue-and-white and pulled along by four mules brandished a towering sign painted on bed sheets and tied taut between long bamboo poles. It read: 'Car of Liberty on the Freedom Road.' Little children dressed in red and yellow shirts hung from the sides of the wagon blowing dandelions out at the crowd that followed along towards the parade grounds where a black officer on a platform shouted loud enough to be heard over the din. They all listened to him to scream out.

"My name's Delaney. We're all the same color to the whites! Whether the light brown or the darkest black."

414

Elsey whispered in Miela's ear, "Or cinnamon."

"Shhh ... I want to hear him."

The officer stopped for a second, looked right at them then kept on shouting. "We need to stop judging each other by the tone of our skin! We're no longer slaves, Mulatto or African. We're free! Free men of color! Unite and help your brothers!"

The crowd roared its approval and broke out in a half a dozen different songs all at once. Black soldiers passed out cornmeal cakes sprinkled with sugar, fried sweet potatoes on sticks dripping in molasses, and hunks of fish. People sang and clapped. Miela and the others joined a huge line of dancers snaking their way through the crowd behind a man with a big drum while the regimental band mounted the platform behind Delaney and started playing even louder. The singing and dancing went on all morning and into the afternoon. Every time one part of the hoarse crowd paused, another group started up with a song. The most repeated verse being,

"We'll hang Jeff Davis from a sour apple tree, as we go marching on. Glory, glory, hallelujah! Glory, glory, hallelujah!"

They all danced and sang and ate the cornmeal cakes and sweet potatoes and laughed until their sides ached. Daphne, Lizette and Miela stayed close enough to the children so no one would get lost in the crush. By evening, they were all exhausted but determined to keep on until the last song, but just before dark, Miela decided it was time to go back. The children locked arms laughing and said they wouldn't budge.

"We're gonna dance all night," Agnes squealed.

"You can stay up and dance 'till dawn if you want to," Miela smiled back.

"Really?"

"Yes, back at Legare Street. We're heading there right now."

"Oh please. Just one more song," Fatima begged.

"Two more," Agnes laughed.

"Three more," Yarrow twirled Grace around.

"NO more," Miela laughed. "Come on, NOW."

The children danced in a circle for another half an hour laughing at Miela, until Daphne helped her corral them, and Jemps threatened to whack them all with one of Yarrow's sticks. They reluctantly obeyed and followed Poins through the throng while Miela and Daphne walked on each side herding them until they made it home. They all pledged to stay up until dawn but were already yawning and, one after another, soon fell fast asleep. Lizette and Elsey carried each of them off to bed, and everyone else drifted into sleep behind them listening to scattered explosions in the distance

In the morning, louder cannon fire boomed from across the harbor. Miela went out to the street to find out what was happening. An officer leading a troop of Yank cavalry galloped past firing his pistol in the air, "Lee surrendered! The war's over! We're going home!"

His white soldiers fired their carbines, waved their regimental flags, and threw their hats in the air. The black troops down the street stood nervously watching as if half expecting their officers to confiscate their weapons.

Elsey came out and took Miela's arm and held it tight. "What does it mean? Will the Yanks leave us?"

Miela patted her shoulder, "It means the old way is definitely over. The rebs have finally been beaten."

"But will we still be free?"

"Yes, of course we will. Freedom's here to stay," she answered matter-of-factly, knowing better than to share any hint of doubt.

Miela had heard about Lee for four years now but never cared much about him one way or the other. She figured there were plenty of other white men around who would be happy to take Lee's place. Whether he surrendered or not meant very little to her as long as freedom remained intact. But she was smart enough to know that the whites hiding behind shuttered doors across the street thought otherwise. Although she never understood Mr. Blessing's almost spiritual connection with Lee, she was also aware that other whites probably felt the same and perhaps blacks underestimated his significance. Lee's surrender marked the end of their old South, and she figured when something that existed for so long ended so quickly, it had to be dangerous Miela made the others keep quiet.

"No use rubbing salt in the wound."

"Why not? They've rubbed plenty in ours," Daphne grunted, cleaning the scars on Fatima's shoulder.

"I know that. It's our job to be decent and Christian in the Jubilee."

"I'm not so sure about that ... "

"Well I am!"

Daphne didn't agree but held her tongue. They listened to rifle and cannon fire all day and well into the night then of and on for the next few days. They were getting ready to go back to Smythes when word came about a boat parade and another celebration out in the harbor. It was to happen the next morning. Miela relented and they all went down to East Bay Street and Adger's Wharf to join the throng to watch.

It was a blue-sky day full of blue uniforms. There was no gray or rebel brown anywhere. A brisk wind blew steadily from the northwest. White Union soldiers and black civilians were everywhere along the waterfront. Everyone seemed to be jostling to get aboard steamers. People were yelling, singing, and arguing for rides from an armada of sloops, coastal schooners, rice flats, row boats, and dugout canoes. Anything that would float would do. Everything was possible. Charleston was theirs forever more.

The memory of Blessing's boat had faded enough so that the sight of all the sailboats didn't bother Miela much. Still, she was quite happy to stay on dry land. She counted sixty five boats as the fleet slowly moved out to distant Fort Sumter for the ceremony marking the end of Confederate rule and the raising of the Union flag. Forever more, she hoped. All the dignitaries were there according to the handbill being given out. Miela read it to them.

Major Anderson, the loyal officer who defended Fort Sumter against the Confederates in '61, will return to watch his flag fly from the Fort once again. Major Anderson will give a salute to the flag. Also speaking will be the son of Denmark Vesey, who was hung along with 20 others, for plotting the overthrow of Charleston back in '22. Robert Smalls himself, the ex-slave who stole the steamer Planter back in '62 and escaped to freedom with his friends and family aboard, and now Captain of the Planter and an officer in the Union Navy, will offer an address to his countrymen.

It was his steamer in particular that thousands were fighting to get aboard. To ride to Sumter on the Planter was like a dream. Miela could hear a few words of his speech from above the din of the crowd. 'Freedom

417

... the future ... emancipation ... ' Most of it was drowned out by all the cheering and by the booming guns of Union warships across the harbor. Their group stayed by the seawall and watched the whole grand spectacle until well past dark then went home and stayed up late that night by a fire in the backyard, eating roasted sweet potatoes and salted catfish and listening to the guns continue to boom.

In the morning Miela and Daphne went down to the Freedman's Bureau office to inquire if there was a word about George, Dye, or Grace. A Yank clerk searched through a stack of papers. There was no word about Grace or George, but he produced a note that said Dye was safe and living in Beaufort.

"She safe?" Miela cried out.

"Yep. Says here that Dye of Blessing Plantation is living with a family of fourteen on a Freedman's grant. Forty acres down near Beaufort." He held up the letter while they danced in a circle until dizzy. Miela thanked him, and they rushed outside wiping away tears and ignoring the clerk rolling his eyes. They met Daphne running up the steps crying.

"What is it?" Miela grabbed her shoulder as she heaved and sobbed. "What's wrong?"

"Lincoln's dead," Daphne whispered in between sobs. "It's true. Shot in Washington by the rebs."

"How do you know?" Miela asked, not being one to believe idle rumors.

"They're reading it out loud down yonder in front of that big Custom House. First Lee's army surrendered then they must have changed their minds. They got Lincoln and shot him."

"Jesus Lord!"

The news spread like fire. Every black in the street stopped in their tracks when they heard it. Women and children cried. Men stood stoically. Yank troops cursed and swore vengeance, churning through the streets jostling citizens, breaking windows, and chanting 'Death to Rebels!' Miela watched them smash in a storefront and knew that it would be a miracle if no one was killed and no homes were burned. White civilians disappeared inside their houses. Whatever they felt about Lincoln, they didn't dare share it now in public.

418

Mr. Luden locked his door up the street, fearing the worst. He figured Lincoln was the one man who wielded enough power to bring both sides to one acceptable peace settlement, and he wasn't happy he was dead. Not in the least. He knew Lincoln, for all the hate spewed at him by the Southern papers for four years, was actually a man who might help the South, and his death might have just destroyed any mercy or compromise.

Miela watched mob of soldiers tromp by. Her mind raced. Would the rebs fight on? Would the Yanks lose heart? Would they let slavery return? She stifled her doubts and hugged Daphne, wiping away tears, "Don't worry. Sherman won't let them get away with it. He'll keep the rebs in line."

Daphne blew her nose. "I know. They say he's on the way here right now. I heard the soldiers say so, right down yonder by the wharf." She sat down and started sobbing again.

"Sherman? He's coming ... here?"

"That's what they say, but what good will that do now?"

They all felt it. Lincoln, the great father of emancipation, seemed part of their family. It was like losing Gage all over again. Miela and Elsey sat down next to her and held Daphne until she felt well enough to walk back to Legare Street. Miela told the rest of them the bad news and announced it was time to head back to Smythe's. She had the feeling that a powder keg was about to explode. Everyone quickly agreed. There were all ready to get back to the farm and out of the city, especially since the Yank officers had suddenly left while Miela was gone and, in their place, an elderly white lady and her two ancient brothers had moved into the big house claiming they were cousins of Mrs. Blessing.

"No telling what they'll do,"Lizette frowned.

"They can't hurt us," Miela took her arm. "Anyhow, we'll head back tomorrow."

"Hello there!" A woman's voice called out from outside. Miela looked out the window at an old lady holding tightly to the banister rail on the second floor porch of the big house. She looked disheveled and haggard. Her white hair was stiff and unwashed and her face smudged with soot. Her once white dress was tinged yellow and splotched all over with large brown stains. She called down to Poins in the backyard. "Do you by chance have our dinner ready?" Her voice cracked.

419

"Dinner? No ma'am. But I can ask Daphne if she can cook you some corn cakes before we leave."

"Leave? Where? Why?" She looked frightened.

"We're going home ma'am."

"Home? This IS our home. We've come all the way from Beaufort. My brothers are ill. You can't expect us to..." She broke into tears.

"What are we going to do?"

"I'm not sure, but I'll ask Miela. She'll know, don't worry." He went inside, found Miela, and pulled her outside with him to speak to the women from the side yard.

"Yes, ma'am. We're leaving in the morning, but we can fix you supper tonight." She actually felt sorry for her.

"All right then. I guess that will have to do," the woman answered curtly, turning abruptly and disappearing inside behind the French doors.

"Once a queen, always a queen, perhaps like Mrs. Blessing," Miela whispered to Poins. "But ... now just an old woman. Kind of pitiful."

"A queen? Really? She don't look like much."

Miela stifled a laugh and found Daphne cooking supper of corn cakes and fried fish and asked them to make up three extra plates. "For the Queen in the big house and her two brothers," she smiled.

"I don't see why the Queen can't fry her own corn cakes," Daphne slapped more batter on the pan.

"Please ... do it for me. It's never a bad thing to be decent to old people. Especially an old Queen,"she laughed.

Daphne shook her head, turning over the corn cakes. "All right I'll do it for you, but I ain't cooking her no breakfast for no white Queen. No matter what."

"All right, I'll make it myself."

"You're too good to those ... "

"Don't start now, please. Let's just be decent."

Daphne rolled her eyes, but did as Miela said. In the morning, Miela took the old lady and her brothers a breakfast of corn cakes and fried sweet potatoes while Elsey teased her. The rest of them finished packing up the wagon and they all headed up Meeting Street, making it to the Citadel Barracks parade ground that was swarming with agitated Union troops, white and black. Freedmen were gathered in a mass in front of the Church across the street. Men were shouting for revenge for Lincoln.

"Kill them! Kill the bastard rebs!"

"Hang the traitors!"

Miela instinctively avoided the square. A mob could do evil things very quickly. She held Fatima's hand and had them all wait behind a low brick wall that curved off of Calhoun Street into a little alleyway lined with single-story cottages that now housed hundreds more freedmen. They waited there for an hour or so until the crowd grew quieter and began to fade. Miela watched a white family come through the square on foot pulling along a cow and a donkey loaded with bulging burlap sacks. No one bothered them, and she breathed a sigh of relief. True revenge meant another round of fighting. Maybe this was a sign that it wouldn't happen after all.

They made it to the ferry landing before dark and huddled under the porch in a driving rainstorm that roared down all night. In the morning, they rode the ferry across soaking wet but relieved to be headed back to Smythes. Miela told Titus about Lincoln and what was happening in the city then she found her bed and lay down, feeling more exhausted than she had in months.

CHAPTER 46 — CONNOR

on the road to Charleston

onner regained consciousness. He quickly checked his good eye. He could still see, thank God. He was alone in a barn wrapped in blanket. His head hurt under a thick cotton bandage. He tried to stand up but fell flat on his face. Then he noticed the plate of cornbread and pitcher of water beside his head. He sat back up, ate it all, and gulped down the entire pitcher. He wedged himself in the corner of the stall and waited.

Just before dark, an old man and woman came into the barn with another wounded man who died soon after. The old couple didn't say much except to ask if he could stand up. Connor nodded, tried again, and promptly collapsed. He woke up in the morning light with the old lady changing his head bandage. Her hands were firm but gentle. The old man leaned against a log post behind her, smoking a pipe and watching. They kept him there another week, changing his head bandage daily and bringing him food and clean clothes. Mr. Plowden and his wife Janet May. They'd lost a son at Sharpsburg and had another missing somewhere in Tennessee.

"Maybe somebody's helping my boy," she smiled, revealing two yellow teeth and scarlet red gums. "He'll come home soon now y' know. Lee surrendered. Mr. Bradley came over from Statesburg to tell us." She leaned away from Connor's face as if expecting an explosion.

"I'm sure your son is fine," Connor nodded. "And I'm glad it's over. Thank God."

She smiled again, checked his scalp and let him look at it with a mirror. A red line an inch wide cut down to the bone on the right side of his head. Angry, red granulation leaked blood but no pus. She let him sleep and he fell back into dreams of his friend William who had been scalped by a solid shot at Sharpsburg and lived to tell about it. At least until Spotsylvania finally put him in the grave.

At first light he thought he heard William yelling to him, but it was just Mr. Plowden calling his cows. Connor sat up, ate more cornbread and drank a half-pitcher of milk, finally feeling strong enough to stand up. Time to get moving. To head home. He gave Mr. Plowden his shotgun and revolver for an old mule, some feed corn and a slab of dried venison.

"I wish I could pay you more than a rusty shotgun and that little pistol."

"Don't worry 'bout that, son. Just get on back home. That's payment enough for that old mule." He puffed out smoke rings then spat into the cow pen. "And be careful. The militia's long gone. The Yanks seem to be drifting back towards the coast, but you never know with Yanks. I think if you're headed to Charleston, you best go by way of Vance's or Nelson's Ferry. Here, I'll draw you a map." He drew it on a blank page he tore out from the back of his Bible and gave it to Connor.

"Thank you sir. You saved my life. I'll never forget you. When I get back to Charleston and get situated, I'll bring your mule back."

He shook his head. "Don't worry about him, son. I can always find me another mule. Doubt he'd make the trip twice anyhow."

Mrs. Plowden brought more cornmeal cakes wrapped in a piece of bedspread. "You be safe now, you here."

"Yes ma'am."

"And watch out for Yanks. You never know ... "

"I already told him, Janet May," Mr. Plowden shook his head behind her and winked at Connor.

"I'll be real careful, ma'am. I promise."

Connor thanked them again, pulled himself up onto the mule and rode off. It took him three days to find his way to the Santee River, but he wasn't really in a hurry. He lived off the spoils of the Yanks. Carcasses of cows and mules that had been left to rot in the fields and byways. Every day he was lucky enough to find one. Hunger made it more tolerable and so did roasting the stiff flesh to a crisp cinder.

At the swamp by the river, an old man came out of hiding and gave him a jar of molasses, a bag of corn, and a few sweet potatoes. More than he could spare. Connor thanked him and promised him he would pay him back in time. The old man grinned.

423

"I've done heard that for four years now. But it's all right. You got to live your life with the Yanks now. And the blacks. That's your payment. Plenty enough too. Old men like me ... Well we just have a while, I guess. I'll be yonder soon." He jerked his thumb up at the sky and laughed. "God willing, that is."

Connor insisted that he write him out a promissary note. "I'd like repay my debts." He tore off the corner of his map and wrote out the man's name. Mr. Lewis Ferguson. "How much do I owe you, sir?"

Mr. Ferguson laughed all the while. "How 'bout a million in Confederate dollar bills. Might as well. Worth about as much as a good shit."

Connor laughed with him. "Maybe even less. But thank you again Mr. Ferguson. You've been most kind. I won't forget you."

"Nor I you, boy, and I will surely treasure your note," he laughed. They shook hands and Connor walked over to his mule. He stepped over our rotting oak trunk and felt a quick tap on his ankle. He jumped away as the rattlesnake lunged again then coiled up with its tail rattle sticking straight up rattling the alarm. Connor backed away ten feet or so, his heart racing as he felt his shoe and ankle. The two fang marks had punctured the leather but not his skin. He caught his breath.

Mr. Ferguson walked up and Connor suddenly couldn't help laughing. To have come through Spotsylvania alive, to have ridden with JB, and now this. A close call with one of South Carolina's nastiest creatures. God indeed had a great sense of humor.

"No doubt the Lord's looking after me."

Mr. Ferguson nodded. "Yep. He's looking all right. Might be messing with you too."

They watched the rattlesnake stay angry for a while then Ferguson dispatched it with one swing of the stout oak limb. "It might be that note of yours. God enjoys a good joke." He sat down on a log and went to skinning the snake. "A fine meal, son. Won't you stay?"

"No thanks." Connor mounted up. "The Almighty might be telling me to get on home."

"Well then. You best listen. And look here. You might want to stay off the State Road. Heard Yanks are all over it. Take the River Road down to St. Stephens then over to Cordesville. Come in the Mt. Pleasant way. You just might save your mule. What's left of him."

"Thank you. I'll do just that."

He waved as he rode off through the trees, making his way down to the ferry landing. No one was about and the flat boat ferry was moored on the other side of the river so he swam his mule over and pushed on towards Eutaw Springs and the back road to Charleston. It took him three more days to make it down to the Mathis Ferry on the Cooper River across from the city where he traded the mule for a ferry ride over and walked into town.

Yank soldiers were everywhere. Mostly well drilled, black regiments with new uniforms following white officers. Connor found a provost office at a brigade headquarters and signed parole papers. He was the only parolee in the room at the time, surrounded by the smiles of the white lieutenant's black bodyguard. But it didn't even bother him. Not at all. The war was truly over. And he'd done about all he could. No use keeping hate alive. It wouldn't change anything. Best to let go and look to the future. Or at least try to.

He made his way down Meeting Street past the burned out railroad depot, the Citadel Barracks now occupied by swarms of Union soldiers, the destroyed charred ruins of the Congregational Church, and the weed-covered yards of battered, once stately mansions. Very few whites walked the streets. An Episcopal minister swept the sidewalk in front of St. Michael's Church, and a lady dressed in silk finery sat on the steps of City Hall selling eggs to soldiers. Each time she took their money and had to say 'thank you' she grimaced.

Connor walked down Tradd Street to Legare and found Mr. Blessings house occupied by Union officers. Poins and Jemps were in the side yard, and he introduced himself. Jemps recognized the name and cautiously let him inside the old slave quarters. Poins stood stiffly in a corner until Jemps reminded him that Connor had given them Smythes.

"Miela's there. So are the others. We come down here once a week or so ... with raccoon and possum meat. Trade it for stuff. Like the rice here. These oysters too." He offered Connor a thin oyster stew.

"Thank you." Connor ate three helpings and laughed. "Guess I was hungrier than I thought."

"That's all right," Poins smiled. "We ain't hungry ourselves. Catching plenty of fish every day when we're here. Caught some nice croakers yesterday. Twelve of 'em. Ain't that right, Jemps?"

"Sure is," Jemps nodded, but he kept staring at Connor, still wondering why he was here. Was he going to take the farm back? Could he? "Mrs. Blessing showed up last week," he said, watching Connor's eyes. Was he here to see her? Did he have some important information? Something that he had to tell Ezekiel? "She stayed up on the third floor the whole time. The Yank officers were nice to her. Nicer than they should have been. She left a few days ago. Said she was headed up to North Carolina. To the mountains. Has a sister up there. Said she wouldn't come back till the Yanks leave."

Connor just shrugged. "I doubt she'll ever be coming back."

Jemps saw no hint of anything and felt a bit disappointed. Poins offered Connor some more stew. "Miela says it's a good thing the Blessings are gone. It's kind of like WE'RE the rich folks now. With the farm and the city house and all. At least the slave quarters, that is." He fetched Connor a cup of sassafras tea.

"Miela and Ezekiel. Are they all right?"

Jemps saw the twinkle in Connor's eye. He smiled back and nodded. "Yep. They're married y'know."

Connor felt his heart leap. He squinted for just a split second, but Jemps noticed. "Everybody loves Miela, but there's only one Ezekiel," he grinned, glancing up at Connor's blushing red face. "You know she's been belonging to him all these years. Ain't you?"

Poins offered more stew, but Connor shook his head, regrouped, and smiled. "They belong together all right. God bless them both." He held up his cup. "To Miela and Ezekiel. A long life and a healthy family."

"Amen," Poins smiled. "To a long happy life."

Connor sipped the tea and thought back on the last few weeks as if it had been a dream from long ago. A dream that was already dissipating with the light of day. He still had the letter in his pocket from the boy who died at Rivers Bridge. He knew he had to go find the boy's mother. It wasn't something he wanted to do, but he knew he had to. He put Miela out of his mind, thanked Jemps and Poins for the meal then walked back up to Orange Street, to the address the boy had given him, and found the house.

The boy's mother, Mrs. Wilson, came to the door and peered out cautiously. She was a skinny lady with sandy hair and green eyes. Connor gave her the letter and said everything he thought might be a help to her.

"He didn't suffer. I was there with him at the end. He was brave right up until the last. As brave as anyone I saw that day, or since."

She listened but said nothing. Her jaw tightened, and she gripped her side as if a cramp had seized her. She had already received word of her son's death back in February. Two of her friends had returned and had given her the details. Seeing the letter was just a hot poker in the guts. Connor saw the tears in her eyes and nodded respectfully, then backed away down the steps, hat in hand.

"What's your name, son?" She called after him.

He turned around quickly, not wanting to be rude and speak to her over his shoulder. "Connor Dumont, ma'am."

She took a deep breath. "Did you know him before ... that day?"

"No ma'am."

"Well ... thank you for coming."

Connor bowed and walked back down the street not knowing what else to say. He walked to the Ashley River found a ride across and hitched a wood train after dark all way to the Young's Island Road. Union soldiers were camped along the railroad, but no one bothered him. He found the Gibson's farm and his Uncle Paul's still intact. Everything was just as he'd left it, which surprised him a bit. Mrs. Gibson hugged him and ushered him inside..

"I'm glad that devil Sherman went to Columbia," Mrs. Gibson frowned. "Glad he left us alone. Had us worried for a while, though." She brought him a plate of fried sweet potatoes and some sassafras tea. "Are you All right Connor? Did you get mixed up in at all?"

Connor shrugged. "I'm fine. Didn't do much. I ... "

She turned and looked out the window at the marsh. "What ever happened to Brig?"

"Brig's All right. On loan to a good man." Then it dawned on him that Brig represented her husband, Mac, so her wound had just been reopened. "We'll see him back here soon, I'm sure of it," he lied, saying what he thought she wanted to hear.

She smiled perfunctorily and asked him to stay for dinner which he did and regretted. The conversation was difficult, even with little Thomas and Peter's laughter. Everything he'd been through was just a painful

427

reminder to Cora and Poppy that Mac, Poppy's son and her husband, and Will, her other son, hadn't been so lucky. He didn't mention Brig again and left as soon as he could, excusing himself to go sleep on the porch at Uncle Paul's, wrapped in a blanket listening to the gulls crying across the marsh.

FOR THE NEXT few days, he played with the children and lounged on the porch enjoying the breeze and the marsh view before deciding it was time to go check on Miela and Smythe's. He was just too restless to sit there idle for too long. He said his goodbyes quickly then walked the whole way to Bee's Ferry landing on the Ashley River, crossed over to the State Road and then made his way across the peninsula to the Cooper. He chopped firewood for payment, tolerating catcalls from a drunk Yank officer with a black sergeant in tow at Dover's Tavern at the ferry.

"Hey reb, where you headed? Shit-hole town?" the sergeant laughed.

"Sure enough ain't nothing across the river there but pigs and reb shits. Except that one light- skinned girl. The one with the big belly. We seen her here yesterday."

"That's it All right," the officer sucked on a whiskey bottle. "Everybody's riding over to pork that big belly. You going to see her too, reb? Is that it? She gonna be your mistress? Some kind of loyal slave bullshit?"

Connor ignored their laughter and took the ferry across. The Yanks went along for the ride without offering to pay. They sat in the bow finishing off the whisky bottle, but Connor figured they were harmless enough. He got off at the Thomas Island landing when the ferry stopped to load pigs and firewood from flat boats coming down Bedford Creek from the Cainhoy Road. The Yanks laughed and got in the way of the loading, poking at the pigs with the sergeant's bayonet until Mr O'Neill begged them to set back down. Connor hurried off up the rood to the farm while they yelled at him.

"Give big- belly my love."

"Mine too," the sergeant laughed. "Hell, the whole army's!"

They started singing an obscene rendition of 'When Johnny Comes marching Home', but Connor kept on walking, trying to ignore them and thinking of the last time he'd come to the island. The old oak tree with a great beard of moss swaying in the salt breeze and leaning low over the marsh made it seem, in one sense, like yesterday but then, simultaneously, like a millennium ago.

He walked up the wagon track to the farm and immediately recognized Miela across the cornfield. She was standing beside a boy and girl by the cistern near the far woods. He watched them turned towards him as he approached. The other blacks in the field, the barn, and stables all stopped their chores and stared at him. He didn't seek Ezekiel anywhere and breathed a sigh of relief. No telling what would happen when they met again. He walked straight towards Miela who stooped to pick a handful of dandelions and blew them on the breeze that came off the marsh which was visible through the trees behind her.

"Hello Miela," Connor bowed a bit stiffly, feeling a lot more nervous than he'd envisioned.

"Hello Mr. Connor Dumont," she smiled and wiped dandelion wisps from her hands. "You've come back from the war."

"Yes, I have." He tried to think of something else to say but felt his mouth run dry.

Miela noticed. "Are you all right? Are you ill?" Her eyes twinkled and Connor wondered if she was teasing him.

"I'm fine, thank you." He cleared his throat. "Just came up to make sure everything was all right."

"Yes. Thank you. We're doing well. Very well. Thank you for the farm ... For the use of the farm."

"No." He waved his hand. "It's yours. You and the others. It's your farm now." He puffed his cheeks out and felt his heart race. "It's ... better this way."

She took his hands in hers. "You're a good person, Connor. We'll never forget what you've done for us. Now come with me and meet everyone."

Connor felt her fingers tightened around his and found himself totally speechless. Miela just giggled a bit as if she'd expected it, and he realized immediately that his predicament wasn't new to her, but neither of them let on.

"Come here everyone," she shouted. "Meet our benefactor, Mr. Connor Dumont." She let his hands go and clapped. She nodded to the children and to the others and they all took it up, slowly at first, then louder after she gave them all a stern look. Connor felt his face brighten into a beet. Fatima and Agnes whispered to each other and laughed. Connor saw the joy in their faces and felt tears well up. He hadn't been sure what he would feel when he came, but now he knew. A huge sense of relief washed over him. The feeling of having cheated death. Of having been granted a new life.

"Thank you." He bowed to the applause. "No, really. I thank YOU." Miela smiled. She knew what he meant. So did Lizette and CumSeh. The others just looked at each other and whispered. Titus scratched his gray, stubble beard. "Thank us for what?"

"Well I ... "

"For tending to the farm of course," Miela laughed, taking his hand then leading him across the field where she had him sit with her on a log bench in the shade of the barn while the others gathered around in a circle to watch and listen. "Ezekiel's joined the army. The Yanks' that is." She patted his hand and smiled as if not wanting to offend him. "Went off with some General named Potter. Said he was coming back in three or four weeks, maybe longer. To be right here. To stay for good. At least that's what he said."

There was a moment of worry on her face and then she smiled again, but Connor knew immediately. As soon as Ezekiel got back, he'd go after Malcolm Blessing. Connor knew it as sure as the sun rising and so did Miela. He tried to think it all out while she went on telling him about the farm and the garden and Jemps and Poins fishing. What should he do? Should he help? Stay out of it? Do nothing at all? But of course Ezekiel didn't really need his help, and he surely wasn't one to ever to give up. As soon as he got back, Malcolm Blessing was a dead man.

Miela abruptly stopped talking and Connor realized he hadn't been listening. She knew it too but didn't embarrass him further. "Let's get you something to eat. C'mon everyone."

"I'll do it!" Yarrow yelled out and ran for shed. "C'mon Jemps. We can fry those silver fish. The ones you and Poins caught this morning."

"They're called whiting," Jemps mumbled, "Whiting for whitey." But not loud enough for anyone else to hear.

"Won't you stay and eat?" Miela took Connor's hand again.

"Yes. Thanks. That would be nice." Connor nodded, beginning to relax, even beginning to feel almost at home. He ate fried fish and collard greens with them and stayed most of the afternoon. Long enough for the children to lose their fear of him.

"Why does your face turn red when you talk to Miela?" Fatima asked giggling.

Connor felt a rushing fire rising up his neck and cheek. "Well I'm not sure what you ... "

"See? See?" She squealed. "Look Yarrow! Just say 'Miela' and he turns all red, just like Mr. Luden." She took Yarrow's hand and pulled him close. "Miela! Miela!" They chanted and laughed.

Connor felt that wave of embarrassment break over his face then gradually subside. The children kept on even when Elsey tried to stop them.

"Miela! Miela!"

"Shush now. Don't bother the boy," Cumseh hissed.

"No bother," Connor started laughing too. It was all just too absurd.

"You're even redder now, when you laugh." Yarrow came up and poked his cheek with his finger. "Does it come off? Does it go back to white?"

"It stays red," Miela tried to keep a straight face but couldn't. She'd bent over laughing, catching her breath as she could, and all the others joined in.

"Miela has a way doesn't she," Daphne came up behind and hugged her around the neck.

"She's a powerful force All right," Cumseh nodded with respect. Connor wiped his eyes. "Yes indeed. Miela is ... "

"Miela! Miela!" The children squealed some more and kept chanting her name and he kept laughing until his side ached.

Yarrow poked at his red cheeks again. "Nope, it comes off."

Connor caught his breath. "My God. I haven't laughed that hard since I don't know when."

"It's the best medicine," Titus nodded seriously. "Better even than willow bark and sassafras."

"It's God's own tonic for sure," Connor stood up and wiped his eyes again. "Here." He waved the children over. "I've got something for you."

He gave each of them a Confederate $100 bill. "It's left over from Columbia. But it's old money. One handful of corn is worth more than all of these. I guess it's a sign of the future ... for this farm and everyone."

431

Cumseh raised her hands behind Miela. "He done said something. Y'all hear that? The boy done said something for all to hear," She waved her hands in the air and started to sing, but the ferry whistle blew, and Connor knew he had a run for it.

"Thanks for the fish. I'll come back when I can."

He bolted off down the road with the children trying to catch him and just made it to the ferry as they were casting off. Across the river at the tavern, he chopped more firewood and paid no attention to the same officer and black sergeant drinking a bottle of rum on the porch. He walked all the way back to Charleston and slept in the ruins of the Congregational Church on Meeting Street, and in the morning, found his sloop, the Aleta, still beached in the marsh grass beside Adger's Wharf where he had left her two years before.

Someone had been living on her and had the hull freshly caulked and cracked transom patched. A canvas tent flapped over the stump of mast. Beef tins and oyster shells littered the hold. A tin box full of coals sat on bricks on the foredeck.

"The Aleta still floats," he laughed, glancing down at the brown stains on the stern seat that brought memories flooding back. The trip to Fort Sumter before he'd gone north with the McGowan's Brigade. His friend , Elliot, hit by an errant shell. He remembered it all vividly, but realized he could actually think of that awful day now without his chest and throat tightening up. Something he hadn't thought possible a year ago. Elliott had died in the stern, his severed arm pulsing blood onto the seat. Connor pictured it all for the first time since coming home and a warmth crept over his chest. But it wasn't the choking feeling of before, and he knew he'd be all right.

"Life goes on. Knit and mend," Uncle Paul chanting along in his thoughts.

It was good advice, and he forced himself to walk over to Dr. Tradd's house to see if anyone was home. It was the first time he allowed himself to think of Henrietta since Columbia. He still couldn't allow the thoughts to proceed much further. Just thinking her name and actually walking to her street caused his breath to be short. What he'd heard in Columbia was still a blur. He told himself she was still alive. She had to be.

432

He walked up the street to the wrought iron gate of the Tradd's home and up the slate walkway to the wide veranda. He knocked on the door and waited. His head felt like he was down deep under water. His ears rang as if a teakettle was whistling just behind his head. He waited there for several minutes. Either Henrietta would come to the door or ... His brain refused to allow any other alternative. He waited for what seemed an eternity then went around back and knocked on the garden door. No one was home. He peered in the window and saw all the Tradd family belongings unperturbed. Furniture, portraits, books and shelves, china and lamps. That was all he needed. Nothing was draped in black. Proof that she had to be alive. And certainly no one had come to the door telling him that she was ... He refused to think it.

He ran back through the side yard out to the street as if he was holding his breath then gasped for air on the sidewalk and looked around. Not a soul in sight. It had to be good news. But somewhere deep down inside, the truth was trying to sprout, and he was forced to squash it immediately.

He ran back to the wharves and quickly found work chopping firewood and carrying loads in a drayman's cart for the Union Navy boats docked along the waterfront. He took shelter in an abandoned warehouse overlooking the harbor. He vowed to save his money to buy supplies to make the Aleta whole again.

First the hull, scraping off oyster shells and barnacles and two years growth of seaweed. Then more caulking and patching. Then a new mast and boom, along with replacing all the lines, sheets and halyards. It took weeks. He worked every job he could find along the wharf to make ends meet. He wanted to thank whoever had kept her afloat, but no one ever came back. The final necessity was a fresh cut and sewn mainsail from the Mr. Luden, the sailmaker, provided in return for two weeks of digging out and rebricking his old privy.

He adjusted the trim on test runs around Castle Pinckney, the old brick fort out in the harbor, then offered the Aleta has a courier and transport service over to Fort Johnson on James Island and Fort Moultrie in Sullivan's. He earned free docking space by serving as night watchman for the wharf. Business was slow at first, but he earned enough within two weeks to repaint the deck and hull. Red and black. The two cheapest paints to be had.

Most of the people he took across the harbor were soldiers or craftsmen working for the army, or ship chandlers for the navy who had been out dozens or even hundreds of times, but occasionally he had someone who had never been out on a boat. Every one of the novices did the same thing. When they first set out, they smiled and waved, yelling to the other groups loading into boats up and down the wharf front. But then, as they got farther away from land, they grew more silent and some even began to pray. Most of the Yank soldiers were courteous, polite and decent to Connor. Only one young private in an oversized uniform was rude, spitting at Connor's feet and calling him a 'damn Rebel Devil.'

Connor just tipped his hat and said nothing. The young man reeked of alcohol and Connor reminded himself that the soldier was just enjoying the fruits of victory. He might have done the same himself. He knew he should have mercy, but he couldn't help himself. It was just too much of a temptation.

He waited for one good gust of wind then let the Aleta heel over unnecessarily to leeward, quickly jibing six times in a row by pretending to have a rudder problem. The taut main sheet snapped and the sails flapped furiously. The private's eyes were suddenly filled with a more contrite expression. Connor restrained a smile then let water splash over the side as he came about. The private started trembling, and Connor knew that any more punishment would just be plain mean.

After docking at the Sullivan's Island pier, he endured a twenty minute tongue lashing before the soldier walked off without paying. But it was well worth it. At least the man's uniform was dripping wet. Connor took two officers back to the city and behaved himself courteously, as did they, paying him three dollars for the return trip. Enough to tide him over nicely for weeks.

Chapter 47 — Malcolm Blessing

Charleston

E zekiel camped with his regiment at the racetrack for three more weeks, waiting for official word that the war was over until he couldn't stand being idle another day. He went to Lieutenant Swails and asked for leave. Swails sat in his tent at a small desk with his bandaged leg propped up on a biscuit box. "I can't be doing this for the entire regiment, you know." He shook his head with exasperation.

Ezekiel nodded. "I really appreciate it, sir. How's the leg?"

"All right," Swails sighed. "Fine then ... 30 days. I expect the regiment will muster out by then anyhow." He signed the necessary papers and Ezekiel saluted. The lieutenant touched his forehead more grudgingly than Ezekiel expected. "Get out of here before I change my mind."

"I'll never forget your kindness sir."

"Get going." Swails waved him off and Ezekiel left quickly, not wanting to press his luck.

He found Esau back at camp repacking his cartridge box. "Just heard that Hartwell's brigade's raiding out from Summerville up to Moncks Corner," Esau smiled. "He's accepting black volunteers, and I really want to go." He looked up at Ezekiel and waited.

"You don't need my blessing, Esau. You ain't a slave anymore. Make up your own mind ... like a free man."

Esau nodded and smiled. "Most of the company's going. The Colonel says we can. Want to come?"

Ezekiel shook his head. "No thanks." He offered no explanation, but he didn't have to. Esau knew the reason.

"Give Miela and the others my best."

"I will. And be careful. Hang on to your rifle. It might be nearly over, but the rebs will still kill a black man if they can."

Esau opened his jacket and smiled. His captured revolver and bowie knife stuck out of his belt. "This here's one black man who'll send Johnny reb to Hell."

Ezekiel hugged him. "Esau, armed and ready. It's a damn fine sight." Esau tolerated the hug. "Damn Ezekiel, it ain't nothing."

They said their goodbyes, and Ezekiel went down to the wharf find a ride up the river to the Thomas Island. Fishermen taking their catch up the river ride let him man an oar until they dropped him off at the landing. He walked to the farm and was quickly swarmed by the children. Elsey, Daphne and Cumseh shooed them off and escorted him to Miela who sat in the rocking chair Poins had made for her from bamboo stalks and wisteria vines. She tried to stand up but the chair came with her. She laughed and sunk back down and patted her swollen belly.

"Thank God you're safe and sound. Are you home for good?"

"Yes. For ever."

He bent over and kissed her, and the girls squealed. Miela pulled him closer. "I'm getting too fat for this chair, Ezekiel. It won't be long now."

"Wonderful." He kissed her again and felt her stomach.

"I think it's a boy. He kicks me like a boy for sure," she smiled. "And what about Esau? Is he ... ?"

"He's fine. Said he's gonna stay on with the Army. Having too much fun being a soldier."

"But you're finished?"

"Yes I am," he lied. "More than finished."

"Thank God." She pulled him to her again. "Help me up. Maybe Jemps can cook up some of his squirrel stew. He made it last week, and it was wonderful." She turned to him. "How about it, Jemps?"

"Give me an hour, maybe two."

Miela walked over to the cottage with Ezekiel's arm around her and the children at their heels. They lay down together just to hold each other while Jemps readied his stew and Elsey and Lizette boiled corn. The supper was as good as Miela predicted, and afterwards, everyone sat around Ezekiel in the barn as twilight fell, listening to his tale of Potter's raid. Yarrow made him tell it all a second time while Daphne and Titus took the girls to bed. Finally even Yarrow's eyes started drooping, and Ezekiel was allowed to go to bed with Miela.

He didn't know for sure if she would suspect he was going after Malcolm Blessing in the morning, but thought maybe not. She was too good a person to dwell on revenge. He'd never said a word about Malcolm since leaving Blessing and neither had Miela, both of them trying to protect the other, but she watched him undress with her head slightly lowered as if she was wondering. He turned away and refused to look in her eyes. Damn her for being so intuitive. He kissed her on the cheek, and she gave him a hug back then lay down on the bed looking exhausted and quickly falling to sleep in his arms.

Ezekiel's plan for the next morning was to slip away early without having to answer any questions, but Daphne and Lizette were already out in a cornfield tending to weeds, and Poins came out of the woods with a cartload of firewood. Cumseh was hanging out laundry, and Titus and Jemps were busy scalding a hog. He felt peeved that he hadn't left before dawn but felt a sense of joy watching the beginnings of a life of freedom. A freedom he'd helped secure. He wondered if it was what fathers felt when their children were born then quickly glanced back to the cottage to make sure Miela hadn't come out. Thank the Lord pregnancy made her want to sleep.

He packed the mule with what he needed. Biscuits, cornbread, and dried ham for ten days. He told everyone he was heading up to Cordesville to buy nails and that he would have to stay there for a while to work to make payment. He left before Miela woke up, and he was thankful for that. She could always spot him in a lie. He tightened the straps of his blanket role, with his knife, his captured revolver, and extra cartridges well hidden inside.

He'd dressed in his old tattered shirt and trousers and rode without a saddle and with a smelly, half rotten sack of corn strapped alongside. To anyone he passed, he was just a poor black man on a worn out mule carrying nothing of value.

He waved goodbye to the others and slipped down the path towards a ferry. He knew that secrecy was the key to success. White men would kill a black man on suspicion of murder, no questions asked, even with the Yanks running things. If the victim was white, there would be no court hearing, just a noose hanging from a tree or a bullet in the back of the head deep in the swamp. His only chance was to escape attention, but he knew he could do it. He didn't have to say a word to anyone.

Malcolm Blessing wouldn't be hard to find, but his dead body would be, and no one would even think about Ezekiel. And he wouldn't have to rely on Conner. He would enjoy the satisfaction of having done it all alone.

That Jemps had seen the bastard while on a trip to the market with Poins was a stroke of luck, but he had to act fast. He knew Blessing would go back to the plantation. His only worry was to get there too late and miss his chance. He figured Blessing would be self-absorbed as usual. Thinking only of the plantation and how to make it run without slaves. He wouldn't be thinking that a black man, one of those he'd degraded and held in contempt all his life, would be plotting his death. Blacks were like horses to Malcolm Blessing. Non-thinking animals, to be used and discarded. His inability to consider a black man as truly a human being would be Ezekiel's opportunity. Blessing would never contemplate that he was the one now being stalked. At least that's what Ezekiel hoped.

He traveled by night and hid in the woods by day. He made a long loop northwards towards Moncks Corner then back southwest towards Walterboro just to be sure no one had followed him or suspect where he was heading. He never built a fire and slept with pistol in hand and knife by his side. He knew the war still wasn't over for some. Maybe it never would be. Some of the rebs were still armed. They might have to submit to the Yanks for now, but he had no doubt that once they were gone, they'd be back at it. Killing a single black man in the woods was nothing. It wouldn't even be reported. So he knew he had to be quiet and careful.

Twice he saw white riders before they saw him. Once they came within pistol shot, but his mule kept quiet and they rode past. He patted her on the neck, gave her some sugar cane, and pushed on, making it to Blessing an hour or so before dawn on the second day. Enough time to hide the mule in the cornfield down past the ruins of the barn and around the tree line from the remnants of the big house. He took food and water with him and hid in the ruins of the cotton press where he had a good view. Then he waited. For three days. He checked on the mule every day just after dark. Once he saw a group of white riders crossing the lower field towards Charleston, but on the fourth day he spotted what he'd come for. Malcolm Blessing, riding up the road like he was headed home from a barbecue. Ezekiel smiled. He had him.

He waited and watched him tie up at the burned-out barn then wander slowly through the charred timbers and the blackened tin roofing of the big house. Blessing stooped and picked up a few things. Ezekiel couldn't see what they were, but he was happy to let the bastard take his time. He enjoyed the wait. Every minute watching him walk around, still alive, was sweet, knowing the bastard would shortly be in Hell.

He watched Blessing pitch his tent and picket his horse in the cornfield stubble. As darkness fell, he thought he heard him singing by his campfire. He smiled. It might have been his mind playing tricks. He was so excited he hardly slept a wink. At dawn, he crept out of hiding and climbed up the big oak tree that hung low over the road.

He covered himself in moss and lay still, along a huge, moss-draped limb. Just another black bump on the old oak, he smiled. Then he waited until just around supper time when Blessing mounted up and came trotting down the road. Ezekiel watched, totally still, but muscles twitching. Just as he passed below, Ezekiel swung around and jumped feet first on his back. The force of his body knocked Blessing to the ground. His horse reared and bolted. Ezekiel was on top of him before he knew what had happened. He put the pistol to his temple with his left hand and pushed his face in the dirt with his right.

"Don't move Malcolm! Or I'll blow your head off."

"What the hell!" Malcolm gasped, his heart in his mouth. "What's going on?" His eyes look back at the barrel and at the black arm pushing him down.

"Shut up, Malcolm. I'll let you go if you do as I say," he lied, knowing Malcolm would calm down just a bit.

"Ezekiel? Is that you?" He didn't dare turn his head with the pistol jammed into his temple.

"Yep. It's me All right. I'm gonna let you go if you do one thing for me." Ezekiel pushed his face harder into the dirt.

"What's that?" Blessing's mind raced, already thinking what he'd do to Ezekiel as soon as he got loose.

"Hold on to this."

Ezekiel let his head go, quickly reached back and pulled his Bowie knife, and just as Blessing raised his head to look around, reached around his neck with the blade and pulled its razor-sharp edge hard across his gullet. The first cut went right through the arteries and into the windpipe. Blessing felt a searing pain then choked for air as blood poured into his lungs. The second cut of the knife went down to his spine and the last thing he realized before he died was Ezekiel whispering in his ear.

"For Miela. Hold this knife in your throat, for her."

Blessing gurgled to death as his blood poured out into the road. Ezekiel held his head face down in the dirt until he was sure he was dead then looked up to make sure no one was crossing the fields. He checked his pockets. Just one piece of blackened, wrought-iron fire poker and two silver Confederate coins.

He smiled. "That ain't much to die for, is it?" He looked around again. All quiet. The fields were empty. He turned him over then he cocked the pistol, put it to Blessing's ear and fired. "Just to be certain." Blessings eyes were still open as he unbuttoned his trousers and urinated on his face. "Join your father in Hell, you bastard."

He dragged Blessing's body out of sight from the road then fetched the mule and pulled him along through the mud a mile into the swamp. He cut off his clothes and wedged the body underwater, beneath a big cypress log. Gator bait, he smiled, knowing it was only fitting that the bastard plantation prince would now be consumed on the land that he had prided himself over. He washed himself off thoroughly, buried Blessings clothes a mile away under another log in the swamp then rode off to retrace his steps back home, forcing himself the whole time not to howl.

Chapter 48 — ASSAULT

Charleston

Miela, Elsey, Poins and Jemps went back to Charleston with the wagon to take Mr. Luden a load of smoked fish and to sell baskets of fresh squirrel meat at the market. They spent the night in the back house at Legare Street which was again occupied by a few Union officers who in the morning paid Jemps and Poins to go to the market and buy them firewood and salt. They stopped to take Mr. Luden the smoked fish for which he gave them a pouch of silver coins in return. Jemps counted them held them up in his palm.

"But sir, you don't owe us anything at all. And this is $12. In silver."

Mr. Luden cleared his throat. "Let's just say it does my heart good. Anyhow, I can sell what you brought me for more than that if I want."

He thanked them again and walked back inside.

"Thank you, sir," Jemps called after him.

"Damn. Let me see it," Poins bent closer.

"We're rich," Jemps smiled, holding up the coins. "C'mon."

They went to the market and finished the buying and selling then carried the load of firewood back to Legare Street. Poins ran to show Miela and Elsey the money while Jemps walked down the block following a growing crowd of freed men and soldiers headed towards the river.

"What's going on?" he asked.

A young Yank soldier on a mule rode past yelling, "Sherman's here! He's coming up the street!"

The crowd started surging forward, "Sherman's here! It's Sherman!"

Jemps ran back and bounded up the stairs, "Sherman's coming! He's here right now! Come on! You'll miss him."

He disappeared like a whirlwind, and Miela looked at Elsey not knowing what to think. "Sherman? I doubt it."

"He's coming to see you Miela. I betcha," Elsey tried to smile, following her to the side yard where they could stand by the big wrought iron gate and watch. "But it can't REALLY be him, can it?"

"Probably just another rumor people want to believe," Miela smiled at Jemps.

Jemps sighed exasperated, "It ain't like I said God the Father was sending Christ up the street. Sherman's just a man ain't he? Why can't he come walking by?"

"Well ... ,"Miela laughed. "Just a man! Some say he's more than that."

"Don't blaspheme," Elsey raised her finger. "Don't be calling him some kind of God. Like Jemps said, he ain't Christ. OR God the Father."

"Well ... all right," Miela smiled and blessed herself, just to see Elsey take a deep breath and puff her cheeks out.

"It ain't right to blaspheme," Elsey crossed her arms and frowned.

"I'm just teasing you," Miela laughed, leaning out into the street to get a better view of the growing crowd.

"Well it ain't right."

Black children ran past them squealing. Adults of all ages followed behind as quickly as they could, yelling, "He's here! He's here! Sherman's here! Sherman!"

Miela climbed up the ladder by the gate, leaned over the wall as far as her big belly would let her, and got a glimpse of a clump of blue clad officers down towards the river hemmed in by the cheering throng. Dozens of soldiers ringed the officers, pushing through the mass of people and wedging their way up Legare Street. They came closer and closer. Miela leaned out farther to get a better look. Jemps and Poins climbed up the gate beside her to see above the crowd. The officer in the center of the soldiers twitched about nervously, puffing furiously on a cigar and leaving a column of smoke to mark his progress. Miela watched the sun filter through a loquat tree to shine on the officer's short-cropped, rust colored beard.

"General Sherman! General Sherman!" The crowd chanted as he walked along, inside the concentric rings of officers. He held up his cigar and waved it to the crowd then glanced up at Miela on the ladder. Elsey was pushing up behind her to see and tipped the ladder, nearly toppling her over. Miela grabbed the top the wall and Jemps grabbed her leg and

442

pulled her back. She caught her breath and waved to Sherman as he passed below. He nodded back then moved on up the street through the sea of cheering people who reluctantly parted. Miela watched the great man puff again on his cigar and called out, "Providence of God!"

General Sherman turned, and his eyes darted once again into hers then he was blocked out by the surging crowd and the entourage of officers on horseback. She knew that God has spoken to her. Jemps saw it too.

"The great man looked you in the eye!" He yelled.

"His power's with you now," Elsey clapped her hands and nearly fell off the ladder herself. "Nothing can take it away. Ever!"

"He's come back to see the rebs grovel," Poins hollered. "Put the hex on 'em for good. He's got the plateye, the demon dog. Gonna haunt them every night from now on. That's why he's come. To lay the root of all of them rebs." He helped Miela climb down the ladder then squeezed her and spun her around. "The root. The root. The magic root," he chanted and laughed, clanging the gate shut hard enough to make it sing.

"Shush up, Poins," Elsey held her finger to her mouth. "Some things are best not spoken."

He nodded but kept on whispering, "Root. Root. Magic root."

"Come on y'all," Jemps yelled from out on the sidewalk pointing to the surging crowd. "Let's go with them."

Miela caught her breath and went along. They all joined the cheering mass, following behind the great man's entourage up to Broad Street past the Catholic Cathedral ruins then over to Meeting Street where they watched Sherman climb inside a wagon and rumble off with a cavalry escort. The huge crowd clapped and cheered for another hour or so until black soldiers came through to open up the intersection.

They walked home recounting every second and talked about it over and over again that night, remembering every detail and every movement of the great man. Miela went to sleep thinking of the sunlight on his rust colored hair and his twinkling eyes and, in the morning, waited by the gate for Jemps who had gone to see if Sherman would be out again. Jemps came back after an hour with news that he'd left on a warship at dawn. They were all disappointed but decided they'd been luckier than most. They had at least seen him and had witnessed what they all agreed was his recognition of Miela, an act quite fitting her stature in their eyes. Miela laughed every time anyone mentioned it, though, and sent Poins and Jemps back to the market to buy rolls of mosquito netting before packing up to head back home. Jemps thought it unnecessary, but Miela was firm.

"Enough to cover each sleeping porch. The mosquitos will be getting much worse in the next few months. There's no good coming from letting children have their blood sucked out by swarms of mosquitoes anymore. They'll bring fever or miasmas for sure. No need for it now, since we have the money for the nets."

"Mosquitoes don't cause no fever, Miela," Poins laughed. "That's just fools' talk."

Miela shrugged, "Well anyway, we'll have the netting for anyone who wants it. If you don't want it ... that's all right by me."

He made a face. "You don't know everything, Miela."

"You don't either. So there." She made a face back and made him laugh, and two hours later they were back with the netting.

They finished packing and headed back home, stopping at Mr. Luden's to share a meal with him before going on to the ferry. Miela made a mental note to raise their price for the smoked squirrel meat next time, having seen how quickly it had been snatched up. Fish and squirrels were plentiful back on the island, but obviously there was a meat shortage in Charleston. When they arrived at the landing, Miela felt the baby kick inside of her.

"He's kicking me. Come feel him."

Elsey did, but Jemps and Poins glanced at each other, and Jemps shook his head. "That ain't right. Ezekiel wouldn't like it one bit."

"Yes he would to," Miela laughed and nearly fell off the stool.

"You're family for God's sake."

"Nope. It ain't right. Not even if Ezekiel was standing right beside you. It ain't ... "

"All right, all right," she smiled. "But I swear Ezekiel wouldn't mind."

Jemps just frowned at her as the ferry came down river on the outgoing tide. A dozen or so people waited by the water, fanning themselves. The land breeze began to die and the mosquitoes came out. Men on the veranda of the tavern laughed and clinked their whiskey glasses behind mosquito netting watching the ferry drift past the landing then turn back up river into the force of the ebb tide to come rest against the swaying pilings.

Poins and Jemps helped her walk up the narrow plank gangway then down the little stepladder to the deck. None of them thought anything odd about the white Yank officer and the black sergeant boarding the ferry behind them along with a dozen others. Only when Miela sat down along the rail did she even get a good look at them. They were sharing a liquor bottle and tipped their caps at her. She nodded back, watching them take their seats in the stern before putting them out of her mind. She fanned herself, feeling a little nauseous and just a bit faint and not wanting to cause a scene by getting sick. The dockhands cast off the line, and the steam engine slowly it built up power and, in a few minutes, the mosquitoes and the pungent smell of pluff mud were behind her. The refreshing river breeze was now in her face. The nausea passed, and Miela marveled at the ferry's speed through the water. She rested against the railing, enjoying the sounds of the boilers churning, the thump and vibration of the engine, the gurgle of water along the hull, and the seagulls gliding along on the breeze just above the stern, occasionally darting down to grab a morsel from the wake. She smiled and thanked God she had lived to see such marvels as steam power. And also that her baby would come into such a marvelous, free and wonderful world.

Up river, the ferry put into the mouth of their creek and slowed down. The mosquitoes rose up from the marsh to greet them, and the sun baked down through the haze. No one waited at the Thomas Island landing as the steamer nudged up to the bluff. The deck hands pushed out the gangway, and Jemps and Poins helped Miela across then helped pull the wagon up to the bank and walked alongside it up the road listening to the crickets roar in the overgrown ditch rows. They didn't notice the ferry linger at the bluff for a while and didn't see the Yank officer and sergeant disembark after they had turned onto the path to the farm.

They were all happy to be home. It was still such a wonderful feeling to have their own place. Titus was the only one about. All the others had gone off to collect oysters. All except Yarrow who had taken Grace squirrel hunting with his newly fashioned bow and bamboo arrows. Poins and Jemps went off through the woods towards the marsh to find them.

Miela went inside her cabin and sat on the bed feeling totally exhausted. She lay back and dozed off for a while then awakened with a start. She heard Titus raise his voice across the yard.

"Hello there. Can I help you?"

No one answered. All was quiet. She listened but heard nothing more. Then the door flaps flew open. The black sergeant appeared in the doorway and threw Elsey inside the cabin. She landed on her hands and knees crying. The white officer stood behind the sergeant.

"What! What are you doing ... !" Miela bolted up.

The sergeant knocked her back onto the bed. Elsey jumped up between them. "Stop it! Stop it! Don't hurt her! She's ... "

The sergeant backhanded her to the floor. He grabbed her hair and pulled her to the other side of the cabin. The officer, reeking of alcohol, snatched Miela by the wrist, spun her around on her stomach then pulled up her dress. She kicked at his legs trying to push him away.

"Be still or I'll hurt you." He punched her hard in the small of the back.

"No ... No. Please!"

He hit her again in the neck. The blow stunned her. She tried to push up from the bed, but the officer hit her again in the head. She felt the room turn upside down. He pulled up her dress, unbuttoned his trousers, and mounted her from the rear. "See here, Sergeant. This is how you poke a pregnant girl," he laughed as he thrust inside her.

"I see all right," the sergeant laughed, holding Elsey by the throat and forcing his legs between hers.

She jerked away and tried to reach a hammer beside the door. The sergeant grabbed her by the neck and choked her until her eyes rolled back and she went limp. He kicked her legs apart. "You like being a reb's servant, eh? After all we've done to free you? A loyal slave? Well, this will teach you." He pinned her down, uncovered her bottom, and thrust hard against her. "Like it, reb lover?"

She came to and vomited. The sergeant pulled away in disgust then punched her hard in the nose. "What the hell? Christ! Throwing up on me?"

The officer kept thrusting into Miela, pushing her up against the wall as he finished with her. She sobbed at the sight of Elsey on the floor with the sergeant kneeling over her, fiddling with his belt. The officer pulled away and slapped her bare bottom. "Not a bad poke for such a fat belly." He pulled up his pants and winked at the sergeant, "You want a turn?"

"Nope. One reb lover is plenty." He drew his revolver. "Best we shoot them now, sir. Whores that tried to hit us with a hammer. Nobody's gonna blame us for that." He cocked the pistol.

"Not this one," the officer held his hand over Miela's head. "She's pregnant."

The sergeant hesitated and smiled at Miela. "Well, I guess she got what she deserved anyhow." He slapped Elsey's bottom as she pulled her dress back down. "Your friend is one lucky bitch. But you ain't." He dragged her out the door by the hair. Miela tried to stand up, but the room turned over violently. She fell on her side.

"Better rest there, miss," the wobbling officer hiccoughed, stooped, and patted her hip. "You've served the Union Army well. You should be proud."

He went out the door. Elsey screamed, and a gunshot exploded. Miela pulled herself up from the bed and stumbled into the wall. The room turned upside down again.

The next thing she knew was Lizette kneeling above her sobbing. "Miela! Thank God you're alive!"

Miela's dress was spotted with blood. Lizette knew what had happened. Her tears dripped on to Miela's shoulder as she helped her sit up, dabbing her swollen face with a wet cloth, and helping her out the door into the sunlight. Daphne was kneeling in the high grass, wailing. Poins and Jemps stood behind her. Cunseh was gathering the children by the barn.

"I'm all right, Lizette. Go help Elsey."

Lizette turned her head, and Miela felt panic rise into her throat.

"Where's Elsey?" She saw feet sticking out from a clump of high weeds. "No. Please God, no."

Lizette held her back and sobbed harder."She's gone. Titus, too. They're dead. Both of 'em. Gone to God."

Miela saw Titus on his face in the weeds. She collapsed on the ground into blackness. She woke up sideways, watching ants climb up a blade of grass just beyond her nose. For a second it was as if she had awakened in a forest with giant ants climbing green trees. She tried to hold on to the dream, not wanting to leave the forest quite yet, but Lizette was calling her firmly.

"Miela! Miela! Are you all right? Please God, wake up!"

Jemps pulled her up and leaned into her face, "Who did this? Who did it, Miela?"

Miela knew immediately she couldn't tell him or anyone. Ever. She would have to take it to the grave. If Ezekiel ever found out who they were, he'd kill them or die trying. Either way, he'd end up in the grave. Her duty, from that moment, was to protect him, to save his life. It was the only way to bear what had been done. To Titus and Elsey, and to her. The only way to salvage something from it. To save Ezekiel and to go on living. For the baby, for Ezekiel, for all of them, especially Titus and Elsey. Lizette helped her up and tried to hold her. She pushed her away, and walked slowly over to Elsey's body in the grass.

"No. I must do this," she cried, kneeling beside her and wincing at the sight of her bloody temple and the congealed blood covering her face. She bent over her and kissed her on the forehead. "Goodbye Elsey. We'll see you again ... We'll be together someday." She wiped Elsey's face gently with her dress then allowed Lizette's help to stand back up. Titus lay a few feet away. The back of his head was crushed in. His eyes were still open and his tongue stuck out his mouth. Miela knelt beside him too, "Rest now, Titus. Thank you for all your help. Go with God." She kissed him and closed his eyes.

Jemps came up behind her, "You've got to tell me, Miela. Who did this? Tell me. Please! Who did this?"

"I don't know!" She felt nausea well up and fell to her knees gagging.

"Why ... Why Lord? Why do you allow such pain?"

Daphne knelt beside her crying, "They're with God right now. They've gone to heaven above."

Yarrow and Grace came back out of the woods from squirrel hunting and started screaming when they saw the bodies. Yarrow curled up on this side and groaned for an hour or so while Grace lay on top of him patting his head. Lizette tended to them while Poins and Jemps carried the bodies to the cabin. Daphne washed the rest of the blood off their faces, dressed them both in clean clothes, and combed their hair. Graves were dug under the oak trees past the barn. Everyone helped. Even Yarrow.

"Goodbye Momma. I'll see you in heaven." He kissed his mother on the cheek. "I'll be right here if ... " Then he cried in Grace's arms with Jemps kneeling behind him holding his shoulders.

"She's gone on ahead of us to heaven, Yarrow. With Titus and all the others. She'll be looking down on you every day and night."

"And her spirit lives inside of you, Yarrow," Poins added.

Yarrow sobbed for a while then wiped his nose and went back to work helping to dig the graves, stopping every shovel full to cry some more and letting Grace hug his neck, weeping, "You're brave, Yarrow. A brave young man."

Cumseh lit a small fire of pine cones and corn husks and burned little pieces of paper shaped like birds. She held up her hands. "They have wings that soar. The Divine calls them up. They live in the clouds and stars now. When the Lord gives us fire then calls us back up in the smoke, we can always smell the burning earth."

She stopped and made a strange noise like cows lowing in the distance then buried the ashes of her paper birds in a little hole she dug by the graves, covering it all up with a handful of acorns. Miela waited for a while to make sure she was finished then led them all in the Lord's Prayer. Poins, Jemps and Yarrow filled the graves, and they all sang *Amazing Grace*.

"Thru' many dangers, toils and snares, I have already come; 'Tis grace has brought me safe thus far, And grace will lead me home."

Chapter 49 — Connor and Ezekiel

Charleston

Connor sailed up to Thomas Island with a small keg of nails, a roll of canvas, and a coil of rope for the farm. He rowed the Aleta up the creek to the landing, tied up to an oak tree on the bank, then walked up the road to the farm with his gifts, passing Lizette and Cumseh in the garden tending to weeds. They didn't wave or look up. Something had happened. Had Ezekiel returned? He felt his heart race as he glanced around. Just Jemps and Poins standing by the door of Miela's hut. But what he would do if Ezekiel came walking out? What would Ezekiel do? Would being the son of Ezekiel's former owner and the nephew to another warrant revenge? He thought not. Not Ezekiel. He was too rational. So why the heart flutter? He put down his load and went inside the hut. He found Miela in bed vomiting up blood and being tended to by Daphne.

"What the hell happened?"

Miela glanced up at him then turned away. "Go away Conner. This isn't your fight."

Daphne covered her with a fresh sheet. "Somebody killed poor Elsey and Titus. Beat Miela Bad. But she won't say ... "

"Enough, Daphne."

"No it ain't," she cried. "Elsey and Titus are dead. We buried them yonder in the field. See the cross?" Her voice cracked and she wagged a finger at Connor as if he was partly to blame. "Ezekiel's still gone y'see." Her hands trembled as she poured Miela a glass of water. "They came when they knew he was gone. They did this ... "

"I said that's enough, Daphne," Miela sipped the water and moaned. Connor barely heard her. He focused on Miela's face. Her eyes were swollen shut. Blood dripped from her badly cut lip. She gagged up some more blood, holding her swollen belly with both hands.

"Please Lord. Please, don't take my baby. Please. Please."

Daphne came over and pulled Connor out of the door. She handed him a knife. "She seen who done it but won't tell. Nobody else saw 'em. We was all down to the creek crabbing." She folded Connor's hands around the knife hilt. "You've got to find them and kill them ... for her. For Titus and Elsey too."

Connor nodded. He'd already decided he would do exactly that. As soon as he'd seen her face. It just had to be done. The bastards that did this to Miela, and who killed Titus and Elsey, deserved to die. He thought of Henrietta and how he'd avenged her death. The boy that he'd killed in the graveyard. It was wrong, but he couldn't take it back. And he knew truthfully that he didn't much want to.

God can send me to Hell, he thought. He can do whatever He pleases. But his gut told him it just hadn't been possible to go on living without having exacted payment for Henrietta. And now he had to do the same for Miela. One deserved no less than the other. Henrietta was revenge, Miela simple justice, but the urge was equally powerful. He would kill the bastards who had done this. Even if he had to rot in prison or go to hell for eternity.

Brave talk! He could just hear his uncle mocking him. But no matter. He damn well would see it through. But first he had to find them. He felt sure he could. Captain O'Neill, the ferryman would know. Or Sean O'Neill, his brother and the owner of Dover's Tavern. Someone would tell. All it took was enough money, and he had the Aleta to make more. He'd find them, and when he did, he'd kill them. He'd work it out somehow. It was a quest he immediately embraced with all his heart. If ever there was a just cause, this was it. To find them and kill them. Before Ezekiel did. He knew Ezekiel would never rest until he found them. Then he'd go kill them without the first thought of consequence. Connor figured he could do it with more planning and a much better chance of surviving. His gift to Ezekiel.

He had the much greater advantage too. No whites would talk to Ezekiel, and no blacks outside of the family would risk their necks giving him information that led to the killing of a white man. Connor knew he, however, could get whatever he needed, no matter how long it took, and he was right. Later that same night, after sailing across the river, he found out their names, just as he knew he would.

451

"Lieutenant Tomlinson and a Sergeant Maxwell," Sean O'Neill, the tavern owner, whispered. "The same assholes that were drunk and poking the pigs when you crossed over a few weeks back. Remember?"

"Yes, I do. I certainly do."

"Well, this last time they confiscated three bottles of rum and took the ferry over with the pretty black girl. You know. The pregnant one. I told them that they owed me two dollars, but that bastard sergeant put a revolver to my face. Said they were part of the 'River and Ferry Protection Command' on 'forage duty'. That they had the right to shut me down if I complained." He took a deep breath and shook his head.

"I'll be glad when they're all gone. Every one of them."

Connor nodded. "Well, the rest of them will be here a while, I guess. But those two, maybe not so long."

"I didn't hear a word," O'Neill grinned.

Connor gave him the last of his gold coins and swore him to secrecy.

"Tell anybody else and Ezekiel, her husband, might find out. They could hang you as an accomplice if he kills them."

O'Neill's red face broke into a huge smile. "I don't give a shit about that. Asshole Yankees can eat my ... " he laughed. "But don't worry none. I can keep a secret. Hell, that's why I'm a tavern owner, for God's sake."

They shook hands and Connor sailed with the tide.

EZEKIEL RETRACED his loop north to Moncks Corner then rode across Biggin Bridge at the head waters of the Cooper River and back down towards Mt. Pleasant. It took him four days, but he was in no hurry. He felt a weight had been lifted. There was no more fire in his belly. McCallister and his grandsons and all the other reb bastards could go to Hell, but he wouldn't be the one who'd send them there. Killing the Blessings was enough as far as he was concerned. The Jubilee could now proceed properly in the light of truth.

He brought rope and nails from Mr. Schuller's stored at Cordesville using the coins he'd taken out of Blessing's pocket and made sure Mr. Schuller caught his name. As far as anyone would know, he hadn't been anywhere near Blessing Plantation. He made it back to the Mathis Ferry in Mount Pleasant the next day then crossed over to Charleston, took the state road up to the Clements Ferry, and watered the mule in the trough

452

at the landing while he waited for a ride across to Thomas Island. A group of refugee blacks with a few pitiful little bags sat alongside the road eyeing him. None spoke. The Ezekiel nodded and stretched.

"It's a fine day, ain't it?"

No one answered. The three men and four younger boys stood with heads lowered as if expecting a fight. The six women, ranging in age from young girls to grey-haired grandmothers, looked wary and ready to flee. Ezekiel glanced around. The only horses tied to the railing belonged to the Union cavalrymen who were inside the tavern drinking. He tied his mule to the rail and walked over to the group.

"What are y'all waiting on?"

The biggest man stood up with clenched fists, his jaw tucked tightly against his chest. He glared at Ezekiel but said nothing.

"Y'all have a place to go?" Ezekiel asked.

"None of your business," the big man replied softly, his brown pants sporting patches of assorted colors and his bulky quilted jacket sprouting cotton ticking from several rips. He lifted his head and Ezekiel saw that he was cross eyed.

"Look here," Ezekiel held up his hand and enjoyed watching the man's eye snap towards it. "If y'all need a place to go, we got a farm over yonder." He pointed across the river. Every head turned and followed his hand. He wasn't sure why he was inviting perfect strangers, but something told him it was necessary. A cure of sorts. One that was way over due. He knew he had the power at that particular moment to help people who might otherwise end up in another form of slavery in Charleston. So why not try? He also had enough sense to realize that by changing their lives he might just be changing his own.

"More than fifty acres." He kept pointing. "Enough land for all of y'all to come join us. We've got a decent sized family there already. If you want, you can ... "

"We don't need no help." The big man scuffed his foot in the dirt and started to sit down.

"Yes we do!" The oldest gray-haired woman spoke up. She wore what looked like a burlap sack, dyed orange. "Caleb, you might think you're overseer now ... But you ain't." She turned to Ezekiel. "Mister, we left PonPon plantation last week. Mr. Phillips ran off when the Yanks came. We stayed there as long as we could, but we ain't got nothing to eat and nowhere to go now except Charleston. Heard the Yanks are giving away some of them white folks' homes. You got something better?"

"Best y'all come with me," he pointed again across the river. "It'll be a lot safer over there with us. Charleston's full of freed slaves from all over. Most with nowhere to stay and no work except the worst kind."

The old woman nodded and rubbed her chin. Caleb sat back down and scowled. The old lady tossed him a piece of cornbread. "Eat something like I done told you, Caleb. You're mighty peckish when you're hungry. Can't you see this man's trying to help us." She nodded to Ezekiel. "We thank you kindly, too."

One of the other women whispered into her ear, but she shook her head and pushed the woman away. "No. I think we'll go with him. God is giving us a sign. His will be done."

Ezekiel nodded back. "I'll work it out with the ferrymen. For today or tomorrow. My name's Ezekiel."

"Cassina," the old woman nodded. She tilted her head back as if to say something else, but Caleb cleared his throat, sat back down, and started whistling. She smiled at Ezekiel and dropped to a whisper. "His way of saying thanks."

Ezekiel smiled, "I see. Well, I might have done the same. Wait right here." He went over to speak to Mr. O'Neill as the ferry came upriver then came back and squatted down beside Cassina. "He says come on right now. He'll take us all across for credit ... and my mule."

"Well then, the Lord has spoken. We'll come with you." she nodded. "I can see Providence in your eyes."

"Maybe I'll come and maybe not," Caleb shrugged. "And maybe he ain't somebody to trust." His eyes wandered to Ezekiel.

"Well don't then," Cassina snapped back. 'Stay here by yourself and don't ever trust another soul. See how far that gets you." She winked at Ezekiel and waved her hands above her head. "But the rest of us are headed to ... a New World!"

The others followed her lead, boarding the ferry then huddling in a clump in the bow while the whistle blew, and the dock lines were tossed aside. Caleb jumped on board as the boat started off. Casinna and Ezekiel looked the other way as if they hadn't noticed, and Caleb sat down with the others for the crossing.

"Well, I figure I just better watch out for y'all," Caleb stretched his arms in the breeze. "No telling what's over yonder."

"Well we're glad you're coming," Cassina smiled. "Praise God!"

"It might work out all right," Caleb shrugged, leaning over the rail to watch the river churn past. "We'll see."

At the landing they all scrambled up the gang plank right behind Ezekiel. Caleb waited to be the very last, jumping off just as the ferry pulled away. As they came into the farm clearing, everyone came out to greet them. Everyone except Miela, Elsey and Titus. Ezekiel noticed right off. Lizette and Daphne helped to feed the new arrivals, and Caleb went with Jemps to help clear a place in the barn and get the group situated temporarily with blankets. Ezekiel found Miela behind the barn feeding the chickens. She didn't turn around when he called her so he grabbed her from behind, kissed her neck then pulled her around. Her swollen eyes and bruised face made his heart jump.

"Christ!" He touched her face, and she pushed him away. "Who did this?"

She shook her head. "I don't know. I don't remember anything."

Her tone was quite convincing, but Ezekiel knew her abilities better than anyone. "Tell me."

"I don't remember. There was a knock on the door and something hit my head. I woke up on the floor."

"The baby ... ?"

"The baby's all right and I'm All right. We're both alive ... And so are you. The others need you, Ezekiel. Now more than ever. Nothing else matters now. I won't have any more vengeance either. I just can't have it. God knows there's been enough already."

He felt his jaw clench. His body shivered all over. Damn this! When would it be over? Who else did he have to kill to protect his people? "All right. Just tell me who ... "

"I DON'T REMEMBER!"

"All right. All right."

Ezekiel kissed her and tried to smile. His arms and legs felt suddenly leaden. He knew the rage he felt inside wouldn't help her, or the baby, now. He had to pretend, at least for a while. Arguing with her or trying to push her to tell him more wouldn't work. He would just have to find out on his own. Without her knowing. So he hugged her and helped get

455

Cassina's group settled. They all shared supper then he lay down with Miela to sleep, being careful to act as if nothing had happened. In the morning he got up early and found Jemps already milking the cows.

He stood over him. "Tell me everything you know."

"I don't know nothing," Jemps squirted milk on his shoe. "Miela won't tell. Wouldn't tell the white boy neither."

"Who? What white boy?"

"That white boy, Connor. The one who gave us this here." He waved his hand at the pasture.

"Connor? Was here?"

"Yep. Came in about a week ago. She wouldn't tell him nothing either." He stopped milking and looked up. "Maybe she really don't remember."

Ezekiel patted his back. "Yep. That's probably it. Knocked her senseless probably." But he knew otherwise. He played along though, pretending to focus on chores and trying to put Miela at ease, thinking maybe she would slip up and talk about it once she felt he wouldn't lose his temper. But she didn't. She wouldn't say a word to him that whole evening then made everyone, including the newcomers, gather together to say a prayer after supper.

"Let us give thanks to the Lord for our blessings and our new family and let us forgive those who have sinned against us. Please Lord, forgive those who keep anger and hate in their hearts. Let your love wash the hate away. Let your light shine brighter than their darkest thoughts."

"Amen," they all answered.

Miela looked up at Ezekiel and blessed herself. "Let us all live in peace."

"Amen," he answered.

Fatima knelt down beside her and blessed herself twice with each hand. "We like crossing ourselves, Ezekiel. See? We all do it now."

Grace and Agnes joined her and blessed themselves faster and faster. Casinna watched to see how it was done then joined in. Her group quickly followed, even Caleb, until they had everyone laughing. Miela looked up at Ezekiel and shook her head.

"You might need to bless yourself a bit more than the others. Maybe a lot more."

Ezekiel nodded. "You might just be right."

456

Neither of them mentioned it again, and the next day Ezekiel went about his chores, tending to the goats, helping plow the fields, putting up split rail fencing, patching leaks in the cabin roof, and helping rebuild the barn into better lodging for Cassina's group. He waited a full week before announcing he needed more nails and tar and would be headed to Charleston in the morning. If Miela suspected anything, she kept it to herself, and he was thankful. He packed a burlap sack with an extra change of clothes and a hatchet then helped Poins load firewood on board the ferry for payment for a ride over. He took him two days to find Connor. When he did, it was nearly dark and Connor was caulking seams on the Aleta.

CONNOR LOOKED UP and saw Ezekiel coming. Head lowered, jaw set, a quick forceful stride. His heart jumped. He knew what was about to happen, but he was prepared for it. Although it had been nearly four years since he'd seen him, it was as if it was yesterday. He wasn't sure what to think. Memories of time spent with Ezekiel came flooding back. Crabbing in the old skiff on the creeks behind Younge's Island and pulling the seine net together. Hunting squirrels and trapping raccoons. All the things any two young boys would love to do. But Ezekiel had been his father's slave. Were all those memories false? What did Ezekiel remember? He watched him come up quickly and stand on the wharf about him. Ezekiel didn't wave or smile.

"Ezekiel. Good to see you, too. It's sure been a while. You look about the same though. Maybe bigger."

Ezekiel said nothing for a second. He looked down at him. Connor Dumont, the white boy who had, at one time, been as close as an owner could be to a slave. He still felt it, the bond that didn't need words and couldn't be put into any if you tried. But in that split second he again reminded himself that all of it, all the years in slavery even as a boy playing in the creeks and fields, were now a meaningless lie. How could he have fond feelings for someone whose father had purchased him as he would a mule. But damn it, he knew he still did, and it tore at him. He stopped for a second and savored the salt breeze in his face and imagined it blowing out the last flicker of nostalgia for something that he knew, now as a free man, had never really existed. He wasn't a slave anymore and Connor wasn't his owner and had never really been his friend. Not really.

Connor watched Ezekiel's second of hesitation and had a glimmer of hope that it wouldn't come to blows."You want to help me with ... ?"

"Shut up Connor. Just tell me who did it ... Before I knock your teeth out."

Connor dropped the awl he was holding. It fell into a pile of caulking cord. He took a deep breath and braced himself, having already made up his mind. Ezekiel could kill him if he liked, but he wasn't going to tell. No matter what. Nothing else mattered. If he gave the names, Ezekiel would kill them as quickly as he could, and without any thought of himself. He'd either be killed in the process or executed afterwards. Either way, Miela and the rest of the family would have to go on without him. And Connor knew he had the better plan. To do it himself. Even if it took months or years. He was already finding out about the bastards' daily routine. He was confident he would find a way. Probably get them down on the Aleta somehow, and drown them both. If he needed Ezekiel's help, which he doubted he would, he'd bring him in at the very last minute and present him with a very good plan. One that would keep him from acting alone and rashly. Ezekiel, even when angered, had usually been sensible, but this was different. This was Miela. If he told him now, Ezekiel would die.

"Now look here. We both want the same thing." He held up his hands.

Ezekiel stepped to the edge of the wharf. "You know who did it, don't you." His jaw worked back and forth like a cow chewing its cud.

"When I know, you'll know. I promise you that," Connor lied.

"Give me the name," Ezekiel sat down on the wharf, dangling his legs over the water. "Just the name. I don't need anything else. Not your help, not your lies."

"I swear I don't know." Connor realized Ezekiel thought there was just one person involved.

"Your eyelids still twitch when you lie. You never were much good at it. Just give me the name."

Connor tossed him his knife. "Yep, you know me pretty well, Ezekiel. And you know I won't give you the name. Ever. So go ahead and kill me now if you want. Asshole."

458

"The name!" Ezekiel growled, sliding the bowie knife out of its leather sheath.

"When I've got it all figured out. When that day comes, then ... "

"Now!"

"No," Connor shook his head. "Kill me now. Go ahead. Or let me do it my way. It's the best chance to get away with it. For Miela and ... "

"I don't give a damn about getting away! Just the name, Connor. I'll take care of the bastard myself. NOW!"

"Yes, you would. But then they'd hang you for sure. Who's gonna take care of Miela?" He picked up a handful of cord and threw it into Ezekiel's face. "It's about Miela and the others, Ezekiel, not you! Stop being so damn ... "

Ezekiel jumped down on him, knocking him backwards into the gunnels. Fists flailed at his head. Thumbs dug into his windpipe. "The name!" Ezekiel yelled, his teeth bared and his face contorted.

Connor struggled to suck in a last breath and choked out what he thought might be his last words. "Kill me now."

Ezekiel punched him in the nose then let him go. Connor gasped for air. "Go to hell, Ezekiel."

Ezekiel climbed back up the wharf ladder and took a deep breath. "You're still as much an ass as ever, Connor. A red-faced, piece of white-shit, rebel ass," he chuckled. "And now with one eye and half scalped. You're more worthless than mule piss. Why don't I just kill you now? I really don't know."

Connor wiped blood from his nose, rubbed his bleeding lip, and felt the whelp that was growing on his forehead. "And you're a dung heap, Ezekiel. Always were, always will be."

Ezekiel smiled at him and laughed for a while. "I swear, Connor. If you die before that bastard does ... If you go to your grave without doing this thing ... I swear I'll dig you up and use your rotting carcass for crab bait."

Connor grinned at him and spit out some blood. "If you do that, I'll haunt you. I'll live in your ceiling and every night drop red ants on your dick."

Ezekiel laughed for a while then sat quietly, watching a thunderstorm grow darker over the James Island shore. Connor went back to caulking. Neither of them talked. Both realizing that it was all more than they could put into thoughts, much less words. Past and present. But Connor figured Ezekiel wouldn't bother him anymore. Not that Ezekiel was above maiming or even killing him or anyone else, for Miela, but now that Ezekiel knew that he wouldn't fight back and that he was willing to die with the names, there was no point in it. At least he hoped that was the case.

"Piece of shit!" Ezekiel stood up and walked off with just a glimmer of a smile.

"Dung heap," Connor snorted out a nose-full of blood and went back to work with a deeper satisfaction.

Ezekiel stopped at the end of the quay and glanced back at Connor stooped over the Aleta. Connor was right, but it irked the hell out of him. Not that he didn't trust Connor to do just what he said. He might be a worthless, scarred up, rebel ass, but he wouldn't let the bastard get away with what he'd done to Miela. Connor had just enough red-faced, don't-give-a-shit, Irish bull shit in him to make the bastard pay.

As Ezekiel walked up East Bay St, he thought of the times before the war, of arm wrestling Connor time and again and never winning. Connor was a slaver's son and a reb son of a bitch, but he was strong as hell when he got his dander up. When that face of his turned beet red, watch out. And now with that half-scalped head and the one eye, he smiled. Conner was truly one ugly bastard, but, he had to admit, truly unique. As Ezekiel rode the ferry back that next morning to Thomas Island, though, he kept wondering if he could wait for Connor to do it.

"God willing," he prayed. "I just have to find a way. For Miela's sake. For Miela's sake."

CHAPTER 50 — LUKE

to Elmira, New York

Pleurisy and another pus pocket on his stump caused Luke's fever return. While everyone celebrated Lee's surrender for days, he sipped laudanum and tolerated the orderlies thumping on his chest and digging more into his arm. The fever finally broke for good on the day word came that Lincoln had been assassinated. Even half dazed with laudanum, he felt sick. It was as if he'd lost his father. Anger boiled through the camp. Groups of soldiers yelled out for revenge.

"Burn Raleigh!"

"Hang the traitors!"

Men pleaded with their officers to let them loose, but Uncle Billy had already made the decision. The war was over. There would be no further eye for an eye. The vengeance and killing were over. Guards were posted at every camp, and officers sent regiments to guard the nearby towns including Raleigh. There would be no more Columbias. Men grumbled and cursed but obeyed. Luke watched angry soldiers burn effigies of Jeff Davis and Lee and wondered if the civilians in Raleigh realized how close they'd come to destruction. He thought of the copper sky that night in Columbia and realized there was still a part of him that actually yearned to see it again. His aching stump helped him push that temptation out of his mind. The last few doses of laudanum weren't really necessary but felt wonderful and helped smother the more lurid thoughts. He drifted off into a half-sleep on his cot in one of the hospital tents, listening to celebratory rifle until jarred awake by a crabby sergeant who threw a piece of paper at him.

"Get up," he snapped irritably. "You're being furloughed with the other wounded. To Wilmington by train then steamer to Annapolis."

"When?"

"Now, damn it! Get up!"

He knocked a chair out of the way and stormed off, either drunk or just ready to go home himself. Luke had just enough time to wash up in the tin basin at the end of the row of cots before wagons pulled up. The whole hospital was evacuated. It was a long, jarring ride to the station at Goldsboro, and the sutured end of his stump ripped open just before arrival, but no one, including Luke, had any inclination to stop and rest. More laudanum and a tighter packing were ordered and the rest of the trip to Washington was a blur. He vaguely remembered a rattling train, a black face bending close with a brown bottle, and a swaying hammock below decks and men all around him vomiting. The laudanum kept him in a warm tunnel until he woke up in another hospital in Washington, on a cot in a long wooden barracks with big open windows overlooking a parade ground that overflowed with soldiers.

Another fever set in the next day, bringing more digging into his stump with repacking and torture until the last pus pocket finally died out. He missed the Army's Grand Review parade but after a few days regained enough strength to start wandering the regimental camps. He found Dave and McMahon at the 137th bivouac just before dark and fought off embarrassing tears.

"Well I'll be damned," Dave took his hand and held it. McMahon touched his shoulder.

"Does it hurt?"

"Nope. Not a bit. Now that the infection's gone."

Dave let go of his hand and gave him a bear hug. "You're a better soldier with one arm than any ten of these new recruits. Look at them." He waved his hand dismissively at the hundreds of bright, fresh uniforms strutting through camp. "All of them ready to fight now that the war's over."

"Sure as hell," McMahon agreed, wiping his eyes.

"Well if it's just the same to you, I'd rather have less pluck and more than one arm," Luke laughed.

They hesitated for a second then laughed with him. "That's my Luke!"

"One arm but still kicking."

Luke caught his breath and wiggled his stump. "Better than losing my dick."

"See?" McMahon put his arm around his shoulder. "That's why he's still our Apostle Luke!"

"Damn right," Dave slapped his back and made him tell all about it. What he remembered at the hospital. What it felt like. How they'd treated him. Everything since he'd been wounded. And he did, but it felt like he was talking about someone else. And most of that, blurred.

"But what about you?" Luke asked, wanting to change the subject.

"Not a damn thing. Just marching along every day. As lazy as could be."

"And no swamps," Dave smiled, fetching a bottle of whiskey. "And plenty of this in Richmond. Them Army of the Potomac ass-holes don't know nothing about true foraging."

"Damn right." McMahon grabbed the bottle from him and plopped down on a bucket. "Ain't been a whole day sober since."

Luke laughed with them. "As it should be, by damn."

"Here's to our greatest Apostle."

"Our ONLY Apostle."

"By God, to all of us ... We made it."

"Hell yes ... we did," McMahon sighed and was silent for a while, sharing their unspoken thoughts of those who hadn't. "C'mon, Dave," he jumped up. "Let's show our Apostle around."

They took Luke on a tour of the huge encampment of dozens of regiments and went on to enjoy a fine evening then another week of sleeping late, warm sunshine, fresh food and new clean clothes. But there was still no news about Jack. They all guessed he was dead, but no one dared say it. Maybe if they didn't mention it, if they just went on with their lives, so would he, wherever he was. Maybe.

Then one morning, a handwritten note came from General Slocum along with Luke's promotion, to be recorded but not enacted until the regiment was mustered out of service a few days later, which was fine with Luke. He knew he'd done nothing more than any of the others and was quite proud to stay a private. On their last night together, they had a decent meal of roasted chickens that Dave scrounged, and drank the last of the whiskey, but no one felt like talking. It was all just too much to think about now that it was over.

The next morning McMahon left on the train to New York City to see his mother. They all fought off tears at the station as he waved goodbye from the passenger car window. "Come visit," his voice cracked. "More to do on Broadway than Elmira." He tried to smile but had to look away as tears filled his eyes.

"Goodbye good friend," Luke waved, standing on the platform with Dave, watching the train disappear around the far bend between rows of neat, well tended, red brick warehouses. He thought of the rubble of the Columbia station and sat down on a bench and cried for a long time. Dave stood his guard, glaring at anyone who dared glance down at him. The next day they took the train together to Baltimore then Harrisburg and Williamsport and then finally home. They said goodbye at the station in Elmira and went their separate ways. Luke on foot, Dave to Horseheads by coach.

"I'll be seeing you soon, Luke," he called from the window. "I bring my Uncle Morris. He can out-drink anybody. We'll have a big old time." "We sure will ... More than once," Luke called back.

He waved then walked down Main Street to the Baptist Cemetery where he stopped and said a prayer for Jack and everyone else who hadn't made it back. Then down Church Street over the Chemung Canal Bridge and past the Presbyterian and Methodist churches then down Lake Street past the Mansion House Hotel to the Black Horse Tavern on Water Street where he sipped whiskey with a group of old men and a dozen other returning soldiers until sufficiently fortified. Then he walked up Davis Street to his parents' home.

The door opened and his sister, Catherine, burst into tears. She couldn't even say his name. She just sobbed. He cried along with her. He couldn't help it. His parents ran up from the back yard and joined in, all hugging and kissing him at once. Soon the entire neighborhood surrounded him, touching and patting his shoulder and arm, but carefully avoiding touching his pinned and empty sleeve.

His Uncle Jim sat alone in the corner with his wooden arm, now freshly painted, and had very little to say at first, but after the crowd quieted down showed Luke how his contraption worked, unstrapping it from his stump and showing how the elbow joint could be set at three different levels. "You should get one of these. It's pretty damn useful. Your arm won't grow back, you know," he tried to smile. "It's crazy, but I kept thinking it would ... for years. Just got this new one about a month ago."

"I think I will," Luke smiled. "It looks good."

His uncle leaned closer. "Enough about that. Tell me about the Henry rifle. How fast can it really fire?"

"The Henry?"

"Yes, damn it. If I'd had one of those at Bull Run ...," he sighed. "Would've changed everything. Wouldn't have been no damned cripple." He tapped on his arm then glanced at Luke's pinned sleeve. "No offense."

"None taken."

"Then tell me about it."

Luke did as requested, telling him everything his uncle wanted to hear and recounting every time he remembered firing it. But as he gave the details, the more despondent his Uncle became, until he abruptly walked out to the back yard to sit alone on a bench for the rest of the afternoon. Luke understood though, as only someone who'd been through it could.

He went back to the others, keeping a smile on his face and answering all of their questions too, however ridiculous. His sister and mother hovered over him the entire evening, despite his father telling them to give him room to breathe. The afternoon, the week, and the entire month flew by in an instant. Friends and family visited daily, catching him up with Elmira news, but he felt a bit lost. He wasn't sure what to do. Time seemed different. Day after day of peace and quiet. No one barking orders, no one shooting at him, no swamps to cross, no death and misery. It didn't seem real, like a daydream that would vanish on awakening. He had to remind himself everyday that the war was truly over.

He grew restless, though, and wandered about town. He visited the reb prisoner of war camp and watched wagon loads of scarecrow rebs making their way down to the station to go home. He heard from a neighbor that over a thousand men had died there and, despite intelligent people arguing that the rebels had done much worse, knew their excuses rang hollow. The Elmira area was flush in food and supplies. To capture a young man then starve him to death in a prison camp, with an abundance of food just on the other side of the wall, was murder, pure and simple. It was like Camp Sorghum in Columbia. Maybe even like the Andersonville prison camp in Georgia that he'd read about in the papers.

But maybe even worse. Yet as he watched the wagons of prisoners rumble down towards the station, a beautiful thought crystalized in his mind and a stillness came over him, bringing with it a purpose that he hadn't felt since waking up from the laudanum. He made up his mind in an instant. He knew immediately that it might be total nonsense, but by God, it absolutely would be the next chapter in his life.

He would go back to South Carolina. To do what he could. To live there and try his best to make something decent of what he'd been through. He knew it was a pipe dream. And probably even crazy. But he figured losing an arm might give him the right to be a little bit crazy. The thought of the copper sky above burning Columbia popped into his mind, and he knew it was God talking. He would sell his share of the freight business, move to Charleston, and set up shop. An ambassador for peace. He smiled to himself at the absurdity of it all but was determined to do it. Better to light one candle and all that. He laughed out loud at his naivete but walked home quickly to speak with his father.

"That's the dumbest thing I've ever heard. You're just not yourself yet... not since you've been home. And no, I will not buy you out." His father wouldn't even talk to him about it further and wouldn't listen to any of his arguments.

"I'm going down there, one way or the other. Money or no money. Even if I have to walk." He surprised even himself at his determination.

"It might be crazy... Hell, it IS crazy, but it's something I'm going to do."

He knew that his father would relent. He could hear him crying at night, and he knew what it was about. His boy had come home missing an arm. And Uncle Jim too. And while one was brooding in the backyard, the other was smiling and making plans to go back and help the very people he'd fought. He knew that deep down inside his father was proud of him, and that in the end, would help him any way he could. He listened for a few more weeks to all of them trying to talk him out of it. His uncle in particular.

"How stupid can you be. Going down there to help those bastards. Going back to rebel Hell. Just to be a carpetbagger. The shame of it. A shame for the whole family."

Luke listened politely until his father cut his Uncle off. He'd already decided not to argue with him or anyone else. He'd just do it. Their criticism just made him doubly determined. He smiled and nodded his head as it went on and on, from one family member or neighbor to another. The whole time thinking about what he'd seen. All the misery of South Carolina. The children in the cupboard, the prisoners being shot, Columbia burning, and scarred face of the boy, Connor, who had saved his life. It all added up to one thing. He would stick to his crazy plan. And he did.

CHAPTER 51 — CONNOR'S REVENGE

Charleston

onnor went about engrossing himself in a rhythm of work on the harbor. He slept on the Aleta and sailed at least twice a day across the harbor to Fort Johnson, Fort Moultrie, or the Mathis Ferry landing at the village of Mount Pleasant across from the city. The new government had set the rate per trip, but he didn't really care. Mostly he carried provisions and supplies. Kegs of nails for reconstruction projects, boxes of food tins for the Army garrisons, sacks of beans, flour, cornmeal, and rice, barrels of molasses, rolls of canvas, and crates of shoes and clothing. He worked the Aleta alone. It was part of his plan. He had her rigged for single hand control with extra pulleys and lines for halyards, sheets, and the tiller. It was just as he liked it, and he refused many offers from men wanting to crew. Dock hands and other boat crews called him crazy and a fool for not hiring men to at least load and unload and make faster trips. They said there was more money with a crew, and Connor knew they were right. But he would just smile and go on doing it by himself. He had it worked out in detail. Even after six months, there would be the occasional new idea. He went over it every day, knowing that even the smallest items, if overlooked, could mean his death.

On full moon nights, he would careen the Aleta on a sand bar ostensibly to scrape off barnacles from the hull but really to work or in his device, in private. It was a simple idea really. A section of planking cut neatly out of the hull, port and starboard, then caulked back into place and held firmly in place with a tight fitting crossbeam under the fore-deck, and a pulley system with strong wire from the crossbeam to the stern where it could be quickly clipped onto the boom. All he had to do was clip it on, pull the iron safety rod from the pulley, jibe in a strong wind, and the wire would pull the crossbeam loose, opening holes in the hull. The Aleta would sink within minutes. The pulley system and clips to the boom of course had to stay well oiled and be free of rust in order

468

to actually work, so he kept a gallon of cotton seed oil under the transom. Also the plank sections that had been cut out and re-caulked had to be checked daily for leaks

But to Connor, it wasn't work at all. He enjoyed every minute of it. He kept the whole system spotless, which was totally unlike him. He knew his Uncle Paul would have been pleased. Dedicating the time and effort to care for something properly. Of course that was the sad part too. Knowing it would mean the end of the Aleta. It was something that he knew had to be done, but it brought tears to his eyes many nights. He tried not to think of it. He told himself that someday in the future he would find her again and everything would be just like it was. He knew it was all nonsense, but he still half believed it. And at least she would go to the bottom in glory, and for a good cause.

In the meantime, what worried him the most was the chance that an engineer officer or civilian contractor would insist on inspecting the hold or the bow compartment. Connor knew his device would be hard to spot even for an experienced seaman, and most of his passengers were far from that, but still, it could happen. Someone could figure it all out before the day when ... Connor stopped himself every time. There was no use worrying 'when.' It would happen when it happened. All he could do was bide his time and wait.

The day would come when one, or both, of them would step foot on the Aleta. He just had to wait. Their faces and their names were seared into his brain. He would pay them back for what they'd done to Miela. And Titus and Elsey. He hoped to God that on that day, they would cross the harbor together. Otherwise he'd have to drown the one and find a way to kill the other later. It wouldn't be hard to do if he was ready to die for it. He could just shoot the bastard. But to do it and live. .. That was why he'd waited six months. He thought every day about Miela and what they'd done to her, but he'd purposely avoided all further contact with her and the others at Smythe's. He knew that if he was caught, suspicion would be cast their way.

At night on the Aleta, he would cook fish that he'd caught that day. He always left trotlines out whenever he could, and nearly every day had spot, croakers, or pinfish to fry for fish sandwiches, which he thought of as his little, edible lures. Most everyone knew he gave them to the Yank soldiers going across on the Aleta. Some of the white dock hands cursed him when the Yanks weren't around.

"Damn Scalawag!" A proud lady had snarled at him from a carriage as it rolled past on East Bay Street.

Scalawag, he grinned. He liked the sound of the word. And he figured it added to his alibi. The blue coats passing by just thought he was a bit odd. But they liked the sandwiches, and he had passengers on days that other boats didn't. Yet in the months that had passed, the only two passengers that he really cared about hadn't booked passage. Connor had seen them down at the wharf-front on many days, and once they'd walked just past him to another boat for a trip upriver. But they'd never set foot on the Aleta, until that one day. It was an overcast Wednesday in November with cold, misty rain. Perfect for what he planned. The two of them walked up together and stepped on board reeking of alcohol and laughing.

"Take us over to Sullivan's Island," Lieutenant Tomlinson ordered. Connor almost fainted. Thank God they'd both been drinking and didn't seem to recognize him, maybe not even remembering him, and, praise the Lord, no one else was with them. They were bundled up tightly into thick overcoats against the cold and wore heavy boots. Connor handed each a wool jacket which they put on as if ordered. He knew that the sleeves were a bit tight. He'd tied them that way on purpose. When soaked in water, they added ten pounds and were almost impossible to get off. He knew he had them and couldn't resist a smile.

The Aleta sailed just ahead of a company of black infantry coming down to the wharf, and he was scared the Lieutenant would order him back. But he didn't. Connor watched them sit amidships, all cozy and bundled up, eating the fish sandwich bait and sipping on a shared bottle of spirits..

Lieutenant Tomlinson leaned his head back against the side rail and lit his pipe. "Maxwell," he handed the bottle to the sergeant. "You've done well for yourself. Maybe you can stay with the Army. Go out west. Fight the Indians. Maybe get an officer's commission."

Sergeant Maxwell shook his head. His mouth was stuffed full of fish sandwich, and it took him a while to answer. "No thanks. I'll stay right here. Ride herd on the rebs. They'll never really give it up. You know that. It's in their blood." He patted his Navy colt revolver. "This is all they'll ever respect." He gobbled another fish sandwich and stared at Connor. "I plan to give back to the slavers just as much as I got. And more. They'll be sorry to see me hereabouts. I'll never let 'em be. Never." The lieutenant puffed away on his pipe, watching Sergeant Maxwell toss pieces of bread to the begging gulls overhead. "That's all you'll get from Sergeant Maxwell, rebel birds! Crumbs!" he laughed, and Maxwell nodded.

"They'll be lucky to get that."

Connor pretended not to listen and quietly clipped the brass hooks onto the boom as he came about. They had no idea what he was doing. The wind picked up, and the Aleta plowed through following swells into the deeper channels past Castle Pinckney. A flight of pelicans skimmed the water just off the starboard bow, drawing their attention. Connor pulled the iron safety rod and jibed without warning. The Aleta lurched to port. As they ducked the swinging boom, the force of the wind on the mainsail snatched the cables tight. The cross-beam popped out of its place below deck and the cut plank sections of the hull gave way with a creak that was barely noticeable even to Connor. Water poured into the hold. The Aleta shuttered, but only Connor was aware of exactly what it meant. It took nearly three full minutes for them to notice. The Aleta was settling lower but still plowing through following swells until water suddenly sloshed over the floorboards.

"What the hell?" Lieutenant Tomlinson raised his soaked feet. "Is the boat leaking?"

"Just slosh in the bilge," Connor yawned, as water poured over the floorboards, suddenly a foot deep. "It's always like this in a following swell."

"Hell it is! This ain't right!" Maxwell yelled in the rising wind. "This boat's sinking! Turn around damn it!" He pulled his revolver.

"Yes sir! You might be right," Connor bumbled about with the jib sheet as if rattled. "I think we might've hit something. Must be got a leak."

"Leak hell! We're sinking for sure!" The lieutenant lifted himself up onto the rail.

"Turnaround! Now!" Maxwell yelled. He aimed the pistol at Connor's head.

471

"If I come about, we'll founder for sure!" Connor yelled back. "Best make it to Haddrells Point up yonder. Tie yourselves to the lifelines. Just in case. See there? The ropes tied to the floats." He pointed to the lines running from the two white float kegs attached to the transom.

He let the jib flap noisily, and water sprayed over the side. They glanced at each other shivering and soaking wet and did as he said, quickly and without a word, cinching the ropes tightly around their waists. It was easier than Connor had dreamed. They obeyed and trusted. And why shouldn't they. After all, he was the Aleta's captain. He untied the white float kegs from their brackets and readied them as water rose quickly in the hold. The bow plunged under a big swell that washed completely over the Aleta.

"Jump! Jump clear!" Connor screamed.

He let go of the sheets and halyards. The boom dropped and screeched over their heads. The mainsail flapped out of control, and the jib snapped as loud as a rifle shot. They didn't argue. Both jumped overboard as if their salvation depended on getting away from the angry sails. Connor threw the kegs overboard, and they went straight to the bottom.

"As fast as kegs of nails are apt to do," he said to himself.

Each 'lifeline' went taut and each waterlogged man went under in a second. Sergeant Maxwell kicked hard, and his eyes met Connor's as he felt the rope cutting into his waist. His arms flailed at the waves then disappeared. The revolver fired from just underwater. The bullet cut through the sail above Connor's head. The lieutenant's hat floated past. The Aleta sunk slowly and Connor had time to cut the stays, trim the mainsail to full power, then harness the wind one last time to snap the mast as the sloop churned lower and lower in the water.

He wrapped up in his rubber vest then glanced around to make sure no other boats were close by. Only two were within a mile. He had at least a half hour. His excuse would be that the wind snapped the mast, and the Lieutenant and Sergeant drowned trying to swim for land. He waited a few more minutes and, as the Aleta dropped under water, pulled up the twine that had played out with each of the sinking kegs. The twine retrieved each 'lifeline' and Connor pulled up each body just long enough to cut the ropes free and let the dead men sink on their on accord, knowing the Yanks wouldn't be too sympathetic if they found two of their own tied to kegs of nails. But now their drowned bodies floated free with the tide. No one could blame him. Men drowned all the time.

The stub of cracked mast disappeared underwater, and Connor swam for the Mount Pleasant shore. He didn't mind the cold and couldn't help laughing as he swam. Yanks tying themselves to kegs of nails! Then jumping overboard! It was too good to be true. No two men ever deserved it more. Miela, Elsey and Titus were avenged. Justice had been done.

CHAPTER 52 — MIELA'S CHILD

Miela waddled along as fast as her huge belly allowed then rested for most of the afternoon in the hammock that Poins had made, stretching between two small pine trees beside a thick oak on a little point overlooking the marsh in the woods behind the farm. The clouds above her turned pink with the setting sun. The sea breeze caressed her face and swirled underneath the hammock to cool her back. Her baby kicked inside of her belly again, but the breeze blew stronger to soothe him. She knew he was a boy. Just by the way he shivered inside her before she nodded off to sleep. Just like Ezekiel.

She curled her toes against the taut ropes and smelled the pluff mud and salt air, smiling and watching the sun peeking through a black wall of clouds on the far horizon and sending a pink ray down across the miles of marsh grass straight to her hammock. She felt it on her arms and watched her palms turn pink then violet. She knew that her son, a gift from God, was being recognized by the Almighty. None of the awful things that had happened to her mattered anymore. Only the child inside her. No meanness, cruelty, or pain could stand up to the peace that she felt. The pink and violet rays covering her belly were a sign from God. A sign that this wonderful gift of peace had to be shared.

The sun's last rays bathed her body and clearly lit the way to a better future. She knew it in her heart. She'd always known it, but here it was in the flesh. And she knew the life inside of her would mark the future for Ezekiel too. She felt the wind, the marsh grass, the earth, and the sun all embrace her. No bitterness, hatred, anger, or revenge could stand against them. She thanked God and watched the last rays retreat across the marsh and disappear across the river into the distant forest.

"Come on Miela," Lizette called from the path leading back towards the farm. "Supper time! Jemps and Poins got us a mess more shrimp."

"I'm coming," she smiled. "We're coming, that is." She forced herself up and waddled back up the path.

She tried to eat but couldn't. Her stomach cramped up all night, and in the morning, full labor pains set in. The women tended to her, and she had the baby that afternoon. A boy. Healthy and whole. Ezekiel waited outside the door until he heard the baby crying then barged in before Lizette could come fetch him.

He knelt beside Miela, "Are you all right?"

She pulled back the blanket covering the baby's head, "A boy, Ezekiel. His name is Smythe."

Ezekiel fought away tears, grimacing as if in pain, "A boy?"

"Your son, Smythe." Miela held up the infant's head.

"Hello there ... son," Ezekiel trembled. "You're just fine! Just as fine as can be!"

Daphne let the girls and Yarrow come in. Agnes peered at Smythe over Ezekiel's shoulder, giggling, "He's kind of funny looking."

"Sure is," Yarrow nodded. "What color is that anyhow? Kind of a brown-orange." He reached to touch him, but Ezekiel pushed his hand away and then wiped away tears.

"He's the most beautiful color in the world."

"That he is," Miela smiled. "That he is."

Lizette shooed them all out except for Ezekiel. He stayed with Miela while she nursed Smythe for the first time, marveling at his tiny fingers and toes and hardly leaving her side the rest of the day and then most of the next week until she started venturing out occasionally to sit in the shade beside the barn where she could see the field and the woods beyond. When he had to do chores, he made sure someone was with her every second, and at the end of the week, as she gradually got her strength back, he helped her back down the path to the hammock as she insisted.

"Smythe likes the breeze. See? He started smiling as soon as we got past the woods."

Ezekiel nodded, "Maybe so."

He figured that either it was true or should've been. Anyhow, Miela thought it was true, and that's all that counted. He lifted her into the hammock and made sure Smythe was nestled safely in her arms then stayed with them for a while until the others came up the path and took turns checking on them. But Miela was quite happy to finally be alone with Smythe, just resting with him on the hammock, enjoying the breeze and keeping one foot drooping over to barely touch the ground, rocking gently back and forth and cuddling him against her breast as he suckled until full then slept as if melting into her.

In the early evening, the massive moss-draped oak limb above her blocked out the sun. Her face and chest fell into the shadows for a while. She reached over and took a handful of dirt from beneath the hammock and let it dribble slowly downwind then watched as the dust blew in the breeze, hovering in the sun's rays for a few seconds before disappearing leeward. The sun crept lower, sneaking beneath the moss on the big oak limb until the light fell fully on Smythe's face. He squinted and closed his eyes then shivered for a second. She covered his eyes with her hand, and he smiled.

"We're truly in the light now. The shadows are gone ... forever."

She kissed his head, watching the sunlight turn a golden yellow and the marsh grass ripple with a hundred colors of green. Puffy clouds changed colors, painting themselves pink and violet as they paraded down river towards Charleston under the endless blue sky.

"See there," Miela whispered in his ear, feeling as content as she thought humanly possible, "They're dressing up and going to town."
The breeze heard her and rustled the palmettos along the bank. Smythe startled with a mock cry and reached out with both tiny hands. She slipped her little finger into his palm. He gripped it tightly and wouldn't let go, making tiny movements against her breasts. She relished the gentle breeze and dozed off for a while until Yarrow's yelling woke her up.

"C'mon Grace!" He came running up the path and climbed up the oak tree above her to a branch where he had a few scavenged boards tied with some old netting he'd found in the creek. It was his special place to hide. A perch where he could spy on the path behind him and the river across the marsh. Only Grace was allowed up. Smythe opened his eyes as he scampered past. Miela bent over close to her son's face and smiled as his eyes wandered unfocused for a second or two and then seemed to focus right on her nose. He startled and threw his hands up. His eyes widened as if he'd just realized she was there. Then he puckered and burped.

Miela couldn't stop laughing, "Am I that scary?"

"What's so funny?" Yarrow yelled from up in his tree house.

476

"Smythe is," she called back, putting her hand up to block the sun so she could look up and see him. "I think he just realized he's not alone."

"He ain't too smart, eh," Yarrow shrugged. "Well, don't worry. Maybe he'll learn."

"Yep. Maybe," she laughed harder.

CHAPTER 53— LUKE

Elmira back to Charleston

Luke said his goodbyes, left Elmira with his saved army pay and the money from his share of the business. He took the train to Brooklyn and then a steamer to Charleston, arriving in December and finding a room with a war widow on Church Street for one dollar a month US currency. He paid double that for food, housecleaning, and firewood so he could use his time to make his way into the business world, setting up a freight shop on Market Street just as his father had taught him. Wagons, horses, supplies, contracts. Things he knew all about. Labor was cheap, but he made it a point to pay more than necessary, and his men, black and white, learned to appreciate him. He wouldn't ask them to do anything he wouldn't do himself, except lifting something heavier than he could pick up with one arm. He joked about it, and they joked back and understood. Two of the men working for him were missing a leg. But, like Luke, they considered themselves lucky.

His shop prospered as Charleston slowly crept back out of devastation. Months went by. He joined St. Mary's Parish and made enough friends there that, despite being a Yankee, he was invited to join the Hibernian Society where he enjoyed hearty Irish fellowship and many a stiff whiskey. He was pleasantly surprised that, although virtually every other member had fought for the Confederacy, they didn't hold his Union service against him. Maybe the pinned sleeve across his chest helped. He laughed as hard as any of them when one red-faced Irishman said that it was the current price of admission.

The Hibernian provided an opportunity, not only for expanding his business, but to help some of the poor Irish families that struggled just to live. All in all, he felt he was doing the right thing, in the right place, and making a difference in a good way. Then, in March, he read in the Charleston Daily News about a Mr. Connor Dumont being held in jail awaiting trial for murder.

"My God!" He called out, suddenly short of breath. "Lord have mercy!"

Linus, one of his one of his black workers, stuck his head inside the door. "Are you all right, Mr. Conneley?"

"Yes. Thank you, Linus," He wiped his eyes and breathed deeply. "But this boy, Connor Dumont, in the paper. The one waiting trial for murder. He might be the one who saved my life."

"You don't say." Linus leaned against the wall and nodded, not appearing the least bit interested. "The Almighty does indeed work in mysterious ways. He sure does. That's what they say anyhow. I guess you should go see him ... Before they hang him."

"I'll do just that."

THE JAIL CELL smelled of urine and feces. The red brick floor seeped groundwater except for the one higher corner where Connor squatted. He listened to the guards laughing at cards down the hallway and the old man groaning in the cell across from him. He figured the man wouldn't live much longer. Cancer maybe, or consumption, by the looks of his sunken temples. The man lay on his side and smiled at Connor, groaning louder as if he'd read his mind, one hand locked under his head, the other holding one of the bars of his cell door. Connor smiled back at him. It was all he could do. Execution by hanging was at least a quick death. He didn't have to worry about growing old rotting in a jail cell

He remembered the men after Spotsylvania with their guts shot out, Barry burning to death at Columbia, Norton dying slowly in the night. If given a choice between deaths ... His brain froze up for a second. All he had to do was avoid thinking of that last second when the rope snapped, but it was hard to do. It made him shiver. He stood up and paced for a while around his little cell. Plenty of time to settle down in the hereafter, he smiled. Plenty of time to do nothing. But now he just had to wait until the day of his execution. The date hadn't yet been set, thank God, but he knew it couldn't be far off.

He thought about Miela and what Tomlinson and Maxwell had done to her and Elsey and Titus and thanked God for having been given the chance to kill them both. It was a huge weight off his shoulders. Going to the gallows with them still alive would have been intolerable. Of course, he chuckled to himself, he wouldn't be waiting to be hung if they were still alive. But he didn't regret killing them. Not in the least. He didn't mind dying either. It was just the price to pay for what he'd known had to be done. Nothing more, nothing less. The two of them deserved to die, as much as anyone anywhere, and he had the satisfaction of being the person who'd done it. All by himself. Ezekiel wouldn't hang with him, and that was the deepest satisfaction of all. One that could never be taken away. As long as he lived, he smiled.

Only God knew what would happen afterwards, and he really didn't give that much thought. Either God waited for him in Heaven or not. But what decent Lord would punish him for what he'd done. If He did, then to Hell with it all. He chuckled louder. Some men deserved to be murdered. Despite 'Thou shall not kill'. And lots of others, better men than him, had gone before him having done much worse. He couldn't believe that all of them would be burning in eternal damnation.

He thought of the boy in Columbia and paced some more, knowing that what he'd done there was truly wrong. It was something that had to be considered horribly evil in the eyes of God. Maybe Hell really did await him.

"Dear Lord, isn't that a confession of sorts?" Again blocking out the thought of the noose until they passed. But, at least God had allowed his drowning plan to unfold about as well as it could have on that particular day. Maybe that was all God would do for him. He smiled. If Hell awaited him, at least he'd have interesting company.

His only other regret was not picking a deeper spot to sink the Aleta. But who could have predicted that two black crabbers would just happen to drop their heavy, wooden crab traps right on top of her, a month later no less, on the lowest tide of the year? The Aleta would have never been found otherwise, and he would have never been arrested.

But why hadn't he planned just a bit better? Why hadn't he thought of that possibility? He asked himself those same questions for the thousandth time, knowing he might have figured a better way. He shook his head and scuffed his shoes against the bricks.

"So stupid of me."

"Yes, Connor, but it doesn't surprise me in the least." He pictured his Uncle Paul agreeing with him, and it made him smile. "A half-baked scheme as usual. All focused on the one thing and forgetting the other that brings you the hangman's noose. So typical of you, my boy."

But he was sure that he'd been in the deepest part of the channel. He just hadn't counted on an astronomical low tide and the Aleta settling upright on the bottom with the stub of mast still intact. Just enough to impale a crab trap and give a hard working crabber reason to dive down 20 feet to free it. He imagined the man's face as he broke the surface to tell his partner of his find, knowing exactly what it was like to come across something of use floating in the harbor or something hidden below the surface. It was like finding treasure. And a sunken wreck was a treasure hunter's dream.

He'd read the papers since then, courtesy of his guards, and had come to learn that the two crabbers had kept it a secret for a while, diving to the bottom repeatedly to salvage what they could. Only after they'd stripped it bare did they report it to the Yank Harbor master, and soon enough, the Aleta had been raised and his device discovered. It didn't take them long to put it all together and arrest him. Plenty of people had seen them get on the Aleta that day. Even without the bodies, the device with the wire still bolted to the snapped cross brace and the cut planks in the hull indicted him. If only he'd figured a better way. He knew he could have cut all the wires loose before she'd sunk. They would have still found the cut hull sections but maybe ... He bumped his head against a brick wall and cursed himself that he hadn't even thought to try. Now he would hang because of his lack of foresight.

He could just hear his uncle laughing again. "You're not much of a murderer are you, Connor. Probably should've let Ezekiel do it. He'd have killed them right off. Yes, he'd have hung, but so will you. All that work for naught."

Connor stood up and paced around the cell some more trying to put the mistake out of his mind. His other regret was not having gone back to check on Norton's grave before he'd killed the Yanks. He should've done that first. He should've put up some kind of marker for him and for Cheshire at the Salkehatchie River, Bucky after Orangeburg, and for Barry at Columbia. Now he wouldn't have the chance. But still. His mind always turned to the pleasing thought that at least Tomlinson and Maxwell were dead. And he had done it. He thanked God again for that small comfort.

EZEKIEL STOOD OUTSIDE the jail for a while resting against on oak tree in the shade, watching civilians and soldiers going in and out the door all afternoon. He knew Connor was in there, but there was nothing he could do about it. Even talking to him might bring undue attention. He decided he'd just keep his eyes open and act if the opportunity knocked, knowing Connor would think it quite fair, and well worth, it to die on the gallows in exchange for killing the bastards and that he wouldn't quibble, no matter what. That much credit he had to give him, he smiled. He was definitely one hell of a single-minded Irishman.

He suddenly felt like laughing. Christ almighty, how much more absurd could life get? If only there was a way to get him out. Maybe just jump the guard and make a break for it. But he knew he couldn't do it and get away. And Connor was right. It wouldn't be fair to Miela and the others. Not now, not ever. Especially with a baby coming. But the thought of it gave him a hollow feeling in his stomach. To be indebted to Connor for the rest of his life.

"Damn you, you bastard," he laughed and walked off.

LUKE GRABBED HIS COAT and walked immediately to the jail and was escorted by a guard to Conner's dank cell. He didn't recognize him. Connor was pale as a ghost and squatting in the shadows in the corner. "Are you Connor Dumont?"

"Yes," Connor nodded, wondering why a one-armed, Yank carpetbagger had a sudden interest in him.

"Do you remember me?" Luke smiled

"Can't say that I do." Connor waited for the next blow. It was what he had come to expect of the last few months. Arrest, interrogation, the charge of murder, and the threat of hanging. A few lesser beatings and one good one that made him spit up blood and lose hearing in his left ear. What would this Yank add?

"I think you're the one who spared my life. Just past the Wateree River. Before Cheraw. You had two others with you. You let me go. You fired your shotgun into the ground. Was that you?"

Connor nodded. "I remember. Your eyes were as big as ... well ... " He glanced at Luke's pinned sleeve. "You had both arms when I left you."

"That's true," Luke smiled. "Lost it at Averasboro." He waved his stump around. "Were you there?"

"Nope. Went back to fight Potter's boys, then worked my way back to Charleston."

"Potter?"

"Yank raid up from Georgetown. After Sherman left."

"I see." Luke shook his head, and they looked at each other in silence, understanding that the particulars might vary, but they were all part of the same thing, the same shared experience. Something that was unexplainable to anyone who hadn't been in the war but obvious to anyone who had.

Connor remembered vividly the Yank kneeling behind the big oak tree. "Luke, from Elmira, New York." He slapped the bars of his cell, and laughed. "You sure didn't know what to expect, did you?"

"Yep. That's a fact. Thought I was a dead man for sure." He offered his left hand, and Connor shook it.

"Well I'm glad you made it back, Luke. Sorry about your arm." Luke smiled. "At least you weren't the one who shot it off."

"Yep. And I'm glad I didn't."

"Me too," Luke nodded. "Look here. I'm gonna do what I can." He looked around to make sure no one else was listening, but the guards were down the hall eating. They weren't paying the slightest bit of attention. "I just need to know exactly what day it happened and well ... the two men in question ... did they deserve to die?"

Connor started to nod yes, but Luke waved him off. "It doesn't really matter. What's done is done. I'll speak to the officer in charge. I just need to know the exact day."

Connor felt a glimmer of hope then quickly pushed it away. No use getting worked up for nothing. "November 17."

"Are you sure?"

"My birthday. I'm sure."

They shook hands again. Connor looked Luke in the eye. "Let me just say this. There's one thing that's as certain as the sun rising. Justice was done. The two men ... yes, they deserved it. Sure as all Hell. And whatever happens to me won't change that truth."

Luke nodded, accepting his word and thinking how could he not. "I'll do what I can."

483

Connor watched him walk down the hallway and heard the door shut behind him. He sat back down in the corner of his cell and tried not to get his hopes up. But it was already hard not to. Six months in jail waiting for the noose and now a glimmer of hope. Maybe he wouldn't hang after all. Maybe.

Luke went straight back to his office and found the note he'd saved from General Slocum that commended his actions at Averasboro. He put it his pocket and then went to the bank and withdrew $1000 US currency, almost all that he had to his name. He walked to the Mills House Hotel, asked to speak to the manager, in private, and was escorted to a small room off of Queen Street where the manager, a Mr. Jervey, stood up and offered him a chair.

He was a small balding man with a long red scar down the side of his face. "What can I do for you, sir?" He offered Luke a glass of lemonade and sat back down.

"I'll come straight to it. I spent this $1000 here in this very Hotel back in November." He put the roll of bills on the table. "On November 17, to be exact. I need for you to give me a receipt for it. It needs to say that I was here for ... let's say, the entire week. Perhaps receipts for each day including meals. Yes ... that's it, That would be good. I need this documentation to save a friend. A young Confederate soldier who saved my life. He's being held in jail now, for murder. They'll hang him if I don't do this. If you agree, and of course I'd prefer this not to leave the room, the money is yours. I just need the receipts dated for November 17 to show that I was here."

Mr. Jervey stared blankly for a minute then drummed his fingers on the desk. "Where did you lose your arm?" he asked gently.

"Averasboro. And your wound?"

"Petersburg. The Crater. Hell of a fight. When I close my eyes, I can still see those bodies in the trench line. Clear as day. Just 11 of us left now. Started out with 157." He scratched the scar. "It still itches. Must still be a stitch in there some where."

Luke nodded. "I'm glad you made it back."

"You too. And about your friend. He's in trouble and going to be hung? For murder, you say. Who did he kill?"

"Two men who deserved what they got."

"And he's southern, you say. Do you know where he served?"

"He rode with Wheeler. He saved my life on the march to Cheraw."

Mr. Jervey sighed. "You came across with Sherman?"

"I did." Luke watched Mr. Jervey strum his fingers on the desk for a full minute.

"Well, all that's over now, isn't it?" He took out paper and pen, wrote out the receipts, and handed them to Luke. "Will these suffice?" Luke looked them over and nodded. "Yes, thank you. Can you enter them into the hotel record? In case the authorities inquire?"

"Of course. I'm the manager," Mr. Jervey smiled and offered his hand. "We should save as many as we can. But you keep the money. Mr. ... ?"

"Conneley. Luke Conneley." Luke shook his hand. "Thank you, but the $1000 should go to helping people like my friend. I can always make more. Please take it. Perhaps you could use it for that purpose? You must have more contacts than me. Will you?"

Mr. Jervey nodded and put the money in a drawer. "Yes I will. And I can assure you it will be well spent. Thank you Mr. Conneley."

"Luke. Just, Luke."

He handed Mr. Jervey one of his hand-written business cards and left quickly then headed straight back to the jail and directly to the commandant, a Major Harrison from the Provost Guard. He saluted and handed him the note from General Slocum that spoke of meritorious duty and promotion to sergeant after Averasboro. The Major didn't seem much impressed with the note, but kept his eyes fixed on the pinned up, empty sleeve. He didn't tell Luke that his son had lost a leg at Gettysburg, but Luke got straight to the point.

"I've just become aware that certain Connor Dumont is being held here on a murder charge."

The major nodded. "Yes, he is," and wondering "What the hell now?"

"Well sir. He can't be the man because he was with me at the Mills House Hotel that very day, on November 17, for a business meeting and for dinner. I've known Connor since he saved my life on the march to Cheraw."

The Major sat back in his chair and sighed. Could this be true? He hoped to God it was. He hadn't ever wanted to hang the boy. Connor's red hair reminded him of his son. And there'd been enough killing ... on both sides. Please, Lord in heaven, he thought, let this be a way out.

"Do you have any proof?" he asked almost apologetically. "The colonel will want ... well, something in writing. Something that would satisfy a tribunal."

Luke showed him the receipts and waited. The major read them both carefully to make sure they would stand up in court. He wanted them to. He didn't care if they were forgeries, which he figured they probably were. The whole thing was just too improbable. He just wanted them to be able to pass the test, if it ever came to that.

"May I keep these? I'll have to very verify these with the hotel manager. They'll have a record of course," he said in warning, wondering if this Mr. Conneley had thought of that.

"Please do. A Mr. Jervey, I believe. And very efficient manager, I might add."

The major smiled, relieved, then handed back General Slocum's letter and stood up. "Thank you for coming forward. We certainly don't want to hang the wrong man. If this is verified, he will be released immediately."

Luke shook his hand, thanked him and left. His gut told him that the Major had seen right through it all, but honestly wanted to help. He smiled to himself. The ruse just might work after all.

A week later, a military tribunal was convened. The three officers looking at the written evidence shook their heads and laughed. They knew it was all a fraud, but they let Connor go. They had heard the rumors about Lieutenant Tomlinson and Sgt. Maxwell and inferred the truth. Their murder although illegal was probably plain justice. But certainly no offer of apology or any restitution to the young reb would be offered, and Connor didn't expect any. He was alive and suddenly free, and that was all that counted. Major Harrison was kind enough to make sure he that he had a new, clean set of clothes, and the guards smiled and waved goodbye like he was part of their family who'd come for a long visit. Connor kept smiling back but hurried away as fast as his persistent cough would allow, not wanting them to have time to change their minds. He realized though, as he walked to Luke's business on Market Street to thank him, that he was much more winded and weaker than he could ever remember.

He found Luke sitting at his desk in his office. Luke stood up, and they shook hands. "Maybe we can do business together, Connor."

"There's certainly a lot to be done. Maybe we could ... ," Connor lapsed into a coughing fit that gagged him. "Sorry," he wiped his mouth, as he finally caught his breath. "That damn, drafty jail cell, I guess."

Luke offered him a seat, a handkerchief, and some bourbon, and they clinked glasses. "To a better world."

"Yes indeed." Connor sipped the whiskey and felt exhausted. "To a better world."

"There's hope, don't you think?" Luke felt the bourbon burn his throat. "The white southerners, I mean. Accepting the blacks as free men. It might take time but ... "

Connor shook his head. "Not in our lifetime. Too much pain on both sides." He coughed sore more and drank another shot of whiskey to calm it. "If we'd freed them ourselves, before the war, or better yet, if there hadn't been a war ... Well then ... "
"But now? You don't think ... "

"No chance. The blacks know Lincoln and the Union Army freed them, and we, the Confederate Army that is, fought to keep them as well as ... the way it's always been." He felt his breath get short again, but the whiskey helped. "They'll never forget that."

"Then what about the whites?"

"The same. They ... WE ... were conquered and forced to do something. It doesn't matter if it was the right thing to do. Only that we were forced." He sipped some more and felt the bourbon sooth his throat.

"I see. But there must be another way." Luke sighed, hoping for at least a tiny bit of optimism from Connor.

"There is," Connor nodded, lapsing into a worse coughing spasm that wouldn't stop until he drank another half glass.

"Better see a physician," Luke poured him another round.

"I'm sure it's just pleurisy. From the damp." He sipped the whiskey and took a deep breath. "What I was trying to say is that there IS a way. But it'll take years. Generations, perhaps. But it's probably the only way." He spit up a hint of blood into the handkerchief but didn't let Luke see. "We just have to treat everyone the same. Black or white. Yank or Confederate. All the same, all the time. From now on.'

"Well ... That makes sense in theory, but ... it could take a very long time and certainly won't be appreciated ... by some."

"By MOST. But nevertheless, that's the only way. No matter how long it takes."

"Well then, if you're right, here's to our first day on the job." Luke held up his glass.

Connor smiled. "It sure doesn't seem like the first day, does it?"

"No, by God, it doesn't," Luke laughed. "It surely doesn't indeed."

CHAPTER 54 — POINS, JEMPS AND YARROW

Poins and Jemps took off at first light with the cast net and the seine they'd liberated from the shed behind Legare Street. Yarrow followed behind. They came back from the river an hour later with a basket full of mullet and dogfish that Jemps dumped out on the grass, "Fish were just begging to be caught," he gushed. "Had to pick and choose. Just waiting for us to eat 'em. They were, I swear. Here, help yourself. Lizette can render them in ham grease. We'll get more if we need 'em."

Everyone gladly set to it. A better breakfast was not to be had. They did the same the next day and the next, bringing in more fish each morning than all of them could stuff down in three full meals until Miela had them limit their catch. "Twenty fish a day. No use catching them all now and not having any left in the fall."

"We'll never catch them all," Poins argued. "You wouldn't believe how many live in that little creek. They must love it there."

"Please, Poins, just humor me if you don't mind."

"But Miela. How about thirty," Yarrow smiled. "Please."

She looked at Jemps. "I think twenty is gracious plenty."

Jemps started to say something then stopped. "All right. You can catch mine, Yarrow."

"Really?" He looked up eagerly. "You swear?"

"That I do."

"Then I can get ten more for today, can't I?" Yarrow beamed.
Miela waved her hands, "I give up. Y'all just go on."

Yarrow took off back to the creek with Jemps and reluctantly went along with the limit of ten more. Every day afterwards they did the same, and their success led them to the next idea of building a creek skiff from a pile of weathered pine boards they'd found back in the woods. Over the next weeks the three of them went hard at it. Jemps figured they could row down the creek with the ebb tide and back up with the flood. He just didn't know how far they could make it one tide, but Yarrow had the idea to add a sail and make the skiff big enough to sleep on, with a little deck in front and benches for two sets of oars. Lizette sewed them a small canvas sail, square rigged from a stout piece of bamboo that could be hoisted up a stubby six foot pine mast, and Jemps rigged a steering rudder for runs with the wind. Within three weeks, they'd finished the hull, caulked it with strips of canvas and pine resin, and dragged it down to the creek for a trial run.

Jemps made Yarrow wait on shore that first time until he was sure it would float, causing him to sulk and frown while everyone else clapped and cheered as they rowed out of sight. A half-hour later, after everyone had left except Yarrow, they came back still smiling but with water sloshing over their feet.

"Leaks pretty bad," Poins yelled.

"You should've took me with you. I could have fixed it."

"Yep, you sure could've," Jemps nodded. "We'll take you next time for sure."

"You promise?"

"I swear to God. It's your boat, ain't it?"

"Sure is!" Yarrow beamed as he helped them pull the skiff up into the woods to be recaulked.

It took over two whole weeks before the hull was finally watertight. Every day from then on, weather permitting, they went out fishing, mostly in the creek to the mouth of the Cooper River, throwing the cast net or pulling the seine, but sometimes with hook and line. Every day the basket was full and the catch a bit different. They caught plenty of mullet, spot, whiting and dogfish to fry, along with spot-tail bass and sea-trout to be stuffed with onions and baked whole. Catfish, with their dagger spines, were clubbed and cut up for bait. Each stone crab was asked to give up a single claw before being thrown back, and the meaner blue- crabs were just dumped into a bucket to be boiled alive later.

Every time the ferry came past, they'd pull to the side quickly, nudging in to the marsh or into a side creek. The two white boys on the ferry would always come to the side railing to watch, and Poins, Jemps and Yarrow would always wave, but the boys would never wave back. Twice they'd been bumped into the marsh grass and nearly sunk, the only two times that the boys ever even smiled.

Lizette and Daphne always waited for them at the landing every afternoon and always escorted by Grace, Agnes and Fatima. Yarrow's eyes lit up every time he came around the last bend, thinking he might have been in heaven, admired as he was by all the girls, and their catch the center of daily attention. He would always hold Grace's hand as he walked up the path while Daphne and Lizette helped Poins with the baskets of fish. Jemps felt it the prerogative of being captain, not to have to actually carry the baskets, and Poins went along.

One blue sky Sunday morning, they decided it was time to take the skiff as far down the river on the ebb tide as they could, just to explore. They made it down to the mouth of the creek and out into the full current of the Cooper River as the wind blew hard from the northwest. White caps danced over the waves. They raced along with the tide, rowing just enough to keep steerage. Poins shared a jar of honey-sweetened sassafras tea, and they ate a few pieces of fried mullet. None of them could have been happier.

They could see the ferry coming up against the current towards them pulling a flatboat piled high with cotton bales. A white boy stood alone in the bow of the towed flatboat, bending over the railing as it plunged heavily into the rising waves. A big swell poured over the boy, and the thick tow rope went taut. They could see the boy reaching down for something then standing up cupping his hands to his mouth, yelling to the men on the ferry boat. They were just coming abreast of the ferry's starboard bow when the tow rope snapped as loud as a cannon shot. The ferry surged forward. The severed hawser hit the boy in the chest and knocked him backwards. The flatboat's stern dropped for a second then lifted higher as the bow sunk into the waves. The boat began to sink quickly. The ferrymen yelled and the captain whipped the wheel around to come about. The white boy lay on his back, not moving at all.

"C'mon row!" Jemps yelled. "We're his only chance. He'll drown! The rope knocked him senseless. They can't get to them before it sinks."

POINS PULLED ON THE OARS with him harder than ever, bouncing across the steamer's wake and closing in on the flatboat as it settled underwater, bow first. Yarrow steered them alongside, and Jemps jumped overboard, grabbing the boy by the collar as the deck disappeared beneath them. Poins held out an oar for Jemps to lock his arms around and pulled them back to the skiff. They wrestled the limp boy onboard just as he started coughing up water.

His blue eyes lit up, and the red hair on his neck bristled, "What the hell?" He jerked up quickly, while Jemps was still climbing back over the transom, then he sat up and caught his breath, watching the last bit of stern disappear. It took him a few minutes to get his wits back and realize exactly what happened. "The flatboat? Sunk?" His eyes squinted into the sun as salt water dripped off his red bangs.

"Yep. Went under real quick," Poins smiled. "Jemps here saved you from the crabs."

Jemps just shrugged, drying himself with a piece of burlap. "Well, I saw they couldn't get to you in time," nodding to the slowly turning ferry. "It was the only thing to do."

Yarrow stood in the stern holding the tiller, smiling. "You would've been crab bait for sure. How deep is it anyhow?"

"Deep enough, I guess," Poins laughed.

"That's for damn sure." Jemps took a sip of tea.

The white boy coughed up more water than splashed some on his face from over the side. "Well then." He took a deep breath. "I guess I owe you."

"Don't worry about that," Jemps waved him off. "All I did was…"

"You saved my life."

"He sure did," Yarrow nodded. "You would've been down on the bottom by now. Crabs and eels all over your face."

A white boy held out his hand to Jemps, "Thank you. Thank you all. My name's Edwin."

"Jemps." He shook his hand. "Poins and Yarrow there," nodding to them.

"Thank you. Thank you all." Edwin smiled then lapsed into another coughing fit.

Jemps slapped his back until it stopped then they all sat there for another ten minutes or so drifting in the current in silence, staring at each other, and watching the ferry make its long winding turn back towards them. Poins started bailing while the ferry came upriver and alongside. Mr. O'Neill and the three other men on board saw that Edwin was All right.

Mr. O'Neill called over to them, "Thank you boys. Can we give you a tow back to the landing?"

"No thank you, sir," Jemps answered. "We'll keep on with the tide for a while," feeling a surge of pride that he didn't need their help in return.

Edwin climbed aboard the ferry and waved as they shoved off. They waved back and watched the ferry turn around to scoop up a few cotton bales that surfaced above the sunken flatboat. Yarrow manned the tiller and steered down river, "I don't think we should EVER let them tow us."

"Nope," Jemps laughed as he started rowing. "That's a fact."

"We won't never need no tow anyhow." Yarrow stood up, wiggling the tiller between his legs. "We got oars and a sail."

"Damn right," Poins laughed, savoring the moment and resting on his oar as the tide took them down river.

They made it all the way to Drum Island, where the Cooper and the Wando Rivers meet, landing there to collect shells and talk about what happened. They wolfed down the rest of their lunch then watch three schooners sail with the tide down the Wando all the way past them towards the harbor. The wind dropped down a bit as the tide began to turn, so the pull back upriver wasn't so hard. Yarrow tapped out a cadence with his bamboo stick, singing the whole way back and making up ditties as they pulled the oars.

They were all exhausted when they got to the landing but told the whole story several times, and it got better with the retelling as the evening wore on. Everyone clapped their hands and took turns blowing into the shell whistles.

"It's a sign from God," Lizette sang out. "Like Jonah and the whale."

"I believe you're right," Miela smiled.

"Of course she's right!" Cumseh waved her hands above her head. "A big whale was waiting to eat that white boy. But he was saved by a brave, handsome ... BLACK ... man." She blew a dandelion at Jemps. "Praise be to God and all His Saints!"

Jemps beamed. The girls made him tell the story again, just to them, before going off to bed. In the morning he went back out in the skiff with Poins and Yarrow, and they'd just finished pulling in the nets when the ferry came downstream. Edwin stood in the bow and waved. He held up a blue bundle tied in twine and tossed it into the skiff as they passed.

"Just a little something to say thanks. See y'all tomorrow."

They all waved back then scrambled to open it up. It was the first gift anyone had ever given any of them. Jemps cut the twine and reached inside. He pulled out a small wooden box and opened it. It was full of copper and silver coins and a folded letter.

"Damn. Must be $20." Then he held up the letter. "What do you think it says?"

Poins shrugged, "Could say just about anything, I guess. No way to know."

"Let me see it," Yarrow begged.

"Why? You can't read neither."

"I know I can't," he frowned. "I just want to look at it. Nobody ever wrote me a letter before."

Jemps passed it around, and they all took turns looking at the scribbles on the page. "Let's take it to Miela. She'll read it for us."

They stowed the nets and rowed faster than ever to the landing, pulling the skiff up, and tying it off to a tree then running back up to the farm and breathlessly handing Miela the letter. She had everyone stop their chores and gather around as she read it. "For saving the life of Edwin Ellis. Special thanks from his family. Please accept this token of our heartfelt appreciation."

"Heartfelt," Jemps beamed. "Well I'll be damned."

Poins took a deep breath, "Special thanks and all."

"What is 'heartfelt' exactly?" Yarrow squinted.

"From the heart," Miela smiled. "From deep in their hearts."

"Well, well. You never can tell what a new day will bring, now can you," Jemps laughed.

"No, you sure can't," Miela agreed, letting everyone carefully take turns looking at the letter. "This is surely proof of that."

"Heartfelt proof!" Yarrow squealed. "The best kind!"

"It surely is, Yarrow. It surely is."

CHAPTER 55 — CONNOR

Miela was nursing Smythe on the hammock when she heard voices behind her and turned around. She recognized Connor with his distinctive limp as soon as he emerged from the trees. Ezekiel escorted him. Another white man in a new brown suit followed behind. She sat up and smiled, watching them come down the path with the sun on their faces. The stranger's face bright pink, Connor's chalky white as he coughed, and Ezekiel's, a rich, ebony black. Richer than she'd ever remembered.

"Here comes your daddy, Smythe. Let's go give him a kiss."

She could hear Connor's coughing getting louder and louder as he came closer. He stopped about twenty feet away and waved to her then bent over with another spasm that caused his face to turn bright red as he panted for air. The stranger stayed beside him. Ezekiel came up and kissed her.

"Luke, his friend there, says he's been sick ever since he got out of jail. Worse for two days," he nodded back at Connor catching his breath.

"You better get him to bed then. Put him in Poins and Jemps' hut. They've gone fishing 'till tomorrow."

"Sorry Miela," Connor tried to catch his breath between coughs.. "I didn't mean to come here sick. Just figured it would pass," he panted, lapsing into another intense spell that gagged him.

Luke put his arm around him, and Ezekiel helped get them back down the path to the hut and into bed. Connor lay there coughing harder and harder. "Damn it, Ezekiel. Didn't mean to be a bother."

"You'll be all right."

But he coughed up a wad of blood and felt something expand inside his chest. It grew and grew, feeling suddenly as big as a watermelon. His heart raced. His thready pulse throbbed in his ear. He prayed it would pass, feeling embarrassed more than anything. To come over for the day, just to visit, and get laid up with some damn fever. "Shit," he mumbled, feeling the watermelon expanding into his shoulder then bursting into a hot poker down his arm. It took his breath away completely. "Shit on this." His heart started jumping and skipping, and he realized it was worse than he'd thought. "Ezekiel," he raised his voice to a hoarse whisper. "Something bad's happening. Shit." Lancing pain ripped into his neck and jaw. "Get Miela. I'd like to tell her ... "

Luke dabbed his forehand with a handkerchief and watched all the color leave Connor's face and his lips turn a dull gray. He'd seen enough men die to know Connor had just a few more minutes. He couldn't believe it was happening this fast and called out the door, "Hurry, Ezekiel!"

A thin, thready tapping grew louder in Connor's ear. His mouth went dry and his lips suddenly felt glued together. Miela appeared beside the bed holding his hand. Ezekiel and Luke seemed to hover above her. She gave him a sip of water, and he panted as if he'd just run a mile. He licked his lips as she dabbed them with a wet cloth. She was crying. Ezekiel and Luke stooped closer to him.

Ezekiel knelt down, "Thank you for saving my life."

Luke nodded and wiped his eyes, "Me too. I wouldn't be here ... if not for you."

"The whole family thanks you," Miela gently rubbed his temple, tears dripping down her face. "For Smythe's and a new life."

Connor cut his eyes at Ezekiel on one knee. He tried to smile and could barely whisper, "Don't need to genuflect ... "

Ezekiel squinted like the sun was in his eyes, "I'll never forget."

Miela kissed Connor's forehead, "Thank you. Your gift helped set us free."

Connor watched her face blur and felt another cantaloupe-like mass grow in his throat. He turned his head and looked out the door and thought he could hear the burning red ball of the sun sinking into the marsh and sizzling into the pluff mud. He drifted off and found himself in a rowboat with Ezekiel who was pulling up a seine from the murky creek. Ezekiel laughed and tossed a dog fish into his chest. He felt pain lance straight through to his back and tried to curse, but his mouth was bone dry. He could still hear Ezekiel laughing when his eyes refocused.

Miela was dabbing his caked lips again. Her face shimmered like a mirage. She whispered into his ear, "You saved us all."

Connor's heart thumped louder then something gave way inside. He tried to smile again, but his face stiffened. Miela was the only one close enough to hear his last words. Just the faintest whisper.

"No. You saved ... me."

CHAPTER 56 — TAKING CONNOR HOME

Ezekiel took charge. After comforting Miela and seeing that she was settled back in bed with Smythe, he sent Daphne to gather up all the salt and Lizette and Cumseh to sew a burial shroud. He refused to cry any more. He would see that Connor was properly buried in the only place that made sense. Right next to his parents on that little point back at his farm on Younge's Island. He felt his heart race for a minute, but he was good at remembering just what he chose to remember and nothing more. The creek out to Stono Sound, the winding salt-marsh creek with millions of fiddler crabs and endless boils of finger mullet. Connor in the bow and him paddling from the stern. It came back as a happy memory, and he let it. His slave days were gone for good, by God, and he would take Connor back to Younge's Island no matter what. All that other hateful misery from the past could go straight to Hell. He was through with it forever.

Daphne came back and knelt by Connor's death bed, carefully washing his body then sprinkling him all over with salt Ezekiel let Yarrow and the girls watch, figuring they'd just imagine something worse if they didn't. Yarrow put his hands on his hips and shook his head. "When we salt the squirrel meat, we clean out the guts first. Ain't you gonna do that?"

"Oh my God!" Daphne gasped. "For God's sake Yarrow!"

"Well, why not?"

Ezekiel knelt down beside him. "It's a good question, Yarrow. But you see, we're gonna treat his body the way we would as if he was alive. The salt on his skin will just keep him cool on the trip."

"Trip? Where to?"

"To where he'll be buried." Ezekiel looked at the children gathered around with wide eyes and made another decision right that moment.

"All of you children will come with us."

"Really?" Agnes smiled. "Is it far?"

"Will he smell bad?" Yarrow rubbed his head. "Squirrels smell when they're not gutted."

"It's not far, and no, he won't. Not after the soap and salt"

"Will he have a coffin?"

"Yes he will. As soon as Jemps and Poins get back. They're our best carpenters."

"Me too," Yarrow argued. "I can hammer better than Poins. Just ask him."

"All right then. You can help too. Now y'all get to bed. It'll be a long day tomorrow."

They all reluctantly obeyed, going off to their huts while Luke and Ezekiel stayed to help the women get Connor's body properly wrapped in the cotton shroud. Luke slept in attendance right there at the foot of the bed all night, and in the morning, Jemps and Poins got back and quickly went to work making a coffin. Ezekiel and Luke helped them strip the widest boards from the side of the barn and from inside each hut until they had enough for the job. Each of them took turns with the sawing until all the boards fit properly. Yarrow helped Poins nail the sides and ends to the bottom while Jemps fashioned a top.

The four men, with Yarrow in the rear, carried it inside and set it down next to Connor's body. Everyone gathered at the door to watch. Ezekiel and Luke carefully picked him up then lowered him into his coffin. Miela led them in the Lord's Prayer as Jemps, Poins, and Yarrow nailed the top down tightly. Ezekiel knelt and blessed himself and everyone followed suit.

"I guess he did what he thought he had to," Ezekiel sighed. "Now I'm gonna do the same." He blessed himself again then stood up and turned to the others. "We'll take him back to his family. Let him rest in peace right beside his parents. It's what he'd want." He wiped his eyes and took a deep breath. "Jemps, could you and Poins hitch the wagon?" They nodded then backed reverently out the door as Ezekiel cleared his throat. "Luke, you could be a big help if you came along."

"I can assure you nothing could stop me."

"We'll take the children too," Ezekiel hugged Agnes and Fatima. "It's something they should be part of. Something they should remember."

"What about us?" Lizette asked, pointing to Cumseh and Daphne.

501

"I'll need you and Cumseh to stay with Miela and the baby. Jemps and Poins can stay for ... Well, just to be sure. Daphne should come with the children. I'm asking for everyone's help with this ... to pitch in. Please."

Everyone nodded. There wasn't even the first hint of grumbling. Each of them had a task and felt obligated to do their part. Only Miela wasn't so sure. She took Ezekiel outside and spoke to him privately. "Are you sure this is what Connor wanted? Why not bury him here? It's his ... it was ... his farm."

"He belongs with his family. I'm sure."

"WE'RE sort of family now, aren't we? You in particular."

Ezekiel felt his jaw tighten at a sudden memory of Connor's father slapping him for dropping something in the stable when he'd first come to Younge's Island. A bridle maybe? Then he stopped himself. He didn't need to go there. "All that's over with. Long over. Connor's not my family. You are. And Smythe and the others. But he does deserve to be buried with his own."

"But are you sure?"

"Yes I am. Absolutely."

Miela realized then what Ezekiel was telling her. He had to take Connor back to Younge's Island not only for Connor's sake, but for his own. It was his way of putting it all behind him. His way of laying the past to rest. She hugged him and kissed him on the cheek. "All right. I'll get your things."

An hour later they were waiting for the ferry with the coffin in the wagon. Everyone remained quiet and respectful, even the children. They realized, without anyone telling them, that it wasn't a time for horseplay. The ferry rounded the bend in the creek and nosed up into the landing. Mr. O'Neill saw the coffin and quickly had his boys help with the wagon.

"Who is it?" he whispered to Ezekiel, not wanting to upset the children.

"Connor. The boy ... the young man ... who came over with me yesterday."

"Connor? How ... ?"

"He'd been sick and ... "

"From that damn jail, I bet."

"You knew?"

"Yep. My brother met him a while back. Told me all about it. I guess I'm still sworn to secrecy. What he said and all."

Ezekiel figured it out instantly. The O'Neill's were the ones who'd helped Connor find the bastards who'd ... He stopped himself. "Well, thanks for your help."

"Glad to."

The ride over was smoother than ever, as if the river and the wind were paying their respects. Everyone at the landing, white and black, either lent a hand or stood by with hats off until the wagon was off-loaded and they were on their way. Mr. O'Neill didn't charge a penny. Even the passing Yank cavalry on the road to Bee's Ferry was respectful and quiet. The Bee's Ferry operator, a squat man with a huge purple birthmark staining his forehead, was the only unpleasant person, charging double payment for the coffin and making them cover it with blankets before boarding.

"Coffins are bad business. And anyhow, one place is as good as the next for a grave. Don't see no reason to pick the other side of the river."

Ezekiel made a point not to get into it with him, but it was hard not to. After they made it across the Ashley river, they got the wagon off the flatboat as quickly as possible and pushed on past the Turnpike Road towards Younge's Island, making it to the Dumont farm well before dark. Ezekiel fought off a smothering swarm of memories as he walked with Luke past what was left of the slave huts, now turned into corn bins, then over to the Gibson house where he knocked on the door while Daphne and the children waited by the wagon. The door opened. Poppy Carr and Cora Gibson stood warily inside. Her two little boys, Thomas and Peter, peeked out from behind her skirt.

"Yes. Can we help you?" Cora asked.

"We've brought ... " Ezekiel wasn't sure how to say it. "I'm sorry to have to tell you, but it's Connor. Connor Dumont. He died yesterday. We brought him home to ... "

"Connor's dead?" Poppy opened the door fully to glance over at the coffin in the wagon. "Are you sure it's him? And who exactly are you two?"

"Poppy please," Cora raised her voice. "They're trying to be decent."

"I'm Ezekiel. I used to ... "

"Ezekiel? Is that you?" Poppy cocked his head back. "Well then, damn. It is Connor. Shit. Excuse me, Cora, but damn it. Not Connor. Shit." The little boys giggled behind him then pushed past and out the door and ran over to the wagon. "Y'all come back here, damn it," he called after them.

"Shush." Cora came out the door slowly, as if facing down a barking dog. "Well, thank you for bringing him home ... Ezekiel ... It's been a long time."

"Yes ma'am, it certainly has." Ezekiel felt a cold chill run down his back at the thought of it all.

"I'm Cora Gibson." She nodded to Luke.

"Luke Conneley. A friend of Connor's." He bowed politely.

"Where you from?" Poppy asked, coming around Cora as if expecting trouble.

"New York ... Elmira, to be exact," he smiled.

Poppy grunted, "You're a long way from home, aren't you."

"Yes, I am. I've come a long way."

"Well, I guess we all have," Cora smiled, letting the door close behind her slowly. "But Ezekiel's right. Connor's come back home...for good. Thank you both for that."

"Yes ma'am," Ezekiel nodded, feeling the chill dissipate. "Is it all right if we stay at the Dumont's tonight? We can watch over Connor and bury him in the morning. If it's all right."

"Hell yes it is!" Poppy walked down the front steps towards the wagon where his two grandsons were facing Yarrow, Agnes, Grace, and Fatima. "You brought him back didn't you? Connor would've appreciated that. He always wanted to be buried on that point over there."

"I remember it well," Ezekiel nodded. "Where his parents are buried."

"And his Uncle Paul. Died just last year."

"I didn't know."

"How could you?" Cora sighed. "You've been....gone. But that's all over now. Please...let me fix y'all some supper. I'll bring it over in just a little while."

Squeals of laughter erupted by the wagon and all six children ran off down the path towards the marsh.

"Y'all be careful!" She called to them. "You here me, Thomas?"

"Yes ma'am," he yelled back at a dead run with Yarrow right behind.

"Don't let those little girls get all muddy, you here?" But she couldn't tell if he'd answered her over all their yelling. She turned towards Ezekiel. "I hope y'all won't mind my boys. They just love to play, and they're always happy to have other children around."

Daphne walked over hesitantly and curtsied like she'd seen Miela do to Mrs. Blessing. "Oh I'm sure they'll be fine. Yarrow will ... "

A loud group -squeal erupted from down the path followed by more peals of children's laughter that made Ezekiel grin. "Sounds like they're getting along just fine."

"I haven't heard that much laughter in years," Cora smiled.

"Me neither."

They listened to the children's wild ups and downs for a while until they were all smiling, even Poppy who was walking over to the wagon.

"How 'bout I help y'all get Connor inside the house."

"Yes sir. Thank you."

Luke and Ezekiel followed him over while Cora invited Daphne to come and help with supper. Cora opened the door for her then turned after Daphne disappeared inside. She called over to Poppy.

"Don't hurt your back again, Poppy. Remember now!"

Poppy rolled his eyes then leaned towards them and whispered, "That woman is a saint, but damn it, sometimes she drives me to drink."

"Yes sir. My mother does too," Luke laughed.

Poppy slumped against the wagon looking at Connor's coffin. "But you know, I couldn't live without her ... or the boys. Wouldn't much want to neither."

Ezekiel stood beside him listening to the children laughing by the marsh. He pictured Miela cradling little Smythe in her arms and smiling at him as he came across the field. He felt a warmth in his chest and an overwhelming yearning that made his skin tingle. A rush of blood in his throat took away his breath for a second. He gathered himself and nodded to Poppy.

"Yes sir. I know exactly what you mean."

PERRY TROUCHE graduated from the University of Virginia and The
Medical University of South Carolina. He is a psychiatrist in private
practice from Charleston, South Carolina, where he lives with his wife
and family.

www.ingramcontent.com/pod-product-compliance
Lightning Source LLC
Chambersburg PA
CBHW022016050726
47499CB00004BA/995